MINO

C000050074

Daniel Dundee

Published by KDP

ISBN: 9781081003043

Any complaints, suggestions, remarks, etc. can be sent to the author at
neepness@icloud.com
He'd love to hear from you.

http://www.smashwords.com/profile/view/minos

Introduction

There is a land called Crete in the midst of the wine-dark sea, a fair land and a rich, begirt with water, and therein are many men innumerable, and ninety cities . . . And among these cities is the mighty city Knossos, wherein Minos when he was nine years old began to rule, he who held converse with great Zeus . . .

Homer-9th century BCE

The history of the Western World began with the predominant acceptance of Classical Greece as the beginning of real civilization. No one, other than ancient poets or dreamers from the lunatic fringe, would have seriously considered that a brilliant civilization of scribes, metalworkers, craftsmen, poets, artisans, and philosophers lived in a world of palaces and industry, grace and artistic inventiveness, more than a millennia before Homer and Plato and the "first" Olympiad of 776 BCE. All that changed with the turn of the century discoveries of Sir Arthur Evans.

Most of the civilization we now know as Minoan, the refined inhabitants of Crete and other islands of the Aegean Sea, still lies beneath the ground awaiting the day when it will be unearthed. At one place it is even paradoxical to think that the very fallout from the eruption that destroyed their civilization also provided their architectural wonders the blanket of protection required to preserve them from the elements, the avarice of looters, and the ravages of time. A century of archaeological excavation and research has recreated much of the former lifestyle that in Homer's time, only a few hundred years after the decline of the Minoan world, was scarcely a dim recollection of shadows and legend, an age when gods walked among men.

This book is written observing the premise that underlying all legend is truth.

Few civilizations have been so completely concealed as that of Minoan Crete. The great city, Knossos, had its beginnings as early as 6000 BC and, although it was abandoned on occasion, it is the oldest Neolithic settlement in Europe. At its pinnacle of greatness, with a population estimated variously at up to one hundred thousand, it was the largest city in Europe and, quite possibly, the world. Thanks to the splendid achievements of dedicated archaeologists we can now pace the perimeter of the capacious court of King Minos's palace, admire the oldest European throne still in existence, promenade the unveiled streets of the volcanic island of Thera, an island destroyed in the most violent eruption in human history, and see pottery of unparalleled splendor. We can imagine ourselves trying to stifle our puerile impulses to climb inside the man-sized storage jars as the legendary son of Minos did, who drowned and was then resurrected by a physician, a tale leaving us the caduceus of modern medicine. We might mature again as we ponder the aesthetic frescoes whose ardent themes make real a world that for thousands of years has lain unknown and abandoned. No thought was given to the defense of these elegant houses of government and theocracy. They were not surrounded with the protective bastions and fortifications of London Tower, but rather with the dignity and pomp of Versailles.

Many of the literary, cultural, and technical accomplishments of the Minoans spread throughout the Mediterranean in the same way knowledge spreads today. Words and ideas from one civilization were passed on in like manner that they were taken from others. The word 'Olympia', as an example, predates the Greek world from which it is normally associated by a thousand years, as do the other place names of Olympus, Kalliste, and Knossos. Everyday words inherited by the Greeks such as 'sandal', 'hyacinth', and 'cypress', were also derived from the Minoan. Farming, smithing, breeding, building; skills adopted and adapted substantively from every realm, the Minoans built their society to heights of intellectual achievement unsurpassed by any previous.

When the Minoan civilization tragically collapsed most of their accumulated knowledge was lost, but portions did endure into the Classical Greek age and we, the successors of Greek conventions and philosophies, are still influenced today from those distant roots of time. In the study of the Minoan past we are only studying our own present and what the future might hold for us, both virtuous and corrupt.

An examination of the beginnings of any civilization begs more vestigial inquiries relating to ourselves. How do intricate and exceptionally ordered nations emerge from inconsequential cultures? Is the catalyst merely an infinite permutation of being in the right place at the right time? What, if anything as in our case, stops the process? How do these past civilizations collapse into a cultural slump after centuries of success and are we doomed to follow in their well-established path? Will the undeniable pressures of overpopulation, environmental and ecological dilemmas, the increasing scarcity and waste of natural resources, the stresses of an all-encompassing world abundant with societal change, the increasing wealth and moral decay of the rich and the oppression of the poor, combine against the people of our age as they have done in every recognized civilization of the past?

Will we be the first to escape this inevitable fate? Will a greater power be our salvation? Or will that greater power suck us into the depths of another Dark Age, an Armageddon followed by a loose order of illiteracy and ignorance?

And the higher the summit from which we plunge, how much greater are our perils of never recovering?

~~~~~~

Forward

500,000 B.C.E.

The rock had been captured during the formation of the Sun six billion years earlier, a remnant from a star and planetary system which had annihilated itself in the process of a supernova millions of years previous to that. Its circuit in the collection of gasses, dust, and debris never brought it close enough to be incorporated into any body large enough to capture it. And so it was relegated to the confines of the Oort Cloud, the virtually invisible collection of fragments left over from the dawning of our Solar System.

The Oort Cloud, existing far beyond the distant orbits of the outer planets at the farthest frontiers of the Sun's gravitational field, is invisible from Earth due to distance and lack of starlight. Even the Sun appears as any other typically bright star in the heavens at that range, scarcely providing any more light. The uncountable bodies of this cloud, with a combined mass greater than all of the planets together and ranging in size from molecular to that of an office desk are forever trapped, confined to their slow journey around a visibly insignificant star.

Approaching the Sun from an even greater distance was a free-roaming wanderer, the size of a small moon, which also had its origin in the destruction of a planetary system. This body had defied all attempts at capture by stars, only briefly as cosmic time is defined, having its course altered enough to be considered a temporary comet, in one side of a stellar system and out the other.

As this wanderer passed through the Oort Cloud, it exerted a gravitational effect of its own on the bodies nearby, swirling them by unseen tidal forces, scattering them wildly in all directions.

The small icy rock which had been in its humble and insignificant orbit in the Oort Cloud was now compelled into a trajectory which would take it on a two million year elliptical voyage through the Solar System, never coming close to a planet, but crossing the path of Earth's orbit around the Sun hundreds of times.

Months after this minor celestial event an observer on Earth might have seen a new light in the night sky. A light that differed from the others in a number of ways. This one grew in brightness as the nights progressed and its position in the sky relative to the others was changing.

Its shape was different; it had a fuzzy, elongated appearance. The Solar wind, increasingly intense as the distance closed, was heating the frozen methane and ammonia forming the gaseous coma and tail so distinctive to comets. The luminous head and vapor trail were about as near to nothing as they could be and still be something, containing less than a gram of material to the cubic mile.

As weeks passed, the object grew in brightness and size eventually rivaling the Full Moon. Crossing the orbit of Earth, it could be easily seen in daylight. Continuing on its journey, the leading edge began to warm further, the growing coma expanding to the size of a planet, gas torn from the glowing head forming the transparent streamer extending to the enormous length of tens of millions of miles and becoming intensely luminous as sunlight reflected off it.

Had any being of even the most remedial intelligence been in existence to witness this spectacle it would have terrorized them. As things were at that time, it barely rated a passing glance.

And so the wanderer passed the Earth, plunging to an ignominious dissolution in the Sun, too early to be appreciated, leaving a legacy of life and terror behind for the future masters of the planet, leaving the small chunk of space debris on its fated journey to becoming a hallowed object, both for good and evil, in the history of mankind.

CRETE

Chapter 1

Deus

2958 BCE

Culture on the island of Kriti during the third millennium before Christ was as primitive as any of the time, the inhabitants shepherds, gatherers of any available and edible growing thing, limited skills as hunters and farmers, and peaceable for the most part.

Deus had been a shepherd for the last eight years of his life, since he had been six years old. He had amazed his father at that early age by showing a responsibility that would have shamed any other lad.

Deus had been one of those quiet children, never crying as a baby, a delight to his mother who had previously exhausted herself attending to the demands of her four other children. He had loudly demanded her breast only once when, in sickness, she had been so weary from her duties of the day that she had not awakened until hours past his due feeding time. Not that she had any concept of that sort of time-keeping. When she had realized that the baby had hungered for hours, yet had not complained as any normal child would, she held him close and cried, thanking the gods for this blessing, vowing never to see this special one need again. His innate curiosity had become the object of conversation among members of his family and all who visited. When he wasn't being held in his mother's arms, or riding comfortably on her back, he would be busily enjoying the antics of an insect, or the caprice of birds circling and diving. Once his mother watched him, enthralled by the bees flying in and out of the blossoms of a fire-flower bush, sitting on the green grass of the spring pasture ever so still, intensely absorbed, never the slightest danger of a bee considering him a threat. She had thought of moving him away to a safer distance but after a while grinned with amusement as it dawned on her that she was watching him with the same unwavering interest as he was lavishing on the bees.

Forever after he would be her "Little Bee".

* * *

The attractive woman watched in comfort from the doorway of the small hut, her young boy clamping her leg, as her husband returned from the countryside with their three other sons.

The flock of sheep in tow, the pregnant ewes were bleating in protest at the walk. Tomorrow they would take pasture to the flatter land eastward where the grass was longer. The ewes would be delivering soon, and they would need easy refection while they were expressing milk. Zeus had learned from his father that the more food available to sheep just prior to birth the healthier the lambs seemed to be, and the more milk produced by the mothers. Milk to the point of excess, milk for his family, milk for curd, and for cheese. Zeus loved cheese, the soft, white, pungent food that his wife made from the curds of the ewe's milk.

Sometimes he could trade his sheep's milk with a neighbor for some goat's milk. He loved the goat cheese his wife would make even more. He had to get some goats, agrimi, with the tough bodies and massive curling horns. But he knew that there was more gain in sheep. And no one but the poorest man would sacrifice a goat. The best trades could only be made for a clean white lamb at the Time of Offering, or a fat yearling during other seasons of the year.

Goats were a nuisance too. A goat he had owned six years ago when Deus was born got into the house and ate a wooden prize that his own father had given him as a youth, a small carving of the fertility goddess which would guarantee him an abundance of strong sons. The omen of the destruction of the idol was so incisive that he slaughtered the creature on the spot, violently dismembering the beast in a rage and swinging its entrails around the inside of the then one room stone hut. His wife hadn't minded the smell, she was used to the stench of a new-gutted animal, but this killing was in the dead heat of summer, and the blood and slime had attracted every fly on the island of Kriti to torment her in her home. It had soaked into the dirt floor and the mud grouting the cracks between the rocks in the wall. There was no way to get rid of it all; it would have to go through the process of thorough decomposition. In the meantime, the family would have to sleep outside. Her man and boys had no trouble with that, they were gone often with the sheep and had become quite accustomed to sleeping under the sky. But it was unusual for her, and she felt exposed, especially with her new baby.

She liked the comfort of the walls around her as she slept. Even during the day she rarely strayed far. Something about the hut called to her, a warmth, a friendliness that had become part of her. Her home was her only possession, if a woman could ever have a possession. Her husband built it, but his heart wasn't in it, and so she seemed to have acquired it by default.

4

For all he cared, it could be filled with badgers. He only stopped by as a central working point, a place to get a meal cooked better than he could manage in the field, a place for the release of his passions. It could hardly be called lovemaking as he had little love for his wife. She was a means to an end, the production of sons, arranged by their respective parents.

Shortly after the birth of Deus Selene asked her husband if he might find the time to build an extra room onto the house. The disaster involving the goat and the idol had slipped his mind, and it would be long before he thought that he would never indeed have another child. He resisted building at first, claiming that his duties in the field took up all of his time. Selene knew better than to press the issue. She had used more subtle methods in the past to get her way and would again. The room eventually came.

Time arrived for the annual sacrifice to the God of Nature and Zeus selected one of the finer lambs of his flock.

He had traded half of the others for what he considered a good profit at the village market and was in good spirits. One of his many trades was for a skin of fine wine, not the best he could have obtained, but it would have the desired effect. He would even share it this year with his family to show the God of Nature that he was above the animals, who typically fought for their own survival only and displayed greed rivaling the most base man.

Selene's part in the ritual was to prepare the lamb. She had used water with sand to scrub it clean, working hardest on the long tail, which was already caked with hardened feces, even at its early age. The lamb hunched its shoulders in pleasure, squirming as parasites that had plagued it since shortly after birth were cleansed from its skin and its itches were relieved. Afterward, she rinsed it in clean water, rubbing with her hands to remove any grit. The lamb gleamed white and was still as she presented it to her husband.

She stood in the circle with her sons as her husband took the leading role in performing the sacrifice, giving thanks repeatedly for the abundance of food, the favorable weather, the lush surroundings, and the privilege of having four healthy sons when others he knew had only daughters. He called for compassion to be on those unfortunate men and asked that they be shown the errors of their ways so that they also might be blessed with sons.

Having displayed his benevolence, he also asked for the blessing of good health to be with his family, especially his wife, who he hoped would be able to give him more children of the right and proper gender.

Now that the form of the sacrifice had been dispensed with it was time for the function, the killing of the lamb.

Zeus wasn't fanatical about religious rites, but he practiced them and taught them to his family as his father had taught him, just to be on the safe side. One couldn't be too careful. The land was fairly peaceful, but he had heard of occasions where unexpected raids had occurred and of the resulting casualties. He'd heard of people in the village found dead in the morning, claimed in the night by spirits, and others who suffered slowly before death.

He truly considered himself blessed. His flocks had always been healthy, not suffering the plagues that often afflicted the shepherds in the more populated areas closer to the village. He wanted things to stay the same, and sacrifice was his way of establishing that very stability that he sought.

He held his obsidian knife high in the air, gripping the well-worn olivewood handle tightly in his right hand while holding the bleating lamb by the scruff in his left at waist height. In one swift stroke, he brought the double-edged knife up and across its throat at the same time as he pushed the animal away from him, almost decapitating it.

Blood squirted out of the carotid arteries, straight up and then landing on the hand and arm of its executioner. He dropped the knife on the grass, reaching down with his free hand and grasping a still kicking hind leg as the air gurgled out of the severed trachea and flipped the lamb over. He held it at the height he had held the knife, allowing the blood to drain out in front of him over the dangling head. When he was sure it was dead he lay the animal on the flat rock he had been standing on and, picking up the knife, detached the head completely.

With another surgical stroke, he eviscerated the abdomen from pubic bone to sternum. There he had to make sawing cuts to separate the ribs on the right side from the breastbone. He rolled the carcass onto its front giving it a shake as he lifted the body by the wool on its back. The viscera spilled out as a reeking stench filled the air. He severed the few ligaments attaching the organs and made a final cut through the colon as they came completely free. With his bloodied hands he centered the wet entrails into a neat mound on the rock, the head resting on top.

Beside the glistening mass, he began skinning the hide from the lamb, incising the inner aspect of each leg and circumscribing above the hoofs before stripping the pelt.

He thought momentarily of the many uses his wife could make of it when he was finished but caught himself quickly as he remembered the words of his father telling him that one must be wholly focused on worship at the sacrifice. As much as he tried, he could not get as absorbed as his father. This worried him immensely as he thought of the ill fortunes that could befall him.

He furrowed his brow and stared into the widening pocket he was now creating at the torso of the lamb with the light scraping cuts of the razor-sharp obsidian. As he peeled back the skin, slowly and with purpose, he spoke thanks once again to the God of Nature for the great plenty in his family's life. He gave one final tug as the skin came free from the bones of the long tail. He rolled it up and lay it on the rock. His oldest son would stretch it on the rack at the ceremony close. On a day like this, it would be dry before evening.

He held the moist carcass in his outstretched hands and stood, turning slowly as he exhibited the offering. His family smiled and nodded in approval.

They had many sheep, more than most of the families in the area. But they, like the others, rarely used the beasts for food. Only during sacrifices, where the animals were killed anyway, did they resort to that.

So it had been for thousands of years among the wiser peoples. Certainly men had discovered the delicious taste of sheep and the warmth of the whole skins long before they found a use for wool alone, but when they began to fashion more comfortable garments to protect themselves from the cold and found that they could repeatedly use the same animal to meet their needs, they learned that sheep were worth more alive than dead.

Older animals that were beyond use for breeding were traded in the village. The injured, the rare ones that may have broken a leg, the ones that had been mauled by predators, would be skinned and eaten. Mixed emotion followed these occasions, the regrets of losing a valued animal alloyed with the pleasure of eating meat that may not have been had for months.

The boys had gathered sticks for the fire. A smoldering flame was maintained in a small clay stove in the hut, the purpose not for cooking but rather to preserve the flame. Fire could be exasperatingly challenging to make by rubbing sticks, although the people were remarkably adept at it when they had to. It was so much easier just to keep a small fire going at all times.

Selene managed the fire, spending a portion of each day gathering bits of wood. The boys had been trained from the earliest age to bring sticks home to throw on the woodpile. This morning they had made a special effort for the occasion and had gathered all of the wood just prior to the ritual. Only freshly gathered could be used. A few thicker pieces had been added to the oven inside, mostly filling the small compartment, and quickly becoming hot coals.

Now it was time for the burning. The members of the circle went into the hut, breathing slowly so the smoke wouldn't bother their lungs. Selene had long since become immune to the acrid atmosphere, and her oldest now was hardly even aware of it. His younger brothers developed watery eyes but wouldn't think to complain.

Selene lay a hardened skin, scraped clean of wool, in front of the oven opening, the red glow from within warming her hands. She reached for the stick she kept beside the stove, blackened and burnt to a point with years of use, the other end worn smooth from much handling. She had stared for hours into the embers when at a loss for something to pass the time, rubbing and turning the stick all the while.

She deftly poked and pulled a combination of small and large embers onto the skin, leaving an adequate number inside the oven and quickly adding another piece of wood. She had a small pile of leaves drying inside and dropped a double handful on top to keep in the heat. Her oldest son took one side of the skin, Selene taking the other, and they gave it one fold, allowing the heavy center portion to drop earthward as they stood up. The oldest son leading the way they took the fire to Zeus who was quietly contemplating the viscera on the flat rock.

He had, while the others had been inside, placed sticks around the organs, pushing some under, some through, making a teepee of kindling. The fire was set beside him on the windward side, the skin unfolded. He pushed the fire, using the leaves to protect his hands, against the side of his pyre, holding the skin up with his left hand for his wife to take.

He covered the embers and now fiercely smoking leaves with a large number of small sticks and bent down low beside them. He blew gently, then harder, increasing the strength of his expirations. Flame burst forth, engulfing the smoking leaves in an instant. The sticks also caught, the smaller ones reddening and twisting, crackling with the heat, a few exploding in a minor way, throwing hot sparks. He brushed one off his arm where it had singed his hair, the smell causing him to curl his nose at the reminder of an incident when he was just a boy.

He was piling the wood on now, it was bone dry and caught quickly, wrapping around the pile with the help of the west wind. They could smell the wool burning off the head of the lamb, then the first scorching of the innards. After that, it didn't smell much different from meat cooking. Occasionally the intestines would heat up at an exposed point and swell, forcing excreta out the end, sometimes bursting through hardened cracks as the kinks refused to yield to the pressure. The stench would be brief as the gasses fed the flame.

He placed larger pieces around the pyre, pieces almost as big around as his leg. Then he heaped more wood on top. The fire would burn for hours now, entirely consuming the scrap parts of the animal below. If it hadn't been a sacrifice, he would have saved some of the organs. He was rather partial to the kidneys, and the heart and liver were nice. He hadn't understood exactly why these were seemingly wasted, he had never asked his father, but that was just the way things were done. He hadn't given it much thought, and it wasn't even worth mentioning. He'd forgotten about it again almost in the same heartbeat.

The fire didn't take long to settle down into a high bed of coals, the offering within filling the air with a tantalizing aroma of cooking meat. The onlookers, and that's all they were, no one spoke, felt their stomachs churn in anticipation of the evening meal. They would fast until then.

Zeus now instructed his boys to place the forked branches on either side of the rock. They dug into the hard soil about a foot, setting the straight ends in and stabilizing them upright with heavy rocks and dirt. The forks were at about waist height.

Zeus pushed a sharpened branch, as long as he was tall, through the anus of the lamb and out its headless neck, centering it and suspending it on the forks. With a strip of soaked rawhide, he tied the hind legs firmly back to the spit, then did the same to the front legs, tying them hard forward. Two more wrapped the flank and chest tight, binding the stretched body firmly to the spit. With the lamb now attached and balanced he could give it a bit of a turn every so often. By the time it was fully cooked the organs below would be incinerated and his family would be ravenous.

* * *

Selene knew that Zeus would never allow his son to have anything of decent quality. His clothes were the outgrown castoffs of his older brothers, and she was forbidden to make anything new for him.

"Why should the youngest have the new? My oldest brother got what my father did no longer need, and when it was not longer suitable for him, then I took my turn at it. Can you say that my father was wrong?"

How could she answer such a question? To disagree meant a beating. Yet he was right to a point. The clothing was not exactly falling apart. Wool garments could remain wearable for decades, if one was not too proud of one's appearance, or smell. But the old ones were quite musky after a rain, and did not keep the wearer as warm. And she was developing a nagging worry that her son might get sick from the damp and cold.

* * *

Deus's father did not have much affection for his youngest son. He had begun to feel that the boy might be some kind of curse, but he wasn't sure. It was just a consideration that had picked away at him lately as he wondered why he was no longer being blessed with more children, even a girl. He had been doing so well with his sons, three strapping young men of great use to him, and Deus.

The boy was smaller than the others had been at the same age, less strong, yet he was already more trustworthy. Zeus had seen that he would always follow through with whatever he had promised and, although he was still too young to do a perfect job of anything difficult, for a boy of his age he enthusiastically put his full effort into it.

Zeus had called him "the dependable one" when the others had chosen to elude their responsibilities one day. His mother hugged him, feeling proud that he had received for the first time the recognition he deserved.

9

The insult to his older brothers did not pass unnoticed, which was just as Zeus had intended. He had hoped that they would feel shamed that a younger boy would take on responsibilities and do a better job than they. To further salt their wounds, he thought he might give Deus the chance to prove himself in the field. He didn't really think too much of his youngest, being thin and weak, but this was an opportunity to teach a lesson. He announced that Deus was to have his own small flock to manage. He could take twenty sheep of his choosing to pasture and have full control over them. The risk wasn't significant as they would only be gone a few days this time and wouldn't be going far.

Deus was overwhelmed at the honor. Only his oldest brother had been given the privilege of flock management, and only when he was five years older. Deus was still only seven years old, and although the other boys said nothing their facial expressions spoke volumes.

Deus had observed closely his father at work around the hut, listening intently to anything he had to say about the animals. When time came to choose his sheep, he was prepared beyond any expectations. Zeus had anticipated that his son would pick sheep at random, or the friendlier sheep that children often find themselves getting attached to, but Deus singled out the finest, selecting a combination of the healthiest ewes with long, tight wool of the lightest shade, one fine ram, and a half-dozen lambs that he felt had potential.

Zeus was amazed at his choice. How could a young boy single out the finest of his flock of over two hundred so quickly and with the expertise that a lad of twenty might find difficult?

"May I shepherd these Father?"

He was sorely tempted to disagree with the selection simply for disagreement's sake. The thought also occurred to him that sending a young boy out in the field with some of his finest was not the best idea. On the other hand, if he wanted the admonition of his sons to have full effect then perhaps the harsher the humiliation the better. With the same vacillation, he resolved to allow his son to manage his selection.

Selene looked out at the hills with some trepidation. "I can have his bedroll prepared by the end of the next day, if he could wait that long."

Zeus had not caught the implication of the suggestion, still wondering at himself for the decision that he had made, and had merely agreed.

She had achieved what she had wanted for her boy for years, and knew that her husband could not go back on his word, although she would likely have to suffer some abuse. She knew that there would be jealousy from the other boys as well, but none of them had ever shown her the affection Deus had and he deserved something in return.

She would make him a blanket. Her husband would be leaving in the early morning with the majority of the flock and her two middle sons. Her oldest would be leaving at the same time, perhaps staying with them for a short while before breaking off to his own pasture.

She would only have to put up with her husband's advances for one more night. She had previously decided that she would convince him that she was unclean and would exile herself to sleeping outside, but with the change in circumstances today it might be wiser to accept his lust.

The sheep had been getting a bit ragged, loose clumps clinging to their sides entangled with the summer coat now replacing it. The flock would have to be plucked soon, probably on their next return. Today she pulled the loosest wool from their sides, gathering the clumps into her apron and pressing it firmly, compacting it. None of the others paid her much mind. The job had to be done sooner or later.

Her movements had to be steady; she was not as familiar to the sheep as the males of her family. Spooking them would send them on a run, maybe scattering them, and she did not want to have to deal with an angry husband at this time.

As her apron filled and could hold no more, she took the load into the hut where the rest of her family would not notice it as readily. This she did several times, plucking the wool quickly with one nervous eye on the others to make sure they weren't looking, slipping into the hut with her loads only when their attentions were elsewhere. If she noticed that one was glancing her way she would slow to a dawdling pace, humming louder, giving the impression that she was only occupying time for boredom's sake. The heap inside grew, the job taking only an hour as she moved through the mass of the flock. With her last apron-load, her twelfth, she felt she had enough.

Her family was fast asleep now in the warm sun, the cool ocean breeze keeping them from overheating. She sorted through the mass inside, picking out the numerous pieces of grass and thistle entangled in the wool. She worked as quickly as she could, hoping to get her project finished before they woke.

She lay an ancient blanket on the floor, her oldest. Swatting the pile of wool repeatedly she scattered it over the square, then picked the smaller fluffs from the perimeter, tossing them to the center. The rougher spots had to be smoothed out, the layer becoming level as she flicked her hands back and forth, knocking the tops of the piles around, poking them into crevasses, skillfully creating an equally dense covering.

When she judged it to be just right, she went over the developing blanket again, moving her fingers randomly, twisting the fluffs, mingling them with their neighbors, incorporating each one slightly into the other.

She had a skin of water inside, enough to dampen the white carpet but little else, sprinkling it evenly from the sides. She felt her bowels rumble a bit as she went through the motions of this clandestine activity. At the same time,

11

her anticipation of her son's happiness with his surprise was making her head feel light.

She made the short walk to the open pit that was their well several times, stirring the water in her rush and making the last skin-full dark with silt. It was enough to finish the job, and some dirt wouldn't make any difference. The wool and the old felt beneath were now well soaked.

She brought in the cooking pole, the spit for roasting animals, straight and just long enough. Starting with the edge closest to the door she began the roll, moving back and forth as she evenly wheeled the poll along, ensuring that the wool was being compacted evenly. She stopped at one point half-way along, jamming a rock under the backside of the enlarging bundle to keep it from unrolling, and poured a little more water onto an area she thought still too dry.

When she was finished she lay out a large bare sheepskin devoid of wool, several skins laced together, and rolled the bundle onto it, wrapping the whole bundle tightly and working it back into the center of the small hut. She then tied it in eight places with rawhide thongs, pulling hard on the knots, squishing the water to the areas less compacted.

Selene was no stranger to arduous tasks, but this was exhausting. She sat on the floor a moment and contemplated what to do next. She had to beat the roll with a large stick. Usually this was a family affair, everyone pounding as long as they could for hours at a time before the felt was ready. A large adult sized felt could take days.

How was she going to do this in time for her son to go out on his first pasture without making noise enough to alert her husband? She couldn't lie and say it was for him. It was far too small. Now what was she to do? She couldn't really start working it until they left in the morning. Even then she doubted if it could be done in time for her son to leave in the evening.

Something of a panic attack hit her. Her arms started to feel as if they were humming inside. Her thoughts became scattered and she had to move her bowels.

The only thing to do was to hide the bundle under a pile of bedding. The afternoon sun wouldn't keep the others asleep much longer and, with that thought, she began to work the heavy roll over to the back wall of the hut.

A floor shadow caught her eye, a dark silhouette framed by the bright sun pouring in through the door opening. She was unable to move, unable to even acknowledge for a moment that it was there or what it was.

She had been caught. The shadow was moving forward toward her. She braced herself for a blow as the sound of the leg movements picked up their pace.

She felt an impact on her leg.

She had prepared for a bolt of pain, but it didn't come. She looked down toward the squeezing sensation and noticed a couple of small arms reaching around to the front, clasped together in a bear hug.

"What are you doing Mother?"

She squatted on the floor, taking in a deep breath of relief. "I'm making you a present my Little Bee. You won't have to feel cold on your nights with the sheep." She spoke in hushed tones. "You must not say anything to the others yet. They do not know about it. Do you promise?"

"Yes, Mother." They each gazed into the eyes of the other. Deus wasn't so sure about going off on his own. He had a spirit of adventure in him that said it was time, but he would have been quite comfortable home with his mother. She was everything to him.

Yet a longing to do something else other than play around the hut had been enticing him to leave. Not for a long time, maybe just a few days, then he would be back. He had explored the area immediately around to death. He knew if a rock had been moved, if the anthill had grown. He wanted to know what else was out there.

He wanted to see the fierce beasts of the imagination that his father had told him about, teased him about. He wouldn't get too close. He wasn't entirely sure if there even were such things. They had never come near the hut.

And why would his oldest brother make those sly faces, showing the whites of his eyes when he thought he wasn't being watched? Deus had fabulous sight and peripheral vision and didn't miss much of what the others around him were doing. He had discovered that if he could observe without being seen to observe, it was more likely that the other person would continue to do whatever it was that they were doing. If he looked straight at them they would often stop, or change their facial expressions, sometimes to a more friendlier look to please him, sometimes, in the case of his brothers, to an irritated look that told him he wasn't to bother them. He didn't know why this was so, but he preferred to know what people were really thinking. He couldn't rely on honesty when looking straight at them and so chose the other course at times. He was well aware that the others didn't know that he did this.

The others didn't know much.

His mother knew about keeping the area around the home in order, and how to prepare good food, but when he asked her questions about his father and shepherding she only replied that she had no need to know of those things, they weren't for her, she was too busy tending to other things.

That made no sense, although he wouldn't criticize anyone for their opinions.

He asked his father about the stars, the Moon, why it was so hot and then so cold, the red of the sunrise, a hundred other things. Zeus didn't know. He made up stories on the spot or told Deus not to ask so many questions.

His brothers were fools. He tried to understand them and failed. They ran around roughhousing all day until they were exhausted and then went to sleep. They had absolutely no interest in anything except their own enjoyment. Learning was a foreign concept. Deus had tried to show them how the ant's nest had grown, and they kicked it apart while he cried. In a rage, he grabbed the youngest of his three brothers and tried to pull him away. The others pulled them apart and gleefully tossed Deus into the broken mass of rich soil and seething ants. They bit his legs as he wailed, more with indignation than pain, jumping away from the pile only to be pushed down onto it again and again. His brothers howled with laughter, taunting him and calling him the "Nature Boy".

As they tormented him, he could see the approach of his father, walking up the hill toward them, with no greater alacrity than if he was going for an afternoon stroll. Appearing unthreatening, the others kept up their mischief, the oldest giving him one final push into the mass but not knocking him down this time.

He sprung out as the bodies of his brothers, a yelp from each issuing forth, crashed down onto the pile.

"You should not have let this happen." Zeus's voice was calm as he addressed the oldest.

As Heltos thrashed about in the ant's nest, kicking up a small cloud of dust in his surprise, Zeus turned quietly and left.

Deus's face was smeared with mud from the dust and tears. He looked sadly at the flattened nest, ants still fanning out in every direction to defend their territory. He had lost, his halfhearted savior doing little to console him. Without a glance at his brothers he followed his father, knowing now that they hated him and not understanding why.

Heltos finished dancing about, flicking and smacking the last of the clinging ants from his body. "I'll get that little field rat, that nature boy." He spat, thinking that he would also kill his father, resolving to do it one day.

* * *

Deus's mother held him tighter. They were sitting on the wet roll, which was now well covered. She clapped him on the shoulder, rising and walking outside. Deus followed her out, noticing that his three brothers were now awake and sitting in a circle a little way off.

Heltos looked at him, scowling, muttering to his siblings. Deus was amazed, and hurt. He couldn't hear that far yet knew what his brother was

14

saying. He could read the older boy's lips. He was calling Deus a "Mother's baby." Why did he hate him so much?

He followed after his mother, keeping the distance between them a little greater than before, not consciously caring what his brothers thought.

No one spoke that night. Dinner was prepared and eaten in silence. There was nothing unusual about this, it was more common than not. They looked down at the food resting on the hard skin as they sat in a circle around it, taking handfuls and filling their mouths. Deus finished first, having the lightest appetite, and was off to view a brightly patterned butterfly perched on a scrub brush in the distance. Zeus didn't notice his departure. He was deep in thought about tomorrow. He would leave early he decided. It would take all day and part of the next to drive the sheep to the rich grasslands he had in mind. And he was having second thoughts about Deus taking the small flock.

Why had he made such a rash decision? How could he have foreseen that Deus would take his finest? He was considering for the hundredth time recanting the agreement. He would have if he hadn't thought that the others would think him fallible for doing so. If only he could come up with some face-saving way to do it.

His full stomach was making him tired. Slipping his backside down off the log and onto the dry grass he stretched himself out full length, his head resting on what was now his pillow, his stertorous breaths amplifying as the sun sank red below the horizon.

* * *

Selene woke at daybreak, the faint glow of early dawn softly lighting the sky, chasing darkness back to the netherworld. The hut door faced east allowing the first trickles of light in through the opening, striking the place where she laid her bed, waking her before any others that slept inside.

Her husband had not come into her that night. She thought she caught the faint aroma of wine before dinner the night before, but she didn't get close enough to be sure. He was steady on his feet so he couldn't have had much. He must have had a skin hidden somewhere over the hill. He had gone for a walk earlier. No matter. It had kept him sleeping through the night.

She looked around the room. Only Deus was present, breathing gently on top of the pile concealing his present. She could get busy on that soon.

Inhaling the warm air she rose, the susurration of her clothes and bedding waking her son. She wagged her head with a smile as she caught his eyes opening. He would lie in his bed but never seemed happy to sleep unless she was also in bed. It made her wonder how he would make out on his new task of shepherding.

She stepped outside and saw Heltos in the distance minding the flocks. His back was facing the homestead, and she could see his buttocks wiggling as he ground against the back of a ewe. At least it looked like a ewe from this distance. What a disgusting creature she had given life to. She wondered, if he had known, whether he would even care that she was watching. In a moment he was done, and lay down amidst the sheep, quite out of sight. It was only a mild curiosity to him, as he dozed off, that the sheep had left him with another small sore, a tiny abrasion really. He wondered if it might develop into another chancre. They didn't hurt, but they were itchy enough to be annoying. He could not see the spirochete Treponema pallidum boring microscopically into the flesh beneath the thin skin of his penis. He curled comfortably with his hands in his armpits, feeling a swelling lymph node that was waging an unseen internal battle against an invisible organism, syphilis.

The others were stirring from their bedding. The boys were becoming most comfortable out of doors, only coming in, lately, when the nights were cold.

Her husband was still propped against his log, pulling his thick beard and jutting out his yellow teeth as he smacked his lips and stuck his tongue out of a wide mouth. He scratched through his matted black hair with both hands, pulling them down his face, rubbing vigorously as he grunted and strained. By the time he was finished his morning noises, he had fully wakened the two boys.

Deus joined them as they broke fast in silence, hoping that his father would not recant his promise. Zeus had obviously been reflecting once again on his offer. "You will choose the flock once more. If they differ from the first, then you are still too young."

So there it was. The sheep had intermingled with the others, and he would have no help in separating out the ones he had selected. As they walked up to the grazing area, he felt some trepidation as he peered through the masses looking for them. He wanted desperately to prove himself. He knew that his father knew each intimately and would also recall exactly. Self-doubt was rising within him. His brothers had smirked at the challenge, well aware that it was too arduous.

Deus roamed the shifting body, easily guiding the ram, the lambs, and the first dozen ewes to an area separate from the others. But the difficult part was pending as the finest sheep departed, leaving the better of the mediocre. Many were almost identical. One by one he made his hesitant decision, trying partly to remember his past selection, trying partly to choose once again the better animal, hoping it would turn out to be the same.

He took several minutes to find the last, knowing that the nineteen previous must have been right or his father would have checked the procedure.

At last he made his pick, moving slowly with it, only easing it along as he kept watch with his side vision, prepared to nonchalantly let go of his beast

16

in favor of another should his father's facial expression betray that he had chosen wrong. That look never came, and Deus was forced to walk the ewe to the smaller group without indication.

Zeus came up to him, his reluctant face cracking into a slim smile. "Well done, boy."

Deus was overjoyed, his insides churning with happiness carefully concealed so as not to raise the wrath of the brothers who had been rooting for his failure.

Zeus charged his boy with attending to the every need of his flock, protecting it from predators, both man and beast, tending the sick and injured, guiding it to the finer pasture, and returning home in three days with the flock in better condition than that in which it left.

With that, the four left, Deus scrambling around trying to block his company from following, clapping his hands to divert the more determined ram.

Rounding the crest of the hill Zeus looked back on the home scene, Selene nowhere in view, his youngest moving the herd closer to the home in what he had to admit was a good formation. The ram only stopped following the boy once, to lap from the urine stream of a ewe in estrus.

As he stood there for a moment, taking in the scene, he wondered at himself. First, he rashly allows a lad of six to take charge of his finest sheep and, then, when the boy chooses a wrong ewe on the last of his second selection, says nothing.

* * *

Selene, secure now that the others had departed, without so much as a word to her, began to uncover her roll. The wet smell of fleece filled the room, instantly raising the humidity, creating a muggy sensation on her skin as she struggled to move it across the floor. She rolled it back and forth, each time changing the angle to get it closer to the door. When the pole was protruding outside, she was stuck. The bundle was too heavy to drag sideways, and the pole was too long to lift up and tip out the door.

Deus, with his flock, moved into the area surrounding the hut. His mother was looking slightly embarrassed as she stood in the door, helpless with the sodden mass that was to become his blanket.

"If you help, perhaps we can get this outside."

They both knew that the sheep weren't going anywhere now. Deus had established himself as their leader, and they would not stray far.

The two pulled and pushed respectively, turning, rolling, changing the angle, both wishing they were stronger, giving up sweaty with exhaustion with the bundle halfway out the door. Deus sat down in the dirt, his arms heavy, a stitch developing in his side.

"We should make the sheep pull this out."

Selene laughed. "My little one. Now my big one. Old enough to have his own flock but still too young to help his old mother move a bundle of wool out the door. Come on. We will do it."

She felt silly again. She could have easily done the job of pounding inside the hut but merely wanted to move it outside for the fresh air and so she could see and enjoy her surroundings. But now that it was halfway out there was no point trying to bring it back in.

Putting their backs into it, they gave everything they had, rolling it back and forth violently now, bouncing it off the door frame, twisting it about as it finally came free from the confines of the four walls.

They both collapsed against the outside wall, complaining that they had never strained themselves so hard. Selene had to get going on her project if Deus was to leave later in the day. She doubted if even that would give her enough time. In fact, she knew it was impossible. Even with another woman helping the roll couldn't be beaten into felt before sundown.

Maybe Deus could stay nearby until tomorrow. Her husband would surely never find out. But what if he did? Maybe she could find her boy tomorrow at pasture; carry his blanket to him. He would be cold, but he could survive one night without too much hardship.

She sat at the bundle, facing the morning with her dark, sunburned skin. With her arms still weighty from their previous efforts she began to drum on the roll with two fat sticks. Deus picked up two others, smaller ones, and did the same. He kept his eye on the sheep, prepared to leave his mother should one make any move at straying. For now, they were behaving. Not even the ram was getting any ideas, but the vegetation around the hut was sparse and he wondered when they would be wanting to go off on a forage.

They sat in silence, soft thudding the only sound aside from an occasional bleating. Deus's arms were so sore he thought they might fall off. There had to be a better way. He lay the sticks down, not able to continue. His mother carried on with her rhythmic drumming, smiling at his efforts and knowing them to be too onerous for a youngster.

"Mother, there must be another way to do this."

She laughed out loud. "Perhaps we could get the sheep to do everything around here."

Deus stood, stretching, windmilling his arms for relief. Contemplating the situation he thought that perhaps the sheep could indeed be used for something.

He ducked into the hut and came out with the collection of rope and leather thongs that the family had gathered over the years. The rope had always fascinated him, the small weaves forming its length. Who could tie knots so small? One day he would meet the person in the village who made such miracles.

"Mother? Why don't we tie the roll to the sheep? They could pull it over the bumpy ground. That would be as good as us pounding on it."

She continued beating. "And what would happen to the wool my Little Bee? It would be pulled apart on the sharp rocks."

He hadn't thought of that. His mother was so smart. "Maybe if we wrap it in skins it will be saved."

Selene lay her sticks down, stretching her arms back in turn. She considered the roll and how long this was taking. She had never heard of anyone doing what her son had proposed but, no matter how she tried, she could not find fault with his idea. Struggling with this new concept, she sat with furrowed brow until she realized that time was wasting.

In an instant she was inside the hut and out again with four skins, the wool scraped off. She untied the thongs binding up the bundle and wrapped the skins around the wool roll, Deus holding them in place and giving the finger of assistance as she worked her way up the length of it and retied each knot.

She tied a fat thong loosely around each hub of the pole and tied the rope to the thong on each side, leaving the rope to balloon out in a broad arc on the ground.

"Now, my Little Bee, we have to harness your sheep to this rope." She was thoughtful but determined. "If we tie it around their necks, they will choke. If we tie it around their legs, they will trip."

She went over to the ram and guided him toward the hut. He came without protesting, a few of the ewes tagging along. With the curiosity of children they had wondered at the proceedings of the morning and had stayed close, not wanting to miss anything.

Selene tied the thong around the ram's middle, snug but not tight, hoping it would hold. He jumped a bit as it was being bound, fidgeting as he was being led into position. Using the loose ends of the thong, she tied the rope at the midpoint, the knot over the animal's back.

"I think it will come off, Mother."

She could see that that would be so. "Perhaps another thong around the front."

She tied another length from the side, around the front of the ram below his neck, and back to the other side.

"This should work." She gave it a push until the slack was taken up.

The ram stopped when it encountered the resistance of the heavy load. She slapped its rear end, and the beast danced about wildly, going nowhere.

"Let's help it, Mother."

The two of them strained along with the ram as the roll began to move forward, slowly at first, picking up speed as they pulled. The rocks slowed them a bit, then stopped them entirely as they hit a larger one.

"We need more help with this. Get the two largest ewes."

They fastened one on each side of the ram in the same fashion and tried again. The going was easier this time, not fast, but at least the rocks didn't stop them. Selene and Deus pulled alongside of the sheep, guiding them through the least rocky areas, areas which were still rocky enough in this rough landscape.

After a few minutes the sheep began to protest, and the mother-son team was getting tired.

"Perhaps a couple more, Mother?"

"I think you have good ideas, my son," she puffed, a trickle of sweat rolling down her temple.

They fastened a sheep to each side of the three already tethered, for a team of five. With Selene on one side guiding and pulling on the rope and Deus on the other side, contributing only a fraction to the forward motion but helping keep the team in order, they managed to move forward with reasonable velocity. They had enough momentum now to bounce over any sizable rock without straining much at all.

This new process of felting continued through the morning, the roll of wool turning and bumping along the ground, the rocks of various size hammering random sections.

Wool fibers have to be bent over twenty thousand times before they break, making it one of the most resilient materials. Even the silk which would one day be produced in the east would have fibers which could stand no more than eighteen hundred bends, and later rayon could stand no more than seventy-five. Wool was far superior to them all.

The wool was being tightly compacted as it rolled, the lubricating water allowing the contorting strands to intertwine, the rough ground bouncing and pummeling the package, crimping the resilient elastic threads into an irreversible mesh.

Unlike other fibers wool is covered with minute scales giving their surface, under extreme magnification, the shingled appearance of pinecones. When the fibers rub together they pull themselves into inseparable tangles, working themselves along like the scales of a snake pulling the serpent forward across a rough surface.

The sun rose to its greatest height in the noon sky, staring down on the unusual contingent unable to continue. They sat down to rest, hugging onto the sheep who also quickly stole the chance to drop to their bellies.

After resting for a short time and catching their breath, they freed the animals. Two of the ewes had gone to sleep and were not even aware of their release. The ram was up and back to the main body of the flock as quickly as his sore legs could carry him with the other two ewes slowly traipsing after.

"Well, my Little Bee, you have earned your name today. Have some water while I untie this roll."

As Deus drank heavily from the skin, his mother struggled with the knots. The continual pounding had yanked them so taught that they were impossibly bound. Giving up in exasperation she cut the leather strips with a sharp flint. She was loath to do that as they had little to waste. The cords had to be peeled off the bundle, having been beaten completely into the wrap.

She evenly stripped off the skins, hoping fretfully that the scheme had worked and the morning's efforts had not been in vain. She saw no reason why their method would not work, but doubt filled her mind simply because she had never heard of such a thing being done before.

As the skins parted from the wool inside they could see that the appearance was identical to that of the hand pounded articles she had made before. All that remained was to unroll it. Would it separate into layers as it should?

She found the leading edge, after some difficulty, as it had been tapered and serrated with the pounding, and slowly picked away at it, working her way along its length. When enough was separated, the rest was easy to pull away. The wool sheet was still damp but not saturated as before, most of the water having been pressed out during the measure of abuse to which it had been subjected.

They lay it flat on the ground, the squarish blanket fully exposed to the sun.

"It is a good felt, Mother." He was very pleased.

"It is, my son. The gods have bestowed upon you genius that not many are blessed with. You will have this wisdom with you always. I can see you as a great man one day. Maybe a leader in the village. Now I need to trim the edges of the felt. They are too thin and rough. Bring us some cakes while I do that."

She set to work on the edges, her sharp flint slicing down from the top, a flat piece of wood split from a wide branch underneath. She worked this arrangement along the four sides, trimming waste away to save for another project.

She then brought out a large bone needle Zeus had found for her in the village. He could be so kind to her at times. She often wondered what other treasures might be there. He had never taken her to the village, but he often spoke of it on his return from trading, as her father before him had done.

She hand spun her own wool thread, twirling it in her fingers as the spinning bobbin whirled at the end of its length, as her mother had taught her so long ago, as her mother had been taught by her mother, all through the generations. She threaded the needle and set to work on the edges of the blanket, doubling over a narrow strip and reinforcing it against fraying. Her supply of thread was large. She often sat with wool she had gathered off the ground or off branches, that the sheep had shed, spinning away the day. She found serenity in the simple chores that others would find life's boredom.

Deus, who never napped in the afternoon unless his mother did, was now unable to keep his eyes open. In a moment he was fast asleep. Selene kept her eyes on the sheep. They would stay with the ram, and he wasn't going anywhere. In fact, he was also fast asleep.

The hours passed, and she finished her stitchery. The sun had done its work drying the felt.

Deus was opening his eyes.

"Mother, it is wonderful." He hugged her tightly around the head as she sat and she responded in kind with a big squeeze around his waist.

"Anything for so wonderful a son. We will eat and then it will be time for you to make off to the pastureland."

They ate in silence, as was becoming the customary habit in their family. Deus drove the sheep into formation afterward and with his mother following to the top of the hill bade her farewell.

"Farewell yourself, Little Bee. The gods have never seen the likes of such a small one working like an adult. You will be blessed above any others. I know it."

And so he went, swinging his crook at times to make that swishing sound, moving the sheep ahead of him. Selene watched until he disappeared out of sight over the next rise, then returned to her little valley. She hadn't been out of it for ten years and doubted she ever would. She had no real desire to, only a dull curiosity of things on the outside. A certain fear as well. Her husband had told her stories. The realms outside of the sanctity of her home were no place for weak women.

* * *

Deus set foot on the green plateau as the sun set in the west, dropping out of sight beyond the low lying hills. He had covered only a few miles, yet he was farther than he'd ever gone in this direction. Normally he would have begun to feel tired about now, but he had that afternoon nap behind him. This was exciting. He might not sleep at all tonight.

The sheep picked up their pace a bit as they caught the scent of the lush greenery coming into view. Deus sat down on the crest of a small rise looking over his flock with a pride that he would not have been able to describe. He was fully aware of his brothers in the distance, where exactly he could not guess, and the antagonistic feelings they must be having. He was so happy and so sad. Could it be that life was like that? Always an opposite to everything? Always someone to dampen any tidbit of happiness one could find?

The sheep had their fill in short order and were bedding themselves down for the night, congregating in a loose group, each curled up like a snowy ball on the ground. The darkness was falling over them quickly, the stars winking into existence starting with the brightest one near the setting sun. Deus's father told him that it was only there when the Morning Star had gone away. He thought that perhaps the two could not live together.

Deus liked to stay up and watch the stars at times. Some of them made interesting patterns in the sky. His father could see the shapes that they made and Deus could see a few of them, but mostly he could only see scattered white dots. And the Moon. Why was it always changing? He could not see it at all right now. He could never tell what it was going to do next. Sometimes only half of it would appear, sometimes barely any at all. Sometimes he could even see it in the daytime, though it was rather faint against blue sky.

He found a flat spot to unroll his new blanket. More than a blanket. It was thick and stiff now that it was dry, the thickness adding to its comfort against the ground. He could feel an emanating warmth, and it was wide enough to fold in half, the extra width curled overtop of him. He swatted the fold to make a crease so it would stay in place.

He wondered if the rains would come back any time soon. They were rather sporadic this time of year. If it rained now he would be fine, his thick felt would keep him comfortably dry in the worst weather. One of the unusual properties of wool is that it actually gives off heat when it gets wet. As it absorbs moisture from the air, as the dew falls, a single gram of wool will liberate twenty-seven calories of heat. His felt was more wind resistant, warmer, sturdier, and more water resistant than any synthetic knitted product of the future. It is the air trapped between the fibers that gives wool such great insulating qualities for its weight, and it feels warm because so very few fibers touch the skin to conduct heat away. Compared with other fabrics, silk, smooth cotton, and linen feel cool, fleecy blankets tepid. While the surface of wool is resistant to water the core is highly absorbent, the most hydrophilic of all natural fibers, and can absorb as much as thirty percent of its weight without feeling noticeably wet. It also absorbs perspiration so one feels dry and less chilled, and as the fibers swell the felt bulks up and keeps out the wind even better than before. Deus had heard that in times of drought people would leave their fleece outside at night and wring the dew from it in the morning, though he had yet to see it done.

He curled back a triangle from over his face and watched the ever-brightening stars. They were brilliant tonight. The Moon was nowhere to be seen. The Moon scared the fainter stars, the weak ones, but tonight they were out in vast numbers, a thick streak of them right across the center of the sky. He wondered if anyone could count them.

He could count fairly well, better than his two brothers immediately older than him. His mother could count only as high as she had to to manage around the house. She started him counting when he was very young, because he showed an interest, but after that he had to bother his father to teach him the rest.

He was hungry for knowledge and his father recognized that in him, but was always somewhat reluctant to teach him anything that would later be considered scholarly. What need did a young boy have of such knowledge? So his lessons were short and to the point. Deus had to learn almost instantly or not at all. He wished his father would teach him all he knew about everything. He knew it would happen eventually, but why not now? He might not remember it all but he would try, and he would get it right the second time around. How he wished his father would have more patience with him.

He was glad that he was given this assignment though. For that, he was very grateful. Perhaps his father was changing. Perhaps more responsibilities would be given him as time went on. If he did a good job with his little flock he knew things would be better between the two of them. Then his father would teach him everything, not holding back just because he was so young.

The stars were beautiful. He hoped he might see a firebrand tonight. His father said they were lucky signs. At least once a year, for a couple of nights in a row, if he stayed up all night, he would see hundreds of them. He took this as a sign that his riches would increase, that his sheep would always multiply. And that is exactly what had been happening.

* * *

The slowly spinning meteor accelerated toward the Sun, increasing its speed from a relative snail's pace of only a few meters per second at its greatest distance to over twenty-eight kilometers per second as it approached the orbit of the Earth.

Eons the rock had existed as a separate entity, but that was soon to end. Its line of approach was converging with the Earth this time, and it would become part of the fifty tons of meteoric dust material penetrating the atmosphere daily.

The Moon's gravitation caused the slightest deviation in the path of approach necessary to seal the destiny of this celestial rock in history.

* * *

His thoughts turned to his mother. He missed her; he wished she had come with him. He felt lonely. He had never experienced such solitude. At least the sheep were nearby to give him some comfort and company.

To the east the sky above an undulating horizon was beginning to change in hue, becoming brighter, the short ribbon of white contrasting against the absolute black of the earth indicating the rise of the Moon. He could see it rising, the actual motion. The sliver grew wider in both directions, the upper curve revealing as it grew. This was not the first time he had seen its ascension, but it was no less exciting for having seen it before.

In no time it was halfway above the edge of the earth, huge compared to its usual size higher in the sky. Last time he watched this spectacle the Moon was a burnished orange, still fabulous, but not like this.

The earth was pinching in on it now, pressing it into its round shape on the bottom. The flat part seemed to flare wider a little, waving in what must have been a gentle breeze in the distance. The Moon must be something soft to be affected that way. Maybe it was made of a pure white wool. It must be. It was wispy like wool, the darker areas shadows like on a ball prepared and cleaned for spinning yarn.

The Moon was giving its last tug to escape the earth, the wider, flat piece clinging, extending, finally snapping free as it procured its liberty.

* * *

As it entered the accession of the upper atmosphere the meteor's surface temperature rose from a mere five degrees above absolute zero to thousands of degrees. It began to glow red, then quickly white as its outer layers began to vaporize, the white trail behind blazing in intensity in the perfectly clear night sky.

The tail grew in width and brightness visible for hundreds of miles in any direction as the meteor penetrated deeper into the atmosphere. Small chunks began to blow off the leading edge, creating a show of sparks shooting out to the side for any to see who were interested enough in the night sky to observe.

Deus gasped. What is that? The Moon was expulsing a bolt of light, flashing in his direction. It was a firebrand, the most magnificent ever.

The fireball grew as the resistance of the increasingly dense air fought to slow the intruder. The lighter composites in the meteor became superheated far past the point of becoming gas. They formed a plasma under supreme pressure still locked inside their rock and iron prison as the surface temperature soared to over twenty thousand degrees.

At last the extraterrestrial structure could contain those pressures no longer. The bolide ruptured into dozens of fragments now on separate trajectories to their permanent homes scattered throughout the waters of the Mediterranean Sea.

The brilliant flare was coming too close, too fast. He hadn't time to blink as the fat shaft came at him, exploding silently into a multitude of blazing bands. One seemed frozen in the air as the others continued on. Everything was moving in slow motion. His heart stopped, he wasn't breathing, a thousand thoughts tore through his mind as it worked with an exhilarating intensity he never suspected possible.

The still shaft grew wider, almost becoming more than one. What was it? He felt his heart give one mighty thud within his chest as the meteorites struck.

The blast of thunder, the concussion wave, almost knocked him over, would have had he been standing. Dust from the impacts, all less than a hundred meters away, showered him. The swelling peal that followed as the sound waves overtook their originator terrified him.

The reverberations faded, the final echoes of the destruction of the bolide rumbling in from the distance. The sheep had gone wild, madness overtaking them as they scattered, running demented in circles, into each other, into the distance. Deus shielded his eyes from the dust kicked up from the strike, fearing the worst as the terrified bleating of his charges rose in volume over the fading timbre.

He uncovered his eyes, squinting to avoid getting dust in them. He could see the light shapes moving about, moving away. They were heading into the depression between the low hills. They would be comforted at the bottom; at least he hoped they would. He thought he could pick out the ram already down there. The others would gravitate to him.

The light breeze cleared the densest part of the cloud just to the west of him. Not thirty steps away he could see a red luminescence. He couldn't fathom what it could possibly be. He quickly rolled up his bed and set forth to gather his flock, taking the slightest diversion to investigate the glow.

As he approached it became wider, his eyes deceiving him as it at once appeared as a mound and a depression. At only a footstep away the horrible reality struck him. The red light at the bottom of the shallow pit was a goddess that had traveled from the Moon on that violent shaft of light.

The impact of the red-hot, softened steel had hammered into rock a foot under the surface, kicking up a rim around the hole, flattening its oblong structure into a collapsed hourglass shape with a knob on one end and a longer portion at the other. To Deus the similarity to that of a woman was stark. One could not cast one's eyes at the gods and live. In fear of his life, he cast his treasured blanket over the scene, gripping the edge as it unfurled in the air and softly floated down.

The light of the full Moon was enough now to survey the immediate area around him. Pieces of wool still attached to skin, and some to flesh, were everywhere. A hind leg was to his right, another ahead. What had happened? What could explain this? The little lamb that he had chosen for its perfect frame and light coat was no more. Its head was lying not far away, tipped against a rock. He recognized the remains of the little creature right away. The animal had been almost vaporized as the entity from another world had taken it in sacrifice.

He could see a couple of other faint glows as he surveyed the surrounding landscape. Strangely, they disappeared when he looked straight at them. He looked away, and they appeared again. Stricken with curiosity he walked toward them sideways, noting that even with his side vision they were quickly diminishing in luminosity.

He moved as fast as he could to the first. Now that he was on top of it he could see that it did have a bit of a glow. The melted ejecta stuck to a rock, flattened, like a glob of clay thrown against a wall. Deus peered at it from only half an arm's length away, wondering. It was only an inch and a half round, tapered on the edges, three concentric rings graduating its ablated face from nothing to a small mound in the center.

He reached out to touch it, feeling that this must be somehow connected to the goddess he had just left. The excitement of the moment interfered with the nerve impulses traveling to his spinal cord, the normal reaction that would have caused the knee-jerk reflex that would have made him drop the tektite without a thought. He heard the sound of his skin searing before he realized what was taking place. The nervous message got through to his brain at the same time as the sensory input from his auditory system, and the reek of burning human flesh only served to heighten the grief of his third-degree burn. He should have known better, cursed himself for touching a holy relic. With his uninjured left hand he made a mark in the earth in front of the button, then set off to the next one. He found five round tektites in all, the last one from memory as its glow had completely disappeared. He was able to find it from the heat still given off as he passed his open palm over the area a few inches above the rock on which it impacted.

In the Moonlight, he could see that they were all the same size and shape. The two farthest apart were only about fifty steps from each other. The overall pattern was in the shape of a 'W', slightly skewed, reminding him of something he couldn't quite compass.

His fingers ached. He had found all he could, his injury calling for attention. He poured a bit of water on them, seeing it wasted as it trickled down his arm, dribbling off and into the soil. The soothing it brought was worth it, though.

He wondered if the goddess had also stopped glowing, as the buttons had. He raised a side of his felt, not high, sighting into the darkness with trepidation. The glow was gone. He lifted the covering higher, allowing the

Moonlight to enter enough to see if the goddess had gone back from whence she came in a more unassuming manner.

She was black now, burnished, magnificent. He removed the covering completely. The Moonlight glinted off her lustrous body. What a thing of beauty.

Had he known, he might have given thought to the seven children buried eight yards beneath his feet. The iron goddess had impacted on a foundation stone of the hut in which they had lived. It had been a thousand years since a small village had occupied this same space. Their buildings had been weak and long since crumbled. Everyone had died when a new virus had been introduced to the island, one to which they had no resistance; everyone had, but they were among the first. There they had been lain, the seven little ones, undisturbed, at rest and never expecting that they would be at the foundation of something new, something great.

The sheep were assembling into their group not far away. Even the ones most scattered were making their way back to the leader of their flock. The ram was coming slowly towards Deus, leading the others of his own volition, knowing where safety lay. He had been under the direction of a human protector his entire life and had an instinctive confidence in the little man now charged with his security.

Deus sat and waited, contemplating the events of the evening. This must obviously be a gift from the heavens, from the Moon. What would he do with it? To what end? He had to tell his family, but what would they think? They probably wouldn't even believe him. His father would probably want to trade these precious pieces at the village. That could never happen, at any cost.

Deus was chosen, that much was clear.

He wrapped himself in his cozy felt letting the warmth envelop him. He hadn't realized in the excitement of the events how chilled it had become. His eyes closed as the exhaustion of the past day overcame him and carried him off to sleep, to dream unimaginable dreams of the glory of gods.

Chapter 2

The Tektites

2950 BCE

The marketplace hummed. Amnisos had been filling with merchants and traders from miles around for the last couple of days, the full Moon being the signal. It could be busy any time of the year, but now, in the middle of summer, the crowds were thick. Zeus had outlined his stall in the middle of the square, arriving early to get the most central location. Deus had told him years ago that the ones in the center got far more traffic than the ones on the outskirts who arrived late. People liked to be in the middle of the action. It only made sense to him that the more traffic the better the chances of making a sale or trade.

Since Deus was eight years old, Zeus had favored him over his brothers for the excursion to the market. The boy showed ever-heightening enthusiasm for commerce, and anything else Zeus cared to mention.

The first year the two of them came together to the village Deus, bored with the slow proceedings, wandered through the crowded midway pulling the cloaks of fleece patrons to gain their attention and extolled the virtues of his father's merchandise. He led them to his father's stall where they found to their pleasant surprise that this shepherd from the hill country had better product than the more respected merchants.

Sometimes Zeus ruined a deal by insisting on a price more in keeping with the prices in the center of the bazaar. "It is only fair. Why should I let them take advantage of me?"

Deus pointed out that he should get rid of the wool for less if he had to, as long as he made some profit. What did it matter? He would do better on the next deal. Zeus reluctantly acquiesced to the advice and soon found that buyers were seeking him out. And why not? His wool was better, and when his supply became low they were willing to pay a much higher price, fearing to miss out on getting any at all.

Deus was becoming a veteran of the trading and selling games now that he had been at it for eight years. His father was still content to sit in his stall and wait for customers to come by, or at the most call out to them as they passed. Deus, on the other hand, could not sit still. He had to get out and mingle. The people of the village fascinated him. They had stories to tell, friendship to give, and goods to trade. Deus regularly made better deals on his walkabouts than he did at the stall, but far more important to him was the information he was able to glean from the older inhabitants.

The most interesting thing that he found out was that the island he lived on was huge. On one day, three years ago, he met two men from opposite ends of the island. The first man had come from Zakro, in the direction of the sunrise, and had taken four days of brisk walking to reach Amnisos. The second had also walked for four days, and swore he had never covered the distance so quickly, from a small village called Kydonia which was from the direction of the sunset. He also told Deus that it was at least another two days walk to reach the farthest expanse of the island, and that was at a speed that was almost a run. There was no way that Deus could cover the distance in anywhere near that short a time.

Both of these men had been well built, they were not weak or slow. He knew they could outdistance him at any opportunity. The island must be enormous. He had never been more than a casual day's journey from his home in the hills. One day he knew he would explore the whole island. He couldn't stay with his family forever.

He felt, sometimes, that he wasn't growing up fast enough. He wanted to be an adult. He enjoyed their company best. He was friendly enough with the youth of his age, but he found them so immature, so concerned with foolishness, with fun and self-gratification. Some were bullies, always spoiling for a fight. Others were crooked, ready to make off with anything left unattended. Always they were trying to get wine, not that the adults weren't, diverting their attentions from anything intelligent.

Deus pulled a wrapped piece of white cheese from his pouch, unwrapping the surrounding skin as the pungent aroma rose begging to be inhaled. He bit off a corner, replacing the chunk in the pouch as he flipped a few of his belongings out of the way. He was hungry. He pulled a tear off a round loaf that a chatty lady had given him on his meandering, pushing some of the soft center into his mouth as he chewed the cheese.

His father was standing at his spot in the row of merchants, chatting with his neighbor on the immediate left when he noticed Deus. "Ah, my son" he gestured with his outstretched arm. "Have you not come back to me with another buyer?"

"I have bread to go with our cheese. We have to devote some time to other things besides bargaining."

"The boy is right." The neighbor thought nothing of reaching in for a rip of bread. He gouged out a scoop of cheese with his forefinger as he held the bread with the other fingers of the same hand, smiling broadly, gauging how far he could push these people. Deus was impressed how he was able to negotiate this maneuver while seemingly not taking his eyes off of theirs, his hand traveling, as it were, of its own volition.

They let this violation of social order go. If it cost a few mouthfuls of food to maintain the goodwill of a contact, so be it. The day had gone well. The last few days had gone well.

They had no more raw fleece to sell. They had made good trades on several rams and ewes and a half dozen lambs that were going to be sacrificed.

Deus objected to the selling of their good young stock and was able to convince his father that perhaps they should keep the best for future breeding. It only made sense that the best would have a better quality lamb. Still, the demand for the finest was high, and a lot could be made. But, as Deus pointed out, if they sold them all then there would be none left to improve their present stock. They would be successful this year, but what about the next?

It was time to go, to return to their home inland.

There was something about this village on the coast that appealed to him, and he found it a bit hard to identify even with a lot of thought. The beauty of the sea was striking, the gentle waves, sometimes low whitecaps that he had heard could get quite frightening in size at times, the smell of the salt air and seaweed decaying on the shoreline.

There were islands in the distance, a small one that was little more than a barren rock not too far for someone to float to on a log if they had such a mind, and a large one far away. Most of the time he'd spent on the coast it displayed itself hazy, but he'd seen it once clearly when the day was perfect. He could see it from the higher rises near his home with more detail than he usually could at the coast, although the distance was double. When he contemplated the offshore island on his quieter days the yearning for exploration filled him.

The island of Dia. As far as he could find out from the people he had met in town the island was uninhabited.

"No one has ever found water there," a fisherman told him. "Without water land is as useless as a cloud without rain."

As they gathered the last of their belongings into their packs and bid farewell to those around them, Deus thought about the fisherman and his stories. Some had been obvious fabrications of sea monsters designed only for the purpose of getting some sort of reaction. Deus played along, feigning astonishment and shocked disbelief in order to keep the conversation going.

He enjoyed even the rubbish that he heard from people, thrilled to just observe their facial cast as they iterated their counterfeit fables. He knew the fisherman didn't believe a word of his own stories, but he also knew that many in the community did. Fear enveloped their existence to the point where they would never think to venture far from the security of their own village. To actually travel or even visualize a sea voyage was inconceivable.

Most of the people he had met, with the exception of those coming for the market, hadn't even the rudimentary curiosity to find out what or who was in the nearest town.

He kicked a stone as they walked, a small puff of dust rising to be caught by the soft breeze.

The first part of the walk was difficult, steep as they climbed the coastal banks, but faster going without the live animals to contend with. Their packs were heavy with new goods, oil, dried fish, olives, wine. Deus had persuaded his father to make what he said was a good trade for a few pieces of pottery and an oil lamp.

His mother would be pleased with the ease at which she could keep the fire going now. He knew the pottery would please her too. She had taken a fancy to dressing her house up now that it was big enough for more than just a storage shed. Deus had organized the men to add a room to it in each of two years.

The area around her home was even more becoming as she was feeling a pride in her little place on earth. With the rocks removed from the ground in the immediate area of the home, she was now able to cultivate easily some of the vegetation and herbs that she used for cooking. The cleaned area was still too small for growing seed crops for bread, that would still have to come from elsewhere, but she thought that in a few years they would not have to get any of their vegetables and squash from the village.

Deus had brought her five olive tree whips several years ago which had come from a grower's orchard. One had died in the transplant, but the others were coming along fine. They had planted the trees near an old gnarly one close by in the hopes that the influence of the new ones would rejuvenate the old beast. Deus couldn't recall ever seeing an olive on it. The old grower had told him that green olive slips always grew into wild olive bushes unless they were treated properly. The best one could expect from one gone wild was a tree with small useless berries. More often what one ended up with was a bush growing out of control into a tangle of limbs and branches that also produced little worthless fruit. What growers did was cut the initial stem back completely after it had grown for two years and then graft a branch from a tame olive tree onto it. It took a while to heal and had to be tended carefully. That is what Deus had brought home to his mother. But the grower had warned him that the tree could not become productive of itself. It had to be husbanded to bring it into production, otherwise it would revert to its wild state. It needed careful pruning and cultivating, and even then it would not give its first fruit for seven years. It would not become fully productive for at least fifteen years. The grower wasn't worried about competition developing all around him because he was selling his whips. Most people would never have the patience to tend them as they required and he could expect most of them to die or go wild. To those who could manage though, they deserved their reward.

The walk home invigorated Deus, in spite of his load. The air changed at the higher altitude, lighter somehow, dryer, the smells of grass and leaves gradually replacing the heavy sea air. It was warmer up here. He started to sweat, noticing that his father was too.

Zeus had never fully recovered from the disease that had inflicted him last winter, along with his oldest son. It had been a raging pneumonia, and Heltos had died after weeks of chills and fever. In the end, he could hardly breathe, too weak to cough out the fluid and puss filling his lungs. His skin was burning hot, yet he had complained that he was freezing even as he was lapsing into unconsciousness. His heart failed, already weakened by an aortic valve insufficiency secondary to his syphilitic infection.

Deus had never known his father to cry before. Perhaps he had been himself so weakened by the pneumonia that he wasn't in his right mind. Perhaps he felt that his son's death could have easily happened to him. Deus tried to talk to him about the event once but he refused, brushing it off with a wave of his hand.

Deus found the whole thing rather curious. He didn't particularly miss his brother, or the inevitable tormenting whenever the two of them were together. But he had never known a person to die before. Death was no stranger to him in the sense that sheep had been killed in front of him as long as he could remember, but his brother dying, that was something new.

The picture of his father wailing, curled in a ball on the sheepskin beside Heltos as his last breath expelled a bubble of sticky yellow expectorant, had always stayed with him.

His mind wandered to other things as they strolled slowly south. He daydreamed of his home, of the beauty and peace of the place. He dreamed of travel. If only even a portion of the fisherman's tales could be true. He tried to talk of these things with his father, his aspirations, his hopes.

"You are a dreamer, boy. Keep your mind on things that matter." Zeus was having no part of it. He wanted his world simple. Who cared about things that no one could understand? Who cared about the terrors of the sea if one was sensible enough never to venture upon it?

Deus could not understand this display of ambivalence. The man was not ignorant. He sacrificed to the god of nature. He was interested in things where a profit could be made. How could he be so indifferent toward everything else?

He kept his peace, choosing to enjoy the beauty of the day without the insipidity of his father. Where would the man be now without Deus's encouragement, his intuitive skills with the flocks, and his trading skills? Where would the family be?

They likely would have been displaced by the increasing population in the area, too poor to buy favors.

The land they held was of increasing interest to others. What had seemed so far from the village in his childhood was merely a walk away now. There was a certain danger in others finding the area desirable. Several times in the last couple of years the family had to put up a front to keep interlopers off their land.

The area through which they walked was far more heavily treed than their own, the trees scattered thinly over the low-lying hills. Some of the olive trees were as thick across as he would be lying down. They must be ancient.

He'd never seen any of these trees bear fruit. They must have lost that capacity ages ago, maybe before there were people. Judging by the rate of growth he had seen in his mother's olive trees some of these must be hundreds, or even thousands, of years old. In fact, that was true. Even tame trees could go on producing abundantly for six and seven hundred years. When the old trees finally begin to grow old and die, sometimes after twelve hundred years or longer, the roots send up new green shoots which, if grafted and pruned in right manner, will mature to full-grown trees again. Thus, while the tree itself might produce fruit only for a few centuries, the roots of the tree may go on producing fruit and new trees for millennia. Some of the ancient trees alive today come from trees that were ancient when Christ was alive on the earth. Also, it is almost impossible to kill an olive. By cutting it down, new shoots are sent up from the root all around the margins of the old stump. Groves of two to five trunks, all from the single root, replace what originally was only one.

The sparse forest thinned even more as they walked in silence inland. The terrain was rough, even though they had developed a trail along the easiest route.

They walked faster now, Deus taking the lead, not even considering that he was subconsciously challenging his father.

There was something perversely enjoyable about a brisk activity, even in the heat of the day. He heard his father curse under his breath as he slid down the side of a small outcropping of rock. Zeus remained upright even under the load, but twisted his ankle and was now in some discomfort, although his stride didn't slow. No son of his was going to outpace him, especially the youngest.

Deus could hear his father wheezing and slowed when he realized that he was going too fast. He knew better than to insult him by offering to take part of his load or to suggest a rest at this point. Even to look at him would have been an offence. Zeus would realize immediately that his wheezes had been heard. Deus was astute enough to know that his father was embarrassed by his physical deterioration.

If Zeus was appreciative of Deus's retarded step, he gave no indication. The wheezes diminished, though a full volume of air was still passing through his open mouth.

The five-mile excursion was rather arduous with the packs, and was probably more like six or seven miles when the convolutions up, down, and around were taken into consideration. They had no measure of distance other than a poor description of time coupled with a conjectural conception of their speed. To them, it was a full afternoon's journey, fully loaded.

They passed the area where Deus had started his career as a shepherd so many years ago. He stopped briefly to contemplate the hill where he had hidden the goddess and the buttons. It was only a matter of time now. He still felt the urge to tell someone, especially his father, at times like this. The feeling overwhelmed him as he passed the place yet he knew it was just one more challenge to test his strength and resolve.

The dream he'd had that night so long ago was specific in that he should tell no man, that he should hide the icons for a future time. He recounted the memory of the dawn of the next day when he had gathered the buttons and placed them in the crater left by the larger piece and filled in the hollow with rocks and earth. No one would find it.

When he returned to his mother, he knew as he was approaching her that he should confide in her. It was a funny thought, that she was not a man. As he described the events of the night her face took on a radiance he had never seen.

"It is from the Gods. I knew when you were born that you were chosen for greatness. This is a sure sign. The dream was a direct message to you, and you must know that if you disobey the will of the gods, you will die. Keep them hidden until you are directed otherwise. Tell no one else. There are those who would corrupt the purposes of this delivery to you for their own ends."

She had clearly been referring to his father. But even though he had not met many people, he had been left with the impression that far more devious people existed. He made an oath with his mother that the icons would stay hidden, not even spoken about.

Over the years the proclivity to dig them up, just for a look, to make sure they were safe, was becoming ever stronger and more frequent. Perhaps his father was ready. Deus was dying to share his find, to show it off, a desire to be thought of as important, to be recognized by others as being one recognized by the gods.

He checked himself. These inclinations were wrong.

He looked behind him noting that his father had fallen back again. While lost in thought Deus had accelerated and was now hundreds of yards ahead. He stopped, deliberating briefly. His father wouldn't even notice a slight diversion to the top of the hill. He would be back at the trail before his father caught up.

He went directly to the spot. After eight years he still found the exact location, recognizing the inconspicuous rock he had left as a marker as if he had just laid it. Even with the dry grass around it he felt he could still have found it in the dark, so frequently had he seen its image in his mind.

The desire to examine the contents of the cairn was too much. Now that he was right on top of it he had to see. He pushed the rock with his foot, applying more pressure and finding it immovable. If he bent down and dug a bit around the edges, he could flip the rock easily. He'd replace it as he found it and no one would know. But he would know.

"What have you found?"

His father's voice almost stopped his heart.

"You've been staring at that rock for a while now. What is it?"

He'd been caught. "I saw a few bees. I thought they came from around here but they must have been from elsewhere. I thought we could take some honey home to top up our winnings."

"That would be a fine finish to the day wouldn't it?" Zeus stretched his arms to the side and scanned the area.

Deus started walking again and his father followed, thinking nothing more of the matter.

The latter part of the journey seemed to pass quickly. The remaining two miles were much easier, the climb from the coast having leveled out some time ago.

They came over the last low rise before their home. Deus stopped. His father came up behind and paused beside him.

"What is it?"

"Something is wrong. Look. The garden has been thrashed. And the fire. There isn't any smoke. Mother hasn't let the fire go out ever."

Zeus changed his facial expression to one of the utmost concern. He hurried forward down the slope to the homestead. Deus was right beside him, surveying the area all around for any sign of jeopardy.

He removed his pack, placing it quietly on the ground. He could move faster now, running, separating himself from his father who was making straight for the cottage. He changed his course to one that would give him a view of the front entrance.

A man's body lay at the front door, prone with its head pushed back hideously, the neck obviously snapped, face mashed into the doorjamb. Deus was crouching now, arms to the sides for balance as he ran, like a wild animal coming in for the kill.

His mother. Where was his mother? He flew through the door into the dark. He discerned the smell of burnt wool. His eyes took a moment to adjust. Enough light came through the door to see that the interior of the room was in disarray. The small stove was smashed on the sheepskin mat on the floor. A pile of clothes lay on the table.

No. Wait. Slowly he advanced. His eyes were dilating now. He could see the bare legs draped over the other end of the table, then the hips. The body disappeared in a disheveled heap of clothing. At the head end there seemed to be nothing.

He reached forward and touched the still invisible black hair. Gently he drew it away revealing the face of his mother. The dim light seemed to highlight her finer features, her high cheekbones, her large, round chin and wide eyes. Her eyes. They stared empty now, in death. Peaceful somehow. He could see her mind was at peace as she died. He could also see how she died. She was at peace nonetheless. A message to him to be sure. She left this face for his benefit, so he would know that no matter what degradation had befallen her no one could harm her spirit.

The tears burst forth. Tears of sorrow, of pride, of admiration. Tears of loneliness. A chill ran through his very bones, up his spine. The light hairs on his arm stood up, goose bumps forming as an image of how his mother must have died flashed before him.

Darkness surrounded him, thick, black. He was breathing harder, heavier, louder. His sorrow was transforming to rage. The sight before him began to fade from focus as a shadow fell across the corpse. He could hardly think. He felt he was being gripped from within, a phantom filling his soul with hatred.

The breathing amplified, grating in his ears, hoarse, irregular, asynchronous to his own.

The disturbing sound gave him something to clutch, something to focus on, something to lead him out of his darkness. A rounded image of the goddess he had secreted away as a boy came to his mind, slowly, as if it were breaking through a surface of black oil. Peace filled his heart as he recognized the form. Its feminine shape gradually brightened before him, metamorphosing into that of his mother, the image loquacious, the message so clear.

He wanted to stay in the presence of the image, to never let go. But the image of his mother, far more than a mother, was not beckoning to him. His time was not yet.

They began to separate, the sound calling him to his own world. In a moment his vision returned, the distressing scene again apparent.

His father was kneeling beside the table, his face close to that of his wife's, cradling her head in his hand, stroking her cheek with the other. Tears ran down his thin face. He sniffed between wheezes and softly pressed his mouth to hers.

In silence the remorse of the scene consumed them. Deus wondered, touched by the splay of tenderness from Zeus.

His father's affection had grown over the years, especially since the loss of his oldest. He was unchanged in most ways but his tolerance of things that really didn't matter much increased markedly. He was warmer toward his family, more attentive to his wife, since then.

They both lost perception of time. They felt they were beside her for an endless age, and for but a moment. Deus had earlier straightened her woven garments, unacknowledged by Zeus who was lost in his own grief. He stood beside his mother, holding her hand while Zeus caressed her face, staring into her deep eyes.

At last they were able to pull themselves away. Zeus stood, signaling that it was time. Another needed an acknowledgment of passing as well.

Ronos was on his back, having been rolled by his father prior to his entering the house, the depressed forehead indicating his manner of death. Dry blood had caked in his ears, a brown trickle drawn down each side of his neck uniting at the front and continuing down his chest. His eyes were closed.

"We must bury them soon. Ronos begins to stink." Zeus looked up at the sun, gauging the remainder of the day. "We will start with him. Get his blanket."

Deus retrieved the bedding from beside the hearth where it had been left in a heap, and they rolled the youth inside it. They slid the pole running over the altar through the roll and tied the parcel. Each took an end and they hoisted him on their shoulders, suspended in the blanket, his casket for the eternities.

There was a small cave, not much more than a hole under a large rock, to the east a short distance away where Ronos could be buried with his older brother.

At the entrance, they withdrew the pole and slid their lost family member headfirst inward without ceremony. They had to push his legs, finally bending them at the knees to make him fit. His upper torso jamming to some extent on the bones of his brother made the insertion difficult. They wedged his wrapped feet up against the rock ceiling so they would stay and filled the entrance with boulders as large as they could carry or roll. When they were done they heaped earth into the cracks of the rocks. Thus sealed the tomb of Ronos.

The usual proceedings would have included a sacrifice and the rest of the day spent in prayer. But today there was another chore left, an onerous one, involving the disposition of a dearly beloved one, far more so than this.

They returned to the house, hesitant to enter and relive their previous apperception. Deus's emotions were whirling. The half saying this is so, accept what cannot be changed, at odds with the vengeful, spite-filled side, the dark side.

His disorientation passed as he focused on his mother's form. Once again peace filled him. Without a word he and Zeus worked as one, preparing the desecrated body for burial. With eyes silently weeping they removed her clothing, replacing them with clean, newer garments.

A mark on his mother's chest caught Deus's attention. He paused to examine it as closely as he could in the gloom of the house interior. He could not understand exactly what it was. It could wait until she was fully dressed.

They slipped a large skin under her, treating her lifeless remains with the utmost reverence.

They lifted the final wrap, pausing a moment to contemplate her serene face before covering it.

Zeus did not look up. "We will have to carry her to a cave farther away. There are no other holes large enough in this area."

"I have been thinking, Father, that something better than a cave would be in order for Mother." He was hesitant. "I think we should make a burial place for her, a place of honor, a place that will forever be a mark of our respect for her."

Zeus was silent. The concept was unknown to him. He had never heard of such a notion. He had only heard of the dead being returned to the earth from which they came. Many were injected unceremoniously into small holes completely stripped of any clothing or belongings. Babies were flung to the back as far possible to leave room for others to follow.

His family had always, as far as was told, shown a far greater respect for the deceased, provided that they were well liked. Even the shunned were given the decency of clothing, although they had been known to be exchanged for other's castaways.

But the special construction of a sepulcher? He touched the wrapped body. The idea was appealing.

"Where would we build such a thing?"

"The rise where you saw me dig for the bees. Mother will rest there. Her soul will be at peace."

Father and son gazed into each other's eyes, the first time of their lives. Zeus felt an almost hypnotic captivation toward the thought of the advent of this new conventionality.

"Agreed then."

They tied Selene and slipped the pole through the bundle as had been done with Ronos. They proceeded slowly, evenly, making sure her body wasn't exposed to unnecessary jarring. The sun was sinking lower in the sky, the cooler rays giving them respite from the exertion of carrying the weight up and down the low hills.

By the time they reached the destined rise the sun had sunk to the horizon, the sky ablaze with crimson wisps in the distance. Laying the body gently on the ground Deus selected the spot. They oriented her so that her head was only an arm's length from where the goddess was buried, her feet pointing east to where the sun rose every morning.

There were only a few minutes of daylight left. Deus had to know what the chest mark was about. With one eye on his father, anticipating but not receiving an objection, he unwrapped the upper portion of the covering, exposing his mother's head and breasts. There it was. The small mark just left of the sternum, two-thirds of the way down her ribcage. It was little more than a dot. A tiny scab had formed on it, a blemish on his mother's perfect form. He picked it off. He could see the spot better now. It was slightly concave, indented, as if something had pressed into her skin.

He placed a thumb on each side of the wound and stretched the skin apart as much as he could, then squeezed it together. A small gelled clot of dark blood emerged.

So that was it. Her heart had been pierced. It wasn't a knife that had killed her but a narrow-gauge weapon of some sort that he had never heard of or imagined.

He stood, his father understanding exactly what it was. They left her chest exposed as a monument to her manner of death, the rest of her torso covered in to compensate for the indignity of her defilement.

They began the labor to which they came. They rolled as many of the large rocks as they could, both of them straining on the irregular boulders. The full Moon was rising as the sun slipped over the horizon, the light more than adequate for the task at hand. They had started placing rocks in a rectangular fashion, surrounding the body, but Deus was inspired by the rising Moon, and memories from far back in the past, to construct a circular structure in recognition to, and obeisance of, the Moon Goddess.

Zeus agreed without much explanation as they changed the shape of the foundation stones, his lungs wheezing in protest even with the aid of a soothing evening air. They piled rocks as well as they could, taking care to fit them into each other, leaving only the smallest gaps between them which could be filled with mud another day.

When the wall reached shoulder height, they leveled the upper surface with flat rocks of various sizes. For the roof, they lay branches across, an abundant supply obtained from a couple of dead cypress trees not far away. They would finish the roof, again another day, with mud mixed with grass, heaped slightly higher in the center to allow for water runoff.

For now, they were finished. Selene was entombed, no door for entry or exit. They sat on the grass, exhausted, contemplating the new structure, the east side lit by the Moon.

It was time.

Deus rose and moved to the place adjacent to the tomb and began digging around the edges where he had started on the way back from Amnisos.

Zeus watched in curiosity. Hadn't they enough rocks? Deus merely lifted it to the side and kept digging, spreading the dirt out to all sides. He used a stick to pick through the hardened, more compact, earth and to loosen some of the smaller rocks. He kept digging, longer than he thought he should. Where was it? It couldn't be gone.

He struck a hard surface. Gripping the stick hard with both hands he reached forward into the hole to channel around the perimeter, clearing more rubble from the sides. He pried up on the side of the flat rock, using another smaller one as a fulcrum. It moved enough to push another stick in to support it slightly. Changing his position and reaching in from the other side of the excavation he strained on the rock and tilted it up revealing the contents that so obsessed him.

Even with the sprinkling of dust from the digging she still shined. What beauty. He reached in and withdrew the prize, the icon, the goddess. He rubbed

41

his palm over the surface, the Moon reflecting off it catching Zeus's attention. He stood and came closer to see.

He was struck. Such a thing of beauty he had never beheld. Its blackness was lost in the night, yet its reflection of light revealed its presence, its shape feminine, seductive, enticing. He knelt before it as Deus continued to hold it high, angling it in various ways, mesmerized by the waving reflections.

"This is the goddess of the Moon. It is she who we will worship. There are no other gods. I know this now Father. She came to me ten years ago, when you sent me here, inspired, although you did not know it at the time. I have been chosen. It is time for her release. I knew it as we were returning home, I felt it so strongly. I knew the time would come." He paused, tears beginning their course down his face. "I had not any idea that it would be associated with Mother's death."

Zeus spoke from his kneeling position. "You are correct my son. I also know this is so. I recall the night this must have come to you. The night when your brother shouting awakened me. I awoke to see a brilliant dragon sweeping the sky, vanishing in a moment, fading from view. His voice shattered the night as he disappeared over the edge of the earth. None of us slept that night. I worried for you. But when we returned to the hut, I made the others swear that nothing would be said unless you or your mother spoke first. We knew it to be a sacred moment, which should not be referred to lightly. Only now have I broken my silence."

"You were wise to heed your promptings, Father. Many times the temptation to come here and dig before it was time was almost too overpowering for me. If we had discussed it I might have given in to those temptations. I think you or my brothers may have even encouraged me to do so."

"You are right. I know that I could not have contained my curiosity. And your brothers were so foolish at times. I fear what they might have done. I would not have been able to control them." He looked away. "I'm not sure I would not have tried."

He felt a hand on his head. "My Father. Sometimes temptations are too much for mortals to bear. Do not beat yourself. Allow yourself to be filled with the joy of this new revelation. This great gift comes not only to me but to you as well, to all people. The spirit of your wife fills this idol. Can you feel it? Her love for all. Her forgiveness. This is Selene, Goddess of the Moon."

Zeus prostrated himself on the ground, trembling, crying openly.

"Rise up Father. Why do you weep?"

Zeus struggled to control himself as he stood, and failed. He was anguished, not able to answer. He hung his head in shame, a hand to his face, wiping the flow from his eyes, his facial muscles contorting his features.

42

He felt a hand on his shoulder. "Father. She understands. You did not know who she was. How could you? You only knew her in the flesh. Now you must know her in the spirit. Feel her warmth. Embrace her. Cling to her with your life."

Zeus sank to his knees, his body wracked almost in convulsions as he grieved. "How can I forgive myself? I treated her like a dog. I was mean to her. I used her. I offended her."

"What has been cannot be changed. But she did stay with you. She had great love for you even though you could not see it." He placed his hand back on his father's head. "Feel it now Father. Feel it through my hand. Let her spirit fill you, warm you to the marrow."

Zeus shook. His body tightened and went rigid. A force of some sort was entering through his scalp, spreading down the length of his spine, and radiating outward to girdle every fiber of his being. It was unnatural. He began to relax as he felt and succumbed to the warmth. His eyes closed, he began to experience a lightness, his soul growing beyond the bounds of his mortal body. He could no longer feel the earth beneath him, as if he were above it. His spiritual size inflated even more, growing to heights beyond his comprehension. He was still within his body, he knew that, yet he was far above it, vast in proportion, encompassing his body at the same time. He observed the scene below, himself kneeling in abeyance, his son with his palm flat upon his head and holding Selene high toward the Moon. He could see the entire countryside, the pastoral beauty taking on a surreal quality with colors that he knew could not have existence in the temporal world. His stature continued unabated. He was in the clouds, viewing the distance, observing as well behind as in front, his own little island merely a speck in the sea surrounded by boundless lands. He could see other nations, scattered all around the sea, with different dress, different cultures, some at war with others. He was a giant. He was filled with power. And then he saw it. His son gigantic beyond belief, unseen because he was too great to see, endowed with power. Beyond him, Selene, infinite, omnipotent, cradling the full Moon in her palm. By way of a voice that wasn't a voice he heard her speak, "A stranger will touch me and build my house."

An inkling of his low standing among greatness crushed him down, collapsing him back to his former self, shooting him into the confines of his body, imprisoning him for the remainder of his insignificant life.

He opened his eyes. His son's arm was lowering, the weight of the steel idol impossible to support even in his trance-like state. Deus knelt, reverently placing the goddess before them.

"Your eyes have been opened, Father. You have seen that things are not what they appear. You have seen the vastness of the world, the complexity

43

and simpleness of existence. You have witnessed an outrage against humanity and seen it defeated. You have been endowed with a knowledge beyond what any, other than ourselves, have been granted."

He paused to rub the object with his thumb, smoothing off a particle of dust that had attached itself. "With that knowledge comes responsibility. We now are charged with leading the people, helping them to develop their society, to improve themselves, to prevent evil actions such as this from happening again. We will do this Father. We will swear to do it."

Zeus flung himself on the ground, clutching the idol. "Forgive me, Selene. Forgive me," he wept softly.

Deus gently removed the hands from their grip, embraced his father and leaned him back into a kneeling position. "The idol is merely a representation of Selene. It sees and hears nothing. Its only purpose is as a reminder, a guide, to turn our hearts and minds in the direction in which they must rightly go."

Deus reached down again into the hole and withdrew the five tektite buttons. "These also are gifts from the heavens. They came at the same time. When they struck, they glowed red, as did the idol. They were easy to find even in the light of the Moon. I found them scattered over there." He swept with his arm to indicate their wide coverage. He lay them on the ground spaced about a foot apart in the 'W' pattern in which he found them.

"Do you recognize this shape Father?"

Zeus concentrated. "Yes. It is in the sky above us. Right there." He pointed to the north, singling out the pellucid constellation of Cassiopeia.

'Yes. That is what I have thought over the years. I don't know the significance of it, but I'm sure that is what it must represent. There is nothing else it could be."

"You have no idea what it could mean?"

"None."

"You think there is a connection between the stars and these little round fragments?"

"I can think of nothing else. Feel their weight. These components are like nothing else, except the idol."

Zeus had touched the idol but as yet had no appreciation of its density. He picked up one of the heavy circular pieces, rubbing it between his forefinger and thumb, flipping it through his fingers like a coin. He examined the back, the appearance lightly pocked from impacted sand. The mound on the opposite surface reminded him of a breast. He quickly banished the thought as he bounced it in his palm.

"It is much heavier than rock, even heavier than copper although it has the same feel, cold, hard. It is black, yet it reflects the light."

44

Deus handed him a second to hold. "Tap them together."

Zeus did this, yielding a brief high-frequency resonance akin to the tinkle of a cat's bell. He was delighted with the sound and struck them together with varying force that affected the volume of sound. He took the liberty of changing one tektite for another, experimenting with the reverberations of each, noting that each had a particular value in the scale of sound quite distinct from the others.

"I am mystified. These are miraculous. But they must have greater value than ornamentation or a musical contrivance."

"I agree, Father. But what? They belong to the idol, that is clear, but I see no connection." He watched as his father carefully placed the dark circles beside the idol. "For now, I suggest we get some sleep, and let the answers come as they may."

They lay head to head on their sides, facing the collection of space fragments with the Tomb of Selene framing the background, blanched by the Moon's illume.

Chapter 3

Meditations

The sky began its routine of brightening, slowly at first, the outlines of invisible things gradually taking shape, forming the tangible objects of daytime existence. The sheep were up, traipsing through the pasture in their endless search for a better patch of grass. Rectus yawned and curled tighter, comfortably warm in his blanket, the moist air cooling his face encouraging his reluctance to emerge from his cocoon.

He thought of home. Home? It was hardly a home. He was away far more than he was ever there. He'd been away twenty days now. He hadn't ever learned to count higher than the number of fingers and toes that he had. He hadn't ever wanted to. His father had tried to teach him on many occasions so he could better tend sheep but could not withstand his stubborn refusal to learn. In exasperation he had ordered his son to count the sheep in groups of twenty, plus the odd amount left over at the end of the tally. This made sense to Rectus. He could say that he had five, or ten, or sometimes even fifteen groups of twenty, plus the odd amount, and that way keep good tabs on his flock.

Zeus was able, by necessity, to add these double-digit numbers and get a correct total. Deus would correct him on occasion, as was warranted, as he had the mind to add the numbers instantly in his head. He had realized a basic form of multiplication, although he could only do it with groups of twenty up to four hundred. That was more than what was required, so he hadn't had to work things out any higher. What Deus had done was memorize the various totals. He had added them up repeatedly to check and double check the values, so afraid of making a mistake and losing even a single sheep.

Deus had been thrashed severely when he was just a boy for allowing a lamb to be killed. He said the gods had claimed it as a sacrifice, but his father hadn't seen the evidence of the exploded carcass at that time. Zeus was full of remorse when he happened to pass that way the next day, curiosity leading him to explore why his otherwise honest son would lie to him so blatantly. The evidence he found was inarguable. Zeus had never found a way to express his distress over his actions. Sometimes he was too quick to anger, he knew that, but what was a man to do?

Rectus realized that he had been lost in thought. The sun that had barely given wind of its presence under the horizon was now well above it, warming the side of his face as he sat as sentinel over his flock.

It was time. Rectus stood, still in his wrap, and took in a draught of the morning air. The sheep below had gravitated into loose groupings, He could never tell like his brother could that they were the same groups each time, and proceeded with the headcount. He was lucky that they did break into groups as they did, they would have been impossible to count any other way. He had fifteen groups of twenty and six more, The same as yesterday and the same as twenty days ago when he left his home. Three hundred and six as his brother would say; as he had said.

The flock had grown nicely over the years, even though Rectus and his family ate much more meat than they had in the past. Even with the trading for fish and pretty things for the adornment of their home the flock did nothing but grow. He was glad his father had decided against goats. He agreed that they were nothing but trouble. They had enough wool, skins, and meat to trade for anything they wanted.

He gathered his belongings, few that they were, and wrapped them in his blanket, tying the bundle and, with his arm through the loop, slung it over his shoulder. He picked up his long shepherd's staff and went down the tempered incline to the perimeter of the assembly to persuade them into a concrete mass. Together they could be controlled.

Assuming all went well and that nothing spooked the animals, he could be home before nightfall. The days were lengthening again as summer came into being. Soon even the coolest nights would be warm.

He loved the heat. He hated to wear clothing and only did so when required by unfavorable weather, or when strangers were about. Many of the other shepherds in the area felt the same way. There was certainly no modesty among them.

The herd was slow moving. The idea was to keep them going in a general direction, concentrating mostly on the whereabouts of the rams. At times the herd would flow to the side like milk spilt on a cloth, a surge taking the path of least resistance. Shepherds rarely ran to control the motion, unless they were making sport of the situation. That had the potential to make matters worse. Besides, what did it really matter? Where were they going to go?

* * *

Deus sat on the bare wooden bench with his father, both stooped forward, heads bowed, clutching their palms together, their mourning of their loss conflicting with the logic of their revelations.

Zeus raised his head, observing the declining sun, a pang of hunger issuing from his belly. They had not eaten since their discovery out of respect for the deceased, planning to break their fast on the morrow at dawn. Their toil of the previous evening was beginning to demand replenishment. Only a diminishing feeling of divinity was maintaining their stamina.

"I smell the sheep. Rectus is returning." The musky waft carried on the barely perceptible evening breeze from the west. They waited, devoid of any thoughts as to an easy way of breaking the news.

The top of the rise seemed to undulate with hot vapors rising as on a hot day. A line spread over the crest and down the side as they came into view, the sheep a variety of hues from white to dark brown. At this distance to Zeus they would have appeared as part of the scrub later in the year had they not been in motion. His eyes were not what they had been in his youth. Even with the contrast against the still green foliage of late spring he still had to strain.

The sheep moved well downhill, knowing this area more than any other. They needed little prodding to come to this familiar valley where most of them had their inception.

Rectus was glad to see his father and brother waiting for him. He had mellowed over the years, the disdain he had once held for his brother passing with time. Still, he felt a bit nervous, having developed an appreciation of solitude more deep than the other two could understand. He had become reclusive after the death of his brother, never able to understand how a person could just stop working, ceasing to function.

Why were they standing side by side like that, watching him advance? They looked neither side to side nor at the sheep, assessing them as those would who had their life invested. They remained focused on him.

He could see the remorse in their eyes but could not place what it could be, Rectus not being a great analyst of facial expression due to his self-imposed seclusion. He raised his arm in greeting. The two merely nodded slightly.

What could be wrong? He didn't like it when things went wrong. That's why he limited his contact with people. Life was just so much simpler. Looking after the sheep was easy, for the most part. And, for his trouble, his family, who didn't annoy him too much, took good care of him. He was clothed, fed well when he returned home, and looked after when he was sick enough to require it. What more could he want?

"Your mother and brother are dead."

Rectus stood there with his staff in hand, staring into the eyes of his father whose place it had been to deliver this news.

"What?" He couldn't comprehend this turn of events. What did they mean his mother and brother were dead? Two people didn't just 'die'.

"They were killed."

Killed. By what? By who? "How could they be killed?" His eyes darted from his father to his brother and back again, searching for a quick answer to this mystery.

Zeus looked at his feet in shame.

"Your brother we found against the door. His head was split open. Your mother . . ." his voice trailed off. "We found her inside." That was all he could manage.

"What was done to her?" Rectus's voice was rising.

Deus was reticent. "She was taken by another man. Then he killed her."

Rectus roared. "No. It cannot be." He swung his staff hard on the ground, snapping it in his rage. The half still in his hand he beat through the air, smashing imaginary enemies, twirling around, killing them by the dozens. Both arms flailing wildly he flung the broken staff into the distance, screaming like a wild man. "You stand here like fools? Why are you not avenging their deaths? Why are you not pursuing the animal who did this thing? What is wrong with you?" He grabbed Deus by the collar and shook him violently.

Zeus placed his hands on his son's arms to restrain him. The two set the trembling man on the bench, taking up position on either side of him, forgiving him and knowing the moment had got the best of him.

Deus spoke. "We have been through this ourselves, and we understand your anger. We found them dead when we came back from the village. What could we do but bury them? If I had found him in my rage, I would have disemboweled him with my own hands, but he was nowhere to be seen. What could anyone have done other than grieve?"

Rectus seemed to see the logic in this. "This is evil. How could anyone do such a cruelty?"

Deus had the briefest flash of a recollection of Rectus tormenting him years earlier. He had little doubt that the world was full of obdurate people who would go through life without the slightest perception of their own cruelty.

"Where did you bury them?"

"Ronos is with our ancestors. He was the last one. There was no more room and so we closed the entrance. Mother is on the plateau not far from here."

Rectus turned his face his brother. "There is no cave at the plateau."

"We built a tomb of rock." He hesitated. The next part was going to be difficult.

"A tomb of rock? You built it yourselves? Why would you do such a thing? Our ancestors have always had the dignity of a cave site burial. Why would you put Mother in a pile of rocks? Are you mad?" His anger was waxing again. "Does she not deserve better than that?"

"She deserved better than a cave. She deserved a monument to show the world what she was, finer than any person we can as yet comprehend. Rectus, we must show you this."

He brought his felt roll from the hut. With reverence he unwrapped the contents, revealing to his brother for the first time the artifacts. He had placed the goddess so that it would be upright when unveiled, centered on the scorch mark made when he draped the felt over it so many years ago. In front of her, he arranged the buttons in a 'W'.

Rectus was mystified but for the moment kept his peace.

"This has come to us, to all mankind, from the heavens, from the Moon. I have been chosen to rule sometime in the future. These icons are to help me do this." He indicated the buttons with his outstretched arm and open palm. "This goddess that has come to us is none other than Selene, our Mother. Her death has given this life. Not life as we know it, but a representation of a higher life. Last night I saw that life, an infinite awareness, an all-encompassing sight, incredible knowledge and power."

"I saw it myself, as well. I felt myself to be an immortal being, wealthy with power. And then I was brought down in humility when I saw that your brother surpassed me many fold, and that beyond him Selene had the power to hold the Moon in her palm. All that he says is true."

"With this almighty power and vision did you happen to see who committed this outrageous affront to our family?" Rectus spoke softly, his sarcasm expressed not as an insult but as one still bent on revenge.

"I wondered that I could not see the killer. I saw the immensity of the land about us, the island on which we live and the islands all about us, the peopled villages, those who are skilled in arts beyond anything I have ever considered, but I could not see a hint of who could have done this thing. I thought about that the entire night. I believe that the reason lies in the fact that it is too late to do anything about it. To Selene, what is done is done. To Selene, it simply doesn't matter."

"You are a fool to believe it doesn't matter. These murders cry out for vengeance."

"In a sense they do. But think about it. If our time was devoted to finding the killer, what then? I have been exhorted to take command of this island and the lands all about. I do not take that charge lightly. Perhaps at some unforeseen time I will be able to delve into the area of pursuing the killer with the idea of vengeance, but that will be far in the future. And yourself. What do you think you can accomplish? You will leave your sheep and do what? Wander the countryside like a vagabond? Will you beg? Or will you steal to survive? Will you perchance kill someone yourself? Or would you prefer your old father to do this searching for you? With his poor health he would be just the match for a killer strong enough to bash Ronos's brains out."

Deus pinched his brow. This was not how he had planned this conversation to go. He was trying to preach peace and forgiveness, and here he was taunting his brother with sarcasm. "I am sorry, my brother. Forgive me. My words are harsh. I grieve our loss too. In memory of Mother let us adjust as she would suggest. Let us build this world and do so in her memory. She is the Moon Goddess and has been before us all these years, giving us life, trying to teach us, in spite of our ignorance, the true things in life. As she has given birth to us so has she given birth to these items before us. And far more than these has she spawned the Earth itself." He was on his feet now, arms skyward. "Selene is the Mother of the Earth. Each day and night, as she cradles the Earth in her circular path, let us be likewise. Let us be in her hands."

Deus's spiritual leadership was blossoming within his own family. He felt his influence growing over them. He could visualize this tenet spreading all across the land. He would begin immediately.

"I am leaving you for a time. I don't know how long I will be away. I plan to tour the island, to investigate the possibilities that it has to offer the future. After that, I will visit some of the distant lands by sea. When I return I will become king and lead this people into the greatest age the world has ever seen, where all will have wealth, all will enjoy peace and freedom from attacks the likes of which we have suffered.

"It will come to pass."

~~~~~~

Chapter 4

The Mission

2948 BCE

Deus traveled due south, not really knowing why. It just seemed as good a place to start as any. As he thought about it, he thought that it made sense to keep bathed in the light of the Sun and Moon throughout the day and night. They would always be passing before him from left to right if he kept on this general tack. He knew that he was on an island and it would only be a matter of time before he reached the limits of how far he could go. He had seen in his vision how massive the island was but, at the same time, he knew he could only get so lost. If he hugged the coast he would always follow it in a big circle and end up back at Amnisos, the village with which he was so familiar.

He had seen these mountains in the distance from his home, not realizing their actual height or how difficult it would be to traverse them. Now that he was upon them he began to feel that perhaps he should have chosen coast travel and made a more sensible loop of the entire island. But a small inkling within him confirmed that this was the way he should proceed and so he carried on, the discouraging thought passing quickly.

The pack he carried was large for one traveling this kind of terrain. He had no idea what to take with him, so he took a little of everything. He had packed heavier loads than this but never with the intention of going so far. He had packed his precious felt, his most significant reminder of his mother as she existed in this life and her exceptional compassion for his wellbeing.

He had the five buttons, they seemed to give him strength, but had left the goddess in the care of his father to guard with his life. He had to swear a pact to that effect before Deus would leave him with it. Its image filled his mind even now as he walked. He hoped he hadn't offended Selene somehow but, in consideration of his mission, he felt he could not carry the weight of such a burden so great a distance. The steel was far too heavy, and the chance of theft was too high.

He packed his waterskin, the membrane tight to capacity. He was following a creek up into the mountains and so far the supply of water was good, but who knew when the water might suddenly turn bad or disappear? No one he had known ever told him of travel any distance inland.

He had some olive oil, also in a skin, along with the lamp that had been destined for use by his mother. His father could easily trade for another if he so wished such a new convenience.

Inside a couple of fleeces he had wrapped a few days worth of dried fish, dried mutton, some figs, raisins, and dried olives. He didn't have much use for the fleece but thought that he might be able to trade for something, later in the journey, if that became necessary.

He really had no idea on how he was going to support himself. He would just have to manage. He had a niggling doubt about this whole thing but tried to convince himself that all would work out, that Selene was watching over him and would provide as she always had. It was easy to have great faith when he was in the midst of an inspiring spiritual experience, but when the reality of the day was upon him once again, he found he wavered somewhat. He made it his personal goal to shake these destructive doubts from his mind.

His enthusiasm rose again, and with it his determination to extend himself to the fullest. He knew he was exhausted and needed to rest, but just as he thought he would have to give in and rest, he got his second wind. The feeling was miraculous. Deus felt it was a needed boost of energy given by the buttons he carried. With such a gift how could he rest? To do so would be to slap the face of the goddess who provided these amulets of strength.

Invigorated, he carried on through the night, euphoric in his newfound capacity. He used the Moon at night the way he used the sun during the day to orient himself. He would have preferred to go in a direct line south, but one didn't go in a direct line anywhere on Kriti. He had hills and mountains to traverse and circumnavigate, forests of oak, myrtle, juniper, tamarisk, and oleander. He noticed several wild trees of quince, mulberry, almond, and pear, but they were either out of season or too untamed to bear. Often a cliff or precipice blocked his progress, once dangerously so in the dark. Only the Moonlight had given a clue to the abrupt drop before him, highlighting the ground that suddenly turned to blackness. As he approached the edge the perspective hints from the land below warned him of the jeopardy he narrowly avoided. His heart jumped with sudden comprehension, but his resolve and determination heightened as he realized that divine intervention had protected him.

He continued walking through the night and well into the next day, stopping very shortly only to unpack food, his meal breaks taken while on the move.

He followed the edge of a long mountain, about halfway up, keeping the same altitude. Sheep grazed in the bottom of the valley. He counted thirty-six. Deus knew that an unseen shepherd guarded them, out of sight and probably asleep. He stopped to test his eyes. Sure enough, a few hundred feet from the small flock, and a little higher up, was a cocoon-like object not quite in keeping with the terrain. To most people that shepherd would have been indistinguishable from the lightly shaded rocks and shrubbery of the hillside. He sat on a rocky protrusion and observed the unmoving guardian. Some not in the business would have thought it odd that a shepherd would be sleeping, especially during the day, but Deus understood fully that shepherds need their sleep too, and that rotational sleep, sleep lasting usually no more than an hour or two, perhaps half a dozen times throughout the course of the twenty-four hour day, was the norm when one was not part of a team.

He knew that the shepherd would be sensitive to any disturbance that the flock made, and would be instantly on the alert at the breaking of any unusual sound whether made by his charges or not. The thought of slipping up beside him unawares, while still carrying his belongings was too much of a temptation.

Slowly, carefully, he made his way down the slope, wary of any loose gravel that might give him away. The sheep had spotted him. Some had their heads up, eyeing him. Some would put their noses in the air, attempting to get his scent, although the breeze was nonexistent and unlikely to carry his smell down into their trough. He knew how to move in a non-threatening way. They would not bolt.

It took him several minutes to work his way to a position beside the man. He looked to be the same age, the same black hair and beard. A strong arm protruded from under the man's wool blanket. This blanket was knitted, loosely, after the manner of some that he had seen in the market at Amnisos. This one was of a bit tighter weave though, clearly superior to the others.

Deus watched him for several minutes, utterly silent. The sheep were completely ignoring him, accepting him readily as a new part of their surroundings. The shepherd breathed on, oblivious to his new companion, his eyes vibrating and rolling as he dreamed. Deus smiled broadly, stifling the urge to laugh as he watched the blissful face twitch.

It was time to give him something to twitch about. He silently unpacked his belongings, laying them about as if he himself had camped there for days, his felt spread upon the flattest patch, his food set on the open sheepskins, the other items scattered about. He was hungry and began to gnaw on the fish, popping the odd olive into his mouth at the same time. Odd, he wondered, how a prepared olive was just fine, but one straight off the tree, ripe or otherwise, was so horrible as to be inedible.

The shepherd's nostrils began to twitch, his eyes made a flurry of movements and then stopped. His lips parted and he began to mouth-breathe.

Suddenly his eyes opened and he sat straight up, staring at his new surroundings, and most particularly at Deus. He gave him a quizzical look, quickly sizing him up and confirming that he was harmless enough.

He put his hands on his hips. "That's twice today this has happened."

They both broke into peals of laughter, the sudden raucous noise scattering his sheep over a small area.

"Forgive me for sneaking up like a thief. But how could I resist a joke on someone so negligent in his duties? Let me introduce myself. My name is Deus. I am traveling to the southern coast where I hope to do a little exploring."

"So you are a sneaking thief then? Running to escape capture no doubt." They grasped forearms in the traditional greeting, trading insults as old friends. "I am Taros. As you can see I am wealthy beyond measure. My vast flock tells it all. Count them. You will see that this is the finest and largest flock under the sun. Rob me and you will have legions pursuing you to the south coast." Again they laughed, Deus tearing the fish in half to share with his new friend.

They discussed the finer points of sheep rearing and breeding. Deus was surprised that Taros had also noticed that mating couples of similar trait tended to have lambs of the same type. Deus had been able to increase the strength and whiteness of his sheep by improving the breeding techniques normally used, which was no technique at all. All the rams needed was a bit of guidance. It was hardly trouble when he was just sitting around doing nothing anyway. He was surprised that no one else ever bothered. He certainly could never get his own family members to do it, except his father who had at least a minimal interest in changing the way things were always done. His interest was more monetary. If he could see a profit, then he could be enticed to participate in Deus's breeding program. But he was a bit lazy too. If the lambs would come faster, he might be more interested. Like most people, quantity seemed more tangible, quality often too esoteric.

"Do you have a family? Around here I mean?" This was a rather dumb question. Deus just wanted to find out more about the man and this area.

"Yes. My family is very close, just over the next rise and into the valley. You would have been playing tricks on them by now, I don't doubt, if you had kept walking. But tell me about yourself. What takes a shepherd on such a journey?"

Deus sat back, his eyes glazing slightly. He related the story in its entirety, the meteorite when he was a boy, the vision he and his father recently had of the world, Selene the Moon Goddess appearing before him as the Earth-Mother. He felt it a point of wisdom to omit the part about Selene being his own Mother in the flesh at this time. That point of doctrine might be difficult for others to grasp. It could wait.

He also felt it wise not to mention the five tektites he carried on his person. If word got out, he might find himself victimized. Not that they would be of value, he was sure, to anyone else. It was just that the perceived value could be the cause of confrontations that he did not need.

Taros was held captive as the story unfolded before him. What a wonder to behold. He could almost envision the apparition of the Moon Goddess as she revealed herself to the two men. Perhaps one day he could be the recipient of such a vision.

Deus could easily discern the interest Taros had for this monumental event. He hadn't actually considered taking anyone with him on his travels. There would be certain advantages, even greater if the other party was as enthusiastic as this.

"Taros, I perceive a certain desire to accompany me on this exploration. Am I correct in assuming this?"

There was no hesitation. "I would be thrilled and delighted. I will leave this flock in the care of my Father, whose sheep they are anyway, and be ready to go with you by sunrise tomorrow. That is if you help me get these beasts back to our camp. We've been talking so long there's barely much of the day left."

* * *

"Father, I want you to meet a new friend of mine. Deus. He is from the north of here. Almost on the coast. He is a shepherd too."

"Are you, then? Welcome, Deus. Always glad to have another of our trade stop by."

"Thank you. You have some fine sheep here. Very well behaved. I've never seen a flock move so quickly home from afield."

"They know where their home is. We treat them well."

"Deus fed me at the field site, Father. He had fish that he brought with him from the coast."

"Is that so? Well, we will have to return the gesture. You will dine with us tonight, Deus. I'm sure your nose tells you our evening meal is nigh at hand. Tell me of your journey. How long have you been traveling?"

"I left my home yesterday."

"Yesterday?" the old man interjected. "That is impossible. I have only been to the north coast once, and that was many years ago, but I have not grown so old as to become stupid, and I know the distance has not become less with the passing of time. Don't take me for a fool, my lad."

"I would never presume such a thing, sir. My home is a normal day's travel south of the coast. I did leave my home early yesterday and have not rested since I left, except for a few hours in conversation with your son. And I might add that driving the sheep slowed me down considerably. I could actually have been here some time ago."

"That is amazing. You are either fool or pompous liar. Why would you be in such a rush? You will exhaust yourself long before you reach the other coast. Then what good will it do you?"

"There is wisdom in what you say. My bones are indeed weary. Tonight I will sleep well and hopefully I will be refreshed enough to carry on in the morning." He looked at Taros. Here was the opening he needed.

"Father, I have been thinking of escorting our guest to the south, perhaps even as far as the coast."

"What?"

"I've never been that far from here, and I would like to see if there is much of a difference. Perhaps I'll even turn back before I get to the coast."

"Or perhaps you won't." His look was stern. He could see the resolve already formed in his son's eyes and knew that he was going to go no matter what was said. If his mind was not yet firmly committed to this adventurous idea, it soon would be. He had disappeared, often for as long as three or four full days at a time, walking and exploring who knew where? He would never tell him other than to say he was climbing mountains or tracking animals. His son had to travel. It was in him.

The men sat at a circle of logs, taking sides opposite each other with a charred pile of ash separating them. A woman came out of the hut with food and water, laying it before them. She smiled at the newcomer, nodding at him, but not saying anything.

Deus felt he should say something, finding her silence a bit uncomfortable. He nodded to the pile of smoked mutton. "This smells delicious. Did you smoke it with oakwood?"

She smiled and nodded once again before departing, disappearing into the hut.

"Will she not join us?"

"Join us?" Taros's father looked genuinely puzzled. "Why would she join us?"

"I just thought she might join in our conversation, enjoy the meal with us."

"You are a strange one. Did your mother eat with your father and you? I have never heard of such a thing. I suppose it happens, maybe, but not that I've ever heard of. Women eating with the men. You have been overexerting yourself."

"Well, now that you mention it, it was a rather rare occurrence up until the last couple of years. But I don't think my mother was too well-loved by my father before. That's all changed now though. She's welcome wherever he goes."

The older man grunted and pulled a face. He obviously held his wife in low regard. And he was beginning to wonder about the person sitting across from him. The beauty of being a shepherd was that you didn't have to tolerate too many people coming by with queer ideas. If they did, they were easy enough to send on their way. However, none of them had ever suggested taking one of his sons along before.

The only thing Deus could get the old man to converse about was sheep. Everything else, any idea, he simply regarded with disdain. This was a man who had no future.

Deus wondered what the point was in living for such a person. He seemed to have a single purpose in life, his sheep, and he wasn't incredibly successful with that. This man reminded him of his own father, many years ago, when he displayed great ignorance. He had changed dramatically, albeit slowly, seeing no pressing need to apply any effort to the transformation. This man seemed a bit different. His eyes lacked the sparkle of intelligence. He had some discernment, that was true, but without an innate curiosity he would go no further.

The man left them, vanishing into the complete darkness of the interior of his hut as the day faded to twilight. Deus got the impression that he typically stayed up a bit later, but had made a special exception this evening.

"Father isn't much of a talker. You were wise not to tell him of your experiences."

"I didn't think he would appreciate them. Still, I suppose I could have at least tried."

"You did the right thing. He might have thought you mad and forbade me to go with you in the morning."

"Would that stop you?"

Taros took in the surrounding landscape, remembering with fondness the escapades of his youth, playing with his brothers, learning from his father. He inhaled deeply. Even the smell of the place told him that this was home.

"No. No, it would not."

* * *

Taros had brought with him a pack little different from that which Deus carried.

The village of Vathypetro was only a small settlement, a tenth the size and population of Amnisos. It was a barter center for the locals more than anything else, a place to meet and trade with whoever else happened to be visiting. A few permanent residents specialized in various crafts, pottery, toolmaking, woolen clothing. Mostly they were aged or handicapped and so couldn't manage heavier work that involved agriculture or hunting. They didn't do well as most people in the area could also make the same things. Perhaps not as well, but there was very little social stratification in these small, widely scattered communities and so there was no impetus to rise above the neighbors.

Forming a class system depends on things that these people were just not aware of. They lived in and were entrenched in the agricultural society, a society in which no one does much more than what is necessary to survive. The creation of an 'elite' depends on wealth, inheritance, privilege, and perhaps, prowess on the battlefield. And since there was no wealth other than the essentials, no wars other than minor local squabbles over women or misappropriated animals, no inherited privilege, and no inheritance apart from the dividing up of the few essentials the deceased may have owned, social stratification was something that just did not occur.

With everyone for miles around making or growing or raising the same thing there is little in the way of craft specialization, and the necessity for trade becomes virtually nonexistent. Occasionally some brave or desperate character will make a go of it and try to develop a special skill. This is seen as a nice thing, but what is it good for? So the things we make aren't as pretty, or strong, but, for better or worse, they still fulfill the same function, and function is all that matters.

Once a society has worked out a way to meld comfortably with the immediate environment it is extraordinarily resistant to change. When the people are comfortable they are happy, and when they stay in a frame of happy acceptance of their lot in life they settle firmly into their survival rut, and generations follow.

How, then, do things change? Something, or someone, stirs up the community, becomes the instigator that encourages it to do things differently. Even more important, this agitator consistently keeps them doing things differently.

No society, regardless of size, regardless of how it tries, successfully isolates itself in a vacuum. The surrounding world is unpredictable. Even internally things happen. A better idea, a new way of doing anything, an epidemic. Hot years cause droughts, cold ones early crop failure. Meeting threats, or opportunities, communities alter their habits to the extent that they must. When crops fail then they have to fish and hunt, or die trying.

When people die from natural catastrophe or disease, they may resort to appeasing the gods with sacrifices, trying various things in varying amounts until the calamity passes. That entails an enormous energy expenditure to procure enough food for the gods, as well as enough for man, and advances may be made. But people being what they are, soon after the emergency passes, the communal society slides back toward the reestablishment of its old, predictable routines.

So things were in the Aegean. Forty-five hundred years earlier, sometime around 7000 BC, the first settlers migrated to the islands, fleeing to a safe haven from the fertile lands east of the Mediterranean. Periodically a new group might settle in the area, introducing a new crop, bringing a new species of domestic animal, a few goats or sheep. Eventually the new groups would mix with the established, slightly altering the way things were once done, adapting their language as they struggled to make themselves understood, sometimes killing the men in frustration, taking the women as prizes.

For the most part, the people of the islands were peaceful. If someone didn't get along with his neighbor, he merely packed up and moved on, if the other party hadn't beaten him to it. There was no shame involved. Chances were that the land over the next hill was as good or better anyway. The population stayed low enough that there was far more land than could ever be used. Still, people liked to be fairly close to a center, a settlement of some kind. There have always been gregarious types that have enjoyed the company of others, strangers or otherwise. Some held these people in contempt, others gravitated toward them. In times of need these convivial people tended to become leaders, unless a more violent usurper took the reins by force, but force was a rarity in the early Aegean.

In the possession-oriented society of today, of the twentieth century, we find it almost impossible to imagine any society where wealth doesn't exist, where there are no savings, and no social distinctions based on property. The strictly utilitarian clay pots, stone tools, clothing, mats, and other household essentials that a family owns have not been accumulated for any other reason than the simple fact that they are necessities. They don't have value, per se, and certainly not any artistic merit.

Although trade existed, the Aegean people, like any other, struggled to get the best deal for themselves at the expense of their brother. Whatever the trade was, wool, food, obsidian, it was at first feeble and painfully slow. Obsidian trade, the very hard, glassy, volcanic stone so prized for knives and scrapers, had been going on in a very limited amount since around the time of the earliest settlers. It held an extremely keen edge and, except for its brittleness, was far superior to flint. A remarkable feature of this close-grained stone is that its characteristics vary slightly from place to place and geological analysis can determine exactly where a particular piece originates. The best was quarried from the Aegean island of Melos, and artifacts are found at the oldest archaeological sites on the Greek mainland, the island of Crete, and the other islands.

Deus stopped to talk to an old lady, the oldest he had ever seen, sitting on a bench in front of her small stone hut, allowing the sun to bath her in its rays. Her bones showed through her wrinkled, brown skin, her knees and elbows fearsome knobs, her arthritic fingers and toes curled up, twisted like an ancient oak. She had been singing the lilting tune of a tempo that he had so far been unfamiliar with, but stopped as they approached.

"What could bring a couple of delightful young men such as you two to such a humble place as this?" she asked in her happy, surprisingly youthful voice.

"We heard the serenades of a Siren and we were compelled against our will to come and worship," replied Deus, remembering the outlandish tales of the fisherman in Amnisos.

The old woman threw back her head violently, Deus fearing she would crack it fatally on the stone wall, a shrill cackle offending his ears and dissolving into a celebration of wheezes as her chest heaved and she rollicked for air.

Deus sat beside her, hugging her tightly with the hope that he could bay her convulsions enough to keep her from falling off the bench and doing herself an injury.

"Calm yourself, woman. You couldn't have reached this old age by abusing yourself so."

"It is you that abuses me. I never thought that I would figure in a fisherman's lies so far from the sea."

She put an arm around him and gave a weak squeeze. "You have made an old hag very happy. But such joy can be the death of one so frail. Admit it. You set out to kill me and are disappointed in your failure."

"Nonsense. You must sing to us again. We have traveled far, and the sound renews us. Taros. Hand me your skin."

She drank the water, savoring the weak taste of wine that had washed off the inside of the bag, giving a light flavor.

With her lips and throat now wet she took the song from its beginning through its entirety, the melody wrapping around the men, carrying them into the past where a younger, more beautiful woman had her love for a man now long dead.

"Your song touches our hearts," said Deus with all sincerity. "I had never known such beauty could come from the throat." They sat in quiet contemplation, moved by the eloquence of the sonnet.

"I have little food, but you have lifted my spirits. I will find a way." She pulled herself up on her brace, a fairly straight branch that forked at her armpit, and made her way, in some pain, into the interior of her hut. She emerged with a small pile of flat cakes and a pot of honey, setting them on the bench before turning awkwardly and sitting down in slow motion, the last few inches a straight flop to the seat.

"You are kind to share with us. You can't have much."

"I am a poor old woman. What have I to live for? If sharing what I have makes those happy that have made me happy, then I am complete, and when my time comes, I can die in peace. Maybe those who think well of me will not leave my carcass to rot but will lie me in a place of decency."

"I think you should have many who would give you a good burial."

They ate the cakes, dipping them in the pot of honey made soft by the warmth of the day. The meal was delicious. The honey filled him with renewed energy.

The kindness of this old woman pierced Deus's heart. She was selfless, even to strangers. "You remind me of the Earth-Mother." He looked directly into her eyes.

She did not respond other than to hold his gaze. Deus began to speak of the qualities of Selene, her love and caring for everything, her long-suffering, her patience, her acceptance of this life as something to endure as well as enjoy. He spoke of the complete joy that would come to those who could keep that peace in their heart, despite all obstacles that might get in the way. "Everyone is to face challenges, that is an important part of life, and with the kindness of others in our path and the benevolence of Selene we will find our trials on this earth so much easier."

A small number of passers-by stopped, as he spoke, to listen to his words. None interrupted.

He seemed to speak endlessly, effortlessly, the words gushing forth as water from an artesian spring. Some of what he spoke he had never thought before, the spiritual enrapturement possessing him again as he expounded the dogma of his cherished goddess.

The sky was darkening. "I have a gift for you."

"You have given me enough, young man. I have waited my life to hear words such as you have spoken to me this day."

Deus removed the lamp from his pack and filled it with oil. "Get me some fire" he directed to a youth who had been listening. The lad ran off.

Now he was speaking to all present. "Do any of you know what this is?"

His question was responded to with blank stares. He thought not. This was new enough on the coast. In an isolated place like this, they wouldn't have seen one. He was probably the first to come by this village in some time and, even if he wasn't, it would have been unlikely that a traveler would have given anyone a lamp.

The lad returned, walking now as he held his hand in front of the burning sticks, sheltering the flame. Deus held the wick up to the fire long enough for it to catch.

"This is for you." He passed the lamp to the old lady who received it gingerly. As you remember me for giving you this light, remember also that you have been shown a far greater light; that light of endless life.

The soft glow washed her face in an orange iridescence. More people were coming now, the crowd increasing in number as the village inhabitants discovered that they had been missing out on some event.

They marveled at the lamp, everyone wanting a closer look. The children pushing their way to the front warmed their fingers close to the flame, not understanding the magic that could make it come from an incombustible piece of clay.

For their benefit Deus described how the lamp had been made, at least how he thought it could have been made, and how it worked. He suggested that the people could make their own as reminders of this new light that had been received in their town, and as a reminder of his passing through.

The clamor was such that he had to repeat to the best of his ability, most of what he had said throughout most of the day. It was late into the night before he had answered their questions and had finally to beg them to leave as he was too tired to continue.

* * *

Morning broke, the light striking Deus on his face, waking him from a deep slumber. Taros and the old lady had been awake for a while but had not stirred for fear of disturbing him. Apparently, they had been watching him and, now, with his eyes open, they felt free to rise.

Deus also sat up. "We will continue south today."

"You must stay with us. The people want you to stay. They said so last night."

"Your kindness overwhelms me. Yet we must go south. I don't know when we will really be able to stop. I feel we must go on a quest. For what exactly I don't know. But I know we must."

He stepped outside into the day. Several small groups saw him at once and started coming his way, shouting their greetings. They begged him to share more of his thoughts with them, not having had enough the night before.

"Please" he begged them. "Please wait here."

He stepped inside and brought the old lady back out with him, setting her outside the door on her bench. "I want you to witness one of the most beautiful things I have ever come across in my short life." He turned to the lady, who was now completely perplexed, knowing he couldn't be referring to her physical characteristics. "Please sing for us."

She was astonished. Still, he seemed sincere. He was definitely not mocking her. Reluctantly and quietly she began a song, different from the one the day before, the ones at the back of the crowd hushed and straining to hear. Deus smiled encouragement, nodding his head as she allowed her voice to rise in volume. Her tongue had never sounded so sweet, not in all her long years.

She sang as one possessed, transported into another realm, a land of harmony, the crowd invisible to her as she vociferated words never before uttered by the lips of man. When she had finished the people of the gathering wept. They too had never heard such beauty. A treasure had been amongst them for as long as any could remember and had not been recognized. Now that her life was coming to an end they agonized, realizing too late that this gift would not be long residing with them.

"Remember my teachings." Deus held his arm high in a farewell salute as the lady cried in protest.

A woman who had been silent, but deeply attentive to the proceedings of yesterday and this morning, presented two bundles to the men. "One for each of you," she spoke humbly, keeping her eyes cast to the ground.

Deus held her chin, tilting her head to meet her eyes. "Your gift is appreciated. Nighttime in the mountains will be cold." He examined the striped blanket. "I have never seen such work. Did you weave these?"

"Yes."

"They are magnificent," he said looking at Taros's as he unfurled his as well.

He turned to face the people. "Your talents are many. An old woman with the voice of a goddess. Another with the skills to weave colors into a blanket. Each of you has a talent, a skill that has to be tapped. Work on it. Those of you who have skills must teach others. Don't hide what you can do, bear those things up proudly. Always work to improve what you can do. The old lady with her gnarled fingers will never weave, but let her teach you all how to sing. You will come to know that such a thing has value as great as something you can touch with your hands. As a blanket warms your skin, a song will warm our soul."

With that they turned and left, the people knowing not to follow.

* * *

It was slow going over the formidable mountainous terrain. They ate as much of the native flora as they felt was safe, not enjoying it, but thinking it wise to conserve as much of their rations as possible. They weren't sure how long it would take them to get to the coast and really had no idea what they would find when they got there. Perhaps nothing.

The nights were terribly cold, as cold as the coldest winter nights Deus had experienced. One morning, before the sun peeked over the horizon, he saw frost on the ground, twinkling like starlight. His breath was visible, like smoke. The slap of cold on his face was refreshing, but not enough to get him out of his wraps. He was thankful that the lady in Vathypetro had given them her thoughtful gift. The supplement to the warmth of his felt was a comfort to him. He'd make a point of staying at lower altitudes at night if he could.

* * *

The thirty kilometers, as the crow flies, to the coast took them well into the third day from Vathypetro. Taros was awestruck, the majestic sea reaching endlessly beyond the distant horizon, bluest of all the world's deep blue seas. Rich cerulean mist whipped up by a stiff breeze washed against his face. He stood spellbound with Deus at the top of the rock promontory, the height of the bluff giving them the advantage of seeing even farther into the distance. Neither had seen such a stretch of water, or land for that matter, so void of anything tangible save the white ripples of small frothy breakers. No one would have thought, from viewing this sight, that there would be other than water until the end of the earth was reached.

It was nothing like the view from Amnisos, the only sea view familiar to Deus. The island of Dia gave something concrete to the sea, made it less fearful, more predictable and welcome, as far as that was possible. This was stark. The high cliffs stretched out to the left and right, undulating but never breaking, giving the distinct impression that this was it, the end. Land stopped here, abruptly. One would be suicidal to venture past this point, other than to do a little fishing, perhaps, within safe distance of the shore.

They rested here for the remainder of the day, indecision on which way to go happily keeping them in this serene and beautiful place. There was no sign that anyone inhabited any area around here.

"I could stay here forever." Taros was serious. He had nothing against the territory inland that he had grown up with, but this was like nothing he could have imagined, sparkling, exciting, invigorating.

He sat with his legs dangling over the edge, like he did as a boy on the ledges of the mountainside near his home. His mother would have had fits seeing him flaunting death like that, his father trying to calm her saying that he was a brave young man and this was good for him. No harm would befall him if she would kindly refrain from spooking him over the edge.

* * *

By dawn, Deus had made his decision. They would go east, following the coast. This sounded good to Taros. He was ready to follow anywhere, but was particularly pleased to be staying within sight of the water.

The coast was rough and irregular. At noon they came across a long beach and paused there to bathe and enjoy a meal. A narrow stream of fresh water broke through at the midpoint and they filled their skins. Deus thought this would be a nice location for a village and, as he thought about it, wondered why no one had settled here.

As much as they enjoyed the beauty of this reach of waterfront they acknowledged that they must be moving along. Deus knew there was much more to this tour than the enjoyment of scenery. He had a compelling urge to meet people, to communicate and discover. To see the land was part of that experience, but he could do that at a glance, or while walking. He really had no need to park himself and observe the same thing for any extended length of time.

They passed several small streams and, later, after pushing themselves, another beach similar to the last one. This was straighter and sandier, hot on their feet. It, too, had freshwater streams feeding the sea. There was obviously no problem finding water if the streams were consistently this far apart. They wondered if that was where all the water in the sea came from. Perhaps over the long years the water just gathered to the point that the world had filled up and only the higher islands were left above. They wondered how long it would be before even the islands would be covered.

What would people do then? How long would it take? They gazed at the sea. The expanse was infinite. The land covered must have been very flat. These little streams couldn't raise the extent of what they could see any significant amount even if they were every ten paces. Relieved at their conclusion, they carried on.

Deus recalled his vision as they walked. He remembered it clearly, every part of it. Yet it seemed less real as it rescinded farther into the past.

Looking to the horizon, much lower now that they were closer to sea level, he would have thought it impossible that anything could be out there. But he knew that his reasoning was false. He knew that another vast land existed somewhere in that direction, out of sight, hidden by distance. They should have been able to see it from their vantage point on that cliff top. Why hadn't they? He pondered that for a time as they walked. Taros surmised that if they had climbed that high mountain, instead of skirting the side of it, they might have been able to see far enough. He had no doubt that the vision Deus had seen had been true.

The day had been long. They had covered more distance today than any other day, and the land had been more rugged. It seemed that the farther they went, the more strength they gained, and the farther they could go the next day. They wondered if there was any end to this secret. What if there wasn't? They couldn't go any farther today, their very bones were weary. But what if they continued anyway? They decided to ensue.

Picking up their bags they hiked up the scabrous incline rising from the far end of the alluvium strand. They replaced their sandals, the sharp gravel contrasting smartly with the comfortable sand of the shore. Once they reached the top of this rise, their travels became easier. The hills lightly rolled, mostly smooth with green grass that they found a pleasure to walk on, even with their legs calling out for attention. Eventually, it was too dark to continue, the hills becoming rocky and treacherous. They could have gone on in desperation but agreed that it was foolhardy without good reason. They spread out their packs and were instantly asleep.

* * *

At last. Taros had been wondering if there were no other people living on the island. As it was, they missed numerous settlements that they could have had contact with had they stayed inland. On a beeline to the village they were now approaching from Vathypetro, they could have reasonably expected to have connected with at least half a dozen.

Deus trusted his instincts and had never been discouraged. This was no surprise to him. The men he saw ahead were simply what eventually had to be. All held up their arms in greeting.

The men were in the midst of unloading packs from their boat to a cache well up the beach. Deus had never seen such a boat, as long as five tall men lying head to foot, a high prow rising from the bow, seats for six oarsmen, or was it twelve? Maybe they sat side by side. He wasn't sure. There were more than twelve men here, but they couldn't have all been in the boat.

The largest came forward to greet them while the others stopped their work to observe. "Welcome friends. I hope you are friends at any rate."

"I should hope that we are. We have no defense against such as you, or so many." Deus made reference to his size, never having seen such a huge man.

He took the compliment with grace and introduced the newcomers to the rank and file of his crew. "I work them hard, and they do well for themselves and their families. No one we know has ever starved to death."

Deus and Taros found that to be an odd comment. No one they knew had ever starved to death either, although they were quite cognizant of a present absence within their bellies.

"Allow us to assist you with your boat."

"Here we have good people, my friends. Already willing to assist us in our struggles. Grab on, men, and lift with all your strength."

Each took hold of the rim at even points around the perimeter, the combined effort just raising the craft above the sand as they moved it up the incline to where the grass began. Deus and Taros barely made it. Their legs felt soft, infirm. They didn't realize that the others had arms that felt the same way after rowing over five hundred kilometers in the last five days.

Deus ventured a question. "What is this long rib down the center of your ship?" He could not understand the idea of such an adornment.

67

"That, my young and inquisitive friend, is a keel. You have never seen such a thing, have you? That is how you can tell a ship I make from any other. With that, I can travel the great waters, straight and unbending. No feeble wind will blow my ship off course. It holds as steady as the sun or moon."

They left the boat, each of the men taking a large pack and heading off up the well-worn trail.

"Come along. You can help us celebrate." The large man motioned with his head as he stomped off after the others.

Deus and Taros followed close behind, the prospect of a good meal tantalizing. The trail led through ever-thickening cedar, the most robust of any forest Deus had yet come across. He didn't know trees could grow so close and not choke each other. The green filtered light gave everything a cool, olive complexion. The air here was fresh, like a sea breeze without the wind, the foliage perfume pure and stimulating, giving them energy they might otherwise have lacked. Inhaling deeply in here was not something done out of necessity but out of pleasure.

They found it difficult to keep up with their hosts. They were exercising this opportunity to work their legs after being too long confined in the close quarters of their boat. Deus was determined to sustain his speed, not wanting to appear weak to these new acquaintances. Taros was also doing his best, surprised at the pace they were maintaining.

They emerged from the woods into an enormous clearing rising up the length of the hill. Stone houses with square wooden beams over the windows and doors and sloping roofs were in abundance. This town was larger than Amnisos, and it bustled. People were coming, seemingly out of nowhere, to laud the arrival of the sea voyagers. The crowd grew as they demanded dissertations from the expedition. The crew dispersed into groups with their families, their friends attracted into cliques to hear stories of adventure and imagination.

Deus and Taros stood quietly on the edge of the reception, thankful to be ignored for the moment in order to catch their breath and take their bearings.

Syros, the captain of the boat, was entertaining the largest crowd. As their strength returned the two outsiders sidled up to his group, hovering in the background as he told his tales. Deus had expected him to weave a fantasy of monstrosities of the deep, ravenous man-eaters that could drub terror into the hearts of the most courageous and smite average men dead with a glance.

He was far more reserved. He extolled his crew for the way they stroked the sea with their fourteen-foot oars, moving the boat as none before had ever done, cutting the water as fast as a sprinter ran on land. They had been welcomed in the land of Egypt, a place of sublime beauty, a flat land with endless sand beaches and green pasture. They could not understand the people, being of a different tongue, but with gestures of mutual regard they were able to secure an amicable rapport with them.

The crew gave them gifts of fleece, superior to anything the Egyptians had, and blankets weaved similarly to the blankets that had been given to Deus and Taros, with a pattern. They gave them olives, figs, plums, and quinces, and skins of the finest wine. Deus thought this amazing as he carried the same things, only in far lesser quantity.

The people had been pleased to receive the gifts. Their most pointed interest, however, was the boat. They had never seen such construction. They used only reeds that grew abundantly on the banks of the river he thought they referred to as 'Nile'. He hadn't known that they thought the heavy construction doomed the vessel to a certain death from sinking, unless they had a powerful magic to keep it afloat.

The Egyptians were much darker skinned than the people of Crete, but nowhere near as dark as the people who were obviously subservient to them. They witnessed the severe beating of a thoroughly black woman who spilt a few drops of wine she was pouring into a goblet. Several of the men had shrieked their displeasure and gave her additional kicks during her assault.

The crew spent two additional days on the northern coast of Egypt. They were well taken care of, given local wine and exceptional food. None would mention the hospitality of the black women that were given them for the duration. They attempted communication with several of the men who were obviously the leaders of the area. They traded names, drew maps and pictures in the sand, and exchanged items of worth.

It was no secret that the Egyptians were the more generous, in an attempt to persuade the Cretans to return with more of their goods. Egypt was a land of plenty, having good crops and advanced agricultural techniques, and being in a good location for trade with neighboring areas of Africa. The prospect of acquiring another trading partner was something most desirable to them.

And so they lavished their gifts, eager to have their wares displayed abroad, at a place too far for safe travel in their reed craft. Why should they attempt travel to some hard to locate island anyway when the foreign people were coming to them?

Syros continued his self-acclamation, passing forward the pictured tales of the Egyptians, the enormous structures, man-made mountains, gigantic statues, and a stone lion more massive than one could imagine. Of course, Syros did not believe any of this. Who did these people think they were dealing with? He countered with tales of tentacled sea demons, one-eyed giants who tore island rocks to rubble with their bare hands, survival of the fearsome and brutal storms that had drowned the other ships that had accompanied them part of the way. It would be no time soon that those people would be trying to conquer the Mediterranean in their silly reed floats.

The crowd howled with laughter, knowing full well that theirs was the only boat to set forth two weeks ago. Still, the achievement was remarkable. For hundreds of years, the people of this town had kept in what could only be called a casual contact with the north coast of Africa. It was something of a test of manhood to go on one of these infrequent expeditions, not truly expecting any riches, just to see if it could be done more than anything.

There was always some old man who tired the younger men to the point of exasperation with his tales of manhood and accusations against the new, weaker generation that had no sense of adventure. His tales would grow wilder with each telling until they could stand it no longer and would go out to see for themselves.

Sometimes the boats would leave in groups of two or three, but more usually it was just one boat with a crowded compliment of men to keep the rowing in full swing twenty-four hours a day.

No one could doubt these men were courageous, even if their courage had its genesis in the form of a red liquid prior to their storming into the blue.

The North Star had long been known as the night landmark that didn't move, the only one in the sky. That was the main reason for traveling at night when out of sight of land. Often a mariner would lose his nerve and start a panic that they were to be forever lost, and it was only the captain who was able to restore order with his calm assurances that all was well, that they were on course and the North Star proved it.

Day travel was more intuition and guesswork. The captain could take reasonable estimates throughout the day, which would keep them on an even track, keeping the morning sun on his left and the evening sun on his right.

The hard part was at noon. As long as they were out of sight of land, they risked arcing in a wide circle. If they had a steady breeze that had maintained its direction, or if the clouds were giving visual clues, they were usually able to avoid problems, but on a windless, clear day it was hardly worthwhile continuing. If the men were particularly tired, this was when they rested for a few hours until the sun could be gauged again, retreating from its high point in the heavens.

That restricted their travel all those years to a direct trip south, to the coast of what is now Libya and western Egypt. Inhabitants were scant, and those they found were mostly farmers with a few sheep. The land in those days was suitable for that kind of activity although they were susceptible to drought. The only reason to bother with these people at all was to bring back some sort of proof that they had actually reached their destination and returned safely. There was hardly any point coming back with nothing otherwise no one would have believed that they had gone any farther than just out of sight and parked themselves there like cowards.

Captains that had made the journey several times, often many years apart, fancied themselves to be quite the navigators and began to run risks. They would let themselves stray a little to the west, or to the east, and try to compensate for that on their return. It wasn't too risky. Kriti was two hundred fifty kilometers long from east to west and gave them a lot of leeway for error. The captains knew their own coast well enough that they would know whether they were east or west of Mirtos. If they missed the island on the homeward leg, they inevitably ran into other small islands that they also had familiarity with and could make their way home from there.

Some of the boats had indeed gone down in storms. There was no lying about that. But they had long ago figured out the pattern of disappearances and avoided the dangerous times of the year. Others had been greeted in a less friendly manner on the distant shore. Tired shipmen were no match for grasping slave merchants who marched them off to Egypt to work in construction gangs. Their boat would be burned and the ashes scattered to the four winds. No one would have ever confessed to ever having seen them, even if they could have spoken the same language. These trends were anomalous so far from the market and therefore rare. No one from Kriti ever found out, and the disappearances only fed some of the fabulous tales that sailors from the earliest times have thrived on.

The stories had been told, retold, and clarified. Syros, as leader of the expedition, now had the glorious responsibility of displaying the substance of their journey.

He mounted the stone wall, backfilled on the other side giving him a broad enough platform, a kind of 'speaker's corner,' and called to the crew to join him for the accolades of the crowd. The assembly had been growing steadily as word spread of the return and was now quite overwhelming to Deus and Taros. They would have lost their position close to the captain if they hadn't been caught up in his family group. They had heard from others that this was the procedure and that they should stay close to better hear the star attraction when he unveiled his inventory.

Syros had a voice like thunder. Proximity was no necessity with this man. The advantage lay in being better able to behold the singular beauty and quality of the effects. He lifted a large urn, corked and sealed at the top, that he averred to be filled with a fine wine. Syros clarified that with an asseveration that they had already sampled from the smaller jug, indeed finished it off just to be sure, and resolutely concluded that it was abhorrent in contrast to the delightful nectar produced in their own vineyards. The crowd roared their approbation, knowing well that his compliment was only meant to secure the jug for his crew's own enjoyment.

"You won't mind passing the tainted venom our way then," cheered an equally loud voice from deep in the crowd. The eruption of approval was deafening. Syros made a great show of reluctance as he gave up the vessel. Even his lion's voice couldn't compete as they collectively pressed forward clamoring for a sample.

Order was soon restored, Syros and his cohorts calling for silence. They each held up a black ebony handled copper knife of sterling beauty, the more fun-loving of the group flashing yellow sunlight from their polished blades into the eyes of the assemblage.

Syros lifted a heavy ax high with his right arm, waving it at the sky, claiming it to be harder and sharper than any blade in Kriti used for carpentry, that there was no end to its foreseeable usefulness.

He passed red blankets into the crowd for their approval, making sure that they were returned and accounted for before continuing.

He held aloft a copper ibis, the body not much larger than fist size, and beautifully worked. Those at the front who could see clearly were amazed at the craftsmanship. No one here had the skills or even knew anyone who could reproduce a work of art such as this. It was almost miraculous, refined and effulgent, burnished to perfection.

The last item was a gold chalice, a fine, thin-walled work with engravings of unfamiliar feline creatures on each side, scrollwork on the rim and base. The magnificence of the copper ibis had not prepared them for the rich brilliance of the gold cup. A gasp came from the mouths of those near at hand, sun glinting off the rim as Syros rotated the stem between his fingertips, smiling in triumph at this splendid acquisition.

This was the end. It was clear that the remaining bundles were the personal effects of the crew; bedding, wet-wear, water skins.

Those in the front of the crowd pushed up onto the rise carrying Deus and Taros along, encircling the crew, clapping them, congratulating them, wanting a closer look and a retelling of the stories they had only just heard.

Celebrating continued into the night, this rite of passage for the younger members of the crew being a mark of honor for their families, the return of the elders a joyous reuniting with their families who had hoped against hope for their safe return.

Families not closely tied to the crew members dispersed early leaving what was still a rather large core to feast into the night. Syros graciously noticed the visitor's feelings of discomfort and was cognizant of them since he had just returned from a not too dissimilar situation. Even as the center of attention he still found time to tell all around that these good lads had pitched in, with no thought of reward, to help with the boat when the crew had thrown up their hands in lamentation of the last effort to beach it safely and were all for leaving it drift back out to sea.

That was as good an introduction as anyone could hope for. They were dined and given drink, some of the party taking enough temporary interest to inquire after their health and the purpose of their journey. For the most part, though, the interest was just politeness and quickly reverted to the theme at hand.

Taros was enjoying his fill of the weakly alcoholic wine that was made available for the occasion. Deus had some but found the taste to have been more accurately described by Syros's pretended diatribe against the Egyptian drink. He stayed with the unfermented juice, which he found to be far more refreshing and which let him observe more accurately the developing antics. He didn't particularly enjoy the foggy effects of wine. It was useful for loosening the tongues of others and making them much more pliable and open to suggestion, as he had found to his delight on more than one occasion at the marketplace, but he did not appreciate that effect on himself.

They were all getting tired, some even sleeping where they were, the activities of the day, and the wine, sedating them for the night.

As the noise waned, and even the happy crew had fallen blissfully to sleep, only a few scattered groups still had the energy to keep conversing. With the exception of a couple of extroverts trying to keep the action going, most of the remaining conversation was in fairly hushed tones.

Something had been niggling at Deus all evening. He had found a comfortable spot next to his friend on a grassy area and lay down beside him. As weary as he was he still could not get to sleep. There was something on the outskirts of his consciousness that he just could not seem to grip.

The haunting voice of the old lady at Vathypetro filled his mind. What a wonderful entertainment she provided. Why didn't people sing like that everywhere? She couldn't be the only person with such an incredible voice. It was more the style, her idiosyncratic approach to the music. It was fabulous. He never would forget it. He wanted it to spread everywhere so he could be regaled like that no matter where he was.

Why hadn't that style of song spread? She was an old lady. She must have been singing for ages. What kept it from proliferating?

His thoughts turned to the distances he had covered over the last several days. The going was rugged, but not insurmountable. People obviously made the trek on occasion, but not often enough for the conveyance of more than the most basic transfer of culture or goods.

Perhaps that was it. Travelers weren't interested in carrying differences around with them. They were too interested in where they were going and their immediate needs to be bothered picking up some new, strange custom even if it was better than what they'd grown used to. That might explain why even everyday things like blankets and pottery were different, why there were words spoken this very evening that he had never heard before. Yet he could understand many of the new words by the context of the phrases in which they were used. Some of the words were technical terms, parts of the boat that had to be explained or pointed out to him, as they were different from the words used to describe the same things on the smaller boats of the north coast.

His eyelids were too heavy to keep open and thinking about abstracts like linguistics was knocking him down. He struggled against the sleep that called to him. There was a connection here that he was missing. People spoke the same language, with minor differences; they wore similar clothes, again some diminutive variation; the food was slightly different as was the wine; customs, fables, songs, buildings, everything; similar but still different.

Each place seemed to have something the others lacked. Each place had something the others would be better off with if they had it.

That was it. Trade. No one had grasped the implications of trade. If someone could set up a system of transport around the island with the express purpose of marketing between villages the wealth of all could be improved. And why stop with the island inhabitants? This Egypt, for example. Could a regular trade be established with these people? They must have liked the gifts that had been brought to them, or they wouldn't have responded so generously. If they liked woolen products, then Kriti could give them woolen products. They must have their own sheep, but obviously the better wool was produced here. They could repay with copper and gold.

And who produced those stunning works? Their metal workers were outstanding. Perhaps they could be persuaded to come to Kriti?

What else was out there to be discovered?

Who else?

~~~~~~

Chapter 5

Copper

"Wake up, my young friends."

They opened their eyes to the image of Syros's huge frame hovering over them. The sun had already risen high, and the warmth had added to their comfort and kept them asleep.

"I should have invited you into my home, but I lost track of you in the dark." This was his way of admitting he'd forgotten. "It is shameful that guests should have to stay outside. You must accept my apologies."

Deus agitated his hair and pushed it back into place thinking he probably looked as unkempt as Taros beside him. "Please don't worry yourself. We have spent many a night outside. And your hospitality has exceeded anything we could have expected."

"Nonsense. Come with me." He waved them after him. "I'll see to it that you get a fine breakfast."

They hurriedly stuffed their few belongings into their packs, draped their blankets over their shoulders, and followed Syros up the lane. They walked past the tract on their left that was the central meeting place of the town, the site where the previous evening's diversion had taken place. Some gulls had discovered bits of food and uncleaned bones that had been left behind and were squabbling over ownership of the remains. The lane had houses on both sides as they passed the park, the outer walls a combination of rough-hewn rock layered alternately with timbers.

"This is my home. Come inside. Here you will be like one of my own family."

The entrance room was bright, the sun still low enough to shine through the large, east-oriented windows.

Several faces were recognizable, being members of the crew that they had assisted the day before. They sat comfortably on wooden benches in a square on one end of the room near the largest window.

"I had been under the impression that you were married, Syros." Deus picked up on the manliness of the home, the complete lack of feminine quality.

"I was married." Syros's countenance momentarily changed to one considerably more sober. "I was married, to a woman more beautiful than you have ever seen." His face bespoke a grief he still lamented but was ready to share with any who inquired. "But she could not bear children and every time would lose the baby. And then the last time," he looked up in the ceiling, remembering the despair, "the last time she bled and would not stop. The midwives tried everything. They gave her herbs. They packed her with moss. I sacrificed a lamb for her. It was all in vain. Even in the darkness, I could see how white she was. She held my hand and told me that all she could think of was sleep. I sat with her, holding her hand all night, until the morning broke and I could see that she no longer breathed. Her hand was only warm because I had been holding it. Her face was ice cold."

"I'm sorry. I didn't mean to bring back such a bad memory."

His smile was impotent, his eyes vacant as his mind returned from another place. "A bad memory? No. Not at all. My memories of my wife are the best memories I have. Sometimes I think about her and realize that it has been a while since I have pictured her before me. And each time it seems a little harder to recall her image. I need to be reminded of her often, and I thank you for doing so. I know that, eventually, her memory will fade away completely and I won't be able to see her face again. Such is the way of things according to the elders among us. No, my friend. You have not offended me. Once again you have done me a favor."

Deus nodded back to him. He understood. His own mother had been before him constantly for the first few days after her death. He dwelt on her memory. Now that memory was fading as well. Life went on. Still, he couldn't imagine not being able to conjure her image at will, even far into the future. Could that happen? Could he ever forget?

No. He could not. Not his mother. She was different from any other mortal.

And he was her son.

His appetite was forgotten. "Your wife still lives."

* * *

The room was very warm, stuffy with the number of men inside the house, the usual breeze failing to blow on this sunny afternoon. They welcomed the shade as the sun was now off the optimum angle to inject its light through the windows.

The men were held entranced as Deus spoke through dry lips, his sentient thirst for fluids abated by spiritual ebullience. The men felt it too and were almost carried away as Deus zealously described his vision. There was nothing they could not see or feel as they listened adhesively to his speech, from the silhouette of Selene's idol to the touch of its cold steel.

"My friends, do you see what I bring you? A truth, a reality that very few others have. We are at the forefront of the most consummate liturgy this world has ever known. The wisdom that will be imparted to us, that has already been imparted, will carry us into a new world which will dwarf anything of the past or present. The minds and ideals of men are but dross. They forever try but rarely advance. Every family, every town, has a better way of doing something but they have no way of getting together, of sharing their wisdom and knowledge. They have been doomed, until now. It is we, my friends, you and I, who will ride the wave of these new thoughts. We will become rulers through spirituality and knowledge. No force, except the wanton embrace of ignorance, can defend against us."

Those present murmured their consensus.

"You are with me then, my friends?"

They all stood, the murmurs now vociferous pledges of fealty.

Syros spoke, lifting his arms to calm his crew members, not purposely trying to dampen their spirited enthusiasm, only expressing a valid concern. "How will we accomplish such lofty goals? We are but a few."

"With the Earth-Mother leading us we are many, a multitude. And our numbers will grow from these few to fill this island, and the islands round about. You feel it. It is our destiny. We are unstoppable."

Deus folded his hands together, his elbows resting on his knees as he sat, his face pressed against his double fist. "Syros, you have a large boat, the finest I've seen. Who crafted it?"

"I did. Boat building has been in my family for generations. Others make them too, but none are finer than mine."

"None could be finer. Are there not any others like it?"

"One old one built by my Father. But it has grown weak and is not fit for the journeys we have taken. Many others are similar except for their smaller size. Fishermen have no need of vessels so large."

"I agree. But we will be fishing for something finer than tuna. It can only be done in your craft."

* * *

Deus and Syros strolled around the perimeter of the town. Deus plucked a red tulip, examining the interior stamens, rubbing the pollen off between his thumb and fingers.

"The people of this island will be like bees gathering pollen. We will take things like this flower that are apparently without use and transform them into treasures. After that, we will take upon ourselves the right and responsibility of transporting these commodities to all who will receive them."

They stopped to accept the entertainment of two squirrels robbing chestnuts from a large tree just ahead of them. They would stow two in their mouths and try to press another in between. The result, every time, was that they would drop one of the others. They jumped and ran down the bark of the tree to their fallen treasure and try the same impossible maneuver, stuffing in

77

the third and dislodging the first or second. They tried to walk as they did this, their avariciousness hampering their progress ten-fold. Each would find a brand new select spot, the perfect place to hide their cache, and push them under the forest floor to be brought up at a later date for an out of season feast. Back they went for more, inexhaustible, to repeat the circuit.

"Ah, to have such boundless energy."

"Even better to have a lesser amount of directed energy. Notice how they waste their time? Their greed gets the best of them. They take more than they can manage which only slows them down. If they would satisfy themselves with only two nuts, they would be far more efficient. Even better, they could throw down hundreds and gather them from the ground later. They could save countless trips up and down the tree. Then they could bury them all in one place instead of everywhere. What animal eats nuts except squirrels? If only they could cooperate." He chuckled at a particularly acrobatic jump from the trunk to a thin branch that flexed violently from the impact of the furry thief.

"You know, most people think that squirrels are smart, that they remember where they stash all of those little piles. They just hide them in so many places that they can't help but find some again." He remembered watching them rob the trees near his home when he was a little boy, not lifting a finger to stop them. "Most little seedlings get a good start because squirrels have planted them and forgotten about them." He turned to Syros. "We as a people are no more organized than these little comics."

"Squirrels will never change. Do you really think that people will?"

"I know they will. Look at how they exist, how we exist. Our parents raise us, we grow old enough to take a wife and raise our own children, we build a hut or house according to our needs, and survive on some basic skill taught us by our parents. Eventually we die, and the world is no better or worse for our having been alive. Did you not notice how the crowd reacted to the copper bird and the golden cup that you displayed? Everyone wanted to have ownership. Those things were beautiful. They would make anyone's home a brighter and happier place. Yet what good were they really? Clay birds and cups serve an equal purpose to the metal, do they not?" he mused. "Functionally, yes. But the beauty is not there. Everyone could have a clay bird if they wanted one, and everyone has a clay cup. They have no value. But gold and copper, that is another matter. People will pay enormous amounts of wool, fish, anything, for what you brought back. You could trade your golden goblet for the largest house in this town, and the man trading would think it a good deal. He can easily build a new house but, ahhhh, where else would he get one of those fine little items?" They continued on their walk. "What you have really traded for is his labor."

Deus mused a little longer. "Tell me, do you think there is any limit to the size a boat can be?"

"How tall is a tree? A boat couldn't be any longer than that. And only the thickest part of the trunk can be used, so that makes the possible length even less. I have thought of building a larger boat than what I have already made. A ship. I think I could make one twice as long. It would also be wider and deeper."

"Why did you make the boat you have? You said it is one of only two of such a size."

"It is much better handling in the sea; farther from land, I mean. The small ones can come quickly to shore if the waves get too high, but I wanted to go farther, to see the distant lands across the water. I had been once before in my father's boat, and once again in a smaller one but the journey is too rough and dangerous. Some of the men get sick in smaller craft, and they are more easily affected by fear. Comfort and safety and bravery come from having a large boat. The larger the vessel, the smoother the ride. And the smoother the ride, the more satisfied the crew and the harder they can work the oars."

"How were you able to cut the timbers for your boat?"

"There have been tools in my family for generations. Copper tools. Axes and adzes. Some better than others, a slightly different color, and harder. They keep a better edge. Without the copper, there would be no way to shape the wood so perfectly."

"Do you know where the tools came from?"

"Some were taken from the eastern shores of the Sea, great distances from here. They were taken by force a long time ago, even before the birth of my Father. Our newer tools were made from ore found on Kypros. The island is named after the metal. The ore is in abundance, but it is such a long way that we don't go often. In places the nuggets lie on the surface, although they are getting harder to find. The distance is formidable, at least as far as Egypt. It is easier to navigate to though. It lies exactly east of Kriti. The people on the island have always avoided us. They are very wary of strangers. I don't know what they think; maybe that we have come to kill them or something, it's hard to say. Maybe they think they are lucky to just have us come and then go without really disturbing them. Personally, I've never seen them. They don't seem to live anywhere near where we get the ore."

"How is it that your family found out where to get it?"

"I don't know. My Father showed me, and his father showed him. How far back it goes, I couldn't say. Maybe an islander showed one of my family. I suppose those people have no use for copper." Deus caught an unsure look in Syros's eye. He wasn't sure what to make of it. There was something he wasn't comfortable talking about.

"You carry a copper knife. I wondered how it kept its edge compared to flint or obsidian."

Syros was happy to suddenly change the subject. "Not as well. But you could never make a stone knife as thin and light as with copper. What is more important is that the metal is easy to resharpen, and it won't break like the stone will. If it bends from straining, I just hammer it back into shape. Heavier tools like axes don't bend though. They are very strong."

"Why doesn't everybody use these copper tools then?"

"Some think they would like to. But there just aren't enough to go around. Not many people know where to get the ore, and fewer have the bravado to get it."

"Why don't you import the ore to here and teach some of the people to make the tools? Or do it yourself?"

Syros laughed. "Only the smallest amount of the metal can be gleaned from a large amount of the ore. The struggle to get it, even to just get to it, is immense. What we do is make most of the tools or knives there and bring them back. It is so much easier that way."

"Why haven't you done this regularly?"

Syros was beginning to see the possibilities. "I don't know. But, as we speak, I envision this as being a good idea. A very good idea."

"Think of the benefits to the community, not to mention yourself. Haven't you had offers for your knife or other tools?"

"Yes. But I have little use for sheep or goats. I am a fisherman. If I want something I trade my fish. I catch larger fish than anyone. I did give some of my copper to a couple of men for building my house. Not that I couldn't have done it myself. But, if I am going to busy myself on land, I would rather the challenge of building a boat." He puffed his chest slightly. "I build the finest you know. Those others you see, it's a miracle they float at all. They are held together with pitch, and so full of leaks the fish inside never die for all the water." Syros wrinkled his nose in contempt.

"Why don't you show them how to do it the right way?"

"Show them?" he bellowed. "Why should I show them?" He thought about this during the pause, changing his demeanor. "I'm not sure they would even be interested. They seem quite satisfied with their little skiffs. A few have taken some of my innovations and adapted them to their own needs, but mostly they think I'm being foolish, a dreamer, going to far off lands when I should be taking another wife and raising children." He looked up at a small cloud formation tearing across the sky, still unable to understand how that could be when the wind where he stood was barely a breeze. "Do you think I am a dreamer?"

80

Deus gave his biggest smile. "Absolutely. There will never be a person of greatness who was any less."

* * *

Taros had never been so miserable. He had been sick from eating bad meat years ago, he remembered, and this was almost as bad, but that thought only made things worse. Why were such evil thoughts filling his mind? He was being tortured without pain, the inside of his head spinning in three different directions at once. He clung to his oar, maintaining the rhythm set by the others even though he could hardly see. The last vestige of his reasoning wanted the others to think that he was not a complete handicap at sea. His recollection, despite his supreme efforts to block the thoughts, of the last three days he had spent on the bench of the rocking ship brought a new wave of nausea which wracked him to the point of wishing for death. His torso convulsed turbulently, forcing air through his sealed glottis in a sustained monody, his neck veins bulging as his face variegated from pasty gray to flaming red.

"Grab that oar" shouted the Captain.

Taros's grip relaxed as his consciousness slipped away once more. His oar trailing in the water was in danger of slipping through the oarlock, the hole near the upper edge of the hull. That wouldn't have been a disaster in these waters; they could easily reverse and pick up the floating item. Still, no one else was sick and why should they have to suffer the inconvenience for one man?

The action of the water pushed the handle forward, hitting Deus, as it started its outward escape attempt. He caught it with one hand and yarded it aboard, fouling his own rowing cadence as he did so. Syros slapped a crewmember who was on his break rotation indicating that he should jump over and get to work.

The rhythm of the others was hardly broken. Deus, who was getting quite used to this after five days, lost only a couple of strokes before he and Taros's replacement got back into the metrical cycle of the other oarsmen.

He wasn't the only one who was stiff. All of them had slowed a bit. But he was determined to last as well as the others, even though he well realized their experience should make them more capable. Syros had singled him out and praised his stamina, which only served to encourage his efforts.

He felt sorry for Taros. He'd had a few waves of nausea himself on the second day, only able to take water in small doses as the boat heaved. He was more fortunate than his friend. He was able to force the sick feeling to the back of his mind and conjure pleasant images of the coastline of Kriti. That still didn't quite do the job as he could yet see the waves breaking on the shore, so he changed the impressions to those of the forested inland mountains. He imagined the rabbits and deer browsing peacefully on the undergrowth, the songbirds and their pleasant arias. He kept these images for the better part of the day and night until, at last, he found his appetite returning. He had refused to be relieved on his turn, preferring instead the physical outlet for his sickness. He wouldn't have felt ashamed if he was simply so sick as to be incapable of working, like Taros, but as it stood he just preferred to be doing something. There could hardly be any point trying to relax and enjoy the ride in that bothersome state.

The swells weren't breaking, but at times Deus realized that he couldn't see over the crests as their boat sank into the troughs between. Thoughts of being encompassed by water in this wine-colored sea with not a speck of land anywhere within sight were at once frightening and exhilarating.

As they rose to top a particularly large swell, he looked over his shoulder ahead and could see plainly the rough outline of a dark bulge on the horizon.

"Not long now, men" Syros called out. He gauged the height of the morning sun as best as he could through the thin overcast sky, looking into the glare for the bright circle that hurt his eyes. It would still be a while before mid-day. The current was with them and, although these swells were impeding their rowing abilities, at least they were traveling in the right direction. If all stayed the same, they should be able to make shore by nightfall.

* * *

"Easy now." Syros was peering over the bow as they pushed slowly through the water towards the beach. There was barely enough light to see the piercing rocks submerged just under the surface. He was thankful that the weather had calmed making his endeavor even possible.

"Go left" he shouted. The rudder man pulled the oversized steering oar to the right. All oarsmen had their poles up, except four still with theirs in the water coordinating their efforts to bring the boat over, two on the left trailing down for resistance, and the men on the right heaving furiously. They slipped past the submerged rock, unseen until the last moment, Syros half expecting to hear a heart-stopping sound of the hull grinding on barnacles, clearing it by a whisker.

The four paddled slowly now until they had sand clearly visible underneath. The depth was down to a few feet, and they were almost ashore.

"Oars out" came the order. "Now stroke." All of the men had their oars in the water for this last fling. They pulled mightily, pushing a small wave up onto the sand, the bow actually clear of the water as it rested comfortably on the beach.

All oars were pulled in, the blades still protruding through the oarlocks. The crew jumped out, even Taros managed a burst of energy for this, each latching onto the hull and giving it a tug up the beach. They only just managed to clear it of the water. Their legs and arms were too stiff to give it any more effort. The boat rolled to the side where they left it.

Syros stood tall, his fists on his hips, elbows out. "Kypros, gentlemen. Another world. Feast your eyes." He felt proud at the end of long journeys. So few attempted such expeditions that he felt an immeasurable sense of accomplishment at their conclusion. Nothing could take from these moments. If he had swum the distance he would still have the energy to stand and look about, as if the new land was a personal conquest.

The others had already positioned themselves for a long and well-deserved sleep. Taros had fallen down in the sand and was crawling to the grassy area where the others were, retching as he moved, the steady land now causing his equilibrium as much grief as the ceaseless undulations of the sea. Deus had brought both packs up to the sleeping area and laid out Taros's wrap for him. Taros was beyond caring and pitched onto it without so much as an acknowledgment, instantly slipping into a fitful sleep which would torment him through the night.

* * *

The noon sun burned hot today, the dead-calm sea like glass. The crew beached their vessel for the second time on Kypros, this time next to a small creek and a large, prominent rock, the first contact being just an overnight rest stop. They had been up at dawn again to continue along the south coast to the place closest to where the ore deposits were known to exist.

"Your health has greatly improved, my friend" Deus said quietly to Taros. "I feared for you."

"Death would have been a welcome release." He was able to poke fun at his own misery now that it was past. "My life now begins anew. I had never thought that feeling normal could feel so good."

"Secure the vessel," shouted Syros. They brought it up the beach as far as was humanly possible and roped the bow to a slim, upright rock. The wide, sandy beach was strewn with pink and white marble chunks and other mounds of black rock prominences undercut by the erosive wave action of bygone centuries.

The oars were brought farther up and buried near the creek, as was everything else that would not be carried with them.

"Fill your skins and your bellies. There is no water where we will be going. We have a long walk ahead of us. I'll guarantee your legs will be screaming as vociferously as your arms did the first days of our voyage. That will be good for you. It means your strength is returning." He donned his pack and was off up the hill with the others in tow.

The clime of this region of Kypros was far drier than Kriti, a scrubland with little in the way of anything green, at least along the south coast. The day was becoming increasingly hot as they hiked inland. The terrain they were traversing was as rugged as Kriti if not more so.

Syros was right. Their legs were beginning to scream, partly from the inaction of the last few days and partly from the physical workout that he put them through as they hurried to keep up. Syros was by far the most physically fit of the lot of them. His bronze skin sweating under the blaze of the sun highlighted a muscular structure that put the rest of them to shame.

Deus wondered if Syros had been fortunate enough to be born of hale parents or if he had become so well formed from heavy labor. Perhaps people were like the sheep he had bred. He wondered. Maybe there wasn't such a difference between the two. His brothers had shared certain similarities with both his mother and father. No one else really reminded him of the two of them. He recalled some of the youths that he had met in Amnisos and they had also born a resemblance to their parents, as had Taros to his father.

Still, there had to be more than just an auspicious birth responsible for that kind of health. It surely must also involve physical stress. Without it, he had seen the result; a person would get soft and fat. He had known a couple of men who would not do anything other than eat and drink, as much as they possibly could. This was a rarity, as most people could not live this way with a family. But these men had nothing, nobody, they were single and so old as to have no prospects. They slept outdoors, except in the most inclement weather when they played upon the mercies of someone to take them in. They accepted and encouraged any form of charity they could muster, and they spent the days slowly scouring the shore for shellfish, crab, washed up octopus, anything and everything, and consuming it gluttonously. They had seemed almost obsessed with eating and avoiding work. Deus knew they had been offered employ on the fishing boats and had turned the opportunities down every time. He couldn't understand it.

Both heat and exertion were getting to him as the terrain became increasingly steep and rough. Mountains rose in front of them, a range that stretched miles in either direction. The center mountain, the one they were headed directly for, was still crowned with a small lid of snow. He hoped that Syros wouldn't be taking them to the top. Dragging the back of his forearm across his brow sweat dripped into his eyes, stinging them and blurring his vision. He was trailing behind the others near the tail end of the line.

Deus resolved to work harder at building his strength. Picking up his pace he caught up and passed several of the crew members. They were equally tired and said nothing as he went by. His legs were exploding, but he kept on. Soon he was just behind Syros. Try as he might he couldn't quite catch up. It was as if the man sensed his proximity and sped up just enough to keep a distance.

Suddenly Syros stopped. Deus was beside him in an instant, elated at the opportunity to give his legs a rest for even a moment if that was all it was to be. Syros looked at him in mild wonder as he stepped up beside him.

"Well done. I was sure you would be far back in the line. You are full of surprises."

Deus only wanted to collapse but held his composure, trying to control his breathing so as not to appear too winded, refusing to let himself even sit down. Syros smiled, recognizing what Deus was doing and admiring his effort. He turned his attention to the scene before them and gestured with his arm outstretched.

"This is the place. We need go no farther."

The others, one by one at fairly regular intervals, dropped their packs and flopped to the dry grass beside them.

Deus noticed a round stone wall a short distance away, only a foot or so high, obviously the foundation of a destroyed hut. Not far from that one was another. They had been there for a very long time, almost completely covered now in dried vegetation.

"Someone lived here in the past."

"Yes." Syros was astonished at the boy's quick perception. "My father said that his father's father was involved in a blood battle with these people. The fight was over the copper, of course. These people spoke a different language and being unable to understand us they attacked. The fighting was fierce, both sides inflicting serious injury. In the end, we prevailed with the greater number of men, and we destroyed the huts in retaliation for the insult." He pointed left. "I think you may have missed the one over there. It was more completely demolished."

Deus could only make out a scattering of small overgrown mounds, not unlike the boulders which were everywhere on Kriti.

" Many of the survivors died later of their wounds. Only four of the party were left alive to row back. It took them twenty days. They were almost dead when they barely drifted ashore, having gotten themselves lost at sea. Somehow they finally came to shore at the place where they lived. Our family rejoiced with a full sacrifice that day. It is still spoken of." His eyes revealed the awkwardness he felt even speaking of another faith, that of sacrifice to a god of nature, which he no longer held true. A twinge of guilt passed through him as he thought of the Mother Goddess and the newness of the idea.

"The other crew members refused to ever leave Kriti again. Our family has always been courageous, though, and my ancestor took his son and a new crew here once again. The copper, you understand. There is no other place that we know of to get it from the Earth." He looked thoughtful. "Yet no one else gets it from here, I can tell. The area is never disturbed. We always are careful to leave this place as we find it so we don't alert others to what might be here. There must, therefore, be other places to find this gift. We aren't the only ones to have it."

This gently sloping valley was surrounded by a thin spread of trees crowning the summit of the surrounding mountains, thick pines warped and flattened by the burden of winter snows. At least there was wood available for a fire. Deus had no idea how high they had climbed from sea level, but his legs were still telling him it was considerable. He refused to rest with the others and spent some time investigating the area. He was particularly interested in the ruins. Who had settled here? Was it for the copper, as Syros had said? He didn't see anything that indicated copper might be in the area although he didn't doubt the captain's word. His legs were feeling better now that he was up and strolling, the added circulation from his movement carrying the released acids away as he moved.

He found an area that looked a bit unnatural, disturbed, like it had been dug away from the side of the slope. He looked back at the group.

"That's the place" called Syros. "You have a good eye." He got up to join the young man.

"We strip the soil off the top before we dig, then replace it when we leave. That way the grasses will grow over it and conceal it from others who might come this way. That wasn't always done, and that is how these people found this place." He indicated the ruins. "They must have found the deposits and set up a permanent camp to begin extraction. When my ancestors returned they put an end to that."

"Why didn't they leave the huts standing? Then they would have a shelter to use for themselves." Not that that mattered to Deus. He was accustomed to the outdoors. But these people had a clear preference for dwellings.

"That would have only encouraged others who might happen by to claim this area as their own. By destroying the buildings, it gives the impression that others had tried and failed to reside here. With the lack of water and the copper deposits covered no one would think to try again."

Both spent the remainder of the afternoon talking as they wandered slowly around the area, stopping frequently to more closely inspect a tree or observe a bird flying by. Deus was pleased that Syros also had an interest in such things of nature, a rarity in most men he had met.

After the crew had prepared their food and then rested for a while, the custom after a meal, they set to work. The good soil was set to the side as Syros had indicated they had done in the past, and the drier, more compact, greenish-tinged soil underneath was carried to the opposite side of the work site. Most of the digging was by hand, the men pulling double handfuls of soil onto flat skins, which were either dragged or carried to the side, depending on the strength of the men. It was a badge of honor to be able to carry the weight in one's arms, and all did this at first. One by one they succumbed to the strain and had to resort to dragging. Wearing out the skins was no issue in this case. They were old, tough, expendable, and brought along expressly for this purpose.

Only the dirt was removed at this point. The dusty pebbles and rocks were tossed onto a pile on the third side of the dig. None of these men, except Syros, had been to this place before, and none would have been able to recognize the copper nuggets here.

Syros opened a flat oilskin and laid it over a ring of rectangular rocks he had scavenged from the area of the ruins. They were the same ones he had used before, but he had always taken care to scatter them before leaving. He pressed the center of the oiled skin down to form a pocket and weighted the sides with other rocks. Into the depression he'd made he poured water, filling it only half way. One by one he swished the rocks and pebbles from the pile through the water, cleaning the dust off, revealing their nature. Most of them, almost all of them, were nondescript and useless. Syros flicked them off to the side a surprising distance with what appeared to be no more than an abrupt wrist action. The limitations of the amount of water they had available meant that he would have to use this same puddle over and over again constantly with little replenishing. He knew that the silt would settle out of the sully mixture overnight and the water could be poured off and used again. As long as he could scrape the tailings off the bottom regularly, he should be able to make this last a long time.

A small number of the green oxidized pebbles and stones were the variegated copper nuggets that they sought, glistening brightly with the film of water adhering to their surface. By the time it was too dark to continue he had enough to fill the leather pouch strapped around his waist.

"This is a surprising amount. We have done well today." He held out a portion of the take to the men who wondered if all this work had really been worthwhile. They handled the oddly shaped lumps, the cold smoothness a pleasure to the touch. These nuggets were a rarity, only the smallest percentage of the world's supply being in this form.

"In my ancestor's time, these were much easier to find, and much larger. I had feared that we had taken most of them. I still do. We have only been fortunate today. Sleep now, and pray for the same smile to rest on us tomorrow."

* * *

The Island of Cyprus stands like a gem above the eastern Mediterranean. Its name reflects its worth, for the word 'copper' is derived from

Cyprium, the Roman word for the island, which in turn came from the Greek Kuprios, and before that the Minoan name Kypros. For thousands of years, the principal export from Cyprus remained copper, and extensive pre-Roman mining works remain today at Skouriotissa.

This localized concentration of copper originated on the floor of the ancient Mediterranean Sea. Here, along an undersea fissure, heat concentrated the copper in an extraordinary process. Below the sea-bed water seeped down toward a massive pool of magma straining to escape the heat and pressures of the earth. As cool seawater met the molten magma, it was heated to the same temperatures. The super-heated water percolated through the microscopic fissures in the rocky crust, leaching out small amounts of copper compounds, and the dissolved copper was deposited in the surrounding sea-bed as the water forced its way upward. Finally, the superheated water burst forth on the sea-floor as white and black smokers, small volcano-like eruptions that grew in dimension with the advance of time. Year after year the copper concentration built in and around the smokers fired by the heat of the earth itself.

Volcanic activity that moves the continents and forces up the mountains has naturally refined copper, gold, and other minerals. Without this first natural step, all minerals would be too scattered to mine effectively.

Over many millions of years volcanic activity in the Mediterranean fissure forced the sea-floor apart, and rich deposits of ore were carried away from the smokers, distributed randomly and diversely as the crust moved. Later the sea-floor was tipped vertically and forced thousands of feet into the air by the vast dynamism of the colliding continents. As the African continent drove north toward Europe, the shallow sea-bed between them was compressed and wracked into an incredible array of folds.

The island of Cyprus is one place in the region where the evidence of the powerful forces at work twisted the rock, turned it upside down, and raised it toward the sky in a formation called an ophiolite. The word comes from the Greek ophis, serpent, because the rocks in an ophiolite are a blotchy green in the same way as many snakes. Copper deposits were brought to the surface along with the mineral-rich sea-floor as it collided with the European plate. In some places, the copper was found right on the surface. This easy access was particularly important to its early discovery and use.

Five thousand years ago miners brought copper to an eagerly awaiting world. It was one of the first metals known to mankind used to form tools, utensils, armor, and art used by ancient Mediterranean peoples to express their dreams and fears.

During the Bronze age, the controllers of the island prospered as the principal source of the metal for the early Mediterranean nations, flourishing because of their copper wealth.

COPPER

On the surface, the earth is a temperate, hospitable place with oceans of liquid water and an oxygen-rich atmosphere. But not too far beneath the crust it is very different. Inside it's hot enough to melt the hardest rock. For millions of years this internal heat has shaped the surface of our planet, mountains, oceans, and continents, and concentrated minerals like copper and gold. Even now, the heat within continues to forge a new world from the material of the old. Perhaps the most important mineral to humanity has been copper. From the first metal tools of the bronze age to the electric wiring in modern homes, copper has helped shape our civilization. Without the unique natural processes fueled by the internal heat of the planet, copper could not have been available to lift us out of the stone age.

But mining copper ore is only the first step in getting the metal. The copper is still not concentrated enough to use. Changing the solid rock into liquid is natural enough below the thin crust of our planet, but on the surface it is not a simple task. Now, in these modern times, the copper ore, which may be only one or two percent elemental copper, is purified in mechanized smelters, great horizontal furnaces that refine it into ingots of almost unadulterated purity.

Prehistoric knowledge of how to work and smelt copper, nowhere near as efficient, was nonetheless one of the crucial discoveries that launched humanity on the road to modern civilization.

* * *

Deus woke first to the chill dawn. The rise of the sun was behind the higher rise of the land on their east side. They would be in the shadow of the valley for some time yet. He stood still wrapped in his felt, the snap of the frosty air spanking his face as he panned his surroundings. The dig that they had worked on so hard yesterday was tiny. This needed to be a massive project. They needed better tools, more men, animals to carry supplies. And water. They couldn't possibly last another two days at the rate they were consuming it.

Syros was next to get up, as Deus knew he would be.

"You look thoughtful, my young friend. What goes on in your mind this early in the morning?"

"I know we worked this dig only a couple of hours last night. I don't want you to think my expectations are too high, but I think we may be able to improve things somewhat. I see several problems that I'm not sure have been attended to if this is to become an efficient and productive operation."

Syros was intrigued and took no offense.

"We are fourteen men. Gathering at the rate we are going, and you say it is a good rate, we will only accumulate enough copper for, say, one ax head each in three days. We will run out of water before that, delaying us another day while we all go with our skins to refill. Perhaps one man could take two

89

skins while the others keep busy here. To further slow us we will need to cut firewood to heat the copper. The cold of last night suggests that would be a good idea anyway, but men will be needed to do the work. That leaves fewer of us to actually do the digging." Deus gazed again upon the site. More of the men were rising to the sound of their voices.

"I envision hundreds of men here. A real organization. Men with specific tasks, laborers, water bearers, cooks, coppersmiths. We may want to include women in this eventually, form a real community." He looked at Syros and the others who had joined them. "Am I holding unrealistic expectations? Am I seeing too far into the future?"

"Nonsense. No one destined for greatness could do any less."

* * *

"Do you really think that this is a problem? I don't think there will ever be anyone coming this way. We are in the middle of a range of mountains." Kirtos was protesting at having to cover the dig.

Syros straightened his back and considered the matter. "It does seem a bit unlikely doesn't it?"

Deus spoke up. "You have said that in the past you rarely came here, neither your ancestors. The cause then for hiding the area was justified. Now things are different. We mean to come here often."

"You are correct, both of you. Fortune has served us well, and I think it will remain thus. This is a very large island, as large as Kriti, and I don't think anyone will find this place either. We are wasting our efforts. The topsoil will not grow anything for the next year and we will be back before then, now that we have our plans made." Syros was no stranger to hard labor nor did he shun it, but he was no more desirous to do something that did not need doing than the next man.

"Away with us then, before we become desiccated." Limbus had his pack in hand and was first to set off along the path they had left on their entry to this valley. It had almost disappeared as the dried grass had sprung up with the morning mist, straightening the brown blades.

The others were right behind, the quicker of them catching up and passing, eager to return to the stream to ease their thirst. Taros walked with Deus and Syros, talking of what they could make with the copper. They had done very well indeed. Deus had felt, since the dig had been worked many times previously and then covered, that they should dig a little deeper past that layer and see what was below. Sure enough, as he had expected, the ground produced a heavier quantity, larger and more numerous nuggets. Syros had planned to show them how to soften the nuggets and beat them into tools by building a hot fire, but they voted to continue mining as long as they could. They could build a fire at the creekside in comfort. This was a fortuitous decision. Just after they would have quit, Lobos found the largest nugget Syros had ever seen or heard of. It was the size, and interestingly almost the shape, of a man's foot. No water was needed to identify this. All stopped to congratulate the man on his acquisition, general harassment following referring to his lack of productivity thus far and how his only redemption was to render such a find to catch up and make amends.

The road back was only slightly less arduous than the journey in. They were without the weight of water and food but had now the copper. Returning was downhill for the most part, but with the burgeoning heat of the sun prevailing on them, and no water for relief, they were sore for respite.

They came upon the stream not far from the beach, its course bringing it in from another direction. Deus was surprised how little time it seemed since they had left the mine, although he could plainly see by the position of the sun that it had taken no less time returning than going. Syros had not been in such a hurry this time, pushing the others hard to keep up. He had felt that they should maintain an even pace to decrease their craving for water.

Tattus jumped in the creek, rolling in it in pleasure, the cold water taking the heat from his body. Another followed suit, plunging his head under, then drinking heartily from his position on all fours.

"Steady, you fools." It was too late. Half of the others, those ahead of Syros, had immersed themselves as well. None had the sense to disrobe completely before jumping in. "I hope you all freeze tonight."

"We aren't in the mountains now. We have a nice warm beach to sleep on." Lobos continued splashing juvenilely in the water.

The others looked a bit dubious as they realized what Syros was getting at. The less enthusiastic among them, the ones with and following Syros who, even so, were delighted to see water, stripped down, following his lead.

This was refreshing. They let the water wash over them in the bright sunlight, having drunk their fill. The contest now was to see who would get so cold as to have to get out first.

Goosebumps were forming on their paling skin. Teeth were beginning to chatter. Those who still had their garments on were better protected but had been in longer. Deus, who now realized this was to be a contest, rued jumping in at all, but was determined to participate now that he was in the middle of it. He forced himself to think of warmth, of the sweltering walk out of the hills. He found he was able, even easier than the last time, to transport himself into another place, all the sensations a part of the experience. He could still hear the playful banter of his cohorts as they challenged and called each other cowards, but it seemed as if it came from another room in a building. His face was out of the water, and the solar warmth radiating upon it was real enough. He focused on that and made it spread down his neck, his shoulders, and his torso. He knew in his mind that he was probably freezing, but that didn't seem to matter. He was able to distance himself. Time seemed to fade. He was in control. He had conquered.

An unusual sound filled his head. He envisioned himself surrounded, receiving the plaudits of the multitudes, cheering, flags waving. He was a king, riding an enormous four-legged creature the likes of which he could hardly have imagined, a long horn jutting ominously out each side of its head just above its huge, saucer-like eyes. The masses were gathered all around him, hanging off balconies on buildings higher than had ever been seen.

He opened his eyes. Syros in the middle with the crew flanking either side were hooting and cheering, clapping and encouraging him to stay in until tomorrow. Not even Syros had been able to endure as long, and he had led the cheer as Deus emerged to the bank, shaking with cold.

Deus realized how cold he was. His joints were stiff and slow to move as he sat up. He was only able to crawl out, the uncontrollable shivering starting as he stood up with the others. Taros threw his felt over him, its instant warmth a comfort.

"Gather anything that will burn. Let us get our champion some heat." The crew scattered, including Deus who didn't want to be seen shirking his part for any reason. He clung tightly to his blanket, barely able to bend at the knee to pick up some broken sticks lying around the base of some feeble trees and bushes native to this part of the coastline.

Syros was a particularly skilled fire-starter. All of the men had this skill, it was a common one, but he seemed to have a smolder going in an extraordinarily short time. With a few puffs of his breath, the flame erupted from the little pile of fluff and grass and quickly spread to the surrounding larger twigs of dried wood. He continued blowing long and gently, adding wood as the fire grew. By the time the last of the men had returned with their armloads of wood, the fire was already a good size.

"Open your blanket and let some of this heat in," Syros advised Deus.

Deus squatted beside the fire with his felt held out like a cape, the radiance augmenting that of the setting sun, warming him.

* * *

The coastline was passing them at a fair clip on the left. They were rowing hard to reach the tip of the eastern peninsula by high noon the next day. They were a long way from shore, taking the most direct route from the prominent rock where they had been to the end of a peninsula jutting to the south.

"I've been there," said Syros pointing to the projection of land. "It's a place of death. Nothing is alive. There is a salt lake in the center that would poison anything. You have to be careful on this island. It was never meant for people to live on, I'm sure of it."

The island of Kypros is one hundred forty miles long, an odd, violin-shaped rise with two mountain ranges and one prominent massif over sixty-four hundred feet high. Its snow-capped peak was visible from anywhere at sea.

The men were able to move at a good pace of six miles each hour if they pulled hard and the sea was calm, as it was today. Their circuitous route around the southern coast would add many miles to the journey as they circumnavigated the curve and the two long peninsulas but, following Syros's guidance, they would keep that excess to a minimum. Syros was an excellent navigator and preferred to keep to straight lines rather than hug the coast closely as other, lesser, captains would.

As their line of travel brought them closer to the coast later in the night, they could clearly distinguish the heavy forestation.

"How do you know that there aren't many people on this island?" Deus asked Syros now that he was on his rest break.

He thought about the question. "I don't, actually. I told you I had never seen any of them. I've been right around the island once and have never seen any sign of anyone. No seaside villages. No fires from inland. Nothing. The only indication of people is the habitations at the mine which were destroyed." He looked down at his feet.

Deus could tell he was uncomfortable about something. "Your ancestors killed the others, didn't they?"

Syros gripped his hands together and gazed out to sea, avoiding eye contact with Deus. He spoke softly, barely audible over the sound of the water washing past the sides of the boat.

"When I was very young, younger than you, I spoke with my Grandfather. I did so many times before his death. He spoke with pride of the situation on this island. Yet that was only when others were around. If I was the only one with him he was more melancholy about the affair, as if it bothered him in some way. The last time we spoke, he told me an imaginary story about a group of people who came upon another group who had something valuable. They waited out of sight for an opportunity to attack, and then did so viciously, slaughtering the defenseless people, smashing their bodies even after they were dead. They gloried in their killing, burning the huts and tearing the charred walls down in their frenzy. They found wine among the belongings of the strangers and then fought amongst themselves for the fruits of their victory. They fought for the wine, they fought for the rights to the collected copper, they got drunk and fought for everything. After the killing of the others it was nothing to continue in the shedding of blood, even among their comrades. Bedlam was the order of the day. The battling went on until only the members of one family were left. They only survived because they refused to be divided as the others had been."

Deus waited through the silence. He could see that Syros was struggling inwardly.

After a few minutes of staring blankly, he turned to the younger man. "You have guessed correctly. I have wondered myself, pushing back my Grandfather's message, not wanting to acknowledge a background of murderers, a background of thieves."

Deus lay his hand on the man's shoulder, words useless in comforting one who has had such a revelation.

"It is time I took a turn at the oars," he proclaimed loudly as he left Deus to continue his rest period.

* * *

They had rowed through the night, Syros believing strongly in getting to where he had determined to go as quickly as possible. Not only did that protect against the surprise of storms sabotaging the voyage, but also it made for stronger, more determined, and disciplined crewmembers.

The sun rose against their backs as they continued eastward along the southern side of the island's long peninsula reminiscent of a violin's neck. They were almost to the end of the prominence, the easternmost point.

"Turn towards land," Syros called. "We will rest here for the day. It will take all night to row to the lands east. They say there are many people there and we will need to be well rested when we arrive. We should get there just after the sun rises tomorrow. That is always the best time to arrive at a strange port. Too many treat new arrivals with suspicion when they arrive at night or late in the day. They want to get to know you before they give you shelter for the night, feel you out so to speak."

Syros steered them to a small, sheltered cove with a sandy strand and pulled the boat up, only a short way, just out of the water as they were not planning to stay long.

The crew was eager to rest. Sleeping in the sun was so comfortable. Some of them were adrift in their dreams almost right away. Even Syros was fatigued and in need of sleep. He had slept less than any of them so far. Deus didn't know how he was able to do it. He only took the shortest naps when at sea, and only after giving the strictest instructions to head for a specific landmark or star followed by an adverse string of threats if he wasn't wakened at the first sign of deviation from that course.

Deus sat on a rock where the white sand ended. A wonderful smell was drifting his way, coming from inland. It was a perfume, a flower of some kind. A gaunt stand of trees convened behind them, interspersed with a few blossoms of color near their bases. He wasn't so wasted yet that he couldn't spend a short time exploring. He had always found a peaceful stroll to be every bit as refreshing as a nap.

He made sure that a couple of the crew saw him leave, he wanted someone to know where he was off to should any wake and wonder. Deus had a shrewd sense of direction and had no worry at all of getting lost as he passed through the woods. They seemed to get thicker for a short time and then thinned out, ending altogether on the edge of a lovely meadow overlaid with the intensely aromatic flowers that had drawn him that way. What a beautiful unveiling. He inhaled deeply, enjoying the incense unfettered from the yellow and red blossoms.

Over to his right, he saw a number of sheep grazing comfortably on the flowers. He was tired but that set him thinking. Where there were sheep, there was a shepherd.

He scanned the field. There he was. Looking right at him. Deus knew that if he tried to duck out of sight now, he would be thought a thief. He raised his arm in salute to the man who was unquestionably older than himself.

The shepherd stood and waved back a considerably less enthusiastic hand, vague on who this stranger might be. He knew everyone in the area, and he had never seen this young man before.

Both stood for a moment, unsure of what to do next. Deus needed rest now that he had found this place of flowers and his curiosity had been satisfied. He had planned to go straight back to the beach, but his curiosity was urging him on toward this new outlet.

Forget his fatigue. He could rest later. He walked, not too quickly, toward this new person, waving several times more and smiling just so there was no mistaking his intentions. As he came close, he said "Hello," stopping a few feet away.

The shepherd gave him a quizzical look and responded with something adumbrate and indecipherable. Their languages were entirely different. This was too fascinating for Deus. Vitality returned as he prepared himself to meet this new challenge. Any concern he may have had for his personal safety vanished as he considered how to defeat this problem.

He gestured to the man's sheep with obvious approval. "Sheep. Beautiful sheep."

"Sheep?" He nodded at his flock.

"Yes. Sheep."

"Sheep."

He couldn't resist the temptation to have a bit of fun. Maybe because he was punch-drunk from want of sleep, or perhaps just the innate fun of youth, he decided to tell the shepherd his name was Minos, a bee. He patted himself on the chest with both hands. "Minos. I am Minos."

"Minos."

"Yes. Minos." He paused and pointed to the shepherd. "What is your name?"

He seemed to understand. "Fazil," he said signaling to himself.

Deus pointed to him just to be sure. "Fazil?" He had never heard such a name.

Fazil smiled, beamed, at the sound of his name pronounced so oddly by this stranger. This stranger named Minos. This stranger with such an alien name.

Deus tried to draw a map in the dirt with a stick, an impossibly inaccurate map of the island on which they stood. Having only navigated the southern coast he had to guess at its actual shape, drawing it almost triangular as Syros had said it was, very wide at the end they started on, and greatly narrowed at this end. He gestured widely with his arms to indicate a large expanse and pointed to the narrow end where he imagined them to be and explained that this was where they were. He pointed in the direction of the sea and made waving motions with both arms, then scratched around the outside of the perimeter of his island drawing. He then pointed again at himself and the stranger and then again at the part of the island drawing where he thought they were. Then he remembered they had navigated past two peninsulas and added them to the drawing. He pointed to the first peninsula and, making gagging noises along with a grimaced face, indicated the place of the salt lake.

Fazil was catching on. He took up his own stick and drew the island in its more correct shape, chattering in his own tongue, somewhat more like a fiddle. He included the salt lake peninsula and also made the grimaced face. He had never been that far from his home but had been made familiar with the basic map of the island by his elders. He drew little triangles indicating the two mountain ranges.

Deus recognized what he was doing and interrupted, "Yes, yes, Kypros", while pointing back and forth from his drawing to Fazil's with his stick and gesturing all around to the whole island. He was excited.

"Kypros? Kypros?" Fazil was laughing. He said this was "Ota Em". Our home. He couldn't believe someone would call his island something so strange. Why would he do such a thing?

"Ota Em?" Deus could see the humor. He had called the place something that Syros's family had named it long ago. Obviously, these people would have a different name for it. "Ota Em" he repeated, forcing a momentary serious face before it peeled back again.

Both he and Fazil thought this a great achievement and laughed, rocking back and forth as they sat.

This exchange of words carried on the remainder of the morning. Deus noticed that Fazil had a hard time remembering many of the words he tried to teach him. Conversely, Deus was picking up the new language easily, seeming to have a natural affinity for this interest. He was able to absorb over a hundred words by the high sun. As Fazil continued to teach him he found it easier, being able to make himself more understandable as he became more fluent.

He tried to describe where he had come from. He drew the island of Kriti a guessed distance from the island of Kypros. Not a bad guess either as far as scaled distance between the two islands went, although he had no way of getting the orientation entirely accurate. The scale of his own island was off too, having only a few people's descriptions of how long it took to walk to any given place.

Fazil said that he had to go to his home soon. He should have left earlier today and would now be late. He shrugged his shoulders indicating that it wouldn't matter too much. Deus knew what he meant. His own brothers had been a day or even two late before, not being good with numbers. Still, a late arrival, especially when it involved more than a day, always raised concern at home. The master worried over the well-being of his flock would be furious, and the shepherd would have to bluff adroitly to avoid a beating.

Deus discreetly inquired over the location of Fazil's home, not wanting to unduly concern him about any possibility of an attack. Fazil missed the possibility of danger against his people completely, fully confident in the trustworthiness of this young man. He was caught up in the interesting challenge of translation with Deus and scratched another, larger scale map of the immediate area of the island, giving an accurate rendering of the beach and stabbing a hole where they sat, speaking quickly as he did so. Deus could make out most of the individual words but found it difficult to put them together into a tangible sentence. It was as if the sentences were said backward at times, the words thrown in the air and scrambled at others. Fazil said many names that Deus hadn't heard which he felt must refer to place names. It was becoming far too much for one day. He couldn't take it all in.

Fazil was still stabbing at different points around his map when Deus noticed that he had stopped, his stick on one point, unmoving.

"Ota Em Eli."

Deus repeated that, puzzled. He thought Ota Em was the name of the island. He pointed to the map of the island, circling it with his stick for clarification.

Fazil nodded. That indeed was Ota Em. This was Ota Em Eli. He pointed back to the dot on the area map. "Our home where we live."

Trying to extract the number of occupants of Ota Em Eli was not so easy. Fazil drew lines in the dirt, twenty of them. That couldn't be right. Deus thought that too large for a homestead, and too small for a village settlement. Fazil wouldn't vary from that figure, apparently sure of it.

Then it occurred to Deus to have Fazil count his sheep. Sure enough, he was using a factor of ten. He counted ten sheep as one line, the line being drawn to indicate he had run out of fingers once. It took only a moment for Deus to add up the number of people in the nearby village.

That seemed like a lot for this area. Where would two hundred get enough water in a place where there were no signs of a creek?

Fazil stood and drew a large circle, about ten feet across, and indicated a depression, a hole. While babbling again, he indicated a wall about knee height.

A well. A spring-fed well. They had plenty of water.

While Fazil was up, he looked anxiously in the direction he should be driving his flock, and then momentarily at the sun. He had to go.

They exchanged a few words of farewell as Fazil, with obvious reluctance, picked up his staff. Deus sat watching as he and his flock moved out of sight, a final wave passing between them. He was becoming aware again of the weariness that had overtaken him. He spent only a few moments longer concentrating on the maps.

Deus couldn't stay awake any longer. He didn't want to fall asleep here in case the others woke and found him missing. They wouldn't know where to find him if they decided to go looking. He had to get up and moving. He found some of the fuzziness leaving his head as his circulation improved through walking. It was so strange that exhaustion could be alleviated, at least partially, by activity. He tried to make sense of it as he walked, to think it through. So few things made sense when one really gave serious reflection.

The others on the beach were snoring loudly, their heads propped against logs at awkward angles. Whoever was supposed to be on watch was failing miserably in his appointed duty. Deus sat farthest from the loudest and made himself comfortable, deciding he would maintain the watch for a while. In a minute he was out as soundly with the rest.

* * *

Deus dreamed of the iron idol floating suspended above him, just out of reach. His hand probed into his belt-pack, his fingers working the five circular tektites as he slept.

The peaceful feeling he had come to cherish had given way to something new, uncomfortable in a way foreign to him. He felt guilt over separating the celestial objects. They belonged together. He should have either left the tektites behind or brought the idol. But she was too heavy, he argued against himself. He couldn't have managed that and kept her safely hidden. And there was no doubt at all that he had to take the 'five' with him.

His thoughts were disoriented in sleep. Logic took strange leaps as he tried to rationalize objections of the Earth-Mother and his reasons for bringing the five irons. He could see her face becoming visible on the image of the idol, the shadow of the backlight shifting around to the side casting dark hues across her features. He thought she was angry at first, the light then sweeping to the anterior giving her a worried look, then an allusion of warning. His uncomfortable feeling had gone beyond to one of anxiety, intensifying as the look of warning became more evident. He struggled against the sleep that had enveloped him. He had to get out.

Deus woke with a start, sitting bolt upright as his eyes opened, fully alert in an instant. He was already looking at the party not far off approaching his sleeping comrades.

He felt for a small rock and without needing to aim tossed it at Syros.

"Wake up," he hissed. The rock hit him at the same moment.

Syros opened his eyes, quickly sizing up the situation as he rose. "Everybody, wake up." He spoke calmly, in a normal tone. The last thing he wanted was for everyone to get excited. "Move slowly. Just sit up and smile."

The two dozen men were only a few seconds away at a dead run. They stopped, observing, as unsure as the mariners. Each carried a weapon, an ax or stone hammer on a wooden handle. Deus noticed that the axes wielded by the two largest men were of copper, and that they wore wide decorative belts with copper adornments. These must be the leaders of the group, perhaps of the village nearby. He looked up at the sun. It had barely moved. Could Fazil have driven his sheep that far and informed these men of their presence in so short a time? Impossible. He must have left his flock with another shepherd, perhaps a brother nearby, and run the distance. He wouldn't have abandoned his animals to their own. And these men, they were sweaty. He could see it now. They were trying not to breathe hard. They were purposely putting on a show of composure, but they had clearly been running also, only resorting to stealth at the end.

Deus stood with Syros, receiving something of an unwelcome look from the intimidating captain. Obviously, he had intended to communicate with these people and was startled that Deus would be so bold. But these men were armed and had caught them with their guard down. There was no room for error.

"Greetings. Peace to you." He hoped he got the salutation correct as Fazil had taught him.

The band of intruders were no less astonished to hear their own language than Deus's comrades. Fazil had told them that they were strangers from a faraway land, that they couldn't speak their language. Several on both sides started talking at once until the leader silenced them all with a sharp word and an abrupt rise of his hand.

"You speak our tongue?"

Deus stepped forward a few paces, making a chest as he did so. He had no idea what the man said, even though he recognized one of the words.

"Fazil is a shepherd." He hoped this was going to work. His company had foolishly left anything they could have used as weapons in the boat, and their defeat would be swift. "I am a shepherd." He patted his chest just to make sure his poor pronunciation was understood. "Greetings. Peace to you." He smiled widely.

The leader took a less aggressive stance, the others following his precedent. Their opposition was making no defensive moves. They seemed harmless enough. There were no weapons about, but who knew what was in that huge craft?

"Let us see inside the boat." Deus could understand this request, partly because the man was pointing in that direction.

"They want to see the boat," he said to Syros. "I don't think they're going to do it any harm."

"And I don't think we really have much choice in the matter." He conveyed his displeasure in a quiet growl without losing much of his smile.

They both waved the men over, walking in that direction themselves. The group sitting on the beach stood nervously but kept their place. Deus and Syros kept the boat between themselves and the new arrivals. They were still carrying dangerous weapons.

Voices erupted as one. Voices of astonishment and admiration. Syros's smile was becoming more genuine as he discerned the apparent praise. Deus was doing his best to concentrate on some of what was being said. This was so frustrating.

As the group were tiring of their exploration of the craft, Deus worked his way over to the leader. He introduced himself and Syros and found out the man's name was Kompil.

A few of Syros's crew were nudging their way slowly toward the intruders. When they were noticed, the others became somewhat tense and a couple of the closest resumed their defensive stance.

Deus caught on to this at once and loudly proclaimed that he was presenting Kompil with a gift, translating in both languages so all would know that he was doing this willingly and not being robbed.

Kompil was instantly pleased with the idea of a gratuity. He watched intently as Deus jumped into the hull and opened a gunnysack stuffed with newly tanned sheepskins. The top one was the largest, from an enormous ram, withdrawn slowly to tease their imagination. He stood high on the bow with it outstretched. Deus described it as best he could, easily remembering the words relating to the sheep industry, trying to build it up into something more than it was, gambling that this was as unusually large in size here as it was on Kriti.

This was working out well. Kompil was delighted to receive it. He felt around its edges, smelled it and rubbed his nose on the supple, pliant skin worked to the softness of chamois.

Deus then reached under the wide center plank atop the benches that the crew used to support them while walking the length of the boat. He extricated a rather wide, light brown vase decorated with red and black ornamentation. This drew nods and grumbles of approval as it was passed down to Kompil's reception and acceptance. He scrutinized the leaping dolphin painted on the side, fascinated at the idea of embellishing a clay pot in such a way.

Deus spoke in a lesser volume to Syros. "Bring a few of the small copper nuggets. Just a handful."

Syros did as bidden and returned a moment later, handing over the mineral discreetly.

When Kompil had finished his descriptive admiration of the pottery, he paused long enough for Deus to divert his attention to the copper, as yet unworked and rough.

He recognized them at once.

"Do you have these on your island?" queried Deus.

Kompil took the nuggets, fingering them with amazement. He shook his head. "None so large as this. We have very small ones." He held his thumb and forefinger close together, indicating the size as more sandlike than these pebbles.

That surprised Deus. He had hoped to discover that these were common here. He pointed to Kompil's ax. "How did you come by this?"

He held his ax head up. "We melt it out of the sand." He had to repeat himself in various ways until Deus was able to understand. Syros nodded as he translated. He had some knowledge about basic smelting, but had yet to describe it in any detail to his crewmembers.

Deus took a bold step. "We like copper," he said, pointing to the mineral in Kompil's hand. "We will trade with you. We will give you more skins and pottery for copper." He pointed at the ax and at the nuggets to make sure he understood that it didn't matter what form it took. "You get us copper, we will bring you beautiful pottery and skins."

This was easy for Kompil to understand, even in this broken speech. He had traded many things. As it turned out he was easily the one with the most equity in the area, primarily through shrewd dealing. He held his ax forward toward Deus, withdrawing it again to examine its quality closely. He caressed it like a loved thing, turning it and extolling its virtues.

Deus understood too. He withdrew another fine skin, mimicking the routine of his adversary. He draped it over the hull and withdrew another quality pot, this one even more elaborately painted with a small-mouth opening and two handles near the top. He rubbed it seductively before passing it down, fawning over each painted object or engraved highlight.

He now planned to hold out, to truly determine what value the man placed on his valuable instrument. To his surprise Kompil handed it over, the decorative vases and the soft skins adequate recompense. He clearly thought that the nuggets were also part of the deal and was obviously not going to be returning those. Still, it was a profitable trade. There had to be at least three times the copper in the ax, and finished into a useful implement.

Deus tried to make it as clear as possible that further trading would be welcomed and that they would like to return another time and continue in larger quantities, as large as they could manage.

Deus instructed all in his crew to make a big show of friendliness at this point, without telling them exactly what it was all about. They complied without questioning, thinking that he had managed the scene well, and eager to continue this non-confrontationally. Kompil had ordered something similar to his company, and the lot of them pressed together in a friendly mass for a few minutes, babbling incoherently to each other as one happy rabble to another.

They gradually separated, the natives stepping back a short distance from the boat as the mariners heaved the heavy craft into the water. They tucked their supplies under the walk and were waterborne, waving with the odd free hand as they departed to the cheerful shouts and waves of their new business partners.

Deus was elated. The thrill of this encounter, of being able to take charge of a difficult and potentially dangerous situation and turn it completely on end into a profitable outcome, was the most extreme form of excitement. He stood at the bow while Syros steered and the others rowed. Syros was only too amused to play the subordinate role and let Deus leave the islanders with the impression that he was in command.

When they were far enough out that observing the social exchange on board was an impossibility from shore, Deus took his guerdon to the stern for Syros's perusal. He wanted the captain to have it.

He spoke loudly but didn't yell. He wanted others to hear without being obvious about it. "This is yours, as Captain of this vessel."

Syros took it in both hands, feeling its weight. He turned it and held it in examination, admiring its workmanship. The double-blade design was one that he had not conceived prior to seeing it in the hands of a potential enemy, a useful design both sensible and doubly dangerous. And here he is holding the weapon he feared in his hand, beguiled from the hands of the enemy by the masterful use of soothing flattery.

He handed it back. He spoke in humility. "It is your prize. You won it fairly."

All were facing them as they made the exchange at the stern of the boat, Syros retaining his position at the rudder. The symbolic transfer of leadership was paramount in this quiet, spontaneous ceremony. Deus had proved his worth. He had probably saved the crew from a brutal slaughter.

That having been done Deus was requested to honor the ship with a full narrative of the events.

Deus told of the inspiration that had guided him to explore inland as the others slept, despite his own weariness, of the shepherd he had met who spoke the unknown tongue and how they sat and tried conversing. He told them many of the words that the boy had taught him as they laughed the approval of the victorious.

"I returned to you sleeping jetsam and fell right in with the loudest of snorers. The weight of my lids no man could lift and, as I slept, I had visions. The Earth-Mother was protecting us. This is her quest, I know not what for. Then fear came over me, a foreboding of danger and the need for utmost caution. I struggled against the grip of the mighty trance, springing up to see the adversaries nearly upon us. We had been defeated without having a chance. I had to salute them as friends, to convince them we were here for their benefit and no other reason.

"They wanted this ship, wondering at its magnificent size. They had never seen such a seaworthy vessel. I had to divert them with gifts to stall their intent, before they pillaged the whole of our goods. I told them we sought after the copper, that it was something we had plenty of but it was useful as ornamentation and held some value as that. They were willing to set up trade for the pots and soft skins, clearly of superior make than they were familiar with. I told them to gather as much copper as they could, that we would be back many times to make exchanges. I think we will have little mining to do ourselves any longer. I think we will be able to depend on these people to do the labor for us. My friends, I can see us wealthy beyond imagination."

The crew threw up their hands in a mighty cheer, the driving oars stroking some of the men backward off of their seats as water caught the dropped blades and flung the solid handles against them. Syros berated them, as elated as he was himself, at their foolishness in letting the oars slide outward through the holes. They were an irreplaceable commodity at sea.

Deus had given that some thought since Taros had almost caused a singular incident of similar gravity.

Enough talk. It was time to continue on. Syros got them back in sync and steered them due east. Deus stood beside him, not wanting the others to think he was aloof from the Captain. Regardless of the transfer of leadership, this was still Syros's specialty, and Deus considered himself an equal now rather than a usurper of power. They would be a team. He had no intention of making any outward show of superiority.

The island was retreating in the distance. He spoke quietly. "Syros, I have been studying the motion of the oars in their holes, and the danger they face in falling through. I have thought of lashing them to the hull in some way to keep that from happening."

"It is a good thought." Syros had every regard for the youth and had no wish to cause him offense. "I think it is important, however, to keep in mind that we have to have the capacity to withdraw the oars at a moment's notice. When the order is given, it must happen immediately. Also, that leaves the blade protruding, and so the oars also must be able to pass outward. Lashing would waste a considerable time doing either of these and would expose the oarsmen to danger. At sea, we can't afford to be packing injured men around. You saw how difficult Taros's illness was for the rest of us to bear."

Deus was tuning his diplomatic skills. He could see that this was a sensitive area. Syros was married to his ship, a craft of his own creation and largely his own development. And regardless of how quietly they spoke, there was a very good chance that those closest would still be able to hear. There was a matter of pride here.

"Yes, I see where that would make things too difficult. A lash that could not be removed quickly could endanger everyone." He paused and looked thoughtful, staring at the nearest active oar as it made its pivoting motion repetitively through the hole. He hoped Syros would see what he had envisioned on his own. "Of course a removable lash of some sort might be more acceptable. Something that was affixed to the oar and merely hooked onto the hull in an easily removable way might do it."

He had said enough. If Syros couldn't figure this out, he would just drop the subject. He continued to look at the motions of the oarsmen. Looking at Syros might put him under too much pressure and he might make a snap decision not to pursue the matter further.

"I think I see what you mean. Yes. I think I see a way to make it work."

He ordered the two closest oars aboard. He removed a length of thin rope, a brownish twine of too small a gauge to be useful for securing the vessel, and more robust than necessary for tying bundles. He tied it fast a hand width above the wear point on the oar, leaving a short length with a loop tied to the end dangling. He cut the excess away.

From his waterproof tool sack, he withdrew an awl with a flattened point and sharp edges. He struck it down beside the hole on the upper surface of the hull rim. Twisting it back and forth and pressing it into the wood he began to drill a small hole, working and blowing out the slivers that filled it from time to time. When he had penetrated to the depth of his first knuckle, he replaced the awl in his sack.

He searched under the floorboard for a small dowel that would do the task. He had to whittle the end slightly, tapering it to make it fit into the hole, and banged it down tight with a large block of wood. The dowel stuck up a finger-length. This would do nicely.

He pushed the oar outward to its rowing position and placed the loop of cord over the dowel. The rope didn't impede the rowing action in any way. He pushed the oar out through the hole and it was stopped, as it was meant to be, by the rope pulling taught. Shipping the oar was as simple as flicking the loop off of the dowel and letting it hang freely. Removing the oar outward would be as simple.

Why hadn't he thought of this? He knew Deus had wanted him to believe it was his own idea, and was grateful as he quietly watched from the rudder position and let him do the actual fitting. It would have escaped the others that the great builder of sea craft had been guided by little more than a boy.

But why not? Hadn't he been the inspiration, and then salvation, of this whole expedition? The shame of not recognizing the contribution was greater than admission. Syros stood with his hands on his hips, striking a strong pose.

"Men. Once again Deus has made a significant contribution. He has deviously led me in contriving a clever innovation to keep your oars in place. I confess that I felt anger in my heart as he tried to show me a better way and," he turned to Deus, "I implore his forgiveness."

Deus smiled at the compliment. "The idea was within you the whole time. I was merely the catalyst to draw it forth. You did the work. I couldn't have used your tools or tied a rope in such a way. No, Syros. Keep the credit for yourself. Your humility belies your skills and intelligence."

"Will this lad give me no peace?" he bellowed. The crew roared.

"You must pay for the lies you tell this crew. If you think that we have a future as rich men and traders, then you must teach us the language of these men of Kypros. And you must start now, or I'll have you back on the oars."

Chapter 6

Ugarit

Unhealing blisters on their palms were causing the greatest grief. Some had tried rubbing wine into their hands, others olive oil. They tried wrapping the oars in sheepskins with and without the wool. But it was little use. The best thing seemed to be a wrap of the softest skins, but they lamented this as these were their finest skins for trading.

They had all expected blisters, but only Syros had known what fearsome sores they were in for and was not one to frighten the crew away before they even started. The blisters formed, swelled, tore open or burst, reformed, broke open again, and hardened into rubbery calluses. Just as they thought their hands were toughened against their labors, the first exposure to seawater would soften the dead skin, which would slough off to expose the painfully raw patches beneath. If, by the greatest of care, they managed to keep the calluses dry after bursting, they split and formed anew underneath the first, the continual abrasion drawing them forth like a fertilizer.

Syros had led them well in learning to man the ship. At the very start of their voyage, he had taken the sternmost bench, the stroke position, where all could see him and try to emulate his timing and style. But, being the biggest and physically strongest of the lot, his best position was the center bench where his great strength was of most effect. He spent most of his time there now that the others had found their own. They had melded together, a unit now. They followed the stern and rarely lost time, an abrasive shout from Syros remedying any dysfunction of an oarsman. The neophyte mariners readily accepted his methods of timing the strokes, relaxing as they swung forward, and controlling the oar blades as they moved through the water. They had established some bad techniques from their fishing excursions, but they became so apparent through sore backs and limbs that they eagerly adapted to any improved methods shown them.

Rowing this twelve-oar galley was far different than rowing the fishing skiffs common to all of the coastal people. The oars they held today were heavier and far more unwieldy than simple paddles. They were cramped together and their legs couldn't be used fully. Sometimes their legs screamed appeals, the only relief being the opening and closing of their legs as they tried balancing on the seat without altering the rhythm of the stroke. Rowing was largely a matter of swinging the weight of their bodies, pivoting forward and back, endlessly, day after day, until repetition dulled them senseless.

They argued about stroke length, Syros let them, some feeling that it should be short and quick, others long and slow. By common agreement, after having experimented with all possibilities, the rowing stroke was kept short.

The worst crime was to swing too far forward at the preparation for the beginning of the stroke, and a fraction too late. When that happened, and once was too often, the man in front would be struck in the mid-back as he heaved backward, his full weight and the motion of his own oar in the water driving him into the hind oar handle like a sledgehammer, the stone counterweight falling to the floorboard jeopardizing nearby feet. In those first days, it was not unusual for an oarsman to be thrust from his bench with a discolored bruise to welt up shortly thereafter. A few hurled threats were the extent of any violence that could have easily escalated. Friendly barbs of the others who now had to lift oars and try to regain their lost synchrony soothed the situation. The men had fostered a camaraderie that could survive most accidents.

Even though the ship was set for twelve rowers, they never had that many. One was always at rest, in his rotation, and another was at the helm. Generally, that was Syros, but he longed to pitch in with the rest. He loved to row. If the others could have been trusted to navigate he would have left it entirely up to them. This crew had a keen interest to learn, however, and he did his best to teach all who were interested.

Food was another matter. They were not going too fast to troll, and a line was out continuously. The only time they brought it in was when they had a catch or when dolphin were around. Dolphin brought any ship luck, and it was an act of wickedness to soil a deck with their blood. They would come close to the craft, sometimes in schools as large as twenty, smiling and laughing and playing in the wavefront and examining the surface-swimming beast before moving off. Syros maintained that they weren't fish at all, that they were some kind of higher creature and that it was wrong to kill such a thing. They were miraculous, the way they spouted water and sucked in air through the top of their heads, magical beasts.

They had brought a quantity of dried fish and octopus with them but had yet to see the need in it. Plenty was caught with the trolling line. Small tuna were their favorite. They ate the flesh raw when they caught it, the delightful flavor a treat that diverted their attention from their stinging palms. It was the duty of the one at rest to maintain the line and check it at the beginning of his break.

A wide ceramic bowl kept smoldering at the rear was always ready for a catch of any kind. Bluefish was most common. The assigned cook lay it over the coals and pulled off chunks as they became ready. The cook ate first, and not much, the fish had to be calculated to reach each member. His main task as he rested was to see that the fish didn't overcook. If it was done before his return to the oar, he was to lay it aside and the others would, as their rest period came up, have sustenance before a short nap.

At night and on occasion during the day, it all seemed at the whim of the captain, up to six men could be off the oars. The others would continue the ponderous task before them a while longer before switching off once again. And so it went, the Captain ensuring fairness as far as food, drink, labors, and sleep went.

The oppressive sun beat down unrelentingly on the men during the day, their salvation a very light stern wind that helped propel them along. Sweat beaded and poured off the men's bodies in rivulets, forming moist patches on the benches where they sat. They rowed naked to let their sweat evaporate and cool them. Those that chose not to sit on their clothing soon found their buttocks red with rash. Those who sat on their comfortable pads of rolled clothing discovered not long after that the soaked material was conducive to producing even worse rashes. Some of the men developed painful boils from the constant exposure to the salts and liquid. Sweat coursed down from their hair and into their eyes where it stung. It was actually painful. They tasted the salt of their perspiration as it passed in runnels past the corners of their mouths.

The coming night would be a welcome time.

* * *

Dawn lit the seaside village of Ugarit. Yaqara raised his arms as he stretched and twisted his head and the rest of his bulk from side to side, his vertebrae snapping consecutively from his neck to his thorax. There was nothing like the early morning. Standing on his south-facing deck, he could contemplate the vastness of the endless sea before him and feel the first warming rays of sunlight strike his back.

He had been doing well for himself this last while. Trade in the relatively rare metal anaku, or tin, was brisk. He could hardly keep it in stock. His donkey caravans to Assur in Assyria kept him in good supply, but they were in constant danger of plundering by marauding bandits. He had wised to their tactics, discovering that every second caravan seemed to disappear off the face of the earth. Taking a string of donkeys and a new group of men by a different route, he was able to circumvent the thievery for a while, a game of cat and mouse ensuing that was still ongoing. He could still buy the anaku from the thieves, for quite a minimal sum since they had no idea what it was they were stealing and had no other purchasers, but why should he have to pay more than he already had?

Now the rules had changed a little. Enough people had increased their wealth through his enterprise that he no longer had to supervise the journeys.

They were willing to risk their own lives and riches to bring the precious anaku to him while he sat in comfort among his assets.

The benefits of being a middleman. If only he could discover where the merchant in Assur got the metal. He had tried everything, bribery, drink. He would gladly have married the man's ugly daughter if she had not already been taken by some vomiting little camel's ass. The mere thought of the twisted beetle made his ulcer agitate. He was responsible more than any other for the ever-rising price of the commodity. And now that the others in the village were assuming the risks of transport his profits were even more marginal. Still, considering that he really didn't do anything other than make the connections, he could hardly complain.

He had thought many times of continuing on with the transport of the anaku to Egypt, but the one attempt he had made was even more disastrous than the eastward journeys. He had lost his only son in that expedition, along with the cargo. The only reasonable thing to do was stay in safety at Ugarit. Adventures were for the young. It was the responsibility of the old and wise to guide them in making a profit for others of more worth. Like himself.

A young girl servant came out with a basket of fruit for Yaqara's breakfast. Her black hair fell over her shoulders as she bent down to place the basket on the table. She smiled at Yaqara before turning and leaving. The cotton dress she wore was becoming tighter as she grew, her slim form revealed inside the blue cloth as it filled out over the last couple of years.

She was a temptation. It wouldn't be long before she would be of the marrying age. She had a conspicuous attraction toward him, but the reasons were different than the attraction he felt for her. She was getting very accustomed to the wealth in this house in comparison to almost everyone else's. Even as a servant she still took part in enjoying the surroundings of luxury.

Perhaps in another year. Marrying a girl less than a third of one's own age was common enough, but there was a certain crudeness attached to it, a baser kind of humor. Men talked about such engagements when they were into their wine in the same way they spoke of drawing pictures in the sand with their streams of urine. Few believed there could possibly be anything in the way of genuine emotion involved between the two. What feelings could a beautiful young girl have for an old man? Not that that mattered one mote. And who would believe that an old man would have any need but one for a young girl? With his notoriety for a bargain, the townsfolk would say that he was just too niggardly to pay the local prostitutes. Yes, any pursuit along that track would have to wait. She wasn't going anywhere, and he could bide his time.

He was halfway through an orange when the pain of his ulcer reacting to the fruity acid snapped him out of his daydream. He squirmed and sucked up several deep draughts of air. That seemed to help a bit, he wasn't sure. This was terrible. He was hungry and he loved oranges. He stuffed the remaining half into his mouth, chewing and swallowing it half whole as juice drooled down his chin.

It was too much, the reaction in his stomach. He would go hungry until his goat's milk arrived. He sat, he stood, he walked around. One would think that a man of such experience and exceptional intellect would know that signs of indigestion in the morning meant that fruit should be shunned like a woman with leprosy.

Sometimes he could lose himself in thought, in daydreams that would make any physical discomfort simply vanish. He leaned over the balcony wall to meditate as best he could on the marine panorama before him. The fishermen had risen as early as he had, their little skiffs dotting the water. From his elevated vantage point, he could see them all.

He focused on a black dot far out to sea, barely visible, an apparition there, gone, and back again in the same breath. Water often played tricks on one's eyes. All the more reason to stay away from it. Fishermen were the worst fools of all from being upon it all the time. Half of them were sightless from the reflected sun, good only for raising the nets at the direction of their sons who were probably going to suffer the same whiteness of the eyes in their old age.

And who knew what invisible terror hid unseen just under the surface. As a boy his brother had gone into the water to bathe, barely up to his waist, surrounded by others who wrongly presumed safety. He could see it all again in his imagination, the boy twisting silently in shock and surprise as the water about him turned crimson, then his arms flailing as he was winched under. The children closest screamed a warning as they jumped away, tackling Yaqara as he rushed into the water to assist his brother, and hauling him against his will to the safety of the beach. He would have missed witnessing the tragedy if he hadn't already been looking that way as it unfolded, so quickly was it brought to its conclusion. He never saw his brother again, the red water being the only remains, and that lasting only a short time before dissipating.

Why or how his own brother could have been chosen over the others haunted him for years afterward, one of the reasons he had for getting away from the area and traveling east to the imagined safety of land. Imagined indeed. He saw more death inland than at any time on the shore. So he returned to his home, his compensation being the treasures he had discovered and imported.

The dot in the distance was more consistent now, closer, not vanishing in the imperceptible haze as it had been. That was an awfully long way out for a fisherman, if indeed that is what it was. He must have been out all night. They did that on occasion with bright torches lit to attract the night feeders, but this was the wrong time of year. As if there could be a right time. Fishermen were generally held to be fools, but only the most exceptionally daft would go so far from land.

Sarai came unnoticed through the doorway with a pitcher and bowl. The quiet thud of her placing them on the low table drew Yaqara's attention to her presence.

"You must have hurried today, or I was deeper in thought longer than I had realized?"

"You seem uncomfortable this morning. Your stomach again?" Her gaze remained on the table as she fussed with pouring the fresh goat's milk into his bowl.

"How could you know?"

"Nothing escapes my notice, master. Is it not my duty to attend your needs?" She allowed a genteel smile and the most expeditious glance at Yaqara before averting her eye. "Will there be anything else?"

"Not presently."

She departed, again attracting his eye as she minced away from him. Even her walk was inviting. She must be acquiring these proclivities in the market. It certainly wasn't from any other of the household staff. They didn't seem to have much use for her. They did little other than order her about; he heard them on occasion. And in the seven years she had served in his house she never, as far as he could know, raised her voice in retaliation or protest. He watched the goings on in his household, and round about, with a keen eye from were he presently viewed the town. Little escaped his eye, or his ear.

If only he could read people's thoughts.

* * *

"I think I can make out houses. One at least, and it must be a large one." Deus shielded his eyes from the rising sun with his upheld hand, the contrast making it very difficult to see the western slope although it was now high enough to cast light on the dwellings. He squinted into the glare, the connected dwellings of the distant town barely discernible, the central white building giving him the best visual clue for the present.

Deus, they established, had the best eyesight. They had held several contests of visual acuity at night using the stars as targets. Only four could see the double star in the handle of the Big Dipper. Had anyone other than Deus and Syros been the claimants to see such a thing the crew would have held the assertion in serious question.

Another of the four was eliminated by his failure to see the extremely faint outline around the dark shadow of the black portion of the Moon, its white part contrasting in a brilliant manner similar but far less extreme than to what Deus was now experiencing looking for habitations on the coast.

Even Syros and Limbus lost out to Deus's ability to distinguish colors amongst the stars. They could get the brightest of the red and blue ones, but anything less than first magnitude was impossible for them. They tried until their eyes were as strained as their backs.

Syros adjusted the rudder and made their heading accordingly as Deus indicated. It was time to add a bit of fuel to the fire again and cook a hearty meal before arriving. They couldn't count on these people being any more hospitable than the last.

* * *

Yaqara was focused intently on the nearing ship, its size even more apparent as it passed the little fishing skiffs about their daily routine. Was that smoke coming off the bow? They carried fire onboard?

He could make out the synchronous motions of the oarsmen as they brought their vessel ever nearer, undaunted, showing no sign of caution. This couldn't possibly be an invasion force. But a precursor to one?

He began to shout, calling for his household staff. He met them at the bottom of the stairway to the second level. "Bring here as much fine food as you can prepare for the mid-afternoon. We will have need for as many as twenty. Prepare baths and scented oils. And have the prostitutes clean themselves and stay nearby."

He ran through the hallway leaving the others in momentary confusion. Dashing through the door of his chamber he stripped off instantly. He poured oil onto his head and massaged it into his hair and beard, rubbing the shining residue on his hands all over his face and body.

He chose the purple robe, designed to impress. Very few had these, the dye being made from a hard to get shellfish that had a preference for water not too near the immediate shoreline. The penalty for any other than a town governor or member of the royalty wearing such a garment was imprisonment. Of course, the edict was almost foolish. Anyone who would prefer a garment such as this over a generous commission from one such as himself for the cloth would have long since been locked up in the interest of public safety.

He almost fled his room. He should have thought sooner about the possible implications here. If only his ulcer hadn't been distracting him. He could sound a horn to gather the men of the town to the sea with arms. But should he? The arrivals could interpret that as a show of defiance rather than one of respect. If only he could know who these men were. Oh, for the eyes of an eagle.

He rushed down the lanes to the shore, looking over his shoulder only once to see with satisfaction that his orders had been understood and the kitchen fires were already being stoked in preparation. Others had preceded him, men women and children, the crowd growing by numbers as stragglers noticed the others already there and, not wanting to miss out on anything, joined the crowd.

Even the fishing boats converged on the vessel as it rushed past toward shore, not having a chance of keeping up with its tremendous speed.

Syros took his place on the bow, using arm signals to guide the rudder man in steering around the submerged shore rocks. There was only one which required a slight maneuver. The water was crystal clear, barely a ripple even from the fishermen who had been floating lazily on this unproductive morning. There were no natural dangers in this harbor.

"Oars up" he shouted. He had calculated the ship's momentum and the water's resistance perfectly. The craft slowed and grounded softly onto the sand below, the stop barely causing Syros any need to adjust his balance as it settled to its rest. He stood tall, Deus doing likewise at the rudder. The men by prior arrangement had spun themselves around on their benches, prepared, without being too evident to those unfamiliar with the workings of a large vessel, to propel themselves forward in an instant.

The man in the purple robe was first to make a move closer toward them, a small triangular cadre of men following him. None of these people appeared at all threatening as Syros completed a snap survey of them and, quickly, of the whole beach. In fact, the overweight man in purple had his arms outreached in welcome.

Deus, having joined Syros at the bow, descended with him, each on either side of the vessel. Syros was nervous, not so much about meeting this purple-clothed man but at the size of the strange crowd. Not a single one bore arms and, oddly, the majority were women and children. Yet, his crew could easily be overpowered by the sheer mass of them should they form the notion.

Deus noticed Syros's hesitation and knew instinctively what he must do. He stepped forward past his captain to accept the greeting of this host. He had sized up this body of people as harmless, greatly curious at their arrival, and eager to find out about them. But to have hesitated and shown insecurity or mistrust could have been seen as insulting or threatening.

Yaqara's gregarious expression twitched slightly as the youth stepped forward. He hoped he had not made a grievous error in reaching toward the older man first. He must be a lesser personage to the youth. Perhaps this young man was a prince. He hoped he wasn't one to take offense easily. But Yaqara was skilled in diplomacy and, barely skipping a heartbeat, swung his direction of focus to the lad, welcoming him in the most fawning terms, gesturing his invitations for Deus and all he would like to bring with him into their town.

Deus clasped arms with the man, letting him take the lead in this. It was a slightly different greeting than he was used to, but he thought it wise to follow this man's lead. The man barely stopped talking long enough to take in air for some time. Deus bobbed his head a few times, smiling when it seemed appropriate, finally getting a few words of greeting and thanks of his own in.

Yaqara stopped talking, still holding onto Deus's arms. He hadn't established up to this point that these people spoke another tongue. He tried three other greetings that he knew, but all were from neighboring lands and clearly made no sense to these people from the sea. He could see that he was moving too fast.

Yaqara stood back two paces and bowed slightly, not so inclined as to make his people think he might be making obeisance to the new arrivals, but deep enough to show some respect in case the lad was royalty. He had known princes to be as shabbily dressed as anyone else on campaigns and after long travel.

He gestured to himself and repeated twice "Chief Yaqara."

Deus picked up on this right away. This was exactly the exercise he and the shepherd boy on Kypros had been through.

Immediately he introduced himself, gesturing as Yaqara had. "I am Deus," he also repeated twice.

"Iam Deus" Yaqara repeated back. He hoped he had pronounced it correctly as he made a slight bow again. His name is Deus, his title 'Iam'. For now, he would consider an 'Iam' to be a prince. What could it hurt? That was most probably correct, although there was the remotest possibility the boy could be a king. He interpreted the wide smiles and sideways glances of the crew still standing in the boat to be encouragement for making such speedy progress with their language. He motioned for them to descend to the beach, turning and slapping his hands together twice for his own men to assist in securing the ship. Men sprang into action, momentarily alerting the crew, but they could see readily that these men were merely eager for the change to grope the vessel in admiration. They would keep it safe, hopefully.

Syros called to the crew to pass the fish that they had caught to this man. It would spoil soon in the heat of the day and relations couldn't be hurt by making the offer. They had caught a number of large bluefish and a small swordfish just before and after dawn. Yaqara made a show of thanking them for their generosity, delighted that now he could arrange to serve fish more impressive than any his locals would have caught this morning.

Yaqara urged them all to come with him to his house, he pointed to it up the slope. He encouraged Deus to walk beside him, and Syros on the other side. He still wasn't sure what sort of relationship the large man had here. Perhaps an attendant, or a slave. He must be highly regarded by this prince, this Iam. He began to talk again, babble really, knowing he wasn't at all understood by these people as he escorted them up the lanes, but needing to put on some kind of a performance for the throngs following him.

The buildings here were dirtier looking, brown sandstone far less appealing than the stone huts of home. But the size. Only the smallest huts here compared. In fact, as they went on one could hardly tell were one dwelling ended and another began. Most were connected, as they climbed the slope they all were. These together must be the one large building Deus thought he had seen from so far out at sea, it was hard to tell now that he was in the middle of it all. He tried to pick up some of the words Yaqara spoke as they walked along but it was impossible, he spoke so fast, gesticulating in every direction. He must be extolling the virtues of his town.

They came to his whitewashed home standing out amongst the others, a palace to these seafarers. It was no larger than many modern late twentieth-century houses, the area of both floors being in total around five-thousand square feet, but never having seen a building of such size, they found it monumental. With their full packs, they obeyed the entreaties of their host and followed him through the impressive entranceway to the large receiving room immediately inside.

Yaqara indicated they should sit on the colored carpets, leading them by sitting himself. Sarai was at the door to the kitchen, watching as they sat, an oversized basket of fruit cradled in her arms. Yaqara saw her, thanking his gods that he had such good help, and beckoned. She came, still winded from running. She had come in the back entrance only just prior to the others entering in the front.

All eyes were on the shapely girl as she entered the circle and offered the basket first to her master and then to the others. She was aware of their surveillance of her body, inwardly enjoying it and hoping Yaqara would notice what they were doing and feel a hint of jealousy. As for herself, she kept her eyes downcast. Her master gave her great freedom when they were alone but when guests were in the house that was another matter. She was to assume her most subservient attitude.

Most of the men were completely disregarding what Yaqara was talking about. There was hardly any point listening. They were feeling quite comfortable about their surroundings now, the desired affect. One by one Sarai swayed in front of them in her esoterically pleasing way. Each could hardly help a slight stirring within, even with the wearying voyage barely behind them. If this man was planning on any lengthy entertainment, he was in for a disappointment. They might have enough stamina left to get through a meal, but the call of sleep was creeping up on them already. As long as they had maintained their labors they were able to fight it off, but now that they were stationary the feeling was becoming irrepressible.

Some of the men were lounging rather than sitting, their eyelids ever so slowly closing, then snapping open again, only to repeat the pattern. If strange people hadn't surrounded them, they would have been asleep with the first touch of foot on beach.

Deus tried again to establish some kind of communication with Yaqara. He had never met such a talker. He must understand that they couldn't understand. It took until now to get him to slow down enough to get a few more words in.

Eventually, while the first of the men began to doze, he began the routine he had followed previously, pointing to things and finding out what Yaqara called them. He was disappointed that none of the words he had learned from Fazil the shepherd were usable here. Apparently, these people spoke another completely different language. He would persevere though. Just like on the Island of Kypros he began to feel invigorated as this dialogue developed.

Syros sat back and comfortably devoured the food and sipped at the wine that was now coming in steadily, served by the attractive girl and an older woman who was probably the wife of a man who on occasion revealed his presence through the kitchen door. He listened as Deus tried to learn the language of this very well adorned host. This was fascinating. Deus had told him everything of his meeting with the shepherd as they slept and how he had mastered so many of his words. That had saved them on the island, and it was likely to be a positive advantage if they could do the same here.

Soon the entire crew was asleep, all with the exception of Syros and Deus, and even Syros was nodding despite his most desperate efforts. The wine, which he consumed in greater quantity, was having an unwanted sedative effect against which there was no defense.

He marveled at Deus's stamina. "Perhaps it is time to present a few gifts to our good host?" he ventured at this point. He wanted to be part of any such presentation before he too passed out with the rest.

Yaqara was almost surprised to hear from him, he had been so quiet. Deus agreed immediately and removed a finely worked goblet from one of the satchels the men had brought from the boat. He had second thoughts about presenting it, thinking that the copper wine bowl Yaqara was using was much nicer, besides wondering if copper was not much more common than he had supposed if people were using it as drinking vessels.

Yaqara exclaimed his delight before the goblet was even completely out of the bag. He could see the craftsmanship integral to the piece, the wide base tapering up to the halfway point where it flared out again as a thin-walled receptacle, the whole of it about nine inches tall. It was fabulously worked, the black glaze having an almost bluish tinge depending on how the light fell upon it, the etched patterns giving the ceramic the rich reminiscence of epicurean wood.

He shouted to the kitchen, Sarai rushing in with wine to fill the goblet, her eyes fixing on the beautifully adorned vessel. She paused a moment after filling it, fascinated by the creativity, before suddenly becoming aware that she was intruding and hurriedly left. Deus caught the ramifications of her movements and wondered. He had never seen such servitude. It was nice in a way, but this girl almost seemed afraid of making a mistake. Why was it that women and girls were so subservient? For that matter, why were there apparently different classes of people? This Yaqara was obviously more important than any others in this area. Why the classes? How did such divisions come to be?

His destiny, he knew, was to become leader of his island, but did that mean that he had to be 'better' than others with them subservient to him? Must people be this way? Syros was very important in Mirtos, but he seemed more or less equal to the others. They looked up to him and followed most of what he said, but that seemed to be more a matter of admiration for his brave accomplishments. There certainly was nothing of fear involved.

He and Syros brought several fine pieces of pottery out to present to their host, each and every one received with greatest thanks. At last it was too much, and they tried to convey their weariness. Yaqara understood at once and called again to his servants. All three came out, the first time they had seen the man other than glimpsed through the kitchen door. He bowed before them, leading the two to a chamber off to the side of the main room while the others slept soundly. They were not disturbed. They could sleep in the reception room until content. Yaqara ordered Deus and Syros taken to his private bedchamber. He would not be needing it until later that night. If they still slept it was no matter, he might sleep on the balcony under the stars. He enjoyed doing that on warm, clear nights. It brought pleasant memories.

* * *

"Master?" Sarai stood in the doorway to the balcony as Yaqara finished his evening meal. He looked up at her without speaking. The smith is at the door. He says you are expecting him."

"Ah yes, him. Are the seafarers still sleeping in the receiving room?"

"Yes. They are as motionless as dead men."

"Very well. See that they are not disturbed. Show the smith up here."

He had forgotten about the smith. That was unlike him. The turn of events today must truly be preoccupying his mind. Trade was in his blood, and this could only be a supreme opportunity. If they hadn't been asleep, he would have had to cancel this meeting with the smith. As much as he hated to break his concentration, he did promise the man, and it was wisdom to expand one's circle of contacts no matter how annoying or simple they could be.

He lost himself in the contemplation of things again as he stared out to sea. The grim-looking man was waiting in the doorway when he returned his attention that way. He must have been there quietly waiting to be noticed for a while. He bowed with a stiff back, keeping his eyes fixed ahead.

Yaqara welcomed him onto his outdoor lounge area as an old friend, the spurious cordiality lost on the suspicious migrant. He maintained his rigid composition despite the condoling of his host. This man in purple was no different from any other man of authority, able to wear the wear, either the fleece of the lamb or the cloak of the tiger and change between the two as occasion demanded in an instant. Their concern lay only in personal gain. Nothing and no one would stand in their way.

"Please my friend, I feel you still do not trust my good intentions. Be seated on this mat. Let me fill your bowl." It was the copper bowl he had been using previously, a complement not missed by the smith. He then filled his own goblet, which had been obscured from view by a basket of fruit. When Yaqara lifted it in a calculated toast of good relations, he enjoyed the sight of his guest's pupils dilating on his new acquisition, although he was disappointed at his control. The man was as unyielding as metal itself.

"I had hoped to get the funding you had promised me."

How bold this man was. How direct, calling it a promise. He excused it because of the man's difficulty with the language. Yaqara maintained his smile, although it took a clear twist to the observant eye.

"I have given your proposal considerable thought. I have done nothing but dwell on it for days. But I have no security, you see. You must see that. I cannot be giving out grants to any who come to me. I would have them lined up to the sea if that ever became common information, and no matter how secretive we were word would get out."

The smith struggled with this. He hoped his interpretation wasn't that Yaqara was reneging. This new vernacular was difficult. He had only been here twenty days, most of it spent with fishermen to maintain his survival. A vital spin-off was that they were the most talkative people, spinning yarns non-stop. They also had the patience to repeat over and over the words and tales until he had a reasonable grasp of the basics of the language.

He tried to clarify what he thought and feared he might be hearing. "Are you saying you will not help me?"

"You must understand it is not so much a matter of me not helping you as asking you to try another way. We have other smiths who are skilled in the use of copper. We are a small town, you see. I'm sure you are excellent, but perhaps we have no need of any other."

So there it was. All this time spent here, struggling with the language, appealing to this oaf, demeaning himself fishing and waiting. All for naught.

He was tempted to scream at the man but, the way he smiled, he thought that perhaps, just perhaps, there might be something in the future, a possibility of a change of heart. He stifled the urge and rose, thanking Yaqara for his time, and left.

He wondered only laconically at the covey of sleeping bodies in the main room as he passed.

* * *

Deus awoke in the snug bedding, a loud vibrato of wind from his friend Syros bringing him into the world of consciousness.

"I was going to go down to the beach to check on the boat."

Deus sat up. He couldn't remember ever being as comfortable as this. "I'll come with you."

The others still slept in the front room and in their exhausted state would until morning. They couldn't see the sun, the long shadows of the buildings in front of Yaqara's falling on them as they left his residence and took the road down. It was cool this evening, more noticeable after delighting in the softness and warmth of the bed.

There were still a number of people around their vessel, as well as a couple of dozen skiffs now in for the night. A rather grumpy looking man sat on the stone wall facing the craft, a vacant stare cast through it to the horizon. He stood out from the other, more animated, town people who shared anything but his gloomy outlook.

The spectators stood aside as Deus and Syros climbed aboard, greeting them in their native tongue.

Syros noticed a place midway along that looked as though it may have been disturbed, a few sheepskins slightly askew from the way they had been left. He brought it quietly to the attention of Deus.

The striped blanket that had been given him by the lady in Vathypetro was missing. He knew that Taros had taken his with him. Deus had left his stowed because he really had no need of it, preferring his felt in any case. Still, it was as a treasure to him, a special memory of a generous and loving person. He felt the loss. Just to be sure, although he was already as much as anyone could be, he made an effort at a search. He knew it was unlikely that one of the other crew came by and moved things around or removed it.

Without a doubt, it had been spirited away by one of the natives. They hadn't taken anything else though, and they certainly had the opportunity if they had been so inclined. He wondered if it was even worth bringing the matter to the attention of Yaqara. Communication was difficult enough without now trying to describe how one of his people had purloined an article of some value from their ship. He might take offense, and that could ruin the good relationship they had been developing. If his people found out that accusations had been made against them, their hospitable temperament might take a turn for the worse, and that could be dangerous anywhere.

"We'll have to keep a guard posted."

Syros nodded. "Yes. I had thought of that, but Yaqara overwhelmed me with his reception. I thought his people would keep things safe. It is my fault for being so unwise."

"We were all caught up in it. It was no one's fault." He jumped to the sand, aware that the people were watching his every move. Even the grumpy man. Here was a curious individual. Deus was drawn to him for some reason. He sat beside him and gave him the local greeting.

The man grumbled back. His manner was completely different from these others, all who seemed of quite good nature. This only satiated Deus's curiosity. As he engaged the man in conversation, it became apparent that he too was not of this place, that he was struggling with a language not of his own. His accent was clearly different from Yaqara's, even though he was speaking the same words.

Hyphes introduced himself to Deus and Syros, not making the obligatory bow he thought so redundant. He was tired of warming to people only to find later it had been a waste of effort, not to mention degrading. Still, he found these two somewhat more appealing. They didn't spill all over him in vain attempts at flattery, neither were they aloof or arrogant. They were friendly without being overwhelming. They didn't seem to be out for gain, more for interest's sake, judging by the conversation so far.

Deus especially had an almost intoxicating effect as he spoke, despite the language barrier. He had the ability to conjure images in the mind that transcended the spoken word. He could express himself using gestures and facial casts as well as another man might use speech.

As light faded with the coming night, the local residents felt they had stayed long enough and meandered one by one back to their homes. The three men were the only ones left on the beach.

Deus described the land from which they came, the island far out to sea, farther even than another island separating this place with their own. He described their quest for knowledge and wisdom. He described the Mother of the Earth, the Moon Goddess, as best as he could using the common language of this area and breaking into his own native tongue when it was the only option. Still, Hyphes could understand him, entranced with his manner of speech. Never had he heard words of such insight and penetration. When the partial Moon rose behind, he gloried in a way never felt before at its resplendence.

They sat in silence for some time after Deus's discourse. Syros too was grateful to hear the oration, not only for refreshing the memory of the first time he had heard the similar deposition, but also for the chance to more fully capture the methods of speaking by these people. Though he was in no way as adept as Deus at language accrual, he was nonetheless more able and interested than most.

He was the first to break the silence with a question to Hyphes. He had gathered from the conversation that he was not from around here and sought to know his origins.

Hyphes pointed to the north, waving his finger and whole arm high in a casting motion. "I come from the sea to the north, the Black Sea, the endless sea as endless as this here before us."

This was of great interest to Syros and Deus. To Syros because he had heard a legend of this vast sea to the north, connected by a small waterway to the one which surrounded his own Kriti. He had thought it little more than another wild fisherman's fable.

Deus found it fascinating in that it confirmed the vision he had experienced when he had been with his father, a vision that was fading in his mind, as much as he tried to keep it fresh by reviewing it consistently. Despite his efforts, he often felt it was little more than a dream. And now this confirmation at a requisite time. This was what he needed. Once again his needs were met just at the right time. This man would come with them.

Voices grew behind them, still out of sight, but there was some commotion. Lighted torches cast an oscillating yellow glow above the houses as they descended the road to the beach. A small crowd rounded the corner, Yaqara in the lead with a number of his men and all of Deus's colleagues in tow.

"We have found them, the gods be praised" he cried. He could walk remarkably fast for so stout a man, staying ahead of the others as they all picked up speed.

Concern and relief were apparent on the faces of the crew. They had awakened to the shouts of Yaqara to his staff, finding his two most honored guests missing. He had almost panicked, worried that they could come to all kinds of misfortune in the night. It was a peaceful town, most of the locals law-abiding, yet they were known to take advantage when they thought they could get away with it. Crimes were hard to prove when they did occur, and Yaqara was not the type to punish someone who might be innocent just to make an example. When the evidence was irrefutable, however, vengeance was swift and harsh.

"We were so worried. And here you are sitting by the water on such a cool evening. Come. I have a fire to warm you."

"We felt it best to guard our boat. Please don't take offense" Deus tried to explain.

121

Yaqara understood. "I will provide you with guards. Nothing could be safer than your ship."

Deus bowed as Syros stood by looking slightly uncomfortable. "I think Syros at least would like to stay. He built this craft, you see. You can imagine it means a great deal to him."

"I would still be very pleased to have all of you stay at my house. But if Syros wants to stay here, then he is free to do so. I will send for wood to build a fire. It gets cold on the beach at night." He called to some men standing behind the crew members. Two ran off immediately. He turned to Syros. "Will you need any bedding?"

Syros muttered in his own language about the blanket being stolen. He made the remark hardly knowing that Yaqara had picked up a surprising number of their words. His face changed.

"Do I understand your friend to say that something is missing from your ship?"

Deus was not prepared for this. He had not expected Syros to say anything about it, not even in their language. Now what was he to say? He could hardly lie to this man, he would see right through it. "It was nothing, a small blanket, a rag really," he tried to explain, downplaying the discovery.

Yaqara understood enough of this to know what had happened. He was outraged, veins bulging from his forehead his face flamed. If his guests had not been diplomatically avoiding the value of the theft, he would have been forced into the position of throwing a tantrum in recompense, maybe tearing his garments. He hated to do that, as with many other cultural habits which were considered 'the right thing to do' in specific circumstances. He could get away with it this time under the guise of dealing with another people who might interpret his actions the wrong way. They might think his rage was directed at them instead of at the situation.

"Do you have another blanket, one similar?" he asked through his tightened jaw. He was doing his best now to speak in the newcomer's language.

Deus was going to again stress that it was nothing and should be forgotten when Taros stepped forward, removing his blanket from his pack as he did so.

Yaqara took it and held it open, impressed by the work on the woolen fabric, the striping as admirable as any he had seen on linen. That worked him up even more. If this Deus was being diplomatic, then he was a rare gentleman. If this really was considered a rag then trade with these people was a must.

He roared. "Our honored guests have been violated. A thief has stolen a blanket like this one from their ship. Bring him to me."

His men were gone in an instant. They would turn the town upside down to find it, pressing other men into service on their way.

There was nothing Deus could do. He was very sorry the matter had even been raised. "Under the circumstances, I think it would be best if I stayed here with Syros."

The crew members agreed in unison. They were not about to leave either. If the boat was not secure, they could not possibly depart from it. Anything could happen with a mob of strangers running around. After all their labors they had no intention of taking more risks than they had to, and who knew what these people would do to the hull of the boat if they took a mind to?

"Please come back to my home with me. You will be comfortable there. I assure you that your ship will be safe. Anyone who touches another thing will suffer for it. And when I find out who is responsible for the missing blanket, they too will suffer." He eyed Hyphes. He had wondered about this humorless man from the northland.

Deus thanked him and asked the others to join him in a bow of thanks for the treatment they had so far received. The thanks were genuine but, as much as Yaqara wished it were true, he could not help but feel that an opportunity was slipping through his fingers. These people were more offended than they were letting on. Why they were concealing their feelings he could not guess, but they must be as filled with anger as anyone could expect them to be. He returned to his home, walking up the hill with as much dignity as he could muster after losing face so badly.

Whoever had that blanket would pay, he would see to it.

* * *

Yaqara had been tossing all night, waking after recurrent dreams of the previous day's events, then returning to the same dreams. His body had achieved more sleep than he thought, but he didn't think it was much. With the first light of day creeping into his room he felt as tired as when he went to bed. Cold air brushing his face was the only thing keeping him swathed in his covers. He felt he should be up, doing something to salvage this unmitigated disaster in international relations.

Enough was enough. He would search each house himself if he had to. Just as he was donning his robe, there was a pounding at the front door. He ran to answer, beating his manservant who always took the night calls.

There was a small mob outside surrounding a youth gripped by two others, terrified by his seizure. Another man held forth the blanket.

"Is this what you seek, Master Yaqara?"

Yaqara took the bundle and let it fall open. The workmanship was unmistakably the same as the other belonging to the foreigners.

"Where was it found?"

"In the house of Sarabel the widow, the prostitute."

Yaqara stepped up to the lad, drawing himself to his full height, only slightly taller than this spindly youth less than half his age. "How did you come to possess this?"

The boy stammered, not able to look at Yaqara in his fear. The men had taunted him on the way, describing the tortures that awaited him.

"His mother knows nothing about this blanket. Her surprise was genuine. She wailed as we marched the thief away."

"Where is she now? Does she not come to stand in her son's defense?" asked Yaqara.

A few of the men shuffled and grimaced. "She has been detained. Some of the men stayed behind with her to, ah, keep her from creating a disturbance."

Yaqara understood only too well the baser instincts of these men, his own people. He hoped they would not be too rough with her. She was one of the nicer widows, only in her trade out of extremity.

"These men mock your mother. Does that not bother you?"

He held his head low, not wanting to see anyone, blocking them out of existence as they held him captive. Tears began to pour silently down his face. He sniffed.

"You know, of course, what your mother does. Have you committed this thievery to bring further shame to her house?"

He would not answer.

Yaqara grabbed his hair, jerking his head back so they were eye to eye. The boy was paralyzed, submitting like a frightened dog.

"Your mother does what she does not for herself but for you, you ungrateful pig. Can you imagine what she endures?" Yaqara's foul morning breath united with the waves of emotion the boy was feeling to collapse his quaking legs. Had he not been supported by his captors was he would not have been able to remain upright.

Yaqara seized his fist tight into Abo's hair, shaking and tearing tufts out of his head. He controlled his rage, his urge to kill him on the spot, and slammed his head forward before letting go. "Bring the pathetic swine." He started off down the hill, the others close behind, kicking at his heels and digging their elbows into Abo as they went.

The mariners rose, some from sleep, as the dissonant mob approached their encampment on the beach. There was little ceremony this time. The greeting was terse.

Yaqara held forth the blanket to Deus who received it with no enthusiasm. He could see the abdication of hope in the countenance of this young man held captive, the loss of even a will to live. This was nothing that had been done over the course of the last evening. A disconsolate mien like this took years to develop.

124

"We have the thief," Yaqara informed them. "We will have him killed of course. The manner in which he dies is up to you. You may carry out the execution yourself if you wish, or have any of your men do it."

"He is the son of a whore. He wants to die," interjected one of the captors.

Yaqara had calmed with the exercise of walking. He did not relish the idea of this youth's death. He was harmless, quiet, a withdrawn lad. Why he had done such a thing was anyone's guess. He would have stood for leniency, a severe flogging, had the victim been any other than the aristocratic leader of these people.

No one spoke as Deus considered the situation. Yaqara was unsure if he understood, but Deus looked at Abo in such a way as to make it clear he had taken in the particulars. Abo trembled as he continued to cast his eyes earthward. His shame was complete.

Deus reached out, lifting Abo's chin. His head came up without resistance, but he kept his eyes averted like a little child.

"What is your name?"

"Answer the question," roared Yaqara appalled by Abo's insolence. He lifted his arm to strike when the answer wasn't swift enough coming.

Deus held up his hand. Yaqara settled, giving a questioning look. He was curious to see how Deus was going to handle this. His right was to have custody of the boy, the boy little older than himself.

Deus bade the young man to sit on the sand, then sat beside him. He asked his crew members to sit in a semicircle on one side and asked the group with Yaqara to sit on the other. He addressed the circle, welcoming the strangers and thanking them for their service to him, in all ways, including the returning of the blanket. He spoke of his pleasure at being welcomed so congenially and was especially flattering to Yaqara, touting him highly as a respected chief of their society. He drifted into the subject of their travels, speaking simply so the imperfect words could be understood by the citizens. He used their language, which left his own crew out of the picture for the most part, yet still they felt the spirit of his speech. They had heard it before and it mesmerized them, even in another tongue.

Deus spoke for hours, elucidating his thoughts on the existence of life, and the life after, Yaqara grasping the contemplations more clearly this time.

The townsfolk wandered down to the beach, as was their want this time of the day. Some took to their boats, wondering at the circle with Deus speaking softly, and their verbose chieftain placidly listening. They had business to attend to though and couldn't spare the time while the fish were feeding.

The few who stayed maintained a respectful distance, not wanting to appear too obvious about their eavesdropping. They moved closer, gradually, as they noted no specific objections. It was a curious, serene sight. The young leader of the wanderers, by now everyone had heard of him, was staring hypnotically into space as he spoke, inaudible from even this short distance. The Chief Yaqara was beside him almost in a spell, as were all the others at hand. What kind of hold did this boy, for he was just a boy, have over them? The foreigner Hyphes was most spellbound of all. They could see it in his thoroughly unmoving carriage. He barely breathed, transfixed on the seer as he expounded on the web of life. For all appearances, he could have been lifeless. Some of the few present on the outskirts felt odd, uncomfortable, and left for their boats or carried on to their other business. Others felt strange in a different way, warm, invited and welcome. They slowly drew in, despite their reserve, like moths to the light.

When Deus stopped, and the blinds to reality retracted, they sat in silence, contemplating the most intimate things of life. Time meant nothing to them. They could have sat for minutes, or days, it was irrelevant.

Deus still held his striped blanket. He looked at it in his lap and held it up. He waited until all had focused upon it.

"This was a gift to me, a gift freely given. I choose, as is my right, to do with it as I see fit. And I choose, as is my right, to do with this Abo as I see fit." He turned to face him. "I choose to give this blanket as a gift, as freely as I accepted it."

He handed over the bundle while Yaqara gasped behind him, not out of remonstrance but astonishment. The justice was so plain and forceful. After that dissertation, Abo would be so wracked with guilt for his crime that no punishment could be greater, and at the same time he could not help but feel the genuine affection that was freely given by his victim.

Abo looked at the blanket in his hands a moment then clutched it tight, burying his face as the muffled sobs escaped. Deus allowed this for a moment then wrapped an arm around his shoulder for comfort. Abo fell in a heap onto Deus's lap.

"You see before you one unsullied. He has stolen nothing from me. He only stole from himself." He turned to Yaqara. "Give me your word you will attend to his needs."

"I promise," he vowed solemnly.

Deus rose to his feet, the others following.

"Take him, then, to your house. Clean and feed him. Find him means to provide for his mother."

Abo held the blanket before him, gazing at it as if this was but a dream. He held it out as an offering to Deus, just to make sure he hadn't missed something in the broken speech. Deus smiled unessentially, and gently pushed it back into Abo's bosom.

Yaqara took Abo by the arm and walked him back up the hill, the group with him not following this time with mean spirit, but with a warm sense of charity and understanding.

Taros wondered. Why would he give that pilfering larcenist the blanket? He had his felt, of course, which was superior for warmth, but not for beauty. He could have given it to one of the crew, who were much closer to him than any thief. Still, it was an oddly warm and satisfying feeling to have witnessed what had been done.

Deus and Syros left the others for a walk down the beach.

"How long will we remain here?" asked Syros.

"I think ten days. We will be fully rested by then. And in that time we should be able to conclude any negotiations of trade."

"Yaqara was impressed by our pottery. He also seemed interested in your striped blanket." He chuckled. The young Abo was interested enough to steal it. "What made you give it to the lad instead of having him punished? You might have given it to Yaqara and further sealed your relationship."

"I could hardly allow him to be tortured, and maybe killed, for taking a mere blanket. What good would it serve? This way these people see me as forgiving, someone who is worthy of their trust." They continued walking. "Also, I felt deeply for his mother."

~~~~~~

Chapter 7

Tin

"Miraculous." Yaqara sat back, holding his pendulous abdomen in both hands, lifting it slowly and letting it drop and undulate. The white powder had completely freed him of his pain. Of all the gifts, this was the most precious to him.

Syros had suspected something had been wrong with Yaqara's stomach. He had a variety of medicines that he took wherever he went, and one that he took on occasion for his own indigestion was given to him in quantity when he was exploring the coast of what is now considered Greece. Magnesium oxide, there in abundance, later gave rise to the name of the place, Magnesia.

"Miraculous," he repeated. "I will pay you well for all that you have."

"You are a most gracious host. What I have is but a small amount. It is yours as a gift. But do not take too much at once. It will make your dirt run like water."

"I would consider even that an improvement. When you return, bring as much as you can spare. You will find me most generous."

Yaqara opened the box beside him. "Have you ever seen anything such as this?" He held forth a small ingot of anaku. Tin.

Deus reached out to take hold of it. It was heavy, lustrous, bluish white light reflecting off its dull surface. He rotated it in the light, its cool smoothness a pleasure in his hand. "What is it?"

"It is anaku. You are not familiar with it? It is very rare. It comes from the east. No one actually knows where, exactly. Every few months I receive a train, I never know exactly how much, which I purchase and negotiate the price per weighted measure of the next shipment. Then I sell it to others for a tidy profit. It keeps me quite comfortable, as you can see. I wish I could get more though. And the cost. It keeps going up. I, in turn, have to raise my costs. There is no end to this." Yaqara felt at ease talking with Deus, even about matters he would never discuss openly with anyone else.

In the short time the foreigners had been here, Deus had established himself as one who was absolutely honest and trustworthy, someone who anyone could confide in without fear. He had become known in the community as 'Deus the Compassionate' for his treatment of the thief, and his later insistence that Abo no longer be known as a thief in the town, not even among the gossips. Yaqara issued an edict to that effect, which all locals were obliged to obey.

"Why do the costs keep rising?"

"Thieves." Yaqara was hesitant to use the word. "There are many who live outside of the control of townships such as this. They prey on the unwary and those who travel unprotected. So the merchants are obliged to arm themselves and hire mercenaries to help protect their goods. With me it is the same. When I send any cargo I am also obliged to protect it. Sometimes I am fortunate enough to have the recipients become so impatient that they send their own envoy to deal with me here. But then they suffer the possibility of loss on the way back. Actually, I have been expecting to receive the purchasers of my anaku for thirty days now. I fear the worst."

"You think they have been killed."

"Yes."

Deus was still holding the ingot. He had considered the dangers of trade but not that it could be so severe.

"The anaku is considered to be quite valuable," Yaqara pointed out to keep the conversation going.

"What does one do with it?"

"I have a plate made from it, beaten into shape." He brought it over. "It has its own beauty, as you can see. It polishes to a bright shine, yet it is not as becoming as silver or gold. And as such, it is not as valuable. How it is presented is irrelevant. My buyers will not pay any more for it regardless of how it is crafted. They prefer to work it themselves. The supplier only provides it in these small blocks, and so that is how I pass it on. Why go to extra work without compensation?"

Yaqara was having a recurrence of the thought that he had pushed out of his mind as unworkable only a few days ago. Unworkable because the stakes were so high. Now he was having a change of mind.

"Keep the ingot," he said almost without thought. "I know you will find a use for it. Perhaps you can find out why it is the others find it so attractive."

"Do you say you don't know what the others use it for?"

"They refuse to say. And I have been unable to guess."

* * *

"We plan to leave tomorrow," Deus told them as they sat in their circle at the rising dawn. Deus felt that he had done enough as far as teaching the townsfolk about the Earth Mother, and had learned their language to a remarkably fluent degree in the process. He had established a need for the medicine Syros had discovered which showed great promise of profit. They had found great satisfaction in the pottery that they had been given, and requested that more be imported, along with a supply of the fine, striped blankets.

And most intriguing of all was the possibility of shipping this anaku. Deus pulled the ingot from his satchel to show the others.

Hyphes gasped. "Where did you get that?"

"You know what this is?"

"I do. I did not know it existed here." He looked fleetingly from face to face, wondering at these people. How much did they know about it?

Deus could see that Hyphes was extremely anxious. "Come. I have been wanting to discuss a few things with you." They left the others for a walk up the beach.

"You were saying that you were from the land north, near a sea such as this."

"Yes. The Inhospitable Sea. Dark. Cold."

"Why did you leave?"

"It is a place of fear, of violence. My family was killed fighting with another family. It was stupidity. A war of words escalating to death on both sides. I am the only survivor of the two families."

"Then you killed." Deus kept his eyes straight ahead as he guessed the apparent.

Hyphes would not answer. They carried on in silence for a while.

"I had a wife and three daughters." He was speaking in a guttural voice through his gritted teeth. "They made me watch while each was raped in turn, then butchered. I broke free too late, but in my rage I saw them join my family in death. They were the last. I barely survived. Only with the aid of the old medicine woman was I able to cling to life. It took ages for my body to recover. But my soul; my soul was as cold and dark as the sea by whose shore I dwelled."

"Were you a fisherman?" He knew this couldn't have been the case but asked anyway. A man of the sea his age would have salted lines etched deep in his face from years of constant spray.

"I am a smith. I work metal."

"That is how you recognized the metal given me by Yaqara."

"Yes. Yaqara. The fool. Had I known he possessed anaku I could have been of the greatest service to him. Did he say where he got it?"

"The east. He would not tell me where it comes from, only that it is delivered from time to time and that he passes it on in trade to others."

"He is the greatest of fools." Yaqara was now glad that he had been turned away. How ironic that Yaqara, a man so concerned with wealth, had ruined his chance to improve his position immeasurably. "Yes, it comes from the east. A place they call Assur. It is a very great distance."

"Are you saying that Yaqara is a fool because he trades this material?"

"I am saying he is a fool because he would not trade it if he knew what it was." He stopped and faced Deus. "It is magical. But it needs to be worked in magical ways, the ways of the smith. Not just any smith, mind, but a smith skilled in the intricacies of the art. A smith such as myself."

They turned and began walking back along the sand.

"If you will have me I would like to join you in your travels. There is nothing here for me."

"You have journeyed on the sea before?"

"Never. The sea where I am from is even feared by the fishermen. They go only the shortest distances."

"Not so different from here. Syros is an unusually skilled captain. That is how we have traveled so far."

"If you had visited the Inhospitable Sea you would know the difference. I have yet to see a storm here."

"This is a good time of year, but you will see one."

They returned to the others. Deus made the announcement.

"Our new friend Hyphes has agreed to join us on our voyage. Will you all welcome him?"

Syros was the first to jump up and clap him on the arms. "Another hand would be very much welcomed." He hadn't told the others, the return journey would not be so easy.

* * *

"I would like you to consider shipping some of my goods by sea. I could provide you with information that you would find most valuable. This would serve my needs and give you, I am sure, the greatest of opportunities."

Yaqara stuffed an oversized portion of beef tenderloin into his mouth. He'd had the tenderest fillet cut from the back of a young bullock for this occasion. The foreigners would be leaving at first light and this was his last chance at a great opportunity.

Deus absolutely savored the succulence of this meat. The crew who had joined him were also in agreement. This was the finest anyone could offer. Fish was nothing in comparison. Even a fine lamb was hardly a match. "You wish us to transport this meat? The distances are too great. It would rot, or be devoured by the crew before we were out of sight." They laughed uproariously. Yaqara saw to it that their cups never went empty.

When the laughter died Yaqara continued. "As for the meat, I am only too pleased to let you choose any of the live animals you care to load on your ship." The crew roared approval again and toasted his health. It was hardly a generous offer, as far as Yaqara was concerned, and he was delighted that it was so well received. How many bulls did they think they could carry?

"Your kindness will not be unrewarded. Perhaps we can indeed be of service in shipping some of your goods." He hoped he knew of which goods Yaqara was speaking. "We must be off at the first light and will have no time to choose from any stock of animals tomorrow. If that is to be done it will have to be now, before the night is upon us."

"So be it then. We will attend to the matter at once." If they had never seen beef on the hoof before, then they were in for a surprise. With that they were off, climbing the bank through the upper elevations of the town and over the ridge to the plains beyond.

"I am taking you to the home of my cousin. In his field he raises the finest cattle in the land. It is his meat you devoured with such zeal."

"Then it is he we will be especially honored to meet."

Yaqara called loud as they came near to the isolated hut. A rumpled man came around the side of the building, a scowling face hardly one which should be greeting a happy group of strangers, especially with a familiar cousin leading the pack.

Yaqara hoped this moody man would not do something to ruin things. He had forgotten that he was more often than not in a miserable temperament, so long had it been since they had visited. He broke into a run to get to his relative first, his robes flying behind him.

"Cousin Jacobah. My dear cousin, how good to see you." He would have but a moment. He lowered his voice as he grabbed his cousin's arms. "These people are important. You will let them choose what they want from your stock. I will repay you later more than fairly. And if you ruin my dealings with them, I will have your hide. If you are in one of your uncivil moods again, I suggest you make yourself mute. You will pay for any rude remarks. Do you understand?"

They couldn't have arrived at a worse time. Yaqara's call had interrupted Jacobah as he was beating his wife for some perceived insult. She would not be seen now that visitors had arrived. The last time she showed herself to a stranger he broke her arm. She stayed huddled in the back corner of the hut holding the disfigured, swollen ears that her husband targeted in his rages, rocking herself between her knees.

Yaqara loudly introduced his associates as they arrived. He perceived that some of them were looking at the man's young son. "And here is young Jacobah as well." He could hardly ignore the youth standing by the corner of the hut in plain sight. And since Deus was about the same age, he thought, in this case, acknowledging him might be acceptable.

Jacobah senior held his temper at the intrusion of his son. How dare he enter into this congregation without being invited. But he had been as much as summoned by his outlandish cousin and, for now, he had to bear it. The boy could be dealt with later.

As they walked toward the circle of cattle a short way off, Deus noticed that the young man was hanging back, curiosity moving him no more than a few steps in their direction. There was something written on his face, an overt desire to be with them overwritten with clear apprehension. Deus signaled him to follow, encouraging him with a few friendly waves.

The cattle were slightly skittish as the strangers approached in numbers larger than they were used to, but they didn't run. The light cream-colored bull snorted audibly, a spray of vaporized slime shooting out of its wet black nostrils on the sudden expulsion of air. A strong beast with broad horns, it had little to fear from these intruders into its territory. But even a simple creature was wise enough to exercise some caution when facing the unknown.

The six cows in its harem stayed close, a survival instinct of great benefit in defense against wolves and other predators. One of the cows urinated, a massive stream compared to that of a sheep, and it made a loud, rather impressive, splashing noise on the soil. The sound caught the bull's attention, and he sniffed her rear and let the yellow flow run over his outstretched tongue. When she was done he tilted his head back and curled his upper lip, slowly inhaling, what to him, was a delightful fragrance. Deus smiled at the familiar characteristic. Yes, animals were all the same, regardless of their form. They could be bred in the same way as sheep, he was sure of it. The five calves also stayed close, a white male contrasting explicitly with the others of darker color. Only one other calf was of similar appearance, a very light tan female.

Deus made up his mind in that instant. Those would be the two, but he would take his time. He felt a need to speak with young Jacobah, but he spoke to the elder first. "Fine animals. I have never seen such wonders," which was true. He had never seen a cow before.

The herdsman scowled. He had no interest in talking with this bunch at all. They spoke with a strange accent, obviously some treacherous foreigners who would slit his throat if given half a chance.

Yaqara cut in to the silence, looking disapprovingly from his cousin and brightening considerably as he spoke to Deus. "These are the finest cattle anywhere in the land. Any man would be filled with pride who could manage to raise such healthy stock. Choose whichever you like. I have said they are yours." He was anxious to conclude this as quickly as possible. He would be fortunate if he could get them all out of here without some sort of scene.

Deus slid aside to speak with Young Jacobah. "If you were to choose the finest of these animals, and you could only take two young ones with you, which would they be?"

This took Jacobah aback. No one was allowed to speak to him except his father, and he had barely been allowed to speak at all even to him. But he knew which he would choose. Should he tell was the question. Deus could see he was hesitant. He was screwing up all the courage he could muster, his father's stare making it all the more difficult. He had heard the admonition of Yaqara to his father just before the others caught up and that was some solace for him. His greatest desire was to escape the torture of living in these oppressive conditions, and his greatest fear was to be left here. Life was not worth living, and he had thought many times in the last while that he should just end his own misery. Maybe he would fling himself off a cliff, or drown himself in the sea. His father hadn't allowed him to see the water since he was a child, but he remembered what it could do. This was his only chance.

He turned from his father's face and inhaled. "I would choose the white bull-calf and the light cow-calf. They are the strongest. They will have the strongest offspring. They will live long and bring many healthy calves."

This Jacobah had learned much by observing. His father disagreed with what he thought was a flawed conclusion and was almost about to upbraid him for his infinite imbecility but was restrained by Yaqara's warning grip tightening around his arm.

Deus sanctioned the choice. "It will be as you say. Yaqara, the two that he has said, they are for us."

The elder Jacobah grimaced, then turned his head away from them all to laugh silently. His son was not such a fool as he thought. Instead of embarrassing him he had sold them on the worst of the lot. And mean little calves? Why didn't they take the fine, full-grown ones? And why would they want these inferior light animals? The dark were the most valuable. The darker, the better. These foreigners were feeble half-wits. Well, he could play this game too.

"You have chosen the finest. You are tearing out the heart of my herd. How can I be compensated adequately? I am but a starving herdsman with barely a hut for shelter. How can I live and provide for my poor family without these, the best of the lot?"

Provide for your family? You supposititious bastard. Yaqara hustled him off a way. "Keep your retarded thoughts to yourself. I warned you." He flashed a polished copper blade from a sheath hidden beneath a fold in his vestment and held it inconspicuously between them, touching the point into Jacobah's belly. "We will settle this later. For now, you will be kind enough to give these people their calves and whatever else they want, and be happy to do so."

Deus was still speaking with Jacobah the younger. He could tell without any special intuition that he was filled with no great desire to stay here.

His situation was unmistakably onerous. The best way to broach the subject, now that his father was privately distracted, was to just spit it out.

"Would you consider leaving this place?"

"Are you asking me to come with you?" His demeanor brightened.

"I would need someone to tend these cattle."

"That would be my greatest pleasure. I am at your service and will come with you at once." He broke from the group in his excitement, running back into the hut to fetch two ropes for the calf's harness.

He had not thought much of his mother until he entered the hut and saw her still rocking on her haunches where she had been beaten down. The poor woman. What a sickening life. He could not have born such trials. How could she? He picked up the rope as she watched silently. Their eyes locked in the dim light for the last time.

* * *

Yaqara was very pleased that his young nephew had been asked to serve Deus. He knew this would be of great advantage later, provided he did not disgrace himself somehow. That was an unlikely event. Jacobah had been made a hard and conscientious worker, the alternative being beaten half to death.

"That is a fine field of grain," Deus pointed out to Syros.

Yaqara overheard. "We grow the finest grains in these territories. We call that wheat. From it, we make the bread which you so enjoyed."

The sun was almost down. "A portion of that splendid bread would be most welcome right now. I have developed a bit of an appetite from our walking." This was hardly so, but he said it with cause. "I wonder if the stewards of that commendable field would indulge us?"

Yaqara bemoaned this request. He had yet many things to discuss before these people left, but he could hardly plead to missing the hint. "They would be honored, I know."

They made for the farmer's hut and arrived as the sun dropped out of sight. The farmer had not seen their approach from the blind side of his hut and was preparing to retire with his family when Yaqara struck the door frame with his stick. The farmer sprang up, terrified for the moment that they might have been besieged with bandits who, when they struck, almost always did so in the night.

From the darkness within he could see by the twilight that it was the chief of Ugarit at his door with an entourage. What could they possibly want of him? He would be obliged to provide accommodation if so requested, but why so close to town? That would be unheard of when more suitable lodgings were so near.

"Chief Yaqara." He bowed to the point of folding in half. "You honor my family and my simple home with your presence. If I can be of any service . . ." The last thing he wanted was to be of any service.

"Good farmer." Yaqara could not remember this man's name, "My honored friend noticed your fine crop from the distance and, having previously sampled bread from its fruits, desired to be filled. I trust you have some prepared and available?"

The farmer barked at his wife. She immediately and silently brought two loaves to her husband who took them from her and passed them on respectfully.

Deus could see that this man, and whoever else was inside, was not going to come out without coaxing. "Your bread is delicious. The finest in the land. You must introduce us to your family so we can know who we are thanking."

The farmer thought it strange that he this stranger should speak so highly of bread that had been half a day out of the oven. It was hardly fresh, he must know from the feel of the crust. However, if he wanted to see the family, so be it. He pushed them out and lined them up side by side, all bowing low until Yaqara told them to stand up and be seen in the dwindling light.

"I noticed an area that is cut. Have you started the harvest already?" Deus inquired.

"Yes," said the farmer. "The weather has been exceptional this year. The most perfect in memory. We have an abundant crop."

Deus eyed a son of the farmer, a man of perhaps twenty years of age, healthy and strong. "Do you farm with your father?"

"I do." This was a quiet one. He wasn't volunteering any information beyond the specific. The man was not the oldest son, being perhaps two years younger.

Deus redirected his attention to the head of the house. "I would like to purchase the grain which you have cut thus far. You will be paid fairly for it."

A purchaser? Already? This was too good to be true. He had just separated the grain from the stalks, a strenuous labor which had taken the entire day, and which left him so presently fatigued. He might not even have to pack it into town.

Yaqara spoke. "I will be paying for the grain. Indeed you will receive a fair price; tomorrow, when you visit my home." He gave the man a look that suggested that he could now drop his intentions of haggling over price. There was no time, and he was not in the mood.

"Your second son looks to be the age where he might be considering striking off on his own. Or did you intend to have him stay on to help?" Deus was finding that much was accomplished by going directly to the point.

His second son? Why would he be asking about his second son? He was a good worker and useful around the farm, but his appetite was huge and something of a liability. He had been wondering himself if it was not a good idea to send him off. This was not often done, sons being considered so valuable, but a second son was still expendable, unlike a first.

"Perhaps you could tell me why you inquire so I may be better able to answer?"

Yaqara could not stand for this. "Impertinent farmer. I should strike you now. Answer the question," he flared.

Deus quickly intervened. "I simply need someone to advise me on the planting of the grain. Do not worry about any competition, the planting place is so far from here you would be unable to imagine."

"I will leave the decision to my son, Abos." He winced, chancing that this was not also impertinent, knowing that he had every authority to order his son to depart with these people.

His son spoke. "I will leave the decision, then, to the honorable Chief Yaqara."

"You have been requested to go. That is enough," spoke Yaqara harshly. "You will come with us immediately. Gather your meager belongings and be quick about it." The farmer's son ducked into the hut for barely a moment. Yaqara turned on the farmer, his patience nearing an end. "We will take as much of the grain as you have threshed with us right now. If we cannot take it all, then you will return as many times as it takes this night to complete the task. Now run."

* * *

Yaqara puffed as he bore the weight of the bag of grain. It would not have appeared well if he had been the only one to refuse to lower himself to such a menial task. Not that it was such an embarrassment. On the contrary, it was a mark of generosity that he knew was appreciated by those with him. It was just that he was in such poor physical condition that he was slow moving compared to the others. They had the decency to move no faster than he was able to walk under his unaccustomed load, but he was still unable to keep up the incessant talk they had come to expect from him.

The farmer smirked inwardly and was glad of the silence. The fat slob. How did he warrant a position of such power? He was glad to have sold all of his grain, but he worried about how much he would be compensated. After this hard walk, he would have loved to just throttle the bulbous lump and take everything he owned. And now what was this enormous boat? This was what they were loading?

It was now floating just off the bottom as they toted out the bags of grain in preparation for the morning departure. They had to wade into water waist deep and toss the cargo over the side into the waiting hands of the crew aboard.

"Thank you, farmer. Take ten men and be back before the night is half done" Yaqara admonished him. "If you do not return in satisfactory time you will not receive in kind. Your son will stay here. Now, go immediately without a word."

The farmer left with his help, vowing vengeance for this indignity. There were many men who were available to be pressed into service at a moment's notice, even at this late hour. The curious had been out to see the boat, and to help push it off the sand. Now they found themselves forced into transporting grain for the growingly abusive and abrasive farmer. Had he not been under the orders of Yaqara they would have cudgeled him for his openly miserable attitude. Who was this, a mere farmer, to be ordering them about like common chattel?

"About the arrangement we were working on to transport my goods," Yaqara was beginning to venture.

"One last thing. The potter Jobah. He makes a fine pot, does he not?" Deus interrupted.

"Jobah. Yes, I know him. His pots are fine enough. They hardly compare with the refined works you yourself have presented me with. Why would you inquire after him?"

"He is old, is he not?"

"Older than I, by some good many years, I'm sure."

"And childless?"

"Indeed. He never did take a wife. Or rather, a wife never would take him." Yaqara suppressed his urge to laugh, not wanting to appear cruel in any way. Deus the Compassionate did not seem to appreciate humor directed at others in that sense.

"He is not what a woman would consider attractive, is he?"

Yaqara pushed his lips out and nodded. Jobah's face was badly scarred from the pox during his childhood. Some said he was fortunate that he didn't die like so many others at that time. Others disagreed. They thought he would have been far more fortunate to die. Few realized that the internal scars heaped upon him from years of vicious torment were the most sorrowful of all. He eventually abandoned attempts at trying to form any association with anyone, be they man or woman, and pulled into his shell of imposed isolation, surrounded by people, yet very much alone. The pottery he produced supported him in a meager way. The women preferred his pots to those of other producers because of their quality, but most would not buy from him because of the stigma of being near him. Some of the more beneficent women, those who had been mothers at the time of his disease and recalled how horrible that time had been, had been the ones to purchase from him, as much out of pity as any appreciation of his skill.

"Does he have any family? Any reason to stay here?"

Ah. He was fishing for another someone to take with him. Why such an interest in these common people? Well, if he wanted Jobah, he could have him. He was nothing in the community.

"No one."

"As he is a member of your town I need to ask if you would have objections against his coming with us?"

"None imaginable. May his life in your hands be something more of a gratification than it has been here." He clapped to get the attention of his escort nearby. "Bring Jobah the Pockmarked."

"Have him bring his belongings," added Deus.

"As you wish. He hasn't much."

"Our needs are small. He has enough."

"May we now return to the discussion of the transport of goods?"

"You wish to discuss the matter of the transport of anaku to Egypt?"

Yaqara was stunned. One amazing thing after another since his arrival here. How could he have known? Neither of them had mentioned Egypt. "You know of this place?"

"The land of the Monumental Lion."

"You have seen the Lion? I did not know whether such a thing could be true." He began to babble, as was his nature, giving Deus no opportunity to interject a correction of his wrong assumption. By the time he had slowed enough to allow for an interruption, the matter of the Lion had been left far behind. Yaqara had heard the same tales that Syros had brought back to Mirtos, only in much more exquisite detail. Indeed trade with this country was going to be a priority.

But one thing at a time. "Yaqara, my dear friend. You have heard my words in the time I have spent with you. I know you accept much of what I have told you about the Earth Mother, about the abundant blessings she provides for those who are attuned to her guidance, about our endless existence after our simple lives here have come to a close. You have felt all that I have spoken. I have witnessed it in your countenance as we sat together. Since then you have been so generous in helping me carry out my tasks, and you wonder if I would be willing to establish trade with you. Yes, my friend. We will trade. You want your anaku taken by safer sea transport, where it will be untouchable by the roving bandits. We will trade with you for it and ship it to Egypt ourselves. We will produce pottery for you equal to that which you have received, even finer. We will supply you with felt and patterned blankets, with copper, with wine. You will not have to worry again about outlaws attacking your supply routes by land, I promise you. They will become obsolete. In the morning I will give you openly our remaining gifts for your hospitality. All in your town will know that we are allied in friendship and trade. Until then, my friend, we must get our last rest before venturing off. I will see you, I trust, at the sunrise."

They stood and clapped arms, Deus watching in respect as Yaqara departed out of sight into darkness behind the closest buildings.

Deus was making himself comfortable. The others had all drifted off to sleep. Anticipation of the laborious days ahead had been a great incentive to be well rested, and the intrusion of the noisy Yaqara on the beach was an unwelcome event to the crew.

Now another was arriving to disturb their sleep. The potter was coming down the hill with two others. They bore no torch but spoke loudly, alerting the light sleepers of their impending advent, the two with him complaining bitterly about the weight of his contraption.

Deus stood to receive them. The others who had awakened pulled their coverings higher hoping to block out any further proceedings. Each wished now that he had gone to the boat instead of one of the two others on deck watch. The planks may be hard but, with the gentle rocking and the silence, they would at least get better rest than here on this all too popular stretch of sand.

"Jobah." Deus walked toward him with his arms outstretched.

No one had ever greeted the potter in this way and he was unsure of the motive, or even if the greeting wasn't mistakenly meant for one of the others with him. One of them could bear the same name. He didn't respond other than to continue in his approach, a very puzzled expression on his face which could barely be seen with the Moon top-lighting his head slightly from behind. The lighting gave his rough pocked face an even more ghastly visage, the cold bluish light blanching further the pallor from years of indoor seclusion.

"Jobah," he said again as he clapped him on the shoulders. "I was worried that you would not come."

"Not come?" said one of the other men. "He would not risk the wrath of Yaqara." They dropped the heavy components contemptuously but harmlessly to the sand.

"Just as well it was downhill all the way. One thing is for sure, you will get no help dragging these anchors back." The two men turned and left, chafed at having had to serve this baseborn defect.

Deus could feel the hurt within Jobah's soul. The two had obviously been tormenting and upbraiding him the whole way to the beach.

"Don't be affronted. If they had but an inkling of your destiny their envy would have rendered them speechless."

"Why have you sent for me? We barely spoke when we met. You do not even know me."

"I know you well enough. One need not always speak to penetrate the depths of another's soul. Your unhappiness here would have been apparent to a simple child. I offer you the chance to come with us when we leave on the morrow."

Deus had to explain what almost everyone else in the town must have known about them. Jobah's ignorance of the recent events was only possible because of his distinction as town pariah. No one ever volunteered to visit and converse with him, with the exception of the scant few of his elderly customers. Even they still would speak little of more than the weather, out of embarrassment at being seen too long associating with him. Thus he was left ignorant as to who these seafarers were.

Jobah recalled, as if the event had just occurred, the kind words offered by this stranger as he stepped into his humble room, the appreciation of skill offered as he briefly examined a few of his pots. Deus's interest mainly lay with his potter's wheel, a fascination which he could not mask as he watched him quickly raise a bowl from a ball of plastic clay. A marvelous device, the pivoted wheel balanced perfectly on another stone with a circular divot in its surface. Greased at the joint with lard it turned easily and, with the inertia inherent in the mass of the stone, kept turning for some time. And he recalled most clearly the compliant pensiveness he felt as Yaqara, embarrassed already that Deus had ducked into the room when his attention was momentarily diverted, hustled him out under the guise of a great desire to show him something of the utmost importance just around the next corner. The insult was inflated when Yaqara let rip a resounding fart as he eased Deus out the door, discharging into the small room of Jobah an opprobrious fetor.

"Jobah, you have nothing here, no family, no ties of any kind. I want you to come with us."

"Come with you? Where?" He was suspicious.

"We are from the island of Kriti, very far out to sea. We are on the threshold of building a nation of wealth beyond your dreams." He paused for effect. "You are going to contribute to that wealth and by so doing will secure a comfortable future for yourself, a future with happiness instead of pain, a future with plenty instead of poverty. More than that, you will have friendship, family, a position of respect, and you will know joy."

Jobah stood silent, observing this young man before him. Neither spoke for some time while he thought about what he should do. He hated this place, but it was all he knew. The desire to leave occurred to him periodically over the years but the thought was always dismissed as unrealistic. As much as he was depressed and dissatisfied, this was still his home.

Deus sensed his thoughts. "Jobah, we will not be leaving until first light. Perhaps it was wrong of me to presume you. I'd hoped you would have some delight in my offer. You will not be compelled to come with us. If in the morning you decide to stay behind you will not suffer because of it. Your belongings will be returned to your room and you will live here as you always have. Know, however, that you will be missed. I believe your place is with us."

Jobah began to nod his head, imperceptibly at first, then with meaning. "You're right. I have nothing here. Nothing. If you are sincere in your offer, then I accept it."

"I am sincere. And I am very pleased that you have accepted."

"Why, I must ask, did you have my wheel brought here?"

"You are not just a capable potter, but also a skilled toolmaker." Deus knelt beside the heavy parts in the sand. "After I visited you in your room I inquired what the device you were using was. I had been impressed at the ease at which you made it work for you, how simply you created a useful object from that which was useless, form from that which is formless. You have made something wonderful, something that will ease the burdens of all who delight in your craft. No more will potters have to coil their links around and around, smoothing imperfectly with their hands. Your method is so far superior to other potter's as to make them lame by comparison. Do you know what I was told?"

Jobah laughed. He laughed for the first time in memory. "Do I know what they said? They could only say one thing. That the man with the face like a full-moon was once again possessed with a fit of madness, that his absurd invention was the invention of a demon. Yes, I know what they said. That my wheel was an unnecessary improvement of a simple technique which has been handed down from generation to generation and which was just fine the way it was. The simple coils that were spun by hand and melded as one manipulated the clay were good enough for our mothers and fathers and so were good enough for us. Never mind that my stones kept the clay spinning for as long as one cared to work the piece and so freed the hands that greater artistry was possible. Never mind that one could produce three in the time it would normally take to produce one." His anger and anguish were spilling forth now to this man with whom he finally, after all these years, felt some mutual regard. "I have wondered if a handsome man, or an important man such as Yaqara, had invented this wheel if it would not have been accepted as the answer to everyone's needs. I have wondered if the reason it is such a joke to the community is simply because I am such a joke." He was weeping now, his face hidden by shadow, turned to the side in shame. He had given up crying years ago too.

"Rest now. You will have to do your share of the work as we travel, but no more than that. When we get back, you will make these wonders for our people who still turn out pottery the way yours do. Let me show you something." He removed a fine, fluted piece from a protective bag. "I will be presenting this, along with several other articles, to Yaqara just before we leave."

Jobah examined it in the pale Moonlight. He turned it around and over, feeling the engravings and the glaze, amazed by the craftsmanship. "Magnificent. This is exquisite. Only a master could have made this."

"Then we have a lot of masters. What we don't have is a potter's wheel," he said as he took the fluted pitcher and replaced its covering. "Jobah, you have the abilities to work clay as easily as the most skilled of our people. You will be shown every technique and then, I don't doubt, you will find ways to improve on them. Rest, now, until the morning. We both need sleep."

They would get precious little. The rest of the grain would be arriving any time.

* * *

Dim light peeping under the blanket and registering as a barely perceived pink haze through his closed eyelid woke the first crewman. He wasted no time in waking the others with a magnificent belch as he sat up, grinning with pride at his feat. On any other morning, following such little sleep, he might have been hit with a stone in appreciation of his efforts, but today all were excited with the prospect of setting for home. Everyone rose quickly, breakfast prepared and inhaled in record time.

"Jobah, Hyphes, Abos, I want you to come with me to the boat. Jacobah, you wait here. Your uncle will want to pay his leave."

They, with the rest of the crew, each took a sack of grain, hoisting it over the side of the craft to the waiting arms of the two who had comfortably slept on watch through the night. Deus had told the packers who had come in the night to leave it on the beach and depart quietly without disturbing the sleep of his crew. They stowed the grain along the center plank were it was above the bilge and sure to be kept dry even should they run into rough weather. The sturdy bags were strong enough to be walked upon in bare feet.

Those in the water helped each other get over the side, getting leg-ups and standing on shoulders to do so. The last few were pulled forcibly aboard like large tuna and dropped hard onto the benches with laughter from all doing the damage. The two lay still for a moment, wincing with pain from the benches hammered into their kidneys, but quickly regained their composure. This was just good sport and they could get their revenge later.

Syros set them to work securing all cargo against shifting. They bailed out bilge for the last time before departure, only a small amount of water having penetrated the swollen hull in these quiet waters. Without the strain and flexing of travel, the hull was almost perfectly watertight. The heavy

143

components of Jobah's wheel were stowed in the center of the boat, low, where it would eventually be competing with the bilge water for space. Water wasn't going to cause the stone any damage.

They mounted the oars in their slots and lashed them in place with the rope locks.

Deus felt assured that they could handle the rest of the preparations without his or Syros's help. The crew could have done all of this without Deus, but he wanted to be sure about their new men. They were skittish about the whole thing, boats being far from their minds throughout their lives.

The early fishermen were coming down for their morning ritual. Deus yelled at them to show their kindness by bringing out the latest deposit of cattle feed in their skiffs. A fight almost broke out for the rights to carry out this simple task, Deus finally settling the dispute by suggesting that if they hurried they could divide the amount between them before more showed up to add to the conflict. The idea was immediately ratified and they now sped into the project, trying to outdo the others in loading their skiffs. The comedy of the performance had the crew cheering the competition unfolding before them. They applauded as the fishermen bulldozed their little skiffs into the water, and stroked like pistons to win the sprint. The distance was short and they bumped up against the larger hull at more or less the same time, yelling in crescendo in tune with the parting foreigners.

There was much laughter as they tossed hay into the boat, flinging it about as Jacobah howled not to get it wet. Very little ended up in the water but the boat was covered boundary to border. Jacobah was at his wit's end. Damned fishermen. He didn't even like fish. At last, they went about their business and left the crew to clean up the mess. He complained to Deus that it really was essential to keep it dry, that wet hay could make the little ones bloat and maybe die.

That warning shook Deus from his brief excess. A loss such as that could not be afforded. The hay took only a few moments for the crew to gather and pile at the helm. They agreed that it should be as far as possible from any danger of fire from the grill at the prow.

Syros and Deus left the ship and waded to shore. The only thing left to do before the inevitable formalities was to get the cattle aboard. Deus thought it most dubious that he would be able to carry either of these to the boat and suggested that they press another of the fishermen into service again.

"Nonsense," said the huge Syros. He grabbed the bull-calf in a bear-hug, his chest to its back with its legs splayed in front as it struggled for release. Deus slipped the knot from its post and walked the rope in his hand, fearing the inevitable and keeping just out of contact by the flailing hooves. Syros slipped in the sand, he almost completely lost his footing, as the unexpected strength of the bullock shook him. He waded into the water with Deus still holding the rope as if he were towing the strangely united couple. The crew thought this was almost as entertaining as the hay fight and debated paddling farther out to more greatly impede his chances of making it. Reason prevailed as it would and they pulled a few strokes to ease the boat a bit closer to shore, gently rubbing the sandy bottom as it stopped. It was not close enough. The terrified calf gave a potent twist to its thick trunk and pushed Syros off balance. He held on only for a moment, holding his breath as hooves buffeted him, their impacts fortunately deadened by the resistance of the water. Deus pulled the struggling animal back to shore, holding tight to the rope and giving thanks that he'd had the foresight to use caution. He was too concerned to register the howling of the crew behind him or the laughter of the assembly now before him on the beach.

Yaqara had arrived in time to see the spectacle.

"Are you starting a new game, my friend? Too bad you saved it for so late a date."

How could the crowd have grown so in the last few moments? They must have come with Yaqara en mass having met him at another location, probably his house. The fishermen had changed their countenances from jovial to respectful, not wanting to appear too familiar with the friends of a higher class.

The Chief held his purple robed arm high, signaling and shouting at the nearest fishermen. "Bring two of your boats. Assist these men in need."

The fishermen ran to help, overpowering the struggling calves by combined brute force and loading them into their skiffs. Two men in each boat held the creatures still as best as he could, mostly by sitting their full weight on them and restraining them in choke holds, while others pushed the little crafts out to the ship.

"Careful passing these beasts over the side. If Yaqara sees them dropped into the water he's as likely to have us flogged as he is to break wind."

There was lots of help from those already on board the ship, all hanging over the sides with their bellies pressed hard against the sides and kneeling for stability and support. They reached into the small skiffs as they pulled alongside and assisted the sole occupants as they struggled to raise the contorting animals.

The men in each boat tried almost vainly to maintain balance. Trussed legs still capable of delivering a mighty wallop bashed one's kneecap in the most painful manner. The men who pushed the skiffs out to the ship held them level as much as it was possible with the thrashing of its occupants. The men on board the ship groped the animals, finding little to grab onto.

Jacobah howled from the beach. "Careful of their legs. The fools. Don't let them hurt the calves legs." He ran to the water, stopping short, as he was afraid of it. He was imploring Deus. He lamented that he should have followed the skiffs out to help.

Deus knew at once what the rancher was talking about. If the legs were broken they would be as useless as any other animal would be, and have to be killed. He could not see that happen to these, the finest of the stock.

"Be careful of its legs," he yelled to the crew in the language they could understand, now regretting that he too didn't follow along.

The crew hadn't the ability to acknowledge what they heard, they were so wholly occupied. Each admired Deus for everything that he was, but this last comment was so redundant that they could do little but shake their heads. Obviously, they had to watch out for its legs. It had just pummeled the poor fisherman again, this time in the ribs below his armpit. He doubled over, almost paralyzed from the crack he felt the bone make, a snap no one else could hear.

As he let go, the crew grabbed the young bull by its legs, tail, and neck, flipping it upside-down over the side and onto a bench where they pinned it under a dog pile of shouting bodies.

Jacobah cursed and danced in frustration. "They've probably killed it. The imbeciles." His fear overcame his anger. He was terrified that his window of opportunity had just been smashed. Without both of these two calves to grow into healthy adults there would be no procreation, and therefore no need for him. These foreigners would probably kill him as some useless appendage if he couldn't produce for them. Just like his father had always threatened to do to him.

Yaqara couldn't hold back his mirth. Neither could the rest of the congregation after he broke the ice. They erupted in cheers when the bull-calf went rancorously into the ship, and the volume crescendoed as the female followed immediately after, kicking a panicked blow to the face of a recoiling fisherman. He tumbled backward into the sea, not even a feigned offering of help to break his fall from the fishermen holding his skiff. The stocky man erupted from the chest deep water, gasping and sputtering the blood away from his bent and fractured nose.

"Jacobah, calm yourself." Yaqara spoke as a kind relative. "I will say goodbye to you first. I expect that I may never see you again and that you will never return. My cousin has given you little reason to do so. I could see that your enthusiasm to escape him was no charade for the sake of our guests. And now you are to become their guest. I admire you. You are on your way to a land of excitement, of adventure. You have seen nothing from that patch of land your Father kept you on like a trapped dog." He moved closer to his first cousin once removed, speaking softly and clutching onto the young man's shoulders. "Remember this. If you destroy what I hope to build, I will hunt you to the ends of the Earth and skin you. You are my kin. Your place is to show me the gratitude I deserve for allowing you the privilege of going on this fantastic journey. Build me in their eyes and ears. Do whatever they ask of you and always speak highly of this place. They must be encouraged to come back, even if it is without you. Do I make myself perfectly clear?"

"I will not disgrace you in any way. You have realized that I am happy to go. That is genuine. I have no need to do anything contrary to your wishes. It shall be as you have said."

"Farewell then," Yaqara shouted. "May the gods be with you." He looked fleetingly at Deus. "Every god. You will learn of more than you know now. Go. Out to the ship while I speak with these others."

Jacobah turned his back and walked to the skiff offered by a fisherman. He did not look back or speak as he was rowed to his new family. His concern was for the calves and not for anything or anyone at his old home. They were passing from memory already.

"And now, my dear friends Deus and Syros. I cannot tell you how sad we are at your leaving. The entire populace has come to think of you as our own. Your acts of kindness, your thoughtfulness, your gifts of charity, all will be remembered here for ages to come."

Syros bowed, leaving the speaking to Deus who he knew was the real recipient of the compliments in any case.

"I thank you, dear Yaqara. Your hospitality to all of our people has been something hoped for and only by you received. It is your kindness, thoughtfulness, and charity that will live in the memory of our people for ages to come. Together I hope we have built upon a future relationship of goodwill that will last forever. You have asked our help in transporting your goods, of establishing trade, of providing you with many of our goods and providing you another avenue of distribution for your own. I wish to declare formally, as the Earth Mother witnesses, that my efforts will not cease in this pledge; that I, that all of my people, will strive tirelessly in establishing all that we have discussed. We welcome this new relationship with your people. We know this will be of the greatest benefit to each of us. In gratitude for your hospitality and to further seal our friendship we have parting gifts to present which we hope you will accept."

Deus and Syros together presented several more pieces of pottery of exceptional skill. Most of those gathered gasped with envy, not having seen the previous gifts.

Deus then pulled the rabbit out of the hat. Copper.

"You have copper to trade? You did not tell me."

"I thought it best to wait. We did not bring any with us, other than this small amount. We had no idea if you would have any interest. Take it. It is but a small allotment, sadly. I wish I could give you more. When we return, if you think you have a use for it, we will bring more. Much more."

"Magnificent. Now, as much as I regret your leaving, the time has come to say our final parting words. I wish you the finest weather, strong arms and backs, and safety from assault by the sea demons. May your ship have speed to outrun them." He held out a silvery bar. "Take this other bar of anaku. I am sure you will find some use for it. Possibly the one isn't enough. My servant is taking wine and a joint of beef out to your men. They have given clear indication that they prefer it to fish. No doubt they will have their fill of that later.

"I thank you again. And now we must go." Deus and Syros turned toward the water and climbed aboard the little skiff waiting to ferry them out.

"Wait. One last thing." Yaqara hurried across the sand. "Deus, I must give you my garments as a final tie." He removed the thin gold chain from around his neck, then disrobed his purple vestment. He hadn't decided previously one way or another if he would give this valuable gift but wore a white linen robe underneath just in case. The murmur grew behind him at this gesture of estimation. He folded the garment neatly and handed the bundle to the much younger man.

"Yaqara. Are you sure you wish to part with this finery? It is a treasure to be cherished."

Yaqara then offered forward the gold chain. "The bond between us runs deep. I consider you my friend. Perhaps more than a friend. A brother as well."

Deus took the chain and draped it reverently over his head, resting it on his shoulders. "Yes, Yaqara. We are brothers. Inseparable now even as the distance grows between us. Should we never see each other again we will always stand side by side. Remember me always as I shall always remember you."

The two stood watching each other grow smaller as the distance between them increased. Yaqara had meant what he had said about considering Deus a brother. He was also sincere about preferring to have him stay. Not many could challenge his mind like that young man could. That he was destined for greatness no one could deny. He no longer thought that he was a member of royalty, he as much as denied that. But the time would come. Not immediately, but it would certainly come.

The old manservant sidled up to Yaqara. "There is some murmuring among the people, Chief Yaqara. A small few thought it inappropriate that you disrobed and bequested your purple garments to the foreigner."

"Let them think as they will. They have not the eyes to see. In time they will feel the benefit in their own lives from that simple act. What was it to me? A piece of cloth that you will have replaced shortly."

"I will see to it at once." He paused before leaving. "Too bad about the Sarabel whore. It has been some time since this sort of thing has happened in this town."

"Yes." Yaqara had only been apprised just prior to the parting ceremony and had still to be informed of the details. He was saddened by the loss. "What exactly happened?"

"She was found by an early riser, so to speak." He tried to stifle the smirk. "When she didn't open her door to him he entered anyway, and found her spread upon the floor. Apparently, she'd entertained someone against her will. They say she has been strangled, but another says she was also lanced through the heart."

Yaqara shook his head. The thought was an obscenity. Sarabel was a good woman. She harmed no one. Misfortune followed her all the days of her life, and now it ended this way. Who knew? Maybe it was better this way.

"Where is the son, Abo?"

"Gone."

"Have you searched the town?"

"Yes, Yaqara. He has fled."

~~~~~~

Chapter 8

Bronze

The crew as one surrendered their efforts at rowing, staring fixed at the horrors as hairs on their necks poised erect. Wakes rolled the ship moderately as they tried to get a bead on the intermittent backs appearing far to close for contentment, the jets of water and steam plangent and hissing as they spouted and fell through the breeze onto the panicked observers.

The drifting spray had only a most diminished sobering affect on the men. Several were passing gas uncontrollably in anxiety and dread, the only sound as they froze to their benches, holding their oars out of the water for fear of attracting the devilish apparitions with their wash.

In spite of the breeze, Taros began to sweat profusely. He saw the dark, beady eye of the monster as it slipped quietly out of the water, fixed on him with malignant design, and vanished ominously beneath the surface. He felt its stare, cold, penetrating to the inner core of his marrow. The back of the beast kept coming, endless ripples of its back like a continuous train of glistening black armor raised with the bumps and welts of endless combat in the invisible depths of an unknowable sea.

How could he keep his senses about him? How could any of them? He could not tell how many of the devils there were, or if these manifestations were the embodiment of only one massive snake-like creation. Those forward-slanting spouts blowing loudly, alarmingly, threatening to envelop them in their shrouds of mist and dew. What was their evil intent?

"Quiet everyone," managed Syros softly. "Be very still." It, or they, was gone, vanished into the rippling blue. The silence and invisibility terrifying the crew beyond measure. A fiend obscured beneath the surface was even more fomenting than one seen nearby. Visions of the monster springing up from hideous depths and coiling its loathsome carcass around their helpless and insignificant vessel twisted their minds into a frenzy almost capable of shattering their physical paralysis.

The silence.

Should they break and run for shore? It would be suicidal.

The bull-calf squirmed in discomfort, wondering at the absence of activity to which it had now become accustomed. The cords binding its hooves together were not too tight, its guardian had seen to that important consideration. He had even laid it on sheepskin to keep the wood from causing pressure sores on its rare and precious hide while it lay bound. But now it had wiggled away the edge of the skin, bunching it up and rubbing its shin uncomfortably along the edge of a bench. This was no position for any beast, not even a domesticated creature, with the hormones to move as much as any young male of any species.

It started bucking against the side of the boat, quick thuds reverberating through the hull as the ashen faces of the crew whipped round on their necks.

"Make it quiet," several farthest away squeezed out through their locked mandibles.

Deus sprung up, along with Jacobah, moving almost without touching the deck as they dropped at the same time on the creature. It squirmed vigorously, but the two had a firm hold on its tethered limbs and it soon mollified in surrender.

The silence.

Even the wind had died since the beasts submerged. All had stopped, even time itself. Only hearts beating against their inner restraints moved, pounding in anticipation of what must inevitably come.

"There it is," Lobos shrieked.

Their heads snapped to the sighting. It was dreadful and captivating, the black bodied monster already risen out of the water, this time straight up. Its fat wings, or were they ears, waved on their slender stalks as it hung suspended before its tremendous bulk toppled slowly sideways, kicking a prodigious rush of white foam and spray into the air. The crack of impact reached them just as another breached the surface, identical with its black appendages swaying, this time falling backward away from them with another sharp strike.

The distance was reassuring. They, or it, was moving away. They were insignificant enough that the monster would not even be bothered with them. Was it a single creature or two? They would never be able to tell. Some thought they saw another burst of spray far in the distance later, then nothing.

No one spoke. No one moved. They slowly scanned all around with only their eyes.

The silence.

The terrifying silence.

* * *

Sperm whales were one of the many reasons, but only one of a few genuinely tangible rationalizations, the natives of Cyprus had for avoiding the water. These very rare observances were enough to keep all but the most fearless, and the most reckless, safely astride the security of land. They were the stuff legends were made of, legends that epitomized the very power and terror of the unfathomable depths.

"See how they dance with the serpents?"

"I see it, Kompil. They hold the hand of the devils, and they touch them not. They plunge their ships over the edge of no return only to come back in greater strength. With the forces of evil as their guides and protectors, there is nothing that can withstand them. I fear for our safety."

"I, myself, see little comfort in this." He pondered the thought a moment. "Are you sure they are the same who were here before?"

"Who else could they be? A strange language, yet the youngest could understand and speak as one who knew us. They bore no weapons when we advanced on them and woke them from their slumber. They were valiant, with no fear of death. Perhaps because they are already dead?"

"Your speech withers my bones."

"Can you deny it?"

"I cannot."

"They must be capable of compassion. Even with our insulting introduction, they withheld judgment against us. They even gave us a gift to see how we would react. We pushed them to the breaking point I know. I could tell by their expressions that they were barely tolerant of us. Only your great gift of the ax changed their countenances. A shame that you traded with them instead of giving it first as an outright gift, but your action saved us from harsh judgment. At least temporarily. Now it is time again for wise decisions."

"Is there a chance they might pass us by?"

"They did promise to return. I had thought wrongly that they would be some time. At least a season. Perhaps many more."

"I, with you, see us in great danger. We have not yet prepared as we had said we would."

"Then I would suggest, Leader Kompil, that we move quickly to secure what we have promised."

"See that it is done."

* * *

Deus had been debating with himself for the better part of the day on whether or not to stop at the settlement at Cyprus. The calves could use a stretch. No animal could remain healthy for long trussed up like an offering awaiting sacrifice. There was much to be said for passing by this area in case of coming into contact with those people again. The first visit had not been too cordial. They had escaped violence, but it had hardly been less than tense.

But the crew was in no state to carry on. The whales had shaken them all so badly that even Syros was still quaking.

There was hardly any point in staying here, bobbing in the sway, frozen for what had seemed an age. The apparition was not coming back. It had released them from all but fear. It had gripped only their minds. The mental exhaustion was worse than the physical of rowing.

"Let's make for shore. None of us will be happy carrying on after that fright. Hopefully, we'll have time to meditate and have a night of peace."

Deus was inwardly glad for the opportunity to give the calves a chance to stand. They needed it. So did the crew. He had convinced Syros not to work them so hard. A little extra time taken getting somewhere was not a problem. They had long lives ahead. With luck.

The crew found their energy and confidence returning as they slowly pulled the oars, driving the ship cautiously toward the coast. None were opposed to the relative safety of shore with the memory of demons still fresh in their minds. They would have preferred their own beach, but this would do. They would take their chances with inauspicious men. The unseen hostiles of the depths were too much, at least for today.

* * *

"They come," declared Kompil.

"I said they would."

"Preparations are being made?"

"The village moves like a house of ants. All copper is being gathered. An edict of death to any withholding has been proclaimed." He looked momentarily unsure under the sudden dart of his chieftain, but only for a moment. "I was sure you would approve. Some seemed hesitant at a time when action without delay is called for."

"You've done well and have my blessings."

His gaze returned to the ship, now closer but turned head on so as to appear as a black urn, wide-bottomed and sharply diminishing to a point at the neck, rising then ebbing into the shallow troughs between wide swells hiding all but the triangular point of the bow.

"It is an evil apparition."

"Yes. See how it rises and falls on a calm sea, dipping into the water then rising out as the leviathans themselves. And something rides with them. See the company which escorts as they show and then vanish." The oars as they worked in unison could be seen on the ascent, the wide paddles at the end blocking enough light from the horizon to appear as elongated levitating phantoms at irregular intervals.

"Their power must be terrible to call up such specters from the deep."

"Make preparations for a sacrifice."

"I have made the arrangements." He was met with another look. "I presumed it is what you would have wanted. If you had decided against it I could have had it stopped at once."

This man was almost too intuitive to have as a head assistant. Men could be dangerous when they could read another as easily as this man could. He did not get a nod of approval this time. Kompil stared straight out to sea.

"Bring Fazil, the shepherd boy."

* * *

"There is a fire burning." Deus was the first to see the building haze, the twisting gray plume, as it convulsed before attempting to climb from its root.

"They see us. I don't know if this bodes well or evil." Syros was ever suspicious of unknown people.

"Do you think they could be the ones we met up with before?"

"I think so. This would be about the right place. If they are, we had better hope and pray that they were not expecting us back so soon. We will not have enough to trade for their copper, assuming they have gathered it already."

They pulled the oars slowly, easily, as the features of the nearing coast grew in clarity.

"Hyphes," Deus called out. "You are a member of our company now. There will be no secrets kept from you. This island is not our own. It may pose some danger, but nothing we will not be able to surmount. It is a land of much wealth in the things of your desire, namely copper. We may have need of your skills here."

Hyphes had been practicing with the men, whoever he had been sitting next to, trying to grasp more fully the language. He was having some difficulty. The repertoire he had learned at Ugarit was confusing him. This was now his third language and he was stumbling badly. He wasn't sure if Deus had said that the copper was rich, or dangerous, or secret, or sensual. It all seemed so garbled. He had to get him to repeat, less eloquently, his statement in the language of the Ugarit.

When he understood, he merely nodded. It was so frustrating, this language difference. Why was it thus? How could men hope to have amity when confusion and misunderstanding were ever so dominant? It was hardly any wonder that tribes and nations sometimes clashed. How could they possibly work out their differences? Men like Deus were so rare. He had never seen the like.

He turned to see what they were approaching as he stroked along synchronous with the others. He lost his concentration and faltered slightly, disrupting the harmony of the concerted action.

"Oars up." Syros caught the disruption before it had a chance to spread.

"Have them raise their oars as high as possible," Deus instructed.

Syros gave the order. The crew pushed the handles down to their ankles, holding the oars high in the air.

Deus told them all to turn, to look over their shoulders to see how they would be met. The whole village, it had seemed, had appeared on the shoreline to greet or assail them. The shepherd Fazil had said that there were two hundred in his village. He had evidently not counted the children, which must have amounted to that many again. This was a dilemma. Should they stop at all? They were safe enough out here in the water. The ship was slowing, just drifting forward now. The safest thing to do would be to leave.

"What do you think?" asked Syros.

Deus inhaled the salt air, the sudden jolt of oxygen euphoric. He had been so caught in concentration that he had virtually forgotten to breathe.

"They are with their women and children. Have you ever heard of any men fighting with women and children under their wing?"

"These are a strange people. They do not speak as we do. Perhaps they don't act as we do either."

"That is wise counsel. But I think that they pose no danger to us. They look stern, but I think this is some kind of greeting."

The ship put to oar again, only two on each side with the rest still raised high. The sight from the island was impressive as Syros slowly maneuvered them along a snaking path ending just offshore, the craft turned backward so all aboard were facing the islanders.

As they hovered with the keel only inches above bottom, Syros gave the signal. The crew had been advised of the possible consequences of this gamble and were prepared for flight should it go awry.

The four oars in the water raised high to meet the others, and all together they fell, paddles turned to the flat, creating a mighty slap and splash of foam. Ten times they repeated this dramatic gesticulation, blinding themselves with spray.

When the mist they had created settled, they were shocked to see the islanders cowering on their knees, some of the women prostrate and pinning their children beneath their bodies for protection.

Deus stood at the stern holding his arm out in salute. He loudly proclaimed a greeting and addressed the Leader Kompil.

Kompil rose and loudly, nervously, returned the greeting in the language of Crete, addressing Deus as "Minos" and thanking all that was sacred that the shepherd Fazil had learned some of their language.

His pronunciation was terrible but still flattering in the attempt. Deus stifled the urge to smile having forgotten his little joke on the shepherd. This was a time to be composed in the extreme.

They noticed that Kompil was wearing a coat of the sheepskins that had been presented to him. They had been cut and laced together to fit. There was no need of such warmth on a day such as this. The sun was bright enough to keep an old lady from feeling a chill even in a breeze. He was wearing it out of respect.

Kompil turned his head to the side, speaking behind him through the corner of his mouth. "Fazil. Stand beside me."

The shepherd came forward, stooped, not knowing what to do. He'd had no idea of the gravity of this situation he was now a major player in. He had thought the pleasant young man he had met was simply another shepherd. A shepherd with a fantastic tale of being from another island, as if that were really possible. Now these people were to be treated almost as if they were divine. The story flying through the village was that they were frolicking with sea devils the way lambs play in the spring. He knew these people, gods, whatever they were, would be seeking recompense for his offensive lack of jurisprudence. He had made haste to alert the elders of his village to the presence of the intruder and had almost caused their attempted slaughter. Only wisdom and compassion, it was clear now, had kept these newcomers from calling forth powers of the deep to destroy them. They had played the elders as fools, toying with them, placating them with gifts and laughing at the playthings they considered weapons.

"Talk to them. Tell them they are our guests and that we are honored to have them with us." Fazil complied with his chief's command.

Deus nodded his acceptance. After leaving Ugarit he had been repeatedly going over the language of these people in his mind. What a great gift he had been blessed with. The Earth Mother had perceived his needs even as she had during his childhood. There was no blessing that she would withhold.

And so he felt, in this moment of rapture, that it was time for these Her sons and daughters to know of Her and worship.

"People of Ota Em," he began.

* * *

Deus had been expounding the teachings of his sacred Mother from the beach-oriented stern while the two oarsmen kept the ship stationary. Words flowed as they always did, his self-mastery of the language evident in his elucidation of the weighty doctrine. How he accomplished it even he could not say. The logic of the matter escaped him. Time stopped, minds linked, hearts joined. All became one.

At length he was done, the silence of the mesmerized congregation inviting him forward, out of his vessel, to touch them all. Even the crew of his ship was entranced, even by speech they could not possibly understand, such was the power of the words he wielded.

The crew disembarked as Deus made his rounds. No words were spoken. None were needed. This young man, smaller in stature than the majority, had become a giant among them. He held his head high, his chest out, not from vanity, but conviction.

He stopped a long time in front of Fazil, staring into the depths of his dark eyes. The shepherd held his gaze unflinchingly. He was not afraid, only full of admiration and respect. One did not avert one's glance from a respected figure who was searching for knowledge through the windows of the mind. That would be among the most contemptuous slights.

He moved to the man next to the shepherd, Kompil. Deus had moved to the high side of the beach, facing out to sea, so that he had the advantage of height from the upward slope of the sand. Still, he was looking up slightly into the eyes of the leader. The man had not the heavy stature of Syros, but he was close in height. He also was able to hold Deus's probing eyes as his innermost being was scanned.

Deus then moved to the man next to Kompil, his assistant. His vacillation bade him not look into Deus's eyes. The man kept his gaze low, or shifted it to the side. Deus stood, unrelenting, not about to move until he had contacted the man. At last his sweeping glances from left to right passed through Deus's and he was caught, fixed immutably for a time as he struggled within. The short time he remained transfixed seemed like an eternity as his soul was penetrated. He was so uncomfortable from the experience that he had to break the visual retention by force, tearing his eyes away to look at the sand once more, deflated and embarrassed by the episode.

His embarrassment spread to the others in the immediate vicinity who had born witness to the encounter. Yet they found that the anger that they normally would have felt at the insult was assuaged by feelings of concavity, of pity, for the man. They could see without doubt that there was no guile in the visitor, Minos. He nodded unessentially, a Mona Lisa smile assuring the man that there were no hard feelings between them, that whatever esoteric thoughts had passed would remain shrouded.

Deus noticed that a couple of men had appeared at the tree line that had not been previously with the group. These were the men entrusted with the care of the fire pit which would be used for the sacrifice, should they decide to have one. The day had gone so far along that they were beginning to wonder what it was they were missing out on. The village was empty, they were left alone with a mindless job tending the fire, and they were getting beyond bored.

Deus picked up on their soot-stained hands and deduced that they had been left behind for that purpose. What other explanation could there be? The purple smoke still wisped up from the coals a short walk through the spindly woods.

"You will sacrifice." His first words to break the solitude a statement of fact rather than a question.

* * *

They had learned previously about the risks involved in leaving the ship untended and unprotected. This was doubly important now that they had the invaluable cargo of calves.

These most unusual beasts were met with looks of incredulity, affirming the sacred status of the visitors. The animals were allowed to graze in the lush grass unhindered by the islanders, who kept a very respectful distance, with the exception of a long rope held fast by their tenders. Jacobah would not chance even the most marginal risk of these animals spooking and escaping into the forest. He knew how easily that could happen without a lead bull to cleave to and no one would catch them if they bolted. Without others of their own kind to attract them by scent or call they would be forever lost and most unlikely to survive.

He was glad, though, for the opportunity that was given these young creatures to stretch and graze. Living grass was always superior to dried, and this interlude would stretch the limited supply on board the ship.

The natives brought water and left it at a safe distance, a concept that escaped Jacobah. He thought they must be afraid to come close out of fear of retribution from their elders, but they were actually afraid of the calves. A rumor had spread that these were two more devils brought up from the deep. They had also left some mutton with the water in case the beasts or the tenders were hungry. Obviously, the beasts were interested in the grass in the same manner as sheep, but who knew with these sorts of creatures? Who was to say they wouldn't like flesh too?

* * *

They sat within the girdle of beehive-shaped houses, the whole population of the village. Encompassed by the circle of bodies of the whole sat the Leader Kompil and a few of his closest associates with the shepherd Fazil. With them sat Deus, now known to them as Minos, Syros, and all except four of the crew who were guarding the ship and minding the calves.

The walls of the rounded cones that provided the backdrop for this assemblage were made entirely of rock and reminded Deus of the cairn he had constructed for the burial of his mother, except for the thatched roofs. Tholoi they called them. Homes. But more than homes they were also the final resting place of the dead. The tholoi were much larger than Selene's tomb to accommodate a family of sleeping bodies and had a door which they kept covered with a skin hanging on the inside of the opening.

The sacrifice complete, the honored guests resting their spread hands on their appreciative bellies, the time had come to present. Hopefully, they would be pleased enough with the meal that they would forgive the meager amount of copper delivered. If only they'd had more time. Kompil's prayer through the entire sacrifice was that it would be enough to satisfy them.

The first man to come brought a sturdy basket, small in size, but heavy and full of raw copper, meticulously separated, granular and sand-like. Deus was urged to run his fingers through the grains, and all smiled when he gave his approval. Two more baskets of the same amount came in unison behind the first.

After that, they came one after the other, each bearing whatever possession he had made of the ductile metal. Some brought hammers, others axes; some had fashioned ornamental goods, simple bowls and cups. The most common implements placed before them were knives. Most had wooden handles, some had the grip wrapped tightly and thickly with fine rope, and one was a rather massive affair being constructed entirely out of copper, thick handle and all.

Hyphes was astonished. That they would be giving their wealth away like this was too much. His suspicions were raised. There must be cunning duplicity at work here. Or these people were so irrational that they would run into the sea if that would please Deus.

What followed he found even more astonishing.

Deus thanked the leader and waved the tools and implements away. Not that he wasn't pleased with them; he was. But, as he explained, they had no use for the manufactured goods with one exception, the outstanding double ax that they had so graciously presented them on their previous visit and for which they were most grateful. It would be as a symbol of their friendship and peace between them forever.

The tools were much better off staying with their owners who undoubtedly had great use for them. He understood that they had gathered their own tools as a kindness and out of generosity. They were most appreciative but simply could not deprive them, their new friends, of things they had need of themselves.

The gift of the granular copper was indeed a gift that they could accept, and this is where Deus was leading.

Kompil had feigned distress as Deus explained that he could not use the tools, and had them removed. Inwardly he was deeply gratified as the work in making them was tremendous. If these powerful strangers wanted the raw material, then that was an ideal situation. If that is what pleased them, then he felt his people got off easy.

"Is this metal easy to gather around here?"

Kompil remembered the large nuggets that he had been shown before. "Our humble gatherings are nothing compared to the richness of what you have accumulated. We cannot compare."

"Your humble gatherings, as you call them, are exactly what we would like to have you provide for us, if you can. As we told you on our first visit, we would like just as much as you can provide, far more than this," indicating the three baskets, "if you can possibly accomplish that task."

"Our source is far from here. We find some nearby, but mostly it comes from the river out of the red hills toward the setting sun. It is a long journey for us. We only go twice each year to hunt. Once when the beasts come down from the cold mountains, and once before they return. We were about to leave on our journey shortly and set about gathering extra copper this time for when you came back. But you surprised us with your early return." He added the last sentence timidly, as a child might confess to a parent who came home sooner than expected.

"What do you call the place?"

"Engomi."

Deus leaned forward bringing his face close to the man. "Is the water good there?"

"Yes, the river runs all year. It is weak late in the year but it never dries."

"Does grass grow there in abundance?"

"It is adequate. Much like here."

"Could you grow crops there?"

Kompil was beginning to see. "Yes," he said slowly, drawn out.

"It would be easier for you to hunt if you were there throughout the year wouldn't it?"

He nodded, frowning and pushing his lips out pursed tight together.

"Are there people there with whom you feel you need to exercise caution?"

"We are afraid of no one."

"We have seen your bravery. But are there other people there?"

"A few scattered wanderers, men who live alone. Some have families but they keep to themselves. We pass them sometimes. We have no quarrels."

"What keeps you here?"

"This is the place of our fathers who go back before anyone can know."

"It is time to break from your fathers, as a boy will leave his home for a woman. The time has come for your people to become great, to become adults, to go forth into a new home with a new woman. The Earth Mother will watch over you and guide you. We will present your gift offering of copper to her. It will be adequate for your protection as you journey and will see you safely there."

"Will we leave no one behind?" His eyes cast over to the spring-fed pool, a place of great importance to the people of this village.

"You are attached to the pool, the teat which supplies your needs as it has the needs of those of untold generations before you. Leave it behind with your cares. You are weaned. If you wish you can visit it as often as you like, perhaps twice a year. You will walk in opposing direction to what you have done before but what does it matter? The distance is the same. If you want to connect with your ancestors, they will be here. But take the living with you."

"Who will give us protection if not our ancestors?"

"You will call on the name Selene."

* * *

Kompil and Fazil were becoming neurotic. The sensation of the gently rocking boat, unstable to them even though the sea was calm and glasslike with hardly a swell, was so foreign, so singularly aberrant, that they could scarcely contain their anxiety. They clung fast to the bench, crouched to drop their center of gravity, fearing to be flung overboard at any moment by some unseen miscreation harboring below.

The scene before them, encompassing them, was out of the realm of imagination. To actually be a part of it was beyond belief. Yet here they were, facing a host of undulating, diaphoretic men who scowled under the vigor of their exertion. The two calves sat curled on the hull behind them separated from each other by the boardwalk, chewing only the spirits knew what. They had not touched the dry grass on board since leaving the green pasture yet continued to eat and swallow. They were veritably magical creatures. Kompil noted the small bumps on the male's forehead that gave him an ominous manifestation. And those eyes. When they fixed on him their blackness bore into his soul.

Kompil was becoming disoriented. He hated this. If he managed to ever again get his feet firmly planted on land he would never concede to leave its safety. He closed his eyes for escape and instead found a loss of equilibrium that left him reeling. He remembered the words of Minos in his distress and followed his admonition to call on the name Selene. As his head spun he did so silently, an outpouring of personal faith in his invocation that would normally have been beyond his personal powers. A wave of calm drifted down and enveloped him, wrapping him like a baby in mother's arms, comforting him in his hour of need. He was still terrified and anxious, but now his fears were assuaged to the point of tolerance.

He opened his eyes, still dizzy but at least now able to concentrate. Was this their destination just ahead? It couldn't be. He surveyed all around trying to fix his position. The land formations were right, he could recognize them even from here. This craft must soar across the water as a bird in flight. It would have taken days to walk this distance and now, in just a short time, they would arrive at their destination.

He summoned his courage to speak. No one had since leaving. Minos stood at the bow, his mate Syros behind them at the stern holding the tail of this wooden creature they had mounted. Somehow he exercised control by easing it one way or the other.

Kompil lifted his arm and pointed ahead and to the right. "That is the place."

Deus barely heard the comment from the bow, recognizing only that it was the foreign tongue. The rush of water pushed before the prow and breaking on either side drowned out any other soft sounds, and the creaking of the oars in their locks greatly diminished those only slightly louder. He turned to see Kompil pointing, and intrinsically knew why he was signaling. He shifted his eyes to meet Syros's, then faced forward again as the helmsman adjusted the angle of his steering oar and altered course for land.

* * *

This short leg of the journey had almost been completed in silence. The experience had not been meant as an enjoyable one for their new guests, and that had been realized. The sea journey had been one of expediency, to get the two here ahead of the others walking, and to give them such a sullen experience that their tales would keep the others from ever considering water travel.

"We will stay the night here with you. Our journey is great and another night of rest will be welcome. While we wait for darkness, I want you to show us the mine. It is not far from here." Deus had made a logical guess from what had been told him before. If he had been wrong, it wouldn't have mattered. He could simply say that what the others considered long distances he considered as nothing. But he was not wrong. The walk to the foothills was completed in a short time, as he expected.

Deus, Syros, and the metalsmith, Hyphes, were eager to see this region where copper was apparently plentiful, the place Kompil referred to as Engomi.

Kompil led Fazil and the others. He was the only one of the group who had been to this place.

They arrived at the side of a steep escarpment, an excavation, where the hardpan had been exposed. Here, over who knew how many years, generations had picked away at the rich copper ore. It was hardly of the quality of the secret place that Syros had shown Deus on their first arrival on this island, there were no nuggets to be found here, but this sheer volume of easily accessible ore was unimpeachable.

The metalsmith was incredulous. He showed no outward signs of excitement, his inward gratification not able to penetrate his deadpan features, and so looked sour when in reality he was just the opposite. This lode was larger than the two he had known near his homeland on the Black Sea. Larger by far than the two together.

"This is magnificent," he said to Deus, his face melting from outward detachment to wealed interest as he recognized the possibilities of this claim. The color and texture of the material he rubbed through his fingers was even richer in content than the ore of his homeland. "There is copper enough here to cloak an entire town." He was on his knees now, lifting armloads of the looser stuff and embracing it to his chest as it coursed out the spaces between. He loved the dusty smell and the gritty feel of it abrading his skin.

"Do not tie your heart to this place. I don't doubt your appraisal of its importance, but when you see the place ahead you will think of this as naught."

How could that be? What wonders did these people possess knowledge of?

* * *

The north wind was picking up, desiccated air passing over the island of Cypress parching their throats as they heaved.

Hot sun pressed on Deus as he rested after his turn at the oars. Those aboard only became more dedicated to him with his efforts. He had no need to row with them. He could assume a position at the bow and they all would accept it without complaint or notice. His unselfish contribution to their cause only bound them further.

He was daydreaming, his eyes half closed and turned up within their lids to give him darkness and solitude. He thought of how well this expedition had gone so far, the trade established with Ugarit, the natives of Kuprios starting an active copper mining operation, the finding of a metalsmith, and the wonderful calves. The Great Mother was meting out blessing upon blessing.

He thought of her wondrous form born by the steel meteorite left with his Father. He focused on it and almost brought its vision to reality.

Suddenly it went dark, a feeling of devastation cast over him like a pall. His left hand resting on his belt pouch slipped inside to grasp the sacred tektites for comfort. His consolation was brief. As he felt through them the wrongness of the perception jolted him out of his pending trance.

He started up and tore at the flap, breaking the thin leather fastener. He spread the buttons with both hands as he simultaneously twisted the bag's position from his hip to his lap.

He was incredulous. The inconceivable had happened, the unthinkable. Only three of them remained, the other two having been replaced by two small rocks.

He howled a wail of despair, startling the rowers who twisted to face his cry. He contorted in anguish with the abysmal realization that two of the most treasured objects, revered objects, on the face of this earth had vanished. Where could they have gone? What monstrous tactic had been used?

163

He glowered at those on board, losing himself in his despondency, directing hatred at everyone and everything as rage welled and fused with his torment.

But no. This was not the way. He had almost lost control, lost the vision. He grated his teeth and fought for domination. Every muscle tensed in his mental clash of arms.

At last he could speak. The others still stared, uncomprehending, as their acknowledged leader pulled himself free of the fit that possessed him.

He displayed the three tektites and the two common rocks that had replaced them. "I know not what to say. My faith is in you, my friends, as much as in anything else. Somehow, somewhere, two of our sacred responsibilities have been removed, stolen from us."

The shock wave discharged through the crew like a bomb. Some were on their feet stamping with righteous indignation and calling for the life of the perpetrator. This would be a curse to any and all who had anything to do with the loss, and all were involved in the protection of their leader and all he possessed.

Syros recognized signs of the impending wrath of the God of Nature, his mind still thinking in that way to a degree. The signs were in the air. The north wind, the dry air. The sky had grayed in the short time since just before Deus's grievous discovery.

"We are to be punished." With those ominous words, Syros gave the command to row.

The wind intensified as they strained their backs, attempting a sprint to the shoreline. There were no safe landings near here from what Syros's eyes could establish, nothing but rocky promontories and dangerous outcroppings. They would have to make haste for a safe haven somewhere ahead. Perhaps the nearest place of refuge would be the place of the mine they had first visited, but that was still some ways off. They would have to follow the coastline, not too far away, not too close.

The boat began to rock with the now breaking waves hitting it slightly off the beam. The calves protested loudly and struggled against their bindings. Jacobah did not wait for an order. He pulled in his oar and leaped to their side, lashing them down with great lengths of leather strapping. He pushed a pile of hay to the nose of each, but they had no interest. He held them tight to comfort them and alleviate their alarm. He was not sure he felt any safer than the calves. He kept his still-developing opinion to himself about men being on the sea.

Deus had jumped to the oar abandoned by the herdsman. Jacobah could not be faulted for what he did. His main charge had always been to the calves first. They were vital. An oar could be lost before a calf.

Hyphes was not fairing better. Within the shortest time he was spewing his vomit over the side, fouling the stroke of the others as his oar clashed with theirs. Still, he was strong-willed and pressed himself back into the fray.

The men had become excellent oarsmen, but their skill as heavy weather mariners was as yet untried. The double roll was giving them all vertigo, the chop breaking all around in no predictable pattern, wind-whipped into a clabber of erratic points.

A breaking sea could easily swamp the open craft, with no deck to throw off a boarding wave. Any loose water slopping up and down the bilge would make it dangerously unstable. And an abrupt gust of wind striking at the same moment that the boat rolled with a rogue wave from the same direction could easily capsize it. After a full day of rowing, the crew was too tired to react with the necessary speed to combat these conflicts of nature.

Some of the crew were experiencing something close to terror. They had to find refuge from this building squall. All bemoaned the fact that they were here at this time. Syros, especially, appreciated the severity of their situation. He had been through one of these surprise storms before, caught too far from land. He had avoided many through his training from his father and only once had to weather one out, but it was in no way as severe as this. And the added aggravation of being so close to land but having no safe place to beach gnawed at him. If the storm got much worse they would surely be swamped. If that began to happen they would have to try a direct attack on the rocky coast and hope to escape with their lives.

"There it is," he bellowed. He had spotted it. The prominent rock that signaled their safe haven. "Pull with all your might and we have a chance of surviving," he roared over the resounding storm and sea.

Here the wind made a strange twist, almost going back on itself, blowing back toward the north with gale force. The waves mounted as they made their approach. They were still cutting across them, terrified, paddling occasionally fouled in the surprising rushes of water. Syros kept up the banter with his vociferous commands, calling time for the strokes with a mastery that kept them from floundering. Without his direction, they would have been lost.

He rode the ship across the waves farther than any thought he should. Why, they thought, didn't he turn them for shore? At last, he pulled the rudder oar. The ship responded at once and the turn was swift.

"Pull now," he bellowed, wishing he had hold of another oar. "Pull with all the strength you've got. Pull. Pull. Pull. Use your legs. Use your backs. Pull for your lives."

They were catching up to the speed of the incoming waves. A large one mounted just behind them, slowly creeping underneath and lifting the boat higher. Syros steered them straight ahead where he could see that the waves were a little lower in height, indicating that the water depth was greater.

"Pull. Pull," he continued.

The spray washed over their faces, the salt streaming into their eyes. They stroked madly, not even able to see, they strained so hard.

Syros was riding the crest of the wave now, hoping it would not break until the last moment. It was working. The end of the channel they had coursed was coming to an end. The wave had broken on either side but remained solid underneath them and they were rising higher on the remaining swell. At last, it too broke and the boat lost height as the water turned to foam.

"Pull." He was almost hoarse now. "Give your lives to it."

The crew moved as one, heaving, working, a single entity bent on a solitary task. They breathed together in vital coordinated gasps and the sound was as if the ship had gained a gigantic lung in its desperate moment of crisis, pumping like a great bellows, heaving with exertion.

Their shoulders were almost dislocating as they squared with the commands. Their last burst of power, a final muscle-cracking stroke, carried them up then grounded them to an abrupt standstill.

"Ship oars. Everyone overboard." He led the way into the water. The others followed, almost falling over the sides.

The ship rose with the lightened load, bobbing on the incoming waves as the still terrified held it and heaved it forward. When they could move it no further they fastened ropes and pulled in unison, moving it no more than another arm's length.

"Fasten the ropes. Get those calves to shore. Empty the ship."

He hefted the first calf, the female, and passed it to Jacobah. The two of them had the greatest remaining strength, not having rowed. He muscled the bull-calf himself. The animal was so exhausted and terrified it surrendered itself limp in his arms. He wondered if the creature would live to see the end of this journey.

When they had emptied the ship they tried again to move it higher up the sand, only with moderate success. They availed in moving it perhaps two lengths of a man. Where they could normally have dragged it up on the dry sand, in their present state they could barely stand.

They secured the ropes anew and collapsed as one.

* * *

"Fools. Why are we not there yet?"

"There is no controlling the wind or sea, Princess. Only the gods claim power over the weather."

Another breaking wave hammered the side of the prototype ship, rolling it hard to the right. It rode the swell and skidded sideways along the crest, slipping down the far face. A rending, feral crack sounded from the steering oar as it snapped, the blade flapping uselessly to one side still connected to the thick shaft only by a few fibrous splits of wood.

"Now what have you done?" shrieked the terrified daughter of Pharaoh.

The priest, and captain, of the ship stormed back to the stern, lashing out at the hapless rudderman with his baton. The merciless beating raised instantaneous purple wheals before he was smote one last time across the eyes and cast violently overboard to fight for his life in the raging sea.

"May the Gods be satisfied with your life and spare ours," called the priest after the drowning man.

"Haul this rudder aboard," he yelled at a spare man. "We may have need of it yet." He envisioned the possibility of repairing it at a later time, somehow. Eventually, they would need it. For now, they would have to manage without steering or steer using only the powers of the oarsmen.

"Turn into the waves. Pull harder on the left side." His commanding voice rose above the exultant winds, the frightened servants breaking their backs to obey. They had seen the example of what lay ahead should they disappoint their master.

Perhaps that was to be their ultimate fate anyway. How could they survive this?

The Princess curled under thick blankets on the bare hull. Her father, Gods bless him, could be the greatest fool at times. What madness had possessed him to force her on this journey? Why her. She had dozens of sisters and half-sisters who could easily have come in her place. Some were even more beautiful; no that wasn't true. She was chosen to be the consort of the leader of some damned island somewhere in this censured sea. If she could get vengeance on the ass priest who suggested that the goods brought to the Pharaoh from the Lower Nile were from any other than men . . . It drove her almost to madness to think that it could be so. Only a fool could believe that dung. She knew how these priests operated. They had her father in their grip in his old age. He was hardly in control of his bladder let alone anything else, they influenced him so greatly with their lies. Oh, he thought he was in charge, so skillfully they manipulated him, but he wasn't.

Perhaps this was for the best. Maybe she would meet her destiny in the wrath of this storm. Better than being taken against her will by the old priests, the perverted scum, as had all of her older sisters. It was almost her turn to service the old bastards, there was no fighting it. If she refused she would have been taken anyway, and then dispatched afterward with some poison. "Taken by the Gods," they would say. Who would dispute it? Who would dare?

She wrapped the blankets tighter against the wind, pulling a corner over her long hair as it began to rain. Her silver hair. The only one ever seen in her country with such hair. The debate had gone on since her birth almost sixteen years ago. They thought her a strange omen at the time. Some thought her hair would change to the normal black, like everyone else's, with time. When that didn't happen some thought she would have a special purpose, a destiny, that could not be foreseen, none having gone before her to indicate a path. Some of the priests thought she should be raised solely as a sacrifice, undefiled and pure until her last breath. They protected her against the most licentious of the others who would have taken her as a child could they have found the opportunity.

Because of her odd but appealing beauty she found favor with her father, seeing him far more than her sisters. Some of them had never seen their father, but he would even speak to her. This was unheard of, and shocking to some that he would so willfully disregard custom. He still had enough strength of will to maintain his right to essentially do what he wanted, in this case, to revise protocol as he saw fit.

At the last, he had seen that his daughter, who was becoming progressively more beautiful, who he was genuinely fond of, could only cause contention in his house. The opportunity arose to make a connection with a rumored group of men from an unknown continent somewhere across the waters of the Sea. Her fate was death at home. At least she would have a chance in another land.

And that chance might bring with it great benefit for Egypt.

Mighty Egypt.

But was Egypt the greatest? These others had supremacy over the oceans, something Egypt had not even attempted attaining. They had reed craft to navigate goods along the Nile, and wooden barges which were used for the priests and royalty, but nothing like the ship that had appeared on the north shore. There was hardly any point. There had been nothing past the shores of land excepting endless water. But now tales were coming in of visitors from lands unheard of, unimagined places of richness and beauty far out in the distant sea. Bearers of gifts, the finest fleece, a delicious and potent wine, fruits that were rumored to be magnificent but which unfortunately could not survive the heat of the journey south.

A tie had to be made to this place, to this . . . Kefti was it? And his daughter would go.

Rain pelted them unrelentingly. The spare man bailed the rising water out the hull. It was amazing this thing was even able to float. The design had come from the recollections of the witnesses who had seen the stranger's vessel where it had been beached. They had all been arrested and compelled to tell all of what they could remember, all suffering torture to stimulate their memories, although they had all been only too eager to cooperate from the onset. A large team of the best carpenters had been put to work, forced non-stop to complete the craft to specifications in twenty days. Poles, which normally were used propelling the barges and river craft, were recognized as useless in the deep sea. Paddles were made in the fashion of the stranger's and were quickly, though inexpertly at first, put to use. Only one test run was permitted, the leaks found patched with a boiled pitch of tree sap. They were then loaded with gifts of gold, wine, and food which was not to be touched by the crew on penalty of death, baser food and water for them to consume, and two soft beddings, one for the priest and one for the Princess.

The crew paddled on under the direction of the priest. He did his best to keep the craft on a northerly course, and had been doing a remarkable job of it considering he had no ability to navigate at night. He had no idea of the concept of a North Star, so they continually got out of alignment, drifting to the east of the mark. During the day they maintained a reasonably straight course but, even so, it was still deviated to the east by a light and constant breeze. Their heading was more toward the island of Kypros than it was toward Kriti, or Kefti as the Egyptians had misunderstood the visitors to say.

Clouds blackened, the effect accented by the coming night. On they drove, pounding the sea with their oars, the cane and club of the priest ever threatening. They were so far from home; how many days now?; that their only hope of refuge was to find the land they sought. They could never find their way back.

Again they were battered by a series of breaking waves, partially swamping the boat.

"Drop oars. Bail the water," the priest was shouting as the craft went maverick, even lending a hand for the first time. He feared for his life. One man slowed his labor, only for a moment to vomit, and had his skull smashed by the priest who then flung him over the side.

"No useless weight in the ship." He began throwing everything overboard as the others carried on bailing with renewed vigor.

He looked at the Princess. To think that he had wanted her for himself, that he had felt resentment and jealousy at the order to take her to this new destination, this destination that probably only existed in the mind of a ridiculous puppet. If only the gods had better judgment and made priests the rulers, the acknowledged rulers. But who could fathom the gods?

They were not meant to transport the Princess to this imaginary place, that much was plain. There only was one way to decide her fate for a certainty, the will of the gods, and with luck they could save the ship in the process.

Bladders of wine floated in the bilge with the small amount of air inside. The priest squeezed the wine overboard rather than just into the bilge, an exercise in futility as more water washed in over the rails. When the bags were empty, he inflated them with his breath and tied them together separated by a short length of rope.

"Let go of me you filthy animal," screamed the Princess as she was lifted to her feet by her hair. "You cannot dishonor me." He tore the soaked tunic from her bosom as she struggled to free herself, the struggle rocking the boat and letting in more water. Her strength was no match for his. He was going to rape her before death took them and the opportunity was lost. She thought he was going to go for her skirt, but he screamed into her face instead.

"Quiet, you absurd virgin. You have one chance of survival." He held her by the hair, turning her back to face him, thrust the inflated bladders under each arm and pulled her arms down tight behind them. They protruded in front of her like two swollen cow udders, strapped across her back by the rope.

"The gods will decide if you will live now," he shouted into her ear. "Be thankful that I have given you a greater chance than the others I have sent to the depths of this cursed ocean."

"No," she screamed as he turned her and pushed her backward over the side.

* * *

The crew, with the exception of five left behind to guard the boat and the calves, tracked their way up the ascending paths to the mine. They had rested through the day previous, nursing their aching muscles. Now that they had recovered they subscribed to gather more copper. Most of them were longing for home by now but the weather was still too inclement. The wind still blowing came mostly from the west, along with a rough chop, frustrating any hope of quick travel.

They climbed the mountains through the dense fog where it had been raining miserably on them, above the clouds to the sunlight above. Deus and Syros both had their acuity bared when it came to tracking ability with limited vision. The warmth of the sun up here was so refreshing, interrupted occasionally by passing, higher clouds.

Hyphes was every bit the embodiment of excitement that Deus knew he would be when they arrived at the mine. He would not even stop to rest a moment but went straight to the soil and began to pull at it with his hands. Luck was with him, and he found a nugget just under the surface.

"It is impossible," he wondered aloud. "Surely no other place like this exists."

"You may be right. But you can see that this is real. I warn you though, that the rest of what you find won't come as easily as that."

"Then I will need clay," he said, seeming not to understand or acknowledge the last part of Deus's remark. "Are there deposits nearby?"

Syros overheard the question and found it amusing. "There is no clay this far from the coast."

"Then how do we make our pottery in the hills of Kriti?" asked Taros. "Did you think our old ladies hobbled for days to bring it that distance?" He was bordering on rudeness, familiarity allowing him to take liberties.

Hyphes agreed. "The world was not always as we now see it. There was a time when all was close to, or beneath, the waters." He looked around. "If we seek clay we will find it."

Deus called the rest around and bade them find what Hyphes sought.

Soon Kirtos returned with a large block, which he struggled under. He dropped the stiffly pliable mass on a rock where it smacked and flared out.

"Will that be enough?"

"Enough to get me started. I thank you. To do this right I could use several more of these."

"I'll find some of the others. How like them to vanish when a labor is found," he joked.

Hyphes had already begun his project, the floor of his kiln. He had found numerous flat rocks in the vicinity, worked by man there was no doubt, a long time ago. He pulled the mossy growth off of them and rubbed them with sand to get them clean. The clay would not bond to any organic material. He lay them in a flat bed, circular, a little wider in diameter than the length of his arm leaving them a finger apart and not worrying about the spaces between the rocks; they would carry air that would only assist in the burning.

On the surface of the circle he lay a thick layer of the clay, not pushing it far into the cracks, leaving a wide, bare circle in the center for air to rush up during the burn.

A few of the others came up from behind, not having found any clay. "Dig a pit, up to your waists," Hyphes petitioned. "Just over there."

Two more came from another direction. Hyphes requested their aid too. "I will need a pile of wood, as dry as you can find. And as thick as you can find. Little branches are fine, but I also need big pieces."

Hyphes continued with his construction, three men arriving with large blocks of the reddish clay. The flat stones which Syros's ancestors had knocked out of the local habitations where ideal for his furnace. They stood perfectly, with a little manipulation, one rock placed next to another sloping on an inward arch with the augmentation of interlaying seams of clay. The walls quickly took form into their dome shape, an opening on the side for access and placing fuel, and a vent left in the top to exhaust hot gasses. He built the small dome with such speed and skill that any could see that he was a master.

The hole the men were digging was now deep and wide enough to satisfy him, and he asked that a large fire be built next to it. While that was being done he modeled the leftover clay into a thick crucible, bending a spout on the edge of the rim and pushing a hole into each side of the rim perpendicular to the spout. On the base he made a thick handle protruding opposite the position of the spout.

The fire was blazing with a fierce intensity, coals from the seasoned wood incandescent even in the sunlight. This was good enough. Hyphes pushed the fire over into the pit with a forked branch. The disturbed pile flared and diminished as the pit saturated with thick smoke, but the coals continued to glow and send out flicks of yellow and orange. He threw in armloads of smaller branches, kindling, which caught and began to glow as a blue phosphorescence filled every gap between. The smoke in the pit stirred and billowed as cool air vacuumed down the sides and into the fire. When the soft combustion in the hole had completely encompassed the wood and it had collapsed into an aggregation of luminescence, he threw in the rest of the larger wood that had been gathered, ensuring that no piece was standing separate from any other piece and that all pieces, although thrown, were just as if neatly placed tight to their neighbor.

"Now you will help me fill this hole."

They thought they had not heard right. Only when Hyphes began to push the dirt over top of the smoking mass did they understand that he was serious.

"Why are you asking to undo what we have labored so hard for? You make a fire in a hole then smother the wood so it cannot burn? Do you also throw your fish back when you spend a day trying to make the catch?"

"I am not a fisher. I am a metalsmith. But I would throw a small fish back to catch a big one."

Deus and Syros smiled at the allegorical wisdom of the statement as they assisted filling the hole, still puzzling over what it was they were helping Hyphes accomplish.

More wood was brought for Hyphes. He started a fire in his kiln with the crucible near the back protected by a couple of larger pieces of wood. He didn't want any of the smaller ones rolling and damaging the soft clay before it was dried.

When the fire caught nicely, he began to brick in the doorway with some of the more square shaped pieces of rock he had placed to the side for this purpose. He wouldn't be using any clay here. They would have to balance by themselves.

The clay had to dry first, so he kept the fire very small. It would take at least the day, but time didn't matter. The transformation taking place within the pit would take at least as long.

"For now," he said to the others, "you can all keep busy digging copper." When they had set about that task, Hyphes took Deus aside.

"Have you brought the tin bars with you?"

"The tin? You mean the anaku?"

"Yes."

The question surprised Deus. Not because of any coincidence, but because he had felt a need to bring the ingots even though it was a weight he could have done without on the steep climb. Because of that, he left it behind, relenting to another feeling he had which was stronger. "I left it with the ship. It is heavy and I could see no reason to bring it."

"How could you see a reason? I am the only one who holds the reason, an understanding I am prepared to share with you. A great secret that only few possess and guard jealously." He took Deus's arm and led him farther from the others toiling in the dirt. There as no way they could have heard with all the scraping and digging they were doing. It was just a formality to magnify the greatness of the magic he would soon work. "Copper is a fine metal, beautiful, easy to craft. But it is soft. It is useful in a woman's kitchen but not in a man's hand, except for drinking wine. A man needs a weapon that will hold an edge as well as a flint knife but won't break or chip." He turned to Deus, to hold his eyes with his own. "That is the magic of the tin. It transforms the copper. It makes it hard but not so hard that it breaks. It makes it easier to reform if you want to. It is what turns copper into bronze."

Bronze.

That was the secret of bronze. Tin. But how? There had to be more to it than just mixing it in. That is why Hyphes was constructing the forge. Not for the copper, the nuggets here could be beaten together without melting, but to melt the copper and tin to mix together.

The possibilities were flooding his mind as quickly as they did when he first conceived of the idea of copper production. This would be even better, except the tin supply was so very limited. How far would a bar of anaku go? Well, he would soon find out.

"Say nothing of this to the others," Deus told him.

"Never. I will leave the handling of that matter to you. But let me tell you, many have been murdered for the secret, going to their graves rather than share it. When that happens whole villages lose. Without means to make good weaponry, they are at the mercy of their neighbors. Many have died because they have killed the ones who could have provided protection for them. Also, the dead have been the ones with contacts and suppliers of the rare metal, and the living would never guess what to look for or how to get it. You, in an unbelievable stroke of good fortune, have walked into a rich supply. It was destined for somewhere else, but you have maneuvered it your way without

173

even knowing the value. Neither does the fool in Ugarit." He paused, catching himself. Deus had been on friendly terms with the man, and Hyphes feared he may have caused offense with his bold remark.

"Never mind," Deus reassured him. "I know he treated you poorly. So much the better for all of us. Remember this, Hyphes. You are with us now, not alone. You are as a brother to me. You will soon come to be as a brother to all of them as well. As for Yaqara, he was no fool, other than in your eyes. He has benefited us greatly and will continue to do so. He will make himself rich in the process. Settle in your mind any problems you might have had with him. Forget them. They don't matter anymore. You will never have to see him again, or even hear of him if you don't want to. He turned you away to something far better. And so you gained mastery over him."

The wisdom in this young man. He had never seen or heard the like of it. If he could push the aggravating fool of Ugarit out of his mind, as Deus advised, he would win. If he thought that the fool had turned away his greatest opportunity, which was exactly true, then he had conquered. He had overcome. That was the end of it. He would never lower himself to think of Yaqara again.

Deus guided the direction of their walk in a wide arc that led them back to their starting point.

He made his announcement to everyone. "I'm going back to the ship. Two of you should come with me to help hump more water up here. We may stay a little longer than we had planned."

That was no problem for any of them. They preferred this to the rough seas. The weather seemed to be turning for the worse again, the wind building and the clouds now high overhead quickly filling the sky in an overcast.

"If you that are staying behind can think of any way to collect water if rains come, maybe by using some of that clay, then you should do so. I will return as soon as I can. Something calls to me. I'm not sure what. But I must return to the shore."

Hyphes thought this was a neat trick, to let them think something spiritual was leading him back when in reality he was preserving his real reason of retrieving the tin.

Deus knew what Hyphes was thinking. There was no point right now letting him know that his feelings were very real. There was more to his return than accommodating Hyphes's wishes, even though he would have gone back for that reason alone.

* * *

Deus and the other two were greatly in need of sleep when they met up with the others on the beach. The wind, at least, had kept them at a comfortable temperature on the walk down. They were sure they had made their way back faster this time than the last. The continual workout of rowing and walking was building a strong crew.

Deus was glad to see the calves on their feet munching contentedly at the grass, the watchful Jacobah at their side.

He had left the potter, Jobah, behind to help guard the ship. There hadn't been much point bringing him along, he was still feeling sick the day after they arrived and would have slowed the climb. Now he was itching to do some work and lamented his uselessness here. He felt he was again being forsaken.

Deus dealt with this complaint as he did all others, by turning it around and making the griever feel as if he were someone exceptional.

"I am glad you are feeling better. We need your skills at the mine. They have found a clay deposit nearby that Hyphes has already put to use. He has some skills that you share in common. I think you will be pleased with some of the work he has managed when you see it. But his time will have to be spent on other things and he will have no time for clay. We need large water bowls, pots, jugs. I have charged the others to find a way, if they can, to catch water but I think only you will have the skills to bring their ideas to fruition. We will be resting the night here but we had hoped that you would join us in the morning for the trip back."

Jobah's pocked face peeled back in the widest grin, exposing his blackened teeth.

"You can even bring your wheel if you want."

The shocked look told Deus that he should have guessed that his jest would be taken the wrong way. Jobah thought he was really serious and wanted the heavy wheel carried all the way to the mine. It could be done but would take several men days to do it. Jobah had heard how long it took them to walk that far and how steep the climb was. He was horrified, unable to reply. He knew he would have a hard enough time keeping up with the others even with nothing on his back. He wasn't a weak man but he never did get about much, what with all the teasing he'd had to contend with.

"Relax Jobah. I was only making a joke. The clay work that is to be done has no need of a wheel." He clapped him on the back as his smile returned, a smile of utmost relief.

Deus had to get away, to find solitude. The loss of the two tektites still gnawed him. He had to think in private. He took a partially empty bag of fresh water, almost drained since one of the men had filled it in the creek. It would be more than enough for him alone and would be less weight to carry than a full one. He rolled his felt tight and made off down the beach, advising the others that he would be back early in the morning.

* * *

The Evening Star glossed particularly bright as the sun dropped out of view, the luminescent nodule in the darkening blue the only star visible until the conclusion of twilight. Only a short time would pass before it too would dip over the edge. Deus remembered his father telling him that something of great significance was about to happen somewhere when the star drew attention to itself like this.

He wrestled with the fact that he had somehow lost two of the irreplaceable tektites. No. He hadn't lost them. They had been stolen. The idea that they had been transmuted into the stones that had replaced them was only a brief consideration. That was too farfetched. Either someone had slipped in the replacements as he slept or when he was in one of his trance-like states expounding the mysteries of life to a small congregation. If it was the latter then wouldn't someone have seen the exchange? In either case it must have been someone close to him, and that was too much to bear.

He entered a dream state, the transition so smooth he was unaware of the change from consciousness to sleep. He dreamed disturbing visions of blackness, or emptiness, haunting but not frightening. He could think, but his thoughts were bizarre, twisted. Five dim rings formed a 'W' dulcet against the dark backdrop, an even fainter silhouette, like a watermark, of the goddess framing them. Two rings faded slowly into nothingness, an absence of ever having been.

Guilt filled his mind, harrowing, acute. His body writhed involuntarily, rolling onto its side. He somehow felt more comfortable curled fetally, more subjectively at ease.

The five rings appeared again, linked this time like a chain, still in the 'W' configuration. They remained for a long time, then slowly unlinked, two distancing themselves from the others. The two then separated and moved farther to the side, one much more distant than the other. Then one of the remaining three separated, moving downward. The two remaining stayed central, the frame of the goddess materializing and surrounding them with her belly, and eventually even those last remaining moved off, one to the other side, and the other to an extreme distance.

And so they remained through the night, occasionally shifting their positions to a greater or lesser degree, periodically becoming bright then fading individually. The meaning behind the dream eluded him as he slept. He had the very real impression that he was capable of conscious thought as if he were not asleep at all. Time, only, seemed altered. The night lasted infinitely, years, lifetimes passing as he lay dormant.

At last, the faded rings brightened again, shifting, drawing closer together. They linked in the familiar pattern and shone with a brilliance.

The very faded outline of the goddess was illuminated from the light, absorbing it, radiating some back. Light grew in magnitude, filling the void, as the form of the goddess took eminence, shining, blinding Deus in his sleep. It was too bright. He tossed his head from side to side but could not escape its all-encompassing rays.

He woke with a start, his eyes wide open. The blinding light was still there. He could not escape his dream even in consciousness, the power of it so great. He shielded his eyes from the brilliance, squinting, raising a hand over his brow. His pupils, dilated from the darkness of sleep, quickly constricted, adjusting to the glare of the risen Full Moon. When he had snapped his eyes open he had been leveled right at it.

The Full Moon. There was nothing like it. Rationality was returning. What a strange dream. Of course it hadn't lasted forever. The night could only be half past. He tried to relax, to give thought to the meaning behind the dream.

The highway of Moonbeams reflecting off the water was the most beautiful sight he had ever beheld. The storm had passed. The water had returned to a calm glassy state, perfectly capturing the scene beheld. The crew would be glad. They could leave any time.

He stared a long while, focused on the white reflection, as it quivered and vacillated with the minute undulations of the water, a black center almost absorbed into the light. The light broke up on a few occasions, ripples from the center spiraling outward and shaking the white image. It was almost as if there was something in the light, but he couldn't make it out.

He sat up, alert now. The black shape was hard to see, even with his superlative vision. It did seem to be moving, coming closer, two small humps. Impossible to gauge how far out it was, if it was anything other than a part of the Moon's image.

The black thing rose then fell, he could hear the splash. Then it rose again, this time staying up. It seemed unbalanced, swaying from side to side as it advanced. Did it have arms? Was that a head? His spine tingled. The dark bulge that would have been its chest fell away.

The Princess felt the sand under her feet with the ecstasy of being lifted to a higher plane of existence. She could see the faint glow and dark shadows of the land ahead, not too far, lit softly by the Moonlight. No thanks to the damned gods. Forget them. This was joy. She cast the bladders aside, the water splashing up stinging her back as the impressed rope peeled away a strip of skin.

Two days and three nights she had been floating, the current carrying her as it would. She had only sipped the smallest amount of the awful, salty tasting water, only when she was desperate, only when her mouth had become dry and her throat sore. The salt soothed her throat but did little to relieve her thirst. She was fortunate. Her aversion to the seawater saved her in the end. Many had, and would, meet their death drinking quantities of the saline that is in such abundance but so toxic.

As she rose higher out of the water on the long and slowly rising bar, the weight increased on her legs. She took it very slow, one step after the other, getting a sure footing and balance before advancing the other foot.

Deus could not believe what he was seeing.

It was a woman coming out of the sea. The sandbar below the surface extended a long way out and she was still some distance away, making her unhurried ascent and advance all the more dramatic. The Moon shone upon her rising torso, backlighting her outline, her wet hair draped firmly over her shoulders. She shook her head, hair flying up liberating droplets and mist. The cloud settling around her caught the light prismatically, refracting light in every hue, a scintillating halo draping and surrounding her form.

He sat motionless, invisible to the weakened and desperate young woman. Her hips were out of the water as she continued closer up the shallow incline.

Deus had a brief flash of thanks as he considered the desperate situation they would now be facing had they chosen this place as a landing point. During the storm, the waves breaking on this shallow rise would have split their ship asunder, rolled it mercilessly and broken it on the bottom. From that fatal error some of them would have survived, but they would not have had the means to return to their home.

The thought was fleeting as he returned his focus on the mesmerizing apparition. She was beyond description, framed by the shimmering white light on the water, the soft glow of her skin almost impossible to adjust his eyes upon with the changing contrast behind. She was like a dream, ethereal and sublime.

He expected to see her legs next, but after her ovate hips, a darkness stretched beyond what could possibly be. Could she not be a woman at all but, rather, one of the man-fish the fishers spoke of? He didn't believe those tales and never had. The minutest doubt fled when he reasoned that a fish-tailed creature could never walk upright so close to shore.

He could see the motion of her legs working enveloped in some sheer fabric to below the knees, light from behind invading the veiled space between, the sibilant sound of the water flourishing around her calves with every step. A few small waves followed her in as if bidden, announcing her advent, gaily breaking around her ankles in jubilation and whipping up a white foam.

She stood motionless, arriving at last at refuge. She wanted to collapse, to sleep forever, but her mind was too schooled and had too much in the way of common sense to cave in so easily. She had to find water and food, and if she only had a bit of strength she should at least make an effort to start in the right direction.

Deus beheld her from only a ship's length away, standing straight and sure of herself, like a goddess in the pale light, her hair and skin glistening with moisture. She put both hands behind her head and shook out her hair. The Moonlight made it look almost white somehow, a trick of the eyes he was sure. She squeegeed the water off her skin, pulling her palm across the opposite shoulder and down her arm, back up and down her breast, side, and abdomen. She repeated the motions on the other side, drying herself as much as she could with her bare hands before the chill penetrated. Bending forward, her back steel straight, she removed her skirt and wrung the water from the material. The foam continued its passionate entanglement of her feet as she rubbed her hips and legs to dry them, the cloth over her shoulder to keep it free of sand. She gave it a final hard twist. That was as dry as she could make it until the sun rose. She unfurled it, placed her legs through, and pulled it up. It wasn't so much that she felt naked as much as she didn't feel up to carrying anything, not even a piece of fabric. Her hips could convey the light weight better than her arms.

Deus was enamored with every movement, every change of position, captivated by every subtle motion. Each burned consummately into the tissues of his mind, deep, ineradicable. He would take these images to his deathbed. His eyes, fully dilated again, began to cloud. He was so entranced he had not blinked and his eyes dried, ruining the focus. He stood as he tried to clear his sight, the motion solitary from anything else, drawing the attention of Aphrodite.

* * *

The rising sun blessed them as they lay wrapped together in the warmth of the packed felt blanket. Aphrodite's body had felt so cold, like a fish caught bright and unspoiled from the sea.

The days spent in the water, warm as it was, still brought her temperature down by excessive degrees. She remembered the protracted shivering that had started not long after the daybreak on that first day alone in the interminable expanse. The shaking was ceaseless as her temperature continued its slow slide. Her body trembled, mildly at first, then uncontrollably during the next night, her teeth clenched and chattering without intermission until she gave them up as lost, inevitably to be shattered or ground to dust. To her great relief, the shivering slowly subsided as her temperature dropped further, leaving her physically spent but mentally not far from euphoric. She had made the transition from mild to moderate hypothermia, a condition which, if not reversed, would lead to her eventual death.

Her arrival on the beach was shrouded in mystery. She had only the faintest recollection, less than if it had been an inconsequential dream. She had a feeling that she had been walking, a nonpareil effort made possible only by her powerful predilection. And here she was, embraced in the arms of a rather handsome young man, despite his weak beard, wrapped in a cloak, and curled on a sandy beach. She allowed herself the wonderment of contemplating the features of her reposing savior before nestling tighter against his warmth and drifting off again into the luxury of sleep.

* * *

Deus woke with a start. He turned his face from its covering in the felt to the sound behind where three of the men of his crew stood looking down at him. He could tell immediately that he had slept well into the morning, the sun too high in the sky for the time to be anywhere near dawn. They had come looking for him.

"We were concerned. It is not like you to be down so late."

Deus thought quickly. He felt very cold, the heat having been drawn out of his body to supplement the little that remained in his foundling. She was real, he could feel her pressed against him still, hidden within the wraps of his blanket.

"I must have been more worn by our travels than I imagined."

He felt the girl tense. She held her breath. His voice had wakened her.

"You look terrible. Your face is pale," joked Abos. He looked puzzled at the footprints on the sand, one pair coming out of the water but none going down. "A swim in the night is not good for one's health." What was that golden wisp across his neck?

Deus mumbled. "I'll remember that. Right now I feel as though I need more rest. I will join you later."

They took this for the dismissal that it was, slightly offended at the abruptness of their prophet, for that is how they were coming to see him. Soon they were gone, disappearing around the point where lay the ship and their camp.

He slowly folded back the corner of the blanket covering the gilded hair. She had tucked herself backward against him, fitting his curves hand in glove. The others hadn't seen her shape, the bulk of the blanket hiding her slim contours against him.

He knew she was awake. "It's all right. They've gone now."

She turned her head up, her profile only a few inches from his face. She was not so white as he had thought, as seen in the Moonlight, but her skin tone was still whiter than any he had known. She had a natural beauty beyond any he had seen, bar one. No. Not even his mother had possessed such perfection during her natural life.

She turned her body supine, the better to view this handsome man who had conferred so freely the warmth of his body. She still felt cold inside and across her front, wishing at the same time he could give more but promptly rebuking herself for the selfish inclination, knowing that if he did he would sacrifice too much of his own life force.

The Sun felt wonderful, its rays warming her face. The rays of the Sun. The giver of all life. More important even than water.

She cast aside the covering, letting in the life-giving light. The body of this man beside her had brought her through the night, given freely of his own life energy to help a stranger, but only the Sun could complete what he had begun. The radiation warmed her skin immediately, no breeze today to carry away the heat. It was wonderful. She closed her eyes and basked in the photonic medium.

Deus lifted himself on his elbow. He was now enjoying the heat of the sun himself. His eyes were drawn, not unwillingly, to the firm body beside him. He let his gaze pan slowly up and down her lithe form, consuming every curve of skin, every pore. He warmed inside, too. His spirit lifted and the congenial affection he thought of as love overcame him.

"Who are you?" he spoke softly, not intentionally, for those were only his thoughts.

She opened her eyes, the sky-blue irises constricting her pupils suddenly to the bright light. Such wide eyes. She locked on to his penetrating stare not a breath away. She would not back down first. There was nothing in this man's eyes to suggest any fear or need for anxiety. He was her savior, her champion.

Their minds locked and bonded. Not a word had passed between them. There had been no need of that. The only need had been for the moment. The need of survival for one, the need to satiate curiosity for the other. He had not realized the imminent danger to her life, but if he had, the need to help another in distress would have contributed.

They basked in the Sun in silence, their minds still entangled in a web of unspoken intrigue. They could never have said how long they held each other's gaze. If simple logic had not dictated otherwise, it could have been days. In that time, a short time that altered all time, they fell deeply and everlastingly in love.

* * *

"We should check on him again. It's been too long."

"It has been. He did say that he would come back after he finished resting. He did not look well, you know. He was too pale."

"I agree. I'm not happy with this."

"We'll compromise then. As soon as we've finished supper, we'll go back. But I don't think he'll like it."

"By the Earth Mother," Tattus exclaimed. Kirtos and Abos followed his gape, shocked themselves at what they saw. Kirtos shouted and waved to Jacobah who was in the grass with the foraging calves.

There was Deus coming toward them, arms linked with a magnificent beauty. She was breathtaking, not another visage like her to be beheld anywhere. Her blonde hair swept back, blown lightly to the side, lifted softly by the gentle evening breeze. She wore only a skirt, cut just below the knee, a cream linen with a simple black band around waist and hem, the contrast to her newly bronzed and slightly burnt skin giving the weathered cloth a whiteness it did not merit. Her wrapped hips below a narrow waist and toned flat belly swayed gracefully with every step. Her head held regal, neither bouncing nor rolling. When she looked to the side her head moved intently on her long, slender neck, slowly, positively. Her perfectly formed breasts held as steady as her head, pointing firmly before her, directly at them. Proud nipples drew their eyes, but only for a moment. Her beauty was beyond all conception and they kept returning to her face. It was perfect, even more so than her body if that was possible, and they could see that it was. Her vivid blue eyes, uncommonly large and deep-set below thin, long eyebrows, nestled above a narrow, undeviating nose. Her mouth opened only a smite, an imperceptible but very real smile disguised in the sensuous heart-shaped lips.

Jacobah stood and moved toward his six brothers, never taking his eyes off this singular vision. He forgot temporarily about his charges, even about the man who walked alongside this living dream.

They stopped before the tongue-tied group, standing august and dignified.

"This is Aphrodite," announced Deus. "My wife."

"Your wife?" They all spoke at once. How could he have a wife on this island? He had never been here before thirty days ago. It was impossible. There were no inhabitants anywhere near; were there? No. There were not. They knew that much.

Deus raised his hand in salute and to signal silence.

"We wed today. Our Earth Mother has blessed me with her greatest blessing. She woke me in the night to witness what even I could never have believed had I not beheld it of my own. Aphrodite rose out of the sea, drawn by the light of the Moon to my very place on the sand, wet and dripping, clad as you see her now. I knew I had to be there but knew not why. Only my instincts took me there. Now I know, and so do you. My eternal companion has been delivered. All we ask of you is your blessings."

"Magnificent."

"Great blessings be upon you."

"Upon you both."

"Upon all your posterity. May they be as the sands of the sea."

They surrounded the couple, slapped Deus and cheered for him. Congratulations to Aphrodite were reserved to a cautious touch or two, pleasant nods and smiles. It was quickly apparent that she could not speak their words but could understand their meaning easily enough. Her bright smile of appreciation and wide, glowing eyes won their hearts and dedication as easily as she had won Deus's. She seemed not the least self-conscious or shy about her beauty or state of undress, even surrounded by these men. She had become used to that in Egypt. She had the grace to keep her eyes on theirs, avoiding the possibility of embarrassing them by noticing their groins. She did not know them yet, and certainly not well enough to make teasing fun of any who were getting too much stimulation from her company.

"We must drink some wine in your honor. Limbus, get a skin from the ship." Kirtos was trying to exercise a little authority by giving the order, though he had no place doing so. Limbus obeyed gladly anyway, delighted with the suggestion, as he took it, to celebrate a fine occasion.

The skin went round many times, the wine of the Ugarit community tasting much better after their ordeal at sea. Deus had to repeat the story three times, clarifying with each rendition the minutest details to the incredulous listeners.

"Came out of the sea?" Kirtos could not believe it. Yes, you said that the first time but it must have been meant metaphorically or in jest. "You cannot mean it."

Deus was amused by their skepticism, and could hardly hold it against them. It was one thing to be told of a wild fisher's tale and let the imagination run with it; it was another to behold the claim standing in front of one's own face. He would have been full of doubts himself had he not witnessed the miracle with his own eyes. Soon he would attempt to talk with Aphrodite, learn far more about her than her name, and find out how she came to be with him, whether she came out of the depths, or fell from a star, or somehow traveled from another land.

For now, it hardly mattered.

* * *

Dark shadows slid through the camp as the flaccid sun slumped down past the intervening summits. They had done enough for the day, passing the time surveying the area fully, digging into the rich deposits and sorting out the easy nuggets. Hyphes was still in awe of the place. He urged them just the same to give all due diligence to sorting out the smaller grains. In bulk they had every bit the value of a large piece, and with patience they found that they could screen out twice the amount of copper in less than double the amount of time. They were coming out ahead.

He removed the crucible from its place in the back of the oven, the slow embers of the little warming fire still glowing. He had restrained his urge to fire it rapidly, allowing it an extra long time to dry thoroughly, giving it the whole day. He held it in a thick piece of hide, rotating it and examining circumspectly for the most minute imperfection. It was flawless. That didn't keep him from criticizing himself for his ill-considered haste in not making a second crucible in case the first was damaged. He would not make that mistake again. A full day could have been wasted.

He had inspected the forge with the same critical eye. Some cracks had developed as the clay shrank around the rocks. They were of little structural concern, and nowhere nearly as important as the crucible, but he could not leave them as they were. He mixed a slurry of clay and water left over from the tailings of the copper separation and spread the paste thinly over the entire structure, working it hard into the visible cracks. When the skin dried, the walls were airtight.

He placed the crucible in the center of the forge for firing, just to the side of the largest opening in the middle of the floor. The fire would be hottest here. He piled an armload of kindling on top and around the urn, the fire from the embers quickly taking hold. He had the rocks away from the side door and he pushed large pieces of wood all around the smaller kindling, and lay half sized pieces crosswise on top of that, then added as much wood as the dome could hold.

He hoped he guessed right about the urn. If the clay had the smallest amount of moisture left in the center of the thick walls it could crack or explode.

He blocked up the door slowly, letting the fire spread, allowing the soft flames to engulf the hardened clay. He would keep the door partially open as yet, letting the temperature rise by degrees. Not too hot a fire. That could be damaging. Just an easy flame for a while. Later, he hadn't decided when exactly but he would feel it when the time was right, he would block in the door completely and let the temperature bloom.

Hyphes would keep this fire going, dropping pieces of wood every so often through the top. It would take all night and the better part of the next day before the magical changes concluded transforming the simple mud into exceptionally hard, durable ceramic.

Where was Deus? It was just as well that he didn't show up as expected. Hyphes had hoped to have the kiln operating and the crucible ready before he arrived back with the anaku. He was now glad for the extra time. He had put too much pressure on himself, allowed himself to be rushed. No. He had rushed himself. Deus was not one to push anyone faster than they could go. He wanted quality, not something that was sacrificed for speed. No. He would not be ready until tomorrow. Maybe.

Lobos humped himself over the last little rise before the mine camp, loaded with the weight of several skins of water. He brought nothing else.

"Am I glad you have a good fire going."

Several of the men started. Lobos's arrival was entirely by surprise. They had no one on lookout, and they were confident that all were accounted for. This was wholly unexpected.

"Lobos. Are you alone?" asked Syros, half expecting Deus to be close behind.

"No. Jobah is just back of me. I didn't think we were going to make it tonight. We left much too late. But just as it was getting dark and I thought about stopping before I got lost, I saw the firelight." Jobah came over the same rise a few dozen paces behind.

"You brought us water. Wonderful. We need it desperately. Labor up here in the mountains takes it out of us faster than near the sea." He opened the plug and took a prodigious draught, passing it then to the next man.

"Did you bring anything else?" asked Hyphes.

Lobos thought that a strange question. They had brought enough food on the first trip to last them several days. Why would he want more? "No. Nothing but water." Maybe he wanted some of the wine. He would when he heard the news.

Syros looked imposing, his high bulk half lit from the fire, half hidden in shadow. He worried Lobos to some extent. No reason, really, other than the man could crush any two of them if he had the inclination. Perhaps not the potter Jobah, who made him feel uncomfortable in the dark and was his true reason for pushing on. And perhaps not the burly Hyphes. Certainly the two of them together would give Syros a run.

"Why hasn't Deus returned with you?"

"Deus has other more pressing matters to attend to at the moment." This was going to be fun. "His wife needs his attention tonight far more than you . . ." He was cut off abruptly.

"What do you mean his wife?" Syros roared. "Have you struck your head upon the rocks?"

"I thought I had when I first saw her." His eyes glassed over. "She is as the sky on a perfect day, a crimson anemone in full blossom. Her hair is golden like the sun itself, her face a gathering of everything beautiful, her body . . ."

"You speak as the damned fishers and their mad hallucinations. If you continue on I will pull you down the mountain by your foot, and we shall see this perfect illusion you conjure in your mind."

"I've not conjured her in my mind. She is as real as any of you." He looked around for support and found none. No one was going to argue with Syros. He had been at the dig with a vengeance, surpassing all their efforts, and as amiable as he was he was too tired for games tonight.

* * *

"We have water enough for another day; two if we don't use too much washing the ore. We have enough food up here to last forever. There are animals everywhere. There are no good reasons to go back today. We will stay at least until tomorrow. All of us." Syros had taken charge, ordering, as he was wont to do when he tired of arguing.

Lobos held his peace and said no more, walking to the dig in a huff. He had been arguing for the lot of them to go to the coast first thing in the morning. They had to behold the miracle. No one would believe him, he knew, until they had seen her themselves. Syros had maintained that the miracle could wait; they had work to do. If she existed, and he did not believe it for a minute, she would still be there when they finally did go back, even if it was next year. Jobah had remained quiet through the argument, not understanding most of it, but nodding in concurrence with Lobos when he did. That he was supporting Lobos and arguing against their sensibilities was meaningless and changed nothing of their estimation of him. They all liked Jobah, thought of him as a brother of sorts, although not exactly as an equal. That would take a long time yet.

Hyphes let the oven fire burn down slowly starting at dawn. He slept as he could, in cat naps, dropping in small sticks to add some heat when he thought it was cooling too quickly. He worried continually, dreading that the crucible could crack under too rapid a temperature drop, fearful that in the roasting coals it already had. He told the others to see to it that he did not sleep for more than a short time, that it was urgent that the fire be tended constantly. They understood, but it was not necessary. His sleep was so fitful that he never stayed down long.

Through the day he gradually let the ember pile get smaller until, by the time of the evening meal it was just a smolder, the heat inside lowered to the point where he could reach in and remove the crucible. He unblocked the door, placing each wedge of stone to the side in deliberate order so he wouldn't have to mentally work at fitting each piece again. He folded the fragment of leather around his hand and reached the lip of the ceramic urn, drawing it carefully out.

It was perfect. He checked it three times inside and out, slowly, to be absolutely sure. There was no joy in his success, only a profound inner peace, a tranquil satisfaction now that the job was done. Jobah was at his side, taking a great interest in the results. He reached forward to feel the work, earning him a stiff rebuke from Hyphes. He would trust no one to touch it. It was too precious for the time being. When he could make more, then its value to them would be less.

Jobah was rightly insulted. He could have made a far superior pot if he had the use of his wheel, even without it. The thick walls were barbarous. But he had no idea of what the end use would be for the crucible, or the need for the excessively sturdy construction. To him it was just a thick pot with some strangely placed holes. He turned his attention to the furnace, used efficiently as a kiln in this case. Again he had no idea of its real purpose but found its construction fascinating. It did the job of firing clay very well; there was no debating that issue. It left the pot black with smoke and carbon, but Hyphes was already polishing the thin layer of creosote into the hot surface, giving it an attractive umber sheen.

A shout from behind triggered a cacophony of discordant voices as all witnessed in disbelief the visitants drawing over the rise.

Hyphes turned to see the others shouting and very nearly dropped his precious crucible, fumbling it for one heart-arresting second before making a safe recovery. The gods of Fire and Earth would not have dared it true. He gasped and pressed his lids together tight. It was his lack of sleep, the stresses and pressures of the last two days. He opened his eyes and focused on the unbelievable.

Lobos stood in satisfied reticence as the clamor abated, replaced by the silence of a group left stunned and dumb.

There they were, Deus and Aphrodite, standing proud on the knoll, motionless as statues. Deus held his chest thrown out, his muscles flexed, arms slightly apart from his trunk. Aphrodite wore the same raiment as before, a skirt covering her pelvis and thighs, all else exposed. She assumed the same stance as Deus, head high and elegant on her long neck, muscles taught, chest inflated. Her lithe extremities were slightly spread, her body turned by degree, in allegiance, toward her mate. A wisp lifted a few strands of silken hair, floating them gently back into place. The pair appeared as ephemeral chimera, dreamlike, wistful in their introspection, intrepid, and self-assured.

Deus surveyed his men, delighted to be with them, delighted to be surprising them this way. He knew from their reaction that they had not believed his two friends who had come the day earlier. Now she was here for them to behold.

As they walked the intervening space, the men pulled themselves free of the trance that held them fast and rushed forward as one to greet the couple. Deus noticed with a restrained smile of amusement that Taros had an enormous erection bulging under his short robe. A fold flipped behind it, between it and his body, as he ran to meet them with the others, outlining it a moment as it danced forward with each step before he fixed his garment, self-consciously darting his eyes about to determine if he had been seen.

He had been. Deus wasn't the only one to notice. It didn't matter that the rest of them had swollen glands to one degree or another, Taros was the only one who'd had himself revealed so patently, and blushed accordingly. Those who noticed paid little mind, minorly amused but quiet, thankful that they had not themselves been betrayed. With all her allure it was all they could do to will themselves down, or keep themselves in place, a difficult thing to do as they walked and jiggled underneath, the stimulus working against them.

* * *

Deus reprimanded them gently for disbelieving the report of Lobos. He munched through the crisp outer portion of the young boar while they sat together at meat. "We will swear an oath to be truthful with one another in all things."

Together they assented, no one letting his tongue linger mute.

"Agreed then. Our bond will be forever, trusting in faith to one another until the end of our days. A lie to a brother is spiritual death, a rejection after all we hold to be sacred. To disbelieve a brother is likewise a similar transgression. Let it be forever told that our bond is solid, our friendship firm, our brotherhood eternal."

"So be it," they swore. "Forever one."

Aphrodite had brought a small skin of wine and passed it to her husband. He drank a little and passed it to her.

She tipped her head back, an enticing sight, and pulled some into her mouth. A large drop rolled off her chin and drove to the end of her breast, clinging tenaciously to her nipple, the surface tension of the fluid holding it suspended in time and in reality on a narrowing stalk before it fell to her skirt, staining red a small spot. Taros squirmed with his knees pressed tight together, leaning forward with his elbows pressed against his thighs as he peeled his riveted eyes to the bright coals of the fire.

The bag went back to Deus, each symbolically serving each other first, then made its way around the circle, the drink ceremonially sealing the covenant they had made. This was most unusual, unheard of, to include a woman in such a ceremony, but she was as much a part of the avowal as any other. They would live and die for each other after making such an oath.

In the end, that is precisely how it would be.

* * *

The dirt was hot while they dug, one of the reasons Hyphes had left it for after sunset. But not the only reason. And now the pit lay open, viewed from above by those who could not understand what it was they were supposed to see. Heat still radiated from the black charcoal below, though it had ceased its transformation from hardwood some time ago.

The discovery that wood could be transformed to the carbonaceous material that constituted charcoal was one of the several turning points in the history of mankind. Its discovery hundreds of years earlier, in many places of the earth and at many times, was a coveted and guarded secret by those recognizing its value. For the most part, people who chanced upon it when they left an unburned log to combust under a covering of dirt just didn't fathom the magnitude of its importance. No different, really, from any other discovery of vast importance throughout history. All it ever took was one person to understand what it was that lay before him in plain sight. All he needed was eyes to see, a drive to perceive, and the intelligence to understand.

In every way, charcoal was as consequential as agriculture, trade, shipping, and government. It allowed for the generation of heat that wood by itself could never produce, not even the driest, hardest wood. Only the hottest, largest wood fires could gather in their centers the heat necessary to melt metals, and those kinds of fires were plenarily impractical. Charcoal solved that problem, coupled with a slightly modified oven.

A low lying smoke gathered at the floor of the hole, a few tiny streaks leaking up from below the surface. Hyphes jumped in and passed up armfuls of the raven chunks, these blocks of broken wood that had burned without oxidizing, split and shattered as the changes to their composition manifested themselves by turning the pieces black and greasy to the touch even though they were as dry as anything could be. He worked furiously, bending over and over into the ink of darkness, as he always did at this kind of mindless labor. This required no thought at all, and he wanted to get on to the part that required intelligent reasoning.

"I am ready now," announced Hyphes, dripping with sweat at the bottom of the hardened, coated pit.

Deus and Aphrodite joined with the rest around the furnace. They had taken another oath of brotherhood and secrecy at the insistence of Hyphes. No one had ever been permitted to know the secrets of the forger, of the metalsmith, without swearing to forfeit their lives rather than reveal their knowledge. Deus humored him knowing that Hyphes had also taken that same oath and now was breaking it. Clearly the smith did not see it that way himself, considering the others to be his colleagues now in all things. The girl was a bit of a sore point. He had some trouble bringing himself to accept her in this group, not that it mattered too much, he justified. She couldn't speak the language even as well as he could, seemingly not at all except for a few words. She would certainly not understand enough of what he would tell them, and probably would not even be interested enough in this manly art to bother remembering. For that matter, who would torture a woman for an answer to the mysteries of metalwork and alloying? No, she would not ever be a problem. Besides, there was something over and above breathtaking beauty to the qualities this woman possessed. Her grace transcended pulchritude, which only served to enhance the flood of blessings with which she was born. He liked her. This was one woman he would trust. Even so, he still thought her incapable of learning the cunning of this black art.

A glow of residual embers still radiated fluorescent red within the chamber. He would build this fire first for effect. They would be impressed, he would have bet his life on it. Only small wood this time. He heaped it in, dry, broken sticks most no thicker than two fingers together, scattering them on the floor. They kindled even as he pushed them to the back, careful to avoid disturbing the embers. It wasn't long before the layer was completely surrounding the embers, tightly packed and growing in height.

Heaping charcoal in, he built a layer of the light material on top of the last. He started popping them in through the smoke hole, dropping them delicately at first, building the pile around the embers which were now burning softly into the kindling layer and the charcoal. The mounting pile built like a volcano, the walls around the center enlarging. A few more pieces and the rim collapsed, cascading gently onto the middle, sheltering the heart. Then he cast in the charcoal by volumes. The fire amplified as he proceeded, licking through the pyre. The chamber was full. He had worked quickly. Now on to the next part while he still could, before the heat would drive him back.

He began blocking up the door, carefully placing each wedge as they were previously fitted, keeping the gaps between them to the minimum. At some later time he would work the rocks even more precisely, he had his pride, but they would be fine for now.

The effect was almost immediate. The hot gasses rising from the top of the furnace began to suck air from the spaces between the rocks below leading to the hole in the center of the floor. A low-key drone built, increasing in volume as more wood caught and the draught increased in velocity. As he lifted the last rock into place, blocking almost all air from entering but by the bottom, sparks shot out of the smoke hole followed by a pure transparent flame that gave every appearance of power driving it from below. The supercharged atmosphere glowed and filled the interior of the kiln, visible to the fascinated onlookers only through the gaps between the blocks filling the door opening.

The jet of fire pressed upward from the inferno, a conflagration of multi-colored streaks of dynamism infinitely variable in appearance. Hyphes had chosen the time with sagacity. The column of power against the backdrop of the stygian hill at night blinded them to all else. Their periphery vanished, freeing them to focus on the raw puissance emanating unopposed from the aperture and to contemplate that contained mostly within.

They were awestruck, filled with wonder and astonishment. And dread. Visions were one thing, this was real. This tangible power Jobah had harnessed, this natural energy, could be used to what end? What purpose could he have for revealing it to them? What good could come of it? What evil? Those questions would be debated for thousands of years to come.

"All of you know that copper can be beaten into shape, that you can pound the nuggets you have found together and form it however you choose. But the metal is weak. It is feminine. I will show you how to make it stronger, masculine."

Hyphes placed copper grains and nuggets into the crucible, filling it halfway. He then pushed the long branches of fresh cut black pine through the holes on the side, lifting it into place at the heat expelling orifice crowning the domed furnace. Deus was given the honor of assisting him. Hyphes would have had no other.

The crucible fit neatly, three-quarters of it hanging down into the inferno, plugging the aperture, sending streamers of transparent fire up and around the lip from the gaps of an imperfect seat.

They removed the branches, warm to the touch at midspan from their brief exposure to the heat.

Now to wait.

No one spoke, the magic of the moment holding them mesmerized. They stood around the furnace as people sit around campfires, warming their fronts and enjoying the panoply staging before their faces. Watching the fire was enough. It always had been and always would be.

The land was sloped, and Syros, the tallest of them, had chosen the highest place. He could see into the container as the contents began to change. The whole crucible itself began to change, glowing as a coal does as it discharges heat, crimson in places, dark in others, but not revealing precisely where the line of color change is.

Vapors rose from the interior of the contents, the metal seemed to shift, a glow coming from deep under the surface nodules. Soon even they radiated softly.

Heat blasted against the bottom and sides of the container. It was translucent now, almost as if one should be able to see through it with the interior remaining invisible. The interior seen from above glowed brightly, too, smoking sporadically as the odd impurity oxidized and rose as gas.

Something was happening. They craned to see following Syros's obvious intense interest. The bright contents again shifted, collapsing a little, then suddenly and completely as they merged together and bound into a single liquid mass.

This was the part Hyphes loved most, the phase change from solid to liquid at nineteen-hundred eighty-one degrees Fahrenheit. He could never see it enough. Everyone 'ohhhed' and 'ahhhed' along with him as they witnessed the change, the lumps of crimson settling into a mercurial puddle.

Brilliant red faded anticlimactically as slag skimmed the surface. It bubbled anomalously, not from heat great enough to boil the metal, but from escaping gasses from more impurities now being liberated from the yet imperfect element.

Hyphes took a wet greenstick, long enough to reach, and deftly twisted it into the metal, only touching the surface. It steamed and smoked together as the slag fixed to the tip, hardening instantly. Hyphes withdrew it before the wood burst into flame and before the residue could fall back into the pot. He repeated this several times, as it was warranted, gradually working the copper as pure as he could. He really needed a skimmer, a copper tool, but that would come in the future. It would all come. Greensticks would be adequate for tonight.

He took a handful of sand and sifted it into the container, a specter of flame rising off the surface as if from an alcohol burner. It sank in and then rose back to the surface, black with the remaining solid impurities. This he pulled off in the same manner as the first few times. He had worked the copper until it was now almost ninety-seven percent pure. Even the purest nuggets and grains had not been this rarefied, but it was still not acceptable to Hyphes.

Through years of preceptorship by the old masters and another decade of trial and experimentation, he had become perhaps the foremost master in his craft. He had the feeling that others had withheld their techniques from him in order to secure a more esteemed position for themselves, but he had always been free with his information and spoke regularly of his experimentations with others of his guild. That, perhaps more than his skill attainment, had placed him, with time, at the head of his league. Those with whom he had shared had shared with him, and his knowledge had become encyclopedic. He thought about it now, an empty part of him that he thought he had cast aside. His memories of his good fellows, the riotous times they had together on occasion, growing more serious as they aged. He admired the ones who could work the metal artfully into not only useful objects but also attractive objects. He couldn't do that. He could work basic shapes but his heart wasn't focused on beauty, other than to briefly admire it. He would always leave the fine crafting for someone else, making subtle and useful suggestions on how they could improve their work. His love was for the fire itself, the earth and its various ores, the forging, the tools and furnaces of power and magic. He loved the heat of fire on his face, sweating in the bitter cold of winter when everyone else was freezing. His hands and arms were scarred with uncountable burns. He didn't even feel the new ones anymore unless they were deep, and when he did feel them they had become almost sensuous, gratifying his senses, the stinging pain drawing him into the metal he worked, binding them, marrying them.

He used the other end of the green pine branch that he had used to remove the slag, the more or less completely fused and vitrified matter separated during the reduction of the metal from its ore. There hadn't been much in this special instance because the copper they had at hand was so untainted with disseminating materials. These good people, his new friends, his new guild, would never really comprehend how precious and rare a find this mine was. There may be no other like it. Most copper ore was little more than a sandy conglomerate, with very little copper at all. The work involved in extracting it was far more difficult than what they witnessed here. And he had actually gone to the effort of making this chore, or pleasure as he thought it, much harder by mixing the most corrupt of their extractions into this mix. If he had used only the largest of the magnificent nuggets then there would have really been very little work to do, and less to impress his friends.

He plunged the green stick deep into the molten accretion, stirring as billows of steam and smoke ripped through the tempestuous liquid. The impurities, mainly oxygen, remaining from the initiatory processes were now stripped from their molecular bindings, freed to combust with carbon from the burning wood, or to rise to the surface as further slag. It was impossible to see through the allotment of escaping steam and smoke that issued forth, but Hyphes could see by feel where the others couldn't even imagine. The metal rolled within the confines of the crucible, kept deep enough below the rim to prevent it from splashing out. In a moment the action stopped, reduced to a slow escape of gas from below the surface.

It was done. He removed the stick, swirling it to capture the last thin skim of slag. He only knew that the copper was now as pure as it was possible to get it. He would have said that it was absolutely pure. He wasn't far off. Using these primitive techniques he had managed, through what amounted to recognized scientific method, ninety-nine point nine percent pure copper. The remaining tenth of a percent was made up of a variety of metals, mostly zinc, which would be assiduously difficult enough to separate five thousand years later.

Hyphes broke the silence. "What is before us is the finest copper you have ever beheld. Notice its shimmer as it gives its own light. It is pure, undefiled, whole. It can be ruined easily, but it cannot be improved in any way. Except one. As it is, I could make for you tools or ornaments finer than any you have seen, even finer than the ax head given you by the Leader Kompil."

He let this sink in as they murmured their assent.

"But there is one metal with a power exceeding copper, a metal that by virtue of its greater abilities provides the greater use. You have seen it. You have been given this gift, I am told," he looked at Syros, "from another distant land which I am unfamiliar. A land by the name of Egypt."

"Egypt?" All eyes snapped to Aphrodite when she uttered the word in exclaimed surprise.

Deus held her arm. "You know of Egypt?" To ask her such a thing had never crossed his mind when he was beginning his understanding of her language.

"Egypt is my homeland," she spoke, incomprehensible to the others.

Deus thought he may have understood but chose, wisely as always, to allay the inquiry until another time. It just could be that Aphrodite had not been spirited out of the depths as they had supposed, but rather had come from the land of Egypt. Wouldn't that be an inconceivable instance? Which was more difficult to believe? It could not have been possible to cross so great a distance of water; no it was too difficult to think about right now. His focus had to remain on the smelting process.

"Continue, Hyphes."

"I will ask you once again, for my own peace, to decide if you want this information passed freely amongst your people."

"They are as one with me; and you. What is revealed to me is revealed to all."

Hyphes nodded. "Very well. Then it is time," he said, "to give me a bar of 'anaku'".

Deus had brought them in his side pack, worn differently tonight, with a strap from his midriff to his shoulder instead of around his waist, like a woman of the twentieth century would carry a purse. He had found the tin bars too heavy, along with the tektites he had remaining, to bear in a waist belt. He unwound the thong securing the flap and withdrew one of the silvery bars, handing it with great reverence to Hyphes.

The bar was elongated, rectangular, as is the manner of bars of metal to this day. It wasn't large, only about the volume of a wrapped square of butter, but it was perfect. Hyphes had only determined through his own exhaustive experimentation that the strongest amalgam of tin to copper was one part to nine. He thought this a logical and poetic blend, occurring to him after a time that it was as the hands, ten fingers with one pointing the way. The way was to the future. He could feel it, though he could see it only as through a glass darkly.

His experimentation had led him to an alloy that was only off by the smallest of margins, eleven percent tin being the cutoff point for what could usefully be considered bronze, and seven percent being the ideal.

With his bare hands, he let the bar slip over the side with a protracted plop, a splash of red metal leaping up and falling again, chasing the other element that was already altering history.

The tin would not take long heating to melting point, the phase change occurring at only four-hundred forty-nine degrees, over fifteen hundred degrees less than the melting point of the copper.

Making good use of the time, Hyphes formed a flat piece of clay, rolling and pressing it out with his palms, making a pancake on a wide, flat, stone. He sketched a large, symmetrical shape into the pliable material with a sharpened stick, then pressed the clay down with his fingers creating a depression into which he intended to pour the molten bronze. The depression tapered gently down from the edges to the center; an inverted, double ax. He filled the depression with water, adjusting the indentation until it was level and proportional in all respects. In the very center he pressed it almost through the clay, and coating a stick evenly with the substance, lay the cylindrical shaft along the depression, ensuring a gap where the metal would flow around, under, and over. When all was to his satisfaction, as much as it could be in these crudest of surroundings, he poured off the water, fearing all the while that he might damage the mold. He would have used dry, packed sand to make the casting as was the way his guild, but he wanted a quick polish to the completed form and sand left a roughness which took longer than he wanted to spend to smooth out. The risks were higher this way. The steam produced from the wet clay could bubble up through or into the metal instead of running underneath until it had a chance to harden, ruining the work.

He sized up the volume of metal needed to fill the depression, judging he would easily end up with some leftover. With another piece of clay he rolled out a long, attenuated form, pressing into it a sword image. He wondered if these people had ever seen such a finished product as he was about to show them.

He thrust his stick into the metal. The quality of the tin was wonderful. Almost no slag rose to the top as he stirred. He waited a while, observing closely. The small amount of impurity was limited to what he saw, a thin, broken layer of dark solidification floating on the surface, easily lifted away.

One last thing. He stared at Aphrodite. Her hair had fascinated him from first sight. A single strand lifted and waved, beckoning, calling to him. He approached her slowly, cautious, his eyes never leaving the wisp attracting him. She didn't flinch as he tugged the stray hair gently, pulling it out by the root. He held it, stretching it between his two hands, rotating it in his fingers as he tested its resilience to breakage. It was perfect for his needs.

He wound the hair around his finger loosely, twisted it into a loop, and launched it into the crucible. Hot vapors shriveled the curled hair before it hit the surface, igniting it in a burst of flame and a crackle. Only an ash struck the surface before disintegrating and rising with the stream of heat.

He needed help with the next procedure and gave Deus and Syros the honors. He slipped a fresh branch through the raised holes at the top of the crucible, skillfully selected by Hyphes's trained eye, the midpoint increased to a thickness so that further penetration would have been impossible. Deus and Syros each took a side, lifting the red-hot crucible out of the vent as flames licked its sides. The branch steamed and smoked, hissing and bursting into flame as they moved precisely to the flat stone. Hyphes placed their hands exactly, the edge of the radiant crucible just at the side of the mold, the bottom just below the side.

He reached a hooked branch into the hole protruding from the bottom, snagging the crucible and tipping it slowly upward. He couldn't see the opening now that it was turning away from him and so got down on his knees, crouching ever closer to the earth as he twisted the heavy urn. The brilliant liquid poured out in a thin stream, growing thicker and heavier as he lifted, not too much lest it all splash out at once. It flowed around the mold, finding the lowest places first, trickling into them in a sidewinding, undulating stream. He kept the pour slow as steam hissed from the border of where the clay contacted metal. It dried almost instantaneously as the area covered grew. Carefully, now. Not too much. He eased up gently, controlling the flow. It was done. The mold was full.

It was so much easier to pour bronze than copper. The temperatures reached had to be considerably higher than the melting point to prevent 'freeze-off', instantaneous hardening of the metal on contact with a cooler object such as a mold, much in the same manner that wax hardens immediately upon dripping onto a table. That was a difficult temperature to reach with copper and often resulted in poor pours. It was easy to 'superheat' bronze, having a much lower melting point than copper, being mixed with tin. The melting point of bronze was only sixteen-hundred seventy-five degrees, varying somewhat according to percentages of mix. Raising the temperature three hundred degrees above that to copper melting temperature was easy, although not necessary. Only a couple of hundred degrees were needed to prevent freeze-off.

He motioned the men to the next mold, the long, narrow indentation. He positioned them longways so they would have less chance of error in the pour. He would have barely enough to complete this and did not want to risk spillage. If he had available to him expert apprentices there would not have been any cause for worry, but with these neophytes the chance of missing, even lengthwise, was high.

The sticks were burning fiercely from contact with the crucible and the proximity to the hot metal. They would be too weak to support the crucible soon. Hyphes pushed them along the mold without saying what he was doing. He rarely spoke during a pour, and was so concerned that, even though he tried, he could not think of any words that they could possibly understand. They caught his meaning, feeling the push and allowing themselves to be guided by it. Syros and Deus could easily see what he was about now that they had witnessed first hand the filling of the first mold. They moved slowly forward, pouring the last of the precious metal into the last portion of the indent.

Deus and Syros moved the thick receptacle to the side, lowering it to the ground just as the branch snapped, weakened by fire to the point where it could no longer support the weight. The heavy container dropped but a short distance, thudding off soft earth. Hyphes had no time to wonder if it cracked. For the purposes of this demonstration it did not matter anyway, its job had been accomplished. He rushed over to the waterskin, taking a small amount into his mouth. He was very thirsty and dehydrated from working so close to the heat, but his mind was too focused to think of such trivialities as his own personal needs. He carried it without swallowing, inhaled a huge chestful of air through his nose, and sprayed the castings with a mist of water.

A high-frequency hiss and a cloud of steam filled the air. But he didn't want to cool the bronze too quickly by dumping water directly onto it. There was too little water to waste on runoff, and there was always a danger that the metal could crack. Five times he filled and emptied his mouth in this manner, each time the noise and steam more diminished.

The blackened metal was hard now, enough of its heat having been drained by the clay and exposure to the air and moisture. There were no visible signs of despoliation. He scrutinized them carefully, biting the fleshy inside of his cheek as he moved his face not a hand-span above the new creations. He could still feel the residual heat reflecting off the skin around his eyes, still smell the weak emanation of the metallic scent touching his olfactory awareness.

He turned each form upside down on the rock and gave them a swift stroke, smashing the dried clay clinging fast to the soft underlayers. The bronze pieces enunciated a musical chime as they contacted the granite surface.

Hyphes picked each up with a piece of skin, thermal protection for his hands, wrenching the clay covered stick from its hole within the center of the double ax. They were still too hot to touch with bare hands but not so hot that they would burn thick hide. He banged them together, a metallic reverberation sounding loud and echoing through the silent night, the scaly oxide which forms on metals brought to a high temperature flaking off.

This achievement was momentous, marking a extraordinary change in the history of mankind. The onset of the Bronze Age.

Bronze had been forged and worked in scattered areas of the world for almost a millennia, but always in small quantity and for a limited time. Tin supplies were sporadic and scarce, and because of the secrecy attached to the metalsmith's field of endeavor the knowledge spread slowly, even dying completely in some places, forever lost.

Not this time.

With the pieces as clean as they could be from banging them together Hyphes dropped them into the shallow of water used for cleaning the copper. Hissing as they broke the surface and boiling only for a moment, the water hushed to a simmer that quickly died. He reached in with his bare hands, removing them from the murky water, the warmth a sensuality that tingled up his arms and into his temples. He rubbed sand into his new creations until all of the black was abraded away and the polished chestnut colored tools, or weapons, gleamed in the Moonlight.

When he was done, he held the dark implements forward for inspection. He tilted them for effect, reflecting the weak beams of the fully risen Moon into the eyes of each in turn. The sides of the double ax and the sword, which had been the upper surfaces after the pour, were perfectly smooth and flat, catching the light with the utmost efficiency.

Deus took the double ax with reverence and respect, holding it before him. He placed two fingers into the center hole, then held it to his eye, aiming it at the Moon. He found a long branch, about arm's length, which had been set aside as a fire poker. It was just the right diameter to fit inside. He pushed the handle in until it was snug and held the ax high.

"This is the symbol of our union, our coupling," he said as he stood beside his magnificent woman, almost touching her as he spoke. "Two joined, separate yet as one. Minos and Aphrodite."

He brought the double-bladed ax head down to eye level as he turned it, admiring the two distinctly separate curvatures narrowing to the center, bound and supported on the long handle. The poetry of the contours, the composition of form.

Aphrodite held out a hand to the shaft of the ax handle, gripping it just below his own. He looked at her, her eyes at the height of his shoulders, her breasts prominent and firm in the cooling night air away from the forge, their association with the double ax patent.

The resolute love he felt for this woman.

BRONZE

~~~~~~

Chapter 9

Minos

There was not a crewmember among them who could not direct the company, calling rhythm or taking the oar in the stroke position to harmonize their rowing style as befitting the protean sea conditions. In a calm, the long stroke was preferable, but on occasion when the water was roused to a chop, a shorter and more arduous stroke was fundamental to maintaining control as the boat pitched and yawed.

Each oar had acquired its own individual attributes. They knew the distinctive idiosyncrasies and which was too stiff, too heavy, or unbalanced and warped. Others were too light or flexible, while the favored few had just the right amount of spring. They found themselves, in the long run, looking forward to the rotation of crew reliefs and the change that put their hands around a good blade.

They had become obsessed with keeping the craft on an even keel. After countless hours at the oar, they had become as cognizant as a spirit level to deviations from the horizontal. If they varied in trim only half a degree off the plane, those on the upper side found it twice as hard to reach the water with their blade and the oarsmen on the down side were easily fouled. The howls of protest were immediate, sending the reliefs hopping to the high side to maintain an even cant.

On the occasion when one slipped off the oar in mid-stroke, caused by a surprise current combined with inattention, the hapless rower would find himself catapulted backward into the bilges. No one laughed anymore. They were dead with fatigue, and it had happened more than once too often.

They had only made one stop at the eastern tip of Kriti, an uninhabited place as far as they could tell with an impressive backdrop of mountains lined up from the southern to northern shores, effectively isolating this part of the island from the rest. Somewhere people must have inhabited the region, but for the day and night they spent resting and grazing the calves they saw no sign of anyone. Except for some cursory exploring they did not expend much effort into locating other settlements.

The surrounding region was lovely, green, meadowed, wonderfully scenic and pensive. As Deus, Minos had contemplated the panoramic vista he had felt inspired to dedicate the area where they camped to the future of the realm, an individual but integral limb of the nation which would become known only by his name, the Minoans, the people of Minos, the 'bees'. The special place where they had stood under the light of the waning Moon, its shape now halved and flattened along the top as the horizon of sunlight continued its twenty-eight day migration along and back across its surface, he saw as a magnificent structure teeming with people of the highest intelligence and ability, an organized society greater than any he had come across or previously envisioned. A society without grandiose yearnings for massive tombs or ridiculous strongholds. The sea would protect them from any enemy, the Mother Selene from themselves.

Jobah had, at Minos's instruction, built a large rendition of the Moon in its precise shape at that time. There they left it, perched on a rock on top of a larger one, a simple monument to their being there, a symbol to the future and an indication of the greater monument to be built at that time.

Now the journey was almost complete. They had taken the northern shore instead of returning to their starting point on the south coast, at the home of these brothers who had born him to the beginnings of his destiny. They passed many villages and in spite of temptation and desire they continued on, passing them for the preference of isolation, stopping again at only one place to rest, give the calves relief, and dedicate the land in the same manner as the last, again leaving a monument this time with a slight deviation to the flattened upper surface, a concave depression pressed measly into the thick, flat Moon. The image of the Moon as something three dimensional was something that would never occur to any of them.

Minos donned his purple robe as Amnisos came into view, the island of Dia ahead and on their right. How small it looked, how close, settled offshore only a short row away by the standards he now found himself inured to. He reminisced about how unimaginably far and unreachable the island seemed in his childhood, even not so long ago.

* * *

The old woman settled to enjoy her view of the sea and the island in the distance. Behind her was a low hill densely covered in carob trees. She was in a quietly contemplative state, finally accepting the loss of her husband. He was a dear man, always kind and gentle with her all the years they had been together. She had lost count long ago, being like most who lost track shortly after they ran out of fingers. She was a dear woman too, much loved by the people of Amnisos. Her husband led them, and judged them when required, always fairly and to the satisfaction of most. He had been the town Chieftain. And now he was dead.

It had been a quiet death. A cerebral artery had ballooned into an aneurysm after years of rising blood pressure. The courteous solicitude of the townsfolk, knowing of his love for the fattest parts of sheep, deer, wild pigs, anything animate and edible, left these parts with his wife for her to cook up for his enjoyment. He thoroughly enjoyed their generosity, and his wife wasn't above sharing in these gifts. The two of them were the fattest people around.

The Chieftain had fished until the day before his death, still pleasantly harassed by the people who loved him most that his boat would surely sink if he brought aboard more than a few extra pounds of fish. The aneurysm growing unbeknownst to him within the confines of his skull had exploded while he slept. He didn't even grunt when it happened. His cranium filled quickly with blood, compressing his brain and rendering any chance of regaining consciousness impossible. As the pressure built, his brain was squeezed out through the only exit available, the hole at the base of the skull where the spinal cord makes its exit from the brain and carries the chemical and electrical signals to and from the rest of the body. The medulla, the brain stem, the respiratory control center, was pinched off from its blood supply as it compacted into the too-small foramen, and like any other part of the body would die from oxygen deprivation. In only a few minutes his breathing slowed and stopped. His heart raced, furiously striving for life-sustaining oxygen and finding none. In only a few minutes more it, too, weakened, fluttered, and then stalled. It was over. He was dead.

And now she sat, picking at her flatbread, still warm after being rushed to her by a kind friend who also knew that the old woman still needed time to herself to reflect adequately on her husband's life. Now that her grief was passing, remembering the good times in a less traumatic frame of mind was an important part of sending her dead on with dignity. All of his friends would have done that for him by now. It was her duty to do the same. Then a new Chief could be chosen.

Normally the son of the dead or infirm Chief would be the first consideration, although the town could veto the choice. But in this case, there was no son. The only child they had conceived drowned while he was fishing recklessly in a storm to show his bravery. She had not born any others. The villagers would sometimes tease her that coupling must be impossible for them because of their size, but it was good natured and no offense was ever taken. It was up in the air, now, who would lead the village. That was part of the responsibility placed on the shoulders of the old woman. She had to make the suggestion to the people of who she would support as her 'son'.

* * *

They stood together at the bow as the ship ground to an easy halt on the sandy bottom. The quickly gathered village congregation stood silent and open-mouthed at the sight. The ship dwarfed anything that floated in their harbor, the young man with his familiar face standing proud in an intensely purple cloth robe, a color never before seen, and the most perfectly desirable golden-haired woman who patently defied even the imagination of dreams.

They had pulled up beside an even, rocky prominence abutting from the shore, the ship skillfully brought to rest against it. Deus dismounted first, giving arm to his bride as she alighted. One by one they followed, first Syros, then the others leading the unbelievable calves.

The abutment made for a perfect stage, higher than the surrounding beach and allowing the carry of voice over a wide area. He made a chest. "People of Amnisos. I have been chosen by Gods to lead you, to unite and lead all of the people of this island. I have left you as Deus, who exists no more. I have returned as Minos."

He raised his arms wide, spreading his legs and stepping to the side to give room between himself and Aphrodite, the drapes of rich purple hanging regally in folds down to his waist. "These before you are soldiers of good will, here to assist all, each and every one of you, in achieving your highest expectations. None shall ever righteously want without having that want realized. None shall ever be found who will have to beg for food or raiment. The great Mother Selene will assure your needs will be met as ours have been, trusting in Her in faith and voyaging beyond the limits of knowledge in the waters of the deep."

He faced his bride. "This woman before you stands as wife to me." His voice amplified and echoed from the twisted rock bluffs. "Let it be known from the beginning that Aphrodite, for that is how she is to be known, is for no man other than myself. She is sacred, a gift from the Earth Mother, risen from the sea as a gift in the night under the witness of the Moon."

Aphrodite stood as her royal upbringing had taught her in civic occasions, head up, chest prominent and full, body straight, every attempt to be made to appear taller than reality would allow. Not a wrinkle in her linen skirt presented itself. She had worked the material constantly from the time they left Kypros, flattening it with her palms, ensuring no fold was caught under her seat which would press into permanence. For all the travel, survival, and rough existence, her form and features were of flawless stature, befitting the princess that she was and the Goddess to which she was now to be endeared.

* * *

Zeus released his clasp on his son. How different he appeared now. It had not been that long, the Moon completing just more than two full cycles. What a surprise it had been, his son Rectus running furiously toward him as he reposed in sight of the flock, shouting that a large contingent of strangers was approaching from the north and that he didn't know who they might be, dangerous or not.

And who should they be but his awaited son? Zeus had known, felt inside the reassurance that comes with hope, that his boy would return soon. But who ever would have imagined a return such as this? A new name, a wife, a solid association of confreres, wonderful wealth, and rich attire.

And these calves. What magnificent creatures. The male had rudimentary horns developing, erupting sideways out of his ridged forehead. He grasped the stubs on the young bull's head, holding firm as it tried halfheartedly in annoyance to break the grip. Zeus stared at it, deep into its huge black orbs with his own eyes, pulling back once as it gave a final flick of its nose upward before settling in complacence. What enormous eyes. He could see, as it were, his own image, inverted he thought, somewhere in the depths of the lens, buried in the blackness of the spherical organ.

"This is a magnificent animal, perfect in all ways that I can see. His whiteness, his strength." He released one horn and let his hand caress the iron sinews of the beast's neck and shoulder. "Even his intellect. See how he stares back at me. There is inner strength as well. And hatred. This animal is capable of killing if given the opportunity. It is our good fortune that he is too small to be of great danger."

Minos smiled at his father. "These calves are babies."

Zeus gasped and stood. "Babies?"

"I chose them both for their perfection, the white male the most perfect of any in the wealth of cattle in the distant lands. The parents of both are the finest animals you have imagined, huge, powerful. And I, too, was drawn by the spirit of this animal and his intelligence. You will see it grow rapidly. I see a difference already after only meager rations and an arduous and unnatural journey. You will see. They will both be enormous, and the male will be the largest with a shoulder as high as yours and a weight as much as twenty rams."

"You have been associating with too many fishers."

"What I speak is true, my Father."

Zeus conceded. "As you say, so it is."

Zeus considered the others now that the formal reunion between himself and his son was concluding. The beauty of the girl had not escaped him, wonderful with her exposed breasts and tapered waist. Many of the women in the village let themselves be seen this way in the summer heat, or when assisting their husbands the odd time netting fish from shore. Usually it was the youngest of the women, still unattached, who removed their tops or rolled down their dresses to the waist, mostly to catch the eyes of the young men who were more often than not far too bashful to be caught looking their way. The only ones who paid obvious attention were the married men who, in this monogamous society, had to suffer the berations of their wives for their mental infidelities.

"The sheep have lambed," Minos observed. These are excellent animals, perhaps the finest yet."

"They are, my son. Your ways of breeding them to purity have paid off in producing the finest sheep in the land. I don't doubt you have similar plans in store for the calves."

"You know me too well. Yes. I will populate Kriti with these beasts. You cannot imagine how fine their milk tastes, how succulent their meat. These two must be protected even at the loss of life if necessary. Of all the animals I was able to choose from these were the best, even unrecognized by my benefactor. The finest cattle in the world will reside here on this island, along with the finest of everything else. You will see, Father, exalted in your place in this world in which we live. And as you will live eternally in spirit so shall your name live forever in the minds of men."

Zeus got that evanescent feeling again, that feeling born of the spirit, tingling the spine and raising goosebumps to the skin. "You know we must visit your Mother's grave."

"I know it."

* * *

They all contributed to gathering wood for the fire. Even Aphrodite felt she should help, careful to choose only clean pieces so she would not dirty herself but still selecting pieces at the limit of what she could carry. She was not about to let these people think ill of her in any way and certainly not because they might by chance consider her weak or lazy. She determined to work quickly, her lean muscles firm and rippling beneath her tanned skin, and with the dignity befitting her standing in life. It would have been unthinkable to be doing this in Egypt, but there who knew what she might have had forced upon her by now? A little servant's work, if participated in by all, was not going to be something she would hold beneath her.

While they busied themselves Zeus took advantage of their distraction and unsealed the secret place where he had cached the iron goddess. He removed the bundle, swaddled in oilskins for protection, and appeared to any other not paying him much mind to be holding only another short section of wood.

The fire swelled in the diminishing light as they piled on more fuel, lighting the dark side of the vaulted stone tomb a few paces away. Venus, the Evening Star, shone brightly, solitary, not far from the western horizon.

The group had been restricted to the few crew members and Deus's family. He knew it was too unlikely to last as the villagers almost begged to be let in on the travel inland. His promises, promises made with the utmost sincerity, to return in a few days only partially assuaged their desire to follow. Sure enough, as he scanned the hilltop to the north, the silhouettes of bodies rose, only visible because of the remaining twilight. There did not seem to be too many, and he could almost feel their longing to be part of the proceedings. With a raised arm he beckoned to them, standing in the bright light of the fire so his meaning could not be misinterpreted. One by one they got up the courage to proceed forward, the trailing ones moving quickly to catch up with the more intrepid. As they congregated, no more than a dozen added now to their number and almost half of them women, he began.

"I am now known as Minos," he said quietly to his father.

"As you were known to your Mother."

"Yes. She knows me best, knows all of us. In time all of our people will be known by that name."

He addressed the now gathered. "Observe the Evening Star. Contemplate it silently as it sinks over the side. You have noticed how it appears alone while the sky is still bright? It is the strongest of the stars, closely associated with the warmth of the sun, following it, embracing it most of the time. Not always may it be seen, usually so closely wrapped in the arms of light. Only at times, when they separate briefly can we see her. She, also, is born of the Mother of the Earth and, as all daughters, has left her mother for the warm emissions of her husband."

He embraced his bride. "The Evening Star was bright when Aphrodite came out of the sea to me. It will always be the symbol of her arrival, always the symbol of her birth out of the womb of the Moon, swollen in fullness. I give the Evening Star her name. The star, when it appears, shall forever be associated with her beauty, her love, pleasure, and serenity."

He kissed her.

"Now then, observe the star until she sets. Then be still. The fire will warm us until the Moon rises."

* * *

During the three days that they had resided with the people of Amnisos, the shadow had continued gouging at the concavity of the Moon. It was rising again, the graduated changes always a miracle, not even noticed by the majority sleeping in their beds. In only a few hours the sun would once again return the day. The crescent of the waning Moon was only seen in the night just before the sun rises, and only for a few days each month before it was eaten completely away by the permanent shadow of its dark side.

The points of the crescent were more upturned than what was normally viewed from more northerly latitudes. Far into the future people of the "civilized" world of Europe, North America, and Japan, twenty to thirty degrees farther north, would hardly recognize a penciled drawing of the Moon if it was oriented with the points upturned to the degree that the Moon presented itself here. They would think that it was rather a rendition of a bowl or would have to mentally rotate the drawing to associate it with the Moon.

"See the rising Mother." Minos spoke with clarity and volume as the others stirred themselves and concentrated on the sight. "The Mother of the Earth, the creator of this land; the Mother of this, her daughter, Aphrodite; the Mother of myself, Minos; and the Mother of all of you. I have taken Aphrodite as a wife and uphold her as a sister. She is one with me, of my blood, united with my soul eternally in this land and the next."

The fire was raging behind them, performing bands of light cast along the ground, long dancing shadows from the surrounding scattered boulders.

"This is the place of Selene's burial." He directed them to the ossuary where she lay. "She exceeded all in her love and goodness. She led a peaceful life, content to guide and raise her family in the ways of living, supporting their needs and staving off contention and danger, danger often found deep within. Her ways were not the ways of man, not given to violence or malicious conniving, rather she gave herself to healing conflict, quiet meditation, and long-suffering. While in this life she had little understanding of her grand importance, the veil of forgetfulness having been drawn about herself while here to experience every joy and disappointment, every pain and pleasure, without the advantage of knowing what lay in wait at her return to the realms above. At last, when all was done, and I was of age to begin my mission, she could return, her life having been taken of purpose and sealed in blood by forces opposing her in every way, by the forces of evil manifest in every creature as the forces of good are. Her mind, if you can let it impress upon you, will always guide you in her ways, the only ways that are acceptable to those who will abide with her forever in the heavens after these feeble impermanent bodies return to dust.

"My charge is to unite the children of this island of Kriti, to bring them into one room in one house, sheltered in the unadulterated faith of the Earth Mother. When that happens, and the path may be long and tortuous, we will rule everywhere from here, Knossos, the central point of knowledge and the spiritual center of the world. Bury no longer your dead little ones under the floors of your houses, not even the stillborn. Bury them with the adults. They deserve as much. Use caves if you must, but for those of you with me this night, you will feel that this is the true way, as you see here, the arching vault in similitude of the arching heavens above."

Zeus passed the wrap to his son who unveiled the iron icon. He held it aloft after reverently considering it in both hands pressed close to his bosom.

"This is the image of Selene, sent to me from the heavens as a portent of the future when I was but an infant. Feel it, every one of you. Feel the sacred substance, the substance of the stars. It came blinding white with intensity and fire, rushing toward me with a speed and volume not matched by violent winter storms. See how it cooled into this invincible icon, this image of the Earth Mother as she lived among us. Touch her. Imagine her with us."

Hyphes, how many times was it now, was amazed. How many more surprises could Minos present to him?

Minos took the idol around, insisting that even the shy and the unworthy should have their turn. "Swear your devotion. Give yourselves in every way to Selene. Use this celestial gift as a focus for your thoughts and imagine it in your minds where you cannot see her in reality."

He took it around again, slowly, giving them time.

The dedication of Knossos began.

He placed the idol on the ground, facing them. From inside his robe, he withdrew the three tektites from their place in his pouch and placed them in a row a hand-width apart. In the smoothed off soil, between and below the other three, he drew two small circles with his finger, the two feet of the 'W'.

"As those of our ancestry before us have resided in this place, living their lives and returning to the ground beneath, let us also live here. Permanently this time, never allowing our residences to crumble without rebuilding, never turning away because of hardship, never leaving for another place of our own desire without direction from our guide."

He did not know, only felt, that here people once dwelt. Beneath their very feet lay the layers of two thousand years of occupation, intermittent as inhabitants came and went, sometimes abandoning the villages completely. The wide meadows were ideal for raising sheep but with random skirmishes and disease outbreaks the area was now and then left vacant, sometimes for a century or more, until times such as this when a family or organized group would establish themselves.

"Of the ten dedicated places on this island this place is greatest, the root and trunk, the head and heart. Selene's blessings are upon it. See how she forms herself." He raised his arms high, the light material of the purple robe sliding down to his shoulders, baring his arms. "We will dedicate this place, Knossos, with an image in her likeness, exactly as we see her observing us."

He addressed Jacobah. "Bring forward the young bull."

Jacobah approached, nervous because he had become so attached to the young bull, worrying that Minos may be considering sacrificing the creature that he knew was the only of its kind on this island.

The calf was placid in the darkness, the Moon and stars soothing its temper.

"This white calf will assume the very semblance of power and strength found in man, exceeding it in every way except knowledge and wisdom. By this animal man will be judged, found complete or wanting, worthy of life or servitude, or death. Only the athletic and wise will able to stand before him. But the choice will always be theirs, voluntary, never to be enforced."

He stroked the calf. He had grown close to it as one builds a fondness and then a love for a pet. He had felt this way about his sheep, remembering how hard it was when they had to be killed. Especially that first time. His eyes clouded, only for a moment, as he recalled that time when his brothers laughed and held him back as he protested and cried. His dead brothers.

He gave his head a twitch as he brought his concentration back to bear.

"As this calf grows its horns will grow, as did his sire's before him. Such is the way. Such has always been the way. The child unites and blends attributes of the father and the mother. Sometimes more of one than the other, sometimes the worst parts instead of the best. In this creature you see the best of both the mother and the father. This creature is perfect. But only perfect for its type. Compared to other things, other people, it is not perfect. And so it will be a measure, whether anon those who choose shall compare to it."

He stroked the stubby horns. "These are as the points of the Crescent Moon. As they grow they will come to represent the Moon as we see her now. The image that Jobah shall construct at this place shall have dual significance, the commiseration and mercy of the Mother of the Earth, and the harsh and unforgiving judgment of the bull. The male and the female. Neither alone. Neither possible, one without the other."

* * *

"I never tire of looking out upon this place." Minos and Aphrodite gazed down from the summit of the hill overlooking Knossos.

Jobah, in the distance, was constructing another clay rendition of the Moon at crescent. The first was unsatisfactory to both he and Minos, not because of quality but position. It had originally been oriented to the eastern horizon in anticipation of the Moon's rising but something about the mountain backdrop appealed to them. Minos had held his peace as he contemplated the surrounding landscape with his ugly, pock-faced brother. It was Jobah who had spoken first.

"That mountain draws me. It calls. It's white dome flashes at me in the brightness of the day, and even in the darkness of the night its silhouette pulls my eyes. There is a spirit there. Something not there before the dedication of this place."

"It is the symbol which you have built. That is what draws the attention of the mountain. This place, without the dedication, was as any other place, no more sacred than anywhere else. Now it has become the center of all. It is only right for the mountains themselves to notice and call to us."

Jobah, the quiet potter, considered this in his usual silence. Minos had left him alone with his thoughts, until the next day. Then he noticed Jobah troubled, arms wrapped tightly around his knees, struggling within with some unexpressed thought or opinion. Just a little longer. Jobah was too reserved to say much of what he thought, his life's experience telling him that it was of little matter to anyone, why should he allow it to be of any matter to himself? Whatever he expressed, his idea would be mocked. Or would it? These people treated him with respect. They appreciated his work. He hadn't used his best skills as a wheel-potter since leaving Ugarit, and even the metal-smith had the capacity to make pottery with skill by hand alone. All he had done so far was live off the charity of those who said they were his brothers. He was having a hard time accepting that, but he wanted to more than anything.

Brothers. It was meant in an ecumenical sense, not a literal one. He could not be the blood brother of any of these people, but as fond as he was of them he found it hard to believe that this wasn't going to come crashing down around him one day. He had given his heart so often only to have it crushed cruelly every time.

Minos seemed so genuinely concerned and impressed with him. Why? Why him? He had been of use though, hadn't he? Minos had asked him at each dedicatory place to construct the Moon images. That was something, and something important, wasn't it? Of course it was.

The crescent was simply facing the wrong way. That didn't matter for now at the other sites. They were a long way from being even started. The images were only markers of an area to develop in the future. They could be changed at that time. But this, this Knossos, was going to be developed now. It was unconscionable to situate the marker in anything but the correct position. It had to be moved, or redone.

"Master," he called him. "Minos. I must speak with you about the crescent." At last he had summoned the courage to speak.

"Yes. You must."

Now what did Minos mean? He was too agreeable. Was he upset about the quality of the representation? He would have to do it better next time. "I am not pleased with the way I have made it."

"In what way?" He had to encourage Jobah to speak his mind.

"The crescent has to face the mountain. Forgive me for saying so." He flushed and looked timid.

"Thank you, Jobah. You know I value everything you have to say." Jobah could not believe what he was hearing. "You may start work at once. We will have further ceremony when the new one is finished." He could see that Jobah was still unsure. All he could do was reach out to his friend and hold him to his breast. Slowly Jobah hugged back. His self-esteem had been so badly crippled over the years that he found it, even now, too difficult to cope with the reassurances Minos was giving him.

"Pray with all your might to Selene. She will guide you in the exact way to sculpt your work."

Minos. Surely he would be the patriarch of all men.

* * *

Aphrodite sat quietly beside her husband, taking comfort in his simple presence. She was bemused by his wandering mind. The vacant expression on his handsome face told her that he was somewhere else. She didn't mind and pressed herself closer, her left arm folded around his right, her head resting comfortably on his shoulder.

The arm squeeze brought him back. He smiled at her beauty wondering how he could have wandered again, as he did so frequently. There was so much to think about, so many distractions. But none could compare with his wife.

She wore a linen cape over her shoulders, pulled around the front with only her deep cleavage showing. Even in Egypt the women didn't walk around with their breasts exposed all of the time. That was for special occasions, or whenever they felt like it, but mainly special occasions, religious rites or public ceremonies. Her skin tanned easily, and wasn't prone to burning from the sun, but the unseen higher end of the spectrum could take its toll on even the hardiest skin if one didn't take some care. And her natural skin was lighter than most and so less protected.

She could feel the irritating sting of the minor burn on her shoulders and the upper flesh of her jutting breasts. Days of exposure, even through the clouds, had burned her on the horizontal surfaces.

Minos unwove his arm from hers and slipped his hand under the covering of the cape. He wrapped his arm around her waist, spreading his hand and following the curves of her tight skin. She tensed a little, a tingle of anticipation and hope sweeping through her loins.

He pulled her closer, tighter, and she lifted her tender mouth to meet his affectionately. He would not make love to her out here in the open, unsheltered by trees, in the daylight where any could see. It was pleasure enough just to kiss and caress.

They lay back onto the padding of the soft grass, continuing in their bridled passion. Minos reached forth with his free hand and untied the two lace bows binding the front of her shawl. He sat up to look at her, to envelop her with his eyes, feasting on the picture as she spread the covering and bared her chest to his view.

The sun felt good on her skin, having been relieved of it for a while. A warm glow spread through her body then rushed back into her hips. She writhed imperceptibly, lifting a knee and spreading it to the side while tightening her muscles, a charge of fresh air inhaling into her skirt, enlivening her, exciting her. She tensed and relaxed her thighs and buttocks, the feelings of exhilaration building in her groin with repetitive undulations.

Minos felt little different. She could see he was ready himself. He was such a handsome man, his chest smooth and bared. His soft short beard was something she could live without, but she would broach that subject at a discreet and more appropriate time.

He pulled at the tucked-in flap of the sarong wrapped tight around her waist, freeing it. He slowly, sensuously, drew it aside, opening the skirt on one side and then the other, spreading the folds of the cloth wide and caring to stretch it smooth like a blanket, forcing the grass below it flat.

He thought it every time, said it every time; she was wonderful to behold. Her narrow hips, narrow but rounder and more full than his own, were offset by her waspish waist at the perfect ratio of seven to ten. Even in older women, heavier women, down through the ages to modern times, the ratio would remain the constant in judging the most desirable, perfect figure. Weights would change according to time, fashion, and culture, but the seven to ten waist/hip ratio wouldn't.

He lay against her and they held their kiss long.

Farther down the sloping incline near where the work was being done by Jobah eyes were keeping watch over the couple. Voyeurism was nothing new nor would it ever become something old. And with that voyeurism went its brother jealousy, a wanton desire for something, someone in this case, that was unobtainable in any normal circumstance.

It was unfair. Unjust. Look at her rolling in the grass with him. Too bad the grass was so tall. It was hard to see. If Minos had been anyone else he would have gone over and taken her himself. As long as his opponent wasn't much of a fighter.

Better to take her alone. Sometime. He could wait. He could always wait.

Just like all the other times. The harlots. They were all harlots. The way they spread for other men.

They would spread for him.

They always did.

* * *

Aphrodite stood with Minos, the right half of the inseparable pair. They were as indivisible as Siamese twins. Syros had joined them, just returned from Amnisos and his ship. He couldn't bring himself to leave it for more than a day or two except under the most demanding circumstances, and there was nothing terribly demanding about this place as far as he was concerned. He did like the walk, though. It did him good, built his strength and stamina, and let him use

212

his legs in a way he couldn't on the ship. And a brisk walk uphill was as good as a steady row across the sea.

"Will it take you long to get to Magnesia?"

"You should come along and see for yourself," he joked. Minos and the beautiful girl smiled at him. "Your journeying is far from at an end. Bring your wife. She'll bring us good luck."

That was a comment. No women were ever allowed on board boats. It just wasn't done. Aphrodite must have been one of the first but, of course, the circumstances were quite different. She was no ordinary woman, but even if she were Syros would have been obliged to transport her to a safe haven upon Minos's request. But he wouldn't have liked it. And now here he was inviting Aphrodite along almost as he would another crewmember. She held even Syros rapt in the spell of her charm.

Minos kept his silence for a while, the eagerness on his wife's face revealing she was all too ready to go along. He looked through the uplifted points of the finished crescent Jobah had finished the day before. The mix of rocks and clay worked smooth was still pliant and its form fragile even though the surface showed a dry skin. Fine cracks were developing which Jobah said he would rub with watered down clay at times through the day. That would keep the cracks filled and prolong and even out the drying process. Who knew how long this sculpture would take to dry? None of them had seen anything on this scale, except Aphrodite who kept any comment, which might appear as boasting, to herself. Jobah had said he was already working on some way to fire the job to an indestructible hardness. Minos was hesitant to tell him that even though it was now oriented to the degree of perfection that they wanted it was still not going to be a permanent fixture. It would last long enough as it was, assuming Jobah could keep chunks from crumbling off in the very long time it would take to dry.

The view was as it had been intended. The huge mountain to the south, rising high, was unerringly framed in the upturned arms of the crescent. Mount Juktas, as it would be known, the bearded man, the dead man. From where they stood the bearded face lay cradled in the arms of the bowl-like crescent Moon, supine, facing the sky, everlastingly contemplating the universe above for this moment and forever. The aura the picture wrought was only partially disturbed by the supporting struts Jobah had propped against the sides of the points to keep them from sagging or collapsing. They could come off when the sculpture was completely dry, and not before, he had said.

"Magnesia," he said again, pulling himself free of the sight. "Would you come with us on another sea voyage?" he asked.

She smiled and nodded once, preferring to keep her voice for when only her beloved could hear. He had been working with her on the language barrier and he was clearly the master at learning. He had been able to remember every word she had taught him, where she struggled to learn his language. She felt she was doing well considering but wished she had the innate linguistic abilities her husband possessed. But it would come in time, as all things must. Then she would have the confidence to speak in public. For now, her silence only abetted the legends that were already being built around her, making her appear more noble and wise.

"Syros, you mentioned an island with a large obsidian supply."

"Yes. It is known as Melos. It is not a large island, and no one lives there for its lack of water. It is a good resting place, about halfway to Magnesia. We always take some obsidian back with us."

"This time we will take some to Magnesia, as much as we can carry. It will be as useful to the people there as it is to ours here. Wherever we travel we should be laden with goods to merchandise. On the way back we will stop for more for our own people to fashion into finished tools. Then, after that, we will be able to take the finished goods to trade and they will have all the more value. In time we will have things as rich and desirable as those offered in the land to the south, the land of Egypt."

Aphrodite pricked up her ears again at the mention of the name. She hoped they weren't talking about a voyage to Egypt. That was the last place she wanted to visit, fearing she would never get away again. She recalled some nostalgic remembrances but had no real love for the place. She missed her father to a degree, but even then not that much. After all, he hadn't protested her removal to an unknown place and she harbored a thought that he had betrayed her. It was only by the greatest of good fortune that she had found a place that was better and a love that could never be equaled. She had been closest to a few of her sisters around the same age and she wanted to see them again, but she didn't want to go back just for them, other than to take them away to this idyllic place where there was happiness, and men who were not offensive. As the thought drifted through her mind, she concluded that they would probably not want to ever leave their security in the royal city. The abuse by the priests would be treated as it always was and in time they would be brainwashed into accepting their activity, and they would embrace it and pass it on as their mothers had. They would have their reward; comfortable living space, good food but not too much lest they get fat, fine clothing, and the adulation of a population who knew no better. All for servicing the sexual proclivities of the priests. As time moved along in its endless progression, leaving them behind to age, they would be passed down through the ranks of lesser priests and, finally, to the members of the public who could afford them, the majority of the gifts and oblations given to sustaining the priesthood.

Only the chosen few virgins would be married off to men who needed to seal their allegiance to Pharaoh. But those were usually the ugly ones, the ones the priests suggested as having the highest spiritual quality, a requirement befitting consorts of royalty. The most beautiful, of which set she knew she belonged, were kept for the pleasures of the priests, and Pharaoh himself, who was hardly above a dalliance or even marriage with one of his own daughters.

Yes, she was fortunate to have fallen into Pharaoh's good graces. And appreciative as she was, she hoped she would never have to thank him in person. His wisdom had dictated that she seek out and ally herself, for Egypt, with the king or leader of this land, and that is what she had done. Pharaoh had kept the ugly ones for those rulers making overtures to Egypt. This was the other way around and so an ugly one simply wouldn't do.

Perhaps there was an unseen, guiding hand in all of this. She was beginning to wonder, listening to her husband as he spoke of such matters. Perhaps she had just underestimated the intuitive abilities of her father. He was, after all, the king of the greatest civilization known to that point in time. Even though Egypt was in its infancy, with mighty construction projects like the pyramids and temples in a future not yet come, it had still been well established for over one thousand years, organized with orders of scribes, astronomers, and arithmeticians who, entrenched by a sanctioned priesthood set in their ways, still managed to make periodic discoveries and achievements.

As the men spoke, the words became too strange for her. Soon she could not decipher them at all, they having drifted into more complex speech. Her mind drifted even more to the past events of her life. She began to scratch in the dirt with the short stick she had taken to walking with. A few circles, a few squares. As she traveled back, she drew hieroglyphs like the ones she had been taught through her own simple curiosity as a child, the pictographic script of the ancient Egyptians where the symbols are conventionalized pictures of the things represented.

Soon she became aware of the silence. She looked up from her writing and saw that Minos and Syros had been watching her intently.

Minos squatted beside the drawings, fascinated by the displayed artistic flair he had not known his wife had possessed. "What is this you are drawing?"

It had only been something she had been absentmindedly doing and she was almost as surprised as he to see what she had done. "This is my father's name. Pharaoh. And this is my name," she said pointing with her stick at the enclosed line of animals. "Each animal has a certain sound attached to it, part of the animal's name or a sound that it is known to make. Together the sounds make a word or, here encompassed by this line, indicate someone's name."

Minos was thinking furiously. "Are you saying that anyone could look at this picture and know what it means?"

"Yes. If they knew how to read. Most people can't. We have scribes who write most things. Priests are fairly able. More people can read than write, although I can't imagine why that would be so. Maybe when they see an image, they are called hieroglyphs, their mind is refreshed in some way and they can recall what they are seeing. If they are writing a word with nothing in front of them they cannot remember. The mind is known for such tricks."

"Yes," Minos said remotely, detached. "The mind does play tricks." He was tracing the drawings with his own finger, imagining.

Hieroglyphs.

Hieroglyphs. Actually writing a name so someone else could understand. He was intense. Something had been nagging him ever since he was a young boy learning to count and having to say things over and over in his head so he wouldn't forget. If he'd had a way to write those numbers down he could have relaxed with the knowledge that even if he had forgotten he could have simply looked at what he had written and all would have been well. Instead, how many times did he count over and over the flocks to be sure he had counted right the first time? The time he could have saved to contemplate the weightier matters of life, lost because he had no way to record.

The ingenuity. The innovation.

The simplicity.

He wanted to scream. Of course. Writing. Symbols. Scribed indicators of other things. How many times had he drawn in the sand? Pictures, maps, stars in the sky? How could he be so stupid?

He saw right away that Aphrodite's way was too complex. If each word was as many characters as she had drawn it would take forever to write even minimally. There should be no more than a few characters for any word, and preferably only one.

And he needed characters for numbers. Eventually, as trade increased in the way that he knew it would, they would all need to be proficient in counting and keeping track of stock. And for that, they would need numbers.

This was too much of a heady experience for Minos. He stood, cursing his own vapid imbecility at the same time as he was giving thanks for this fervent revelation. He was chagrined as much as he was elated. What an emotional upheaval. Another debt of gratitude was owed to his beloved. The thrill of excitement embracing him made him want to take his woman far away so he could ravish her. That is how they spoke of it although there was more aggression on her part than his. She had been a virgin but had been schooled in the arts of lovemaking, and there was very little she hadn't heard, seen, or dreamed about. She had been trained in the skills of experts from a very early age, techniques Minos had never heard of or imagined.

He wanted that now. Her touch.

But he restrained himself, putting up a reserved front. He would not appear rude to his brother Syros. As important as this new great subject of writing was, as important as his feelings and needs were for his wife, he was still in conversation with his brother about their next travel.

~~~~~~

Chapter 10

Reflections

2899 BCE

The ewe bled tremendously as a lamb issued forth from its vagina.

Minos knew the little creature had no chance of being properly nurtured by his dying mother. She made weak attempts to lick clean her blinking newborn, the poignant feebleness of her effort heart moving. Not ten feet away was a ewe who had given birth to a stillborn lamb, fully and perfectly formed, but devoid of life. As Minos contemplated the irony of this, the exsanguinating ewe passed quietly into unconsciousness, her breathing becoming shallower until it was no longer detectable.

Minos felt for the little lamb. He was so fragile, so comely. How sad that he was doomed to a certain death. The chance of him surviving was hopeless, yet he felt a need to at least try.

He picked it up and presented it to the ewe with the stillborn, but she ignored the lamb for her own, still licking it, trying to stimulate it to suckle now that it was clean and dry.

The limp, pathetic body remained inanimate. The strange lamb tried to get close, to bond with the nearest animal, but the ewe nosed it away in irritation.

Minos found this the most terrible thing, even though he had seen it before and knew this would be the sure reaction of the mother. Ewes had an intense drive to suckle their own and no other.

The saddest reality was that the little lamb was going to die. He picked up the carcass of the stillborn, melancholy, contemplating the tragedy of this situation as he carried it away.

The mother stood and tried to leave the annoying little pest as it continued to bleat and poke for a chance to suck. She was still weak and could move only at a slow, deliberate pace, her kicks at the invading creature lacking the vitality to do much damage.

What a tragic waste, thought Deus. If only he could make the ewe think the living lamb was hers.

He held up the carcass.

An idea came to him. He withdrew his knife and removed the skin of the unfeeling lamb, cutting neatly around the neck and legs and making a cut, only through the skin, the length of the belly and chest. He peeled the little body out of the bellycut to the sound of connective tissues separating, and gently lay the carcass on the ground. He would never bring himself to be disrespectful to a body, not even that of an animal.

He took the lambskin over to the still bleating lamb and slipped it over its back, pulling its four legs through the holes he had cut, fitting it like a shirt. When he placed it on the ground it ran, or wobbled, toward the ewe he had bonded to, in spite of her confusing abuse. This time the ewe hesitated in rebuffing it. She sniffed and prodded, sensing something was not quite right, but being too simple to figure out the ruse she dumbly accepted the lamb's presence without further objection. In a very short time she began to nuzzle the little one as her own, sniffing and licking its face, offering her teats which were accepted with enthusiasm.

Minos was old now. He had been known as Minos for fifty-one years, and Deus for fourteen years before that. That put him in his sixty-sixth year; zeros hadn't been thought of yet and a person's first year of life was considered to be "one"; and that was a very old age for anyone to live to.

Only in the last few decades had people in general begun to count, and they counted everything. And one of their primary interests was their age. Many of the older people had not learned to count until they were well on in years and either exaggerated or underestimated their age according to whom they were trying to impress. The men had a tendency to make themselves out to be older because, thanks to Minos, old age was no longer associated with dotage but rather wisdom.

The women, on the other hand, could go either way. Most were quite honest when discussing their ages with others until they started to notice a decline in their physical attributes. Then, as if to ward off the effects of aging, they either refused to tell their age or they undervalued it. This became something of a joke among the other women. The men simply didn't care. It didn't matter how old they were, but how they looked, and actual age was irrelevant.

Aphrodite was more sensible. Until her dying day she maintained to her closest friends that she was decades older than she really was. She laughed with Minos over their friend's adulations, hearing that they commented amongst themselves that she looked so good for her age.

Aphrodite.

How he missed her.

Five years now. And she was every bit the beauty when she died as when he saw her that first time emerging from the surf.

His life was incomplete without her and he was only biding his time, waiting for his turn to pass through the gateways to eternity. It couldn't be long. The aches of old age were with him constantly, although he would never let it show. He had been in the finest physical condition for most of his life, hard-tuned by the rigors of sea voyages and long foot travel by land. There was not a village or settlement that he had not visited on the island at least once, leaving his messages of peace and hope, prosperity and health. Every person heard the narrative of the "Vision" and, with Minos's signal skills as an orator, most believed. Those who didn't were hardly antagonistic to those who did and enjoyed the benefits of a developing society along with the majority. Everyone benefited.

The only major problem he ever encountered was the one recently. It tugged at his heartstrings when he found out through his trusted Brothers that his family was the subject of some jealousy, a jealousy that he could see destabilizing the peace of the nation given the wrong emphasis.

The issue was almost an absurdity. Aphrodite's children had all been exceedingly fair. Lighter skinned, handsome or beautiful, and blond. No one else was blond. It had become the standard with which to measure beauty and everywhere everyone was coming up short.

Suitors hovered as the children came of age, eagerly vying for the hearts, or at least the bodies, of the inheritors of such godly features. On the more remote parts of the island, the inland settlements, and the smaller coastal villages, these children were even more deemed children of deity.

The problem started with a brief insult to the populous about thirty years ago. One of their sons took another of their daughters to wife. They were so caught up in the beauty of each other, both closely the image of their mother, that they could have no passion for any other. They insulted the appearance of the other island inhabitants, verbally only in secret to each other, but the message was clear. They were thoroughly repulsed by the appearance of the dark-haired men and women, most of whom were still not shaving. A life with any of them, and the thought of any kind of sexual liaison, was wholly repugnant and out of the question. The only choice was to join themselves to each other.

The scandal had passed quickly enough, fortunately, and for the most part was forgiven. The suitors retired to other avenues of pursuit, as they always will despite the bemoaning of their fate for the interim. The children of the coupling, and numerous they were, all looked the inch their parents, as anyone would have expected.

The other four children of Minos and Aphrodite, two other boys and two girls, did settle comfortably and lovingly with other island youth. They were, however, not left to their own devices in making an independent selection. The competition was as fierce for them as for their more aloof brother and sister. With such a bounty of possible mates, they had to rely, and were forced to rely, on the guidance of their parents.

Minos, with his experience in breeding sheep from his earliest years, and having kept himself involved in breeding all kinds of animals including the ever more prolific cattle which were becoming so popular, felt strongly that people were little different and proper breeding was essential to improving the lot of mankind, or at least the nation of people here on the island. Mankind would come later. Right now it was imperative to breed, just as in sheep or cattle, the strongest, comeliest, most intelligent people anywhere. He had become fabulously wealthy and satisfied with life raising the animals and surmised that it could hardly be different with people. He had spoken of this lightly with others, merely mulling the idea over in his mind for years, and thought that it must surely bear similarity to the mating of animals. After all, how different were they? They ate and slept, breathed and grew, just as we do. They didn't live very long, but that was the failing of animals. Mostly they were to serve mankind in some way and didn't need to live longer than their purpose served anyway. And if the traits of animals could be coaxed into different directions just by manipulating their mates, then it should logically be assumed that the qualities and characteristics of people could be managed in the same way. How many children looked like their mother or father? How many shared the same family eyes or had the same muscle build or got as fat as their parents?

So they let the word go out that they were searching for the best mates for their children.

The suitors appealed to Minos and Aphrodite in person. The repulsive were rejected out of hand, without telling them exactly why, also the weak, the diseased, the patently simple. These were mercifully few, as most of them, from all around the island, had something of an idea of what was expected and generally knew if they were fit to be considered or not. Still, the hopefuls from all walks of life turned up in a seemingly endless stream.

Some of the young men and women were saddened at their rejection, having come so far. Others had only been using the exercise as an excuse to get out and travel. It gave them a purpose to their journey. Travel was becoming ever more conventional as the tales of other lands, and even the sights around their own island, were brought to them by the colorful language of sailors visiting the shores of their villages in increasing numbers every year.

But the rejected were not so gravely disheartened and, now away from their families, were now more inclined to take risks that they never would have contemplated isolated from the rest of the world in their own villages. With the added compulsion to attend to their personal needs, food and shelter, they were able to be lured into the business of sea travel. There was always a boat these days to be powered to some distant shore, and oarsmen were a necessity. The mariner's trade had been increasing for years, no longer sporadic but organized. Syros had determinedly built a boat every year since he had landed on the shore of Amnisos with Minos and Aphrodite. More than that he had been persuaded to share his wealth of knowledge of navigation and shipbuilding with others.

Only a few of the ships constructed were of the size Minos originally traveled in. There was no need for such a vessel to ply the local waters around the island and that is where most of the seafaring was done. Men still got nervous out of sight of land and most of the trade was local, almost like a regular ferry system, going in circles in opposing directions around the island.

Sea traders established themselves because they found that travel by sea, although slow, was far faster than walking the rugged terrain of the island with heavy packs on their backs. In season, when the fishing was more prosperous, they could still fish out of the larger vessels and sell at the villages. That rankled the local fishermen who had no better equipment than fishermen ever did, the little skiffs that had been used for hundreds of years. But the villagers were willing to trade for the larger fish from deeper water that the local fishers only rarely caught so close to shore. Sometimes even the local fishermen were the buyers, negotiating out in the bay, away from land, and transferring the stock to the skiffs right there knowing that they could get a better trade in the village and thus make a profit for no more than the trouble of moving the fish to shore. The captains of the larger vessels had been instructed by Minos to keep the peace at all costs, within reason, and only the reasonable were given charge of seaworthy vessels. It was almost as hard to get charge of one of these as one of Minos's children. Comely appearance didn't matter as much, but stature did, and intelligence. Every captain had to have been a strong and unwavering oarsman, have excellent vision, and had to possess a photographic memory for navigating. And only the best of the best would be given the crafts capable of traveling across the sea to Egypt, Cypress, or the Levant, through waters where storms could arise out of nothing; or through waters leading to the island menagerie to the north, the puzzle of the thousand islands where anyone could go hopelessly astray.

Minos recalled his memories those days with fondness. He always felt he should be able to make the choice of which he preferred, land or sea, and never could decide. They were like the earth and sky or the night and the day, nothing without the other; a mated pair, as man and woman.

He loved nothing more than visiting with the people and teaching them. Inwardly he felt a deep revulsion of the ignorance most people possessed and longed for them to learn and know as much as he did. But even the ones who could not grasp any but the most rudimentary concepts he still loved. And with his wife, Aphrodite, he traveled everywhere around the island perimeter, mostly by sea, where most of the populace were discovered to be, but also by foot to catch the landlocked settlements which were far less peopled but more numerous and scattered.

They longed to see the growing town of Knossos, the center of their religious beliefs and philosophy. Everyone had been encouraged to make a pilgrimage to the graveside of Selene, and leave a gift of something they had skill in, a finely crafted chair perhaps, a pot turned on one of the new wheels, a colored blanket. Anything, or nothing if the person had nothing to give. It didn't matter to the deity except what was in and from the heart. However, it didn't take long for it to become something of a contest to see who could craft the most attractive offering.

These items, these devotional offerings, were left with the full expectation that they would be used by the keepers of the temple built beside the mounded cairn. The priests, the ones who had dedicated themselves to the functioning and management of the temple, had less time to work in the fields and as fishers and around the home and it was expected that they would have a semblance of support from the devotionalists.

Almost as many women as men were interested in the pastime and were an integral part of the priesthood. Their function had developed along a different line, and there weren't quite as many of them involved, but nothing unusual was thought of them that wasn't thought of any of the men. It was understood that offerings were not to be actually owned by any of the priesthood bearers but rather would be held in common and would return to the temple treasury upon their death or resignation of service. Some families of the priesthood, not caught up in the spirit as much as they were hoped to be, clung to the possessions, which in many cases, had been in the family so long that they were considered to be a part of the estate. Several bitter debates were exacerbated by claims of friends or neighbors that the families were not "correct", to be polite about it, in their covetousness. Most of those who kept the goods explained it all away by claiming that they never knew, or that they had simply forgotten over time. They were the ones who were deeply embarrassed to have been discovered or remembered. This became one of the first uses of the new hieroglyphic writing, to track temporary ownership of temple oblations.

It had always saddened Minos that otherwise good people could so easily justify their occasional dalliances with dishonesty. They always came up with a reason. So it came about, by necessity, that he found himself in the position of judge of the people. It had started easily enough as part of his acclimation to the position of Chief of Amnisos. The Chief was expected to judge the people of the town and the surrounding areas, including any transients, on everything from rowdiness to encroachment on another's land. In between, there were petty thefts, assaults that only seemed to happen when the men got drunk, and mischief or vandalism. These incidents were rare in Amnisos, usually involving only the male youth. For the most part, he dealt with the delinquents with a stern public rebuke, public because most of the village turned out for the trial, shaming them into conforming to accepted standards of behavior. It was a rare thing to see anyone appear before Minos more than once.

The most difficult cases for him to judge were those who justified themselves in simple dishonesties. Minos was a master at reading faces and often could tell that the accused before him were lying. But since there were no substantial facts to be used in evidence against them, and their defense when caught was to say that they had forgotten, nothing could really be done against them other than to chide them to use their minds more effectively. When they refused to confess that they had even forgotten but challenged the charging party to prove that they had, for example, a pretty pot that was not theirs, something that did not belong to them, the verdict was often hung because it was a case of one word against another. It was not unheard of for people to lay false charges and so he had to let the accused keep the article under dispute. That was not easy for him. He agonized over some of the most trivial issues, things like the rightful owner of a pot. Sometimes it was so difficult to make a perfect ruling that he reserved judgment, citing lack of sufficient evidence. No Chief had ever done that before, fearing to look indecisive in the eyes of the people and glad to wash the issue from his plate regardless of whether he was right or not.

One of the biggest shockers was when he once deferred judgeship to Aphrodite when he was busy with seminal contemplations at Knossos. He was going through one of his spiritual revivals and did not want to leave, and she was more than willing to serve in his stead having grown comfortable with the language; indeed she had become perfectly fluent.

The task set before her was to determine if a fishing skiff lost through neglect should be replaced by the borrowing fisher who lost it. Drunkenness, as usual, was involved. The two fisher friends now at odds with each other had been into the wine and consumed far too much. Each owned one of the little fishing barks and one thought he would take the other's for a spin around the bay in the middle of the night. The idea was riotous. Off he went while the others laughed and spurred him on. But he stayed out so long that the others tired of the fun and faded to sleep. The owner of the boat, discreetly nervous about the situation though he was, nonetheless eventually passed out along with his companions from the effects of the alcohol, the late hour, and fatigue. The rower, drunk as could be, fell over the side and could not get himself into the skiff without filling it with water. He gave up, floundering so much that he couldn't even raise a cry for help, barely able to ride the current back to shore without drowning.

The first of the others to wake in the morning found him face to the sand, snoring away with the wash licking his heels. The skiff was nowhere to be found. The fishers looked as far as they dared, but the current had changed and carried it away.

And although the skiff involved was rudely constructed it was still precious to the fisher, his livelihood being utterly dependent upon it. Building another was far from an easy task, the regular people mostly having access only to sharp flint or obsidian tools. He might possibly be able to borrow one of the new bronze axes or knives to speed construction but he wasn't friendly enough, he thought, with the owners of those tools to pull that off. It would take months of labor, splitting wood, shaving it down, shaping the planks; even then it would just be another ugly skiff, nothing like the magnificent ships that now visited the harbor. How he would have loved to go along on one of those voyages, he would forget all about his little skiff, but he was too old. In the meantime, what was he to do?

Aphrodite listened intently to the story told from each involved, including the witnesses. There was no doubt or conflict to the story. The only objection was that of the party who had lost the boat. He said he was not to blame, was drunk and therefore not responsible, and had been given the blessings of the owner because he did not stop him knowing that he would fall out in his state. In short, it was not his fault.

The owner, on the other hand, wanted the other man's skiff in compensation. If anyone should have to build another boat it should be that man.

The heated argument that ensued almost had the old friends coming to blows. Only the immediate intervention of the closest in the crowd prevented it.

Normally a judge would decide who had presented the best argument and grant the claim of the winner.

What Aphrodite did was almost inconceivable. She called for silence. Then she pronounced that the two old friends would become friends once again and that nothing would get in the way of that; not her decision, not the skiff, nothing. The two would have to sit facing each other and would have to smile. The first to stop smiling, other than for brief flinches, sneezes, or to pick his nose, would lose and would have to grant the other his claim. They could talk if they wished, but only to each other, and they had to keep smiling, whatever their thoughts may be.

The crowd loved it. There was an uproar of immediate approbation and two stools were spirited into the center out of nowhere, passed overhead, hand to hand. The two were seated as the surrounding assembly chanted, "Smile. Smile."

The two fishers were too dumbfounded to comply at first, thrust into their seats like so much baggage. They both came to the realization that this whole affair was serious and everything hinged on the ludicrous demand that they have a smiling contest. It was mad. The first grimaced. The second did a little better.

Aphrodite rebuked them. "That is not good enough."

They tried harder, the smiles obviously forced while everyone around them embraced their bellies and guffawed. Everyone was leaning on those in front for support, straining their necks and pushing for a better view, the ones in front jealously defending their positions. It was too fabulous, these hardened leatherskins having a face-off by smiling. Who would win? The bets began to fly. One fish says he does. Two fish says the other. This was the most fun any of the villagers had had in ages.

Aphrodite calmly watched the two men. She had wanted to smile herself, but her ruling was serious and she had no intention of ruining it by joining in with the jocularity of the crowd. They had always held her high above that sort of thing anyway. They only saw her on occasion, usually when they went to pay homage at Knossos; rarely when she made an appearance here at Amnisos to ride the waves with her husband.

The two men were both getting sore at being brunts of the crowd's humor. They would have preferred to get up and fight each other and everyone around them, and would have if not for the unwavering eye fixed upon them. They knew that if either challenged her, they would lose. Each did all he could to wish it to be the other. So they sat, smiling. Each took advantage of the ruling that allowed them to twitch and cough and pick their noses; but in the end, they had to keep smiling. The hardest thing to adjust to, and they tried bellicosely to make it stop, was that they actually felt a twinge of happiness brewing inside. Their long lives had been spent smiling only when they were happy, and at no other time. Here they were now, smiling, and it was impossible to keep that inbred feeling from tagging along. There were periods where both of them wanted to scream. But what could they do?

They began to feel foolish, grinning like Cheshire cats, neither speaking. Finally, the oldest could bear it no longer.

"I hate this," he confessed, still grinning.

"I do, too," said the other, likewise.

"I'm going to outlast you, you know. You might as well give up and give me your boat."

"You old goat. I'll slice a smile into my face with a knife before I do that."

"Perhaps you would give me that honor."

"Carve a smile into your own head, and I don't mean the one on your shoulders." He was taking a chance saying that, and was relieved that Aphrodite remained silent though her eyes flashed daggers.

Neither dared talk for a few minutes, sensing they were treading dangerously. Still, they sat smiling.

The youngest could take no more. "This is torture," he screamed. Catching himself and fearing what he had said would inflame the wrath of his judge he quickly said, "Isn't there another way? Can't we share my skiff and both build another together?" He had just blurted it out of panic but instantly realized that what he had said was what Aphrodite was expecting one of them to eventually say.

"That would make sense," affirmed the older. "We would both be able to fish. And we would both build the new skiff. Would I be able to keep the new one?"

"Yes. Anything. Let's just end this madness."

The older looked at Aphrodite who was harboring a pleased countenance. "Since you both agree, this court is concluded."

The crowd cheered. Not a single person had decamped out of boredom. They pressed in, careful to give the lady space but crowding as close to the men as they could, slapping and pulling them both away. Drinks were the order of the day. This was a trial to relive over and over.

Now the two fishers were pleased to be the center of attention. "Listen," called the oldest to his friend. "I'm getting on in years. When we build the new one you can have it."

The crowd roared its approval once again, picking them both up bodily and hurtling them into the sea in a baptism of cheerful goodwill.

What a fond memory. Minos found he was weeping. That tale had been told so often that he almost felt as though he had been there. He could fully imagine his wife in all her dignity presiding over the trial, as he had known she had every capability of doing. Many had said after that she shared the wisdom of Minos. He did not disagree. Her ability to be comfortable in the tensest situations or to delight in the peace of an afternoon sunshine excited him, held her fast to his soul.

The contrast between her handling judgment and quietly gardening at the old family homestead, later their retreat when they needed quiet time together, was something that only he could truly appreciate. She had become

227

personally attached to the five olives growing by the old stone hut. Minos and his mother had planted four whips just out from each corner of the structure not long before her death. They had grown better than he had hoped, a testament to her life-giving powers.

Aphrodite had tended them with care, pruning a bit here and a bit there, artistically shaping the trees without really understanding how the cutting back of the branches actually contributed to their overall health. The way they were growing, they would be as large as the first old gnarly beast in another generation. She took the same interest in the rest of the garden and especially the vines. Zeus praised her grapes as the finest anywhere; not that it was the grapes but rather the seasoned juice that he really cared for. He always praised her, appreciating deeply that the young beauty would have any interest at all in providing for an old fool. He loved the food she grew, a skill he could never really master, and was only too pleased when she would let him repay her, sometimes accepting his sheep or his wool as a gift. Even after Zeus left for good, she still kept the garden flourishing and organized.

The trees were still there. Others tended the garden now, but not with the same knack. Minos thought he might visit the old homestead soon. It had been so long. Zeus had asked that no one change the hut after he left. Its purpose had come to an end with his leaving. The walls were cracking anyway. Who would want the place?

Minos stood and stretched. Stretching eased his aching bones. He still had the triangular, muscular frame of a strong man half his age but now his gut was beginning to sag a bit, no longer rock hard like in the old days. He was disappointed in how his body was becoming so decrepit. There was nothing to be done, of course. The seasons came and went, and age was inevitable. He was thankful to have lived this long.

There were so many people he had known that had enjoyed much shorter lives. One of his favorites, the ugly Jobah, barely lived five years before succumbing to a paralytic stroke. It happened while he was hard at work turning one of his enormous pots, which he was becoming quite well known for. No one else had the strength or dexterity to work such massive blocks of clay. The pots he turned out were big enough for an eight-year-old boy to curl up inside. He had suddenly collapsed against the pot as it was spinning, the momentum throwing him down and sideways onto the stone that ground a hideous gash into his face as it turned under him, his bodyweight braking its rotation. There he lay until one of the old ladies who he felt comfortable with came by with his dinner. She found him crumpled and drooling on the ground, his pot sitting above him on the unmoving wheel, half finished, a testament to his life.

The old lady summoned aid, moving Jobah to his bed with the first to arrive, and washed his wound. She had seen many people die of wasting paralysis and, even in her experienced old age, found it hard to adjust to. Jobah's eyes were open, there was even a vestige of consciousness within, but he wasn't able to respond to them at all. Like the others she had seen, his whole side was flaccid, not even responding to hard pinches twisted into his tender inner thigh. The other side responded at first, just a little, his leg twitching and half of his face grimacing with the induced pain.

His whealed face was repulsive. The frozen droop on the one side with spittle dribbling out the corner of his mouth, and the jagged laceration on the other side, gave him such a disfigured appearance that Aphrodite had caught her breath when she saw him stretched out on his bed. Minos had been filled with sympathy for his friend and brother. Jobah had never gotten used to the idea that Minos had really loved him. Saliva filled his mouth and he inhaled some, sending his chest into a spasm that was no more than a weak cough, not enough to clear the fluid from his lungs. Minos asked the old lady tactfully if it would be of benefit to turn his head to the side to let the fluids drain from his mouth.

Her response was curt and to the point - "To what end?"

He understood her meaning right away. Jobah's condition was miserable and irreversible. He could die of thirst and emaciation over the next few days or he could drown in his own fluids now, in front of his friends and family, in a short time. It would be better for him this way.

It had been the hardest thing Minos had ever done, and hard for his wife to witness although she stood by his side and would not leave. It took longer than they thought. Jobah's capacity for survival was greater than the old lady had assumed. Even with his lungs filling with saliva he still continued to breathe, the long gurgle accompanying each expiration sawing away at their nerves and hearts. Bubbles formed, a white froth blooming up from the depths of his airway, receding into his throat with each breath inhaled and emerging farther with every retraction of his chest. Foam spilled over his chin and cheeks, bubbles popping and leaving a sticky, glistening layer adhered to his face. Sometimes a spasm would send up a little geyser of goo that dribbled down and matted into his hair.

Then he retched and his spew erupted in a fountain, covering his face entirely and spreading out on the bed in a circle of congealed pollution. Aphrodite cried and took a rag to his face, wiping the emesis, unable to bear the sight of a friend so defiled by his illness. Her heart was filled with compassion for the man. She had admired him so much for his great works of art, his kindness and humility, and his shy disposition. Now he was dying in front of her very eyes. No one she cared for had ever done that to her.

A good deal of the vomit had been drawn into his lungs and the powerful stomach acids went to work. Chemicals rapidly broke down the tender lining, burning it and raising blisters filled with blood and plasma. In minutes all air was cut off and his colour changed from pale to cyanotic. His lips and ears, already dark from the insult of low oxygenation, went completely purple, a sickly hue promising an imminent death.

His right eye slowly closed, not quite entirely, before his heart convulsed erratically and ceased all effective pumping action, his left eye solidified in a crooked, wide open stare.

Minos had tried to remain staunch throughout Jobah's final trial, but now that his friend was dead he broke down as well. Even the old lady who had seen her share of death cried for the gentle troll who enriched the village with his talents. Minos was further saddened that the burial would have to take place without his shipmates. They were out at sea without him this time, and although Jobah was not really a crewmember he had still been part of that first expedition that was still the crowning glory of their lives. The potters in the village, those who had been interested enough to take up the craft on almost a full-time basis now that the fundamentals of trade were allowing for such a thing, were the ones Minos chose to assist him in the burial proceedings.

Jobah had said many times that he loved the area just up the slope from where Selene was interred and that he would like to have a workshop there overlooking the plateau. The walk to Amnisos was something that he had come to enjoy and so the smaller items could be carried easily enough. He had planned to teach the local potters his methods of throwing the big lumps of clay and working them into the huge pots like that of which he was working on when he died so that they could be made in the town and not have to be brought down from so far up in the hills. He was going to do that soon. There was so much he was going to do soon; experiment with colors and glazes, shapes and techniques. He was really free and appreciated here, and could never figure out why or if it was for real.

Jobah's bearers carried him in a linen roll beyond Selene's gravesite up the gentle slope to the top where the tree line began. It took all day to do it and the men spelled each other off. Except Minos. He clung to his adopted brother and, although he sweated profusely and fasted even drink until the site was reached, made the entire distance. There he helped the others gather rocks and entomb him in the manner of his mother.

Dear Jobah. His memory was still so fresh in Minos's mind. He wondered what effect he might have had on the local society if he had survived. Would his artwork have influenced the styles of the island even more than it had already? Jobah was forever learning, forever improvising and developing ideas. Some were strictly practical like the oversized storage jars; some were

230

purely artistic and practically useless, little figurines of animals or people, jugs in the shape of animal heads which were impossible to pour from.

Minos recalled the time he took Jobah to visit the old woman in Vathypetro near the place where he had met his first friend and brother, Taros. Taros had wanted to show off his new friends to his family and Minos complied, thinking it was about time that they exerted some effort into meeting with the landlocked people of the interior. When Jobah was introduced to the old woman, he boldly, before they even had time to sit down, requested that she sing for them. The dear old soul. She was taken aback, but complied with the ugly man who seemed so genuinely enthralled just with the tales he had been told of her nightingale voice. After seating them all, she too sat down on a stump, not having the strength in her old age to both stand and sing. When she opened her mouth the most delicious sound emanated, softly, but piercing to the very marrow. The quiet reverb off the surrounding trees added a rich texture that filled their senses. Jobah, with his eyes closed, found it impossible to tell from where it came. It was everywhere, the full soprano ringing indescribably as she sang, improvising the words as she went, bearing the feelings of her deepest soul. As he mused on the words he sang an accompanying melody along with the old lady. Perhaps it was the humid, cool air, but he sounded better to himself than ever before.

Minos forced himself back to reality. Those two dear friends. Word reached him soon after Jobah's death that the old lady had died on the same day, even at the same hour. The two had connected in the singing of that song. And why not? Both had changed everything; the old lady's modus of song had caught on in the same way that Jobah's style of clay working. Both were of the same mind. Both had given so much, and both were so humble. The old lady had even refused to tell Minos her name, believing herself to be so unworthy in her old age that such recognition was nothing more than an unnecessary indulgence.

He inhaled deeply, filling his lungs with the cold, fresh breeze suddenly welling up from the coast. He wondered at his thoughts. He prided himself on never forgetting a fact but found that these days he was dwelling more on the past than he used to.

The bath looked ready. Wisps of vapor lifted from the water surface into the chilling air. He poked his hand into the water to test the temperature and found it just right. The heat passed through the copper tub readily, the embers below the one end doing their job nicely, heating the water. A thought of tossing a bit of dirt over the coals to slow them quickly passed. If the water heated more, so much the better. He slid off his robe and slipped in, crouching in the warmth that enveloped him.

Beautiful. Everything was beautiful. The warm sensation of the water, the view, the breeze on his face. Life had become such a joy. There had been tribulations, but they had been transient and quickly passed. For everything bad that had happened there had been ten others, a hundred, that had been good. Only two grim events had truly pierced him; the death of Selene, and the death of Aphrodite. The first had been so violent, and yet such good had come about from that, the greatest good the world had known, that even now he could barely fathom that he had played such a role in it all. The second, his beloved Aphrodite, was still an incomprehensible mystery. Coming home to her leaning back in her chair, he bent forward to kiss her and found her face cold and unresponsive. His heart stopped for that instant as the reality drenched him like ice water. A pain ripped across his chest and into his arm. Her expression was placid and untroubled, as if she had left it that way purposefully to comfort him, knowing he would be the one to find her. Her eyes were open; in death still filled with bounteous life. He knelt in front of her and wept. She was so still and quiet. He reached out and took her hands in his. They were cold but still soft. She hadn't been dead too long.

Then he saw it. The small stain on her tunic. He moved closer, fixing his eyes on the spot, a tiny hole in its center where the fibers had been pushed to the side. He body-shook as he lifted the fabric off of her breast. A small puncture had been made over her heart, with only a trickle of blood dried to her skin below where it had seeped out of the raised rim. His legs gave out as he fell to the ground, hurting his hip. His head was spinning. Everyone said he was sagacious and understood everything, but he could not understand this. How did it happen? Self-inflicted? Impossible. Murder? The thought paralyzed him. No. There was no struggle here. An accident of some kind? He looked around. Nothing could have done this.

The injury, the cause of death, was exactly like that of his mother. Without the rape. And where his mother's death was brutal with evidence everywhere, this was a serene picture. His head was reeling. Was there a connection? There had to be. Could it be that Aphrodite's being was so closely tied to that of Selene's that this was a spontaneous act of deity? That she had been spirited to him by the powers of heaven had never been in doubt. Aphrodite herself had come to believe it after a time, since her memory of the ordeal she had faced alone on the Mediterranean and her life previous to that seemed to her little more than a foggy hallucination. Yes. She had been taken by the Gods; taken home by Selene who watched over the Earth and sky, the Earth Mother. She could now reside as the Evening Star again, the illustrious orb gracing the heavens with a beauty for all to enjoy.

Minos relaxed in his bath. The water, still being heated, wrapping around him in comfort. He pulled himself tight into a curl as he thought of his wife. God, he was lonely. His face reddened in a flush. As a frog will stay in water that is slowly heated, so Minos stayed in the tub, lost in reminiscence, his core temperature rising dangerously high. He was only minutely aware of a twinge in his chest, just another one. He paid no heed. The beauty of the valley below, the comfort of being so close to his mother and his wife entombed at the temple at the bottom of the rise, all served to compose his spirit.

He felt as though he were rising out of himself. It was hardly a new feeling, but it was not common. But whereas the other times were identifiable as visions, this one seemed more tangible, more real. His heart gave a final, audible thump as a flash of worry over things undone coursed through him. He looked down on himself in the bath; how he loved the bath; and now basked in a different warmth that flooded over and inside him. He rose higher, gratified to see that he had left the expression he had seen on his wife's face, a peaceful serenity that told whoever might find him that he too had, overall, been pleased with life.

A fundamental light and heat as of the Sun washed over him, and ahead he could see the backlit silhouettes of those family and friends he loved most.

* * *

(End Of Part 1)

<center>~~~~~~~~~~~~~~~~~~~~~~~~~~~~~~~~~~~~~</center>

Chapter 11

The Labyrinth

2898 BCE

Zeus had emphatically asserted before his death that he be interred in a cave in remembrance of the history of his ancestors. He wanted to be the last, the very last at the end of a long line stretching back to the beginning, before this new era completely took root. Minos, out of respect for his father's age and ill health, granted his only wish. Zeus had felt that he was being called to the mountain with the face south of Knossos. In fact, he had been living up there, alone and hermit-like, for most of his life after Minos returned from his first voyage with his new wife, returning with his flock only on occasion and for short duration to the hut he had built for his family.

After seeing the unparalleled beauty of the girl, the calves, and hearing the tales of the limitless copper supplies, the populations of the other lands, and the new ideas Minos had on trade routes and writing and manufacturing, and a hundred other things, he bowed his head and declared softly that it was a new world, a world which he would never understand. Zeus had simply, and humbly, said that he was immensely proud to have brought such a fine son into the world. It would be a better place because of it. He had forgotten much of the intensity of the vision he had experienced with his son, and no matter how much they talked, he could never recapture the feeling that told him he could be completely forgiven for the manner in which he had treated his wife while she lived. He felt a twinge of pain and guilt every time he passed by her cairn. As the years marched on he found he felt the same way even being around the family's homestead, and so spent less and less time there. He knew he deserved to suffer those feelings; he wanted to feel them; at least that much.

He stayed in the vicinity for the first few years while the calves grew, fascinated by their growth as they continued to mature. There was a time when he thought they might never stop. Jacobah, the boy from Ugarit, had taken an immediate liking to Zeus and the two could be seen together far afield with the cow and the white bull grazing cooperatively amongst the increasing flock of sheep. Then they mated and gave forth two new calves. He'd seen the lambing process a thousand times, but it was newly miraculous with these novel beasts.

But after a time even that fascination wore thin. Zeus never thought it would happen, that he would tire of everyday living. But he was intuitive enough to know that he could not keep up with the skills of his son or his young friend Jacobah. A new generation of shepherds, farmers, and ranchers was in its inception. He was happy to have been a pioneer but now resigned to them.

Zeus had been making more and more frequent trips to the mountain, staying longer each time. Minos would visit him regularly with his wife, taking with them oil and supplies of vegetables and dried fruit to supplement his all meat diet. They often stayed days at a time with the aging man.

He was happy in his solitude, finding the quiet and meditation most satisfying. At night he could sometimes see the yellow glow of a fire at Knossos, and in the day sometimes a column or two of smoke; more in the winter. The visual connection was all he needed for comfort. His small flock of sheep kept his belly comfortably filled, and now he even had a nanny goat for milk. They weren't so bad after all.

His isolation from everyone made the rumors fly about his communing regularly with the Earth Mother. Everyone had heard repeatedly of the vision that he'd had, and a more relaxed telling of his marriage. Years into his self-imposed exile he had become an icon himself, a legend among the people. Sometimes one or two might make a pilgrimage to Mount Juktas to visit with him. Often they returned disappointed, unable to find him. He moved around with his sheep, grazing them here and there, not always on the same side of the mountain. In the winter, in particular, he mostly stayed away from the north side facing directly to Knossos, the perpetual shade being too cold for his aging bones. Then just when some would begin to doubt if he was still alive; or wonder, unsaid, if he had ever been alive; someone would find him and enjoy days of communion. When they left, usually unfed the entire time, they would marvel at how Zeus could live without eating and keep his physique so substantial, not realizing that he had been eating and drinking while off on short meditational walks. The visitors went away thinking that the sheep were not a food source but rather more like pets doting subserviently on their master. And when they finally made their departure Zeus ever more actively encouraged them to tell whatever they wished when they returned home but discouraged them from inviting others to share in the experience by coming to see him. He was quite complete seeing only his son and his wife.

At last, the time came, as Minos and Aphrodite knew it would, when they found Zeus dead. He was lying in the mouth of the cave where he had previously made it known he wished to be buried, his head and shoulders slightly propped by the rock wall. His appearance took Minos back to the times he would sleep like that against the log outside their little hut, his bearded face rumbling in a deep appreciation of sleep.

They carried him to the back of the cave, only a short way, and covered him with stones, sealing him up against the elements and marauding predators. Minos was glad he came when he did. He had almost ignored the compelling feelings he'd had to come up here. Other matters had been pressing; the union of his two eldest children; arguments about style in crafts, a surprisingly contentious topic of discussion; numerous little squabbles about who owned what now that people where embracing the idea of private rather than communal ownership. In the end he had gone with his instinct, something he had learned and relearned to do long before.

He and Aphrodite had stayed at the mountain retreat for a ten-day week, the week he had established as a standard for the people. This had become over the last years the appropriate mourning period. As part of the funerary Minos sacrificed a ram in his father's memory. The meat kept them well fed during their stay at the place where "the partridges sing more sweetly than anyplace else," an observance of Aphrodite.

Minos never did tell much about his father's stay on the mountain. He left that cloaked in mystery. Tales would be weaved all by themselves; tales of the imagination that would be improved upon, line upon line, time upon time.

Minos the Second would only be party to the embellished tales told by the people; the strong man, almost invincible they said, who ate no food in remorse over the passing of his beloved wife yet lived for years, who dwelt on the mountaintop often communing with deity and engulfed by clouds, who dealt harshly with his family when they deserved it but always only with wisdom and instruction. A man who secured a place with deity and so, in the end, became one himself.

* * *

"Great Father Zeus. Receive this ax with our expression of respect and reverence."

They stood before the entrance of where Zeus had been interred, the shallow cave, among the largest of hundreds which had been etched into the soft rock by eons of wind buffeting the slopes of the mountain.

Minos held the bronze weapon firmly beneath the head, the weight of the metal balanced at the top end of the long handle touching the ground, both blades pointing oppositely to the east and west. It was heavy and had been cast especially large in consideration of the greatness of the man to whom it was now dedicated. He had only heard from his grandfather, the Great Minos as he was now known, about Zeus's life.

Minos, the second Minos, the grandchild of the first, was now in his twenty-second year. He had been appointed to the position of leader of the people and High Priest of worship while only in his ninth year. The Great Minos had seen in him wisdom and intellect far beyond his years and had taken such a personal interest in him that the boy was virtually by his side continuously from that time until his death eleven years later. In that time he had learned all that his grandfather could teach him about languages, numbering, writing, spirituality, farming, herding, breeding, navigation, leadership, judgment, and improvisation. His ability to grasp both the obvious and the enigmatic was equaled, it was said, by only his grandfather. Even at that, with the man growing in age and caring less for the things of this mortal life and gradually divesting himself from it, Minos the Second had become more closely endeared to the hearts of the people that he served. Not that they loved the older man any less; he had become so much a legend that, had he lived forever, they would have followed his direction without question on any matter. No, it was that Minos, the husband of Aphrodite, had preoccupied himself with fundamentally deeper matters than what this temporal world could provide. He had passed the cares of mortal man.

The parents of Minos the Second had been married earlier than Minos would have liked, but the pressure of the people had persuaded him that the time was ripe. After the illicit liaison of his first two children, he could not refuse. He and Aphrodite had selected the young man's wife by the standards they had agreed upon; to choose the most physically fit and attractive intelligent girl of a logical childbearing age who was able to converse wisely and did not seem to be in possession of an ornery or overbearing temperament. They had been delighted in their final selection.

The girl, two years their son's senior, fit in like a member of the family right from the beginning, even having come from the south coast where customs were slightly different. She had gone out of her way to conform and was curious about everything, from the everyday activities of the women to the occupations and avocations of the men. And she was beautiful. Except for the dark hair, she could have been an immediate relation of Aphrodite, not such a farfetched idea when she considered the memories of her Egyptian sisters all being dark. But this girl had no tales to tell of being at sea. She took to it though, an unusual thing for a woman, traveling on occasion with the men although not as frequently as Aphrodite herself.

The two women formed a close bond, Aphrodite finding to her unremitting guilt that she wished her own daughters could be more like this young one. She had decided quickly that this girl was the one to marry her son and dismissed the other applicants. No other really came close.

They spent weeks together before Aphrodite introduced her to her potential husband. He still had every right to refuse her if he wanted. Minos and Aphrodite spoke ever after about that first meeting with a bemusement reserved for parents in situations such as this. Their poor son. He knew that they were planning his marriage and had been nervous about who they might decide to stick him with. Mostly couples were left to themselves to arrange their own lives, but there were parents who arranged marriages for their children and they were not always to the mutual satisfaction of the pledged spouses. But when the girl, a woman to him as she was older, was introduced to him he became so nervous and overwhelmed and embarrassed that he could hardly speak coherently. Words failed him as he tried desperately to think of even the simplest things to say. He was fortunate in that the girl retained her composure quite well and found herself to be quite genuinely attracted to him. He didn't treat her rudely, certainly didn't fawn over her, he was handsome, and had a laconic allure that she found rather disarming. If she hadn't heard so much about him over the last while she might have dismissed him as a bit of a dolt and not have had much further to do with him, but she was able to carry the conversation and soon had him more or less himself. His mother was right. He was far more the man than he had first been able to present himself. That only added to his charm and she quickly fell for him.

Yet she had a secret she hadn't told. An ominous secret she was sure no one knew about, but still she was plagued by doubt that one day someone, some way, might discover. She could not go through with a marriage to someone that she truly cared for without revealing the secret. Moreover, she had come to consider Aphrodite as such a close personal friend, as well as a future mother-in-law, that to not tell her would be tantamount to living a lie. She of all people had to know. She demanded that much respect. In fact, she would leave it to Aphrodite to decide if her son should ever be told.

She was risking everything by doing this. She could be sent back.

Aphrodite had known that the girl had something on her mind when she faltered in speech and became tongue-tied, completely out of character. Her downcast look told her that something unpleasant was forthcoming. She bode her time, reclining naked and soaking in the spring sun with a cup of last year's wine in her hand. At last the unaccustomed silence drove her to speak first. Clearly, the girl hadn't the courage, even with a few cups of wine in her system, to bring forth the subject of her concern.

She faced the girl directly, penetrating with her eyes and a serious gaze. "What troubles you?" she asked.

There was no escaping the fact that the query was more than that; it was a demand. She knew that she could have said anything, or nothing, and her falsehood would be immediately exposed. It was widely known that no one could lie to either Minos or Aphrodite, that they could see into the very mind of those with whom they communicated. She felt completely exposed mentally, compounded by her own nakedness. Sunbathing for leisure was something she had never heard of until coming here and she was still a bit reluctant, although certainly more comfortable, than she had been. At the moment, she found herself wishing for clothing.

It took her a few moments to gather her thoughts, even though she had been preparing for the inevitable confession for some time. Now that it had actually come down to it she felt muddled. She received a smile of encouragement, and it was all that was needed to get her started.

The words just seemed to gush out. She found it hard to keep hold of Aphrodite's pervading stare and found herself looking away frequently, crying at the first interruption. It was too painful.

She told of how she had been in her grandmother's hut, isolated from the other huts in the tiny community. She was in her eleventh year at the time, and her family had left for a long walk as they often did. She was going through a rebellious stage of life and refused to go with them, preferring to be left alone in her snit. Her family was only too willing to accommodate her, not wanting her along to spoil their good time. So she sat, mad and lonely, forcing herself not to wish that she had gone along. It had still been fairly early, but the sun sank behind the western hill that cast its shadow on the little hut well before it got dark everywhere else. Inside the hut it might as well have been night.

And then it happened. Almost too fast to comprehend. The rushing sound behind her was too fast to react to, and her hair was ripped and her head smashed against the hard wall. The darkness of the room exploded into a fusion of light and color. She flailed her arms at nothing as she was tossed about by the phantom, no more than a shadow himself in the darkness. She could hear him muttering incomprehensibly as her head spun, still reeling from the blow.

He was tearing at her clothing and getting frustrated because it was skin and wouldn't rend. He picked her up and bodyslammed her onto the hard dirt floor, knocking her almost senseless, but still she struggled to resist. Then he punched her hard in the stomach causing her to heave forward in a suspended curl before collapsing flat as he hiked her skirt high around her chest. She couldn't move but was still not quite unconscious as he forced his way into her. The pain was awful but not enough to make her unaware of the hurts everywhere else. She knew what he was doing to her; she had seen her parents do that before but hadn't imagined it might be painful. Then it seemed to be over almost as soon as it had begun. He was on top of her, motionless, panting she thought with the exertion of beating her into submission.

She was dimly aware of a familiar voice calling out her brother's name in the distance. The man on her startled. He heard it too. He jumped up and leapt for the door, peering around the corner of the jamb. She saw him pull something long and very thin out of his pocket. All she could see was the silhouette against the dim light still highlighting the doorway.

He was coming closer, too fast for her to do anything. He took a swipe at her chest and she felt the prick of the thing enter her skin at an oblique angle and ride along the outside of one of her ribs, grating the bone as it went, hurting even more as he yanked it out than when it went in.

Then he was gone.

Just like that.

He was gone.

It hardly seemed real or possible. She lay there trying to move, her body not responding to her will. Finally, she pushed the dress down over herself and rolled onto her side. The pain of the spike inserted through her pectoral muscle was the worst now, the pain down below nowhere near as bad. She took a deep breath. It would be all right she decided. She twisted a bit and took more deep breaths, testing to see how badly injured she might really be. Her head was clearing rapidly from the blow and she felt she could now sit up. She put her head into her hands and just held it for a while.

She could hear her family talking outside the hut. They had come back. She hoped none of them would come in and find her like this. She crawled over to her mat and lay down, pulling a skin over herself for warmth even though she could tell the air was warm enough, and curled up in shame. She sobbed, squeezing herself, holding her knees tight.

Then she felt terrified that the man might have left marks on her that her family would notice in the morning. The thought almost panicked her. She felt her head for wetness and was relieved that there was none, not even any crusted blood. The bang against the stone hadn't broken her scalp, only left a big bump that would be invisible under her hair. She felt her chest and, amazingly, that wound hadn't bled either. There was a raised welt along the path that the spike had traveled and the flesh below it felt tender and hard, but no one would see that.

She stayed awake most of the night, she thought, isolated in her anguish as the others filtered in one by one to retire. How could she tell anyone what had happened to her? She wanted to. But how? And what was the point, really?

She was the last to get up in the morning. She tried her best to put on some kind of a normal face but felt incredibly self-conscious as if they were all staring at her. They weren't. They just put off her recalcitrant mood to her still being in yesterday's snit, and ignored her.

They might have not noticed anything wrong at all, except for her mother seeing a dark stain on her rear. She smiled at that. Now she knew what was wrong with her daughter.

She took the girl away from the others and, without really looking at her, explained that this happened to all young girls. There was no predicting when it would happen, but it happened as surely as night followed day. And it would continue to happen, the only respite given when the woman became pregnant. The bleeding had happened to her so many times she couldn't even begin to explain it. No one knew why it happened, it just did. It was just an annoyance that women had to put up with.

She had heard that before. At first she was terrified that her mother might have meant that the assault she had suffered through was what she was talking about but, fortunately, she possessed the good sense to realize that her mother was completely ignorant of what had happened to her and naturally assumed she was having her first period.

She chose to keep things that way.

"And so you kept this inside all these years." It was a knowing statement not requiring an answer. Aphrodite was moved by the story, her heart filled with compassion for the girl. They embraced, forgetting and unashamed by their nakedness. Aphrodite stifled a tear as she remembered what she herself might barely have escaped in Egypt at the hands of the foul priests.

They pulled apart and Aphrodite noticed now the faint scar lingering on the girl's breast.

"You will marry my son. If that is your wish, of course."

She fully burst into tears, her relief and gratitude so complete.

"You may tell him of your rape if you wish. That will be your decision, I can't make it for you. But, unless you fear that someone who knows might tell him, there seems little point. I assure you I will not breathe a word of it. I also assure you that I have seen enough love in his eyes that he will not reject you because of the knowledge. He wants you as much as you want him."

And so Minos's parents were mated. Even now they were still happy together, rarely fighting or even disagreeing, as far as he was aware.

He was told that, at Aphrodite's urging, they had refused to name him until he was "old enough to deserve a name." Both she and her husband had felt from the moment they had witnessed his entrance into the world that he was different, the one who should accede as heir to his grandfather.

That is why they didn't want him named. There were too many unexplained and petty jealousies developing all around. If they had named him Minos there and then, his life could have been in jeopardy. It wasn't likely, but it was possible. Also, there was enough doubt that they wanted to wait and see.

It would take years for him to show enough development that they could make any rational, logical decision.

It took nine years. Nine years to confirm that he would be Minos. The people rejoiced when they were told the news at his naming ceremony outside the small, one-room temple at Knossos. And as far as he was aware, all had been sincere. Even his two uncles seemed to support him. There had always been the supposition that one of the brothers, most likely his father, would be Minos's successor. The man was indeed wise enough, but it didn't seem logical to promote him to the island's most powerful administrative position at a time when he was half-way through his life. He agreed. It made far more sense to give the inheritance to one young enough that he and the people would enjoy a full lifetime of leadership.

And now he was overseeing this simple ceremony at his great-grandfather's burial place, Zeus's tomb. For, just as his namesake before him, the people loved Minos and would follow him in any endeavor. The leader of the people: king, judge, priest, and exemplar. He rotated the double ax slowly to face all directions and handed it off to his wife who stood beside him. She was the High Priestess representing the embodiment of the Earth Mother Selene who had been married to Zeus. Her dress was simple and modestly covered her figure, not even belted at the waist. She was actually a renowned beauty in the area, but out of respect for the Earth Mother kept herself covered. This was a substantial change from the way Aphrodite, and later her daughter-in-law, performed any religious ceremony. They had always exposed their upper torsos, which sometimes distracted the less spiritually inclined men from the real meaning of the ceremonies. But it did have the effect of keeping their interest, albeit in an errant way.

She repeated her husband's actions and sang the Song of Vathypetro, now something of an anthem left as a legacy by that nameless and now forgotten old lady.

The hymn done, they together gripped the shaft of the ax and forced it into a crack in the floor of the cave near to the back. They then took turns pouring wine over it, passing the decorated wine jug between them. This they would do at this place every nine years, in remembrance of Minos's choosing at that very age, holding converse with mighty Zeus, deriving laws and inspiration, and expressing fealty to both he and Selene. Here they would demonstrate their colloquy with the greatest of deities. There was no separation of priesthood responsibilities between the two of them. The High Priest and Priestess were together responsible for enacting any ordinance which may be required and either could call for whatever ceremony or sacrifice they thought necessary for themselves, privately or publicly.

Minos had become synonymous with King, and any king of Kriti would forever be called Minos. He could be king without a wife, but when he took a wife she would share in his power equally and it would be expected that she would possess an equal portion of wisdom and intellect. This was in keeping with the general societal system of the island.

The men had never truly usurped the powers of the women as in other lands. At least no more than a strong man might take advantage of a weak man on occasion. But, as with weak men, if the more intelligent can find a way to win with argument rather than brute force, and can avoid violence by strategy and guile, then so it was with the women.

Minos had from the beginning encouraged all people to be interested in everything, to take chances and discover new ways to do all things. That didn't always work out. For instance, some of the younger men and women came up with ideas on dying blankets and coloring pots that were nothing less than repulsive. People bit their lips and nodded without saying anything detrimental; unless they were younger brothers or sisters who mocked the work unmercifully. The disasters could not be traded for more than a fraction of their functional worth and the budding artisans soon realized the value of sticking close to traditional and commercially successful norms.

There seemed little that women weren't interested in involving themselves with. The more physical tasks like mining or woodcutting had few participants, but the few that attempted it were rewarded by a welcome from the men. It was usually only the younger women who were going through their rebellious years who had the stamina to carry out that kind of work and not admit defeat. The work was hard and hot and meant that they usually worked naked or with only a skirt or loincloth. The work was mostly far from home and the men found the reminder of a hard, supple body fulfilling. Sometimes the women were more than accommodating, and the idea was often sported that every site should have a woman for recreational needs. Not too much later, that humorous expression would evolve into something of an expected right. The men worked hard and, although they liked the company of the few women there, they sometimes got frustrated at rebuffs aimed at them in favor of other men, especially when the other men boasted unabashedly of their conquests. The women weren't above teasing the ones they had no intention of lying with either. They might arch their back and stretch, all at the appropriate time, with the man nearby just inside their peripheral field of view craning his neck for a better vantage. Considering the time, it was almost surprising that rapes were rare and almost never happened at organized sites. That was something specifically condemned by Minos from the earliest times. A rapist had to give all that he had to the girl that he had attacked and banish himself to another corner of the island. Should news of a repeat offense make it back to Minos's ear the man would be set upon the nearest island and left to his own. Many of the little islands nearby had no water and little edible vegetation, unlike the bountiful Kriti with its broad plains, high rain-condensing mountains, and long seaboards. That was of no concern to the nervous local fishermen who had to take the man out in their little skiffs. They were not going to go any farther than the nearest island, and that was that. Everyone knew the law, especially the repeat offender. If he died thirsting, or if some horrendous sea thing from the depths came in the night for him, that was his problem. He should have known better. Everyone else did.

Then there were the rape-murders. Minos had spent much time puzzling over the rumors of these.

He shook his head, a habit he used to restore his concentration when he was drifting. "It is done. Begin your task." He and Helene, his wife, stood back from the entrance as the others, anointed and ordained to assist in priesthood duties, began the labor of filling the cave with rubble. Twelve men assisted, with twelve women. Only two couples were actually married to each other. The others had mates who kept themselves removed from this deeper aspect of the theology.

Zeus was being completely sealed up, something grandfather Minos had assured his grandson he would feel inclined to do at some future time. The red iron ore was tumbled into the opening and pulled to the back by sleds. More of the ruddy ore was exposed from the vein and used to fill the cave. It didn't take very long. They worked hard and the labor was a joy. When the exercise was finished, the entrance was indistinguishable from the surrounding scar on the rocky slope. Minos pondered the unusual ore as he gave some concluding words, and scattered the dust of the ground on the finished grade. It wasn't copper ore, he knew that for a surety.

They stood on the small plateau, where Zeus had stood a thousand times, regarding the covered entrance. Minos and Helene stood closer than the rest, in front of the semicircle, all contemplating what they had done, each searching their souls for meaning and enlightenment.

"Rest forever, strong and mighty Zeus." His words were soft, barely heard by those behind, dulled by a sudden wind curling off the rock bluff and blowing against their faces. It was as if the great man's spirit was suddenly liberated from its rocky confines and rushed out to meet its emancipation.

* * *

Word of life at Knossos was spreading. More people were coming to the area than could reasonably be sustained. The fact that they were coming was not the problem; visits for the purpose of paying homage were welcomed.

Selene's grave was the principal attraction, its simplicity lost on a people who still thought it extraordinary that a circular rock structure would be constructed by a young man in honor of his mother, regardless of who she was.

There were some who still clung to the practice of burying the dead inside the home. It was almost exclusively stillborn or very young children now, when it was done at all, some still not able to let go of such long-held tradition. Everyone else was placed in the numerous caves found far and wide. So far only a few chiefs had rock tombs similar to this built for them in their honor. Slowly it was catching on though, especially in and around Knossos.

Minos had ordered a large circular wall built, covered by a flat wooden roof, a short distance from Knossos. With the floor sunken by three feet, it would hold many dead and would take years to fill, even with the growing population. He hoped this would become the norm for the area and spread from here of its own accord without him having to decree it.

The people who visited Knossos on their pilgrimages were encouraged to find Zeus on Mount Juktas. An impossible feat to accomplish physically, the encouragement was to find him spiritually. Having already paid homage to Selene they were expected to have something of her spirit communing with them so that they would intrinsically find it easier to combine their souls with Zeus. They could be one with him anywhere on the mountain, and that was the idea behind concealing the cave in the first place. A specific location of worship was not necessary. They could be anywhere, and the gods could be everywhere. It was a difficult concept lost on many. To be everywhere. If nothing else, it made people think.

Those who did feel that they understood were becoming more numerous, having been told by those returning to their villages of their experiences and having had to retell the tale so many times. The new pilgrims had so much the advantage of having an idea of what to expect, and having the time to prepare themselves. Finding it easier to grasp the implications and relationships between mankind and the gods, they wanted only closer association, and with that desire went a longing to dwell close by in Knossos. Many had gone back to their villages after their pilgrimages and returned the next year, or the year after that, with all of their belongings and their entire family in tow.

It was becoming too disorganized. Minos had to post qualifications for status as citizens in the town. It was the only way to curtail growth. Development could not be stopped, but it could be more selective.

He had considered limiting the population by the same standards used to select his wife, the same standards he would use for his own children. It was a good idea, one that he would have preferred, but he didn't think the people would be up for it.

The greatest supporters of a strict selection process were his own family, with the exception of his wife, Helene. His own blood relatives, however, were firmly in favor. All blond, they had come to see themselves as different from the other people of the island. They began to carry themselves differently, more haughtily, some taking to wearing the purple dyed linen from the Levant as everyday garb rather than for special events.

None of his blood relatives were part of the select twelve couples representative of the twelve men who accompanied Minos on the first sea expedition. He just didn't feel good about having them as members of that council. They participated in other ways, and he actually got on with them quite well, being masterful in the arts of social discourse as taught by his grandfather. He had to wonder about them. Though they had the blood of gods in their veins, they seemed so frivolous. One day they would take life so seriously, and the next they would become riotously drunk, obnoxious and uncontrollable. They would sometimes insult the people of Knossos by belittling their lineage, thinking they were inflating their own social status by doing so. The people stood for it at first but, with time, began to resent the abuse and mutter complaints among themselves.

It wasn't long until those complaints reached Minos's ears.

He lost his temper for the first time. He gathered his family together, calling them to the old homestead away from Knossos where they could be isolated from the rest of the inhabitants of the town.

Most objected. "Why are we out here? What a ridiculous place to be."

"Young Minos flexing his will again, I'll wager. Just trying to see if we'll do what he tells us to."

"And here we are doing it." A few laughed. Most had an irritated air of boredom, especially the eldest of them. Minos's uncle and aunts were the worst. They looked up at the sky, rolled their eyes around, and made great exaggerated movements to show their displeasure. Neither spoke for or against this assembly, but their actions signaled their true feelings on the matter.

Minos swept over the hill with a retinue of his closest supporters. They only slightly outnumbered the members of his family but those with him were all men, and they were armed. Each had a long knife, almost like a sword, made of bronze and sharpened to a razor edge. The blades were sheathed, but ready for use in an instant's need.

Minos held up his hand when they were a few hundred feet away. He spoke a few words and then continued toward his family alone. The ones who had dedicated their lives to him if necessary kept careful watch, ready to vault into any danger that may present itself to their king.

Minos's eldest uncle stood as he came close, not out of respect, but as a matter of form that he had merely adjusted to.

"Minos. Welcome." He spoke halfheartedly and didn't even bother to forge a smile. The others stood up behind him, taking their time and stretching impolitely. A few nodded or made feeble bows. Some didn't even meet his eyes but made a pretense of focusing on something interesting in the distance.

Minos knew they would not have been so blatant had his entourage come closer. They made a big production about praising him publicly when in close scrutiny from the common people. After all, he was the king. And through him, or rather his grandfather, they were all part of the mystique that had to be preserved until such time as their numbers increased to the point where the inferiors could be put in their place.

If only Minos would see that. If only they could get him to see that his association with these second-rate mongrels would lead them all to ruin. He must see it. He chose an exquisite wife; he came from better parents; he must believe it.

"You welcome me with your lips, but your hearts are far from me." He stood before them holding a long staff topped with a thinly cast double-bladed ax of bronze. It was decorative rather than military in strength but could be wielded dangerously if needed.

"You speak harshly against us nephew." There was no disguising the underlying tone now. "You have summoned us for a reason. Will you engage in pleasantries all day or will you occupy us with your reasoning now?"

Most did a good job of concealing their thoughts, but a few could not hide the coruscations of sarcasm pulling at the corners of their mouths.

"You speak harshly against the people of Kriti; the people who we serve," cautioned Minos.

"Serve?" he exploded. "Precisely the problem," he yelled. "These people are less than us, can't you see?" He was waving toward the group of men grimacing back at him after having heard clearly the outburst.

"I see everything."

"You see nothing. You are as a blind man," he spat venomously. Some of the ones behind him were taking their weight off one foot and then the other, shifting nervously. "We are the inheritors of greatness, the children of Gods. Do you not believe your own ancestry? Look at you. Look at all of us." He swept his hand behind him. "What do you see?"

Minos held his tongue. He was fighting a fierce struggle within. He wanted to let himself submit to the fiery intensity of the anger seething inside. He wanted to shout them down, to smite them with his staff for their ignorance. That such disdain and conceit was coming from his own blood was unendurable.

He forced his voice to maintain a regulated volume. It quivered just the same. "It is you who have misinterpreted the goals of our Parents. Yes, I see you in your glorious blond hair and finery. I see you in your handsome and muscular frames. I see you with intelligence and understanding lacking in others more simple. I see you with the advantages given by the Gods to better the world in which we live. I see you have missed the point of it all. You are vain and self-important, intolerant and prejudiced. You have no love for any other than yourselves, and barely even that. You are so personally arrogant that you hardly even consider your own anymore. Each of you desires the state of godhood reached by your ancestors based only on rights of bloodline but you fail to understand that it was not their physical or mental perfection which led to their exaltation but rather their spiritual perfection."

Audible insults were grumbled. Many faces flushed in anger as Minos enumerated their faults.

"You anger at my words. So be it. You are insulted because I do not couch my words in flattery and false praise; because I speak truth, not lies."

"Truth? You speak truth? The truth is Minos was deceived in his old age. He suffered the same weaknesses in the flesh as anyone so old as he might be. He suffered the same weaknesses of the mind. You are nothing more than an impostor, an impersonator deceiving yourself as much as your simple people who have allowed you to be lifted on high when you should be grazing with their flocks. Only the pure should have reign in this world. I and my sister, my wife, are the only ones capable of keeping the blood pure. I should be in your place, but I was unjustly deprived of my right due to the deception thrust upon the strength of the ignorant people. Your blood is tainted no matter how careful your father's selection of a wife. She had black hair and so has your wife. Your children will be so far removed from purity that they will be little better than the stains you defend as 'your people'."

"You insult the people who have supported you, who have toiled more than their fair share to make your lives easier because of their respect of who you are, who have quietly tolerated your insults until they could no longer stand it? You dub them stains? They are the people from whom sprang both the blood of Selene and Zeus. Do you forget that? Aphrodite may have been sent directly from the Heavens but she was wed directly to Minos who, in case you have forgotten, had hair as dark as any on this island. We share her traits, and there is no way of knowing how long it will be before her traits pass from us. But this I do know, you will not be here to see it."

"Do I sense murder in your thoughts, Nephew? Are you planning to kill my children and those of your Aunt's as well? Do you think that such a notion could possibly be approved by our ancestors?" He was cock-sure of himself.

"I have no intentions on your lives. I will not harm a hair upon your heads unless you fight me, that I promise. But you have no place here. You do not belong with the people of Kriti. You would destroy them in time."

Minos called to his men. They came and fanned out on either of his flanks. They had not drawn their weapons yet but stood threateningly with their thumbs tucked into their belts.

If the drawing of blood had to be sanctioned it would be a first on the island. Bloodshed had been explicitly forbidden amongst the people. Only the Chiefs could make recommendation to Minos, and only he could authorize it. So far it had never happened.

Minos beseeched his family. "Are there any among you who will reject this man as a fool?" Minos would not dignify his uncle by using his name, an unconcealed insult. "Are there any who see him as an aversion? Who will stand with me and the people of this island?"

He waited only a moment. A few shuffled but no one moved toward him or spoke. They knew he wouldn't have them killed, there never had been a danger of that, and so they let it become a standoff. Minos was saddened. Even his younger brothers were so indoctrinated on their own superiority that they could not think to their own advantage. His only relief was that his parents had been away and had not been forced to endure this gathering. He knew their minds were not as one with this group.

"Very well. You have decided. You have chosen the bitter herb of your own free will, and I will not stand in your way." He lifted his staff high and vertical. "Your rejection of all that is sacred leaves me no choice but to banish you from this soil." He brought the staff down with a thump on the sod.

A tumult of exasperated exclamations erupted from the blond relatives. The twenty dark-haired men and women with them, previously considering themselves so fortunate to be tied maritally to them, now broke down. The women wailed knowing that they would never see their real families again. They protested that it was so unfair for the little children. How could he do this to them? He must be a monster. The dark-haired men protested in shouts along with their in-laws, uttering oaths and decrying the unrighteousness of the judgment.

This was getting far too tense. The men with Minos unsheathed their weapons. He didn't ask them to, but as soon as the first did the rest followed and he would have appeared as if he were not in control had he chided them for it. He understood their apprehension. The men in his family were larger than most men and could easily do them bodily harm, with or without a weapon.

"You have no right over us," stormed his uncle again. "He is but an impostor," he shouted to the men with the knives. "Lay down your weapons."

He could see they would not. In a frustrated rage, he charged Minos. He was only a few feet away and plunged into his nephew before he could prepare for the collision. There wasn't any way to step aside in time. He was thrown back and the staff underpinning the double ax snapped.

249

"No," shouted Minos to his men. The nearest were making moves toward his uncle. "Stay back."

Minos was much younger and had kept himself in such superior physical condition by working with the crews when on the sea and walking and carrying great distances by land, that there really was no contest against this older man. Even his bulk had been no help to him. He tried to get at the ax and take a swipe at his nephew, but Minos blocked the assault with his arm before it was given momentum, and then wrenched it from his grasp. He headlocked his uncle and twisted himself to the dominant position, pinning the kicking and protesting man under him. He was looking the fool all right. He couldn't even beat Minos in what had amounted to a wrestling match, and he was puffing and sweating with the exertion.

Minos released his grip, prepared to engage it again immediately if he had too.

It was a humiliated and self-conscious man who tried to regain his composure as he regrouped with the other detained.

Minos spoke. "You will be confined here. All of you must now get into the hut."

They protested again. "That hut is not fit for animals. It might fall in on us. Look at the cracked walls."

Minos shook his head sadly. Yet not all of them were protesting. Perhaps he was being hasty about banishing them while in a moment of anger. Maybe a few of them could use a second chance. He might discuss that back at Knossos. For now, he had to keep them incarcerated.

"Those walls have stood for generations. They won't fall in just because you have chosen this moment to go inside."

The roof had caved in years ago, but that didn't matter, all that was needed was the walls for control. The cracked and crooked walls were actually to the advantage of the men guarding against escape. If the detained tried to climb out en masse, the wall would undoubtedly collapse and seriously injure them. The only way out was the narrow door and only one at a time could come through that way. It was easy to guard. The men encircled the hut, staying back far enough to give themselves time to react in case of an incident. They were more concentrated at the front where the door was. They would allow one woman or child at a time out to evacuate their bowels. That was all. The men would have to use the back of the second room. It was humiliating, and it was meant to be. Be they men, women, or children they had to urinate inside if that's all they had to do.

"Give them wood for a fire inside. It will blind them to the night, and you will see their silhouette if they try to climb out one at a time in the darkness. Don't light a fire yourselves." Minos took one man with him and went back to Knossos.

* * *

Helene was happy to see Minos returning. She had been worrying that there would be fighting.

"Where are the others?" she asked, embracing him.

"They're overseeing my relations. We'll go to them tomorrow with food and drink, and a few more men. I don't trust my uncle. He has a smooth tongue, and I know he won't accept his defeat."

"What have you done with them?" She wondered at his use of the word 'defeat.'

"They're safe. No one came to any harm. We are holding them interned in the hut." Helene knew where that was. She had visited the place often, fascinated by the olive trees and their history of being planted by the Great Mother, a marvelous feeling to know that they lived not far from where she had resided.

"What are your plans? Are you going to punish them in some way?"

"I've banished them."

"Banished them? To where?"

"Somewhere off the island. I haven't decided yet. I wanted to have the council decide. I also want you to help me decide if I've done the right thing."

"You're unsure?"

"Yes. Not about exiling them but exiling all of them. I think some of them may have a change of heart. I think that they have been coerced and that they might not have realized what it was that they were actually doing. That doesn't exclude them from all responsibility, but it does perhaps lend itself to some leniency."

"You were meeting with us today anyway. There is no reason why this can't be added to the agenda of issues to discuss. Unless you want your family to sweat about their predicament for a few days."

Minos was too concerned for his family to find humor in her remark. He gave her a polite smile anyway and led her to the meeting place, hoping to find the others arrived early. They were. They liked to come early and discuss all of the events and share the news from all over. Unlike Minos's family, these men and women weren't sponges on society; they worked as hard as anyone else in the fields or in the workshops. They took time off in the afternoon once a week to attend to the business of governing the affairs of the nation, and met one entire day every week to attend to religious functions. On occasion, they found they had too much to do and would meet on consecutive evenings, often until late in the night, until all of the work was complete. They worked harder, in the end, than the other people. They received no pay for what they did, other than to borrow the oblations left at the small temple. Even those they shared out to any who were more in need.

The people were appreciative of what these select volunteers were doing. At night, if they had been meeting long, they could almost expect a group of the local women to come up the hill with bread and meat, knowing that they would be hungry. No thanks were ever accepted. The women were honored to serve those who served them.

Everyone stood as Minos and Aphrodite entered the circle. They met outdoors high up the slope where Minos the Great had been found dead in his bath to be close to his spirit and consume his wisdom. The bath still stood where he had placed it; still a marvel of ingenuity how it had been cast.

Minos's parents were absent, and several of the men guarding the extremists, but almost all of the women were here. It was unusual for so many of the Chosen to be in Knossos at one time like this. Usually they were scattered widely, around the island and at sea dealing with the affairs of state. These were the representatives of Kriti. There were no finer people anywhere.

They sat in a large circle, a warm fire already quietly burning in the center. Everyone had a personal goblet, bronze or ceramic, and the wine was passed along in several large and highly decorated pitchers. Minos held the new pitcher up with both hands to get a better look. This was one of the newer designs that so many were touting as superior over the older ones. The incised patterns scratched through a single color were now becoming passé, and potters were favoring the multi-colored glazes. This pitcher was black with a secondary bluish hue decorated with faint lines to give it a wood-grain look. This style was making a comeback after many years, only this time it had a baked-on glossy finish instead of just a flat stain. It was wonderfully done, thinly turned with great skill and very light. Another pitcher, just as masterfully done, had emphatic dark rust patterns, crisp lines laid on top of a lighter background. It had a portly, more bulbous, contour. It was easier to use than the other pitcher because it had a fluted handle riding from the spout and looping to the center point half-way down the container. It was a more useful design, but Minos thought he liked the artistry of the other better. It was more pleasing to the eye. He understood how people could argue on the variety of styles.

Usually these meetings warmed up with a bit of small talk, the weather, children, discussion of the most recent oblations, like these wine decanters, left at the temple. But there was just too much to do and Minos wanted to get on with it. He had tremendous patience, but today he was still wound up from dealing with his family.

"There is much to accomplish today. Let us commence this meeting."

He spoke loudly, a natural capability that he didn't even think about, overcoming the soft buzz of conversation between those sitting closest together.

"You must have heard that I, early this morning, met with the members of my family. We met at my ancestor's land, a land sacred to me. I called them particularly to that place to get them away from the people here, and to give them the opportunity to bask in the spirit of the location. I had hoped that they would cast off their scales of blindness and see what it was that the truth of our doctrine might reveal to them." His eyes were downcast and they were all intuitive enough to see that he had failed. "I had the greatest hopes for them. You are all aware of the problems that they have been causing, the curdled feelings left in their wake. There has been no excuse for their behavior to the people. When I found out how they have been treating others, I could not stand for it. I have to say that they have never shown such a disposition of malfeasance in my presence, although now that I know how they have been behaving I fear that I should have seen it in their eyes long before now."

There were grumblings of acknowledgment that Minos's relations had indeed been awful, that he shouldn't feel personally responsible, and that it was good that he was addressing the issue so promptly after it had been brought to his knowledge. He found great encouragement in their support. He had never known an instance when they had not sustained him in a decision. He counselled with them in most important issues, the ones that could wait. Their advice, even when it differed diametrically from his final decision, had always been welcomed and a necessary part of everything he had to consider to make what he confidently considered to be a righteous judgment.

"I have acted somewhat out of character," he continued. "I have pronounced sentence on them without your counsel. I fear that I may have judged them over-harshly in my indignation. I'm not saying that I want to change my mind or that I want you to help me justify my doing so. What I am saying is that I need your input even now, after the fact, so that if I have made a mistake it can be corrected before it is too late."

"What have you done with them?" asked the aged Taros.

"I have confined them in the old homestead."

Taros pressed out his lips. "A wise decision. They are guarded?"

"Of course. I left them quite vexed and shouting bile at me. They would not have stayed voluntarily."

"I know your uncle. It would be like him to attempt escape."

"Where would he run? This island has become a small place."

"He may try to overpower a captain."

"He may. But he would have to escape with everyone in the family to accomplish that. And none of them have useful experience at sea. That would be the death of them."

"There is much at sea that could sustain as well as destroy them. You may underestimate their chances."

Taros's words carried a great deal of weight at council. He was known as the only one yet alive who had journeyed with the Great Minos on his earliest voyages of discovery. In fact, he quietly let it be known on occasion that he was with Minos on that very first voyage in their early youth before he was even known as Minos. He was very old. But he had maintained almost a magical youth. He still walked for miles every day. He still traveled on voyages, although he kept to the local excursions and was never far from the shores of Kriti. Sometimes he still walked the island adventitiously, gone for months at a time as he toured incognito. He preferred to be just an old man of no consequence, keeping his past adventures and experiences secret from the many. He preferred to hear the unbiased words what others were saying about him, about Minos, and the men of old. He was a legend among them and, even though he had a humble exterior, he loved to hear of himself and his old comrades built up larger than life.

Taros took a slurp of his wine, neglecting to let the customary few drops fall to the Earth as oblation before raising it to his lips. "You haven't mentioned your judgment."

"I was hoping not to just yet." He clasped his hands. "But on reconsidering I will tell you that I have banished them all from the island."

Everyone gasped and started talking at once. Some thought it a marvellous idea, others were not so sure.

"As I have said, I want your counsel on this. I have considered giving reprieve to those who will swear allegiance to me. However, I am not blind to the fact that if I make such an offer some may go through the motions without meaning it sincerely in their heart. On the other hand, there may be some among them who have been genuinely led astray and should be given another chance. This is too difficult a judgment to make so quickly. I erred when I did so. I am asking you to sleep on it tonight, as I will. We will convene in the morning and you will give me your opinions then."

They saw the wisdom in this. When emotions were prevalent judgments were almost always too vindictive.

"We have the issue before us once again about the influx of people into Knossos." It was Taros's position as senior member to act as secretary and bring issues before them for discussion in some coordinated order when he was present. Minos managed just fine when he was absent, but it was a courtesy extended to the eldest because of the esteem in which he was held.

"Yes. It has gone past the point of tolerance. In the beginning, it must have been good just to have people come to colonize the area, but now the population has grown to the point where there are more than enough to do every routine thing that could be imagined.

"To start, we have an overabundance of shepherds. Some grown men are managing flocks the size a child could manage. Part of that is that everyone wants our sheep because they are the purest and most suited for sacrifices. It has been a blessing for us that this was so. But now it's time to spread the fine sheep which we are known for out to the other temple sites. It is time to develop them as the Great Minos said would happen. We will be fulfilling prophesy by doing this. I propose that we select ten shepherds who have proven themselves capable as fine breeders and assign them locations to start as Knossos was started." He paused and looked around indicating that if any had anything to contribute this was the time.

Helene sat silent beside her husband. They had discussed this matter at length and were of one mind on it. That was her greatest advantage over the others; the two of them would engage in conversation about all of the matters of state as a matter of course and so far had always come to a consensus between them. Usually when she spoke, it was when someone had introduced a surprise subject or when an issue required her verbal support.

Mostly the others sat silent as well. They usually only spoke to give final approval or when they were specifically asked to express an opinion. Taros was the only one who openly contributed to everything in this forum. It was something that everyone expected and enjoyed listening to. They knew they were welcome to speak if they wanted to but rarely took the liberty, preferring to defer to the wisest.

Taros spoke, as they knew he would. There would have been the utmost surprise if he and kept silent on this subject. "I was with Minos when he dedicated six of the ten temple places. It was a privilege granted to only a few. I can tell you that there was a magnificent upwelling in my soul with each consecration and that every person present was witness to the same perception. Few of those places now have people numbering more than two hands. This was because Minos knew that Knossos, the highest, had to be built up first. Here it is."

He stood and swept his arms out before him to symbolically embrace the town of Knossos. There were over two thousand people here now, by far the largest concentration of people on the island.

"Now it is time. It is time to act as Minos had wanted. I'm not sure that even he could have seen at the beginning how this city would grow, how people would flock here with their gifts and oblations, how they would clamor for the right to stay, how some would stay even without that right. The other temple places have been eschewed long enough. Some have grown and are fine places but not all. They all must grow and now is the time. Do you all agree?"

Helene was the first to do so, expressing her approval of the plan even as the word 'agree' was passing from his lips. The others followed suit in a united chorus.

Taros could not be stopped. This was common and delighted them all. He continued on in his prolonged speech, all the more acceptable because of his age. His hair was perfectly white now, and gave him an air of veneration, glinting in the sun as he gestured and turned.

"I am so gratified that this is happening in accord with prophecy. It will interest all of you to know that Minos foresaw that I would see the onset of the great kingdom before my time was ended. He knew that I would outlive them all. And now it is coming to pass. My friends, it signals that my time is nearing an end. When that end will be, I cannot say, but it beckons and I must answer one day. Should it come in another year or on the morrow I want you to know that I have been delighted with my life, that I have no unfulfilled desires, and that I can be carried to my final bed knowing that I have seen the beginning and the beginning of the beginning, and I am filled with peace."

A touching sentiment, although riddled with untruth. Minos thought he caught an indication of that in Taros's eyes while he spoke but passed it off while the symphonic accolades of the council rallied to adjoin what they perceived as the old man's final testament.

Taros had seated himself. Minos had to respond with a rejoinder.

"Our dear friend and colleague; should the day ever come when we ever have to lay your body in the ground be assured that your immortal soul will be ever with us. And when the day comes that we too meet our destiny, we will be pleased to have you standing in wait to guide us to our next domain."

He saw it again, a flight of apprehension that disappeared the same instant it was manifest. He felt uneasy for some reason. He thought it best to get back on track.

Minos returned the discussion to the migration of people to the temple sites around the island. Taros seemed to have bowed out of the conversation, lost in thought. There was a conclusion developing in everyone's mind that he had passed his time formally now, had made his statement, and that he would be content to sit and watch. They hoped he would participate again but, for now, they would help him along by participating in the discussion more than they normally would have to ease the silent pauses.

"The movement will include every craft and trade, their equipment, and families. It will mean that soon not everyone will be clamoring for our goods, that other places will be turning out quality perhaps as good as our own. That will alter trade between towns."

The suggestion was politely submitted that such a thing might be taken wrong by the locals of Knossos, that they had grown accustomed to the lack of serious competition. It had been a fact that with the movement of people this way that a great number of the most skilled had also found their way here. That had made Knossos more desirable, and even more skilled people had followed.

He responded to the concern. "Knossos will not be sacrificing so many as you might think. These other places are small yet. They do not require twenty potters; only one. They do not need more than one skilled mason; only one to direct the men in building the new town. They will not need more than one herdsman-"

"Herdsman?" The reflex interruption was unintended but unstoppable.

"Yes." Even Helene was shocked. Minos had never brought this up with her. "The cattle are numerous enough to spread around. The land is becoming overused and we haven't been clearing enough for both the sheep and the cattle. Both will have to be thinned while we make room for more. Again, we will not be sending too many. One bull and two cows to each place will be adequate. They can manage fine with that. They can raise their stock in the same way that we have. Over the years they will be as successful as we have been here, only, by then, we will be even more advanced. They will never catch up. Knossos will always be in the forefront. Knossos will always be the center of Kriti. Knossos is the center of the world."

This was incredible news. The cattle were almost sacred, at least the bulls were. No one had ever envisioned the bulls being moved from this place. Great work had been done to secure pastureland from the forest by cutting trees and spreading grass seed. The benefits of that were more wood for building and for making charcoal for smelting. It was laborious work. Digging out the stumps and pulling the rocks was hard and tedious. But it was for the cattle, and they were worth any amount of effort. The incredible power symbolized by the bulls were part of the central theme of the still-developing Minoan religion. If Knossos was the center of brilliance, of thought and reason, of spirituality, then the bulls must stay here where they belonged. Everyone had something to say, and many spoke at once. It was a rare occasion, and they shocked themselves.

Minos and Taros quietly sat and listened. Helene stopped first. The others slowly began composing themselves.

Minos held up a hand, and all became quiet.

"You see beside the temple the emblem of the Moon at crescent. There is more to it. When the Great Minos placed it, he had with him the White Bull of Poseidon, one of the many gifts of the sea, along with the Princess of the Moon, Aphrodite, by his side. When they arrived at Knossos with Father Zeus, they erected the emblem of the Moon. Little was said about it. It was said that it was altered soon after it was constructed, turned from the framing of the rising and setting of the Moon to the framing of the mountain Juktas, the dwelling place of Zeus and the giver of strength. It was for the White Bull that the power had to be focused. The emblem of the Moon was much more than what people had been told. It was symbolic of the horns of the Bull. Every year, at a time when the Moon is in conjunction with the crescent shape of the horns, I and Helene, and before us Minos and Aphrodite, alone, stand silently before the horns. Many have seen us, but no one knows what we do. I will tell you."

They were all deadly silent, even Taros who had no idea of any of this except to recall that past events weren't exactly as Minos had spoken.

"We stand before the Horns in communion with the Earth Mother. No one could know, as we stand there undisturbed by any who see us, that it could be so. We ask when the time will come when the kingdom will go forth. When Great Minos came to this island with his bride and the White Bull he stopped in many places and consecrated the ground to receive a future temple. There was more than that. He had crescents, or horns, built at each site. Each site had to have a bull to precede the construction of a true temple acceptable to the Earth Mother. My friends, I tell you the time is at hand. It is now. Can you not feel it within you? Can you not feel the spirit of the Earth Mother enter you and assure you that this is so? Close your eyes and see. Cover your ears and hear her voice crying in silence. You will be the carriers of the kingdom. You will be the leaders of the new temple cities that will grow and fill the world with light. Which gives more light; one lamp or ten?"

"Ten," they shouted at once.

It was done. They had agreed. They were the only ones who needed to. The temple council controlled the cattle, even if they only played an incomplete role in handling them.

"And now the subject of citizenship in Knossos. This comes up repeatedly.

"As we have agreed we have too many people in the city to currently sustain. In time this won't be a problem. With work done in the tight areas, better organization of works that will be for the common good of the people, those problems can be worked out. With the moving of cattle and sheep to other areas, we will have land available for grain and vegetables, for olives and grapes. Not so much food will need to be imported, and carriers will be able to use their efforts to transport other goods that will be of greater benefit to us. We will have a superior and more varied food supply to perhaps trade for more useful things. And it makes no sense at all for our junior smiths to be carrying copper from the coast. The completely unskilled people are carrying food when they should be spending their energies transporting the copper. That would free our smiths from the burden and let them do the work they specialize in.

258

"Besides efficiency, there is the matter of worthiness. How do we select the elite among our people who can carry on after us upon our deaths? Everyone aspires to that capacity, once they are accepted into this town, in the same way that they stay here and expect to be accepted.

"I propose that we establish a 'higher order', the most competent and desirable among the people. Everyone would be welcome, and encouraged, to petition for acceptance. Once accepted, the applicant would be given the special status of Citizen and would have the right to attend special meetings pertaining to our temple ordinances and sacrifices which would normally be veiled to the ordinary people.

"There will be two social stations between the ordinary people and ourselves.

"The first will be the skilled workers, the masters, the craftsmen and artists of great merit, exceptional farmers and breeders; any producer of quality. Among them will be the beautiful, the strong, and the handsome who will be subject to direction of the council on who they will be mated with.

"The second will be above them. They will be the intellectuals. They will have passed through the gates of wisdom and been accepted into the special circle. There will be only one prequalification; they must believe and accept the Earth Mother as a fact and not a superstition. It will not matter where they come from be it this island or another land. Nor will it matter if they are from the hoards of ordinaries or from the first social order. All that will matter is that they have the capacity to pass through the gates of wisdom."

He let them absorb this. His mouth was dry from speaking, and he took a long draught of wine. It had not been long in the crock and had not matured fully, still sweet, and not very alcoholic. He preferred this incomplete wine served at the council meetings so their heads would not be clouded. If they wanted to get drunk after the conclusion that was fine with him. He liked a good drunk once in while himself, but avoided it mostly because of the 'next day' effects. He thought it must be something like seasickness, something he had never experienced aboard ship. It had past occurred to him that the malady must be even worse on board a moving ship and he felt for any who fought against it after imbibing too fully. As many as were prone to it he banned from future voyages. There was no point in having a useless body taking up space and not able to assume his fair share of responsibilities.

Glaukos set down his own goblet and ventured a comment, hoping that it didn't sound like a criticism. He cleared his throat. "Are we to understand that you contemplate others, outsiders, coming to this island? That is to say, they will have the full rights of any who have been born here?"

"Yes. Remember the tales of Great Minos. Many of our benefactors came from distant lands. They taught us metalworking, the secret of bronze which has been isolated in this place of Knossos; they improved farming and brought us grains which have provided increased sustenance for us; they have brought us potter's wheels; they continue to come, on invitation, to live with us and improve our lives with their different, and sometimes improved, ways of doing things."

"I welcome these changes too. But I worry that one day one of these foreigners might betray our people. They could live here for a time and then go back to their own. In treachery they could reveal any weakness we might have and mount an attack against us."

"Against Kriti? Impossible. You have seen the walled cities of the distant nations. How afraid they are, with good reason now that we are supplying weapons of strength to their neighbors. They are concentrating so much on fears of their own, and our, making that they have no mind to attack us. Even should they come to that inclination, the sea is our wall, our greatest protection. And wherever we go we spread ever more grandiose tales of the dangers of sea travel. They are so deathly afraid of sea monsters now that we will never suffer a danger from any of them. The respect we gain from them for our bravado in plying these dangerous seas makes us immune from even being in danger in their own lands.

"Still, I understand your point. Immigrants could see that the journey here was no more dangerous than a long walk and that our towns and villages are not fortified. Yes, you make a very valid suggestion. Therefore anyone coming to this island will not be permitted to leave. That will be regardless of gained citizenship. It will not even matter if they attain council status. Once here they can never leave. Will that satisfy you?"

"Yes, Minos. Your wisdom is evident once again. Forgive my concerns."

"Your concerns are why these councils are held. I depend on all of you to bring before me all things that I have not considered. Wise judgments cannot be made with incomplete information."

"How will the selection of applicants to the second social order be ascertained?"

"I have discovered a cave unlike any other. As all of you know, there are innumerable caves on Kriti. Most were only good for burial in the old times. Quite numerous are the ones large enough to be habitations. I have met many who live in such caves. But more rarely are found caves that are enormous. I have been shown three that are so large no one has ventured into them far enough to find the end. Recently we found one not far from here that is at least equal in size. I suspect that it may be the largest of all."

"You found it yourself? Does anyone else know about it?"

"Helene and myself only. Its entrance is well concealed. It was only by the most extraordinary chance that we came upon it. We found a quiet place to enjoy our solitude with blanket and wineskin thinking we would have a nice evening together, perhaps spend the night under the warm summer sky. The ledge where we lay looked over the sea in the most contemplative way, as it does at sunset. We felt so idyllic. The most beautiful singing started from the sumac bush just behind us, bursting out loud as unexpectedly as a clap of thunder on a rainless day. The song was so exquisite and penetrating we were held bound by its spell until late into the night. It called to us, yet we could not move. We were paralyzed by its incantation. On it continued, splendor unspoken by human voice, calling, always calling. I noticed the Star of Aphrodite appearing and falling, most incredibly bright. Just as it was passing away, the song changed timbre, becoming wilder and more urgent. As the star slipped over the edge, a nightingale thrashed in the branches and made its escape from our company.

"In the darkness we could see nothing that the bird could have been calling us to. But with the rising Moon, we were able to find an opening in the rock wall behind the thick bush. It was narrow, barely as wide as two men abreast, and along an in-turned section of the wall where it was completely blocked by the boughs of the sumac. With the shadows from the bush the way they were, it was almost totally unnoticeable. We broke a few of branches around the back of the bush, careful to maintain concealment of the opening, just enough to let us in unhindered.

"The cave is a maze inside. We went in without a lamp and got lost almost immediately. It branches and twists like no other cave we've been in. Although we knew we had only gone a short distance the cave spoke to us that we had descended into the bowels of the earth. We were so disoriented that we had to stop in the darkness and compose ourselves, to think of where we had come and how we could find our way out. Only by the most concentrated effort were we able to find our way back to a place near the entrance. In the nighttime it did not reveal itself as it would during the day, and so we curled together for warmth and slept until then.

"As the dawn broke, light filtered in through the bush and showed us, to our great surprise and relief, that we were lying in the very entrance itself. We tore down the offending bush that darkened the entrance and caused us to sleep in the wretched cold and damp of the rock.

"It now lies exposed for all to see who get close enough to it. Helene and I have returned to the cave on two occasions and, with torches, found our way to the end and back. One of the endings, at least. We dedicated it, thus making it whole in the manner in which the greatest of memorable places are dedicated. With prayers to Selene and the consecration of the double ax, we set it apart for our bidding. It is now named the Labyrinth, the Hall of the Double Ax.

"This Labyrinth is a network of convoluted paths which lead around and over, often crossing, forking and rejoining. At one point it opens into a dry cavern. Another cavern holds a wide subterranean pool of purest water.

"My brothers and sisters; this cave is the place where the selection of worthiness will be held. One at a time they will enter. One lamp to get to the end. At the end will be an item, singular in appearance, which they will have to recover. If they have the intelligence we seek, they will be able to recall the exit route, and they will have a lamp that should last long enough to escape. Even with an expired lamp, they still may be able to feel their way out. During the day, as long as light penetrates the entrance, it is visible from a short distance inside. Should they tarry inside until nightfall they would be lost, unable to find the exit. At that time they will have failed the test and will have to be rescued.

"This is not onerous. I have done it alone, as has Helene. The second time there we challenged ourselves, and did the quest without the aid of light in both directions. We have no doubt as to your abilities to do the same."

There were several nervous glances between them.

"I will not make such a requirement of any of you. Should you volunteer as a matter of personal fulfillment, then that is to your credit. The experience is worthwhile."

* * *

Minos had started a popular trend of having herbs steeped in hot water as a morning tonic. The styptic fluid wasn't the greatest for taste but he had grown accustomed to it and, in fact, looked forward to his morning drink. Others who had withstood the first several tries felt the same way. The health benefit certainly outweighed the minor disadvantage of bitter taste. Lately, someone had taken to adding honey as a sweetener and that had caught on surprisingly fast. Several must have conceived the notion at once as many were taking credit for the idea. The astringent tea, now so much more palatable, was invigorating and stimulated the bowels, which everyone found beneficial. Minos had never liked that full feeling soon after he rose or the urge that went with it. Best to get elimination over with as early as possible. Foul stuff; far worse than what came from cattle or sheep. The sooner he could get it out the better.

No one had previously spent much time contemplating the vile mess exuded daily from their nether eyes. No one liked the stuff, but until recently no one had given it much thought. Now bowel cleanliness was becoming a focus of attention. They were realizing how detestable it was and they were becoming obsessed with ridding it from their system.

262

After they enjoyed their morning tea, Helene warmed the shaving kit. She was happy that Minos let her shave him each morning. So many men offended her with their beards. If that was their wish, and their wives didn't mind, then it probably didn't matter too much. But how could they stand it? Those whiskers, often spotted with bits of food and drink, must be terribly rough on the face when making love. No, a smooth man was much better.

She placed the blade of the bronze razor in hot water, beside an ornate floating dish of warming olive oil.

"Bring your whiskers over here, my love."

She always called him 'my love' when they were alone. He rose with his mug and sat next to the stove, leaning back in a recumbent position, and took the last of his tea. Helene swabbed his face liberally with hot oil, rubbing it vigorously with her fingers. His sharp night's growth abraded her fingertips uncomfortably as she thought again about the unattractiveness of bearded men.

"Why don't all men shave?"

"You might ask why all women don't shave."

"Do you find hairy women as unappealing as I find unshaven faces?"

"I was talking about faces."

They laughed.

"Careful. I could slip with this."

"I don't know why people think or act the way they do. Some people don't care much about beauty, that much I do know. At least, if they do, they don't think that laws of attractiveness apply to themselves. I've yet to meet a man who didn't recognize a beautiful woman when he saw one."

"Does the man, then, not think that women look at men the same way?"

"Clearly not. Or else they think that they are attractive enough the way they are."

Helene shook her head. She started to scrape his neck, the most delicate part. He tilted his head back and stretched the skin taut. Neither spoke. This part was unnerving even with his wife doing the shaving. A man was literally entrusting his life at this stage. It had never happened, but a man could be killed in an instant by a deceiver. She finished quickly and rinsed the oily emulsion of dead skin and whisker ends from the blade.

She rubbed more oil onto his face and neck before going over it again. There were still little whiskers that had been missed in several places. They would have to be tidied up.

"I still don't understand how they can see the difference between beauty and ugliness in others but not themselves. Hairiness is so unhygienic. If it were only their beards it would not be so distasteful, but they let their nostrils sprout like carrot tops and their armpits like fields of wheat. Their eyebrows grow together and their ears fill with moss. Do they have the right to offend the sensibilities of others as they do?"

"I cannot argue on their behalf. I don't know the answer. Perhaps it's too much trouble. Maybe they think it's too dangerous. And they would be right."

She raised the blade threateningly above her and made a quick slash, coming nowhere near him.

"See. They have heard how you try to murder me daily."

"I'll do worse when I shave the rest of you. You're lucky I don't have to do that every day."

"Not so. I would have you do it twice a day." He reached for her breast.

"So you say." She squirmed back on her knees, keeping herself just out of reach. "Stop that. We have to meet with the council soon. How would it be if we both showed up grinning like newlyweds? Now hold still and let me finish."

"You have to let me shave you next."

"Oh, won't you stop. You just did that. It will be days before you have to again." She went over his neck again to shut him up, and to make him go limp. Going out in public with an erection was always unseemly. Bad manners. He was quiet until she finished.

She dabbed at a small nick on his neck. "You were wise to have this made." She dropped the bronze razor gently into the hot water.

"Yes." He toweled himself off. "The obsidian blades left me with worse than this." He continued dabbing the tiny cut, minute dots of red spotting the cloth tens of times over.

"Amazing how they bleed," she said. "If I cut your arm it would have stopped long before this."

"Necks are like that. It's the best way to kill an animal. It's no different for a man." He dropped the cloth into the water.

Minos went over to the chamber pot and squatted. The drawn-out tone, amplified in the commode, was at once relieving and amusing. He tightened his anus and bore down as the wind passed raising its pitch to a high whistle.

Helene parted her lips to say something then changed her mind. She merely looked away.

What an amazing organ. Minos bore down again and felt it expanding, a squishing, cracking sound preceding the dull tot of a turd hitting bottom. Then another. The rank fetor offended him. He noticed that Helene was no longer in the room. When he was done he washed his rear with water and let as much as possible drip into the pot. He smeared on a bit of the warm olive oil. He couldn't help but see the brown coil inside the pot as he carried it to the door and placed it on the ground outside. One of the collectors would come by later in the morning and empty it into a skid, a shallow box on tracks something like a sled. Urine drained through gaps between the planks and soaked into the dirt but at least the solid components of the waste were taken away. It was dumped in a heap just outside of town where prevailing breezes carried the smell salubriously away.

Minos donned his loincloth and skirt and went out to find Helene. He couldn't understand how she could go so long without purging herself. He had to shit at least once, and often twice, daily. She would go for at least three days and longer. And in the years that they had been together he had never heard her make a noise. When they traveled by sea she never emptied her system and wouldn't even urinate more than once a day. But she bled. Maybe that was what women did instead. He didn't think too much of that either. No one was able to answer why these disturbing things came out of their bodies, least of all he.

* * *

The special council meeting got underway early. They broke fast together and attended to the business at hand while eating.

"I have charged you with judging the traitors to the people of Kriti. I have given you all of the facts and complaints of the people against them. I have told you that when I met with the traitors, they were unrepentant. I have given you the night to sleep on it and make your recommendations. What say you?"

"Banishment," said the woman and her husband to Minos's left.

"Banishment," said the next couple.

"We agree with banishment but would like to see them given another chance to recant their disdain of the people."

Minos pursed his lips as they said this. Many nodded and expressed the same sentiment. Several more said that they should not be given any chance at all and should be banished without delay. Helene was among them.

Taros had so far been silent. Minos looked at him and waited. At last, he spoke.

"You have already pronounced sentence on your family. You seek our opinion on this matter, but I believe you have already made your mind firm. I believe you will indeed banish them. I do not think you have a choice. They are rebellious and in time they would usurp your power. I have heard what they have said. I have heard you tell of their own perceived nature. But having known them and having known their ancestry I must ask this: Are you absolutely sure that they are not superior to the average person as they claim?"

Taros had a way of shaking the council and making them consider unpleasant conceptions that they would rather not.

"You are suggesting that they may be right."

"I am suggesting that you are not convinced that you are."

"I have said as much. That is why we are here in discussion."

265

"Do you hope that we will uphold your decree, or justify your changing it?"

"As they are my own blood I can neither be seen to be acting in their benefit for fear of the people saying that I have acted with favoritism; nor can I bring myself to banish them without your support for fear that I will always think that I have judged this way simply to win the support of the people. Our relationship is too close. I must have direction from the council on this."

"You have not answered the questions."

Minos put his face in his hands. After a moment he looked up. He was obviously stifling his tears. "I do not know the answers."

He had said it. The truth. The others murmured. This was not wisdom on his part. As king and judge, he could not be seen as equivocal.

"I think you do," Taros said helpfully. "You have already discussed it. You have said that they are not what they claim they are; superior. We have at the same time said that we have a way to determine status of people here in Knossos. If your family is what they say they are then they should have no difficulty passing the test."

"Put them through the Labyrinth? Taros, I hope as I grow old I will be granted increase in apperception as you have. I then propose that the members of my family who will accept the challenge be given the chance to defeat the Labyrinth. Those who prove their worth may stay. The others will be banished. Do you all agree?"

The response was loud. Most did. A few murmured quietly that they thought banishment should not be avoided by those clever enough to pass the test, but they would support Minos's decision no matter what it was.

* * *

It had been a short meeting. Minos had decided to give the prisoners a final chance to repent. In the meantime, he needed to pay a visit to the master smith.

He and Helene stopped in the doorway of the furnace house and thumped their oak staffs on the sill three times together. They had the act well synchronized and could do it without even looking at each other. Just the whisper of a shadow of movement in the periphery was enough to clue each as to the first stroke and, after that, the remaining two were just timing.

The dripping wet men turned suddenly at the sound, all standing except for the two crouched in the middle of a pour.

"Minos. Helene. You grace my shop. Setos bring some wine." The master snapped his fingers at the apprentice. "Come in. Don't stand in the door like sellers of fruit. Come in and sit. Or is it too warm in here for you? Perhaps I will come out."

Minos held up his hand to silence the fast-talking man. He could talk all day about nothing if allowed. He was worse when he was nervous, as he always seemed to be around Minos. There was no reason for it. He knew without a single doubt he was the most talented smith anywhere, turning out the most exquisitely crafted works. That was why they had come.

They stepped inside. The torrid atmosphere pressed into their lungs and stemmed their spontaneous respirations for a moment. Helene wondered how even the strongest men could stand this for any length of time without succumbing. They drank copious amounts of water to compensate for that lost through the pores. Still, the heat.

"Caphes, it is a wonder you do not ignite in this inferno."

"Ah, but it is the love I have for the working of the metals. They are magical. They are wondrous. They make me one with the Earth Mother who supplies us with endless ore. The Mother gives us water to quench our thirst. She gives us stamina to not faint. I would not sleep, but I must. I would work all day and all night if only she would give me more strength. But I am a weak man. I pray that I will live long enough that I may become stronger and more able. I pray that I may gain perfection through my work. She has blessed me with everything. She has given me skills that have been passed to me from the mind and hands of Hyphes himself. If only I can begin to fill the place he left vacant. I . . ."

"Caphes, please." Minos had been holding up his hand but the sign was being ignored.

Caphes was particularly manic today. Minos had heard that sometimes Caphes would ruin a work and fade into the depths of remorse, hardly speaking to anyone for days as he pined over some mistake that would have happened to anyone if it had happened to him. At other times he was uncontrollable, running around in the shop, ordering the works of five different pourings at the same time, confusing the other smiths and apprentices as he drove the furnace hotter and spurred them on at a frenzied, intolerable pace. But his work was magnificent. Not only was he able to make the hardiest bronze, he was able to shape it so exquisitely that no one was ever disappointed. He had taken to embossing designs on his work if the castings were for special people. And carrying that one step further he was now creating small, artistic works, engraving them with sharp instruments and polishing them to a glassy finish.

"I want you to make a seal for us. Not large. About the length of my finger. It should be square, with a raised image. I want it of fine metal. Do you have any?"

"Fine metal to make an image of that size? I should say I do. I have that much gold. I have much more silver. I could make a hundred of anaku. There is nothing I have not got. If you want anything larger you will have to supply me from your guarded stock. This is all I have for now. I . . ."

"Thank you Caphes. Could you have such a thing made by this afternoon? Out of silver?"

"Silver? Yes, I could make something out of silver by this afternoon. Even sooner. By lunch, if you will tell me what I should make for you. You want a pattern? A tree? Grapes? Tell me what you would have me make. I will make you anything. I . . . "

"I would have you make a puzzle, Caphes. A Labyrinth."

"A puzzle. Yes. A Labyrinth. I didn't know they were the same. I'm sure I could make a puzzle without too much trouble. I will get to work right away. A Labyrinth you say. Is there any particular type of Labyrinth you would care for? One like a puzzle perhaps? If you could just give me a bit more of an idea of what you have in mind I'm sure that I can make something to your great satisfaction. I . . ."

"A Labyrinth is a place where a person could get lost. He goes in, tries to find the end, then tries to find his way back to the beginning. The way is contorted, but not impossible. If he remembers each turn then, when he gets to the end, all he has to do is reverse the turns to find his way out. Can you make a design which is simple and at once elegant?"

"Yes. I see what you mean. I will portray it as a Labyrinth. That will be the best way. I will show you." He was giving the idea his full focus. His speech slowed noticeably when he concentrated like this.

"If I take my stick and draw a square like this . . ." He was talking more to himself as he sketched on the dirt floor, although he would respond to anything they would have to say. "If I draw the square like this and start the pathway at the top . . ." He pulled a line downward a short way. "But then it should end in the middle if it is going to end." He poked a center point. "And now it needs to be joined. Yes. That's what it needs. Hmmm. Yes. Hmmm. I need to draw a round square. That's what I need to do."

He drew a large circle on the dirt beside the square. Starting at the top, as with the square, he pulled a line down a bit then took it counterclockwise right around to the top again, leaving a small section blank equal to the distance he pulled the first little line down from the top.

"Hmmm. Hmmm." He extended the little line at the top right the way down to the middle. "Yes. Yes, there it is." The first line circling inside the outer circle had made a path, a roadway. Starting just below that, equidistant and going in a clockwise direction this time, he drew a line right around, again stopping just before the straight line going to the center. He repeated this process five times, creating a zigzag path that finally ended in the center of the circle.

"This is it. This is perfect. Now I will do it with the square."

It was exactly the same. He extended a line from the middle of the top down to the center. At equal intervals he drew lines right around the inside of the square, making a series of five squares inside the first. The last box was quite small. Then on alternating sides of the line that extended from the top to the center, he wiped over a short portion, erasing it with his fingers. It was the same zigzag path that he had drawn in the circle, only now it was square, as Minos had requested. One last little erasure at the top, which would be where the door would logically be, and it was done.

"Caphes, you are an artist. It is perfect. Don't you think it is perfect Helene?"

"I do. It is just what you had attempted to describe. You said he could do it and you were right." She turned to the smith. "Your design abilities make you a master. Show us how you will make this seal."

"Ah, it is easy. This is not hard at all. If it were not such a beautiful design so full of meaning I would not even attempt such unchallenging work. Yes, this is easy."

He unwrapped a wet cloth soaked in olive oil. Inside was a brick of very fine clay, still pliable in spite of the heat. He pulled off a handful and rewrapped it as if even brief exposure would be detrimental to its preservation. He slammed it on the table several times, rotating it after each assault. In seconds the mass was shaped into a brick. A short stick, almost the required size, he pressed into position, pressing it in and out and moving it a little side to side until the square depression was of just the right dimensions. He almost threw the little piece of wood away in his excitement, reaching for another tool. This was a sharp piece of copper, a long pencil-like implement with a curved point on the end. He pushed the end rapidly up and down as he drew the lines into the dark clay exactly as he had outlined them on the dirt floor. By dabbing, instead of drawing as one would a picture on a piece of paper, he avoided the raised ridges that would have been created. He held the evolving creation close to his face as he rotated it and poked away. Helene could not fathom how he could see the lines developing in such poor lighting, but he was obviously used to it. She wondered if he ever came out of here. Now that she thought about it, he was one person she had never seen on the street. She had never seen him at the temple, or anywhere else for that matter. She wasn't even sure when he had arrived. It was like he was born in here and had never left.

It was done so quickly. He showed the negative to them for their approval. It was as hard to see as she had suspected. A few faint lines, that was all. Some appeared, and others faded, as the angle of the little light that there was changed over its surface as he wiggled it back and forth. They thought they could make out most of it and nodded, having to accept some of it on faith.

Caphes took the mold over to the pouring table, a high box filled with sand, and placed it close to one side. Then he reached deep into a box hung on the wall, after removing a peg holding its door closed. He removed a small leather pouch, and from that a small piece of silver. He held it out to Minos for inspection.

"Will this be of the quality you desire?"

"Silver. Yes. That will be exactly right."

It was all that Caphes had. "Setos. Remove a small crucible."

He kept several of them heating in the kiln which saved considerable time in melting the metals. They were always ready to be used.

Normally Caphes would have found something to do while the phase change from solid to liquid took place but, because of the presence of his most important guests, he stood with them at the kiln and talked.

Helene could not believe the heat, dry and penetrating, far worse than the sun on a fiercely hot afternoon. She felt the raw intensity of the furnace on her face as she peered inside. The crucible had reddened to a bright glow, losing its form, melding into the fire itself.

The silver liquefied fairly rapidly. When Caphes removed the crucible from the fire they saw it jiggling like mercury at the bottom, edges raised ball-like from the powerful forces of surface tension acting upon it, repelled as it were from the very surface of the smooth lined container.

Carefully he began to pour. This precision changed his whole demeanor. His facial expression swung from one of gregarious sociality to a deep furrowed frown as he concentrated. Not a precious drop was splashed or spilled. He could not hear as he was pouring; he could not feel or see anything other than his work. A thin line of silver trickled into the mold. Caphes bent and arched his whole body. The crucible was not heavy even at the end of the copper fork, and his arms were amply strong. He twisted none the less, as a musician contorts while playing, feeling the music. He could have poured faster but preferred to keep the slow dribble constant. A continual hiss of rarified steam boiled out from under the hot metal, aiding the cooling.

Caphes stretched his neck forward to inspect the empty container for remnants then placed it back in the furnace. He picked up the mold and flipped it upside down, bending the clay backward and ejecting the ornament. It dropped the short distance to the thick leather-covered table with a thump. Amazing to Minos and Helene was that it was already hardened. The change must have been almost instantaneous.

It was duller than he hoped, the sheen stripped away by the steam which had a poor effect on the finish. Caphes noticed the difference between this and the finish that could have been achieved with a dry mold, but his customers were in a rush. There was no time to let the mold dry as he typically would have.

Minos reached out to pick up the square, allured with the raised image of the Labyrinth design laid on top of the flat surface.

"Careful," warned Caphes. "It is still very hot." Minos withdrew his hand, wondering what he was thinking about. Caphes had just prevented him from severely burning himself.

The smith took a short bar of bronze, a tool much like a pencil except it had a wide, arced flare at the end instead of a point. He worked the curve of the tool back and forth along each depression between each raised line on the ornament, smoothing the metal while it was still hot. The shine came up nicely, improving the dull, microscopically pocked surface. Caphes worked quickly, a flurry of action with his face pressed against his hand as he added extra pressure to the smoothing implement. The perpendicular corners slowed him down. The tool was becoming less effective as the silver cooled, resisting the manipulations of the smith. He finished up by buffing the silver with a cloth soaked with olive oil and wood ash. The oil brought the silver to a temperature that was handleable and Caphes picked it up for the final polishing. It was still fairly hot and he kept it moving through his fingers to keep them from burning, and his furious burnishing lent a lambent finish to the surface.

Minos received it with wonder. Helene bent close to his hands to examine the detail. She had a great attraction to articles of this kind; detailed works of precious metals. This was just the sort of thing that appealed to her. She took it into her own hand, surprised that it was still so warm. She felt along the smooth raised lines outlining the path, tracing it all around until it ended in the center, then retraced her path to the beginning again. It did remind her of the Labyrinth. Symbolically it was a perfect representation.

* * *

The council gathered in front of the doorway of the old house in which the prisoners still remained interred.

"Have you had any problems with them?" asked Minos.

"Other than a battle of wills we have had none. They realized our superior strength and complied with our restrictions. Keeping them quiet was another matter. Your uncles were the worst, attempting to stir dissension among us by calling speeches into the night."

"What did they say?"

"They accused you, Minos, of being an impostor and Helene of being a seeker of fame. They said that Minos the Great was infirm and addled in his old age. Only because of his affliction did he make the demented decision to name you Minos. They caused quite a commotion, yelling and arguing amongst themselves for what they perceived to be our benefit."

271

"How did everyone react?"

"As you would expect. Minos, we are among the closest to you. Each of us is loyal to a fault. They could say anything or offer anything." He waved his hand at the hut, dismissing all inside. "They have no influence over us. Absolutely none. We are saddened, if anything, over their treachery. They could be among the finest people. They are born to be so. But they have rejected our ways. So be it. They have made their decision. We have made ours."

"They may have not made their decision yet. We will be giving them another chance."

"Another chance? But they have rejected you completely. Forgive me for saying that I think you are making a mistake. You were not here to listen to them last night."

"You may be right. I did not say that they are forgiven. Only that they will be given the opportunity of that. It will not be easy for any of them. Probably it will be impossible for most."

Several skins of water were flung over the wall with terse orders to the prisoners to drink their fill. Then the family was rounded up at knifepoint and the men tied together by rope around their waists. The restraints were pulled tight enough so that they could neither slip down over the hips or be lifted over the chest. None of the men had a pot-gut, so this was neither difficult nor painful for them. The rope chafed some as they walked, but it was not too uncomfortable.

The going was slow with the children. Both the mothers and the fathers carried them for spells. All complained bitterly about the abuse they were enduring, but none balked completely by refusing participation in the move. The line proceeded voluntarily, if reluctantly.

Because the line moved so slowly the cave was not reached until after dark. The armed escorts maintained a scrupulous vigilance as darkness fell. Before the cave was reached even the vociferous women had to be tied together in a second line. The protests were becoming more vehement. Minos was afraid that they would have to use force to compel them to maintain the march but, after a few moments of tense standoff, the line again began to move.

Everyone was tired. The cave was reached just in time. The prisoners would not have kept moving much longer without enforcement by some form of brutality. Fortunately, they were so tired from the journey that they fell to sleep almost as soon as they had eaten a small ration. The children were given as much as they wanted to keep them quiet through the night.

"Do you think those ropes will hold them until daylight?"

"I think so. The knots are difficult," said Minos. "Probably too difficult in the dark. They won't even try. Even if one or two did get loose they would still have to get past the guards. No. They won't go anywhere. There isn't anywhere to go. They won't leave the family."

The camp was relaxed that night. Minos was correct in his assumption that the prisoners would be no trouble. All of them slept soundly after the long walk. With the exception of a couple of babies crying to be fed and their mothers attending to them, no one stirred.

First light signaled the beginning of the trial of worthiness. One by one the members of Minos's family were brought before him. One by one they told him to kill himself. They were so antagonistic that not even the women, not even his own sisters, softened to his words. They had a malignity for the dark-haired islanders that could not be assuaged.

Minos felt a sadness beyond parallel. His own sisters. They had not been brought up this way. They had been raised by the counsel of their father, and their own mother was a regular islander, a beautiful woman of high intelligence and integrity. How could they condemn her too? He was glad his parents were away for this. It would crush them to know of the secret thoughts their own offspring were harboring.

Even more lachrymose were the children who would have to follow their mothers in exile. They could not be separated. Once the decree was prescribed this time, it would be final. With not a single woman willing to renounce her disloyalty to Minos and chance the Labyrinth, it was a surety that no man would.

Except one man. After interviewing each of the male members of his family, and having endured their unveiled loathing and curses, he was averse to see the last of them, Seth, his uncle. The man would not sit, but stood defiantly before his nephew.

Minos rose in strength before him, not willing to sit while the other stood. "You will not even sit with me? Your own blood?"

"You have rejected your blood."

"I have rejected only what you say you believe. Your blood is precious and belongs here. Yet you make it impossible for me."

"Why have you called us to you separately? Did you hope to sway us individually when assembled it was unachievable?"

"Yes. That was my hope.

"And was your hope realized?"

"I will make the same statement and offer to you I made to the others. You are superior to the people of this island, I agree. Further, they are superior to other people of this earth. It is their destiny. Yours is to help them achieve it. Without you their destiny will still be fulfilled; it cannot be altered. But it can be achieved faster with you than without you."

"You tell me nothing new. What you haven't told me is why the banishment? We can be great. We are great. We can lead these people into the greatest force ever known and from there enslave the world. Our dominion could be endless. The Children of Minos could have complete supremacy. How can you dispute this?"

"I can't."

"Then why do you fight against us?"

"It is you who conspire against us."

"For the greater good."

"No. For your own ambitions. You care not at all about any of the other people, the people who make up the world. You want to see yourselves as the only ones in authority with all others subservient to you. You cannot see that everyone can be equal to you. You cannot see that you don't have to lower yourselves but must rather raise others higher. That is the objective that has escaped you. Mankind has such a great destiny. You would destroy that destiny with your megalomania, with your greed and selfishness. Did you really think that Selene's gifts and messages were meant for you alone? Did you think that her laws were meant for everyone except you?"

"Selene. What do you know of Selene? I don't care a sheep's tail for any of the eloquent offal vomited by you or the 'Great Minos'. You speak only words with no truth. Meaningless words. Words to palliate the multitude. Words to control. You don't believe them any more than I do. Confess. Tell me it is so. You don't have to lie. We are leaving anyway. No one except you and I will know."

"You traitorous filth." Minos fought to control his temper, but the only thing he had to replace it with was sadness. "I have invited you before me to give you another chance, and you spew out all that we hold sacred? You have corrupted so many that your iniquity can never be forgiven."

Minos breathed deeply. Grief was overwhelming him. He had thought so surely that some at least would consider taking the test he had devised, and here he had barely been able to get as far as the offer with most of them because of the venom of hatred barricading the way. Yet he felt within that he had to make the offer to Seth. Of all who had made themselves his enemy, Seth had to have the chance.

He made a fist. Somehow that helped him break through enough of the barrier that he was able to force it out. "Seth. Listen to me. You say you are perfect, or closer to that ideal than any other. I want you to prove it to me. I have devised a test of intelligence that shows clearly the superiority of any who apply themselves to it."

"You want me to take your asinine test? Is that what you want?"

"I have put myself through it. Helene has done it as well. I think you could too."

"Your troglodyte has been through it and you 'think' I can do it? You insult me with your speculations."

Minos fought to control his wrath. No one had ever spoken of his beloved wife in such an insolent manner. "I will pretend I heard different."

"Because you are a pretender."

"I am making you the offer which I promised I would deliver. My word is aggregate. I would send you away now if I was not bound."

"Bound you say. Yes. I believe you would like to see me go off in disgrace. It must be destroying you to have to make offers which you would rather not make. You purulent faker. Tell me about your test then. I will take it. I will never swear allegiance to you and will fight against you at every opportunity. Nevertheless, I will accept your challenge if only to show all that we are as we say."

Minos rued the idea of having to endure the company of this man. How vile he was. He wondered how he could have kept it secret for so long.

"There is nearby a cave. We are almost upon it, yet you cannot see the entrance. This cave runs deep. It runs not straight but twisted, with many turns dividing and rejoining enigmatically. At the end there are several unimportant items that I have left. You will bring one back to prove you have been there. You will be given light that, if you hurry, will be sufficient to see you to your return. If you linger, the light will fade and die. Even so, you might find the exit while the sun shines. But if you stay too long in your efforts to escape, darkness will fall upon the entrance and you will not find it. You will have failed at that time. You will not die in the Labyrinth. You will be rescued the next morning."

"I will hardly need salvation from you. I will only take your lamp to get it over with faster and show you your own inferiority."

"You may take any of our relations who will go with you. But I will tell you now that they have all declined my offer."

"Of course they did. None will accept it should you make it again either. However, I will take one with me."

Minos led him to the prisoners.

"Arita," Seth called to his daughter. "You will come with me."

Minos nodded, signaling the keeper to release her. She was young and extremely pleasing to the eye. Like most of the young women in Minos's family, she held back on marriage far longer than what was the norm. She was in her eighteenth year, seventeen years old, and held herself with an arrogant conceit that spoke only scorn. She hated this place. Resigning herself to exile was not an issue. She welcomed the event.

She came up to them, presenting a scoffing sneer as she looked down her narrow nose, taller than any of the women and most of the men. She crossed her arms under her breasts and inflated her chest, then held her breath and stared crossly. Her carnal sensuality had afflicted more than one of the men there, a rough tempered girl who they saw as one in need of a good taming.

Helene came with a lamp for them to carry into the cave, a small palm-held oil lamp with a little hole through the top to fill it and another at the end of an elongated extension that was upturned at the end with a woolen wick protruding.

"Only one? There are two of us. Each of us must have a light," he demanded.

Helene was justifiably critical in her retort. "Only one. If you had another, you would put one out and use it to return. Your opinion of us is low but credit us some intelligence."

Seth was disappointed that he had not been able to pull that one off. Not a problem. They would still find their way back in record time.

"Very well. Let it be known that you place us at an unfair disadvantage. It only proves further your unjust grab for power. You will try to show that we will not be able to accomplish this task laid out before us. But we will prove you wrong. We will show that we are capable indeed of what you ask of us. Not that that matters. You will still exile us at the end despite what you say. Nothing you say can be believed."

Minos was exasperated with the accusations Seth was levying against them. He could not get used to the blatant lies. He could not understand how anyone could be so outright mendacious and still live peaceably with themselves. Maybe it was wrong to be giving this man another chance. Maybe he himself was the one at fault for turning a blind eye to Seth and his spurious rhetoric all these years. Doubt was filling his mind again. This whole thing could turn disastrous. What if Seth passed through the Labyrinth easily? What if he changed his mind and did swear an allegiance to Minos? He would be lying but, without any proof of the future, he could claim the right to stay. All he could do is hope that Seth would not go that route. For now, there was no stopping the test.

"Let's get on with it then. Or will you stand in a daze until death takes you? Light the lamp."

They were not used to tolerating such insolence but said nothing, enduring the impertinent cheek. They were now convinced that this was all a waste of time. No good could come of it.

The fire walked across the minute gap between the torch and the wick as Helene touched them together. She would have preferred to pass the lamp to

Arita, who at the moment was less vitriolic, but Seth was clearly master of his daughter and it was only proper to give him the light.

She expected him to make a rough grab for it and was surprised that he took it so gently. He would not spill even a drop of oil. One quick glance into the top to satisfy himself that it was full and the two of them disappeared into the cave entrance.

"How do you think they will do?" asked Helene.

"I have no doubt that Seth will be up to his word. He will be almost running through the course. He may not even take Arita with him. She will probably stay close to the entrance while he carries on to the end and back."

"He will be able to move more quickly that way. And he would be without the added distraction of his daughter tailing along. Still, the agreement was that they would both go to the end."

"Yes. The agreement. There is no way of knowing whether or not they are fulfilling it or not. They will bring two artifacts back with them, but who is to say whether they each brought one or if Seth brought two?"

"May I make a suggestion?" They turned to look at Taros who had been listening behind them. "If I was to enter the cave you could not be accused of spying on them yourselves. If I was to do it of my own volition, without your specific approval, you could not be accused of showing mistrust. Should I find the young girl near the entrance, I will be surprised and tell her that I had come in out of curiosity and that I just wanted to see why the cave holds so much mystique, that I didn't believe that it could be so grand and challenging as it has been portrayed. It will hardly be a lie. While I don't disbelieve you, I have never seen such a thing in all my years and surely am curious, a perfect reason to enter."

"Thank you for your offer Taros. But I would prefer it if you did not follow them. The girl might see through the ruse."

"As you wish. I did not really expect your approval. It was probably not a good idea."

They stood in silence for a while. There wasn't much to do or say until Seth and Arita returned, or darkness fell.

"Perhaps you would like to leave the entrance for a while. Glaukos and I can guard the way until you get back. It will still be a long time before they find their way out, if what you tell us is any indication."

"I am in need of a walk. How about you Helene?"

"I wouldn't mind the opportunity to stretch my legs."

He felt a stirring. Her play on words escaped no one, but he thought it did. This was not the time to be thinking thoughts like that, but recreation was as necessary to life as eating. He took her by the hand and led her up and over the hill.

"How long do you think they will be gone?" asked Glaukos.

"Long enough to satisfy themselves. I'm glad. They have always been a perfect couple. They need time away from affairs such as this. Minos worries continually. I've not seen anyone so concerned about the goings on of lives around him since the Great Minos died. In time he will be as great." But not for a very long time, he thought.

"You're going to go inside, aren't you?"

"Is there really any choice? Seth and the girl must be discredited if possible. I won't lie if I don't find her, but I may bring her back with me if I do. Then they won't be able to dispute that Arita stayed behind."

"If she screams Seth will hear, no matter how deep the cave."

"I wonder what she will do myself. I'm still assuming that she is near the entrance. I could be wrong. The gods know how many times I've been wrong in my life."

"You speak an apology for all who live. But do you think she would alert Seth while he descended deeper into the Labyrinth?"

"That is the question. She may remain quiet in the hopes that I won't find her. There will be ample places to conceal herself. She will know that if she is discovered she could ruin the statement they are trying to make."

"Not much chance of your surprising her either. She will see your light. Even if you went in darkness she would hear you coming, and you would never find her."

"There is only one way to find out."

Taros filled his lamp with oil, the same lamp he had carried faithfully with him since his youth, the same lamp that had accompanied him on every adventure. How many years had it been? He cursed his memory. He couldn't even remember a simple thing like that, and he was never able to manage the calculations to figure it out. No matter. He took a long guzzle of wine and threw a blanket over his shoulders. It was warm outside, but he knew the chill inside a cave.

"I won't be long, Glaukos."

He stepped through the entrance with his hand cupped over the small flame and was at once sheathed in darkness. He had to stoop as the ceiling drew closer to the rough floor. The short, low passage twisted and opened suddenly into a hallway he could stand in upright leading perpendicularly in both directions. He checked behind him. Only dimly lit rock gave away the passage to the outside. Minos had accurately said that it would be impossible to find in the night. It seemed to vanish as he moved away from it, passing down the hall to the right. He had no particular reason for going right, it just seemed more natural. He went slowly, checking into every crevice. He looked behind him frequently, a trick he used everywhere he went, by land or sea. Things looked so different on the return trip. When people got lost it was almost always because they didn't remember to check behind them. He knew Seth would not make that mistake.

The passage divided into two smaller corridors. Again he stayed to the right. If he kept doing that then he could find his way out easily by just keeping left. This tunnel sloped downward at a noticeable incline. Taros was careful to take consistent regularly sized steps, and to count them. It was very tempting to take small cautious steps, but that would not have given him an accurate measure of the distance he covered. He maintained his caution, his old bones couldn't withstand a fall on these rough rocks, but he also maintained his step.

The rock walls were beginning to press in on him from the sides, and he was beginning to think that he might turn back and try another way when suddenly the rocks dissolved into nothing and he stepped into a huge cavern.

The magnificence of the chamber took his breath away. He wondered if Minos and Helene had been in this part. They hadn't mentioned it. The light from his lamp may have been the first light this cave had ever seen. Purple stalactites hung down to their contemporary stalagmites rising from the floor. There were dozens of them, most quite small in size, but some larger and more deformed.

In the middle of the chamber, a large object caught his eye. It could almost have been a man standing there, wearing a dark cloak wrapped loosely about him and spread wide at the ground.

He held his lamp higher, his hand shielding his eyes from the flame as he warily approached. As he came closer the form became more discernible, a pillar of rock about his size, rounded and smooth at the top with a cleft starting at the apex and running down the rounded portion. The part below that was rougher, almost wrinkled, in appearance. At the bottom there was a bulge on the front where he thought he had seen it flaring. It looked for all the world like an erect penis. A penis inside a dark cave.

A tear fell from the ceiling, a small hanging stalagmite losing a drop of moisture gathered from the humid atmosphere, landing on the tip of the glistening phallus. He saw it fall, reflecting his light. It splashed evenly in all directions, sending minute droplets all around. The mineral water blended evenly with the moisture already there. That was why the tip was so smooth. The minerals had been building for centuries, smoothing the end into a purple helm.

The sight of it excited him. What was it doing here? Minos should have made mention of this. Unless he hadn't found it. It was possible that he hadn't come this way. He did say the place was huge but it hadn't occurred to Taros that it might still be partially unexplored.

He rubbed his hand on the slippery surface of the phallus, sliding it around. He moved closer, sidling up to it, and stood on the bulge that rested at the base of the vertical oblong, representative to Taros of the scrotal sack. He breathed heavily on the wet end, intent on the mist that formed for a second, altering the sheen of the rock from gloss to satin.

Suddenly he wrapped his free arm around the upright rock and clutched it tightly to his breast. He was breathing hard. He could smell the rock. He could taste the mineral solution as he ran his tongue along the glossy finish. This thing was taking hold of him and he was submitting to its spell. His head began to swim. Part of him fought against it while the animal side of him wanted to let loose, to embrace it further, to fling away the lamp and let the darkness consume them as he would devour the standing organ.

Something caught his eye. He didn't turn, but it brought him out of his reverie. Someone else was here.

He relaxed his firm grip on the phallus, stepping off the bulge and back a few steps as if that was a perfectly natural thing to do. He moved his hand over the flame as he did while entering the cavern, protecting his eyes and limiting the light. He closed his eyes a minute, listening in the perfect silence for movement or breathing, but was aware of none but his own.

He opened his eyes. His hand still shielded the light. He kept the lamp down near his waist, allowing the light to shine without blinding him to movement from the sides. He learned from Minos so long ago that one's eyes worked best in the night from the sides, not from the front. He kept his eyes fastened on the phallus, as anyone watching might expect, but the stare was blank. He was consciously working on making himself aware of his peripheral vision, preparing for the slightest movement. He couldn't make out any specific shapes, nothing that could be distinguishable from the surrounding rocks, but that was not the purpose of peripheral vision. It was solely for the detection of movement.

He could wait as long as it took. Anyone watching would eventually have to move. He could sway back and forth to circulate his blood in this cold environment, move his legs and arms slightly, tightening and relaxing his muscles to relieve tension, taking a few steps in the right direction. It didn't matter if he moved. If he was right, he had already been discovered. How long could the other party wait without moving before their limbs cried out in needle pricks and pain?

A dimly effervescent shape moved to his left, small and disappearing into the darkness. He would have easily missed the movement if he had not been trying to see it. He was impressed by how quiet she was.

He still didn't move or give any indication that he might have seen. Gradually he stepped back and placed his lamp on a stalagmite where it would be out of view of his surveil but still casting light and shadow as if he were standing with it.

He moved with stealthy silence closer to the unseen opening where lay the intruder in hiding. The blond hair had been an easy giveaway. It had caught his light as perfectly as a mirrored pond.

An outcropping of rock was all that separated them. The rift was just on the other side. He paused, deciding on the best strategy. Quick or slow? He couldn't have her scream in surprise, at least not before he could catch hold and muffle it.

He thought about his approach a moment. It was a sure bet that she didn't know that he was so close, or even that he knew she was here. The young man in him wanted to spring quickly, but reason prevailed.

"Arita," he spoke softly. "Arita, I know you are here. It will be best if you just come out."

He was met with silence. She knew where he was now, so there was no need for the game of keeping the lamp where it was. He made the few steps to retrieve it and went to the place where she hid.

He held the light high and shielded as before, peering into the darkness of the crevice, a long tunnel curving up and to the side.

She was gone.

* * *

"I distinctly told you not to pursue Arita in the cave." Minos was controlling his temper, a task to which he was being put far too often these days.

"You told me you 'preferred' that I did not. I took that as a blessing to do as I wished; not that you forbade it."

There was no point in arguing with Taros. What was done was done. Seth would protest, and have good reason for doing so, but it would avail him nothing.

The prisoners were behaving themselves still. They were not so splenetic without Seth to provoke them. All of them had been fed and given drink. The children had been turned free to run around and the women their bonds loosed. Even the men were remaining phlegmatic.

The day was growing long. Minos was actually surprised that Taros and Arita had not returned. They were well past equaling his and Helene's time. He had been so sure that they would be able to do it, especially now that it was as good as confirmed that Arita had stayed behind. Maybe she had gotten herself lost when she ran from Taros. That was more than likely the case. Seth's light should be running out just about now. There was hardly any point in waiting for them.

"The sun will be down soon." Helene made an unnecessary observation.

They were finishing their last meal of the day, preferring to wait until after the prisoners had finished up theirs.

"They look rather sad, don't they?" She was speaking of the prisoners.

"Yes. They do. They are still high minded regardless. They may be thinking less of Seth, but they are thinking no better of us."

"Will we go into the cave to get them out?"

"Eventually we will have to. I don't want to drag the process of this exile on for too much longer. We'll set a watch for the night, just in case the unexpected happens and they do find the exit by chance. At dawn, we will go in search of them."

* * *

The search party of six men, each bearing a bright lamp, and each armed with knives, wended their way through the corridors of the Labyrinth. Only Minos had been in here before. Taros had insisted on coming but Minos had been firm; he was to stay behind. Minos took them on a convoluted path so that none could find much of an advantage should they one day try the challenge. He didn't make it too meandering lest he himself get lost, and doubled back in a few places to regain his orientation, which only further served to disorient the others. He knew full well that he had not covered all possible routes in here and Seth could be anywhere.

He shouted out his uncle's name at intervals while they all stopped and listened intently for an answer. What could have happened to them? The sound should have carried far enough. They must not be answering for another reason.

Minos was suddenly on the alert. He withdrew his knife and the others, when they saw what he did, mirrored him.

He stepped into the entrance of the cavern. They had wound their way to a place not far from the cave entrance. The pathway to the exit lay on the other side. He knew the way but felt caution take him by the hand. This was the place of the phallus. He had discovered it with Helene and they had coupled here, in the cold, in front of the sign. This was a cavern of mystery, of meaning, of life. And right now he felt a bad spirit here, a feeling of something being wrong. It was not like this last time when the cold was present but of no accord. Now it was penetrating, chilling cold.

Something was very wrong.

He held his knife blade where he would have placed his hand to shield the lamplight from his eyes. He warily examined the rocks immediately around him for ambush and finding none stepped completely into the open. The five behind him stepped in and gave audible gasps but returned to silence, also feeling the uneasy tension in the air. The light thrown by the six lamps threw eerie shadows on the ceiling, walls, and floor. The hanging and standing pillars moved with every flicker of flame. It was hauntingly uncomfortable. The men found themselves forcibly controlling their rate of breathing, slowing it and finding their lungs inadequate as their racing brains demanded more and more. They were breathing but felt as though they were underwater starving for oxygen.

Minos reflected a beam of light into the cracks and crevices off of his highly polished blade. It was dim but still enough to reveal anyone hiding in the shadowed cleavages.

They walked forward together, slowly and grouped, Minos leading. The cavern was kidney shaped and they could not see to the other end because of the curve. They rounded a large column where a stalagmite and stalactite had grown together, dividing the cave in two.

Minos stopped fast. He could not believe what he saw, but it became real enough when the collective light grew brighter. The men could not restrain their exclamations of shock.

There, on the tip of the phallus, lay the body of Arita, supported on her lower back, bent over backward. Her spine must have been broken to be folded over so completely.

The men circled her, holding their lights forward timidly as if to ward off some unseen evil. Could she have done this to herself? She was an invidious bitch but none of them wanted to see her dead.

Her clothes were at their feet. She was a beautiful girl in life, but in death she was grotesque. Her blood had descended to her lower legs and head before coagulating, blackening both, a hideous contrast against her blond hair hanging down with her arms. Her face looked pained, her mouth hung open in a silent scream. There could have been nothing voluntary about this death.

Minos felt weak. What had happened here? He looked around, tearing his eyes from the mesmerizing sight.

The rest of the cave was bare. Except . . .

Except for small white pottery shards over against the wall. He walked over to them and bent close. It was the lamp Seth had been given. He recognized the elongated portion still intact. He must have impelled it against the rocks when the oil burned out. There was no oily patch indicating any was left when he threw it.

A shuffling sound caught his attention. A shape hurled itself toward him at lightning speed screaming insanely. Minos flung himself backward to ward it off, dropping his own lamp in the reaction, running back low in a crouched semi-sitting position, not having time to recover from examining the broken pottery. He fell against a stalagmite, bashing his head and abrading his back painfully. The roaring apparition thrust down its arms violently, targeting his head with a sharp boulder. Minos twisted to the side just as the rock smashed down, sending broken chips flying into the side of his face. It was hard to see. Most of the light had diminished.

Suddenly the eidolon was torn away from him, picked up bodily by his companions rushing to his defense. They pulled the attacker back as he writhed and they almost stumbled, letting him fall away from their grip. He dropped the rock and stooped to pick it up while they charged him again. In a fantastic whip of strength and speed he recovered it and straightened, bringing it sickeningly down on the imploding head of one of his attackers. The man dropped, tripping one of the followers who fell into the bloody pulp that was the top of his friend's head. The others had their knives out now. There was bloodlust in their hearts. This being had killed one of their companions.

They fell on the assailer with a vengeance, driving their barbs into him over and over. At last he stopped defending against them, and fell into a limp and endless sleep.

Minos caught up behind them sweating profusely as they all were, as much from fright and tension as exertion.

"Seth."

They stood up, away from the traitor. He lay still, slumped in a pool of blood that continued to leak and spread from his multiple wounds, an inerasable rage permanently chiseled into his face.

He had planned to take them out violently and not suffer the indignity of exile. His final statement of rebellion.

"Let's get them out of here." Minos went to the girl as the extinguished lamps were relit. A couple had spilled their oil and would not last much longer. He held one up to her face. She had been such a beautiful young woman. His cousin. Now that she was dead it was hard for him to think of her with enmity, even after all that she had said and accused him of.

"Help me get her down."

They straightened her and lifted her clear of the phallus, lowering her to the ground. She didn't look so ghastly lying on her back, stretched out as in sleep. But now that her breasts had fallen back to a more natural position Minos thought he saw something.

He bent closer with the light. It was hard to see clearly with only the light of the small flame, especially on the darkened upper chest. In sunlight it would have been more conspicuous but, in these conditions, only the keenest eye would have picked it out. He placed a hand on her left breast and moved it to where it would be if she were standing.

Shaken, he let go and it shifted back to the side.

"Earth Mother, save us from these evils."

The small hole had been directly over her heart.

284

* * *

Minos emerged first from the cave followed by the other men bearing the three traumatized bodies.

Taros and Helene ran to them.

"What has been done?" Taros appeared mortified. They had unequivocally succumbed to violent deaths. What was ghastly inside the cave was doubly so in the light of day. He knelt beside them. "Seth's brothers will riot over this."

Helene held her hand to her mouth. All the times she had spoken with Arita. It was bad enough that they were to be forever separated by distance, now they were separated by dimension. Arita would probably have been a perfectly acceptable citizen had it not been for the protracted influence of her pernicious father. For a fleeting moment she thought that the blackened face could not have belonged to Arita, that she still walked the Labyrinth. Her face was that unrecognizable.

Minos gave them a moment, a short time of silence to consider the deaths and send any good feelings they may be harboring along with their souls.

Only Taros knelt. Such a shame that they had been killed. This was going to make the rest of the prisoners far more challenging to handle. When they found out about the deaths they were more likely to rise up in united revolt and outrage rather than retain the reasonable calm that they had maintained over the last day. It could go either way, as all things could, but he felt certain that there would be open insurgency again, and this time with more than words.

Taros observed closely the signs of death, and the causes. He wanted to roll Seth to see if any blades had been thrust into his back but left him untouched rather than commit what might seem to others an indignity to his body. He counted eleven stab wounds on his front and sides. There were probably more masked by blood. Interestingly there were no wounds on his face and none on his limbs. The stabs, if they were administered in panic, were at least well aimed.

Taros repositioned on his haunches, looking now at Arita and placing a hand on her forehead. Her beautiful blond hair would stay here on Kriti after all. He had never seen a corpse quite like this. How extraordinary that her upper and lower parts should be so blackened while her belly and thighs should have become so white. The only exception was a purple bruise barely visible radiating up the sides from her lower back. A severe blow would have done that. He didn't need to bend closer to see the tiny hole on her breast. He wondered if any of the others had noted it. He looked back at Seth. For now, he would not disturb the dignity of the scene. Respect for the dead, even one's enemies, was of great importance if one expected the same in kind.

"This will cause great difficulty," he said. "How do you propose to deal with it?"

Minos answered as he often did, listing possible resolutions before letting it be known which he chose to be most right. "They will not be set in stone, but buried in soil as traitors. We could inter them right away, without telling the rest of the family. We could display the bodies and allow the family to mourn. We could say they were lost in the cave; not an untruth. We could say nothing at all and banish the others without delay. We could tell them exactly what we had discovered and the events following." No one outside of the search party had been given the details yet. All present were tantalized by a desire to know, and their anticipation was almost tempting many to ask.

Minos looked up at the sky, his habit before rendering a judgment regardless of the time of day or night.

"The respectful thing to do would be to give the dead back to the family. In this case I will be considered the family, and they will be buried. We will bury the traitors nearby but not too close to this place. It is sacred. I realize that now for a certainty where I only suspected it before. As for the prisoners; they will be escorted under guard to Amnisos where they will be loaded aboard three ships and taken away. No one will know except the captains of the vessels and myself where they will be freed. They will not be advised of the deaths of Seth and Arita though they will ask. I don't doubt that they will guess, but I want to avoid any more bloodshed if at all possible."

Minos's word was law. The bodies were carried a respectable distance and kept out of sight from the nearby prisoners. After lowering them gently into a hole and backfilling it, Minos offered a prayer to Selene to be gentle on their souls, especially Arita's. He also asked for protection to be with the exiles that they would be able to fend for themselves in their travels and eventually find a place where they could be at peace with their environment.

Now it was time to deal with the prisoners. Word had been sent ahead to tie them securely again, and they were tightly bound when Minos and his small group came up to them.

"Where are Seth and Arita?" they shouted at him.

"Take them to Amnisos," he ordered the men.

The line swayed as the men shouted blasphemies at Minos. The women joined in and children cried as the cords bit into their skin as the adults jostled.

The guards withdrew their knives and threatened the line, garnering obedience but not respect. The epithets continued unbroken as the expatriates were marched away.

Minos led with Helene. They kept a fast pace, a pace impossible for a string of bound captives to keep stride with. They moved far ahead in no time and escaped the abuses hurled their way. The taunts thrown at him he could take, but the things they shouted at Helene, it was too much. After the mix-up in the cave he was still feeling bloodlust he knew shouldn't be there.

Three ships were tied to the pier jutting into the bay, their high prows a stirring sight. Every time Minos saw a ship he longed to leave, it didn't matter where, for any adventure. The mission of discovery was something inherited from his grandfather. He had explored so many places, but there seemed to be no end of others he had missed. He had to be satisfied with reports from his captains. But he wasn't. No matter how well they told a tale, it was nothing like the experience of being there.

The ships had transported everything from livestock to tools and weapons, raw minerals and metals, finished works of art and utility, dry goods and food, workers both veteran and unskilled; the list was becoming endless in both variety and quantity. Now, for the first time, they were tasked with transporting exiles.

The banished were divided up carefully, mother placed with child to keep her busy and not able to scheme, fathers separated from their families to keep them civil. Enough doubt was with them that they might be forever separated from their families, so they kept a reasonable behavior that they might have the opportunity of seeing them again. Men who were tight-knit friends were partitioned to keep them from gaining the upper hand conniving in the same way that the women might. Moreover, they were spread to both ends of each ship with their leg bindings attached securely with munificent knots that could not be untied but would have to be cut. Even the children were so bound. In addition, the men were fastened by the wrists to the gunwale. They were not expected to help, and they were expected not to complain. Any disturbance was quelled with a pot of water over the head, even the children. If the women protested they to were subject to the same treatment. Sea water was warm, it was not a cruel subjection, and the youngest children not liable to the treatment found it entertaining and encouraged it, even when it was often not appropriate, just to relieve the boredom of travel.

Before they left Minos stood on the pier and addressed them.

"You are exiled," he called out in his loudest baritone, "to the north countries yet unexplored. Stripped of your citizenship you are forever forbidden from occupying or visiting any isle of the sea. You are also banished from living in regions, which on occasion and from time to time may be visited by our people for the purposes of exploration or settlement. You have rejected all that we hold sacred and so are thusly rejected by us. You are anathema. You are reviled. When you are placed ashore you will not be welcome there. Do not think that you are. Keep ingrained in your minds that you must continue north beyond where there is any chance that we may find you. I hereby put forth this decree, which is temporarily postponed to give you fair chance of escape, that you will be hunted like wild boar should you be seen. Your families and your family's families, in perpetuity, shall forever be at enmity with us. We will kill you as we killed Seth in the Labyrinth."

It was said. They roared and foamed, struggling against their bindings, abrading skin and bleeding at the wrist as the ships rocked.

"You have murdered Seth. You hold yourselves high and you murder with the ease of butchers of sheep. Have you murdered Arita too?"

The curses and expletives peaked in crescendo and showed no sign of abating.

Minos roared back at them. "You vile and cursed expatriates. Do you not realize still that you have so damned yourselves? With all your intelligence can you not see that you have turned your backs on the greatest kingdom to ever have been born? You are obscene in your stupidity." He took several breaths.

Minos withdrew the silver ornament with the Labyrinthine symbol from his pouch. He fingered it, poised to do something with it. In his rage he could easily throw it into the sea.

He held it high. "This is what your damned Seth led you to and finally rejected. It is the Labyrinth. Remember it well and always. It will be symbolic not only of his arrogance and inability, but also of your long, long journey, which will seem as a never-ending search for something you once had. In this time you will come to realize that you had everything and exchanged it for dross. Your decisions will haunt you with regret endlessly, plague your posterity, and cause you so much unnecessary discomfort. You will encounter those on your journey hostile to you who will continue to drive you north. You will not stop, without suffering painful death, until you pass them all and find land clear of any others, an unoccupied place where you can settle and find peace. But even the peace you shall find will be of little value and short lived. You will be at once lusted and the butt of jokes. You will be forever cursed with high opinions of yourselves, to your last generations, reviling others and being reviled in return. Your people will be subject to, and the initiators of, the bloodiest wars."

Minos threw the ornament into the bow of the first ship. It landed on the lap of one of the men. He stared at it with fascination, not having paid the least attention to Minos's prophecy. It was pure silver, shining and new, a most remarkable pattern on its raised face. He could see it and understood its representation at once. It was the Labyrinth; more than just a cave, it was the path of life, the crooked, convoluted path of life leading first to pleasure then to pain, to happiness and then grief, to love then hatred. The world was summed in this simple design. This thick embellished wafer would preserve the memory of this place and every place they would travel. Its motif would keep them stable when they finally found a home. They would be safe at that time, snugged in the center of their Labyrinth, safe at last.

This marking they and their generations would leave as a sign everywhere they went, etched into rocks, carved into wood, from the coast of the north Aegean Sea to the shores of northern Europe and the Scandinavian Peninsula. Others would find it and in their measure also find it fascinating. The pattern would turn up on everything from Sumerian seals, Babylonian clay tablets, and Etruscan wine jugs to Roman mosaic floors, and pillars in the ash buried city of Pompeii. In northern Europe they covered rocks, megaliths, and burial monuments, including one of the oldest surviving structures, Ireland's forty-six-hundred-year-old Newgrange tomb. Later the chiseled illustrations occurred also in the New World and in Asia. Every culture unvaryingly expressed the single most captivating and enigmatic facet; meandering paths leading inextricably toward - or away from - the heart. They became metaphors for the womb's fertility and the supernatural means of procreation; entombment and spiritual resurrection; hypothetical diagrams of the underworld within the bowels of the Earth to which lies only one precise course. They stolidly depict the concept of exclusion. Any educated in the labyrinth's mystery could nimbly track a direct course to center. For the uninitiated the test was hardly so basic, frequent incorrect turns made wide of the mark before attaining the objective. In time labyrinths became associated with Christianity, tortuous lines depicting onerous and trying paths of righteousness to the end goal of Heaven that devout individuals strived to travel on their passage through the vicissitudes of life.

The ships untied and pushed off. The oarsmen synchronously stroked the deep blue sea, driving the ships farther away, due north as if on an exploratory expedition. Minos wished it were so. Such an unpleasant task he hoped with all his might he would never have to face again. He wept openly. There was no shame in this. Many were of similar mind, crying and thinking to themselves, "What a waste."

They stood on the beach and on the dock, some climbing higher up on the shore, as if in denial, thinking that the ships might turn and come back and that all had changed and the blondes who had been so instrumental in establishing an organized society might return.

In a surprisingly short time they disappeared, vanishing into an invisible haze unnoticed until a ship passes into it, slowly disintegrating into a wavering and shapeless mass of graying mist.

* * *

Several weeks have passed since the exiles had been taken away. They had been transported without incident through the Cyclades and Sporades islands to the very northern limit of the Aegean Sea. Their exit from the ships was somber and grave. Wordlessly they limped ashore with a bare minimum of supplies and the clothes on their backs. They had their task set forth; to follow the North Star until a haven beckoned to them near the waters of an unknown sea. With the extra ballast of the people reduced the ships rose in the water. The captains had no words to say; they had loathed even having the traitors aboard. It was a relief to have them gone, a waste that they would have just as easily dumped into the sea.

The ships returned to Kriti with an enormous bulk of raw materials picked up along the way. The captains had reported back with a supply of magnesia so heavy that the ships had come dangerously close to having water splash over the freeboard. They were wise enough to stay close to island shores whenever possible, but the last expanse between Melos and Kriti had been nerve-racking. A few of the oarsmen new to the trade had been wrecks the whole way, even though the water had been glassy smooth. If they had only known that even the captains had been wishing that they had not entered into that contest of courage, each trying to outdo the other's bravado. They were chancing a sudden squall, a very rare occurrence at this time but not an impossibility. Even a lighter wind could have submerged a ship loaded to this extent had the crew and captain been of lesser experience.

Minos had reprimanded the captains privately. Two ships lost would have set them back considerably. They had lost one last winter, and it had not only slowed commerce but also created an unreasonable fear in the oarsmen. No one had seen the ship go down, only heard in time that it was overdue and then missing. Tales of sea monsters made the rounds, again raising the fears of all and their families. For a while it had been hard to find new oarsmen, and many of the experienced ones even began to have doubts about their life expectancy.

Publicly Minos had congratulated the captains on their bravery and efficiency and saluted the crews for their valor in moving such loads. The crew, as well as the community, needed the reassurance that they were doing a valued job and that their efforts were recognized.

In actual truth, Minos was sincerely delighted with the volume of magnesia brought in. It was an extremely valuable commodity, its worth dependent upon the desperation of the purchaser and they were most desperate during the citrus season. All it needed before export was a thorough pounding to pulverize it to a fine powder, then bagging. When it was taken to coastal towns all around the Eastern Mediterranean it was unvaryingly the first thing to go, even before the bronze weaponry.

The day was brutally hot, being mid-summer. Minos had called a special council together. All had stayed in Knossos for the weeks following the expulsion of the exiles to hear news from the captains when they returned. They knew it would be a long wait as no one would expect them to go that distance without doing trade or bringing a cache of minerals, just as they had done. Even Minos's parents had returned. For the first time in anyone's memory, with the exception of Minos's coronation, all councilors were present at once for a meeting.

A ship's captain had been invited to give a summary of the journey and the events of it. He did his best to stretch the tale, but it was so uneventful that even with his hyperbolizing mariner's blood he could not make it last. He judiciously abbreviated the part about the two captains precariously vying for superiority over who could carry the most cargo. That would be a story for another place, nights of wine at shore, blended with other tales of fearlessness and mettle at sea.

When the captain was dismissed, Minos recounted the business of Seth and his daughter scouting through the Labyrinth. They found it odd that he should go into such detail, musing over every particular. Not that they minded. A good recounting of past events was one of the surest forms of entertainment, although they had grasped that he must have had more in mind than just their diversion.

Minos left nothing out. He even told them of the doubts and regrets he felt throughout the entire episode, the fear when he thought he might die at the hand of his violent attacker, and the heterogeneous emotions of commiseration and fulfilled vengeance when Seth died under the knife. He openly expressed the shame and hurt he felt, piercing him deeper than any sword, as he had walked ahead of his own kin while they reviled Seth's lifeless body. Even now, as he thought of his family trekking through unfamiliar lands with their little ones in tow or in arm, he was saddened. It should not have had to be so, but that it was could not be changed. In his heart he wished them well. He wept openly, tears streaming down his face. There was no shame in this for him. Others were equally moved by the long oration.

"We have had so many troubles. Yet how long past was it that we as a people were as nothing? How many generations back were we simple, with no thought for the morrow other than survival? In spite of the few problems that have been set upon us, our people have come to know that there are far greater things to be done and thought than have been considered in the past, and even still lie waiting.

"Yet, with the telling of such tales as I have just related, we cannot escape the fact that there are devils among us. Something has always whispered to me in warning and, like a fool, I ignored the voice. Had I listened years ago, this whole disreputable affair may quite possibly have been stayed. I vow to you all, I will never stand in the way of the promptings coming to the depths of my soul again. To do so would be to slap the face of divinity, a deed to which I plead my guilt to my eternal shame.

"The girl Arita, a woman yes, but little more than a girl, was cut down barbarically in the Labyrinth. I told you of her wounds, of how we found her. Her injuries were shocking, and I left out nothing to give you the full impact, as unwelcome as you found it, so that you may judge the killer who so long ago must have died in spirit. I told you of the small prick in her breast, almost unnoticeable among her other injuries. Remember it. You have all heard tales of murders of women, young and old, around our fair island, some only tales reaching us years after the fact from settlements not regularly contacted. As our communications improve with more frequent travel and trade, we hear more of these things. I have been wondering for years about these murders. Most of them, almost all of them in fact, have had no mention of this prick in the breast, but all of the women had been raped. All of the women died at the hands of their assailant. Be the men attacking them one or many I never knew, and still don't, but I do know that those with confirmed stabs to the heart are the work of a single man. When Seth found us in the cathedral he must have been sure, up to that time, that finding his daughter would be an impossibility. He had thought wrongly that we would have told him of the magnificence of the cathedral and the phallus had we known about it. I told him that we had completely covered the inside of the Labyrinth, but he thought we had been mistaken. He was right. No one yet has known the Labyrinth, and I know, as he did, that it will be a long time coming before all of the passageways will be fully explored. Leaving her where she was showed brilliance on his part. He thought that only by the remotest chance could we have stumbled upon her as we did."

Glaukos had to ask. "Why would he kill his own daughter in the cave? To what end could it possibly serve him?"

"Such a question has nearly driven me mad, and the answer has taken me to the brink. Seth could have left Arita inside, never to be found again. Think of it. He comes forth with any tale; she fell into a crevasse, she panicked and ran into the darkness never to be found, she rebelled against him to find her own way. Any story would do. We would be moved with compassion, and the exile would be stalled. In the meantime, he is able to raise public sentiment in his favor, and the exile postponement is extended by public demand. As he raises the ire of the people his power increases, and soon the country is divided. We could have been at war with ourselves in no time."

"But we found her body. He must have known we would."

"You protest what you know little of. The Labyrinth is immense. The passages leading to where we found her are small and unassuming. The natural inclination is to follow the largest passages. That is the surest way to get lost. But in answer to your question, it hardly mattered. Should anyone find her, they themselves might never emerge to tell the tale. That is surely what he was thinking when he attacked me in his demoniacal frenzy. No one knew the caves better than I and if he could have felled me and escaped the others might not have found their way out. If they did, he would have accused his accusers of murder and lies.

"His reasoning is not what I want to speak of, however. It is the manner in which Arita died. Not her gross injuries, but her more subtle. The almost unnoticeable mark on her chest. I have already said that it is distinctive. No one would have noticed it on her chest but myself." His voice dropped an octave. "It is the same mark which was found on Aphrodite's chest by my grandfather Minos." There were shocked murmurs around the circle. "You have not been made aware of this secret. Aphrodite was murdered. A sharpened spike was thrust into her bosom, straight into her heart. Had one not discovered the small wound, her death would have seemed as natural as any other. I tell you also that many women have died similarly, though no one exactly alike. Some were beaten severely, some were strangled as well. Some may not have been viciously raped, but I think that some were more discretely done than others. I tell you what the Great Minos told me, a great secret of shame. Selene, his mother, the Earth Mother herself, was martyred in this very way."

The tumult was deafening at close proximity. They all jumped up from their seated positions, shouting in outrage, the men tearing at their tunics and rending them. It was too much. The evil of the villain. Minos let them wind themselves with their ranting. It took longer than he expected but he was grateful for the time to compose what he would say next.

"Please sit. Please." When they had brought themselves to order he continued. "We stripped the traitor Seth before burial. Did anyone find the spike he could have used so many times?"

Everyone shook their heads and looked at each other.

"He would not have left so valuable a tool in the cave would he? And so effective a weapon he would have chosen to use against me, not an insoulary rock. I implore you to think, to use your minds as Great Minos has taught you. Would he not have attacked me with such a weapon? Am I, as an adversary not worthy of receiving the point of a weapon only used previously, singly, and cowardly, against women? Moreover, I ask you, how old is Seth? You can count enough, each of you. He is a grandson of Selene. He was not even born at the time of her death. Do you think he might be the one?"

"Who then? Tell us," Glaukos shouted.

Minos wrung his face in his hands, raising a flush. "Taros. Stand before us," he directed.

Taros was stunned with surprise. His mouth gaped. Not only he. It was inconceivable. The others flew to his defense, their emotions getting the better of them.

"What are you saying?" they called.

"Not Taros."

"Impossible."

"Stand before us, Taros," Minos repeated louder and with the voice of authority.

Taros did as he was directed. He set his face rigid and straightened his back. He looked as dignified as he could. One leg trembled a bit but he fought to control it.

"You entered the cave, did you not?"

"As I have said."

"And you encountered Arita?"

"I supposed. It may have been Seth, or even both together."

"But they escaped from you in the dark?"

"As I have said."

"As you have said. You did not actually see anyone then."

"No."

"Yet you had light."

"I did. But it does not have the power to light every crevice." A moderate impatience trespassed into his voice.

"In darkness she, or he, or both, fled."

"Yes."

"You did not pursue them."

"Not far."

"Because you caught them?"

"I did not." His voice firmed with denial.

"In that impossible Labyrinth, with jutting rocks and unsure footing, you did not overtake whoever was escaping you. You with the lamp and they with utter darkness."

"I am old." And I did not feel safe, he wanted to add but knew that would not be accepted as an answer from a man known for decades of bravery.

"You are old. Old but still skilled in the arts of battle, both of word and sword. Old but still known in all parts as the man who walks like a youth."

Minos went silent, waiting for Taros to say something in reply. They both stood and stared at each other. Taros had seen that penetrating gaze before. It had been so long ago, but he still remembered it as yesterday. He shuddered and held it. This Minos was as the reincarnation of the last. It took all of his will to withstand it and not break the intensity of what he among few could return.

Minos spoke accusingly still not separating his eyes from Taros's. "You know how Arita was murdered."

"I know because you have told us."

"Take off your clothing."

"What?" Again a buzz from the circle arose. None could believe it.

His voice rose again. "Take off your garments at once."

"Have you gone mad?" He wished he hadn't said that as soon as it was past his lips. The circle spoke their discontent with his comment, defending Minos and chastening Taros for his disrespect. Still, they did not understand how Minos was leading toward proof of his accusation.

Minos continued to stare down Taros. There was no getting out of this. Taros was beginning to acknowledge his fear. Slowly he untied the tunic he wore, a formality he was known to observe even on hot days. He dropped it down beside him. Hoping that would suffice he stopped momentarily. Minos continued to stare into his eyes. No signal had been given that Taros could stop. His hesitation was temporary. He undid the tie securing the skirt he wore and let it drop to the earth around his ankles. He was feeling embarrassed as his old body lay exposed in front of the younger of the women. In the old days he would have been considered a sight. Now he wasn't worth a second glance. The damned women. He loosened his loincloth. He was one of a growing number of men to wear them, a custom imported from the Levant and becoming more popular even without the skirt. It too dropped around his ankles.

"Step away from your clothing."

Nakedness was not something that many would consider shameful or embarrassing under normal circumstances. There were times when it was more appropriate or acceptable than others, but Taros felt exposed in other ways as well. During his entire lifetime he had never liked the feeling of being naked in front of company. It had never felt right.

"Helene," he directed his wife. "You will search his clothing."

She retrieved the bundle and began to sort through it. There wasn't much. He hadn't been carrying a purse. In fact, other than the three articles of clothing themselves there was nothing. She unwound the loincloth, which had a heavy twisted binding for around the waist where he had rolled it into a thick rail. It was an attractive way of keeping it she thought.

As she unwound it she began to feel through the thinning layers something firm. From the loosening wrap a bronze spike fell to the ground, tinkling off a stone. The moment was lost on no one. Another item, a worn and shiny block of hardwood dropped out beside it.

Arita, herself quaking with the confirmed revelation, picked up the two items, one in each hand. The dark spike had fit neatly along Taros's back inside the rolled cloth. It wasn't so long that it would ever poke out either side even with the pin-sharp tip working through the fabric. The removable handle concealed against his belly shortened the spike and made its concealment simple. She rolled the evil contrivances in her fingertips thinking of the women

295

she had worshipped who had died at its sharpened tip. She fit the dull end into the flat handle, pressing it easily most of the way in, then increasing the pressure until it touched the end of the hole. It was a formidable weapon, used expertly.

When she passed it to Minos she was weeping.

He fingered it for a moment then stabbed it into the wood he sat on. It stuck fast. He glared at Taros whose head was beginning to droop along with his faltering gaze.

"Why such deception? You of all men who have been one with all of the sacred ones before us. Our most trusted member of council. How could you?"

Taros refused answer. He stood defiantly proud as he could, but his muster was fading. He could see his own death hanging before him. What did it matter? He had lived a long and filling life. He had lived wealthily, eating and drinking to his enjoyment. He had traveled endlessly. And he had left a trail of corpses ravished to his pleasure until this end of his life. He was filled. If they kill him, he would go peacefully. Nothing mattered anymore. He smirked. Nothing ever had.

"Have you nothing to say?"

"Nothing you care to hear. Do with me as you will."

"You disgust me." Minos ordered him tied inside a stone hut while they discussed his fate.

"He is the last of the original ten. He has been integral to the building of the faith and the establishment of truth everywhere we have traveled. What are we to do with him?" Minos thought of his grandmother suffering under Taros's hand and found mercy fleeing.

"He is a murderer," Arita breathed. It had not taken her long to conclude that her attacker in her youth also was Taros. She had barely escaped and the horror of the moment filled her mind again as if she were back in the darkened hut of her childhood reliving the violent assault. Sweat secreted in volumes from her pores as her past played before her. Her face dripped, blanching at the recollection of a shadowed phantom beating her, tearing at her clothes, knocking her senseless. Taros it was who had gripped her. She remembered now. She had seen him only days before the attack. He had visited the settlement. He had looked at her and she had felt so privileged to be noticed. Such an important man, they had said. So many wonderful words he had spoken. Then he had gone, and her family had changed. Changed for the better, becoming kinder and more pleasant to grow up with. Except for that single night which she had spoken to none about except Aphrodite and her fiancé Minos. Her mind was filled with visions becoming darker and more macabre. The shadows played before her, a shadow she recognized as her own being buffeted about like a leaf by a storm. Arms gripped her tight as she struggled uselessly against her own body stalled by an incomprehensible paralysis, refusing to respond to her will. She opened her mouth to scream but nothing came out, no help would come, no escape was possible. She shook, not from her own doing; it was the invader, the evil incarnate depravity reaching through her skin tearing pieces from her mind and heart.

"Arita." The voice was grating under the disguise of sweetness and concern.

"Arita." Louder and more urgent. If she could only move; fight against it. She shook again.

"Arita," Minos shouted into her face.

She saw light coming in from the periphery, the darkness deliquescing. Minos coalesced in front of her, his expression pervasive with apprehension and distress. It was he, she realized, who had been shaking her, calling out her name. He had torn her from the clutch of her incubus. She embraced him with the violence of her relief, sobbing, and squeezing him until he felt pain.

Minos knew what this was about. He knew that Arita would not tell the others, and he would not either. She would be mortally shamed by such a disclosure. He held her tight with one arm around her shoulders, holding her hands together on her lap with his other hand.

"You can see the damage the evil of Taros has caused," he announced to the council. "Not only to those who have directly suffered but to those who feel the pain indirectly. I leave it to you to vote if he should be killed as he has killed, or if we should be compelled to show a vestige of mercy and leave him to another fate. What say you?" Minos wanted the man to die, to die a slow, excruciating, and bitter death. But he also acknowledged that his emotions were high and he was riding the back of vengeance.

There was no organization in this. The council members spoke as they felt inclined, in random order dictated only by their urge to express. Some declared similar feelings to what Minos was experiencing. Others said that he should die swiftly with mercy. Others wanted even more charity to be shown in respect for his past works and association with the Great Minos. Flare-ups occurred between council members as they began to argue and throw their reasoning, and then insults, at one another. Minos had to stop this before contention fully reigned and more damage was done from the debate than from the crime. If the council ever fragmented so would the whole of society.

"Enough," shouted Minos over the din.

The silence was immediate and absolute. They had been hoping that someone would call them to order, ashamed and remorseful over their own unruly conduct even as it was happening. They had never been so intransigently fractious at any meeting.

"There is no consensus here. Taros will therefore be dealt with in a manner that will satisfy each of us, I hope, by leaving him to the higher order of the gods. Whether he lives or dies will be out of our hands. He will never be set free, but his life will be passed from our protection to those who must ultimately decide for each person. Taros will be set before the black bull and will be painted with the blood of its offspring. If the bull shows mercy then so shall we."

Heads nodded. All seemed to agree that this was the best way to reach any conciliation. Those who thought he should die knew that the bull would surely kill Taros while those who thought he should be given mercy knew that the gods with whom he had lived in life would favor him enough to preserve him.

Minos ordered an enclosure of stone be constructed before the end of the next day. Minos paced out a flat area of fifteen long strides by forty-five and placed each cornerstone. Every person in Knossos who could be spared from other duties helped. Men, women, older children; it was a community project and duty which they all had a responsibility and desire to assist with. None knew what it was all about, other than that it was of great importance. There was no shortage of rock to make the dry wall. While the area was fertile, it was also plagued by an undue abundance of rocks that hindered plowing and planting grain crops. Piles of rocks that had been randomly left were now brought to the site and used for the wall of the enclosure. It began to take shape quickly with all the help. Hundreds of men and women took the largest rocks that they could carry, making a contest of strength and endurance out of it, walking the distance to the place set apart just at the edge of the town.

Minos was pleased with the speed at which the wall was being erected. They would be finished so far ahead of his intended time that he told them to rest and resume the next morning. The next day went just as well, and the shoulder-high wall was finished by noon. Only a wooden gate for the opening on an end wall had yet to be completed. One of the town's best woodworkers was busy with that, and he promised it would be finished and fitted shortly. All that he had been told was that it had to be a strong gate.

Even arrived. The people of Knossos had their usual supper of grains boiled with small chunks of spiced mutton and watered wine. Tonight they had been ordered to their huts. No one was to come out for any reason. No explanation had been given other than the goddess Selene was to show her will tonight. She would be sitting in judgment, and anyone who dared interfere would bear the weight of her wrath. The Earth Mother, normally peaceful and the seat of mercy, would be violent when necessary and would not hold back tonight if provoked.

The black bull's hooves thudded against the ground as it tramped up the hardened dirt track through the town center. It was the mightiest of the bulls now alive, a direct descendant of the white legend brought to the island by Minos and Aphrodite. Taros, it was said, had been aboard that same ship.

People could see the bull passing their doorways and craned their necks as far as they dared to watch it pass. The children were the hardest for the parents to control. The young ones amplified their own strong desires to follow and witness for themselves what was going on. The bull had to be going to the enclosure. The two had to logically be connected.

None of the huts faced the enclosure, also none of the windows. Even if some braved the warning and slipped out of their abodes, they would find it difficult to see through the cover of darkness. The bull lay down at the far end from the gate where a trough of water and feed had been left for it; just a small amount to get it to settle in that area. It had been fed nothing else that day to put it in an ornery and judgmental mood. The small amount given was just a taste for such an enormous and powerful beast but, as it was not accustomed to being up and about in darkness, it settled with a less than satisfactory feeling of want in its belly, and a sour disposition.

Hours passed. The midnight hour came and went as the council sat in joyless contemplation and prayer. Some prayed for a speedy death, others a miraculous salvation. All prayed for fair and just retribution until the Moon rose.

"She shines with fullness above us. It is time. Lead Taros inside."

Taros was brought, still tied, and pushed through the gate. His bonds were loosed and he slipped free of them, giving them honorably to his guard who stepped out through the gate and closed and fastened it tight. The 'W' or 'M' of the Great Minos also shone down upon the scene in conjunction with the Full Moon. It was almost time. The bull snorted at the far end sensing that something was about to happen. The voices woke it from sleep and it could see the shadows of the men and women of the council spreading out around the outer perimeter of the stone enclosure. Each had a long knife in case Taros tried to jump the wall. He would be confessing his guilt and readiness to meet death in that event and would receive it swiftly.

The bull was on guard now. It stood in anticipation. Of what it did not know, but its senses had been alerted.

There it was. The final judge. The morning star of Aphrodite.

"Taros," Minos addressed him. He was holding the three of the tektites hard in his fist. We have passed judgment. That is to say, we have passed judgment to a higher order. You hear the snorting of the bull. Beloved animal of Minos and Aphrodite it will be the harbinger of your fate. Whether you live or die matters not to me. Not anymore. I have made peace with myself. I dare to say I doubt if you can make the same claim."

"You are as arrogant as your uncle said," Taros snapped. "He was right. You dare to see into my mind? You have no idea what thoughts lie there. You dare to think that you have any idea of what life brings? I tell you, for most it brings nothing but hardship and misery. Only for the few who take what they want is there any peace or happiness. And now I see that you have devised a scheme to relieve yourself of any responsibility for killing me. You are wickedly clever. These of your council will no doubt agree that you have arranged my dispatch with the slyest aplomb."

The bull scraped ground, loudly stomping, and snorted a stream of snot toward the intruder on the other end of its pen. It pranced to the side, holding its head high and defiant, looking down the length of its nose as it circled close to the walls that held it captive. It zigzagged back and forth toward Taros, closing the distance between them, knowing the intruder was inside but not seeing him well with such poor vision. He was there though. The bull could sense it. An intruder that was a danger. An intruder that bore a hatred. A hatred that made it an enemy. Not like the keeper who fed him every day, who rubbed the bony pate between his horns when it itched and tickled behind his ears and scratched his back. This one smelled different. He stretched his neck and took another sniff. The bull put his ears forward as he continued the dance, circling closer, curious but wary. A shadow had taken form in the light of the Moon. It was discernible now, so close, a man by its smell but a stone by its want of movement. The bull swung its head from side to side giving each eye the full benefit of a direct view. It took another step forward, lowering its head and stomping again, pawing great chunks of turf out of the ground. It snorted a mighty blast, another prodigious squirt of mucal slime ejecting across the short distance and all over the front of the intruder. It moved now, a guttural protest cursing the earth and stars, running to the side, twisting and writhing, flapping and wiping.

The sudden movement startled the bull. It flung its head down and half squatted on its front legs. The spring off of the powerful recoil of its legs almost shot the bull fully into the air. It sprung back, then forward like a cat on the attack, overtaking the fleeing intruder in a second.

Taros, even in his old age, was lithe enough to avoid the bull's first charge. He took advantage of its poor night vision, falling and rolling to the side as it stormed past. The thunder of the massive hoof beats only a step from his ears rammed home the danger he was in. He had played up his nonchalance at the specter of death, but that had only been because he was in a hopeless situation and he refused to give satisfaction to his judges by displaying the fear he kept leashed inside. He forgot about them now. Only the bull filled his thoughts. This was going to be the end of everything if he could not escape. He had run closer to the center of the ring in his first attempt to avoid the horns of the great beast and now was as far from the walls as it was possible to be. His thoughts lay exclusively in hurtling himself over the wall in an attempt at escape. But he had to get there first.

The bull had turned and was thundering back at him. He could see its mass clearly in this light, his eyes so widely dilated in alarm. He had barely picked himself out of the dust and the fiend was bearing down on him again already. Time slowed. The great head grew wider, closer. Taros's body felt like a heavy stump, and his legs as immovable. He felt himself sway to the side in a reaction to dive that way for safety, but with his thoughts racing knew that he would only place himself far enough over to be raked by a vicious horn.

His legs grew fluid and began to fail. Then in a commanding maneuver of supreme desperation he willed strength into his limbs and, in what looked to the observers as an outstanding deployment of artifice and bravado, he vaulted upward. His timing was exquisite. In his futile attempt to protect himself from the impact of the bull, he pushed his hands forward, contacting with its rushing brow. His bent arms cushioned the shock but, with his inertia still carrying him upward, the effect was as one vaulting off a springboard and over the gymnastic horse. His legs swung upward until he was doing a handstand on the forehead of the bull as it passed underneath him. The forward momentum of the bull and the upward thrusting arch of its neck had the effect of flipping him through the air and, as Taros twisted in panic, he landed feet first on its back facing its direction of travel. Only one of his feet planted firmly, the other hanging in the air as the bull continued on. Taros was only carried, as he balanced, another step as his supporting leg buckled. He slid off the bull's rump, and both feet contacted the ground. Miraculously to the witnesses observing this feat, he remained standing. Taros had appeared to take the bull by the horns and vault over its back with virile purpose, twisting with the grace of an Egyptian dancer, and stepping off as if the act were nothing more than descending a stair.

In truth, as frightened as he was, and as filled with wonder and terror at what he had just somehow done, he did find a fleeting moment of self-gratification before the bull turned against him once again.

Dirt flew as the solid hooves bit the turf. Every muscle worked. Flanks rippled with tension and power as the bull targeted its prey and fell headlong toward him. Taros was in fine physical shape, but the rigors of the last minute had drained him and all he could do was stand transfixed as his enemy bore down upon him. Even the rush of fear was not enough to compel him to carry on this futility. The fence was still too far distant. He knew that the silhouettes on the other side were waiting with weapons should he make a break.

Resignation was the only way. Loss was inevitable. He would go with grace before fear overpowered his reason.

He stood resolute and puffed his chest to meet the opponent. The impact came painlessly. Taros felt his chest cave to the force. His limbs snapped forward and flailed as he hurtled through the air. A most incredible sensation, he thought. He maintained a full awareness that he was mortally wounded. Bone ends grinding at fracture sites attested to the severity of his injuries. He thumped to the ground, his leg folded under the weight of his torso, his jaw hanging uselessly from the concussion of the horns. Breath was impossible. His trachea had been crushed along with his jaw.

He lay stunned, drooling into the dirt, immobile. His ear pressed to the ground picked up the clumping of the bull as it turned to find him. The sound stopped only for a second while the bull zeroed in on his cynosure. Taros felt the quiver of the earth as his enemy stampeded toward him, the sound growing against his ear.

Everything shook and he felt the force of the driving hooves stamping and kicking at his body. Horns pricked his side and tossed him like a rag. It felt as though they were passing right through him, the force and power were so great.

But he felt no pain.

* * *

Fully half of the Council members had left to points on the island. It was important that they carry the news of the recent events personally before word traveled by way of merchant and trader. It was vital to the integrity of the nation that not only the basic information be spread, but also an explanation.

The episode with Taros was easy. There were no witnesses apart from the Council. No one had spied clandestinely on the event. He had simply died in his sleep. His body had been cleaned and wrapped in extra layers of linen. His blood had been drained through a small slit in his neck and allowed to seep into the ground before dust was kicked over it. No leaks would appear in the cloth; no one would be the wiser. Taros was given full honors in keeping with his station.

The blond relatives of Minos were portrayed as treacherous usurpers of power who, had they been given more of a chance, would have forced the islanders into a submissive condition of slavery. That they had been speedily exiled was hailed as great a judgment of Minos.

The news was further spread that the opportunity for life in Knossos was only open to those who faithfully believed in the endowments and vestiges of Selene. They would continue to display acceptance of her sanctified existence by bringing gifts and oblations to Knossos, and for those who thought themselves worthy and desirous enough they must demonstrate their capability of finding their way through the secret complex of the Labyrinth. Those who succeeded would be granted the special citizenship of Knossos and would be obliged to separate themselves from their friends and family, all of their loved ones, until such time as those people could themselves prove worthy. Special exceptions in extraordinary circumstances could be made only by Minos himself. It was hinted that if a man or woman had impressive physical attributes they may be accepted with limitations even after failing the Labyrinth. Still, everyone was invited and encouraged to make their devotional sojourn and stay as a pilgrim in the city for a short time.

With half the Council away Minos's thoughts began to peregrinate about the three remaining tektites. The larger issues had dissolved with the passing of time and action. Now he was finding time to concentrate on his greatest pleasure, far from administering the country, delving into the supernal matters of life. He found a quiet place away from town, taking only his beloved and a day's ration. How peaceful it was away from the interminable procession of people and voices, the cries of wanting children and the questions of seeking adults. The truest religion was that of peace found under the sky and in the midst of the groomed oasis of nature. Here they could meditate without interruption. Here they could be together, enjoying each other, pleasuring each other. Here they could recline and watch the cloud formations as they passed and inspired.

Minos delighted in reflecting on the various peoples of the world, of Kypros where the copper was, of the Levant where his nation was known by the name of Kaftor, of Egypt where they were known as the people of Kefti. The Great Minos had been wise in giving their names differently to each nation. Should they ever get together they might never discover that they were dealing with the same island power.

He had been pondering Egypt. His visions had revealed to him that, in time, it would be a mighty nation. It was already sowing its own seeds, people with a love of art, a graphic form of expressing thought, a firm leadership by way of their Pharaoh. Still, they lacked. Egypt had changed not one iota for hundreds of years. They had found a niche from where they had concluded they could advance no further. Kriti, under the leadership of Minos and the inspirational guidance of Selene, had progressed and surpassed their standards in only two generations. Egypt was ready for the next step.

Minos had visited the length of the nation once, just before taking on the mantle of 'Minos' at the death of his grandfather. He had traveled to the place of the Great Lion, the Sphinx they called it. It had been described to him as something more than it was, as things often were. The immense feline rose out of the grassy plain solitary to a grand height, without peer, its rubicund stone shifting hue with the passing of the sun. It was an inspiring sight to behold and he had lingered the entire day watching the progression of the subtle shade variations. There were times when man needed to lend a hand to nature to perfect it, and this was irrefutably a time that cried out for such intervention. The natural rock formation still begged a great imagination to see the lion within the rock. Truly it had the general configuration of a reclining lion with a large, maned head but it was coarse, lacking the finesse that it called for.

Imothes, Minos's brother, had been along on that expedition. He had talked endlessly of the beauty of the land and even in his dreams had longed to be there. As much as his heart was full for Kriti he knew that something was calling him back to Egypt. He knew he would die there, he had seen his own future, and Minos only had to give the word and he would be on the next ship. He told Minos of the visions he had, of freeing the Sphinx, carving it out of its limestone hillock, of making it a wonder and symbol of strength to the eternities, a mainstay of fortitude and security, a monolith of stone in the image of the most magnificent of beasts. He told of a vision of a towering, stepped pyramid made of stone higher and wider than anything previously conceived or imagined, a first of its kind. The place called Memphis was where he must build it. For years all Imothes could do was think and talk of the great works he would do in Egypt. Now the Egyptians were ready for him. Right now. The Pharaoh Zoser had complained of the increasing famines prevailing in so many parts of Egypt. The grains were inadequate for the people and many precious things were having to be traded away for necessary imports. Kriti had profited well from excess supplies of wheat and barley, gratefully received by Egypt. The best was always sorted for shipment directly to Pharaoh's house, and the gesture was never lost. Pharaoh would respond in kind with gratuities of scarabs, beads, pendants, and ivories, and eggs and plumes of ostriches, most finding their way to placement within the Minoan temple sites.

Six years the annual floods of the Nile had failed, each year contributing to a more critical drought. Imothes predicted that one more year lay before them without relief and that they would build the pyramid, out of desperation, to their gods, if they could be convinced that it would be of benefit. They were in desperate straits. They would do anything. They would be easily convinced that even beginning of the mighty project, with the promise of completion and uninterrupted labor, would suffice. When the rains and floods finally brought respite, they would be convinced that their great expenditure of public effort and funding had been of avail, and the gods had shone upon them with mercy. Their gratitude to Minos and his people of Kriti, the people Kefti as they were known, for sending the guidance of Imothes would be without parallel. The Egyptians already held them in a higher esteem than any other peoples who were openly regarded as barbarians. The Minoans were smiled upon by the Egyptians for many things, not the least of which was their legendary reputation as seers and astrologers. No other race or civilization was worthy of recognition to the Egyptians. Only the Kefti had been smiled upon by Pharaoh, and Pharaoh would smile on Imothes. His scientific mind, his erudite knowledge of medicine and healing, his architectural aspirations; all would seal Pharaoh Zoser's place in history as the Pharaoh who led the Egyptians into the age of the pyramids. And it would seal Imothes, who they would call Imhotep, with deification by those of the Ptolemaic era two millennia into the future. By then the tales of his monumental architectural feats, his powers of healing, and scientific achievements would not have dwindled in the retelling, but instead magnified to the point of magic. By then he would be deified as the son of the great god Ptah and as himself the god of medicine. Imhotep's tomb in modern-day Sakkara, near Cairo, became a shrine two thousand years ago where people flocked in search of cures as they come today to Lourdes. Imhotep would be the first, and the last, scientist to uniquely be made into a god.

Minos would miss his brother. Imothes could do great things here in Kriti, but his calling was elsewhere. Such sacrifices had to be made.

Such changes to his life could only be accepted with divine mediation. Though the parting anguished and tore like a garment, he would abide Selene's will.

And there was a greater separation.

He would send with Imothes, a tektite.

Chapter 12

Great Expectations

2193 BCE

The constant background drone of the living mass of people in Knossos was hard for those from the perpetually quiet countryside to appreciate.

Paras had arrived only the day before with his wife to pay homage at the shrine of Selene. He believed in the Earth Mother. He saw her almost every night. Even through the cloudy skies, he could pick out her light behind the mists that would have him miss her blessings. Even on those nights when she could not be seen, having transformed herself from a pregnant whole to a sliver of her former self, he would still enter the night with his arms upheld in supplication and meditate with his eyes closed imagining her there in all her resplendent fullness until his arms fatigued and dropped. He had developed strong shoulders almost solely from this nightly exercise.

Paras was a scribe. His vocation kept him busy recording every kind of business transaction and negotiation. It was no way to get rich, not like the merchandise traders and traffickers, but it kept his family well fed and healthy. He loved the news that his clients brought with them of Egypt and Libya, the ports to the south. Egypt had been having trouble with bands of raiders randomly pillaging their personal property and water, cowards who would not stay to fight but would flee after netting their gains. They had proven themselves unstoppable despite the efforts of the most capable people. The stories of these land pirates were so interesting to him with his love of history. They reminded him of the tales of yore when trade was developing in the Mediterranean and Kriti's ships were occasionally attacked. But in spite of the pirates and their harassing uncertainties the water routes from Europe and Africa to Asia, through Kypros, Sidon, and Tyre, or through the Aegean and the Black Sea, became cheaper than the long and arduous land routes that had carried so much of the commerce of Egypt and the Near East. With their ships that were so much larger and faster and more easily handled than any that had previously sailed the Mediterranean, trade took new lines and created new wealth. Kriti was blossoming like the watered rose. In Egypt, a high foundation had been struck along the entire length of land from the Red Sea to the Mediterranean, the same route that would be followed later by the Suez Canal. Slowly the wall was being built up to allay the threat of roving bandits. It was halfway complete and with the skills at massive construction projects to which the Egyptian were renowned the project should be finished within thirty years. Contemplations of a waterway to join the Red Sea with the Nile were also being considered by the engineers although as yet no one could imagine how such a feat might be accomplished. Other news reached Paras's ears, too, from the sailors, the few who came to this port from the east, news of the expansive cities of Ebla and Ur far east of the Levant, cities which, unknown to any but Minos and his closest advisors and ambassadors, were the places where the two tektites had found their rest.

Paras's spastic, intermittent work gave him enough time off to pursue his love of athletics. His wife, Carthea, shared his enthusiasm for sport. They would leave his parents and her mother and race each other up and over the surrounding hills of Phaestos, an important south coastal port dealing directly with Egypt and Libya. There were many from there who ported goods by foot and ox to the larger Knossos saving the limited number of ships to pursue their trade more lucratively rather than oaring around the extra distance of the island to the northern coast. The port was weak though. Soft sandstone eroded at an incredible rate. Paras remembered it to be quite different in his childhood from how it presented now. Coastal shapes changed slowly by the standards of humans concerned only for the day, but it was persistent and accelerated dramatically by the annual storms that scourged the shoreline. Escaping the attention of all but the older and wiser men who plied the seas in search of sustenance the erosion continued unabated. The old men noticed. They noticed everything. And Paras dealt directly with those men.

Paras was also an accountant as part of his calling as scribe. The purpose of the strange lines and pictograms which he kept on air-dried clay tablets was to present proof that a transaction involving a certain amount of any merchandise or commodity had indeed been received and that payment had been returned in kind. Money was not used by Minoans but they were lovers of minutely recorded detail when it came to commodities. Thereby they could use gold or silver balanced against lead weights as payment, or trade commodities of differing value such as wheat against olive oil. The transactions were not always simple, straightforward, or even efficient.

Clay was hard to come by in that area of the south coast. All of it had to be brought in from miles away, and clay was heavy. He kept the tablets for one year, unless there was a special request or on the occasion where a dispute was in progress. After that time he soaked the archived tablets in a pool of water poured into the hollow of a rock. He kept throwing the tablets in until it was full and let them soak for a few weeks. He added water as it evaporated and the tablets slowly softened and fell together as new clay requiring only kneading and rolling into new tablets.

The system worked well for him. His occupation was enjoyable in that he found himself involved in trade that would otherwise have escaped him. He might have appreciated a more physical job but Paras actually preferred the purity of physical exercise for its own sake. He felt there was something demeaning about profiting by the improvement of one's physique.

Carthea's arm touched his. The touch was without purpose; she had not noticed he had been lost in retrospect. The Priest was speaking again after a long meditative silence. He spoke in a monotonic drone that was at once mystic and instructive. This elucidative juncture of the daily observance followed the opening religious rituals and gave explanation to the people attending, mostly pilgrims, what exactly they had just been through and why.

Upper clothing was forbidden in the temple. It had not always been so except for some specific rituals. Now it was mandated even for simple entry into the enclosed area. Disrobing was done inside the gate with clothing left there. The women were expected to have a long skirt or dress extending from the waist to any point beyond the knee; the men either a short skirt or loincloth rolled and tucked around the waist or held up by a belt depending on their standing in society. Pilgrims were to wear the longer kilt. Members of the higher order wore the loincloth of starched heavy linen, folded out on each side of a stiffened codpiece to cover the upper thighs, which was provided only by the temple upon confirmation. On informal occasions the garment was often simply wrapped around like a miniskirt. There were those involved in military training who developed shorts by sewing the front to the back between the legs and to further set themselves apart even went so far as to crop their hair, both in the name of safety. Those of highest military rank wore double-layered shorts in parallel with the flounced, or layered, skirts worn ankle-length by women of high standing.

It was a sight. Paras caught the eyes of even some of the women casting upon his wife. Their fleet glances were precipitous, involuntary. The men, too, averted their eyes as quickly as they could. No one was here to see breasts or hardened torsos as a purpose, although the Priest seemed to be speaking more often in their direction than in others. Paras wasn't sure if the Priestess beside the speaker was actually his wife or another woman assigned to the part today. They were about the same age. Maybe they were a married couple. If so Paras could understand why he may be distracted somewhat by Carthea. It was difficult to tell. The loincloths with which the worthy arrayed themselves betrayed nothing, so stiffly formed were they at the front.

The service ended with the Priestess thanking them on behalf of Selene for their oblations and the Priest doing likewise on behalf of Minos. The dominance of the Mother-Goddess meant that women were involved in all rites and ceremonies, priestly associations of women being formed at palaces and holy places. With that concluded they left by way of a concealed exit at the curtained rear wall.

The pilgrims followed the lead of the few worthy, evident by their vestment, and left by the larger doorway.

Paras wanted to become one of the worthy. So did Carthea. They had brought several oblations instead of the obligatory one per couple. They could attend services as often as they wanted once they had made the first offering and as long as they stayed in Knossos. But they wanted their dedication to be manifest to the Priests and Priestesses. They would take a gift each time. They had used their entire wealth trading for this expensive pottery. There were a number of skilled artisans in Phaestos, equally adept at the manufacture of exquisite work as the potters at Knossos. Some would argue that the finest among the masters was even superior. It was speculated that it would not be long before she would be recruited for membership among the worthy and transferred to Knossos. For now, Paras and Carthea were grateful that she was still in their hometown and that they could obtain her work. It was only after a long and pleasant relation of friendship and professional service that they were able to pay for the finest of her work. Many traded well for the rights to take her goods to Egypt were it was held in the highest esteem. It was said, not too loudly lest the price go up, that even the Pharaoh had some of her wares at his table. In truth, he had commanded that upon his death several pieces would be entombed with him for his exclusive use in the next life.

Paras was inwardly glad that the first offering had been received so well. The Priestess behind the table fixed her sight on the magnificently crafted bull, a rhyton, a stylized ritual vessel, which decanted fluid through its mouth.

Each gift was placed on an alabaster table, a slab low to the ground. The gifts were as many as the couples attending but varied in actual value as the incomes of those presenting them. Each brought the best they could afford; there was no shame in being outdone. No one would make the journey unless they were sincere in their hearts and that was all that was supposed to matter. The gifts were not a requirement, only a custom that demanded attention if it could be afforded. No one would ever be turned away because of poverty. Of course, that grace had yet to be tested.

They left the temple gate, donning their shirts as they passed. It wasn't particularly warm today. The sky was thick with low cloud, overcast and gray. A viscid humidity had been building all day. At this central place the most fashionably adorned women gathered, as much to be seen as to see. Although women often had their own means of income the men of Kriti provided them also costly means of enhancing their loveliness, grateful for the polish and adventure women gave to their lives. Every adoration was provided them; stickpins arrayed with flowers or golden animals or heads of crystal or quartz, hairpins of copper or gold, rings or spirals of filigree gold with fillets or diadems mingled with the hair, rings and granulated pendants dangled from the ear, plaques and beads and chains hung to the breast, bands and embossed bracelets on the arm, finger rings of silver, steatite, amethyst, carnelian, agate, or gold beautified the hand. The men kept some jewelry for themselves, the poor carrying necklaces of polished stones, the wealthier bands of precious metals on their biceps and wrists inlaid with bangles of agate.

Mount Juktas rose framed between the upturned Horns of Taurus. All male bulls had taken that name from Taros, the first to challenge the horns of the charging bull and dance upon its back unharmed, conquering and subjugating the animal to the will of man. No one had known of his manner of death outside of the Counsel. As far as the rest of the population was concerned the man had died following his remarkable feat, not during it. The work was outstanding, all clay by the look of it. But how could it be made so large without breakage? It was at least twice the height of a man and each horn as thick as a couple locked in tight embrace.

A spool of thunder voiced far in the distance. The storm seemed to be coming in from the south, opposite to the usual progress, as far as Paras could judge the ill-defined clouds. They seemed to be almost touching the summit of the mountain, darkening to a blackness far beyond. Yes, they were definitely coming from the south.

"I'm glad we found a warm place to stay tonight," said Carthea as she clutched tight to her husband's arm. They were lucky. The woman who agreed to take them in, and feed them, had taken them on a promise of help for the next few days. They could still have plenty of time to worship. The old widow just needed a bit of muscle to help with a few chores which she found difficult since her husband passed away. Normally she didn't take in boarders, but her need was great now. Women in her predicament usually depended on their neighbors and friends to assist them when they have a need, but she preferred to make her own way in the world where she could.

They walked past the walled-in area where they supposed that the ritual bull leaping took place. They had heard of the fantastic feats of bravery that even some of the heartier women attempted. Anything to avoid the fate of exile, they supposed.

This really was an enormous city. As they climbed the grade to the outskirts they enjoyed a beautiful panorama of the community. Smoke was rising from many chimneys as others who had seen the signs prepared for what was sure to be a cold evening. Wood must be getting harder to get, he thought, as he scanned the surroundings. They had been so excited when they arrived that they hadn't really paid much attention to the countryside. The trees were quite distant, far from where they stood when Knossos was established, far from the meadow that could not now be distinguished from the extended fields and orchards surrounding the city. Paras's accounting eye estimated that the population must exceed twenty thousand, an impossible number. Could they all be worthy? No. There would have to be those who did menial work here just as anywhere else. How is it they were able to stay and not pilgrims?

A ripple chased itself along the fields of grain, a whipping undulation sweeping back on itself and then speeding again toward them. The tops of the olives shook and then they felt the first winds. It was the second year and the olive trees were heavy with fruit. Olives bore only on alternate years and whole districts tended to be in phase. Harvest would be starting soon. It was the longest harvest of any of the crops and ran from November to early March. Paras could envision the beaters as they hammered away at the branches, knocking free the ripened olives, gathering them up on the dropsheets laying around the base of the trees, and amassing them in huge baths to soak up water. Then they would be pulped in wooden mortars and put in a settling vat where the water and oil would separate. Some of the farmers preferred the hot water method that made for a faster separation but changed the subtleties of flavor significantly against the purist who preferred his oil slow partitioned in cooler water. Either way, the water was drained off through spouts at the base of the bath and the oil was stored in huge, full-bellied pithoi for grading and sale to licensed merchants.

A gust whisked against them as it passed and died. All was made still again. The air was filled with the crisp scent of the last crop of grain and the refreshing cool essence cascading down from the mountain.

Someone was coming from that direction, two people carving their path through the fields. The farmer would be upset about their trespass, tramping down his grain like that, though he could hardly expect them to walk the considerable distance around with a storm nigh on their tails.

Paras waited with Carthea tucked in against him for warmth. They were both curious to see who this might be making so bold and coming straight toward them. They carried nothing but a small bag so they must obviously be citizens. There was no reason to suspect, in fact, that they were anyone but the farmers themselves. If that was the case it must be a wealthy couple indeed, as the farm was huge. That was most unlikely. No, these people would be suffering the ire of many farmers for their blatant trespass. Of course, the crop could be flattened if this turned into a real storm, in which case the point would be redundant.

311

They came closer, following a straight course. They must be high people. Their clothing certainly suggested it. Both of them wore a very appealing blue which was expensive anywhere. They clenched their garments tight about them, lightly dressed, as unprepared for the brewing weather as any. Storms from the north were predictable according to the skills of the Minoans for a thousand years, but the southern storms were so rare that no one could forecast them.

The couple bore themselves high against the irregular winds. They walked a fast pace. The grace they sustained conveyed that they were most certainly of high standing. Coming from the valley they must have been spending the day on a peaceful walk, a common thing to do, a recreation of all people who did not exclusively work every day. The weather was changing so suddenly that anyone could have been caught out.

"What shall we say to them," Carthea asked her husband, overly concerned about their social status.

"I don't know. They are clearly one of the chosen. If they didn't want to speak with us they could have deflected their path a little and missed us by enough that they would not have to acknowledge us. But see how they come directly toward us. It is as if they want us to meet."

The wind became less erratic and rushed firmly against their faces. The smell changed. No longer was the scent of fields present but that of the farther evergreen forest.

"Perhaps they are in need?" said Carthea holding her hair back with her arm. "They could be. They have nothing. They may have been away for longer than just a day hike."

The answer came soon enough.

"Hail," shouted the man as they drew near.

"Hail," shouted Paras in return.

"You will have to get out of this storm."

"Yes. We were waiting to find out if you were in need. We wanted to make sure that you got safely across the fields before the storm breaks. It won't be long." He looked up and pointed. "Here it comes now."

An angled curtain of rain fell over the mountain and rushed toward them, a gray wall of shimmering liquid. The line followed the contours of the mountainside and the valley casting its pall on the flora behind. They could hear the sweep of the pelting rain even over the stir of the windblown fields and orchards around them. Of a sudden they were drenched, as if they had fallen into a pool, so great was the deluge. The darkness of black clouds rushed along behind the rain and overshadowed them.

Paras and Carthea wondered what they were lingered for, but they waited for the other two to make the first move. It was their city. The way to fit in was to behave as the natives, and their objective was to stay. If it took standing in a downpour, a cold one at that, then that was what they would do.

Oddly, the two new arrivals faced each other and held hands. A strange look of comfort passed between them. They both inhaled deeply with their mouths wide open and held their arms to the sky, seemingly feasting together on the tempest, only for a moment, then their fete was over. They returned their attention to the pilgrims.

"Come with us. You cared about our well-being; it is only right that we should care about yours," yelled the woman over the rising gale.

That invitation would have pleased Paras and Carthea even if the weather hadn't been so inclement. They followed the pair to the gates of the temple-palace, surprised that they just walked right inside as if it were their own. They observed no formality, no more than anyone would ducking into their own home to escape the elements.

"Wait here," instructed the woman again. She was about to turn but changed her mind. "I have neglected to ask your names."

"I am Paras. This is my wife, Carthea."

"Very good, Paras and Carthea. I will return with warm clothes and you will join us for some hot drink. We will be back shortly."

"You haven't told us your names yet," called Carthea as they passed through the doorway.

"My husband's name is Minos. I am Rhea," she said, distinguishing herself by her ecclesiastical investiture.

Paras and Carthea were left alone. The shock of this chance meeting was just setting in.

"By the gods. That was Minos and Phaespae," whispered Carthea.

"What could they have been doing out in the weather like that?"

"Do you think they treat all visitors with the hospitality that they have shown us?"

"Of course not. How many people have we known to make this pilgrimage? How many have even seen them?"

Down the hall where Paras and Carthea dared not even to look Minos and Phaespae were changing into dry clothing.

"Take some garments for our visitors, and some hot tea," she directed the servant. "Remember they are not sanctified yet."

"I will find something appropriate for their standing." The servant bowed and quietly left the room to do as bid.

"You said 'Yet' my Priestess. Are you so sure that they even want such an honor?"

"I know that they do. And you know that they could be appointed even on their physical attributes alone. Don't think that I don't notice when a woman

313

is beautiful. As for the man Paras; he is more of a man than most around Knossos."

A double peal of thunder shook the room.

"The storm is a fierce one. That bolt must have struck close."

"There won't be many who will be inclined to observe the bolts of Zeus. Most of our people will be sheltering inside."

"But not us, my beloved." Minos took his wife by the waist and pulled her hips against his.

Phaespae gripped his loins and squeezed hard, until Minos rolled his eyes with the pleasure of pain. He relaxed his hold and she slipped away from him. "Come then. We will take these new guests to view the tempest." She shook the rain out her long black hair and tied it behind, into an informal ponytail.

Both of them wore long robes of purple, their winter clothing. They bound the heavy material, wool lined with linen, at the waist with colorful silk sashes. There was no need to embellish themselves with the adorned garb of royalty today. The storm would keep any but the residents of the palace away.

"Come with us then," Phaespae said to the younger couple. Carthea started. They had not heard their king and queen coming up the hall in their felted slippers.

"Bring that hot tea with you. It's getting even colder outside."

They grabbed up the hot decanter and the only two cups and followed after. The hallway was long and convoluted, turning seemingly for no reason and then turning back again. There were no doorways off of this hall. It just seemed to keep going. It ended at an open breezeway without walls, straight columns on either side supporting a heavy roof with a wonderfully painted ceiling decorated with spiraling geometric patterns in white and red. Paras noticed it right away and stretched his neck to see above and almost behind him. The chilling wind made him want to pull his chin back down and tuck it in for warmth, but one look at Phaespae, her hair as wet as his, told him that he should endure any discomfort that she could. They were very fortunate to have the simple robes the servant had left them with the tea.

Minos took the decanter from Carthea and poured their cups. Then he filled their own left at the ready on a small pillar of stone. They came here regularly and always had their golden matching goblets on hand for wine or hot beverage.

"This is our place of meditation, the Hall of the Winds."

They didn't have to ask why it was called that. Surrounding structures had the effect of focusing the drafts up and at them. A powerful blast hiked up Carthea's robe and blew it behind her. The wrap held it at the waist but she was fully exposed below. She twisted and reached out to grab the billowing robe, reeling it in, bunching and pushing it down in front as the wind picked it away again and twisted it into a whip.

Phaespae was right about their physical attributes, thought Minos as he caught an unobstructed view of Carthea's hard legs and buttocks. "Come over here. The wind is blocked from below."

Carthea held the robe tightly at the front, the wind breaking and not able to grab at her in the same way as she got nearer the stone railing.

They stood leaning forward onto the high balcony rail. They overlooked the north section of the city from where they stood, the panorama complete at this height. To the left and right they could see the expanse of the city in those directions too. Somehow they had come two stories high. Paras was sure that they hadn't come up any steps. The long corridor they walked must have been a gentle slope up to this level, unnoticeable to them because of the length of the rise.

The roof overhung the balcony just enough to prevent rain from falling on them, except for a few gusts where they received a dose of cold drops. The mountain rose in the distant south. This platform must have been built with the view of Mount Juktas specifically in mind. Its porphyritic skin rose high above the darkly verdured treeline to coalesce with the frenetic clouds above. Brands of lightning stroked the earth all around, followed by fervent detonations of thunder.

A servant appeared from out of nowhere, the sound of his approach obscured by the tumult. Suddenly he was just among them, and clearly on edge. The sky flashed blindingly, sheet lightning illuminating the clouds as a mighty bolt arced unseen between opposing polarities high above the earth and still within the cloud layers. The rip that followed shook the earth and the foundations of the palace-temple where they stood observing. The servant almost dropped the new decanter as he was placing it, tipping it and knocking the empty, lighter one off of the column. It smashed noiselessly, fully muffled behind the prolonged roar of thunder.

Another bolt struck with a single ripping noise like torn calico. An entire tree had been stripped. Balls of electricity rolled along the ground, violent spheres of haze moving softly through gates and even through walls like hypnotic specters daring any foolish person to come close.

The flustered servant cleaned up the pieces of broken decanter unseen and unnoticed by those he served, thankful for the distraction at the same time as he was escaping from it to the relative comfort and safety of the indoors.

"The focus of the bolts," observed Minos, "if you have noticed, is around the mountain. There is a message from the gods in this."

"What do you think it is, my husband?"

"I don't know. Only by observing can we find the answer to such things."

"The astrologers are out," Phaespae noted.

Minos looked over to the lower covered shelter. There they were, the men who stargazed every night, even on overcast nights in hope of seeing through a break in the cloud cover. The astrologers of Knossos had become the most widely known and regarded of all of the astrologers in the world. They shared much of what they knew with other nations, even as far away as Babylon, but what they shared was incomplete, leaving those nations to fend for themselves in certain instances. That tended to discredit them to a certain extent, but there was political wisdom in the withholding of information on occasion. Now they were watching another wonder of the heavens, and it was happening during the daylight hours.

"Setuei," Minos called above the wind. The Egyptian servant came out from behind his place down the hall, just inside the doorway.

"Setuei. Call the Chief Astrologer. He is on the landing below. Escort him here."

Setuei left at once. Running was not permitted within the boundaries of the temple-palace but Minos knew the servant could reach the landing in astonishing time. His strides were long and fast, and he knew the building as a mother knows the cry of her child. He would never know the personal privilege of being 'select,' but he was better situated than his father who was a slave. Setuei was fortunate that his father had married a citizen and so he, as an offspring of the union, was a citizen also with the only restriction placed upon him that he could not be fully sanctified. When he married though, if he married a citizen himself, their children would have the opportunity of proving their worthiness and being 'selected.' That was Setuei's dream, his only real wish.

He routed down the long corridors, finding his way to the lower concourse. Many had told him how difficult most of the servants had found the palace architecture at first, and applauded him on how quickly he had been able to negotiate the winding passageways. How he lamented that he wasn't able to take the ultimate test of the Labyrinth.

"Master," he called only loud enough to be heard above the wind. A few of the gathered astrologers turned to the interrupting servant, then a few more followed their motion.

"Master Deukalios," he repeated, now that he had raised their attention. "Minos requires your presence."

Without a hesitation, the Chief Astrologer girded his warm robes about him and followed the servant. "What is it about?" he asked.

"I haven't been told, Master."

"Where is he then?"

"At the Hall of the Winds, Master."

That made sense. He was probably witnessing the storm and wondering what its portent was. He could guess well enough, although this was a far cry from analyzing the celestium.

He needed no guidance through these halls. His abilities were renowned. He had made his way through the Labyrinth so quickly he had become renowned as the record setter, establishing a new mark to overcome. Following the servant was only a matter of form, but if the Egyptian half-breed took a wrong turn he would not hesitate to go the proper way without letting him know.

"Is he alone?" he inquired.

"No Master. Minos is with Phaespae and two others. I do not know them."

"You don't know them? They are not from the temple then?"

"They are not from the temple. They are not from any temple."

"What are you saying, man? That they are not of the Order?"

"They are pilgrims."

"Pilgrims?" Deukalios was shocked. Pilgrims this deep into the temple? They were not to be anywhere beyond the Place of Oblation. Not without the express exemption of Minos. Without doubt, they must have had that release. But why?

"Describe them to me."

"They are hardly different from any bright couple, Master. Both very attractive, very athletic. I have not spoken with them other than to receive their thanks for a change of dry clothes and a decanter of hot tea."

"They were out in this weather then."

"Yes."

"And Minos and Phaespae?"

"Also."

"They met outside then."

"One would surmise." Setuei should not have spoken like that and regretted it instantly, although Deukalios let it pass with nothing more than a sour look of reprimand. "Through this door, Master." The servant stepped aside to let the astrologer pass. He would stay his place until bidden, happy to be out of the wind.

Minos caught the movement behind him.

"Ah, Deukalios. Stand beside us."

Deukalios looked at the young couple, wondering. The servant was correct in that they were very attractive. The girl ventured a civil smile, weak but polite. No attempt was made to introduce them.

"The gods are angered," he said.

"I had wondered," said Minos. "There is more to this storm than any usual. Everything about it is different, singular."

"It comes from the south, Minos. An ominous portent when this severe."

"As I thought." Another fork of lightning struck the side of the mountain. "Have you been watching it closely?"

"Yes, Minos. Since its inception."

"What do you mean by 'its inception'?"

"Since the first loud thunder shook the earth."

"You did not observe, then, the formation of the clouds."

Deukalios shuffled. "You know that I sleep during the day, normally."

"Of course. I had not meant offense. As you slept the clouds appeared from the clear sky, coiling around and above Mount Juktas. They rose and fell with the winds but touched upon the mountain continually, darkening as clouds from the south were ushered in to couple and bind with them. They rolled and tangled, spreading across the sky, growing more dense and impenetrable, obliterating the sun and frustrating the penetration of daylight. Lightning struck far in the distance, long before its resounding broke loud enough to disturb your slumber. But it came undaunted. The wind. The rains. The most powerful of the blasts were the ones that woke you. I have been watching them carefully since then. Have you noticed anything in particular about them?"

Minos was testing him. Deukalios was up for the challenge, and liked it that way. It kept him astute. "The strikes have centered on the mountain."

"Your powers of observation have not diminished with age, Deukalios."

Another wide fracture opened in the heavens, letting the light of the higher world blind them. The speed of the flash tearing up through the atmosphere from Earth to sky, faster than any eye could see, generated an enormously powerful shock wave transforming intervening air to plasma. The trillion watts of current bound to the north side of the mountain and refused to release its grip. The blinding surge held, five times hotter than the surface of the sun. The bolt thrashed through the sky, but held on to the iron vein where Zeus had been entombed. The shock wave reached them in forty-four seconds, needing four seconds per mile.

The prolonged electrical charge vanished as suddenly as it appeared. They felt, as well as heard, the deafening report. A gust of wind focused on them at exactly the same moment and had the effect of blowing them back, their ears reverberating painfully with the blast.

"It is Zeus. I knew it to be," shouted Deukalios over the din.

"Yes," yelled Minos back, wincing and nodding his head.

The tumult stopped, leaving them all dazed and with ears ringing.

"Yes." He was still yelling, half deafened by the terrible sound. "I thought it must be Zeus. There could be no other explanation. But why? Why does he plague the mountain?"

The astrologer was silent. He stared at the mountain in wonder. He knew the spot where the focus of the charge lit. He had seen fires of worship on certain nights at that very place. It was where Zeus was said to be buried. No one knew precisely where that was as the grave was unmarked, but people had a general idea. Zeus was trying to tell them something, that much was clear, and both Deukalios and Minos were sure they knew what it was.

"He marks his grave."

* * *

The storm passed quickly after that last lightning strike, as if all the pent-up electrical energy had been spent at once and none remained. All went quiet and the wind died away. Minos and Phaespae, along with their invited guests who had shared in the experience, and Deukalios made the hike that night to see the damage wrought by the terrible discharge. The going was slow through the soaked fields and trees, a speed quite suited to the astrologer's age. Moreover, he was used to being up all night. The others were tiring, he could tell, and he was just warming up. The overcast sky stayed with them the remainder of the night, a mixed blessing. The cover kept what heat there was in, but the stars were obliterated and he longed to see if there were any celestial signs indicating what they presumed the daytime storm to have disclosed.

Paras fell back with Carthea. He touched her arm and slowed his walk.

"Why are we slowing down?"

"I wanted to speak with some privacy." In truth, he was feeling a little inadequate.

"About what?"

He didn't quite know how to phrase this. "Why do you think we are here?"

"Here? You mean here with Minos and Phaespae, or here at Knossos?"

"I know why we are here at Knossos. It is where we have longed to be. I mean here with them. There are so many. They don't need us for anything. There are at least ten priests and priestesses. Why have they taken us with them? They haven't asked us to carry anything. There are enough servants for that. Why even did they take us into the palace? You know that twisted hall we went down? It goes nowhere. I looked at the building from the outside. It is much smaller than it seems, no bigger than the temple we were in earlier. That narrow hallway must make up the entire lower floor. We doubled back on ourselves so many times that we only got the illusion of a huge building."

"Why would it be made in such a way?"

"I don't know. Here. Let's fall back a bit more. We can see them better in this twilight. They won't be getting off the trail."

The narrow path led to the mountain. It wasn't as wide or as worn as the one they had been on before this one branched off a little while ago. The wide one was obviously the main road used for travel to the south points, making a wide circle around the mountain, staying on the flat as much as possible to make the transport of goods all the easier. This narrow one had been amply traveled, though. It was still hard packed even after the torrents, except for a few places where it had washed away.

They were going uphill now, the ascent growing steeper by degrees.

"Are you not pleased to be taken in by Minos in this way?"

"It isn't that. I'm not sure what it is. I just don't understand it, that's all."

"Then thank the Earth-Mother who has provided. There is a reason for this. You know that. You can feel it. I know you can. She has given us everything. Don't let doubt creep into your thoughts."

Paras stayed silent a moment.

Carthea continued. "Think about it. Phaespae is Rhea, the earthly manifestation of the Earth-Mother. She does as the Earth-Mother would do. She has welcomed us from the beginning. It was even her who invited us on this journey to Juktas."

"Things do seem to be pointing that way. There is too much coincidence in this to be anything other than fate. Everything, from the time we chose to come here, to the walk where we met them, to the storm and the lightning; it all combined to place us in their midst. You are right. It can't be anything other than divine guidance which has conveyed us here."

They picked up the pace a bit to work their way back closer to the others. Several whom they had not been introduced to were in the group ahead. Some of them were bearers, carrying supplies, others without doubt members of the ranking 'Order'.

Minos took a look behind. He and Phaespae preceded the file. The rest were fairly close, with the exception of two.

"I may have been wrong about our pilgrims. They seem to be lagging."

"Not for want of strength or stamina, Husband. I turned to see them, as it was light enough. They dropped back to have privacy talking."

"About the singularity of being with us, I must imagine."

"What else could it be? It is rather amusing to bring pilgrims into the fold in this way on occasion. Their gratitude is boundless, and they make for the most dedicated followers."

"They still have to pass the Labyrinth."

"Only to attain the highest rank. I am convinced that they can do it anyway."

"So am I, actually."

The trees were getting smaller as they climbed. The slope was getting very steep, with large boulders that looked unstable enough to roll down the incline. The green glades they passed through on the way up echoed to the drills of the cicada.

A young shepherd sat fascinated by a copris beetle, a scarab, rolling a little ball of dung across the ground to a hole it had dug. Considered with fondness they were given the status of lucky charms rather than the high religious significance attributed to them in Egypt. Where there were sheep, there were copris beetles, little companions to the shepherds to entertain them with their antics and help them pass the time. But here was another more engaging sight. A string of people, an enormous concourse to his untutored eyes, passing into and through his field. Fabulously attired they passed by on their mission at a higher elevation. He longed to join them, but he knew where his responsibilities lay.

The climb was slowing all of them down. The old astrologer was affected most of all. He was staying with the pack as best as he could but was falling behind. Paras and Carthea stayed just behind him. They would have liked to pass and get closer to the main group but felt it was surely not their place to do so. They knew that servants were ahead of the man, but familiarity had its privilege. They would stay behind unless invited to do otherwise.

The trees completely disappeared. Neither Paras nor Carthea had climbed to such an altitude before. It was like stepping beyond a curtain and finding one's self leaving a green room and entering an empty, desolate one. Rising above them was the mountainous rock that was Juktas; bleak, scrubby, ominous, and powerful to behold. They did not stop.

No one had eaten since dinner yesterday, a greater burden on Deukalios and the other stargazers because of their backward hours. All were hungry, but none complained. To attend Minos and Phaespae and fast on this quest for enlightenment was their privilege and pleasure.

It was mid-day before they reached the meadow, or what was left of it.

"Mother Selene," gasped Phaespae.

"Great Zeus." Minos fell to his knees.

They had expected some form of destruction from the lightning, but this was unimaginable. The entire meadow was blackened. The surrounding area, shrubbery, scrub brush, it was all gone, just a memory, leaving only a wet smell of the sodden, burned streak up the side of the mountain. Only heavy rains and the sparse nature of the growth had confined the flames and kept them from spreading. The ore where, centuries earlier, Zeus had been sealed up had fused and run liquid into rivulets of iron-gray metal. Solidified into freakish formations the anomalous lumps lay about an area most focused near one place at the foot of a short cliff; the place where they said Zeus was buried. No one had ever been absolutely sure, it was only legend. But now they knew that the unverifiable tradition was reality. Here was the confirmation. The violence Zeus had inflicted on this place signified his displeasure on the ignorance of the people. This would have to be remedied right away.

"Oh Great Zeus. Great master of the powers of nature. Mighty one of the heavens. Fearsome wielder of shafts of light who smites unmercifully thy place of entombment. Thou hast demonstrated thy wondrous potency, creating metals from sand, incinerating life, leaving ash and destruction following in thy indomitable wake. Shield us from thy wrath. Forgive us our offenses against thee. Wrest us not from this Earth before our time. Show us only thy will; reveal thy desires by way of this intrinsic sign."

One of the priests brought Minos his double-bladed ax, the first to be made with the oval instead of round shaft hole. He received it, clutching it tight to his breast, his eyes closed as he embraced the symbolic weapon of the father. He lifted it high and with a cry brought it down hard, driving the long shaft like a stake into the scorched earth.

Far below, miles below, the plates of the Mediterranean shifted a few inches, tension having built along the fault line over the last year since the last minor quake. The relaxation of pressures and the slide of compressed plates sent a tremor rippling up through the solid rock. It had been an easy release of energy, a slip rather than a snap, generating a soft rumble and a prolonged, docile tremble.

Minos felt the ax quail and gripped it harder. The pulsations of the earth massaged his legs as he knelt.

"He speaks," Minos shouted. "Listen. Feel."

Coincidence was lost on them. They knew that it was Zeus. The servants were the first to fall to their knees, terrified. The priest class were more restrained, more circumspect because of their learning, but also knelt in reverential fidelity to their deity.

The rumbles stopped as soon as the last man, the old astrologer, had lowered himself stiffly to his knees.

"Zeus has spoken," called Minos.

"He has spoken," echoed Phaespae.

He held his hand out to his wife and Priestess. Together they rose while the others remained kneeling with heads bowed. Hand in hand the holy couple walked the perimeter of the scathed and burnt out vicinity. After pacing the periphery they returned to the steepest place, the place where the lightning had obviously focused. It looked like it might have been a higher cliff at one time but that part of it had collapsed. All around there were the large, bizarrely shaped iron casts, some of them very long. There were even more, now that they were closely inspecting, little tear-shaped beads all full of holes and bubbled like lava.

There was more to this material than they could fully understand. Minos bent to pick one of the smaller pieces, surprised to find it heavier than a bronze piece of comparable size. From a distance the pieces had appeared a homochromatic gray, but close up they could see that the metal was as scorched as the earth around them. There was a gray underlying the mists of jet that had tacked onto the surface as the igneous metal consolidated. Minos wiped his fingers together, rubbing the ingot as he twirled it. The act of moving it around in his hand like that reminded him vaguely of something, but he didn't focus his thoughts. The sooty veneer was coming off on his blackening fingers revealing the underlying mousy gray of the cold metal.

Phaespae caught her breath, realizing an instant before Minos the significance of what they had.

"The Drops of Heaven," she whispered.

Minos could not believe it. Could it be that after so very long the gods had sent it again? But this was different. The legends of old were that the Goddess and her five guides fell at night from the Five Stars of Heaven, the Throne of Minos. The Goddess herself was said to have followed them down with intense light and overwhelming sound, similar to lightning and thunder but definitely not. Shooting stars seen in the heavens were not lightning. This difference was the difference of the deities; one female, the other male. It would be like the male to leave his tailings in a spectacular and violent way, boldly in the clear light of day, blowing clouds with his mighty breath, incinerating the side of a mountain, and venting drags of undestroyable ejaculate.

But it was the same. He picked up another piece and tapped them together. The ring was the same. It was the material of Heaven. These signs were all pointing to a new age ascending over the horizon, the age of greater strength, knowledge, and influence that had been promised since the beginning.

The age of fulfillment and distribution.

* * *

"How is the work progressing?" asked Minos.

"Every stonecutter in Knossos has been sent to Juktas. Fifty laborers have been assigned to help. The most enthusiastic has been that young man you allowed to come with us after the storm. His wife stayed with him too. Neither has left the site since that day and neither has flinched from their work. The woman cannot work as fast but she refuses to do lighter duties, insisting that her love of Zeus fills her to the marrow with strength. Indeed, she outperforms some of the men. As for the man, he also keeps track of the material used, tallying the stones in his head and writing quickly onto clay tablets before going back to his harder labors. Both of them are useful and have worked with greater dedication than anyone. They have also hinted frequently that I might remind you of their desire to pass through the Labyrinth."

"They will get their opportunity. When do you anticipate a finish to the sanctuary?"

"The main structure will be finished in a few days. The white stone is softer than what we find closer to Knossos. The masons can shape it much faster. And we are trying a new type of cement, different from that of the Egyptians. Instead of gypsum mortar we are using lime mortar, composed of lime, sand, and gravel. Mixed with the ash of the island of Strongyle it has the strength of stone when set."

"And the roof?"

"The carpenters have been cutting oak for weeks. The roof will be done. And as soon as the walls are complete, they can get to work on the inside of the sanctuary. The five Horns of Consecration will be completed by then. I had ten stonecutters from Malatos brought here to do those works. Each set will be identical and they will sit high upon the walls."

"You have great praise for your own work. I have seen it, and I agree. The Full Moon is tonight. Will you be finished in time for the next?"

"That depends on when you can finish the final pieces; but yes, our part can be completed by that time."

"Return to Juktas, then. I have no doubt that things flow much more smoothly when you are there."

Wonderful, thought Minos as he walked away. This was going much faster than he had expected, far ahead of schedule. The soft stone was a lucky break. The rumbles from deep within the earth were increasing in frequency. He still could not imagine why the gods were so displeased. Even the astrologers were not of any use in interpreting the peptic complaints. All they could advise was that the completion of the mountain sanctuary would end the disturbances. They needed the peak sanctuary to worship and plead the deities controlling the heavens. Pastoralists, in particular, moving about in the high meadows with their flocks, would make great use of the sanctuary supplicating the gods who controlled the weather and thereby the lives of both man and his beasts.

Minos had to check on the new forge to see how it was coming along. He took the winding road from the palace to the new structure almost completed, set next to the old forge where bronze had been smelted for centuries. The range of tools manufactured there had made the progress of civilization possible for the farmer, the leather-worker, the mason, the carpenter, the gemcutter, the shipwright, and sculptor. Axes, sickles, plows, adzes, hammers, chisels, knives, gouges, gravers, borers, awls, nails, drills, tweezers; these tools transformed the Minoan world and, with the shields and weapons, provided the means of establishing the palace economies. The old forge had been updated, repaired, and improved on since its construction, but it was still inadequate for the task that had been recently and unsuccessfully attempted; the melting of iron.

The lengths and pieces that had been left by Zeus's coital ferocity had been brought to the temple for safekeeping and veneration. It seemed indestructible, but they were determined to create the intense heat required to melt this substance into a reverential form that could be adapted for the glorification of the sanctuary.

The new cone-shaped structure was much larger than the forge beside it. It rose almost twice as high and was double the diameter. Piles of charcoal were being heaped under the new covered shelter next-door. Miles of new fields had been cleared of trees for the conversion of wood to charcoal over the centuries. Much of the oak was taken to the coast for shipbuilding but it was much fought over, as it was also the best wood for charcoal. The other varieties, beech, black pine, sumac, and fir, were fine for smelting copper, but for the searing heat needed for this undertaking they knew they were going to have to use unadulterated oak charcoal.

Variable vents in the floor for outside air to blast into the combustion chamber were included in the design. The higher chimney made for an increased draft to create more of a vacuum that more forcibly drew in the unburned air.

Smoke was already coming from the stack, a gray fume that hovered and fell after rising from the chimney lip only a few feet. There was thermal inversion today pressing down the smoke stream into and around the dwellings, layering the area with a thin smog of misty haze. This was an objectionable condition to some people and fortunately only happened on the rarest days when there was a complete absence of wind.

Minos stopped outside the door before entering and inhaled a deep lung-full of the gentle scent. He was noticed from inside.

"Minos," called the voice from the darkness within.

A short, muscular man with a balding head sprang from the void that was the door. He was covered in grime and soot, his hair frizzed and static where the flame of the forge had come too close. His filthy tunic was a subject of much discussion and some derision in Knossos. But the man was a genius, they said, and could be forgiven his slattern ways. He was almost never seen outside of the foundry, never in the light of day, so what did it really matter? As long as the pilgrims didn't see him. They might think that just anyone could set up shop here.

Hyphesteus, the name a variant of Hyphes, the first metalsmith, was very excited to have Minos come to the new foundry. It would soon be time for the blessing of fires where the full council of priests and priestesses, at least the ones in the area, would fill the place and give it their benediction. As the chief metalsmith, he would be allowed inside the foundry with the holiest people and participate in the consecration. Not many people, even among the select, were given that honor. And not many buildings were given that honor either, only the palace and temple buildings, shrines and sanctuaries. This was considered one of the most important new structures because they were needing to produce ever more weaponry to feed the increasing needs of nations demanding newer, harder, sharper, and better instruments of death.

But more immediate was the need to shape the sacred ejaculate. It had been whispered to Hyphesteus what the need of the higher heat was about, but it was enough for him to know that the project was of extraordinary import to his sovereign.

The last few weeks had been almost painful, so great was his desire to get the forge working. But he couldn't rush things. The chimney was so tall and heavy that the ground beneath needed at least that long to settle, and the clay used to cement between the shaped rocks had to have plenty of time to cure naturally. He gave extra time at every stage just to make sure, even though an anxious desire to get on with it burned within him. Even the warming fire radiating for two days under his careful eye was kept low. The kiln was going to be raised to temperature very slowly. He'd seen the disaster of exploding rocks before, and the collapse of chimneys that had been brought to temperature too quickly. It didn't happen all of the time, but the risk was great. Too great for a project like this. A fault now could set them back another month.

Hyphesteus was alone in the large room that was the forger's workshop. The size of the room was out of the ordinary, but the extra area was allowed for specifically for what they had in mind. The very first works to come out of it would be sacred, and it would be the only way that the works to be commissioned could be kept under the security of a roof. Minos followed him inside. The room was already taking on the odor of the other forge. It didn't have the scent of melting metals yet, but it did have the sooty sniff of slowly combusting charcoal. The humid, mossy aroma of drying clay had passed since he had last visited. A long, altar-like table stood in the middle of the room. It was of incredible value and made of necessity for the special project. Cubic rocks, each a cubit on every dimension, had been shaped and placed next to each other in a row of ten, and set two high. The long supportive base was ground perfectly flat and absolutely level on the surface. Then a thick casting of the strongest bronze was laid on top, fifteen feet long and one and a half wide.

It was magnificent and easily the largest and heaviest bronze casting ever made. Such a work should by rights go straight into a temple. That was impossible, so the forge would be sanctified as part of the temple, an extension, or annex.

There was something appealing about a forger's workshop, even to one who loved the light. They were dark, magical places where something could be made of nothing. Lumps of metal were turned into works of art, tokens of sacred reverence, useful cooking or eating utensils, or fearsome weapons of violence. Almost anything was possible if the temperatures were high enough and the skills and strengths of the master and his apprentices combined to overcome the limitations of time and energy imposed by nature.

Neither spoke for a moment; they just stood before the gate of fire, a soft glow imbuing gentle heat against their bare faces.

"I will be tending this fire with the care a first-time mother gives her newborn." He caressed the rock walls of the forge and ran his finger along the dry warmth of the joints between the stones. "I judge the chimney to be ready now for a higher temperature," said Hyphesteus as he tamely, one lump at a time, tossed a few baskets of charcoal through the gate with his black hands. Sparks showered upward in defiance of gravity with each strike of a new chunk, pursued by transparent flickers of white and orange.

"How long?" asked Minos. He was referring to when the forge would be in full operation.

"Tomorrow morning," he said without hesitation. "It will be ready then."

* * *

The entire city had come. Paras and Carthea had even made the long journey at night from the sanctuary where they labored after begging permission to attend. Phaespae had seen them from a distance and she had instructed an attendant to escort them to the front of the crowd. They were astonished at the consideration of the Priestess Phaespae. Still, they wondered why they had not been invited to take part in the selection of the Elect. They obviously held favor and they knew that many others had been through the test recently, several even passing. Why were they being delayed?

There wasn't much to see at ground level outside of the forge, but the thoughts in the minds of the spectators of the doings inside the workshop were alone enough to hold their interest. In addition to that was the voluminous column of smoke. There was no inversion today, although the air was absolutely still. The misty-white pilaster rose to unbelievable heights, driven by the intense heat of the pyromantic engine below. It was invisible at the chimney lip, nothing but a wavy absence of focus that fluctuated and veered and made the eyes water to look at it. Above that transparent ether it took shape and

327

altered itself gradually to a white column of pillowy gas that was recognizable for what it was. On it spired, like nothing could curtail its transit to the heavens. They craned their necks to see the ending of its passage but could not. It stretched into a cerulean infinity without disseminating. It just went on forever.

Inside, the dedicatory intercessions were coming to a close. Wine was spilled on the altar which was, in reality, an extended anvil. More was splashed along the walls and cast onto the fire. Little was drunk. Minos wanted the work to start today. This ceremony, as solemn as it was, was also the prelude to a practical application that had to be attended to.

The manufacture of the four Spires of Zeus.

* * *

Fires were raging in the hottest inferno yet to be under the control of man, the thick ceramic cauldron filled with the wrought iron emissions set amongst the heat of a fervid blaze.

Hyphesteus opened the door after a time to check on the process. If the cauldron contained bronze, or even copper, it would have long melted by now. He pulled on the door, the hiss of the vacuum drawing in air around the perimeter and making the job harder as if there were another smith inside pulling against him. Suddenly it released its grip and let the door fly open. A precipitous backflash discharged in a singeing fireball that caught him as he fell away with his arms across his face in a defensive guard. He caught the unmistakable effervescent hiss of hair searing away from his arms and pate. He could feel burns on the backs of his forearms. He thought himself blessed to have had the reflex to protect his eyes so quickly. In his eager curiosity he had forgotten that the flames sometimes attacked without warning. It had been so long since the last time that he had gotten lax in his guard. He'd have to put up with the stinging pink burns that now chafed at his nerve endings. He lay his forearms in the cool water of the tempering tray, giving him quick relief, but not complete. He was too busy to stay like that, bent over the tray, although his arms would have appreciated it. He would have one of the apprentices get him some olive oil to massage in later.

The stench of burnt hair filled the shop, and the temperature rose suddenly as heat from the open door radiated outward. Even with the furnace now sucking air in through the door heat still escaped in surfeit profusion.

The smith worked his way closer against the heat, wincing and squinting as he adjusted his eyes to the bright oven interior contrasted against the dark room. The cauldron glowed inside the confines of the stone walls with luminous intensity, flaming red, almost invisible against the fires. And the emissions still rose above the lip of the cauldron, still resolute, still solid. He had left a long one poking up and supported by the others so that he could tell when they melted. This was astounding. He threw more charcoal in through the opening by the basketful, careful not to strike the cauldron, and closed the door.

The tone of the furnace changed again as the needed air was sucked up from the floor and into the pile of charcoal. He left it for a good while, knowing the temperature inside was growing ever hotter and more difficult to manage. A thrill of concern swept through him in the time that he waited as he contemplated the dangerous new ground he was traversing.

A priest, a member of the Council, stood silently among the apprentices and with the newly appointed chief metalsmith from the old forge. All were keenly interested in this new furnace. The priest's purpose was to call on the powers of heaven to aid the process, the chief's to satiate the priest's curiosity and perhaps aid in his understanding of ways to improve what was here available.

The temperature rose ever higher within the confines of the chamber; beyond the two thousand degrees Fahrenheit which would have quickly liquefied copper, beyond even the twenty-one hundred degrees which, had they thought of it, would have melted the iron out of the ore found at the small vein on Juktas. But no one would think to smelt iron ore for another thousand years.

Twenty-two hundred degrees, an unheard of temperature for a man-made furnace to have reached. But still not hot enough for the wrought iron ingots created and purified by the subjugating power of nature's electrical energy. The internally fibrous structure and evenly distributed slag content that sets wrought iron apart from the pure element, demands a temperature of twenty-seven hundred degrees to melt it; an impossibly high temperature.

Hyphesteus opened the gate. He prepared himself this time, shielding himself behind the door and opening it carefully when it felt as though it would spring open again. Only a small lick of fire swelled out. The heat was unbelievable. He could barely stand the proximity, peering into the conflagration. The sacred emissions were still standing. It was inconceivable. They still had not melted.

"Bring it out," he commanded.

"Have they melted?" asked the Priest, coming closer and shielding his eyes.

"No," was all he replied.

"Then why are we removing it?"

Hyphesteus hadn't much patience when he was deeply involved. "Because it is never going to melt."

"How do you know?"

"I know because I know," he said testily preparing the removal equipment. He picked up the long bronze bar and laid it on the anvil, lining it up with the furnace opening.

The priest had suspected as much. This mysterious substance was so different from anything in anyone's experience that it would naturally not behave as a normal metal. Anything, that is, except the remaining three of the sacred Five and the Goddess. He only saw them once every year at the annual celebration of the Earth-Mother, the special event attended only by Council and their closest associates. He had never touched them, but he had viewed them close up. They were the same substance, or at least similar, he was sure. All had come from the Heavens.

Two apprentices muscled a heavy wooden round to its place a pace back from the furnace opening. They laid the end of a long bronze pole onto the bronze Y support fitted into the center of the massive stump and smoothly inserted the rod through the door. The rod was cold and wet from its bath in cool water, a necessary precaution to give them a little more time in a furnace hotter than the metal's melting point. Carefully they moved it, guided by Hyphesteus who directed its tapered end through the holes near the upper fringe of the cauldron.

"Everyone. Now. Lift it," he called. Normally he kept his voice reserved and calm during the cauldron pull, but he was too excited.

All of the apprentices and assistants piled on to the bronze rod and pushed down, the leverage of their combined weight barely enough to lift the hefty load.

"Now back," he ordered.

The apprentice at the back was in the best position to pull, as well as push down. He gave it his all while the others did their best to contribute by leaning sideways and giving small jerks, unsynchronized, together amounting to a surprisingly continuous removal. The load grew easier as the rod emerged with the cauldron coming closer to the fulcrum point. It radiated so passionately it glowed almost white. Only a hint of red added to the illumination gave it any semblance of color.

"Slower now," he said as they removed it. "Now swing to the side. Around. That's it. Steady. There. Let it down." The cauldron rested on a high stump with a flat rock set between as a thermal break.

They withdrew the rod, not careful enough not to burn their hands. The heat had traveled up the rod farther than they had anticipated. "Drop this in the trough and bring the other," called Hyphesteus, thinking several moves ahead.

Hyphesteus pointed to the spot he was eyeballing as he mentally calculated the exact distances for the next move. "Quickly now. Get that support over here." The apprentices pulled it over and laid the cool rod onto the Y support again and inserted it through the holes. The reach would not be so far this way so they would have an easier time lifting it.

A loud crack sounded and they felt a sudden lift on the rod that they had not prepared for. The rock beneath the cauldron had exploded under the combination of heat and pressure. It had completely split apart, pieces tumbling off the stump and falling to the sandy floor. No one was ready for the cauldron's sudden lurch and warrant to tip and fall.

"Hold it," Hyphesteus cried out. "Don't let it drop." He lunged onto the bar and put his full weight onto it as others grabbed on and assisted. The combined effort was too much and the cauldron rose too high, swinging and shaking the pole. It slid a few inches toward them.

"Gently. Gently," he panicked. Let it down a bit. That's better." Perspiration broke out anew on all of the men, even the ones near the back.

Hyphesteus felt his heart palpitating. "Swing it now." His voice rasped, dried with the apprehension of the moment. "There. Now down."

The cauldron rested safely on the long anvil. Hyphesteus let go, and the apprentices withdrew the pole and placed it against the wall. One apprentice placed a bar in front of the base of the cauldron and firmly held it along with another apprentice on the other side of the table. This would keep the cauldron from sliding. Four other apprentices took long bars with hooks in the middle and fitted them into the holes where the long removal pole had slid through. Two on each side of the table tipped the large ceramic over, wincing at the incredible heat still emanating from it. The iron ingots spilled out, glowing and bathing the entire room in their light as they were fished from the bottom of the cauldron and hooked along the table. It was miraculous how they had resisted the heat that had been thrust at them.

The cauldron was removed with the two hooked grapples and placed safely out of the way.

Hyphesteus had prepared for this. The packed sand mold for the liquid that never materialized was against the wall and would not now be used at all. It could be discarded. The anvil was the only way they were going to achieve their objective, if they were lucky. How resistant these ingots were going to be was still conjecture. They might not be forced into malleability at all.

They spread the ingots, all sizes and shapes, along the table. They were cooling fast, especially the smaller ones. They had already reddened from their brilliant white.

Bronze hammers were distributed and the banging began, a rhythmic, coordinated progression that filled the room.

"It's working," cried Hyphesteus unable to contain himself. "They submit."

It was true. The metal was yielding to the impact of the large hammers. They pounded the metal until it grayed and yielded no more. The small pieces had been completely flattened, the larger ones only partially so.

But they had won.

They had prevailed over the magic of heaven.

* * *

Almost three of the ten-day weeks had passed; twenty-eight days if he wanted to be precise about it.

Paras was glad to see the project end. He had never worked so hard and he was stiff from stem to stern. Carthea too. She had been unforgettable, exciting to watch, keeping up with the men the way she had. Neither of them had been oblivious to the looks of desire that other men had thrown her way. It was funny, really. They were all too tired to do anything about it, but she was a sight, all sweaty with her clothing clinging tight. It was when she bent over that she got the most scrutiny, her hugging skirt separating her taut cheeks and delineating the solitary cleft between while her breasts hung forward and prospered magnificently.

All of the sanctuary workers had been invited, required, to come back to Knossos for preparations for the ceremony. The dedication would be far above what had occurred at the foundry; a celebration, a holy day that would involve everyone from Knossos.

The workers were catered to for the day, scrubbed in a seemingly endless supply of hot water that filled every tub in the city. They were oiled, their bodies shaved and scraped with strigils, perfumed and, for those who were single, servicing was available on request for both men and women. They were showered with compliments and congratulations for a job well done, even though most people had only heard about the sanctuary, not actually seen it. Everyone was excited about it.

If the people of the city could have carried the workers back up to the mountain, they probably would have. If they had been asked they certainly would have tried. Everyone had packs on their backs, even the little children.

The only exceptions were the members of Council. They had an even heavier load and divided themselves between the four long wrought iron poles that had been formed with such industry in the dusk of the foundry. Helping them carry were those who had labored hardest on the rods, the metalsmiths and apprentices who had served in the foundry.

Hyphesteus was the talk of all who knew and saw him. He was barely recognizable. Minos himself had to intervene and assure the smith that a thorough cleaning, a bath, was necessary and would not kill him and that, yes, he would indeed have to submit to body shaving. The sacredness of the coming event could not be overemphasized and he, along with everyone else, would have to fully prepare. To be less would be an affront and a sacrilege. And, no, he could not be excused for any reason. Minos had no time for argument. The man was coming and he was coming of his own accord. Hyphesteus had seen the controlled displeasure in Minos's eyes and experienced the stare that pierced deep. He did not like it and knew that Minos did not appreciate his ill-timed humor.

The sacred procession took the entire day, led by the couriers of the iron, fifteen to each one. They didn't require that kind of combined manpower at first, but everyone had to have a part, and the road was long. By the end of the day they were sore holding the irons against their shoulders, especially the Priestesses of the Council.

Hyphesteus was proud as he walked under what he perceived as a light weight. He wished he could carry more. These irons were his creations more than any other, with the exception of Zeus. The work involved. His thoughts wandered repeatedly over the production that had taken so many months, from the inception of the powerful furnace and its construction to the final polishing of the rods themselves. How he had labored, pounding with his hammers, exhorting and cajoling the smiths and apprentices to harder toil. The iron yielded to their relentless basting, flattening and extending, folded over and over, stretching longer and longer as the flattened pieces were hammered into each other before being folded over again. The poles grew so long that to heat the center parts a small hole had to be chipped in from the outside of the furnace to let the pole protrude through. Daily they worked, the banging of the hammers and the ringing of the brass on iron pervading the shop and their heads, carrying to the surrounding neighborhood and comforting those who lived or worked within the sound and knew of the sacred nature of the métier. They stopped only in the late darkness of night when laws required quiet for all but religious observances so that rites could be undisturbed and all people of Knossos could have time to sleep or contemplate in peace. But even through the night the furnace was fed, keeping the temperature to the heights required for their precedential work. Massive amounts of charcoal were consumed, keeping the charcoal-maker's apprentices laboring at the forest edge as busy as the carpenter's apprentices cutting trees. The oaks were protected from the carpenters and shipwrights within two days walk around the area of Knossos. There were a few minor grumbles, but none that ever made their way back to Minos's ears. There were eight pits going in rotation to produce enough charcoal, and even then they were falling behind once the fires were underway. It had been a good thing that they had started stockpiling months before. As they cleaned out an area, they moved on to another so that they would not have to haul the heavy logs so far. A huge steer was put to work dragging those unwieldy cuts for them. The oak was such a hard wood that they could use only the sharpest and hardest bronze axes, and the chopping took a long time. They even used the branches of the trees to get the initial fires going in the pits before burying the stacks of trunk-wood. They used dead oak as much as they could, bringing it in from far and wide. There was no danger of any carpenter or shipwright making off with any of that. It was useless to them. The whole operation had been a good opportunity for the young men of the city. Numbers of them were put to work porting the charcoal from the countryside to the foundry, assisting in bringing smaller sections and branches of oak out of the forests, and digging pits. Prodigious esprit de corps grew between all who participated. They were participating in a significant project of great value for all of them. The self-worth that they felt for their efforts, echoed by the citizens of Knossos, made them feel as consummate as the gods themselves; minor ones anyway.

The long line came to a stop, more slowly the farther back in the line the people were, as they bunched up in reasonable order.

Minos and Phaespae, releasing the rods and taking the lead started the procession of the High Priests and Priestesses anew. The metalsmiths also stayed behind with the multitude. They were to wait until all had been given the opportunity to relieve themselves wherever they could and take some wine. There would be no food here, except a little for the children. This was a fasting occasion.

The Council had broken the treeline and were passing through fields of anemone and cyclamen to the more barren area where grasses grew thin, and mosses and lichens layered the rocks. They were coming into view of the sanctuary surrounded by its decorative low wall. Wonderful it was, the temenos perimeter wall extending across the front of the view for twenty-four hundred feet. Nine feet thick and twelve feet high, it was the closest thing to a defensive fortification on the island. But there was nothing defensive about it, only a need to express on a larger than usual scale the majesty and power of the divinity honored. The workmanship had been unparalleled, and the ones who had not laid eyes on it prior to this grieved to voice their approval, but held their tongues reverent.

The four rods were laid upon the ground within the temenos wall, hallowed ground, a scorched area that still had not greened with any living thing. The bearers separated into two groups, male and female, and parted to attend to any needed toilet functions. It was as much a matter of smell as elimination. The members of the Council were fastidiously clean, and body odors were offensive to them. That was why they could not stand to be at the foundry for more than the most abbreviated visit. Black water pots had been left by couriers two days before, heated since then by the sun. It was hardly the hot baths they were accustomed to but, since their bodies were already hot from the long walk, mildly warm water was a cooling refreshment.

Flagons of scented olive oils and phials of imported perfumes had been set for them, including rare and precious myrrh from the small, thorny bersera tree of southern Egypt. They changed out of their sweated garments and towel bathed, running curved copper scrapers over themselves to remove the perspiration and excess oil. New garments were packaged for them in protective boxes placed in advance. They donned their new raiment; brightly adorned purple skirts for the Priests, long blue dresses for the Priestesses with the traditional open bodice gathered tightly under their prominent breasts. Gold threads highlighted the borders; gold braiding for Minos and Rhea.

The men oiled their long hair, almost as long as the women's, which coursed down their backs to their waist. It was a rare thing indeed to cut one's head hair, the crown being the most sacred part of the body. Only the criminal had his hair cut as a public humiliation. The men let their scintillating tresses hang front and back. The women bunched their hair high into a pile with combs and pins, gathering it into a ponytail looped back on itself and tied three times behind their heads with the remainder hanging behind them and tied again in several places down the length of their backs. They didn't oil their hair but kept it rich and free, soaping it with a mixture of boiled-down beef fat and extracts of barren sandy soil from where nothing grew. The alkali solution leached out of the soil was enough to break the hot fat down into a soap and, mixed with herbs to alleviate the deterring odor, made for an acceptable shampoo.

Minos, when all were ready, took up a triton shell and blew a long note signaling the women to meet them at the rods and the multitude to begin their final ascent to the sanctuary. All would be prepared by the time they arrived.

The full Priesthood met, the divine couple leading the sorority of Priestesses in pairs with the Priests behind, five to each two poles, hefting the rods upon their shoulders. They passed the gates of the temenos wall and took their places beyond the raised stone fire-circle. Minos and Rhea stopped at the entrance and turned to face the followers. The double row of Priestesses separated and fanned out on either side forming a semicircle across the front of the shrine, also turning their backs on it. The Priests were last, sweating again under the strain of carrying the weights uphill without help, and grouped themselves in the center of the semicircle in front of Minos and Rhea who now were in representation of Zeus and the Earth-Mother.

Minos blew into the great triton shell again and again, inflating his lungs and sounding the onerous tone from earth to sky. The Priests bowed low and then raised up the rods, directing the enlarged apices heavenward. As an afterthought, when the poles had been completed in the foundry, Minos had ordered the tips to be widened like a spear, pointed at the tip and not flat but conical, giving them an appreciably oriental look. Hyphesteus had not been impressed, having just completed the most formidable project of his life, and then having Minos change the design when he thought he had concluded his work. He was chagrined that his work had not met with complete approval, but he acquiesced and set to task, thanking the gods that he had not let the furnace run down. It had taken the rest of the day and most of the night to complete the labor, laws of silence at night be damned. No one complained. He had been concerned about the loss of length as he doubled the poles over on themselves at the end several times to get the prominent head, losing a cubit on each in the process. He'd had his doubts that the iron could even be worked that way, but he had done it. The smith-gods of ancient times, the Telchines, had been with him, speeding him along and assisting him in completing the challenge just in time. The result was satisfying to himself and to Minos, and he was glad, in the end, that he had been asked to do it.

The priests climbed the structure, easily done with the steeply sloping mountainside behind it. The sanctuary was twenty-five feet high at the front but only six at the back, effortlessly scaled. They raised each rod up in turn and inserted them into their brackets, right through the height of the sanctuary, to be planted into the earth itself. It was a balancing act when they raised the poles, almost losing one of them, but still managing to maintain their grace as they recovered and dropped it into place. The forty-foot poles still rose above the highest point of the sanctuary by fifteen feet, or ten cubits. It had worked out perfectly. Hyphesteus had made the originals too long, supposing it would be easier to drive them into the earth than it actually was. By removing a cubit and curling it into the swollen end, he had inadvertently made the lengths symbolically correct. Ten.

The priests stood among the five horns of consecration adorning the roof of the sanctuary, similar but smaller than the horns at the larger temple sites. From there they could see, and be seen by, the hordes coming up the climb. They assumed the pose; legs spread, arms out with fists on hips, back straight, and head high. Minos and Rhea climbed the steps to the arched entrance. There was no door to close, inviting all in at any time. They stood before it then turned to greet the multitude swelling into the immediate vicinity inside the wall. On they came, welling up the slope and around the back, spreading out to the sides and stretching for the best view. The pilgrims fortunate enough to be at Knossos at this time stayed at the back, along with Paras and Carthea who did not expect to have favor curried again in getting themselves ushered to the front.

When the masses had stilled and quieted themselves the ceremony began. Minos blew the first note, an astoundingly long tonal report that, just before his lungs failed, was joined by the ten trumpeting Priests holding their own shells. They initially aimed the blast at the crowd most before the sanctuary then, when Minos rejoined, swung their trumpets around to herald all in attendance. The notes were not all the same, some high, some low, all in perfect harmonic pitch giving the most balanced illuminating effect. When the

Priestesses, after a few minutes, lifted their shells to raise the volume and add to the tonal variance the crowd was in rapture.

Rhea held up a decanter of liquid honey, symbolic of the hard-working bee, and spread drops of golden amber at either side of the entrance, then trailed a string of it down one side of the steps then up the other. She stood full in the doorway and began to undulate her body. Running a finger around the rim of the honey decanter she withdrew a dollop and placed it to her lips. She withdrew it, a streamer stretching from her mouth to her uplifted finger. She tilted her head back and opened her mouth, letting the honey slip down as she wrapped her tongue around it and pulled it into her mouth. All the while she let her pelvis gyrate to the changing music. It had taken on a tempo, different from the initial constant tone. It now carried a pacing meter that was increasing in momentum. The Priests above carried a background note that varied little beyond subtle changes in tone and volume but the Priestesses weaved inflections and diversity, pausing then starting again, contributing a drum-like bass enhancement that drove Rhea to a frenzy as she contorted and pivoted about on the steps of the sanctuary. The priests took up the changing sonorous reverberations and one by one the Priestesses, the Klowiphoroi, the Key-bearers, joined Rhea on the steps, passing their horns to lesser Priestesses who were not of the Council. They took up the dance along with their mistress, cavorting and flailing in sensuous abandon, whirling with their hands on their hips, then flung wildly out into the air, then energetically waving high above their heads while the music called. They reeled to the point of depletion while their tresses flew, and suddenly they and the vibrant music stopped, instantly and without warning, the synchronous silence as startling as a sharp and unexpected noise.

Pilgrims embracing the spirit of the moment threw their votive offerings into the pyre where they were swallowed by the embers. With the fat of sacrificial lambs feeding the inferno, they were quickly consumed in acceptance. The ashes and votive remains, still fiery hot, were swept together and loaded aboard a wooden cart which erupted in flame as it was rolled to the edge of a deep fissure in the rock to the west of the sanctuary. There the cart was completely immolated, and the ashes and non-combustible offerings spilled into the void.

Beautifully decorated urns at either side of the sanctuary entrance had been filled with wine, and the Priestesses collectively had their fill. Likewise, at each place where a Priest or lesser Priestess stood with their horns, there was also a smaller urn. The effect was almost immediate with the amount they consumed in their thirst. In fact, most wine was consumed in temples, sanctuaries, or shrines. The warmth they felt inside at this time verified that the great Zeus was smiling upon them, and confirmed that their offering of a sacred sanctuary to his name was accepted.

Minos blew a deviating tone through his shell, loud and beautiful to the ear, masterful in its variance. The Priests filed off the roof and took their positions alongside the Priestesses while he blew. The consecration of the sanctuary was concluded. The celebration by public dance and music would now begin.

* * *

"At last. I didn't think the day would come." Carthea was musing as she walked the road to the Labyrinth.

"You knew it would," said Paras in his practical way.

"I still don't understand why it took so long for us. We've been here six months."

We've been over this before. For some reason, we have been singled out for special treatment. That doesn't mean things move faster. The contrary. Everything has to be just right. Don't you feel it? Our setting apart will not be ordinary. Members of the Council will be there. Didn't you hear them? Not just one, like usual. Members. Plural. Something extraordinary is going on."

"But why? Why us?"

"I don't know. I can't figure it out. We've almost been treated like members of the Elect since our arrival here. In the time we have been in Knossos no other pilgrims have been treated as we have. I am as puzzled as you are."

"I wish I knew. I'm getting nervous about the test."

"Nervous? You? I didn't know you could ever get nervous about anything."

"Well, I can. What if we don't make it?"

"Don't make it? How could we not make it? Thousands of others have. Lesser people than us." He caught himself and bit his lip. He wished he hadn't said that.

Carthea looked at him. "You know you can do it, don't you." She wasn't asking a question.

He wanted to keep silent but couldn't. "Yes I do. I do know." He was getting angry. "Why should we stay behind in that stupid seaside town while I count inventory all day and get little in return for making other men rich? I make them rich. They would not even know if they were being stolen from if not for me. I myself could have defrauded the unsuspecting fools, but I didn't. What good is a fortune in a place like that when we could be rich in Knossos?"

"Is that what you think? You never told me that before. You think we can become rich here?"

"Of course we can. Nothing can stop us."

"Some would be wary of your words."

"Some should be."

"Me?" she questioned.

He turned to her and held her arms. "No. Not you. Have you seen these people, these Priestesses who fancy themselves so fine? Have you taken a really good look? They are nothing to you. Nothing. I would have no other but you." He smiled as he reassured her. But she wasn't so sure.

They walked in silence the rest of the way, each lost in different thoughts.

There seemed to be an unusual number of people above at the cave entrance. Ordinarily there wouldn't be more than a dozen or so on a busy day, when the families of those who lived in Knossos would sometimes attend and pray outside the Labyrinth for the success of their relative inside. When a pilgrim went through there were usually only a couple of people, including the Council member who would oversee the challenge and assure nothing went amiss. No one had ever died inside the cave, unless one believed the old legend from the past. But that was surely just a tale.

There was nothing to be afraid of at this place. It was a sanctuary too; a cave sanctuary. Instead of being sanctified for the reverence of Zeus this was a place mainly of worship of the Earth-Mother. Many gifts were brought here in recognition of her, laid in cracks and clefts just beyond the entrance. Few went farther in than that except the Elect and those on their mission of passage. The entrance was guarded by two labryses, double-axes of brass, a golden-like metal imported from Egypt. The metallurgists of Knossos longed for the secret of making brass, just out of curiosity, but the line of Minoses had continually stayed of the opinion that the Egyptians had to have some secrets. All of their science had so far come from Kriti. They had to leave the Egyptians with something they could call their own. The labrys used to symbolically guard the entrance was the root of the word, Labyrinth, used as the name for this cave. In time the word came to mean any maze-like structure.

Paras and Carthea had visited here on several occasions, almost able to taste the challenge. They had not entered past the first oblation, the place just inside the entrance where tributes for favor were left. They had heard that past that place was another of great magnificence, a place where there was a vast chamber where rituals were performed by only members of the Council; the Cavern of the Phallus. No one knew exactly what went on there. All they could coerce out of one teasing young priestess was "Use your imagination." They would get a chance to see the Phallus. It was unrestricted to any who were going through the challenge, although the cavern would be empty except for them at that time.

Carthea could not repress the anxiety she felt as they came nearer. She felt cold even with the exercise of walking the miles from Knossos, even though this last stretch was uphill. The overcast sky had been darkening all day and it looked like they might be in for a storm. At least they would be inside the shelter of the cave by the time it broke.

They rounded the last corner before the cave and to their utmost dismay were greeted by the entire Council. Their arrival had been watched, that much was obvious. Not one of the Council members was surprised to see them.

Rhea stepped forward. "Welcome," she said. "We knew you would get here early."

"Early?" said Carthea. It was all she could think of to say. Paras wished she had stayed silent. He, too, was overcome by the reception but didn't want to appear imbecilic.

"Most people are not of your physique, your athletic capacity. Almost any other couple would have taken longer to get here. We have watched you, you know; your work on the sanctuary. You, Carthea, amazed all of us. And you, Paras; as a scribe you missed your calling. You have great abilities as a worker of stone. We can only assume from your education and your physical abilities that you will excel at any task put before you. But we are being inconsiderate." She turned to another Priestess. "Give them drink."

The woman poured freshly pressed grape juice into two wonderfully crafted ceramic beakers. "We would offer you wine," she said, "but you will not be needing anything to befuddle your sense of direction inside. This fresh juice will quench your thirst. Drink as much as you want before you enter. You will not have anything once inside."

They drank thirstily. Carthea thought she could feel a rumble or a vibration beneath her feet but kept drinking. She hadn't realized how thirsty the hike had made her.

It was then that she smelled the unmistakable scent of mutton. Burning mutton. Behind the congregation was fire, small but burning hot. On top was the oblong charcoal carcass of a lamb, prepared not for eating as in most sacrifices, but for incineration.

Rhea saw the realization in her face. "We were having our annual gathering here. Perhaps you have heard of it?"

"Something of it, yes."

"Then you may also have heard of the Cavern of the Phallus. You will see it when you pass through the way to the end, depending on which way you go. Every nine years we gather there and hold worship to the Earth-Mother and to Zeus. It is part of the devotion that we hold here at his birthplace, and later at his place of interment. We have spent the last day inside, even through the night. I represent Rhea, or Selene as she is sometimes known. Minos represents

Zeus. Together we ensure the fertility of the people of Minos. We do this in front of the Phallus and in front of the Council. Do you understand?"

Carthea felt a twinge of embarrassment. "Yes. I . . . I think I do. Why are you telling us these things." She knew that this could not be other than privileged information.

"It cannot have escaped you that you have been singled out for treatment which we do not disseminate liberally. You are different. We knew that before we even met with you that wet day months ago. While on the slopes of Mount Juktas we envisioned just you two coming to us. We did not know exactly why but we knew that it was foreordained and that you would play a vital role in life as we know it on Kriti. You yourself have felt it in your dissatisfaction with your previous lives."

She looked directly at Paras who trembled inside. How could she know?

"You want to be important, don't you Paras?"

He didn't know how to respond. To agree would show his inner self too clearly, expose things he wasn't sure he even wanted to acknowledge to himself. To stay silent might reveal even more.

"It doesn't matter. Your destiny is at hand. You will be important; both of you," she said swinging her penetrating gaze from one to the other, "in ways that none of us can foresee."

Carthea felt a cold chill at the nape of her neck. Paras felt warm inside. It was coming to pass, just as he knew it would.

And even sooner than he had presumed to hope.

* * *

"What did she say we were looking for again?" asked Carthea as they pressed on through the dim light of their white marble oil lamp.

"A scarab."

"That's right. A beetle of some sort. An Egyptian beetle."

"They need it as proof that we have been to the end."

"That's why. Of course. Do you think anyone has lied about being to the end? Is that why they need to have proof?"

"I can't imagine anyone doing that. No one could come into this place and have no respect for the Earth-Mother. We are as if in her very womb. For someone to blatantly commit fraud such as that would deserve the worst retribution.

Carthea gasped, almost dropping the precious lamp. A skeleton lay among the jumbled rocks.

Paras was more composed although inwardly shaken at the sight that came just as they were talking about divine punishment.

"Let's carry on. Try not to think about it."

They carefully moved along the tangled corridor, making good speed they thought, shaken by the bones but trying to divert their attention to anything else. There were a number of choices they had to make, divisions which went to the right or left. The second time they had to decide they took a path that rapidly terminated at a dead end. They hoped that wouldn't happen again.

They had agreed that if one of them made an obvious mistake then the lamp would pass from one to the other. That was what happened when they went down the dead end. Paras had taken the lamp at first and had to relinquish it to Carthea when they discovered he had erred. Now she was leading the way, and so far without becoming disoriented.

"I wonder where the Chamber of the Phallus is?" she wondered aloud. "Rhea said that it was not far from the entrance."

"Only if we went that way. We must have taken the other route at the first division."

"I hope it was the right one."

"As do I. We cannot fail at this. You know that it has been directed now that only one chance be given."

He was getting concerned. If they were defeated in their attempt to do this their hopes and dreams would be dashed to pieces. Try as he might he was getting confused by the twists and turns of the convoluted passages, bifurcating arteries leading them deeper into the heart of the cold stone ridge.

This was more difficult and taking longer than they thought it would.

"I'm getting worried Paras."

"How is your oil?"

"Low. I don't think it will last much longer."

That was not good news. They stopped at another decision point. The way divided again, one passage leading upward, another narrower way leading down.

"Which way?" asked Carthea.

Paras knelt down close to the ground. "Bring your lamp down here."

Carthea knelt too.

"Hold the light out in front, close to the ground."

There was a conspicuous wear to the path leading down. More importantly, there were indications of traffic returning from that direction. People who had taken the upper way to the left had not come back. Those who had gone down to the right did.

"That way. Let's go. There is not much time."

They hurried, a sense of urgency filling their chests with unsettling anticipation. If only they had been given a second lamp. If they could find their way back out even now, it would be a miracle.

"I think I see something up ahead," said Carthea.

"What is it?"

Carthea thought she would cry. "It is light."

"Light?" Paras's hopes and dreams collapsed. There was only one place where they would find light.

The entrance.

With grieved hearts and withered countenances, they carried on toward the glow ahead. Carthea was crying. Paras was not of any mood to offer comfort. How could this have happened? What disastrous breath of ill fortune could have blown such disappointment their way? It was too cruel to contemplate. Everything, lost.

They rounded the last prominent rock to the entrance, filled with remorse and self-reproach.

Carthea stopped cold. Her head whirled and she buttressed herself against the rock.

Before them, the tunnel opened into a chamber large enough to swallow numerous houses. Everywhere there were objects that would only have been found in shrines or in homes of the wealthy. This place was a repository of rich votive offerings. At the back, on a natural stone altar, was the gilded life-sized head of a bull, its horns raised in threatening censure. Above it, mounted on the smooth wall, were adornments of the most curious workmanship. The first was a sharp-cornered symbol, a golden cross with arms of equal length and an odd continuation of each at right angles. A swastika. Above that was a more recognizable sight. Five silver circles spread apart, not touching, in the orientation of a 'W'. The symbol of Minos.

Many things came together in this cave, the cave where it was said a boy named Kouros was born, Zeus Velchanos, The Boy. Subject to an untamed temperament and violent acts of rage in his youth he was only calmed in his adulthood. The jagged lines of the swastika represented his violent youth and adolescence. To bridle and subdue him, the Earth-Mother took the form of woman, and tamed him as a woman eventually tames any man. From his weak and inferior character she led him, from his small and unimportant status, to assume the role of consort to represent the critical principle of discontinuity in nature. Always subject to the goddess and always imaged in attitudes of adoration, the Divine Boy grew in stages from Kouros, to Velchanos, to Zeus. Still, even in adulthood, as in youth, he stood erect with arms raised in a gesture of worship and submission subject to the restraints of the Mother Goddess Selene, Rhea, her name so sacred it could not be written. 'Potnia,' they called her in print, 'The Lady,' the 'Magna Mater.' Contrasting the hideous symbol of the jagged fury of self-righteous perspective and intolerance were the smooth, welcome lines of the five circles. Apart, the circles sought each other, naturally striving to draw each other in until they touched and merged into a unified whole. Friendship, fellowship, against exclusivity and prejudice.

An enormous steatite lamp burned beside the bull's head, feeding a wide wick from the urn-sized container of oil and blessing the small cavern with its luminosity. A lamp that size could burn for weeks without having to be refilled. Their little lamp was woeful by comparison, its pale light washed out completely by the incandescence of the other. Paras tipped his head forward and blew out his little fire.

"What are you doing?" Her voice was a stifled scream from a tensed throat.

"Settle down. We need to conserve the oil."

She thought about it a moment, realizing to her relief that they could light it again from the flame of the other lamp. She was getting jumpy in here. She didn't mind going into cave sanctuaries, but this was far beyond that. Knowing she was far into the heart of the earth was hard for her to accept. Even in this holy place she did not feel at peace.

Taros was poking around the altar, quietly, not wanting to disturb the idol. There was a distinct odor of old wine and he wondered where it came from, suddenly feeling thirsty. He hadn't expected to find anything to drink inside the cave; the Priestess had said that they would not have refreshment while inside. Of course. There had been wine offerings here.

"Is this the Cavern of the Phallus?" Carthea wondered. There didn't seem to be any phallus anywhere.

"No." Paras turned around and held up a palm-sized copper beetle. He spoke with the excitement he felt. "We have found it Carthea. The scarab."

"The scarab," she echoed. "Then this is the end. This is the place we have been seeking." She rushed into Paras's arms and embraced him tightly. The floor of the cave vibrated for a second, a sub-bass resonation manifesting itself through the tactile, rather than the auditory, senses.

Carthea leaned back still holding her husband. "Did you feel that?"

"Yes. I think so."

"We should get out of here. I don't like this place."

Paras kissed her. "Don't be afraid. This place has given us what we came for. Still, we should be getting back. I hope we have enough oil."

Carthea looked inside the lamp. It wasn't far from empty. "There is no way we could get back on this much oil. Even if we made no mistake, I don't think we could do it. No one could get here and back with the amount of oil we have been given unless they were absolutely familiar with the way."

Paras looked for himself. "We will have to hurry and leave it to the gods to guide us in darkness."

"No." She looked at the big lamp on the altar. "That has been put there for more than lighting this cavern. It is there to feed our lamp as well. That is why it is so big. That is part of the test, isn't it? To see if we can figure that out. I don't think it would occur to most people to take oil from there."

"You may be right. You must be. Even if a hundred of our lamps were filled there would still be enough oil left to keep that flame burning for weeks."

He took the lamp from her and dipped it into the oil, filling it. He removed the dripping lamp carefully, wiping off the residue with his finger and letting it dribble back into the urn. There may be plenty, but it would not be right to let any fall wastefully onto the ground.

He looked inside his little lamp. "We don't really need this much."

Carthea understood. "Then you should put some back. The Earth-Mother has given. It is fitting that we should give some back in gratitude. It is as it always has been."

Paras replaced as much as he dared, then lit the wick. It flared up and burned with a streamer of lampblack shooting straight up until the over-sodden wick burned off its excess.

Paras held the Egyptian scarab like a treasured heirloom. The lamp he returned to Carthea. "You found the way here. Now take us back."

* * *

"The storm comes," shouted Rhea against the winds.

Another etesian wind was blowing south, carrying with it a black thunderhead raised solemnly to the heavens.

They had climbed the promontory and were standing on the highest elevation above the cave entrance. Another lamb was near them, a female this time, engulfed in fiery embers for quick and total consumption. From here they could see the storm rushing toward them. It climbed high over the supine face of Zeus, the Mountain Juktas. Bolts of lightning flashed across a maddened sky, illuminating the cumulonimbus pile from top to bottom.

A multitude of slim brands joined earth and cloud too fast to see and converged into a single, terrible thunderbolt focused precisely on the location of Zeus's mountain sanctuary. The wrought iron poles had acted as lightning rods, attracting and conducting the lighting to earth without causing damage to the surroundings. The rod's affinity for lightning was in part caused by the Minoan smiths pointing the masts like spearheads, the form recommended by Benjamin Franklin when he reinvented them after his famous kite experiment of 1752. The sharply pointed terminals of the metal rods closely concentrated the lines of force of the electric field so that ionization of the air around the points took place. Electrons became dislodged from the atoms of the rods with the result that the latter were left with a positive charge, making the air around them inordinately conductive to electricity, and providing the path of least resistance for electric discharges.

"Call him, my husband. Call him now."

Minos blew on the shell, beckoning to the god assailing his own place of worship and veneration, calling him to unleash his power and accept their sacrifice.

* * *

Two hundred feet below, Paras and Carthea were quietly stepping along a passageway that they prayed would lead to the exit.

"This doesn't look right," worried Paras.

"You're right. We haven't been here before."

The narrow passage that they had before sworn was the right path was widening, the ceiling rising steeply, the rubble on the ground loose and tripping them up. They had wandered into another cavern, an elongated curve much larger than the one they had retrieved the scarab from. There wasn't too much loose rubble after a few more steps. A small section of ceiling must have given way, littering the floor. They could still smell the dust so it could not have happened long ago.

Paras was getting a bad feeling about this.

"Let's go." He went ahead of Carthea even though she still had the lamp.

"Are you sure this is the way? I know it's not the way we came."

"I know. But if we retrace our steps we will of a surety run out of oil. And we might not find the lighted hall again to replenish it. We have to go on."

She caught up and gave him the lamp. He was leading anyway so why not? She couldn't lead any better.

The cave seemed to be widening even more, curving around a large outcropping of rock.

"We did it," Paras shouted. "We are almost back."

"The Phallus. Oh, Paras." They found it. The symbol of procreation. The Cave of the Phallus. If it was as near to the entrance as Rhea had said, then they would soon be out, and full members of the Order.

Paras clenched his fists and curled them into his chest. He wanted to roar with satisfaction. His dreams were so close they were as good as fulfilled. Carthea embraced him from behind.

Slowly, and with foremost reverence, they drew themselves nearer to the upthrusting stone. The need to hurry was over. They had oil enough for at least an hour. Plenty of time to stop for a few moments of devotion although they both felt an urgency to receive confirmation of the blessing that awaited them. The power of the stone called them to touch it, though they dared not. It was hypnotic the way it reeled them in.

Paras felt the inevitable stirring in his loins. This was not the place; not the place for that. It might be appropriate for Priests and Priestesses but not for them. He had to resist. They had to be going.

Two sacred symbols eyed them in miniature. One, a votive colonnade, a bird epiphany consisting of three pillars with beam end capitals each surmounted by a dove. Bird epiphanies represented the presence of the Mother-goddess, though the couple needed not another visage to remind them of her. This quiet indication of the divine spirit contrasted so much against the grandiosity of the foreign nations. Minor monuments such as these were everywhere and were ever enough to keep the people from losing contact from natural processes, always able to find in the wilderness of a cave or the splendor of a mountaintop a talisman against priestly confusion and meaningless talk. The doves were the emblems of love and fertility, and they were having their effect on Carthea.

She was at his back again. She rubbed his sides and pressed herself against him.

"Do you feel it?" she asked in a whisper.

Paras didn't answer. He was willing himself away. They had no time. He turned.

"Paras. My true love," Carthea said gazing deep into his cerulean eyes. He returned the gaze to his inamorata. He felt such love for her that there was no room left in his heart for more. No increase in capacity was possible. Alone neither could have come this far. Together they had done it. Only joined were they complete.

"Paras, I must tell you, now that we are in this place. . ." Her voice drifted off as she looked down and lightly bit her lower lip.

"He took her chin and tilted it up. "Tell me what, my love?"

"I am with child." A tear settled in the corner of one eye.

"A child." Paras almost dropped the lamp. They had wanted a child for a long time, or he knew she did. But a child might have interfered with their plans and aspirations of being accepted into the Order. But now not even that mattered. The news could not have come at a more perfect or meaningful time.

"A child," he repeated. "How wonderful."

Paras embraced his wife and she burst into tears. She had been so worried that it was not a thing that he wanted. Only the Phallus had given her the courage to disclose the news. How filled with joy was she at his approval.

They kissed, long and delicately. The stirrings of lust Paras had felt only a moment ago melted to feelings of tenderness and affection.

They parted their lips. "We cannot stay," Paras said, regretting that he could not nestle up to Carthea and hold her for a long time. Even in the cool, humid air of the cave, he felt warm. He wanted to stay in spite of his mind telling him to do otherwise.

"Come on then. I can see you want to go," she teased. She took him by the arm and guided him forward. "I wouldn't want to spoil your day by making you late."

Paras wanted to stop her and say something nice, but common sense agreed, and he just followed her escort.

"There it is. Another tunnel. That must be the way."

He barely heard his wife. A baby. He could not shake the images playing in his mind. What a time for daydreams. He had to regain his concentration. The Phallus still held him spelled. He would be all right once he was out of here.

The second epiphany gazed after them as they departed. A black raven balanced on a small double-bladed ax. They had not noticed it perching in shadow. The two epiphanies together bespoke the two aspects of creation, light and darkness, life and death, good and evil. The antithetical, paradoxical essence of divinity.

* * *

Above, on the surface, stood the Council encircling Rhea. Minos stood as the link in the circle facing south toward Juktas. The wind where they were worshipping had slowed to a breeze, but farther up it was a different story. The higher altitude jet stream made dark clouds fly past like black vultures on the wing. Lightning flashed at irregular intervals all over the island. But where it struck Juktas was always at the site of the sanctuary.

"Accept our sacrifice, oh Great Mother," called Minos to Phaespae, who stood as the earthly representation of Rhea.

The Council chanted in a low tone; male, then female, male, female. "Great Mother. Accept our sacrifice." To appease the deities the Council changed their note and sang their lavish rites of prayer, sacrifice, symbol, and ceremony. Flute and lyre accompanied the reverent chorus, the Hymn of Adoration.

"Intercede with Zeus on our behalf. Accept these perfect two into thy birthplace and link them to thy burial place." Minos's tenor voice carried as loud as an opera singer on stage.

The earth rumbled beneath their feet for a few seconds, then stopped.

There was noise following the rumble this time, roaring like a locomotive, and it filled Minos with dread. This was completely different from the thunder harmonizing in the distance. This was not the sky speaking. It was the Earth herself.

"Oh, Great Zeus. Hear the Earth-Mother. Again we beseech thee. Take these two as one offering into the bowels of thy Diktaean Cave. Take them now. Wait no longer we implore thee."

For weeks the animals had been acting up, nervous, unstable in their behavior. Frogs croaked warnings and jumped madly and without purpose. Rodents and rabbits would flee from their holes with every tremor, even the ones unfelt by man because of their weak disturbances. The animals could still feel them in their dens. They were inside the earth.

Minor waves caused by small slips occurring fifty miles below the surface made the little tremors, exciting the animals, and made themselves manifest to those who monitored such things by way of the vibrations under their feet. Tremors were common in Kriti. But when they hadn't been felt for a long time, and then of a sudden came at an increasing rate, a big one was sure to follow. It was the god's way of letting the people know of some displeasure.

The African plate subducting under the Aegean seabed doesn't do so with a smooth or steady deportment. The rock crust sticks. Irregular slips relieve some of the pressure of the entire African continent creeping and boring under the weight of the fractured smaller plates of the Mediterranean, but not all. Over centuries the relief falls far behind the buildup of potential force and only a catastrophic movement and release of energy can return the tectonic plates to another temporary state of equilibrium.

The little quakes, the tremors, which would only show as a mark of around 4.2 on the Richter scale are nothing to worry about. But quakes of 8.4 are. The Richter scale is logarithmic. Each increase of one represents an increase of thirty-two times the energy of the tremor, and of ten times in the size of the seismic wave measured by a seismograph. That means that an earthquake of magnitude 8.4 is not double the intensity of magnitude 4.2. It is one million times the intensity.

The focus of this quake was ninety miles to the north, near a Cyclades island known to the Minoans as Strongyle; Santorini or Thera to the modern world. A strange island, queer because of its periodic venting of smoke from the summit, forbidden of old as a place of residence but still valued as a source of ash for cement. Only an uncivilized rabble of people lived there, altogether unrelated to the cultured Minoans. The sudden subduction at the epicenter where the fault let go dove eighteen feet under the upper plate. Primary shock waves, or P waves, spread outward like the ripples on a pond. Always the first to arrive, the compression waves, pushing and pulling surface structures in the direction of wave travel, made themselves known by trembling under the feet. And because the P waves travel like sound waves, vibrating back and forth, they set the air in motion when they leave the Earth's surface and produce a roar proportionate to the strength of fault slippage. At a speed of five miles per second, or eighteen thousand miles per hour, the waves reached the feet of the Council in less than twenty seconds. This was the vibration and sound that struck their hearts with fear.

The vanguard of secondary, or S, waves traveled slower. They hammered the island with a violence that only nature can impart. Traveling at two and a half miles per second their advent was delayed by another twenty seconds. Slamming home at 9000 miles per hour, Minos barely had time to voice another sentence after the first rumbles had subsided. The ripples of the S waves heaved the ground up and down in rapid succession, this movement being even more destructive than the side to side rocking common to most severe earthquakes. More waves arrived and pumped in more energy. The Earth grew alive and danced. All around the island, first at the north coast and last at the south, geysers of sand and water blew skyward. All loose material, and some entire cliff sides, crumbled into valleys. Picking up the rhythm, soil and rock swayed to the strengthening beat like partners in a dance. The island was driven ten feet straight up before being punched back down, over and over again.

Council members were prone and scrambling, terrified beyond anything any factitious monstrosity conjured by the mind could effectuate. Had they not been impelled to the ground by the puissant vitality of the seismic thrills, they would have hurled themselves down in abject fright. All around, rocks rolled and tumbled, rocks that seconds ago had not even existed. They sprouted from the earth like peas spilling from a newly opened pod. Men and women were tossed as ably as any inanimate. Unable to grasp any foot or handhold, they bounced frantically, terrorized by the hammering of the Earth beating them from below as they fell to meet it and the drubbing of loose rocks flying like they were thrown by the hands of giant marauders.

A third type of wave, the surface waves, arrived last. The low-frequency waves found the soil in tune with their own vibrations and strummed it like a guitar string. The ground was rolled and whipped sideways. After the horrible shocks of the S waves had diminished, the surface waves continued to bruise the landscape and shake loose any rock or building not wildly toppled or smashed and battered to smithereens by the previous shocks.

By the time the quake finished, less than a minute after it started, the cities, towns, and villages of Kriti had been utterly wasted.

Phaespae fought with all of her might to stand during the quake, calling out in supplication for the Earth-Mother to intervene and stop this catastrophic disaster that was threatening to tear the world apart. Time and again the jackhammer motion of the Earth felled her, and time and again she willed herself onto her legs. Her balance was exquisite as she attempted to counterpoise the heaving beneath her feet. The other members of the Council, who still had the capacity to observe, noticed with disbelief the attempts of Phaespae to intercede on their behalf and heard her words shouting merciful pleadings over the tumult. When the minute-long eternity finalized she was the only one standing, arms spread to the heavens. Her face was bleeding from a cut over one eye, and a tooth was missing from her initial blow against the rocks. Her wrist was deformed from a fracture, and both knees were bruised purple and starting to swell. Phaespae was becoming conscious of the pain that had been obliterated temporarily by her religious ardency. The sacrifice of Paras and Carthea had been consumed with greater vitality than even she could have supposed. The omnipotent expression of the gods had been far more than ever imagined, their satiety endless.

Phaespae's head swam, and her body began to weave. She was being taken too. She could feel it coming. The island had been destroyed in the sacrifice, but for a greater good. It had been cleansed, and after the time of cleansing would come a wondrous new era that would surpass all others.

She swayed and attempted futilely to obtain her footing. Minos leapt toward her as she fell backward, missing her only by inches. She fainted back against a pointed rock and smashed her skull at the base.

Her death was instantaneous.

* * *

No description could adequately portray the horrors of the night that followed. Paras had lain awake at times in the night and wondered at the oppressive silence, but he had never imagined what a vivid and tangible thing perfect silence really is. On the surface of the Earth sounds and motions, imperceptible as they are, blunt the serrated edges of absolute silence. Here there were no such anodynes. They were buried alive in the bowels of the Labyrinth, under the insulation of rock, in the interior of the Earth. A hundred feet above them fresh air rushed over rocks, shook boughs, and swept against clothing, but no sound reached them at their depth.

The choking dust of the collapsed Phallus Chamber had finally settled. It had been so close. The smaller passage they had just entered had remained perfectly intact while the larger cavern had buckled and failed under the massive earth shocks. They had hung to each other tightly and utterly screamed through the chaotic clamor of the earthquake. Blasts of wind following bounding drumbeats deafened them and knocked them over, blowing out the lamp and leaving them encompassed within a barrier of concrete blackness.

How long they huddled and fed off one another's warmth and remnants of courage they could not judge. They could feel their pores plugged by the fine dust that had almost done them in, and their skin crawled in filth that they had not endured even during the building of the sanctuary. If they had not had the good sense to filter the air with their clothing they would have succumbed to the intolerable atmosphere and their lungs would have been permeated and destroyed by the copious particulates.

Mercifully their fears were to some extent mitigated by sleep. Even in such dire positions, consumed and wearied by fatigue, nature will sometimes come to assert herself and offer some measure of palliation. But the sleep was fitful, stressed with dreams of terror and dread, and they couldn't sleep much. When they lifted their lids they were as blind as when they slept, disorientated as to whether they were still asleep or awake, still alive or dead. The bravest on Earth would have quailed at the fate that inevitably waited. Thoughts of impending doom tortured their minds as they waited for the air to clear, amplified by the uninterrupted silence. The crashing and banging of all life on earth could not have reached out to their ears in that deep and living tomb.

They were cut off from every echo of the world, every voice, every scent, every touch, as if they were already dead.

Paras was wakened by a trembling from his wife, not a shiver of cold but a convulsing of her chest that told him she was crying and inconsolable. He held her closer and she fell harder against him.

"We have to get out of here," she sobbed in jerky spasms. "I can breathe now. We have to try."

Paras thought the idea beyond hope. But if they didn't at least try they were destined for a slow death, preceded by madness.

He felt blindly above him as if the ceiling might have fallen half way. Satisfied that such a thing had not occurred, he stood and helped Carthea to her feet. They stood stooped over and bent their knees more than normal, waving a hand and protecting their heads as they slowly made their way away from the cavern. They knew there was no point in even trying to go back that way. The last thing they had seen was rock filling in the opening only ten feet behind them just as the lamp was blown from Paras's hands by the wind.

Paras stepped on something loose that rolled under his feet and made a distinctly ceramic sound grating against a rock. This was the closest thing he could have had to a laugh in here. He bent over and picked up the lamp, wet on the sides from spilt oil, useless with no way to light it. He was in the motion of tossing it when his fingers tightened at the last second and held it from escaping his grasp. It wasn't broken. He fingered it completely. There wasn't even a crack. It could still hold a flame if they could fuel and light it.

"The Bull's Cave," he said. "We can get light at the Bull's Cave."

"But it is behind us." Carthea was thinking now, distracted from her morose gloom. "Wait. All of these passages are connected, aren't they? If this takes us back anywhere near the entrance, as we thought it would, then we can also find our way back to the Bull."

"Yes. Of course, if we get near the entrance we might also find our way out without light. There is still a chance of that."

Paras pocketed the lamp along with the scarab. They might still have to prove their passage to the end. They picked their way carefully along, moving painfully, slowly. There was no need to rush. There was no light to preserve.

Time did not exist in here. Paras was becoming aware of his hunger, but did not say anything lest Carthea begin thinking the same thing. If her mind could be kept from such thoughts she would have one less torture to suffer. Paras stopped.

"What is it?" asked Carthea.

He took another deep whiff through his nose. "Do you smell it?"

She did likewise. "Fresh air. I smell fresh air. The entrance must be close." She could not conceal the excitement in her voice and would have jumped if she had not been so concerned about the low overhead.

They moved even slower now, aware of their own heartbeats as they pressed blindly on. Every sense amplified a thousandfold. They felt the walls with their hands, the floor with their feet. They weren't just walking anymore, they were touching and examining, feeling and building their understanding of the little clues around them. There were small bits of gravel on the floor, and musky air was giving way to the mild refreshment of outdoor venting. Gravel quickly changed to stones and then boulders. The passage narrowed and they silently feared that it, too, would be blocked. But they got past the stricture and the rocks on the floor got smaller again.

"Stop." Carthea was sniffing.

"What is it?"

"Shhh," she hushed as if the sound was interfering with her sense of smell. She kept sniffing. She wet her finger and held it up. "Paras. The draft is coming from behind us. That caved-in area must be the way out. That is the exit."

"Are you sure?" He sniffed too.

"Wet your finger."

Sure enough. There was a draft. He leaned against the rocks and made his way along them. A few loose ones rolled down and he lost his footing, bashing his shins painfully. He had to be careful. An injury would be disastrous. If only he could see. He spit on his palm and spread saliva over his face and felt the draft more acutely. It wasn't long before he zeroed in on the opening. It was near the top of the wall and very small. He reached in and felt around. It wasn't big enough. Fury and desperation roiled within him.

"Arghgh." Paras roared in frustration. He began to fling rocks behind him as he dug. This was the way. He knew it. The smell of fresh air went arrow-straight to his brain like an intoxicating drug. And now that he had a whiff he wanted more, he wanted it all, and right now. Nothing could stop him. He tore at the rocks, breaking his fingernails and cutting his fingers on the jagged margins.

Carthea wanted to slow him down, but the air was having an effect on her too. When she smelled the dust kicked up by Paras's efforts a loathing of the place overcame her good senses and blinded her to the dangers of digging so frantically. She stood back as the rocks flew around her. She wanted to help, but she would wait her turn for when Paras tired himself.

"I'm in," he shouted. He was laughing. "Praise the gods, I'm in."

Carthea cheered and jumped, and did knock her head this time. Faint and shapeless myriads of color danced in the darkness. She wondered about praising the gods. She climbed the loose rubble and very warily followed her husband's voice. She felt the narrow opening, stopped, took a deep breath, and plunged forward as if diving into cold water.

The passage opened just inside, but not much. She crawled on her belly, snaking herself along, unable to rise to her knees because the passage was so low. Ahead she could hear the scraping noises Paras was making as he cleared smaller rocks to the side.

"Arghgh." He followed his guttural expression with whispered curses, as clear to Carthea's enhanced hearing as if he had muttered the oaths right into her ear.

She caught up to his foot and stopped. "What is it?"

"Another rock. I can't move it. It is too big."

"Is there no other way?"

"What do you mean 'Is there no other way'? You stupid woman. Of course there is no other way." In his fury he heaved against the offending rock. It refused to budge. He licked around his mouth, tasting the dust, and felt the draft again. He was going the right way. He felt all around in the blackness. The roof was solid. Except for a bit of loose gravel, all of the rocks around him were bigger than the one he was trying to move. He gave one last mighty effort and thrashed himself against the rock, squeezing himself tighter into the restricted conduit, a pointed prominence digging uncomfortably into his belly. It was hopeless. He gave up and began to weep.

Carthea reached forward to hold his foot, the only part of him she could reach. She understood his frustration. It was so claustrophobic in here it was hard to think. She wanted to curl up just to stretch her muscles, but there was not even enough room for that. It was like being in a pipe just wide enough to pull one's self through but having the additional contention of having to scrape against sharp rocks. She rested her head on her arm as a pillow, unable to hold it up any longer.

She must have slept, at least for a moment. She was sure she was somewhere else, someplace green and full of light. When she opened her eyes she still could not see but was instantly aware of where she was. Paras was wiggling. She was no longer holding his foot.

"Paras," she said softly.

"I'm stuck."

Those awful words would haunt her to her death.

"Stuck? What do mean stuck? Can't you move?"

"I'm stuck. I can't back up. I can't do it." His skirt had bunched up with his loincloth. His tunic had also pulled up around his chest and hooked on the rocky prominence that had been pressing so uncomfortably into his abdomen. He could not bring his arms down to adjust them and had only been able to pull himself forward again and then work his way backward as carefully as he could, hoping to keep the clothing straight. The hope was of no avail. He was in the same terrifying predicament children and dogs get into when they force their heads between banister rails. Their heads go through, but can't be pulled back.

He began to scream. The sound focused and echoed back to Carthea's ears as if she were within the dark helix of a great trumpet and she began to scream herself.

"No Paras. You have to get out." She latched hold of his foot and pulled. He thrashed in response to her touch and she lost her grip as he pulled away, kicking at the rocks imprisoning him. A spray of gravel struck her in the face, and she winced and backed off. Then she recognized her own predicament. She too was having a hard time backing up.

A wave of paranoid anxiety paralyzed her and deafened her to the wailing pleas of her husband. She seemed to swell inside the passage until her body filled the cavity like a plug. Terror and panic cascaded through her in the blind tunnel. She flailed and screamed and skittled backward like an insect fleeing the light into the security of a narrow crack.

She tumbled out of the hole and down the loose rocks to the hard floor of the larger passage. Finding herself outside of the unendurable claustrophobia of the conduit she regained her senses. The horrible sounds of her husband's plight again came to the forefront. There was nothing she could do. His screams penetrated and echoed throughout the cave like a banshee wailing in the night. His notes were driving her to madness. She stood and felt her way along the walls of the cave, running until she tripped or slammed into a turn. She fell among the bones of the dead man, tumbling them like dice, and felt them fracture under her weight. Her arms and legs were bruised and bleeding. She could feel the wetness against her skin. It didn't matter. She had to get away, away from the torture her husband, her love, was enduring. Another piercing lamentation keened the air. She screamed again in the darkness and ran the faster, arms out for protection, running until she was immersed in the silence of the cave again, the cries behind mere ghosts in her mind.

Through her tears she thought she saw something. She ran toward the light ahead, impervious to the pain of the beating her feet were subjected to on the rough floor. She burst into the Cave of the Bull, miraculously still intact, immersing herself in the glorious palliation of the golden radiance. The gilded bull's head had fallen to the ground, bounced off the altar by the tremors, but the lamp still burned. It was balancing precariously on the edge of the table, threatening to fall with any breath. She rushed over and eased it back to safety. It was wet, and she noticed a slime on the surface of the altar where some of the oil had leaked out through a crack that had extended from top to bottom of the urn. She stood on her toes and peered in through the top, pulling and leaning on it in such a way as to support herself. The strain was too much for the urn. The whole back half separated cleanly away and the remaining oil splashed out and poured off the table to the floor. She gasped in newfound terror and hopelessly tried to right the piece, but the weight of the oil pushed the bottom of the fragment out and she could not do a thing to stem its flow. Weeping with frustration, she let the two pieces of pottery crash to the altar, and again to the floor, as she tried desperately to catch some of the flow cascading off the table. She caught some up in her palms, but threw it out of her cupped hands in aggravation when the logic of the futility of it all was rammed home. Paras had the lamp. She stepped back from the altar and sat down in a lump.

Had the fallen bones of the dead man she had kicked through on her passage here suffered the same fate as she? The bones would never tell her. In this awful labyrinth there was only death, and the dead make no noise.

The irony of the situation forced itself upon her callously. Here around her lay treasure enough to set herself and her family up wealthily for the rest of their days, and yet she would have gladly bartered it all for a chance of escape. Very soon she would be glad to exchange it all for a morsel of food or lick of water, and after that, for the privilege of a speedy close to her suffering. Truly, wealth, which most men spend their entire lives amassing, is a valueless thing at the last.

The flame spread along the length of the wick now lying on its side in a snake. The light grew blazingly bright to one who had strained her eyes into the darkness for so long, almost hurting and causing her to squint. She turned her eyes up to avoid the glare and focused on the precious-metal symbols still firmly affixed to the wall. They reflected the light of the burning flame back at her as if they were extensions of the deities they represented, five eyes beaming from the black face of rock, a twisted mouth with jagged lips.

She hugged her waist, the unborn child within who would never know his first breath or see the breaking light of day in this, this birthplace of mighty Zeus.

The flaming wick consumed the endmost slip of oil within its fibers, flared its final light and faded, slowly, painfully, into darkness.

And Carthea screamed in solitude, perfectly desolate, perfectly alone.

~~~~~~

Chapter 13

Daedalus

1910 BCE

Daedalus disembarked from the square-sailed ship at the harbor of Amnisos. Bless the Gods it was good to be in a place like this, long sung of civilization and peace. Unlike the damnable Acheans who bickered and fought constantly among themselves, spending more time drinking and farting and threatening their neighbors than building works of lasting beauty. Ignoramuses; that's what they were. Garbage people. No more sense than fish. Curse his luck for having been born at Athens. Twenty-five wasted years. Had he been raised in an environment of opportunity for learning and personal growth like Kriti then he would have been so much better off. Why couldn't he have been born here?

A fetor of boiling pitch wafted across the bay. He knew the smell. Somewhere around here, they were shipbuilding. He sniffed and let his eyes be guided sideways against the faint breeze until they rested on a sturdy shed at the far end of the beach. It was one of the only buildings to be constructed entirely of wood, and it looked like it had fared well. In fact, it looked like it hadn't even been touched by the quake. Almost all of the other buildings had suffered hurt, especially the largest. The smaller ones with wood beam supports and lintels had escaped major damage; it was the larger stone structures that had been destroyed.

"It's the second time, you know."

"What?" He hated having his cogitations interrupted like that but thought he had better make an exception when he saw that the person talking to him was not one of the oafish fishers that were in such abundance around here. In sharp contrast to himself, and the short-tressed Egyptians, this exotic stranger wore his hair as the others, in long locks falling over his shoulders. Bare-chested and slender he was dressed in high boots and wore a stiffened, intricately patterned kilt longer in the front than the back. With rich gold bracelets on his wrists, he was obviously of the Elect. "Sorry," Daedalus said. "You surprised me."

"I shouldn't have come up behind you like that. I was saying that it is the second time that the earthquakes have been wild enough to cause such widespread destruction. The whole island has been hit."

"The entire island?"

"Yes. Just two weeks ago. You're probably wondering why we aren't too busy rebuilding. Today is the tenth day of the week, the last day. Everyone has the option of doing anything they want; relaxing, playing, sports, or working if they want to. That is why you see some of our fishers still out. Hard workers. They would rather do that than play. Same with our shipwrights. Normally we don't allow them to stink up the town on the rest day but so many of them have been assisting with rebuilding the town on every other day that we have turned a blind eye."

"A plugged nose, more like," he said through wrinkled nostrils.

The man laughed. "Very good. My name is Androgeus. Welcome to Kriti."

"I am Daedalus. I thank you for your welcome. I must ask if you are always so open with newcomers? It doesn't seem the height of wisdom to be telling your misfortunes to the extent that you have."

"Why do you say that?"

"It occurs to me that a hostile adversary might seize the opportunity to take, ah, advantage of this time of calamity."

"You are thinking like someone from the mainland. In such a place you would be correct. Not here. You will be amazed to know that we have not even a single walled city. We never have. And we have no intention of building them. The sea and our laws protect us. No one living within striking distance of Kriti has the desire or capability to take us on as adversaries. The people of mainland Attica, where you are from, are landsmen and no military threat to us. In like, the people of Egypt are in no position to challenge us on the sea. Invaders, well, we have had a few. Rather pathetic attempts. But they are only pirates bold with a few successes or drunk enough to raid shore villages at random. There will always be those who think privateering and brigandage are the more acceptable alternative to business. Fortunately, none of them are any match for our ships. Our merchant navy has no equal and is trained in swordsmanship and spear. Usually it never comes to that. Our arrows eliminate opposition before we get close enough for hand to hand combat. And, of course, we are widely known in all waters for our mercy. When we catch up with piratical buccaneers, they often surrender before we completely cut them down. Their other option is abandonment in the water with a lacerated vein to attract the sharks." He smiled.

"I don't suppose many choose that option."

"You'd be surprised. It really depends on how much wine they've had."
He laughed. "But we aren't cruel about it. That's why we cut them. It would be
too prolonged otherwise. We aren't interested in having them suffer. In fact,
any who will surrender and can demonstrate to the captains that they aren't too
obnoxious or difficult to manage are brought back as slaves. Especially at times
like this, we need able workers."

"So the ones who capitulate become slaves. You are merciful."

"Yes. But not too merciful. We still cut their balls off."

"Ah."

"Most of them live through it. We use a sharp knife."

"That isn't something widely known."

"No. Our emissaries, including the very least of our oarsmen, are
coached on what is and is not to be said off of this island. Propaganda is one of
our greatest defenses. Do you understand?"

"Very much. Getting back to my question on why you are telling me all
this?"

"You know that you are not permitted to leave Kriti once you have
come. Not even foreign Kings are granted that option. Everyone knows that. It
keeps fear high in their minds. It engenders respect. Do you understand
Daedalus? Do you understand our laws? They must have been explained to you
before you were allowed passage to immigrate. If you had arrived by chance on
some hideous off-course bulk from Attica I would understand ignorance, but
you have arrived on one of our ships. I know what has been explained to you."

"I have begged for the opportunity to immigrate for ages. Yes, I am
familiar with your laws. Please forgive my distraction but the revelation that
my balls may be in danger has me concerned."

Androgeus exploded in laughter. "My dear man. That is for slaves. And
only criminal slaves. All pirates are criminals. It calms them as a bull is calmed
when he is made a steer. Not only that but we can't have distempered
reprobates hatching children, can we? No, your fears are groundless and
unfounded, though they make me laugh. Zeus knows I've needed one." He got
serious again. "Come with me. I'll see that you are fed, after we see how the
ship is coming. I can at least see to that for you. You must have paid enough to
get here."

That was true, Daedalus thought. It had cost him a fortune. Everything
he had, and he had been left a considerable wealth by his father. How fortunate
he had been to be the eldest. After selling his house for sheep and shrewdly
trading those and everything else he owned for trinkets of silver and gold he
was at last able to come up with enough. His family must be in a fury. They
would never forgive him if they ever discovered his whereabouts. He wondered
if they would ever find out or if they would just assume he was killed by

bandits and dumped somewhere. He sighed deeply. He would never know. Because of the situation back there he could never go back, even if he were allowed to leave this place. This was his home now; forever. Only his children might get the chance to leave, and only if they happened to get involved with the merchant navy; if he ever had children.

The reek got stronger as they came close. Dull noise of chipping and hammering on wood grew loud from inside the barn-like structure. Blocked from view, until they rounded the building, was the upright hull of a ship.

Androgeus closely watched Daedalus to see what his reaction would be. Very good. The man was cool. He barely blinked. His reaction was one of intense curiosity and scrutiny rather than amazement. He could see that Daedalus was impressed more with the methods of construction than the actual size of the ship; that it was actually possible rather than done. Considering that this was the longest ship that the man, as an outsider, ever could have seen he was showing signs of great profundity. Either that or he was a complete dullard, and so far he had not given that indication.

They had come just in time. One side of the hull had been finished. The whole of the ship was canted over on its side, the exposed ribs of the unfinished half supporting the rest. Excessive strapping affixed to the ribbing kept the spacing intact while the planking on the other side was completed. Shipwrights bustled up and down the length of the ship, tying on a fanatical number of struts and crossbraces, all intended to keep the green timber from warping out of true as it dried, an absolutely essential precaution because fresh cut wood twists and bends as it seasons. Unless the keel and ribbing were trussed up and immobilized, they would contort out of shape, and finishing the boat would be impossible.

Historians would puzzle over how classical societies could replace their damaged fleets so quickly after major battles or losses due to other causes. They could only assume that vast stocks of spare aged timber were warehoused in the ancient shipyards, all set and ready to build new ships as the need arose. But that being the case, how would they have been able to calculate for their future needs? To inadvertently stockpile would have been an incredible waste of resources that they simply could not have afforded. But they did not use seasoned timber. They used fresh green wood, cut as needed and preferred because of its inherent suppleness. The shipwright's peerless skill was manifest in knowing the characteristics of each piece of wood and the manner in which it was likely to behave as it dried. Only the master shipwright could understand the nuances of the material he lived with, to what extent it would shrink and twist and bend, consider that, allow for it, and take it into account whilst the vessel underwent construction.

The planks were attached one at a time, fastening the first to the keel and then working up to the top of the rounded hull beyond the deck-line. In that way, the entire side was finished before going to the other.

The planks were fastened to each other by way of the mortise and tenon. Slots were precut along the lengths of the yellow beechwood planks at intervals. The tenons, of the same wood, were fitted into the slots so that each tongue protruded and, with mallets, were beaten into place. When the next plank was laid over top, the projecting tenons fit exactly into them.

Holm oak bushes were used for the treenails, the wooden pegs used for pinning the structure together. Holes into each plank, at the place of each tenon, went right through the hull above and below the joint. Into these holes went the oak pins locking the tenons to the planks and joining the planks of the ship together into an interlocking hull. It was exceedingly laborious, and equally strong.

The finished yellow hull, freckled meticulously with the heads of mated pins, was a bona fide piece of art. They were not the only passers-by to stop and admire the curving sweep of timber made smooth with bronze scrapers, the subtle, exacting lines of fitted plank seams, and the tawny yellow sheen of the wood, glowing and splendid, systematically dotted with the darker heads of wooden pegs interlocking the tenons.

Then the master ship-wrights would take torches to the wood, as if they had become inexplicably crazed under the stress of creation, threatening to burn the ship to cinders. But the instant the planking began to char and smolder from the flaming heat they would wave the torches like feather dusters, teasing the wood free of moisture. They were using the fire to dry out another series of holes into which they wanted to drive more pegs. If the wood at that particular point was dry, the pegs would hold better. Both the planks and the pins would swell later and create an impossible embrace to rend. The wrights used a drastic means of drying the timber, but it was effective. Unfortunately, it had the effect of leaving the beautiful hull looking as it if had been dragged through an ash pit.

That didn't matter. It had to be covered over anyway.

The bitumen byproduct of charcoal manufacture had been brought to Amnisos from far and wide. Every port had need of it. It boiled and stank in the sheet copper tub heated from below with bright coals. Two strong men pulled it out of the kettle on flat planks, dipped in and removed coated with the sticky black tar. They rapped them straight down on end, and most of the goo oozed like adulterated honey onto the flat stone slab blackened from years of use. They scraped the remainder off with sticks and went back for more.

The procedure moved quickly. Four other men, much older, scooped up smaller portions from the slab with trowels and placed the dollops onto hand-held wooden floats that had been layered with fine ash from the fire. With the trowel, they smoothed the pitch flat. The ash acted like a releasing agent and the layer was easily rolled up, like a little carpet. With the layer of ash on the outside, it could be picked up by hand, and the men tossed the rolls up to other men standing higher on scaffolding. They, in their turn, slapped the rolls hard down on the hull and, with rolling pins, worked the slime into the cracks and pores. The dust was incorporated into the mess as it was applied and spread. This was the second and final coat. They were just finishing off at the bow when Daedalus and Androgeus arrived, too busy to notice the presence of a couple of new observers.

"It is done. Remove the scaffolding," shouted the oldest. He had to be the master shipwright. The men on the ground quickly scraped their tools and placed the unused tar back into the boiling tub. Then they set to work with the rest tearing down the scaffolding. They were miraculous to watch. Even after the exertions of a full day they still had the stamina to pull the heavy planking down with accelerated kinesis.

A loud shout from the master and more men came out from inside the barn. They all began yelling and calling to everyone within sight, including Daedalus and Androgeus. By the time they had stopped shouting at least fifty men were around them, leaning on the underparts of the hull, the ribbing. Daedalus got the message. They were going to right the ship so they could plank the other side. He pressed his weight against a rib along with the others, all bellowing encouragement to each other, and the ship began to move.

Daedalus was worried about this. There was no longer scaffolding on the other side to hold the ship upright. They couldn't balance it on its keel. That would be impossible even if the sides were of equal weight. It was too big, and the keel too narrow. What were they thinking of? The ship was going to tip and be destroyed. "Stop," he shouted. But he was calling in his own tongue, not knowing what to say in the Minoan language. A few smacked his shoulder as they would a slacker when they saw him back off on the help. He could not believe this. Well, if they wanted to destroy what they had toiled for, then it was a lesson hard learned. He put his shoulder back into it and heaved. It would serve them right.

The ship creaked and straightened and actually did balance for a moment. Most of the men backed off, including him, but the shipwrights stood close still applying pressure against the wood frame. Then it started to go. Slowly, ever so slowly, it began to list. It was magnificent up like this, enormous out of the water. Far higher than a man at the low sides, and doubly high at the long prow extension, the ship gave one the impression of an immense sea dragon. He could not get over the dimensions. It could easily take on twenty-five oarsmen each side, with plenty of room for cargo and passengers.

The shipwrights stepped back. They seemed casually unconcerned as the ship tilted sideways and impelled itself toward the ground. It crashed down on its side, the barreled-out midsection striking first, and the keel whipped up as the whole ship rolled right to the gunwale and back again. The half-built hull rolled back and forth as the crowd hooted their approval. This was entertainment, and they were as pleased as could be to have lent a hand.

Daedalus was still shaking. He had been sure that the ship would have broken to pieces under those stresses, but it was so well constructed, not because of any excess of bulk, so perfectly engineered, that strength was lent to all the right places. A ship like this could never be destroyed by even the fiercest storm at sea.

Before the hull had even stopped rocking the carpenters were out of the shop with lengthy planks and others were setting up the scaffolding. These people didn't quit. Their work was pure quality, and they were fast. It was no wonder they were so regarded around the world, even if a lot of it was propaganda, as Androgeus called it.

"You look shaken, Daedalus. Come with me. We will have some wine and a bit of food. Tomorrow we will put to work, but today you can tell me your mind. Tell me what you thought of the ship you just helped with."

It was kind of Androgeus to acknowledge his little contribution. In Attica, no one would have noticed, except to force him to help if he wasn't.

"I am amazed at the size. I have always been impressed with the ships of Minos, but I have never seen one of such length and girth as that."

"You are observant. That is good. Especially for one not familiar with the sea."

"Why do you say I am not familiar with the sea?"

"I know a newly sunburnt nose when I see one."

"You, too, are observant."

"One gets to be. This ship is of the type used for open waters, not the waters among the islands. Far better to have smaller and more numerous ships for that. Like the one you arrived in, the thirty-six footers. Our pirate problems are almost exclusively among the hundred little islands. When we travel in groups we are not only safer, we are able to more easily cut them off and subdue them. That isn't required far from land where no one goes except us."

Daedalus followed Androgeus's lead and they strolled down the paved and newly swept road. "You have fine carpenters to make all the planking for the ships. But I don't see many trees around here large enough. Does it come from far?"

"You can see them from the top of the ridge. Off in the distance, mind you. Every kind of tree we need for shipbuilding grows here. Our highland forests are of oak, cypress, fir, and cedar. It is the shipwrights themselves, far more specialized than carpenters, who cut the lumber for masts, keels, and planking. They study the wood more than any carpenter ever would. Carpenters are for building furniture, and roofing houses."

Androgeus picked up a rock laying straight in the middle of the road. Some playful youngster must have thrown it there. It was the only rock on the pavement. Clearing and repairing the damaged roadways after the quake had been the first priority, even over the buildings. The weather was perfectly clement and anyone could stand to sleep outside for a while, but trade and commerce could not wait. He threw a precision shot at an old man snoozing against a wall. The smack of the igneous bullet ricocheting off a stone wall inches above his pate startled him to life.

He looked like he was going to utter an angry oath but changed his mind when he saw the only person around who could have thrown the rock. "Can't you let an old man sleep on his only day of rest?"

"You're to close to death. You cannot waste the last days of your life sluggish and lethargic," Androgeus yelled in fun as they walked past. "Get to the games at least, and try to remember your youth."

"My youth," the curmudgeon huffed. "No one has a memory that long."

"Such rot and decay you speak. At least go to see the young women."

"I would only frustrate myself. Why look at something I can't have?"

They were past shouting distance.

"A friend of yours?"

"My Uncle. More like a Father really. He raised me. He's a good man but, if I don't kick him a bit, he just sleeps all day, his mind drifting in the salt air. Even on working days he doesn't really do much. He loves it here on the water. He has a place at Knossos but hasn't used it for years, preferring this Amnisos to the great city. You would not guess that he was a member of the highest elect, would you? Of course you wouldn't. You aren't familiar with any of our classes yet, but you will be. Ah, the things old age besets people with. Still, I feel an obligation to stimulate him whenever I pass. I've seen what idleness does to the aged."

"I see," Daedalus said wryly.

"You are thinking that it is ironic, perhaps, that a man should have to coax his father to action? You are right. It was he who dragged me forcibly through my lazy age, and now I must do the same for him in his second. I owe him that debt."

Daedalus wondered if it was a good debt or bad.

"Are all of your ships for the open waters of that size?" he asked to change the subject back to one more interesting and pertinent.

"Some are smaller. The ride becomes rougher as the size diminishes, so most are close to the size you saw under construction. We have made larger ones, of course. The shipbuilding industry on Kriti goes back hundreds of years. There was a time when ships of one hundred fifty feet were made here. Interestingly they weren't for us but rather for Egypt. You have heard of the land of Egypt haven't you?"

"Some news does reach us."

"Yes. More reaches us, as you will find, if you are interested in the events of the world. Even hundreds of years ago we made two ships of cedar wood, one hundred cubits long. 'The Pride of Two Lands' we called them. They sealed the peace we have enjoyed with Egypt forever. The Egyptians were poor shipbuilders, you see. In the time since then they have managed to copy some of our skills in that area, but not to any great ability. Their ships are still small and still leak. Almost useless outside of the Nile. That is their river, the Nile. The ships we make for them are freighters. That is why they are so long. They are for carrying wood, you see. Sometimes we send them our timbers, but we found it too much trouble carrying the long beams to suit them from the mountains to our coast. It was far easier to set up markets for them in Phoenicia. That is what we call a segment of the eastern coast of the Great Sea. It means 'purple.' That's where we get all of our purple dye. All from an insignificant little mollusk they call 'murex.' The people living there call themselves Canaanites."

It had just occurred to Daedalus that Androgeus was speaking a broken tongue almost half Minoan and half Achaean. That's probably why his speech sounded so choppy. Androgeus had perfectly assessed Daedalus's proficiency of Minoan right from the start, and when he had words to say that were too complex he went right into the Achaean language. It was so brilliantly done that Daedalus had not realized until now that it was being done at all.

"We took cedar wood and meru wood from Byblos to Egypt in endless amounts. Forty ships worth, absolutely laden, before the ships were no longer fit for use. The Pharaoh Snefru was the one who was so pleased. He recorded the event between us for all time. The Egyptians are odd that way. They would rather write something and forget it. We are the opposite here. You will see. We destroy almost all of our written documents, all but the most complex arrangements. Better to speak of it than hide it away on tablets. People in Egypt are never heard to talk about the magnificent cedar doors of Pharaoh's palace or the five magnificent ships of cedar and sycamore wood that we built for them the same length as the freighters. They were far more opulent, of course, so they ended up being sealed in stone chambers around the Great Pyramid to see the Pharaoh Cheops into his afterlife. And they would be crushed to know of their ancestor's cowardice at sea travel. It is still our people who have to captain their ships even to this day. And their crews will not leave sight of land. That is why they can have such long ships. One is always safe near shore. Fully loaded the ships can weather most summer storms. They become quite stable when they are loaded. I bet you didn't know that. The Egyptians still don't believe it. They think an empty ship is safest. And they are quite content to plod the water in their slow freighters. Barges really. Only the upturned prows set them apart."

"Why do you build these ships for the Egyptians. Why don't you leave them unto their own?"

"Trade, of course. Not so much ships anymore. The woods of Lebanon are being pushed back so far that, again, it is hardly worth bringing to the coast. It is just a matter of time and forestry there will come to an end. But we trade for everything. Oh, we have enough rock to build anything we want, and enough wood, although I have heard tell that our island was once completely covered with forest. You would never know that now, though, would you?" he said sweeping his arm across the pastureland. "We have the finest sheep anywhere in the world, and our woolens are in the highest demand. I should show you our workshops. We have spinning machines and looms the likes of which you will see nowhere else. But some of the most prized work still comes from the isolated villages where clay spindle whorls are used, and weaving is all done by hand. Then, of course, we have our pottery, the finest in the world. But we haven't much else. Metals we have to get from afar. But what we do with it, and how, is scarcely imagined among other lands. Our works are esteemed as treasures. When I visited Tôd in Upper Egypt, what did I find but one hundred fifty-three silver cups and one gold one imported from Byblos, sent to the Hyksos as tribute from the king. Such irony, don't you think, that they should send us our own produce as a gift after having paid a handsome price for it? Gold, silver, copper, bronze, perfumery, paints, dyes, linens; all come to us through trade. Egypt gives us our spices, our turquoise, and large ivory. Their linen is magnificent, though I must say that from Ugarit and Byblos is better. Our ladies need the lapis lazuli powder to blue their eyelids, the stibium to touch up their eyelashes. Every country has needs, or wants, that cannot be provided adequately by their own. This is where we come in. This is where we prosper. Let others battle and plunder. We gain our fortunes by trade. We act as intermediaries between countries and keep a bit of every transaction, gold or product, and we become rich."

"Even with Egypt?"

"Of course. The people there have never shown great love for strangers, but they respect the Minoans for our prowess as seafarers and traders. Other foreigners, in general, are known as Ha-unebu, which diplomatically means 'people beyond the seas'. Really it means 'barbarians who are an abomination to God.' Only the people of Kriti and its colonies have been honored and distinguished with a separate name - the Keftiu; the people of Kefti. The name means 'capital,' or 'pillar,' and denotes that we are from the island of the lofty mountain that helps support the dome of the sky. The Egyptians believe that a goddess bears the heavens on her back and the four sky pillars are where her arms and legs touch the earth. The Egyptians believe that this island of Keftiu is the place of one of the four pillars of heaven."

"They don't call you the people of Kriti?"

"It is important not to allow people who may have contact with one another to agree on who we are. To you we are known as the people of Kriti, or the people of Minos. To the Egyptians we are the Keftiu. To the people of the Levant we are those of Kaftor. Each have been given different stories about us so that if, by chance, they should get together they may think that they have been dealing with different people. This is of great benefit to us. However, should they chance to determine that we are the same, then the stories will combine to make us even greater in their minds than they had ever thought before. Information gleaned surreptitiously is of far greater impact than information bombastically spread about by foreign diplomats. It is fear of the unknown that keeps us powerful, masters of the highest order and respect. No foreigners come here without invitation or purchase and, as you know, there is no going back. Thereby we retain our mystery. Our emissaries are in every country, giving freely advice on trade and conflict resolution, even religion. All issues important to any nation are under advisement by our people, and we see to it that those under advisement always prosper. With the right men in office, with the right palms greased, there is never an objection raised to us profiting alongside them. Egypt is especially vulnerable to our services. We have been able to exact greater influence there than anywhere else and have profited accordingly."

"You speak of Egypt as if you have been there."

"Indeed I have. In fact, I have just returned. I am needed here more than there because of the recent disaster. In Egypt I am known as one of the Hyksos, the Rulers. Sixty-five years ago we subjugated the government of Egypt and made them submit to us. The Pharaoh was corrupt, following a lineage of corruption, and through his foolhardy ineptitude, and likewise of his advisors, was bankrupting the country in a civil war with his own people to the south. It was becoming disastrous for us because of the resulting trading inequities. We had to relieve him of his charge. So we created a league of administrators who would maintain the traditions of the Egyptians, with the exception of the massive and hugely unaffordable public works they engaged in, while keeping better control over their treasury. Interestingly, it was easiest for us to have the Egyptians believe the Hyksos were people from a previously unknown country in a far eastern land rather than from Kriti. Along with the oath of fellowship from the known people of Minos to the invaders, confidence and acceptance from the Egyptians was clemently proffered." He gave a low chuckle. "The Hyksos, offering as persuasion and indemnification, introduced a wondrous animal to the Egyptians, one they could readily appreciate; the horse. They took to the new beasts right away, seeing in them greater possibilities than either the ass or the camel could offer. Peace has been established and trade is once again flourishing. This is especially important for us as we also do trade with nations on the east coast of Africa, and the only way we can get to them is via the canal between the Nile and the Red Sea. Others can war. For now, Egypt will abide in peace."

Androgeus picked up another rock and hurled it at a man squatting on the side of the road. The whack was like a fisher's death slap to a fish on the rocks. The man yelped in pain and leaped skyward holding his broken skin. A turd half-emerged from his brown eye broke off amidships and tumbled through the air. He took one look at Androgeus and scuttled off.

"Of course, we could do without these earthquakes. They are good in a way, but they have wrecked the plumbing. None of the drains work. Everything will have to be repaired, or rebuilt. That idiot had too much to drink. He knows better than to crap on the city streets. It's not that far to walk to the cesspit outside of the town limits. He's lucky I hit him. If I'd missed I would have had to have him flogged. He would have liked that a whole lot less. Did you see him step in his own dirt? That was funny. He'll be scrubbing his foot for a week. We're a very clean people, you know. By the way, we'll have to get you into a bath. You Atticans, well, you don't make friends too readily without a bit of friendly guidance. You're lucky we don't have too many of our baths in operation right now. I've noticed that even our own people are getting somewhat ripe. In time though. All it takes is time. We will restore all, and then some. First the roads, then the drains and plumbing. Then the shops and foundries. After that the houses. Last the shrines and temples."

"You surprise me. I would have thought shrines would be the priority."

"To what end? Few would give thanks until they had something to give thanks for. If they want to worship they can do that anywhere. The whole Earth is a place of worship."

"But don't you appeal to your gods for blessings? To further your cause? To better your situation?"

"Of course. But who is to say how much of that we should do? This earthquake for instance. Who is to say if it was retribution for not appealing sufficiently for blessings or if it was recompense for enough? Perhaps it was a show of strength to quiet us from endless appeals for more when we should have been satisfied with what we had. Perhaps the gods were bored and wanted to shake us up. Who are any of us to interpret the mind of the gods?"

"You don't care?"

"Of course I care. It's just that it is irrelevant. Nothing can change things to what they were. All we can do is get on with life. We will rebuild, and we will build better and stronger than before. Those who say we have been punished will be satisfied. Those who say we have been blessed will also. They will argue the finer points for years to come, and those who don't care will sit back and be entertained or disgusted for as long as it is done. In the end, nothing matters. What is, is. What isn't, isn't. We love the gods and devote much to them. But we cannot know what is best for ourselves. Only they can, and all we can do is hope and pray that they do what is best for us. Whether they do, or don't, we will never know in this life. We can only be given that knowledge in the life to come."

Daedalus ruminated over what Androgeus had said. It did have a certain cogency.

Suddenly, shouts of an unseen crowd caught their ears. Daedalus was on the alert, but Androgeus remained unaffected as they rounded the corner of a row of wood-framed buildings that had not collapsed. A large gathering had assembled in a clearing, bordered by Egyptian date palms, which must have been the town square. There were at least three hundred men and women, no children, all pressing tight into the circle. The ones closest to the center were sitting on the ground with the ones behind them kneeling to gain greater vantage. Only the ones near the back had to stand, and any behind them had to crane their necks to see.

Surrounded by the excited congregation the encouraged wrestlers had at it with great enthusiasm. Daedalus was pleased that a few people surrendered their places to him and Androgeus. He had seen these scenes before, on the magnificent vases imported to Attica, reliefs of a variety of contests, pugilists pounding with their fists, lightweights sparring with bare hands and kicking feet, middleweights with plumed helmets battering each other manfully, and heavyweights coddled with helmets, cheekpieces, and long padded gloves fighting until one falls spent and the other stands above him in the concise grandeur of victory. Both wrestlers were furiously tangling with one another, punching, pulling, throwing each other into headlocks and trying to lift the other off the ground at the same time. They spun in circles and when they came too close to the fringes of the ring raucous and cheering members of the audience pushed them back. The long-haired men twisted and tugged, finally freeing themselves from the other's solid grip.

They dove at each other, their skulls striking with a sickening clap. Androgeus had been fairly dignified up until now, but with the blow of heads even he began to root acclamations. The larger of the two slipped over the top of his opponent, wrapping his arms around his chest and heaving him upside down before dropping him head first to the ground. Before the man had even hit the ground, the victor was falling on top of him with his elbows out to inflict that one last bit of pain as he made the pin.

The crowd rose to their feet cheering congratulations and calling for another to come forward and challenge the winner, who now had to defend his position. No one seemed to be forthcoming as the loser crawled a bit before struggling painfully to his feet.

The winner's victory-face fell when he saw a new competitor stepping forward. Daedalus was surprised to see that Androgeus was no longer beside him and was entering the ring. The crowd fell silent with the exception of hushed whispers. Those at the front lowered themselves, and the fight began.

The contestants threw themselves together with fists flying. Androgeus had the upper hand, being larger in stature and fresh in constitution. The defendant gave an exceptional performance protecting his face but lost terribly to fast blows to his midsection. He curled over after landing no more than a few defensive and feeble return punches. Sometimes the thrill of the bout led the competitors to continue fighting on the ground, flailing their legs and reigning blows upon one another with foot as well as fist. Today was more staid. This was no annual event but a friendly joust. He was down in seconds, the fight concluded.

Once again on their feet, the congregation clapped and roared. Daedalus lost sight of what was happening but, after a moment, when it appeared that there would be no further challenge, the crowd pressed inward to fill the ring. He could see now. There was Androgeus, receiving accolades and working his way among the throng back this way.

"You hadn't told me you were such a warrior."

"Warrior? I am no such thing. I am an athlete. If called upon I could certainly defend my country, as could any man, but that is not the purpose of these events. We worship the gods with our bodies. Look at us Daedalus. What do you see? Look around you. You see the straight nose, the almond eyes, our wavy hair falling to our shoulders and farther. Do you not see our tanned bodies, athletic and tense with nervous energy? Look at them; strong and muscular arms, shoulders and thighs. Have you not noticed their lower legs and waist, slim and lithe. See their grace Daedalus, whether in repose or athletically engaged. We wear little when weather permits, in tribute to our gods. And it is to the gods we sing a physical song in our boxing and wrestling. All things involve the gods, and in all ways we venerate them." They passed by a family working on repairing their house, stacking the beams and blocks of stone and brick in neat piles. "You see," he pointed out "Even in the repair of our buildings there is order and worship."

"I have noticed that the wooden structures seemed to have fared the best against the earthquake," Daedalus offered, grateful to change the subject from that of self-aggrandization.

Androgeus pondered that observation a moment. "That is the case. Perhaps the gods have a message in this. I can see many possibilities."

"And that structures constructed entirely of stone or brick have collapsed entirely."

"Again, many messages may be interpreted from this observation."

"Also that buildings constructed by a variety of methods have withstood damage better than others. For instance; that building over there." He pointed to a stone house that was built with wood beams going both vertically and horizontally. The plaster had peeled off the outside, assumably during the quake, and was in a continuous length, a low burm at the bottom of the outside wall. "It has sustained some damage, but you will notice that it is still mostly intact. A few rocks have fallen out of place, but the beams have held it together. The wooden lintels over the doors and windows have not given way, neither have the posts struck deep into the soil. This house must have shaken with the rest but because of its construction has survived where others have fallen. Even the wooden roof has not come down."

Androgeus studied the house reflectively, analyzing what Daedalus was suggesting.

"A place with so many of these quakes, severe or not, would do to adopt the most logical building techniques suitable to its needs. Wood post and beam seems to be the most suited for this island. From what I have observed every other method of using inflexible material has failed. If that be the will of your gods than perhaps that is also their message to you. That is their lesson."

Androgeus stopped in mid-stride. He turned to face Daedalus and held one fist within another, putting them to his mouth in thought. He furrowed his brow as he studied Daedalus. With his head to one side, he interlocked his fingers and rested his chin on his folded hands.

"Tell me, Daedalus, where exactly did you live in Attica?"

"Athens."

"I know the place. What was your occupation in Athens?"

"I sculpted. I designed and built some homes."

"When I visited Athens, and I've only been once, I noticed some statuary there that was among the finest I have ever seen. There were only a few pieces of fine white marble, carved with realism so fantastic that they seemed as if alive. At night, with the Moon shining bright upon them, they looked like they needed chaining to keep them from running away. I swore that should I ever chance to be there again I would bring the sculptor back with me. I would have at the time, but I could not locate the man. The informants that I had there were too envious of the works themselves, but would have told me, I know, if I had been prepared to pay their bribes. They were asking too much, but I have since regretted not taking them up on their offer. Wouldn't it be ironic if you were the one I was seeking?"

Daedalus's face flushed, giving away the answer. Curse his luck. If it weren't for the greed of a few people whom he probably knew he could have saved his wealth and brought it with him instead of spending it in desperation to get here. Even if he could have waited a little longer he might have found free passage, and maybe even payment, to come. But waiting had been out of the question. After what he had done he had no choice but to flee. Only the good favor of those few in high places who had admired and befriended him over the years had saved his skin. Another man would have been put to death on sight and without mercy.

* * *

Such a splendid woman. She turned and danced with a slow, pulsating meter, gyrating her pelvis sensuously and inviting him with her eyes. The Minoan's horror of flabbiness was certainly apparent in this woman.

Daedalus had heard only vague descriptions of the religious rites and had no idea they could be so enticing. She was perfection in a woman's form, flawless to his critical architect's eye. Her skin was tight, smooth, and oiled with the sheen of polished marble and looked for all the world as if she had been sculpted from living stone. Her face had been painted with lapis lazuli blue around the eyes, giving them wide and penetrating allure. Her rich sacred vestments tightly bound about the waist with a double-wound girdle drew her mid-section in, and separated her chest and pelvis as a wasp's are separated by a narrow stalk. A girdle extended over her hips, trimmed them, and accentuated their symmetry and form, the knotted ends of the wrap falling loosely from her constricted waist over her intricately printed dress. The striped and layered skirt was open at the front revealing the braid decorated robe beneath. Only glimpses of her bare feet could be seen under the fringes of the hem brushing along the floor as she performed to the music. Minoans only wore sandals and boots out of doors, the interior of any building being considered too sacred to dirty with the trampled dust picked up while walking. Starched blue fabric matching her glorious eyes and frontiered with gold brocade bodiced her prominent breasts to consummate exposure and plunged deep to the navel. A heavy belt tying her skirt drew the bodice edges in around her bare breasts and lent them support from the sides and below. Her hypnotic dance embraced his mind and siphoned his will. He was aware of nothing else. The overall effect, with headdress, necklaces, bracelets, and rings struck him as barbarically opulent. The two snakes she held in either hand coiled up her arms over her short, tight sleeves and wove their way to the space between the bodice rising high-peaked behind her neck as she moved them with a wave-like motion reminiscent of the motility of the sea. The snakes entwined their tails around her neck for anchor and let their bodies fall to her supported breasts, pushing into the cleavage and seeming to enjoy the massage as they were kneaded between. They coiled and writhed as she did, as if they themselves were in some libidinous rapture.

Other priestesses wed their souls to the dance and forsook themselves wholly to a pitch of religious ecstasy, inspiring awe among the beholders; but to Daedalus it was if she was all alone, surrounded by a secret darkness separate from the cloak of night. His faint awareness of the Full Moon, the Goddess Selene, illuminating her wonderful sashay, was the only other thing in his life.

Priests and Priestesses chanted prayers and invocations to the deities, pressing their lips and calling through the chiseled openings of the triton shells they held to amplify and distort their voices.

Until now she had not looked at him, oblivious in her reverie. Then, of a sudden, their eyes met and she held them, and through them his mind, in a vice-like grip. Even her body withdrew into a faded halo leaving only her face, her hair, and her neck still entwined by the moving snakes. In the center of his vision were her eyes, almond shaped, lids highlighted blue, and lashes long, curled, and black. So far away they still filled his whole field of view.

The eyes. Nothing could be more striking. As the Priestess abandoned herself utterly to the dance leading to the epiphany his heart leapt as he fully became aware that they were real, not just a vision. She really was looking at him.

His heart fluttered and began to palpitate as a rush of adrenaline increased its rate and strength of pulsation. He could hear and feel throbbing blood in his ears, and his eyes began to tear. The picture distorted and misted over. He was barely aware of his knees collapsing against the stone paving, incognizant of the grit abrading his skin, as he fainted into the black of unconsciousness.

* * *

"You have been sleeping well, my friend."

Daedalus squinted into the light but still could not see. It took him a moment to place Androgeus's voice and another moment after that to clear his eyelids of the muck that comes with long sleep. He was outdoors; that is, he was within walls but not under a roof. He lay on a soft bedding of sheepskins. Odd, he thought, that he couldn't smell them. Outside of the shipyard not many things associated with people smelled in this country, unless it was of a purpose to please the olfactory senses.

"I've been dreaming."

"Of course you have. We all dream. It is a vital part of sleep where we journey to places unknown and unheard of; where we visit people nonexistent; and where we are unquestionably convinced of the reality of the impossible until we wake up. Tell me your dream."

"A magnificent woman. A Goddess. I cannot describe her beauty. She held snakes in her hands and wore the clothes of a queen. She danced like a lily waving in the field, but more lissome and exquisite. Ah, such a dream. It is burned into my memory like no other. Almost as if it was real."

"It was real."

Daedalus sat up. "How say you?"

"I assure you it was quite real. Dream-like to you perhaps because of your exhaustion and your imbibing. I wondered if I should have taken you so far after such a long sea voyage on so little sleep. No first-time seafarer sleeps much on the water, so I was surprised that you accepted the invitation to come with me."

That's right. He remembered now. His head was still a bit fuzzy, but he recalled the long walk to Knossos after Androgeus boxed that man down in the square. Then the revelry and drinking in preparation for the celebration of the Moon. The wine had been altered in some way, he knew that much. It was no mere alcohol that gave him those sensations.

"The Priestess with the snakes."

"Yes. You remember."

"Why did she have snakes?"

"The serpent is the arcane symbol of both earth and water. Like a river winding its way, the serpent creeps silently along the ground without limb or wheel. It wields the adroit manipulations of its body in such a way that no person can fathom its powers of movement. It dwells in the earth and issues forth like a spring or new shoot from its hole. Above all, it can penetrate a tomb. And in sloughing off its own skin, it epitomizes the resurrection of the dead. Its representation was of life, death, the hereafter, and the gods. Its peaceful display of sensuality with Pasiphae, who in the liturgy was the embodiment of Selene, represented the connections between mankind and the gods, and through the gods to everything else."

Daedalus struggled to understand. He would give the analogy of the ritual further thought later. Right now he didn't feel all that well, hungry and nauseous all at once. This was more than just a mild hangover.

"I see you are feeling some malaise. That is a common thing after witnessing the formalities of a divine veneration. First-time witnesses always experience it. Even those who only infrequently come do. With more exposure, the symptoms pass. Have some of this. It will help."

Daedalus took the wine mixed with watered grape juice. The alcohol content was quite dilute but the blend had a very pleasing taste, even to his sour mouth.

"I would offer you a bath but, as I told you before, we have other priorities at the moment. This is a working day and everyone will be busy with rebuilding. You were lucky I was able to find you a place to have a short soak last night before the observance. But really, I just couldn't have taken you otherwise."

Daedalus rubbed his stubble. It was an odd sensation not having a beard, but he hadn't minded the pretty girl who had shaved him before his bath. A few things were going to take some getting used to if he was going to fit in. The bath was tolerable enough, refreshing actually. But he wasn't sure if he liked the idea of shaving every day. The perfumed oil helped a bit against the stinging, but it certainly was an uncomfortable process. Still, if that was what it took.

"It is not particularly right for me to not be working, but I wanted to take you on a tour of Knossos. There wasn't much to see in the dark, and it is important for you to know your way around."

Daedalus put on a show of tenacity against his ails and followed along. It was the last thing he wanted to do but he felt an obligation to his generous host. He could hardly have come so far without his guidance.

"I'll show you the temple first. It's just over here. It's where the formalities were last night. We didn't take you far. No one wanted to lug your weight a long way."

All around gangs of workers, male and female, were struggling with rocks and loads of rubble. Beyond the wreckage a half dozen pygmy elephants, native to the islands, grazed placidly. Not all of the foundations were completely destroyed. Some were remarkably intact, even the ones entirely of stone. It was like some random force had just decided that this building should fall and this one should stand. There was hardly any logic to it other than the observance that he had made before; the wood reinforced structures overall fared better.

"Here it is."

There was absolute devastation. This was the widest and highest pile of destruction within sight. Only a few of the perimeter walls had survived, short sections and not very high. It was terrible. All the work that had gone into the building before was now gone. Such a waste. Several hundred people were at work on the site clearing debris and sorting materials that could be used again. Wagons of rubble were constantly being loaded and taken away by steer teams. This was material that may still be good for houses but hardly for a new temple.

It was all very organized and the work was moving steadily. Already they had cleared small areas right down to the base floor.

"I see that this building was entirely built of stone."

"Yes, Daedalus. I knew I could trust your eye. Even with your condition not exactly at best you see what is most important."

"You said that you weren't working on the temple until last."

"Quite so. The reconstruction will not begin until all else is done. However, the cleanup has to be done at the same time everywhere. Already we have rats moving in. They are intolerable. They come for the grain, the fruit, anything they can lay their nasty little teeth to; but most of all, meat. There are still pockets of food stores about, and most have at least some dried meat. We have cleared out most of it, but we can't yet get to it all. We will, of course, but that will take time. The rats have the advantage. They can sniff it out and move easily between the cracks. And between the rocks, they are safe from us. Filthy little beasts. There is a bounty for their bodies, should you manage to kill one. A flagon of wine; real wine, not the watered-down fare."

"Quite an incentive, I'm sure."

They picked their way over the humps of rubble and detritus, careful of the loose rocks. A gang of laborers was removing the last of the ruins from a wide circle of what looked like wheat. The opening went down a few cubits, a round pit that had a staircase winding around the inside wall to where men and women were removing small rocks and gravel and flinging them up and out of the pit, heedless of where they might fly. Androgeus was almost hit with a larger stone, but didn't flinch as it zipped past. His judge of trajectory and his quick reflexes told him that the projectile was of no danger, even though it only missed by inches. Even if it did hit, a lightly tossed rock was nothing. Not like one hurled with intent.

"This is the temple grain repository. It is a priority not just because of rats and mice. It has to be covered before the rains come. There is enough here alone to feed the twenty thousand people of Knossos for at least four weeks even if we had nothing else to supplement our diets. Do you see that staircase descending the perimeter? It doesn't stop where you see it end. It keeps going right down to the bottom, thirty-four cubits below the rim."

With a depth of fifty-one feet and a diameter of thirty-three feet, the storage chamber held over fifteen hundred cubic yards of grain, although at the moment it was not entirely full. Another underground silo, which had not lost its vaulted ceiling in the quake, had remained undamaged and it was full.

"All temple sites have large repositories where grain and other dry foodstuffs are collected and then redistributed fairly and according to need. No one is allowed to go hungry, and no one is allowed to have too much. If a citizen is noticed to be getting too fat, their ration is cut. If they value their food above all else, then they have to trade their own precious commodities for more. That is their choice, but the temple does not condone it. Fat is frowned on as a sign of unhealthy intemperance and, if seriously uncontrolled, the offending citizen could be expelled from the city. Temple cities are, above all, the residences of the Elect. The unhealthy are welcome as visitors and pilgrims, but are not welcome to stay. To allow such people as residents would be correlative to inviting desecration."

Daedalus was impressed with their organization, not only for prioritizing their needs but also for having the foresight to cache such large stores of food for the future. Being grain, it could be used for emergency rations or taken back to the field in case of crop failure. It was brilliant. No one had considered such precautions against natural disaster in Attica.

"Come this way. We will have our chance now to do some work."

Over on a few more piles was a smaller group of men working isolated from any others. One looked up as Daedalus lost his footing on the loose pile and slid a little. The noise had alerted them.

"Androgeus," called the tallest.

"Minos," returned Androgeus.

Great Gods. Was he going to meet King Minos? Daedalus felt his stomach knot. A squirt of acid burned his esophagus. He never thought this would happen. What was he going to say? If only his head was clearer.

Minos was about the same age as Daedalus, young and healthy with a physique equal to, or better than, Androgeus. He was the twenty-sixth Minos, a fact known only to the inner circle. To everyone else he was simply 'Minos.' They remembered his grandfather who passed on the lineage, but it was not thought of in the sense of a new man assuming new responsibilities, rather as a continuation of the same king, the same thought processes, the same person, closer than any other man to the gods. Having assumed the helm, he was the virtual embodiment and reincarnation of the Great Minos. He shared the wisdom, the ability, the prowess, and the nobility of the original. And in keeping with the original, his obligations lay in serving the people, his people. Working alongside them in this time of national exigency was as natural as a bird in flight although he couldn't labor equally long hours at the physical work with the administration still required. Fortunately, he had a competent base of skilled builders who had taken charge of most of the work. Coordinators were managing crews with great efficiency, and the captains of the merchant navy were able enough to handle trade without much guidance for a while at least. No one outside Kriti need ever know of this disaster. No one would. Precautions enough had been taken against that. All first-generation immigrants, be they bond or free, were ordered inland under the guise of administrative need. They would stay there until this chaos of destruction was

378

attended to. Daedalus fell into that grouping, although Androgeus didn't tell him that.

"Have you had success yet?" asked Androgeus.

"Not yet. But we are not far off. That smashed amphora was in the Cardinal Treasury, so we know this is the right room. We will have found them before day's end."

Daedalus was surprised to hear that they were excavating the treasury. There should be guards here to protect the riches. It was beyond his comprehension that so few men could defend against looters even with others working at other places on the site. An organized attack could be richly rewarding. But he discounted the notion as quickly as it had come to him. What was he thinking of? He had to change his lines of thought now that he was here. Of course they were safe. In this jumble the bandits would have as hard a time digging out the treasure as these men before him. The labor was rough and escape before reinforcements arrived would hardly be possible. Even if it were, where would they run to on an island? It was huge, but it was still an island. By the time they got to a coastal port where there were ships to steal, watches would have been posted and a defense in place. No. It was impossible. These men were as safe with their treasure as if an army guarded them.

Everyone seemed to be ignoring Daedalus, immersed in their work as they were. Androgeus had stepped close to Minos and was speaking in tones hushed enough that his words could not be made out. Minos spoke a little louder, but the few words that Daedalus could hear were so unfamiliar to him that he could not understand even the gist of what they were discussing.

He cast his eyes about while the two men talked. Then something glinted deep inside a breach between two larger blocks. The sun had struck it just right and reflected a brilliant yellow sparkle. He walked closer. It wouldn't hurt. He crouched down and looked into the crack. It was a golden urn. He could hardly believe his good fortune. If he told them he had found their treasure he would surely secure their trust in him. He began to stand and, as he did so, he saw another golden object even more exposed, and not as deep, in another crack. Then he saw another.

"I have found it," he cried. "It is over here."

The men looked at him with blank faces, as if he were a boor interrupting a meeting to which he had explicitly not been invited.

He felt something was terribly wrong but, more out of a pending embarrassment and an inner defense that told him that his instincts must be fallacious, tried again.

"I have found your treasure. Your gold."

Minos looked at Androgeus as much as to say 'You deal with it,' and went back to his work. The other men turned their backs on Daedalus and returned to their efforts too.

Daedalus was stunned. Androgeus came over, holding his arms out to the side for balance as he wandered over the tumbled wreckage. He was watching where he was stepping, but Daedalus was twisting inside, thinking that he might be refusing to look his way just as the others were.

He pointed down the cleavage where a golden lamp could clearly be seen just out of reach. "It is gold. Right there. They are digging in the wrong place. See that foundation wall there. They are in the wrong room."

Androgeus sighed. "What do you think they are looking for?"

"The treasury. That is what Minos said." He hushed his voice when he said Minos, afraid that the man might hear him.

Androgeus looked down the crack and saw the gold lamp. "You have indeed found a treasury. Good for you. But this is where a few gold and silver objects are kept when they are not required for the shrines. I believe that they will be uncovered later. Minos was referring, when he spoke, to the Cardinal Treasury. It holds something of far greater importance than gold."

"Here it is. Help me move this rock." The words were loud, and Minos had spoken them.

The men with him crowded close, and Androgeus was on their heels. Daedalus considered only for a second and then followed. The call for assistance had been generic. If he hadn't been invited he would plead ignorance. No one objected as he helped roll the larger rocks and threw the smaller ones out of the way.

Minos lifted an alabaster box out of the hole. He was a strong man, but he strained in his bent over position. The heavy stone lid had broken and fallen into the box, still covering its contents. He placed the box onto an askew block as gently as if it had been his own newborn child. Tossing aside the fragments of thick white stone like so much trash he removed a small purple pouch inside. It clinked as he lifted it. Still inside the box was a large object also wrapped in a purple bundle. He ignored the large item for now, clutching tightly to the small purse. He squeezed it in his fist and held it to his face, inhaling deeply as if he were breathing in emitted vapors.

Daedalus stretched to see without being intrusive. No one spoke, and all eyes were on this prize esteemed far above even gold. Inside the box was a folded towel of the same rich fabric, which he removed and laid out on the tilted rock. Slowly he opened the flap of the little bag and tipped out its contents. Three shiny black buttons slipped onto the cloth. The men clenched their fists and inhaled fully through their noses. This was almost akin to a rapturous experience for them.

Daedalus was bewildered. He must be missing something. Those black things were the object of this hunt? There must be more to this that the larger bag would reveal.

They were still oblivious to his presence. Minos removed the purple wrapped weight and placed it upright on the block at the center of the cloth. He loosed the bottom as he moved it and lifted off the skirting. It was another black object, much larger and heavier than the little buttons. It was surely of the same material. It looked metallic with a mildly polished sheen that varied with its angle to the sun. Its hourglass shape was reminiscent of a female form, tapering in at the center and again toward the feet. On the top was a small knob, which could be a head if one used their imagination. It had an enigmatic charm that appealed to his esthetic endowment. The form was simple, elegant, and somehow universal. As Minos turned it, the resemblance became more apparent. It was posteriorly flat, but the front was bulged out in the right places. It was a perfectly surreal cast of a woman; not a specific woman, but all women.

Daedalus found himself caught up it the hypnotic effect the icon was exuding. The others, though standing dignified, were fawning over it with their eyes. As Minos withdrew his hand from the figure, another came nearer. Before any could stop him, Daedalus had his fingers on her.

A collective gasp sounded from the men. None but Minos were ever permitted to touch the Earth Mother. Daedalus got an immediate grip on his senses when he heard them and broke his touch. What had he done? He could see that this representation was held in the highest, most sacred esteem. How could he have been so obtuse? This was their temple. He could lose his life anywhere for less than this.

Two of the men grabbed him about the arms and held him tight. Expressions of bristling malevolence raked their faces. Androgeus was poising himself to strike, his arm reared in preparation.

"Hold," shouted Minos.

Androgeus relaxed his arm.

Minos stepped close to Daedalus, staring straight into his eyes. He was far to close for comfortable endurance. Daedalus began to sweat and, in spite of desperate striving, was unable to assume control of his breathing.

"Your name is Daedalus?"

Oh God. "Yes." It came out like a squeak, a clot of phlegm having risen into his vocal cords. He had to clear his throat but desperately fought the urge.

"You are an architect; and a sculptor."

Androgeus must have been talking about him during that time when they were speaking softly. "Yes." It was barely a bubbling whisper of an affirmation. He tried to swallow the interfering mucus but found it impossible.

It was in the wrong passage. But if he coughed it up, or even cleared his throat normally, that would seal his precarious position. These people were wonderful in their way but also capable of anything. To insult them, especially their king, would have to end in the death throes of torture; probably by way of a vicious infection following a slow and purposeful orchidectomy.

"Release him."

He felt unsure hands cautiously relaxing their constricting hold.

"The stranger will touch me and build my house." Minos recalled the quote as he pursed his lips and touched them to his fingers. "He is the one." He was looking at Daedalus but obviously addressing the others. "He is the one who will build the Labyrinth."

Chapter 14

Obsession

1890 BCE

Daedalus picnicked with the multitudes outside the court of the palace. It was unusual to have so much meat at one sitting. A hunt had brought back an abundance of wild goat, deer, and wild boar. The wild boar was what they were really after, a vicious pest that had been growing too readily in number. They had to be eradicated. And while they were out, they might as well take advantage of a few milder pests like the goat and deer. Farmers were becoming ever less tolerant of those animals too. The hunters had even caught a few prized hoopoes and partridges, which were by law set aside for the Council's private enjoyment.

He picked at his food, wishing he hadn't taken so much of the herbed and spiced delicacies. The aroma of baked mint and cumin blended with delicious meat got his saliva flowing even now that he was full to bursting. Still, he forced himself to swallow the last bit before returning his bowl to the table. It was as much as an obscenity for an adult to refuse to eat his meal at the sacrifice. A child might be forgiven, but an adult was expected to appreciate the sanctity of whatever creature gave up its life for one's sustenance and enjoyment. He helped himself to a small draught of honeyed wine to wash it down, swishing it through his teeth to clean the food out of the spaces. The children were getting active and noisy with their stomachs full and eating no longer on their minds. They wanted to play and roughhouse. One of them got into a pile of discarded pistachio shells and threw them at a brother or a friend who retaliated in kind. It was enough for Daedalus. He had to retreat to quieter quarters.

Daedalus had aged gracefully in the twenty years he had lived in Knossos, and the nation had grown fabulously wealthy in those prevailing two decades. Even he marveled at the wealth of those who should be the poorest, the ordinary farmers. They typically lived in well built durable houses of stone with wooden pillar and beam supports which could have only been built by the rich few in the country of his youth. The ground floor of their homes was for storage, cooking, and other work, the upstairs for the living and sleeping quarters. Living rooms twenty feet square with six or more rooms off the sides, windows glazed in translucent parchment, shelters for animals, and storehouses for grains, made for very comfortable accommodation. They lived comfortably with every tool available for purchase at their disposal. The more successful farmers could even afford a bronze cauldron, a prize in anyone's home. Considering they could produce almost a ton of grain per acre in the fertile soil, it was no wonder. With a hundred thousand acres in grain production, the farmers were among the greatest benefactors to the people, allowing them the opportunity to get on with their other avenues of pursuit.

Now in his forty-fifth year, Daedalus had a brindled graying of his black hair, which the women spoke of as being most attractive. Even the younger ones lamented his lack of interest in women. With his handsome good looks and his renown as the most celebrated architect ever, even though the official credit went to Minos, he was the catch of catches, the sex symbol of the day. Many of Knossos's young beauties had tried their full allure to beguile him, none with any effect. Several watched him now as he walked, past the circular threshing floors where they guided oxen dragging flinted wooden sledges in an eternal circle over tufts of wheat. Others smiled and giggled as they tossed winnow from their forks at just the right time, letting the breeze blow the dusty chaff in his path to get his attention. Their pains were for naught. His heart lay elsewhere, with a woman, nay a goddess, whose position made it impossible to have her as anything other than an occasional secret consort.

Every waking moment, every dream while he slept, was filled with her vision. The temple-palace he built was inspired by the beauty of his paramour, by his infatuation for her every curve and line. It was for her he built it, not Minos.

Pasiphae had matured even more beautifully than he had. Her role as goddess during religious ceremonies was only heightened in the public's eye by her incomparable attraction. Her characterizations of Selene the Moon Goddess or Earth Mother, then Rhea the Mother Earth, was finally eclipsed by her personification of Aphrodite the Evening Star. Her finely trimmed figure suited the role perfectly; the embodiment of sensuality, sexuality, and beauty. Even in her adolescent youth she had not been the creature she was now. He still remembered her, dancing before him while he was in that opiated alcoholic haze, two decades past. She was beautiful then, but she was transcendent now. She carried herself with a stature and bearing that no young priestess could realistically hope to equal, though they all tried.

How many times had he made love to her, secreted in one of the thousand rooms of the palace? His obsession was to visit every room with her, covertly enjoying one another's bodies while Minos was none the wiser. The Labyrinth it was called. And within it a Labyrinth within a Labyrinth. A thousand chambers and he knew every one, every hallway, better than any. He, after all, had designed it.

The summer heat was alive with complaining cicadas. He remembered when he had to keep a towel over his shoulders to keep the sun from burning them, but his skin had toughened and he could stay exposed for days straight if he had to now.

The view from the West Court was his favorite. Access to the palace by visitors was gained this way via the road approaching over the south viaduct. On the other side was the aqueduct he helped improve. The expertise of the Minoan's hydraulic engineering was one of their most impressive achievements. At moving water their abilities were unsurpassed. They had constructed a sophisticated system of jointed earthenware pipes linking the palace with a spring seven miles away, the three-foot pipeline sections tapered so that one interlocked snugly into the next. The clever tapering design of the pipes increased the water pressure, preventing sediment buildup and eliminating the need to ever have to disassemble the pipes to clean them. Handles or lugs on the outside were laced with ropes drawn up tight to bind the sections firmly together, and the joints were cemented to prevent leakage, an ingenious system where the terracotta pipes could be laid straight or in curves. Stone aqueducts raised the water across gullies and ravines along the route to the palace. For the residents this made for a cleaner, more accommodating life, allowing them to surrounded themselves with fountains, pools and streams, and bathing rooms; a never-ending supply of fresh water.

Since the island was deluged with torrential rains at times during the autumn and winter seasons, the architect gave careful consideration to drainage. Within, and around, the Knossos palace an elaborate system of ducts, gutters, and catch basins funneled runoff into larger underground terra-cotta conduits, with manholes at intervals for convenient access. The main channels, made of stone and lined with cement, were so large that a man could stand comfortably inside. The violent rainstorms that periodically hit the island during the winter months would funnel into the intricate network of sewers and blast them clean.

Steep channels beside the outer stairway on the east side was a particularly challenging problem. The staircase was broken into flights set at right angles. Fast flowing water, unable to make the sharp turns, would have poured out over the landings, but to prevent that kind of flooding the water was slowed by forcing it through a gutter of gentle baffles, a series of zigzags and small rectangular sediment traps and basins to retard the speed of flow, and a final course into a cistern for storage.

Visitors were immediately struck by the loveliness of the setting and the trellised path that winds through the grove of black pines to the stately entrance of the West Court. That broad area paved with irregular stone slabs was crossed with several raised walks, one leading directly to the West Porch, the entry to the main reception rooms of the palace.

To the north of where he stood the Royal Road was nearing completion. This road was of the same design, his, used throughout Knossos during the intermediate and final building phases, a center lane four and a half feet wide, or three cubits, made of two lines of large rectangular stone slabs. On either side, there were slightly lower and narrower lanes made of smaller unshaped stones. The elevated center lane was always dry even in the most torrential rains and the separation of outer lanes made for ease of traffic congestion during the busy months when pilgrims flocked in their droves to the temple. The Royal Road would soon be lined with premises for the guilds of ivory carvers and stone vase makers and other master craftspeople under the aegis of the temple, many of them already well underway, and would be the progression used for the reception of foreign dignitaries, a gesture to those once excluded. It would start with the visitation of the Hyksos king, Pharaoh Khyan of Egypt, who would present a gold filled alabaster chest scribed with his own name of 'Son of the Sun' on the lid. Although Khyan was of Minoan decent, and under Minoan control, he had still never sojourned to the island. Khyan was Minos's eyes in Egypt. An entourage in full regalia would attend him, some who were of pure Egyptian stock and who would be allowed to return to their land. This was a paramount deviation of the fundamental laws of the island, acceptable only by the combined authority of Minos and Pasiphae and accorded by the Council. This event, scheduled for six weeks from today, was to signal the official inauguration of the Labyrinth even though there would be no more changes. The building itself was completed. Hundreds had worked and dwelled inside during the construction period that had merely been adding addition onto addition over the decades. As the building grew, so too did the numbers of inhabitants until they now reached one thousand.

A distinctive feature of the West Court, and the model of the smaller palaces of Kriti, were the three large koulouras, meaning round and hollow, the domed circular pits used as granaries. These were put in place outside the enclosure to impress visitors with the abundance enjoyed by the ordinary people. The koulouras supplemented the prototype of these structures, the underground silo on the south edge of the palace that was held strictly secure for dire emergencies.

Daedalus was ready to do his tour. He tired of the noisy children playing in the greenery. There really wasn't much he could find to like about children; loud, dirty things. The only great miracle he could see about them was that they could eventually grow into adulthood. A greater miracle would have been to start them out that way. At least they were banned from the Labyrinth during the Central Court festivities. And a side benefit was that the adults involved or spectating would all be at the Central Court watching the proceedings. They never seemed to tire of the events. That was fine by him. He liked solitude inside the palace when he could find it. Solitude in almost any room was not hard to come by, but to have free roam of the whole Labyrinth and not see anyone, that was real pleasure.

He entered the West Porch entrance, one of six ways into the palace, and nodded to the bored guard who only acknowledged him because of his renown. To have Daedalus notice you was almost equivalent to having Minos do the same. Even so, the guard would rather have been at the Central Court. It was his lot today to keep the children from sneaking in and to stay any wandering pilgrim. At least he drew the ceremonial entrance. It was of an interest great enough to hold him through the day. The sparkling alabaster facade carried high above him to the layers of open balconies belonging to the main reception rooms. Some of the finest wall paintings in the palace were here, and a prurient white marble statue of Aphrodite said to have been sculpted by Daedalus himself. Something about it reminded the young man of Pasiphae. It was an exciting, stimulating statue. Standing here alone made him want for his new wife; how bothersome that she could attend the events without him.

Daedalus passed under the guarded portal and through the substantial double doors into the narrow Corridor of the Procession. He always felt a pang of guilt when he came in through the West Porch and was glad to pass through it quickly without having to talk. It was the alabaster veneer that caused him to make the insufferable connection to his nephew, the reason he'd had to run from Attica.

On either side of the doorway were solid bronze figures of worshippers in attitudes of adoration. Daedalus smiled and forgot his hostile thoughts for a moment when he saw them. They were one of his favorite developments. They were rough and bubbly on the surface because of the small amount of tin he was able to garner for the project, and the resulting alloy did not flow well. But when the finished products were exposed, they had such interesting quality that they were received with enthusiasm from all who beheld them, and thus were given a place of honor gracing the door to the corridor. A little too unusual for reproduction on large scale for more temple ornamentation, they were nonetheless requested in numbers as smaller figurines for votive offerings to be left in caves. What he had developed that was so exciting, far more so than the rough-textured skin, was the 'cire perdue' method using lost wax which made it possible to go into quick production of figurines. The original model was made of wax and then encased in a clay mold. The molten metal was poured in through the top, which displaced the wax, filling the mold and creating the figure. The mold had to be broken away and was lost, but the wax could be used over and over indefinitely. The little statues for the small votive offerings had a symbolic, not esthetic role to play, and so did not have to be as perfect as one would have required for something decorating a home or shrine. But in spirit they were perfect, having a soul as any other inanimate object be it rock or metal, and as such welcomed by the gods. In the dark caves and crevices, these offerings were not intended to be seen by mortal eyes.

His thoughts were uninterrupted as he walked the long corridor south, then east at the corner of the palace. He was taken back twenty-one years to the time when he was such a proud young man in Attica, so able, so omniscient in his own mind. He worked so hard, ever learning, never sleeping, always seeking more skills and knowledge in even the most seemingly insignificant things. His fame grew and he thought he knew it all, thought he could do it all.

Then his younger nephew found a way to do something he couldn't. Talos had picked up a fish's backbone discarded on the beach and had seen something so obvious that it had been there all along for any with eyes to see. He had played with the skeleton at first, sawing through wet sand buildings he had made for a couple of children. They laughed with delight as he cut wedges out of the parapets, in the same way one makes the undercut when felling a tree, and let them topple one by one. All the while he entertained he was thinking. If something similar could be made of metal, bronze preferably, it would work on wood just as well, maybe even stone.

He had taken the idea to his Uncle Daedalus first, but due to his weak powers of speech was unable to convince him of the merit of the idea. Daedalus had to admit later that something inside told him that it was worthy of the credit the lad was giving it, but his bias against the youth's age and his stutters prejudiced him to the potential value of anything he could have come up with.

Talos then went to a coppersmith who was having a slow time of things and convinced him, as a matter of curiosity at least, to try the idea. That very day the smith hammered out a long sheet of copper and notched teeth into it. A bit of sharpening on a whetstone, and a final heating and plunging to improve the hardness, and the saw was ready. They were astounded at how quickly it cut through wood, far easier than a sharp ax. And instead of splitting wood into lengths and chipping the planks smooth with an adz, or peeling the wood away with a spokeshave, they could just cut the planks directly from the tree with the saw. It was faster and there was almost no waste. They tried the saw on soft stone but it dulled instantly, not that that mattered one whit. The teeth were easy to reshape and resharpen. The only problem was the copper. It was too soft. Even for prolonged usage on green wood the teeth dulled. Bronze would have been perfect but, of course, it was impossible to get raw. Only the people of Minos had bronze, and they only traded finished products. Too bad. It was highly unlikely that even the coppersmith would have the powers of persuasion to convince anyone to sacrifice their bronze goods for an experimental saw. Yet that is exactly what happened, and the few who had made that wise speculation reaped enormous profits.

When Daedalus had heard what Talos had done, and the success that he had, his jealousy raised to a fever pitch. To think that he could have paid heed to his nephew and developed the saw himself. He was absolutely wroth. The stuttering imbecile had outdone him. It was too much. That the boy was his nephew only made it worse. The smith he could forgive, but not Talos. To exacerbate his aggravation his friends hectored him with taunts, all in good fun, but furtively tormenting to him. He took the heckling with an outward bearing of reluctant tolerance and good temper, but inside he seethed for vengeance.

When he heard by way of his proud sister that her son was taking the invention to Athens, it was all he could do to control himself long enough to exact his revenge. He lay in ambush on the road until the lad came by, wholly innocent and unsuspecting. Talos had been glad to see Daedalus, who he admired and loved, and reached forward to embrace him. That his uncle would strike a fatal blow with the rod he held was as far from him as the stars of heaven.

Daedalus had flung the saw down off the side of the road and kicked some dirt and rocks over it. The saw was valueless. He could make another easily. Talos's corpse was something else again. This was a well-traveled stretch and someone would surely be along any time. There was no time to bury him. A rock cairn would be too obvious and still take too long. Carrying him away from the road and across the rocky terrain would not work either. A traveler might see him packing the body a long way off. He had planned far enough ahead that he had anticipated this problem. He put a sack over the youth, thankful that he was still a youth, skinny and short. He tied the opening and flung the sack over his shoulder. He would hope that he could get to a place where he could dispose of the body unobserved, but as he suspected, luck was not with him. Only minutes later he saw a man coming toward him. Daedalus slowed, debating exactly what to do, glancing behind as he deliberated his stratagem. Two more men were coming from the rear and would probably catch up at about the same time he met the one in front.

There was no escaping the situation. He was going to have to confront them. That he had a body was quite evident. There was nothing overtly suspicious about carrying a corpse in this manner; that was how it was done. Daedalus just didn't want to have to do the usual explaining that men in this position always found themselves having to do. The man approaching hailed him, as was the requisite mannerism. Daedalus hailed in return, softly and without spirit. Surprisingly the man looked abashed and hurried on. How fortunate. He didn't want to involve himself, fearing perhaps that Daedalus would compel him to assist in carrying the deceased.

Then he heard the hails of the men just behind, almost beside him. He could tell by their caring ventilations that they aimed to help. Curse them.

"Tell us brother, who have you there?" they inquired properly.

"It is, alas, a dead serpent." This was the imperative reply. Attican law required that he respond that way and in order to avoid suspicion he maintained custom. The snake, as in Kriti, was a hope of the resurrection. All dead were labeled as snakes in ritual hope. That was one of several customs common among the people of the Aegean. But Daedalus was so caught up the atrocity of his crime that he could not think straight. He said his destination was Athens where his son would be united with his mother before burial. Of course, he was going the wrong way and the men immediately became suspicious. At first they were only concerned, but when they tried to turn Daedalus around and he hesitated a moment with an unsure look of anxiety lining the orbits of an otherwise youthful face, they took him for what he was; a murderer.

Daedalus had dropped the body and bolted. The men, unsure of his potential as a dangerous highwayman, alone with the body and not willing to leave it out of respect, and not getting any aid at all from the man who had just passed, had to watch as Daedalus ran headlong over the rough.

How opportune that a Minoan trading vessel was just preparing to leave port. It had only been unusual good fortune that he had settled his father's estate and liquidated enough to make his move. With his gold and silver, he bought his way onto the ship. His lead on the men could only be a matter of hours. They might stop to perform a burial, assuming that the victim had been throttled by a roadside bandit that could have as easily done the same to them, or they might bring the body into town. Either way, they would not be long. A third possibility was that they would leave the body to someone else's care and continue without it, packing only their own belongings. If that were so, then they could arrive any time. They would not find him right away, and would not think to search the ships first, but they would raise the alarm. Such an alarm might be enough to prevent the ship from sailing. He had never known terror before, but this was surely it.

The vivid recollection and wave of age-old guilt washed Daedalus's skin in a sweat that even the noon-day sun could not beget. Damn the ingenious Talos. Was this memory to curse him for the rest of his life? It was, after all, the bronze saws copied after Talos's copper invention that enabled him to cut limestone blocks so sharply that they could be put together without mortar. The alabaster veneer, the fine-grained, marble-like variety of gypsum, could be cut thin with such precision that there was virtually no difference in thickness from one sheet to another. As long on all sides as the tallest man, the interior walls of the Knossos palace were not plastered and frescoed but were completely sheathed in this lustrous thin-cut stone, all made possible with Talos's saw.

That was why he was afflicted with guilt these long years. The lovely veneer was everywhere in the palace. Daedalus had constructed a place to inflame his own conscience; a place where he lived, loved to live, and which consigned him with sustained affliction of his own creation. There was a sense of spontaneity and naturalness about what were complex, labyrinthine constructions to everyone else, but to Daedalus this living beauty only served as an interminable reminder of his horrible crime.

The Corridor of the Procession was long, as one could expect in a palace covering an area of over four and a half acres. Outsiders duly fortified their appreciation for the priestly role of the king from the brightly painted portraits on the wall of the corridor. There were none of the grandiose depictions of other powerful countries; parsimonious lion hunts, bloody battle scenes, prisoners cowing beneath the lording executioner. These frescoes showed long processions bearing gifts to their king, their representative of their most powerful male god. This tranquil atmosphere left room for the human spirit to breathe, contrasting the overwhelming presence of the contemporary statues of the Pharaohs or the depictions of the military prowess of the Semitics. No vehement deity or scene of brutality would find honor or respect in the Minoan kingdom. Conversely, the processional fresco hinted at a gratification in the fullness of life, a free civilization unfettered by man-made walls, a people of composed serenity in their semi-rural setting living in a palace city at ease and intimate within its natural surroundings. And like the indistinguishable line between town and country, so was the blurred separation of human and divine. In the wonderfully rendered art depicted on the quixotic frescoes one could never be sure that one figure might be immortal and the other not. Minoan art ignored the distance between the human and the transcendent that tempted men to court sanctuary in abstraction, and to create a form for the significant, remote from time and space. It correspondingly ignored the glory and futility of single human acts, time-bound, space-bound. The artists did not give essence to the world of the dead through an abstract of the world of the living, nor did they immortalize proud deeds or state humble claim for divine assiduity in the temples of the gods. Here, and here alone, the human bid for personal everlasting renown was disregarded in the most complete concession of the grace of life the world has ever known. Nowhere is the name of an artist to be found.

At the South Propylon, the formal inner entrance, he had the choice of ascending a courtly open staircase to the extensive upper halls or, instead, going to the sunlit Central Court. He could hear cheering but wasn't in the mood for sport right now. He just wanted to be alone.

He took neither of the choices but, rather, a third. To his left was the entrance to the West Magazine. The north-south corridor took him past batteries of rooms containing huge pithoi, enormous storage jars as tall as he was and into which even the largest man could easily climb, if he had such a mind. This was the largest of the storage magazines inside the palace. Four hundred and twenty pithoi there had a capacity of one hundred twenty thousand liters of oil and wine. Further, cists sunk into the ground between the long rows of jars were filled with the cleanest, purest grain to be used, not for food, but for planting the following year. The highest quality was always sorted from the rest, painstakingly, to ensure unsurpassable growth later. All Minoan palaces laid aside considerable ground floor storage space for foodstuffs. The corridor Daedalus walked was far longer than the Corridor of the Procession. It traveled almost the entire length of the west side of the building. Blended aromas rising from the rooms, wine mingling with oils and grains, reminded him of his favorite time of year; the harvest. There were actually several harvest times but the most productive, the one just finished, was the one he liked best. Tremendous wealth was generated from the produce, wealth that had been poured into the ten palaces of the island. The others were nowhere near finished nor of the size of Knossos, but in time they would come to have an importance in accordance with the wishes and blessings of the first Minos. How deep in time that was. A thousand years ago they said. Back when people really were gods.

Situated in between the Central Court, which he was avoiding, and the West Magazine were a cluster of office and cult rooms. The smaller rooms were for the clerks who kept records of the goods available, of what was due their king, and what he might owe to others, as they scribbled on their clay tablets. All was accounted for. Not only was the temple the center of Knossos geographically, but also economically. Agricultural produce flowed into it from the regional estates and from the surrounding rural territories owned by the temple. The rest, a lesser part, came by way of tribute and offering from owners of private estates. The central priesthood administration redistributed the produce, earmarking it for particular deities or sanctuaries, and therefore to the priesthood and servants of those shrines. In other cases, the dedicatory offerings were more general and allowed the administrators to use the produce in any way that would benefit the temple-palace and the community as a whole. There was no money as such, so all wages were paid according as they were deserved in the form of rations or produce, and it was the accountant's place to enumerate everyone's record. As always, those who could establish that they lacked enough could lay claim to a portion for their sustenance. As continuation of tradition in Kriti, the only writers of any great skill who were not priests or priestesses were the accountants.

Inside one room were the large scales used to certify the weights of the incoming copper ingots, a stone off one arm weighing exactly twenty-eight point six kilograms.

The king's, Minos's, religious duties may have made him godlike in the eyes of his people, but he had another role to play which was the true seat of his earthly powers. As the island's chief administrator and businessman, and as supreme commander of his fleet, he was master of the flow of commerce between Kriti, the several island colonies, and other peoples and nations. Massive volumes of trade made him eminently wealthy. Vaults of stone beneath the mainframe of the palace veritably overflowed with precious metals, and the coveted stones of lapis lazuli, carnelian, and amethyst. And not only Knossos secured these riches but also the other temple-palaces.

Yet, for all their all their wealth and power, the Minos's, from the very first to the present, had an equitable modesty. No stately monuments or effigies celebrated any statesman or power. They built no imposing architectural landmarks to themselves as the Pharaohs did. Not even the frescoes of the Knossos palace hinted at the ruler's achievements. The people knew through their love of history and news of current events. That was enough.

Two of the cult rooms had stone posts, similar to the sacred pillars in the limestone caves, marked with the sacred symbol of the labrys. On either side of the pillar nearest the Central Court were shallow stone trays set into the floor. These receptacles for sacred libations of harvest grain, wine, and oil, revealed a cult of generation and regeneration; the cycle of birth, growth, death, and decay that encompasses plant, animal, and man. The phallic association of the posts in these Pillar Crypts was passed down from ages untold, the dark cave-like nature of the shrines recalling the dimension of the sacred grottos where intoxicating drinks prepared from honey would be consumed on festive occasions. As in the innumerable natural recesses and their forests of stalagmites and stalactites with their myriads of votive offerings wedged into crevices, so here there was a wealth of similar oblations; bronze double-axes, startling urns faced with gold leaf, and elaborately decorated vases with graceful handles, delicate bowls and ewers of gold and silver, long necklace-like chains, and trinkets of every description. Fabulous stone vases, laboriously crafted of chlorite schist, serpentine, mottled breccias, and orange stalactite, even rarely ground out of hard obsidian and rock crystal, demonstrated the passionate dedication of the bestower. Here, as almost everywhere else in the temple-palace, the stately column rose erect as a potent symbol of vitality emerging from the Earth, the eminent source of life and, paradoxically, the adumbrate abode of the mortal dead.

Enough of this place. Thoughts twisting to death and the dead and dying were not what he felt like contemplating today. What he wanted was his love. But she would be tied up with today's events. She could have slipped away if she had wanted to; anyone could, even the first wife of Minos. If only it hadn't been her. He liked Minos. His guilt at having such a long affair with his wife was just another guilt heaped on the pile. To make matters worse, Minos never broached the subject with him, though he was sure he must have known. No one could see into minds of others like Minos could. It was said he could read a man's thoughts just by looking into his eyes. Daedalus had seen evidence of it. That it was true, he had no doubt. Minos must know. But for how long had he known, and why didn't he say anything? Probably because he needed him. No one else could have accomplished this marvel of engineering and beauty. And it wasn't as though Minos didn't have his own selection of women on the side. He had his choice of any young beauty he wanted, and often took the opportunity, usually after imbibing of the opiated honey liqueur that was so exclusively popular among the Council. Those were the times when Daedalus found his chance to escape into one of the rooms with Pasiphae. She also was under the influence of drugs and alcohol after these closed rituals, something he objected to but tolerated in quiet reticence. What was one foible?

He passed by the Pillar Crypts and walked the long promenade, the longest in the palace. It doubled back on itself at the end, swinging all the way around to the right. Unlike the builders in Sumer or Egypt, the Minoans spurned the conformity of symmetrical design. Daedalus had galvanized his talents to reflect their artistic genius and filled the palace with rooms of different sizes and shapes, connecting them with hallways that jutted off in all directions. Many of the interior walls consisted of multiple doors that could be opened or closed to change the shape and dimension of a room. The multiplex levels of expansive staircases, columns, corridors, porticoes, and colonnades, all encompassed the spacious central courtyard. To visitors unfamiliar with its layout the palace seemed an enigmatic jumble, indeed a Labyrinth.

There is a great swing in seasonal temperatures on the island of Kriti. Summers can be stifling, but it can get uncomfortably raw in winter. By incorporating many open courts and light wells in the palace design along with the colonnades, windows, and connecting doorways for cross-drafts, Daedalus had solved the problem of making life tolerable in the hot weather. He'd even invented a silk screening for the doors and windows fine enough that light wasn't impeded in the slightest, but durable enough to act as an effective barrier to birds and flying insects. The living rooms were large and airy, some with partitions that could be erected in winter thus shrinking the space in a given room so that it could more easily be warmed with portable braziers.

At the end of that shorter passage it rounded to his left and progressed to a termination at the Central Court again, this time at the opposite end from where he had first made the decision to avoid it. The Throne Room was to his right. That would be a pleasant diversion. He could imagine himself there with Pasiphae, as he had been in reality many times before.

He entered the antechamber to the Throne Room, another throne room in and of itself. The great beamed ceiling frescoed with clouds of the open sky gave the illusion of being outdoors, belying the fact that another five stories were directly above. The fresco masters had adorned the walls as well. This medium had become the nation's predominant art form. Fresco artists were widely patronized by the wealthy, the interiors of villas and palaces on Crete covered with fanciful impressions of life and nature in the seagirt Minoan world. Apprentices prepared walls for painting with a thin layer of white lime plaster then, while it was still wet, the artist outlined the main features and sketched in important details with an obsidian chip. Before the plaster had time to dry the colors were applied. The pigments soaked in and the images became more durable, a process that placed a high premium on speed and spontaneity. People not as financially well-off had their walls painted dry, not as brilliant or permanent, but lovely still. The colors were contrived by the artists from available minerals like copper silicate or ground lapis lazuli for the blues, carbonized wood and shale for blacks, hydrate of lime for white, ocher for yellows, and hematite bloodstone for reds. Close inspection revealed the sharp detail for which they were so regarded. Different textile patterns in men's kilts were painted with the most dexterous ability. Geometrical, stepped outlines of garden walls include subtle elements not at all evident except under the closest scrutiny. Exhilarating red backgrounds highlighted every aspect of the murals. A wall's cornice might have seven or more separate zones of ocher, some of them textured with subtle and expertly detailed criss-cross textile and basket-weave patterns imprinted into the wet plaster with taut string. A honed eye for explicit precision is what gives Minoan art its singularly appealing allure. And they used colors with a freedom not seen in many cultures, choosing to portray everything somewhat unrealistically. Portrayals of plants and animals indicated religious devotion and solicitude, the artist unconcerned about capturing a fleeting moment in the manner of a realist or impressionist but rather imparting the idea of spirit and vitality to the subject depicted. People were regarded in the same spirit as that of the animals, doing that which is natural for them to do, boxing, wrestling, chatting animatedly, dancing. It is an otherworld shown on Minoan murals, with species of flora and fauna not at all existent in the everyday world. The dream-like, poeticized effect was deliberate, part of the exotic thought-world that the Minoans inhabited. Vegetation was painted in a variety of colors, but only rarely green. In one scene a blue ape is set among an array of beasts in a royal menagerie, picking flowers of iris, rose, and crocus all tangled in wreathing ivy. The same imaginative creativity managed to work its way into every order of Minoan art. Artisans styled the bowls and vases around the Palace with serpentine handles, queues of spiky studs, and attenuated spouts. Metalworkers hammered thin sheets of gold and worked them into adornments of animals, insects, and flowers. Even personal art was worn in the form of jewelry, miniature scenes and geometric delineations etched onto seals, rings, gems, and beads. Some of the engravings were almost microscopic, barely discernible with the naked eye. Produced in abundance many of these artistic renderings would last the balance of the next four thousand years.

Minos's stunningly crafted throne, exquisite in its simplicity, graced the rear wall. It was recessed into a space left vacant by the stone benches flanking either side. The four-legged wooden throne stood on a low, square block of stone, protruding in front so Minos's feet reposed at a higher elevation than the rest of the floor. The front legs arced inward and grew in width as they climbed toward the seat, forming a narrowing arch at the upper margin. The chair back rose higher than his head and the outline waved with the suggestion of ripples on the sea. Three paces in front of the throne was a wide stone basin for offerings of obeisance left by the pilgrims who insisted on visiting Minos himself when paying homage. Once each week he would receive commoners who were earnestly gratified to have audience with him, no matter how brief.

For the Minoans, religion and government were closely related. Behind the throne, visitors were confronted with a giant fresco of a charging bull that dominated the room. The bull symbol, associated with both the religion and its ruler, pervaded palace artwork from the storage chambers to Minos's throne room. Stylized horns carved from massive blocks of stone, smaller than the huge copies outside the south wall of the temple, consecrated rooms and hallways and reminded all who saw them that this throne room was where the one closest to Rhea received audience, where that one was as if he were the Great Minos of antiquity. Palace officials would pour libations from vessels fashioned into the shape of a bull's head and on the most special of occasions, when Rhea, the Earth, aligned with Aphrodite and Selene, Venus and the Full Moon, Minos would wear the mask of the bull and enter the chamber of Pasiphae, his divine consort.

The room was befitting of a sovereign but was only the preparatory antechamber for the real power, the real spiritual head of the country. Minos might be the international savant gifted with administrative perspicacity, but Pasiphae was the attraction to whom all were imbued with the greatest devotion.

The left opening led into the real Throne Room, where only the pilgrims who had laid the most generous proportion of their wealth at Minos's feet would be granted entry. There they kneeled upon polished gypsum flagstones before Pasiphae, known at various times of the year and suiting the occasion as Rhea, Selene, or Aphrodite. Queen of the High Priestesses she was the combined sum total of all that they were. The room was even more opulent than Minos's reception room, befitting the esthetics of a discriminating recipient. Daedalus had attended to every detail of the construction of this room himself, chosen the color scheme, drew the cartoons for the frescoes adorning either side of the throne, and selected painters and sculptors with skills enough to do it justice. Two couchant griffins, half lion and half eagle, crouched in a field of lilies and kept watch with their haughty beaks and feathered necks over the Throne of the High Priestess as her heraldic attendants. A symbolic peak, the regal back support of the stone throne itself, was planted in a whimsical backdrop of fresco mountains. On the floor opposite, a bath, a lustral basin - a sunken purification chamber surrounded by a balustrade - and a collection of sacred stone vessels waited to be put to use in the lustration rites. Light from above traveled down the well into the lustral area, brightening it during the day, offering a view of the sky at night. Opposite to the throne, a slender, bare-breasted ivory statuette representing the Earth Mother reached forward with snake-coiled arms toward the seat of her earthly surrogate.

The Priestess's throne. A throne that would survive everything the Earth and man could throw at it to become the oldest throne in Europe. Minos's seat was almost a mockery of this. Carved from a solid high-backed block of alabaster, this was proportionally the same as Minos's, but the center was not hollowed away. The image of the wooden legs had been carved in relief at the front according to the same measure, a slow inward curve increasing in arc as the surface of the seat was reached. Because the throne was a solid block an additional marking was sculpted in, a marking not possible in the vacant space under Minos's chair; a foreskin line. The rising shaft teasingly threatening to penetrate the seat was the product of Daedalus's genius lost all but subliminally on visitors to the room when it was vacant. The marking would never be seen when she sat upon the throne, covered by the long skirt that covered down to her ankles.

The secret was his alone; and hers. It was he that she sat upon.

As he pulled himself back from his fantasies he was dimly aware of a sound coming from the room he so revered. A whispering, rhythmic panting.

The sound was unmistakable. Softly, with his feet bare as was normal on the soft gypsum floors of the temple, he toed up to the entrance to steal a glimpse. It was none of his business who was sneaking a few moments of privacy. On the other hand, if it was a younger couple or one of the lesser order, he might have something to say. There were many who had no right to be in the Throne Room unescorted at any time.

He stood a moment at the door frame listening. They were certainly enjoying themselves. He let himself fall forward a few inches while holding the projecting jamb.

He caught his breath, thankfully not making a sound.

How could she do this to him? It was Pasiphae with another Priest of the Council. He didn't even remember the man's name; he had just been appointed after the death of another. There he was, rapturously mounting her croup while she knelt before the throne and clung tenaciously to the back, breasts pillowing her weight pressed into the cool alabaster seat. Daedalus was so wounded by her transgression that he could not peel his eyes away. Yet why wouldn't she do this thing? She had with him. Was it so unthinkable that she would with others too? He could not stand it. He fell back and slipped away, shamed and insulted. Once into the hall, he broke into a run, determined to escape the proximity of the place with all speed.

He ran the convoluted route through rooms and halls, staying as far as he could from the throngs at the Central Court. He passed inside of the North Entrance, the images of her transgression flooding his thoughts, and wended his way along until he came to the Grand Staircase in the domestic quarter.

He burst into one of the many palace light wells, openings in the roof where sunlight was channeled into the building, stopping when he saw two women sunning themselves in quiet conversation. The patter of his feet alerted them to his entrance and they broke off their discussion to look at him. They hadn't seen him run in. But there he was, interrupting something. Their clothes were typical of Minoan women of the higher order, not the clothes of women kept in the purdah of other countries, but of women who were expected to take the center of the social stage. They wore the elaborate dress of wealth, haughty girls, young, highborn and contemptuous of much. That was likely why they were here instead of with everyone else, seated across the causeway from the frescoed display of Minoan shields painted like the dappled hide from the sacred beast, the bull. The shields, pinched in the center like a figure-of-eight, indicated the area was under divine protection and shone upon the girls with a prophylactic preserve.

One girl, the prettiest and healthiest looking of the two, was feeding a tidbit to a monkey imported from Egypt. The little simians were extremely rare here, not considered with particular fondness by most. Both of the young women had an arrogant air and neither greeted Daedalus, rather looking down their noses at him, their upper lips pushed out with a pretentious conceit. Their feigned curiosity belied a derisive attitude that as much as said 'you are disturbing our privacy.'

They made him nervous for some reason, their perfection of form something that he only ever hoped to achieve in his art and architecture. They were magnificent with their lifted breasts trussed underneath. It made him think, only fleetingly, of the women of Attica whose breasts became flabby after a few years of hanging unsupported and drooped unappealingly with nipples pointing straight down and areolas stretched with time to pancake proportions.

He could have shrunk away, turned in his nervousness and fled the way he had come; but he was Daedalus. No sophomoric maiden was going to cower him. He made a chest, and with as much dignity he could muster against their disrespect, walked the three sides of the brightly frescoed light well.

Huge wooden columns supported massive oaken lintels underwriting the weight of the multistoried structure above. The girls sat at the corner beside one and they were temporarily lost to sight as he passed by each column in turn. Each time they vanished, even though it was only for an instant, he felt a wave of relief. He tried to pull himself together. He thought of the discreet ubiquity of his round columns, a wonder of design, perfectly original. Unlike any other, these at Knossos tapered gradually down from the top, a daily reminder of the chthonic power of the gods, augmented from a design he came up with in Attica where the trunks he used to support roofs were inverted to keep them from taking root in the earthen floors. There had been doubters who had said his columns would topple under the weight of the multi-storied structure at the first earthquake. That was one of the first things he had taken into account. To stop the foot of the columns from slipping sideways, he designed the stone bases to have a roughened top surface and a shallow mortise pit into which projected a tenon from the foot of the fitted column. Painted bright red up to the crown they then flared wildly out and then back in like two shallow black bowls pressed together. To assuage the fears of the doubters who questioned the strength of the uprights they had been consecrated by the painting on of the holiest symbol, the labrys. A raised fret of yellow partitioned the black distention from the red pillar. The illusion created was one of supreme strength, the mass of the structure pressing the colonnades like titanic nails into the stone foundations. The bulging capitals at the top appeared to be caused by the weight of the building deforming the very stone it was quartered from, a symbol of the unbreakable stanchion that joined man to the soil, the seed-bed as well as the death-bed of life.

He passed the girls, almost unaware of them now. Even their stiff display of themselves like fashion models wasn't worth his notice. He ignored them completely, which utterly turned the tables. Now it was they who felt repudiated, rebuffed by the great Daedalus passing them by with never so much as a nod to segregate them from the dust.

He climbed the gypsum steps where, at each of the four landings, he could look down to where the girls had resumed their highbrow patois between the lush inner garden and the backdrop of great frescoed figure-of-eight shields. He loved the idea of shrubs and blooming flowers inside the confines of a building; the milkworts, hyacinths, and tulips attracting little hummingbirds, and the ration of seeds left out each day for the songbirds filling the shaft with the music of life. A background drone of bees working at the task of pollination enlarged the euphony of the echoing birds and invited any who felt inclined to partake in quiet conversation or reflective contemplation. On any upper level one could go into a foyer, and an arrangement of rooms that ended at the colonnaded verandahs, overlooking gardens laid out from the eastern side of the palace to the Kairatos River. That gentle water supply never ran dry, it seemed, even in the hottest summer. Fed by snow lying deep in crevices and clefts near the summits of the highest mountains, the stream was always adequate for the people of Knossos.

He climbed the stairs right up to the flat rooftop, a flock of turtledoves scattering off another part when he surprised them. Minoans favored the flat roof. The light roofs were a framework of wooden beams on which thatch was laid and covered with an impervious clay with only a slight slope for drainage. Sacral horns were spaced all along the perimeter of the temple, on every roof of the multi-level split structure. His eyes took a moment to adjust to the bright reflection off the whitewashed stucco he walked on. Far in the distance he could clearly see the blue of the Mediterranean, much better from this height than the shallow angled view from ground level. How many people over the ages stood at Knossos and wondered about life and its mysteries, its fell blows of disappointment and heartache? They said that Minos was the twenty-sixth of his line, an ancestry going back a thousand years. Hard to believe. Minos was smart, but was he so much smarter than anyone else? Daedalus could think of numerous people, including himself, who could just as easily manage the commerce of the nation; and the theological dogma was one of repetition as much as anything else, something even more men were capable of. Was it so important to be high born? Was that all it was?

His wandering ruminations returned to Pasiphae. Had they finished yet? The thought galled him. He had to find a distraction.

The clamor of the congregated Elect drew his attention to the wide aperture in the roof. They had gathered en masse on the courses of balconies around the arena. Below was the usual sight drawing their howls of approval; the bull leapers engaging in their repertoire of spectacular and dangerous stunts. What struck them with amazement was the dramatic contrast between the unbridled power of the beast against the vulnerable suppleness of the toreros. Acrobatic skill, not bronze weaponry, ensured a successful performance. It was not just a game, not mere entertainment, but an ordeal, a central and serious ritual in the Minoan belief system. The bull was a manifestation of Zeus and dancing with the most powerful male god was no light matter. While the spectators cheered, there were limits to their reverie. They cheered, not only for the acts and the bull but also for the succession of the rites of passage that ensured the athletes higher status. The bull dance expressed the interweaving of human and divine destinies, the elements of collusion and the elements of struggle apportioned with all deities.

He leaned through the rift between the upturned stiles of the sacral horns for an easy view. Three of the young acrobats were teasing the heavy animal toward them. The man was the first off the mark, purchasing the white bull by the horns and flipping up and over its back as it tossed its head in anger. One of the two slender women, their skin painted white, followed suit, actually running at the bull and vaulting over its horns, flipping, springing off its back and landing with the aid of the man who had proceeded her. The final show was from the remaining young woman who attached herself to the animal's horns and lifted her legs, riding the bull until he flipped her up with his powerful neck and flung her through the air. Her course was a slow arch which landed her hands first on its back, her vulnerably supple body arcing rearward into the outstretched waiting arms of the two recipients. They steadied her descent and guided her to her feet, scattering as the bull turned on them, confusing him enough for them to make good their escape.

The watchers shouted accolades and clapped approval. The riled bull fixed its wild eyes upon the last of the three athletes to dishonor his back, snorting its flared nostrils, and pursued her to a gate that was slammed behind her by tenders.

Another gate was opened and the bull galloped through, thankful to escape the congregation's assaulting cheers. He would have a short time of peace before he was called upon again. He hated the torment of the arena. How much more peaceful it was in the field. He had been a wild animal, different from his contemporaries in that he had escaped the pasture after weaning and had lived in isolation away from his tame herd. Three years he had foraged as a wild beast avoiding the strange creatures who kept his parents, and him when he was but a calf. The men chased him, lured him with food, did everything in their power to call him back, but he would not go to them, would not allow himself to be captured. As he grew, changes happened, urges came that he couldn't understand or control. His body changed. Smells from his herd that he could not as yet identify summoned him. He lurked at night nearby, wishing to be with them, but caution stayed him where he watched, hidden on the forest edge. Then one day he saw one of his own, alone in the woods, a beast so like himself, but different. He sniffed the air. Her scent was somewhat inconsistent from the cows he had observed in the pastures, almost like there was an underlying corruption. It was beyond his understanding, but the smell was

401

intriguing enough that he took a few steps closer. She didn't move. Closer he came, surprised that his stealth was so perfect that she still did not notice him. He cozied up beside her and leaned just as he heard the rustle of leaves behind him. Distracted by the scent, his reaction was too late. A rope had been secured to his back leg before he could turn his broad horns in defense. He flung himself sideways, knocking over the decoy cow and charged the fleeing man. The rope pulled taught against the tree where it was secured and his body momentum sorely tore his back leg. Still he leaned against the grappling hold, his leg almost straight out behind him. In a combination of fear and bravery, another man sprang out of a leaf pile and fastened another loop around his other leg. As he spun around the ropes tangled his hooves and he fell. With practiced expertise, four men descended on him as he lay struggling and bound him hoof and horn. He was theirs.

Wild all his life he could never be fully tamed. Scavenging and browsing gave him strength and endurance that none of his kept cousins could match. And with his scrotum intact he had a foul temper that was perfect for the ring.

To execute the precise timing required for a non-fatal performance the bull-leapers trained with tame bulls. To face a wild bull the athletes needed a great deal of practice and natural skill, as well as an almost foolhardy courage. There were often injuries and athletes had been killed. From the perspective of the spectators the most coveted routine was that of the female jumpers, who exclusively performed in the temple. Only the male leapers would perform for the general population in the Bull Court not far from the temple. Only the most gifted and seasoned performers attempted the frontal assault on the bulls. Usually they leaped sideways across their backs, even trying to ride them for a time. Standing on their backs was always greeted with a cheer as the bull ran and bucked trying to dislodge his parasite. Acrobats cartwheeling and somersaulting around the court distracted the bull while the leapers prepared for their stunt. The bull had no way of knowing in advance which of the people in the ring would come at him.

Minos drank from a golden cup depicting the capture of a wild bull sidling up to a dummy cow while a quick-handed Minoan tethers one of the bull's hind legs. In an extraordinary fresco at the Palace a poised female acrobat has seized the horns of a tremendous bull at the onset of her speculative launch, an airborne male is already upside down in the midst of a fantastic vault over the bull, keeping himself afloat and from off its back with his hands, and another female has arms outstretched behind the bull to check her fellow's fall. Attesting spectators were alive with the thrill of witnessing the sensation and appeared to emerge out of the wall in mid-shout.

But as breathtaking as the entertained crowds found the exhilarating stunts, they had far greater significance. This was a sacred ritual observed in honor of the Mother Goddess. Like dance and prayer, athletic competition was considered to be a form of worship. To honor the deities athletes competed in not only bull leaping, but running, jumping, wrestling, and boxing.

Daedalus had missed the other events, the bull leaping being the climax of the occasion. He tired of them anyway, not that they weren't exciting. Only protected to a degree by thin gloves, helmets, and in some cases leather leggings, the fighters used both fists and feet to thrash each other in boxing matches. Daedalus had carved three such depictions, in his spare time, of boxers exchanging blows, having been fascinated by the sport at one time. In the first a fighter cocks his fist over his prostrate opponent; in the second two boxers exchange blows and one is on the way down; the third shows a pair of combatants on their backs but still fighting it out with their feet.

Below, the music lit with the strumming of stringed harps and cithara. They shook rattling sistrums, tambourine shaped instruments with crossbars of beads. They blew double flutes with fourteen notes, sending shrill peals of harmony into the night air. Tumblers and dancers coursed into the vacant court in a choreographed dance. Daedalus looked down on the balconies of spectators. Athletic and tense with nervous energy after the leaping, they chanted and swayed theatrically to the music.

Minos, in the Royal Box, eyed the proceedings. He wore a stiff cod-piece, wider and more prominent than its predecessors, with a rear kilt falling from the belt and curving up smartly at the bottom. He had the long curling locks of the aristocrat, one on each side in front of his ears with the rest behind, a broad golden diadem across his brow keeping the hair back from his face, and a brightly colorful feathered headdress. His tanned body was as athletic as the male leaper just seen, his arms, shoulders, and thighs strong and muscular, his waist and lower legs slim and lithe. His physically attractive build was typical of the other male spectators, graceful in a self-conscious way with the poise of a matador or ballet dancer.

The women were as lithe as the men, narrow waists pulled in tight with belts of linen, chests pyramiding out to exposed breasts held aloft by richly embroidered, constricting jackets. Their hair was piled on top, knotted and laced with silver and gold chain, pearls, and bands down the length of their backs. They clapped to the music animatedly, wide almond eyes stealthily sweeping for others surveilling them more than the entertainment.

Minos was prominent among his coterie of High Priests and Priestesses of the Council joined with him in the Royal Box. On either side of the combine were ritual urns decorated with shields, wheels, swastikas, and stars. Pasiphae was conspicuous by her absence. Any time now she would come.

Music swelled louder as players set their hearts and strength into the work. Dancers grew manic and whipped around the ring in frenetic delirium. Acrobats catapulted themselves through the air, flipping forward and back, pirouetting and twisting in impossible physical gyrations.

Instantly, and somehow with the utmost precision, all stopped. The dancers stood at stone-like attention facing the Royal Box. In the all-pervading silence they even strove to control their breathing, even with their protesting muscles starved for oxygen.

A quiet drum roll echoed off the palace walls. A bell began to chime.

Two High Priests in the Royal Box parted and held aloft the purple curtain, and behind revealed Pasiphae. All eyes focused. More glorious and bedecked than any of her sister Priestesses, she never failed to draw whispering awe. She stepped under the valance and onto the portico with all the grace of an established queen, her arms wide, a snake in either hand and a white dove perched upon her head. She wore an open fronted jacket and a seven-pleated skirt of different colors reaching to the floor. A heavy apron of woven gold cloth hung from her hips and rested down her front.

Other musicians fused their scores with the bell and drum, and the dancers slowly moved around the ring. Again the tempo increased by degrees until the dancers had returned to the frenetic velocity of their climactic celebration. Even the spectators could not contain themselves and rhythmically gyrated in time with the cadence.

A baritone bruit from the lower gate was barely heard above the din. But it was enough to signal the end. The gate was low enough to see the horns of the returned bull waving over the top. The music continued while dancers spun and zigzagged their way nonchalantly to the far end where they disappeared through the other exit. He would go now, the bull, to the city Court where the proceedings would continue for the benefit of the rest of the population. The Priests and Priestesses would follow the privileged audience, arriving lastly to take their place at the head of the continuance there. The members of the Council left their places at the Royal Box and took up position outside each gate around the Bull Court, relieving those on duty to go to the Public Court. They had one responsibility, to theatrically open and close the bolts on command, after which they would be charged with turning a blind eye to what followed.

As the mezzanines cleared and quiet returned to the Central Court, Minos and Pasiphae took their positions alone at the railing of the Royal Box. Exactly below them a door opened, and seven men and seven women were expelled into the ring. The sound of loud bolts being driven home in the doorways around the Court signaled their locking. At that point the Council members turned their backs, able only to listen without seeing.

No one was aware of Daedalus observing from the rooftop. To the north, he heard the clamor of the exiting celebrators moving out of the temple to the streets on their way to the Public Court. His proper place would have been with them, but his mind was far away. He had seen enough acrobatic antics for one day. He did find his curiosity mildly piqued with the entrance below of the seven couples, though. This was something he had never heard tell of. He had assumed, along with everyone else, that the temple festivities were over when the crowd went to the public arena.

On the lower level, a High Priest who had taken the place of the bull handler released the gate to let a new beast into the ring. The white bull had been pressed into a small enclosure, trapped by a second set of doors just behind the first. There was room enough only to stand, and movement was impossible in the confining space. Although it didn't like being in the ring, it was preferable to this cramped trap. The bull bounded into the court with the energy of a frisky calf, but stopped dead at the sight at the other end. Fourteen men and women. More leapers, it thought.

The bull pawed the ground. It could not tell that these were here for another purpose.

Pasiphae plucked the dove from her hair and pushed it to her bosom. It cheeped in fear as the snakes coiled around it. It pecked at them a few times and the snakes pulled away. Pasiphae kissed the dove and released it into the air. She heaved her chest and pressed the snakes passionately as she gazed upon the powerful strength of the bull. Under her heavy apron she flexed and relaxed her thighs, arching her lower spine as an electric thrill rode her vertebrae up to the base of her skull.

On the Court floor, the condemned criminals were becoming intimate with fear. A few huddled together. Two of the men split off and consulted. One of the women exhibited her cowardice and screamed, the first running alone to a corner where she quailed in fright. The rest then scattered, unsure of their next move but knowing that they would be running for their lives in only a moment. All seven of the men, this time, were murderers, and one of the women. The rest had stolen, an intolerable offense in a society where every genuine need was guaranteed to be met. Ambition was encouraged; avarice was not.

Past were the days when offenders were sent to uninhabited islands. It was too cruel to let them die so slowly, of thirst or starvation. Yet they had to suffer in penance for their deeds. How much better that they should die quickly, at the horns of Taurus, the incarnation of Zeus, the maker and defender of the law.

No one but Minos could normally witness their deaths lest the people think it entertainment instead of the tragic and serious loss of life given by those who should have known better. For the first time, Pasiphae had joined him. She had suggested at first, but later insisted. While in the throws of matrimony he had consented. Now here she was. He was not sure it was for the best. His prophetic reservations would be realized.

Still excited but unfulfilled from the encounter in her Chamber she fixed her eyes on the prancing bull. A wave of raw energy filled her groin and exploded outward. The bull's power and energy was something she could grasp even from this height and distance.

Daedalus could not divorce his eyes from Pasiphae. She was wholly bewitching. Even from here she lifted him. He was forgetting her promiscuity even as he took in her loveliness. He had no interest in the leapers below, although he wondered again momentarily why they were there. Unusual that they should display such unprofessional conduct. Perhaps it was a panoramic stage play for the singular enjoyment of the king and queen. Pasiphae seemed to bleed an alluvium of sexuality. She wasn't looking at him, didn't even know he was watching her, but he felt as if she was contacting him empathically in some way. He could feel her longing, her need.

The bull charged the largest huddling group. They scattered. It was of little use. They were mowed down like strands of blowing wheat. Daedalus was horrified. The leapers had never had accidents like this before. They didn't appear to even be trying. Then it registered that the women weren't painted white. These weren't leapers. Hooves trampled the people knocked to the ground, snapping their ribs and avulsing their flesh like it was being torn and crushed by a vice. One was skewered on a horn and borne around the ring, the bull infuriated that he could not shake her off. He whipped his head to no avail and charged everything that moved in his frustration. A man wailed as he tripped while looking behind as he fled. The bull was on him in an instant pummeling him into the stone floor with his bony forehead, the woman's arms and legs whipping against him. The bull reared up to shake her again, but still she would not leave go of his horn. His wrath surged to heights unknown. He bucked and kicked, slipping on the hard floor and hurting himself. The pain only increased his fury. Blind with rage, and with the woman doggedly riding his spur, he galloped around the perimeter, goring all along the wall. Any humped object on the floor attracted him. He stomped each in turn, be they dead or alive. Some played possum in hopes that the bull would leave them be, but they were disillusioned. None could withstand the pain of being trampled underfoot. With their screams came reinforced assailment until their protests ceased.

Pasiphae leaned her forearms on the balustrade, unable to stand. Minos knew he had been wrong to allow her to attend this bloodletting. She was faint with aversion from this brutal display. He admired her, in a way, for sticking with it and not begging to leave. At least she would not want to attend again.

Pasiphae throbbed inside, one uncontrollable contraction after another. They would stop for a short time as she began to recover, only to start again, small contractions at first, rapidly growing in intensity and overwhelming her so that she could only stand with the aid of the loggia railing.

Minos was standing staunch witness to the deaths. What was going on? Daedalus could see that Pasiphae was almost overcome. Her snakes had escaped and she was clutching the rail for support. She was so disgusted she was almost swooning. He squinted and focused as clearly as he could. Was he seeing right? She was kneading one of her breasts, the one distant from Minos. She leaned that elbow on the rail and her arm farthest from her husband fell to her side. Her hand slipped under the apron covering her lap. Minos didn't notice, his eyes fastened on the slaughter. Her hand penetrated the slits cut in the many-layered garment and she pressed it into herself. She could not control her panting except by holding her breath and bearing down, her chin buried in her bosom. When she rolled her eyes to see the powerful beast strutting imperiously about the ring, finally free of the woman impaled by his spike and satisfied that his tormentors were finished off, she fainted away.

Daedalus was incredulous. Amidst the pogrom of carnage Pasiphae had exulted in the rapture of overwhelming multiple orgasms.

Minos was bending to her, shaking her gently as she moaned. He did not call for help; there was no one to call to. And there was no real need. She had just been overcome by the antipathy of so much death. She still trembled, but she would be fine.

* * *

Daedalus rarely went to Amnisos. His work at Knossos kept him too busy. Right now he felt he had to take a break from the Palace, the duties of his work, and the people there. Most of all he had to get away from Pasiphae.

It was startling how the difference in the air only a few miles away could be so dramatic. Here the salty scents were so strong that even with the flower gardens in full bloom he could still smell the sea. A big fish catch had been brought in today. He could smell that too.

The town had been completely redone since his arrival at the port years ago, as had all of the harbors around Kriti. Piers, warehouses, dry-dock facilities, lodging services, and full administrative and accounting capabilities were all provided for. As the pre-eminent sea traders of the time, the Minoans developed their ports and kept them in exquisite condition. Through the ports, the seafaring islanders used their ships and their strategic location in the eastern Mediterranean to link the major centers of trade. The Cyclades and the coast of Asia Minor lay just a few days sail to the northeast. Mainland Attica, to the northwest, was only one hundred ninety miles away. The rich Nile beckoned four hundred miles to the southwest, and Kypros six hundred miles to the east, and the Levant also lay within reach of Kriti's stout merchant vessels. They were making full use of the sail now, as opposed to the way they managed in the past. Only on the most urgent commissions did they row with a strong wind to increase their speed. Whenever they could, they coasted with the wind, limited only by the wind's direction. During the calm season there was no choice but to row, but come autumn the winds picked up and were fairly reliable through the winter and early spring. With the square rigging they could not vary more than about seventy or eighty degrees to either side of the direction of the wind. This was a serious limitation that necessitated the circuitous routes that they took. The only alternative was to row into the headwinds, which was very slow and laborious and added to the expenditure of the merchants. The speed of advancement was cut not just in half, but almost to nothing. Rowing against the influx of even a mild headwind, barely imperceptible whispers of a breeze, had an onerous effect on the progress of a ship. Depressing to the crew, the effect was like walking endlessly uphill on a steep sand dune, sliding back in the shifting sand almost as far as the step taken. If there was no anchorage the ship could only slither backward, with the captain deciding if the crew should try to maintain position, or just give up and let the wind carry them back to their port of departure. Either choice was discouraging, but it was left to the proficiency of the captain to decide the lesser evil. Flogging the oars against a contrary wind was only worthwhile if anchorage was near, for no crew could battle on for very long, clawing away at it until their strength ebbed to nonexistence. A good captain, however hesitantly, would always abandon the struggle of a wasted effort and coast with the wind to a safe haven, even laboring with it if the winds looked as though they might turn even more unfavorable. Since moving the heavy vessels against swelling waves, especially when laden, was a futile exercise in nine cases out of ten, this was a choice all too familiar to any of them.

At every port along their established network of commercial maritime routes, the Minoans exerted their influence and succeeded in sowing some rootstock of their culture. Many were no more than outposts for traders, havens from sudden storms, or meeting places to pick up and drop off cargo from other mariners, a place to keep up on the news and ungleaned opportunities. Other ports had evolved beyond simple trading posts to bona fide colonies, officiated over by civil representatives and governors, under the auspices of Kriti. Scattered colonies were conceived in political opportunism and exigencies. If a leader of an island or territory within the orbit of Minoan trade, assuming they were also within the sphere of influence and close enough to Kriti, found himself under pressure from neighboring malefactors, organized or not, he might send out an appeal for aid from the Minoan fleet. If the odds were with them, and they carefully calculated that with brilliant strategists, they would send the assistance required. But being mainly traders, they would give their aid by way of supplying bronze or copper arms at a reduction, or even gratuitously. They would provide strategic military training or naval reinforcement, but on land they would rarely see any of their own go into battle. It was the other nation at odds with their neighbors. If it was so essential to maintain their sovereignty it was the locals who could enjoy the bloodbath, or die in their own savagery. The Minoans would advise, and make a profit from arms, often to both sides at once, but the help would come at a higher price than any paid by way of commerce. Allegiance to Minos.

Colonies had been established throughout the Cyclades, the islands of Thera, Melos, and Keos, and they were influencing the mainland Greece. They hopscotched to Kasos, Karpathos, Rhodes, Telos, Kos, and Samos, and thence to the mainland of Asia Minor. Eastward they had scoured the coast and islands of Siciania, Malta, and Sardinia, to the gates of Gibraltar.

Amnisos was one of the busiest of all the Minoan harbor installations. Here, as at any other, the single-masted ships loaded and unloaded cargoes directly onto the shore. Stevedores plied the sandy beach shifting goods to and from warehouses in the which mountains of commodities were stored. Administrators worked hand in glove with accountants adjusting schedules and tracking the progress of inventory. Ships rarely went directly to point of destination and most property was transferred at least once to smaller shuttles that circled the island in both directions. Roads had been built and carts were hauled, either by man or beast, to nearby inland towns where those inhabitants became the chief beneficiaries of the port's trade.

Daedalus took a meal at a waterfront taverna. He chose to sit at his leisure on the patio, soaking in the sun. A shuttle was coming into the harbor at full sail using a different course from any of the ships he had seen enter before. The south wind coming off the land was such that she was being blown to the cliffs. Generally in such a wind the captain would have dropped sail and had the crew row, but he kept the sail up. He was making some inward progress, but his motion was carrying him past the port to the other side of the bay. Then he turned sharply, heeling the vessel over so that it might capsize. The crew fought with the sail, righting immediately, and worked their way back across the bay. It was discernibly faster on this crossing, yet the wind hadn't changed direction or speed. What was he up to? The captain threw her into another turn and again crossed the bay. Five times he tried this maneuver, gaining only slightly on the beach when he could have been here by now with only a few men rowing. He submitted to the inevitable and dropped sail for good. Oars were extended and the men heaved the ship into the landing.

Daedalus ordered a second mug of wine, one for the Captain. Marching down the beach with both in hand he was determined to find out what the man had been up to crossing back and forth in such unseamanlike character.

Daedalus had become accustomed to dealing bluntly and to the point with anyone, as long as they were men, even those whom he had never met.

Thrusting the mug at the older captain he asked him without hesitation, "Take this and tell me what, in the name of any god you care for, were you doing out there?"

The captain was somewhat taken aback by this abrupt approach, but his responsive arm reached out on reflex and took the wine. He recognized the lingering accent that Daedalus had never shaken and presumed rightly that he must be a foreigner who could hardly be expected to have the essential propriety of a native-born.

Not forgetting his own manners he thanked Daedalus and introduced himself. "I am Pilot. What I was attempting, my kind partisan, was the impossible. I was ahead of schedule due to the favorable winds. It changed direction just as we were coming up to the harbor so I took it as a personal challenge and thought I might try to tack into the wind. No one has ever been able to do it although there are some who say it should be possible. I am one of them."

"Still? After the valiant attempts which I just witness so arrantly failed?"

"Even still. Not with these ships though."

"Then which?"

"Ah, you ask that which I cannot answer. And now permit me a question." He quickly drained his mug. "Who might you be?"

"My name is Daedalus."

Pilot handed back the mug. "Daedalus. Hmmm. I believe I have heard the name though I cannot remember where."

"Have you been to Knossos?"

"Not for many years."

"How many?"

That was bold. "Five or six. Why do you ask?"

"I built it."

"What? The Palace?"

"Yes."

"You're the architect?"

"That is one of my talents."

"And you sculpted the Aphrodite? It is known from Egypt to Athens. You must tell me; why do you meet me here?"

"Where else would I meet you?"

"I mean why do you meet me at all?

"I told you. I wanted to know what you were doing. Watching your escapades fascinated me."

"I was just sailing. Why are you interested in that?"

"You were more than just sailing. You were attempting that what you know to be impossible. You were attempting it because you think it is possible. You contradict yourself."

Pilot was having enough of this. A gifted man he may be, but he was still a damned foreigner. The conversation had become insulting. He turned to direct the unloading of his ship.

"Wait. I was not trying to be rude." Daedalus caught up to the captain. "Come dine with me. Your crew can unload themselves. Look. The stevedores are taking care of everything. There is nothing for you to do. Come with me. Please."

"I have to put my mark on the shipment."

"You know you can do that any time." Daedalus took him by the arm. "Come to dinner as my guest, I beg of you."

The captain made a great show of reluctantly acquiescing but, in the end, went along.

"You raise my curiosity about ships. Did you know that I had been on one?"

"By your accent, I had guessed."

"Of course. Only once, mind." Of course only once. "I am no experienced sailor. Ah. Look ahead. They are getting ready to launch."

At the shipyard, a shuttle the same size as the one Pilot captained was supported on its keel. It rested in a greased stone trough running the distance between the boathouse and the water where it disappeared into the depths. The balance was precarious. Only a few struts wedged on each side kept it from tipping. Ropes hung loosely at points along either rail. The keel was white with fat, and another fetid layer of rancid mutton grease was being brushed onto the race and finally anointed with a spray of olive oil along its full length to the sea.

"They are about to launch," observed Pilot. There was no need to suggest that they stop to watch. Daedalus was already pulling him in that direction.

The master shipbuilder gave the order, and from a skin he squirted a drenching of red wine over the prow. Ropes were pulled tight on either side, and the supports and retaining chocks were sledged away. Ropes at the front were yarded forward as two strong men put their shoulders to the keel. The slipway groaned and the ship lurched. The push and pull of the men was all that was required to launch the black-hulled vessel. Slowly it coasted forward on the slippery lubricant, the sideways pull on either side by the rope handlers enough to maintain an even balance. The practiced feel of the shipwrights kept the ship perfectly upright. Nevertheless, the master kept his precision eye on it from his vantage point at the front. The balance-men could not contain their urge to assist achieving speed down the ramp and their ropes had a distinct forward lean. The momentum increased until the men were running with the ship down the incline. As they got their legs wet they halted in uniform and snapped the ropes, leaning outward and letting the prow carve a furrow and fire a wall of white froth over them as it settled comfortably into its new element. The men cheered as it bobbed from side to side like a duck on a windy lake.

"Wonderful. Fabulous," exclaimed Pilot. "There is nothing so exciting as the birth and baptism of a new ship." His voice noticeably cracked and he looked, for a moment, as though he might cry.

Daedalus had to half agree. He imagined that Pilot must get the same satisfaction from seeing such an event as he would from the inauguration of a newly completed building.

"Let us celebrate with a drink and dinner shall we?"

"Let us."

Passing marketers with their pithoi filled with roasted snails, buns, sesame seeds, and grains, he led Pilot to the public house where he had been drinking and ordered dinner for two with a prefatory jug of wine.

A slapping line of young boys were beating octopuses, the 'boneless ones', on a stone wall to tenderize them for their family dinners. Daedalus could smell them, not exactly fresh, having been caught the night before by torchbearers according to the ancient method of pit-lamping. Down from the boys, a woman gathered a spread of sponges left to dry in the afternoon sun. That was something they hadn't done in Attica, he thought, gathering the soft sea-plants for padding in pillows, cushions, and mattresses. Useful dry, they were even used for swabbing background color-wash onto plaster and scrubbing clean walls and floors.

The evening was young and the two men were first to come demanding food. They were alone on the patio. The few afternoon drinkers had gone home for their meals.

Their only company was a white pelican holding his mouth open. He was eyeing their table from a few yards away, knowing that they would soon be eating and perhaps toss a scrap his way.

"You've met our friend, I see."

They turned to the woman who had replaced their mugs and set a jug on the tripod table.

"His name is Petros. As white and beautiful as a seagull, and every bit the scrounge. The old boy has been with us for five years. Never leaves, except to go down the beach to beg from the fishers. He doesn't like them much though, do you boy?" she said changing her direction of speech from them to the bird.

A flapping of wings alerted them to the arrival of another bird that landed next to Petros. He flared his wings and dove at it, snapping his beak and driving the interloper back.

"Petros has never been much for sharing. This girl has been chasing him for over a year trying to win his affection. She even brings him fish, but he always spurns her like this."

"I'll bet he eats the fish first."

"Of course."

Petros took another swipe at the amorous female but she held her ground, not retaliating but withstanding the abuse. He continued the attack and the woman was poising herself to go to her defense. Pilot tried to watch both their server and the two birds, amused at the possibility of a confrontation. Petros snapped hold of the female's head as it screamed peals of defiance. It was too much for the woman and she jumped in to the rescue.

"Petros," she yelled. "You bad bird. Let her go." She was waving her arms and gave him a soft kick to the chest, actually more of a rude push with her foot.

He spat out his mouthful and stood high with his head back and his chest inflated, giving the woman an annoyed look as his paramour flew off.

Pilot laughed. "I believe Petros has taken umbrage at your interference."

"Damn pelican," she blushed. "Who does he think he is?" The bird followed her back to the table, imitating her walk.

She huffed back into the diner.

"You do not find it amusing, my friend?" questioned Pilot.

Daedalus managed a weak smile. "Just thinking of something else, that's all."

"Look how she circles," he said, indicating the female rising on the currents above their heads. "Trampled upon. Treated with contempt. Still she will not leave. Do you see the parallels Daedalus?"

He nodded, not wanting to express his inner feelings to this man he had only met. They returned to their wine goblets, admiring the freedom of the sea in silence until their food arrived.

The woman's temper had fouled and she let the plates drop to the table with a thud loud enough to break less sturdy flatware.

Pilot was starved and glommed a red mullet, all steaming and smelling of coriander. He had the small fish stripped of meat and swallowed in seconds.

413

"Fabulous. Have a barbounia. It is wonderful." He tossed one over to Daedalus landing squarely centered on his plate.

The captain helped himself to a handful from the bowl of calamari and some of the steamed greens inside a red pottery crock. It was unbelievable the appetite one worked up at sea. The woman was back again with a bowl of pistachio nuts and a piping hot stew of barley, asparagus, celery, carrots, and beans simmering in a meat broth and seasoned perfectly with cumin and fennel. Daedalus couldn't stop his belly rumbling in anticipation when he got a whiff of the heavenly soup.

An accelerated whooshing drew their attention just before a piercing screech. They barely had time to look up. All three raised their arms at the sight, fearing that they might be struck by the diving flurry of wings and beak zeroing in on them from the heights.

A dull splat and crunch followed in the wake of the airborne noise. Her amorous attempts having failed to woo the affections of Petros, the disconsolate female had torpedoed to her demise at his very feet. Petros squawked and fled. The female pelican's broken body lay smashed in a heap on the stone deck, a single wing extended in death.

* * *

Daedalus pondered the unprecedented action of the suicidal pelican. He remembered losing his appetite after that, which didn't matter since Pilot enthusiastically gobbled the remains. The town was ablaze with gossip of the love-struck bird and its self-inflicted death. Some surmised it had also been a murder attempt and that the fortunate Petros had successfully sidestepped at the last possible moment.

What stuck in Daedalus's mind, however, was the dead bird's jutting wing. He had never paid any heed before to the fact that every bird he had seen had triangular wings. He had seen them, to be sure, thousands of times, but he had never really noticed. Birds flew at will and with, seemingly, very little effort. There were some now, a small group of scarlet-beaked gulls cavorting in the sky, calling to each other as they played and swooped. They were flying in every direction, riding high, diving low, looping and curving in defiance of whatever force held other creatures hard against the earth. When they lost momentum they flapped their wings and drove themselves faster.

They were obviously held aloft by the same winds that impel ships from sea to sea yet they suffer none of the same restrictions as to direction. A bird could fly any way it pleased.

Could it be that the wing was that inherently different from the square sail? Was that the only reason that Pilot could not maneuver his ship into the wind as any bird can?

He finished his small dinner inside the residential section of the Knossos Palace. He ate alone tonight. He didn't really feel like anyone's company. In the solitude of his small apartment, he drank his barley beer and chewed a bland salad. He was not in the mood for any more.

A knock came from his door, the last thing he wanted to hear. He noticed he had left it unbolted and hoped the unwelcome intruder would simply pass.

Slowly the door hinged open. He rested his forehead on his right fist and closed his eyes, emitting a grunting sigh. Why couldn't people leave him alone?

He heard the door close. Hopefully the invading presence had left, assuming he was at prayer.

His heart leapt when he looked up.

"Pasiphae."

* * *

After their intertwined love-making, they uncoiled and settled for a comfortable cuddle.

Pasiphae still seemed wanting although Daedalus knew she had been satisfied, many times. She wrapped her legs around his bent knee and continued to pulsate against it.

"I don't think I can go on," he said. "You have drained me."

"You would not continue for me?"

"I have given you my all, more than I could give any other. Still it is not enough for you?"

"How could it ever be enough? Don't you know what you do to me?" She pulled his face to hers and kissed him hard. He pushed his hand down her thigh and pulled it up between them. She fell back a bit to give it room. She began to pant again, feeling the dilating sensation inside her. He worked his hand harder. Time after time she came, thrusting herself against him and enveloping his entire hand. He made a fist so he wouldn't slip out. She was so big inside. Her tireless rhythmicity bore down on his arm until she finally collapsed. He was drained himself, his arm and hand muscles thoroughly enervated.

"Taurus," she whispered. "Mighty Taurus."

Daedalus could barely make out the words. Was it the bull's name she uttered? She was opening her eyes and looking at him with a loving sensuality that beguiled his sensibilities. No. He had heard her right.

He laid himself beside her, stroking her gently. She closed her eyes and smiled.

"I saw you at the Central Court," he ventured.

She opened her eyes. "Did you? Were you there?" she asked. "I didn't see you."

"I came late. I was not in my place."

"I had thought you were missing a purpose. Perhaps working, as usual."

"I was. You know I don't think too much of public assemblies." He wanted to continue but his tongue wrapped. He averted his eyes.

"You have more to say, my love."

He continued hesitantly. "Before the exhibition, I was touring the Palace." He felt her stiffen. "I saw you. I saw you in the Throne Room."

She exhaled. "Daedalus." She put a hand to his face. "He was nothing but a transitory diversion. I had a need. He was there. I would much rather it had been you."

"Was it me you thought of when you were with him?"

She started to speak but paused. "I could say that it was, but I cannot tell you an untruth."

"But you must tell me something."

"I needed someone, do you understand? He was only passing by and I pulled him inside the room. He could have been the chamber boy. It wouldn't have mattered, my need was so great. I was thinking of the Ceremony. I was thinking and reliving the experience of Minos, as the Taurus, coming in to me with the mask and mounting me as an animal." She held his face. "It was as if I was actually with him. I felt it. I could see it. It was real."

"Who was it you saw? Minos or the bull?"

His comprehension startled her.

"I watched you from the rooftop," he confessed.

She pulled back. "The rooftop?" She could not believe it. "You stayed after the congregation left?"

He nodded once.

"You know the penalty for such a thing. Only Minos may watch the blood reparation. Only at my begging was I able to gain a singular exemption."

"And why did you beg?"

"Your questions are piercing."

"Are you afraid to say?"

"How much did you see?"

"Everything."

"Tell me."

"I saw the killings, the slaughter. It was repugnant. Only your attractive beauty kept me still. I watched you instead of the massacre."

"Don't stop. Tell me what you saw."

"You got pleasure from the killings. With each death you reeled in climax. Is there something inside of you so cruel?"

"Cruel? No. I did not even see the killings. I saw only power. The raw, unbridled power of a magnificent creature. I was lost in his spell as I have been for years. Why do you think I was so insistent to be there for the supreme manifestation of his power?"

He could not answer.

"The Taurus comes to me in the night. At first, it was unbidden; he just took me. There was no resisting such a potent force. Then it was I who called him to me. It was I who was taking control. He needed me. Larger and larger phalluses I would mount in the privacy of my apartment, sometimes leaving them in for the night while I slept. He had his way and I had mine. Had you not noticed?"

She could tell that he had.

"I am ready for the real thing, Daedalus. I want you to help me."

"What?" He could not believe the request. "What are you saying?"

"You must find a way to help me couple with the wild Taurus."

* * *

The Theatral Area had been readied throughout the day with garlands of every growing flower. Curtains of purpled felt sashed the odeum pillars. Singers and musicians were lining up in front of them and on either side in preparation.

"It is a fine work, Daedalus. Perfectly worthy of the Palace grounds."

Minos was pleased with any addition Daedalus made to the Palace or its surroundings. This special Theatral Area was just outside the north-west Palace corner and, now that the Palace was as good as finished, they could concentrate on these supplemental projects.

They were speaking from backstage where Minos's daughter, by his second wife, was readying herself for her coming-of-age cotillion. A curious young girl. Daedalus thought it strange that she alone among all of the people had always kept her hair covered, even as a little girl. Minos took Daedalus by the arm and led him outside. The women would take Ariadne from here and complete her preparation. They parted at the curtains. Minos had been somewhat taciturn these last few weeks. Daedalus was glad to be away from him. He took his place outside the portico of the theater, below the wide steps. He would have a place as an honored guest at the front of the open square of the agora but could not actually be on the stage with the Priests and Priestesses. Even the singers and musicians had higher official status than he and were allowed up as theological servants. Strictest protocol was routinely dropped for Daedalus because of who he was and how he had helped with the rebuilding of Knossos. He would not have to stand at the back with the other slaves, or even as far back as citizens like his son Icarus. He wished his boy had been born of Pasiphae and that she could have been his wife. Instead, he had settled for less and had a son by her. He never did love her. She was just a convenient companion on lonely nights who offered him the adoration he longed for, but he couldn't return the earnest compassion she gave to him.

Minos had promised Daedalus that someday he would be able to waive the national requirement of 'citizenship by birth' in his case to ordain him to the Priesthood, but thus far it had not happened.

Ceramic bells rang signaling the ceremony commencement. Lyres strummed and a soft, steady beat struck from a coordinated marshal of drummers. Eerie double tones broadcast from the collective throats of the vocalists. They alternated respirations so the monotonous sound never ended; just a steady murmur reverberating from the ceiling and unadorned rear wall. The uninterrupted drone was reminiscent of a hive shielding its queen.

The sound suddenly became electric. Fires volleyed up from bowls at either side of the stage as singers strained their vocal cords and musicians laid into their art. A chorus of singers danced out from backstage and cavorted back and forth across the floor, adjoining their voices to the perfect harmonizing of the pure vocalists. Elaborately dressed, bejeweled priestesses glided across the floor as the rite unfolded. Against the backdrop of rich curtains, bright pillars, and multi-colored frescoes the overall effect was one of dazzling opulence. To the dance, flutists played in sublime union with the strumming and plucking lutenists.

And then she materialized out of nothing. Somehow she had mingled into the dancers unseen and, when they parted and fell before her, the music stopped as sudden and sure as the impact of an ax embedding a tree.

Pasiphae. Wearing the adornment she had been seen with all too briefly at the closing of the bull ceremony, standing pomp and sure at center stage, splendid, honored, and supreme.

She began to move, swaying in silence. Slowly, as at the first, voices began their chant and music softly merged. As she waved her torso the music became harsh. Minos came forth, wearing the bull's head of the Taurus. The men shouted over and over again as the shriller cries of women singers backgrounded to a more melodious song from chorus dancers. The dancers rose and flew around the stage in a figure-eight, flashing between one another with perfect functional interaction. Minos stood within one circle. The other enclosed Pasiphae. The tempo quickened, the volume increased. The dancers changed their formation from figure-eight to hourglass. Slowly they widened the gap at the central neck until the shape became ovular, and then a circle. Still they ran around the central characters; the embodiment of all of the female goddesses, and Zeus appearing to the humans as a bull.

Minos stamped his feet in rhythm to the music and strode back and forth, increasing his speed to a run. Pasiphae continued her private dance without noticing him. He charged at her in lunges intended not to wound but garner her attention. Every time he leapt at her she turned away, ignoring his advances.

Louder the shouts and singing grew, and they could be understood now to be voicing "Submit. Submit."

Finally, Pasiphae turned to Minos on a charge and embraced him. The moving dancers swooped in on them, hiding them from the view of the spectators now so absorbed in the performance they were as if swept away to another spiritual realm.

As suddenly as they appeared, they vanished. The dancers scattered to the sidelines and black blankets of wool were draped over the fires, casting a pall of blackness over the setting. The blankets were hurled back before the flames could be extinguished fully and the light returned bright to the dilating irises of the spectators.

The girl standing in the center was not Pasiphae. Exclamations of wonder from the congregation were heard above the singers. Her face made up she was every bit the equal of Pasiphae as far as beauty went, and her youth hinted at an innocence long lost on her elder. But her hair. Her hair, which had been concealed so many years, was blond.

Ariadne. The fair-haired Ariadne. The girl of the lovely tresses. Even her name meant 'utterly pure.' Behind her neck was the Sacral Knot, a length of patterned fabric with a tasseled border at either end, a knotted eye in the middle, the two ends freely suspended like a modern dinner-tie. The knot binding a small knurl of her long hair behind her head symbolized the tie between a communicant and deity. The mantle of Selene, Rhea, had been passed from Pasiphae in the ritual dance to the younger Ariadne to separate it from the increasingly sexual idiosyncrasies of Aphrodite.

The energetic music had soothed to a slow waltz, the accompanying vocals now but a whisper. Ariadne chasséd across the stage, her intricately choreographed movements, her winding and unwinding executions finely effectuated. Those who were of the Elect, those who had passed the test of the Labyrinth, knew the secret of the paths she traced on the dance floor. In her purity, she performed before the assembled nobility the celebration of the natural flowering of life. Surreal, she was the vital element moving across the flagstones. She was the life within every animate thing.

Her dance also gave entrance and exit to the mysterious Labyrinth, the place of life, death, and rebirth. She was guide to the spirit on the dangerous journey from life to afterlife, the Elysium, the pleasant heaven awaiting them at the end of their earthly lives.

419

* * *

He thought he must be losing his mind. To build such a contraption was tantamount to murder. Yet perhaps she could survive it. Maybe. Her increasing looseness had not escaped his notice. Her preparations were obviously continuing, but he did not want to talk to her about it. The reason, mainly, was that he could tell that he was not really satisfying her anymore. Always she begged for his arm and always he obliged, but it could not help but disturb him that his manhood should be so disregarded.

Pasiphae had first used her specially made dilator immediately after giving birth to Ariadne. Her vagina fully dilated from the delivery and she didn't want to lose the opportunity that would never come again. She had no intention of having another child so the moment had to be seized. Almost the size of the child's body she inserted it and waited. Only moderately uncomfortable after passing her daughter's head she left it in for days, only removing it once at the insistence of the surgeon to allow passage of the placenta. Still, after many years, she seemed normal to Daedalus. He never really liked the constricting tightness of other women. He wondered if it was that or if it was that he was so infatuated with Pasiphae's beauty over all others that her looseness was simply of no account.

But she'd obviously been up to her vaginal stretching again. She had many stone dilators of differing sizes upright on the floor of her cloister and he pictured what she must be doing with them. He envisioned her going up the line of lubricated dildoes, squatting on each in turn and gradually working herself larger. He wondered how much it was possible for her to take. Did she get sexual satisfaction from something that surely must be painful? If not, why would she do it? If so, why would she even bother with so many men?

Daedalus had labored personally on the hollow cow for over a month. A full-sized replica, it could easily accommodate a person concealed inside. He had cast the legs of copper with a leathern hammock between them to support the wooden forgery. Entry was through a trap on the creature's back.

It was finished. He hoped he had thought of everything. That it would cozen the bull, he had no doubt. He had covered his creation with the hide of a real cow and mounted its head on balancing gimbals that it might sway realistically.

He had measured his love as best as he could, without her realizing that he was not doing it for her pleasure. There was no way that she could take the three-foot length of the bull's assault no matter what her fantasy. He had contrived a long canal, which would absorb half of his penetration. The inside of the canal was lined with fleece saturated with a grease concocted from olive oil. The sensation was as close as he could devise to the genuine channel. Hopefully, the bull would not care about any small differences.

He pushed the wheeled animal to the middle of the Central Court. How he wished that she had not insisted on this place. But she insisted on the open forum so her goddess could be witness. He only hoped no one else would be. The greased axles between its legs made not a sound as he pushed it. The wheels wrapped in thick hide gave barely a whisper against the stone. He locked the wheels into position.

No one would be awake, but the bull might make enough noise to alert someone. He hoped not. He hoped the bull would just do his business and that would be the end of it. No chasing or play. He could just have his way with the cow and go back to his pen.

There was no Moon tonight. With no lamp in the Court it was near pitch black. The Morning Star would be up soon and then they would have about a quarter of an hour before twilight began to lighten the sky. She would not come until she could see the Star from her place on the roof.

Her star.

Pasiphae watched the nearly invisible shadow move across the Court below her. She wore a black robe that belied her presence. It wasn't too likely that anyone would have seen her anyway. No one was ever allowed on the delicate flat roof. It was too easily damaged. Not even children snuck up there.

Her star would come any minute now; any minute. She could feel it coming.

There. Just peeping over the eastern horizon.

She ran her hands hard up her flanks, against her breasts, and twisted her bent arms outward with her palms out toward the rising planet in the Minoan habit of prayer.

Her bosom filled with warmth as she tensed her arms and squeezed her breasts between her outstretched arms. A tingle of expectancy washed down her spine, down her nerves to her very toes. Every muscle contracted in a thrill of anticipation.

On unsteady legs, she walked the steps to the Court level. How silent the Grand Staircase. How wide. How sweet its smells. She was inhaling too deeply and becoming giddy.

The narrow gate was left open for her. Daedalus had done his part well. He was nowhere to be seen but she knew he was in the darkness. He would be at the Bull's Gate, waiting for her to get in position.

Her heart was palpitating, racing, bursting from her chest.

She closed the gate behind her and heard the latch quietly fall into place. The walk of only a hundred feet felt like a lifetime journey. Yet when she stood beside the cow and felt its rump she could not recall anything else, as if she had been transported instantly from before her birth to this place, this time.

She stood back. Inhaling deeply she turned her arms and shoulders out and let her garment slide off her back. Still holding her breath she stretched her head back and closed her eyes.

Her moment of ecstasy would soon be at hand.

She spread her fingers and reached out to touch the cow. Rubbing her hands hard into its hide she became one with it. She embraced it and pressed tight against it.

She was the cow. She was its womb.

And the womb had a place.

She felt the opening on its back and pulled herself up. The hatch was open, waiting for her entry.

Daedalus could just make out the lighter skin of his love climbing up and disappearing into the hollow. He heard the light thud of the lid sealing.

The cow was no longer barren. It had life within.

All he had to do now was open the gate. The bull was becoming anxious in his pen, jostling uncomfortably when normally he would be sleeping. After Daedalus had locked the bovine mannequin in place, he spread the secretions of a cow in estrus on its rear. The bull could smell it and was wanting.

Daedalus wiped his nose. He was crying. He asked the gods for forgiveness and cursed himself. She was a god. A Goddess. The Goddess of the Morning Star. Aphrodite. He had to do as she requested.

He lifted the latch and eased the gate open. He walked it back as if he were letting out a domestic lamb instead of a wild bull. Had it blown the gate and killed him he would not have cared.

But he was fortunate. The bull was suspicious, having only tasted blood and never pleasure in the ring. When he was put to mate it was always outside the Palace, never in. This required caution. He could see no better than Daedalus.

He snorted. As he walked toward the scent of the cow the smell of the man he knew had opened the gate subsided. In an instant, the white bull had forgotten about him. He circled the cow, bobbing his head and waving it from side to side to better catch the scent. He stopped behind her and inhaled. The scent was inviting him. He threw back his head and curled his lip, shaking his massive horns. He put his nose back to her vent and inhaled again.

He jumped back and broke into a short trot, his head high and looking behind in the darkness as he fled, terrifying Daedalus with the noise of his hooves of the flagstone surface. He stopped. Something hadn't been right, smelled right. He stood contemplating. The cow hadn't moved. He had a faint recollection a cow in a forest that hadn't moved, but he couldn't organize his thoughts enough to bring the image back.

Slowly the scent of estrus teased him. Caution vaporized in proportion to his excitement. Another sniff and he was convinced that this immutable target was for him.

Daedalus had masterfully wrought the inside of Pasiphae's artifice as well as the out. It was softly lined with fleece, warm and downy against her skin. The belly was doubly padded and her knees and forearms soaked deep into it. She pressed herself against the end of the canal and settled her lower legs into the cavity below. Fitted carefully into place she could barely squirm, so beautifully had Daedalus crafted the hollow to her shape and size. She rested her chest on a raised portion, like a platform with two holes in it for her breasts to hang down. Her shoulders butted against padded yoke that held her back tight against the canal. She was fixed in place. Paroxysms of elation filled her as she waited.

Pasiphae felt the cow pitch forward.

She was being mounted.

* * *

Minos looked down from the munificent mezzanine. One of his consorts was being a little too demanding and he wanted to get away from her. He could have sent her away but why hurt her feelings? It wasn't that he disliked her company; he just wanted his beloved Pasiphae. She often spent nights away from him. She went to great lengths to make sure that he was accompanied to bed with the most exquisite women, trained by herself in the arts of love-making so that he might feel at ease with them. She had even personally chosen his second wife. But they were not the same. Nowhere near the same. How could she think they could be?

She was probably with another man. Her cavorting was not totally secret from him. He had known about it for decades but what could he do? She had told him on the first occasion that she would not stop. His only option was to kill her, and that he would not do. She would be his, she had said, as wife, as lover; but she would have other lovers too. It would be best if he would just look the other way.

He leaned against the balcony rail, bent over on his elbows. Dawn would not be long off. It was incredibly dark in the Central Court. He didn't like the dark. Moonless nights were unnatural somehow. If he could change anything about the natural order of things that would be it. There should always be light in the sky. The stars without the Moon were just not adequate.

He thought he could make out the soft plod of an animal below. He couldn't see anything but he was sure there was something down there. The sound faded. Was he mistaken or did he hear the catching of a latch?

Daedalus thanked the gods that he had been given the foresight to grease everything, even the hinges of the gates along the path the bull would take. They were virtually silent opening and closing. He cursed to himself when in a moment of forgetfulness he had closed the first gate without lifting the latch first. The metal striking metal had made a noise. There was nothing he could do about it now, like there was nothing he could do about the step of the bull's hooves against the stone. He could only hope that no one had heard.

There was barely any time left. The bull had taken longer than he thought it would. Not much longer, but it seemed an eternity. He wanted to check on Pasiphae but she had been strict with him; he was not to release her in the Court. He would push the cow to its room first and let her out there. To do that he had to get the bull back to his pen outside the Palace first. It wasn't far. Calmed by his frolic the bull was as tame as a plow animal. It only took a few minutes to drive him down the hall and along the cordoned path to his stable outside of the grandstand where the general public viewed their own entertainment. Already dawn was breaking, the Star of Aphrodite the only light left in the sky. Daedalus undid the ropes along his outer path as he backtracked to the Palace entrance, thankful that the bull was spent and hadn't turned on him and made things difficult.

His Pasiphae. How had she fared? He ran the rest of the way. He had to push the cow back. He almost leapt over the gate; would have if he'd been younger. Instead, he had to stop and open it.

But he didn't. Across the Court, he could see a man closing on the cow. It was still too dark to make out who it was but he was sure it must be one of the Council by the silhouette of his dress. As he came up next to the cow he slowed, obviously wondering what it could be. He could almost hear the man's thoughts. A cow with wheels? What sort of contrivance is this?

The intruder surveilled the mannequin, ducking to inspect the undersides and the wheels. He resumed his perusal around the cow and touched it. He pushed its head so it bobbed up and down. Finally, he stepped up on one of the wheels and felt along its back.

Daedalus could not stay still. Who was this interfering clown and why was he here? Where had he come from?

The figure turned around, curiously trying to comprehend things for himself.

Oh, the Gods, the Gods. It was Minos.

Daedalus ducked behind the gate. He was panicking. He would be killed for this. He would be put before the bull as the others had and slaughtered. And what would he do to Pasiphae if he found her?

If he found her. What did he mean, if? Minos was not a stupid man and Pasiphae could not stay inside forever. He would find the hatch and open it. How would Pasiphae explain herself?

He waited. What else could he do?

"No." He heard the wail. "No. No. No." Louder and louder came the screams. He looked over the gate. Men and women were appearing with haste at the east mezzanine of the Domestic Quarter, their faces riveted on the sight below.

In the middle of the Central Court, Minos was pulling the naked bleeding body of Pasiphae out of an imitation cow.

* * *

Minos kicked over the amphora vase, smashing it to pieces and spilling its contents of fragrant potpourri. Another rage was prevailing over him as he anguished over the personal loss of the one he loved most. His suffering was eternal; not to time yet, but to magnitude. He refused food, hadn't slept, wouldn't participate in the administration of the country, and would not attend to his duties as principal High Priest. He was not leaving his apartment, was not bathing, and was eliminating his stools into a chamber pot instead of availing himself of the flushing toilets. Neither had he shaved, and he spurned his attendant who had stopped by to perform the weekly tweezing of his body hair.

He would take no visitors but only sat in his room, the curtains drawn day and night, only opening them to see the Morning Star rising in the east before fading from sight in the light of the trailing Sun and illuminated blue sky.

Pasiphae. His glorious Pasiphae.

He could not concentrate enough to make any decisions. He knew he was psychologically distraught and that in time he would at least partially recover. But even Pasiphae's commemorative funeral had not lifted his spirits enough to deal with the realities of living. He, as the highest of High Priests, had been obliged by law and tradition to conduct and preside at her requiem, but he had eschewed his responsibility. He had cursed his weakness as he grieved with all of the others afflicted by Pasiphae's death.

It had not been possible to contain her manner of death. That she had willingly entered the hollowed cow no one had ever doubted. Tales of her ardent liaisons surfaced everywhere. What were careful secrets became whispered gossip and, finally, open discussion. She had lain with almost every man in the Palace, and enough of the women, swearing each to an oath as if they were the only ones. Minos, who thought he knew about all of her amorous affairs, had been grossly underinformed. The truth had shocked and sickened him. Yet, even in corporeal death, she held him in such tight reign that he could do nothing but forgive her and long her resurrection. He wanted no more evidence about her furtive life and, so, sequestered himself from the reality of the past.

The treacherous Daedalus he locked in the highest tower of the Palace. Treacherous.

Daedalus was no more treacherous than any other man, so it would seem. Had any other of sufficient skill been propositioned to construct the demonic contrivance, they would have done the same for her. He would have, himself. He choked. He finally admitted it.

He would have; for her.

A knock at the door. He ground his teeth. He had given strict instruction to be left alone. Another knock. He pinched his nose until it hurt. Damn and curse them.

After a polite pause, the knocking resumed, a little louder and more persistent.

"What do you want?" he screamed.

The door crept open. A Council Priestess injected her head. The Council had together decided that a woman would probably be served a softer hand than any of the men.

"I am terribly sorry to have to bother you in your grief Minos. I have distressing news."

"Nothing could be important enough to disturb me. Get out." He turned his back.

"But Minos . . ."

"Get out."

"It is about Androgeus."

"I told you to get out."

"He has been injured Minos. He may die."

"What? Where is he?"

"He is being carried here from Amnisos. A runner says that he is just over the hill and will be here very soon. His bearers do not want to carry him too quickly lest the aggravation to his injuries cause him to expire."

Minos snatched up the copper stand that had fallen when he kicked it and smashed it against the wall. Its shape collapsed into a twist of metal banding. He roared and hurled it across the room.

Throwing a robe over his shoulders he shoved past the Priestess, and stormed through the winding halls and past fearful groups of residents, to the West Porch where any arrivals from the south would come. He stood between the trees and waited.

There were others about waiting in fearful silence, none daring to look at him let alone speak. They had never seen Minos so dissonant.

Androgeus's litter was hauled over the rise. They would be another half hour at the rate they were moving.

Minos turned. "Go help them," he shouted to everyone and no one in particular.

The Porch emptied. Men and women sprinted down the Royal Road to the crossroad and on. All seasoned runners, they would meet the bearers and relieve them in minutes. Even at the end of their hard run, they would still be in better condition to finish the transport than the men who had born him the first six miles from the coast.

It was still taking too long. At least the bearers had the good judgment to bring Androgeus on a litter instead of a cart like he had seen done before. The road was smooth enough for transporting most goods, but jarring wheels against the imperfect paving stones created too much vibration for a seriously injured man.

Minos paced while they brought Androgeus closer. He had missed him terribly in his absence; except for the last few days when Androgeus had failed to even enter his mind. He realized he hadn't thought about him at all since the horror of Pasiphae's death. He excused himself for that.

As the litter crossed the bridge and was ascending the slope toward the Temple Minos ran down to meet them. The bearers stopped, laid the bed on the ground, and Minos knelt beside Androgeus.

"What has happened to him?" He was horrified at the sight of his sick friend. He lay gray and unconscious, his skin old and worn like the hide of an ancient, balding animal.

"He was assaulted in Athens. They tried to kill him. They ambushed him and left him for dead. They think he is dead."

Minos felt himself losing his temper and did everything within his power to regain what little control he could muster.

"Take him to my chamber. Now. Tell me the rest later. Go."

They raised the litter on his command and positively ran with it. With fantastic coordinated effort, they kept the movement to a minimum while still carrying on at unhesitating speed.

"You," Minos shouted. "Run ahead of them and have the physician prepare my apartment for Androgeus. It will become his ward. The physician will see him immediately. Understood?"

"Yes, Minos." The man dashed away and passed the running bearers in seconds.

Minos, too, ran. He loped beside the litter, not saying anything and terrifying the bearers by keeping his silence. They feared they might accidentally stumble and that Minos would unleash a whirlwind of fury upon them.

They carried Androgeus to the Royal Apartment and laid him cautiously on Minos's bed, not entirely sure if he wanted them to take things this far. Minos did not object as they hesitantly guessed his wishes and slid Androgeus carefully sideways to the soft feather mattress.

427

The physician ordered the bearers out of the room with a wave of his staff, leaving himself alone with Minos to minister to the injured man. Without a word, he leaned over and felt Androgeus's head. He spent a great deal of time palpating every bump and prominence under the thick black hair.

Asclepius lifted his patient's eyelids and peered closely into the inky depths. One pupil reacted to the introduction of light by constricting; the other didn't.

He pulled the jaw down and blew into Androgeus's mouth, inflating his lungs, and smelled the exhaling air. The physician looked into each ear and felt firmly around the back of his neck, feeling each muscle in series along each side and pressed his fingers into the pulsations on either side of his windpipe. He then went to Androgeus's feet and pressed the point of a sharp pin into the pad of each great toe. Both feet reacted by languidly pulling away.

The practitioner removed a razor from his bag and began to shave off Androgeus's hair. Carefully he rolled his patient's head to the side and removed what was on the back, then tilted it the other way to shave the other side. He bunched the long tresses into a bag and placed it beside his physician's bundle. Then he rubbed a fragrant saffron oil on his hands and felt again the skull of his patient. There were two deformed areas on the left side. Now that the scalp was clear of hair and shining yellow from the oil, Minos too could see the disparity. Just above the ear was a bulge that seemed more than a bruise. A sharp edge under the skin indicated a protruding fracture. Slightly above that was a depression from the normal plane that sunk inward.

"Androgeus has suffered a severe blow. His skull has been smashed." These were his first words. "How did it happen?"

Minos called for the captain of the vessel that had transported him. "Tell the physician what happened. Leave out no detail."

The nervous captain had never been to Knossos. He was merely the captain of a small trading vessel that circumstantially happened to be in the area when the events unfolded. His words faltered here in the very chamber of Minos, in the richest bedroom of the nation.

"Speak up so we can hear you," Minos commanded.

The captain forced his voice louder. "Androgeus was at the Games of Athens. They say he had gone there for that purpose."

Not entirely true, but that was part of it. "Go on."

"I heard that he had taken several competitors with him. They won every contest. Every one. And in the end, all of those winners conceded to Androgeus rather than compete openly against him. The Atticans had to declare him the champion and bestow all honors upon him." He was worried about how he was making the story sound. "But he deserved the championship. He won every event against the Atticans that he did compete in. They were just resentful. It's not only the games. They have been very difficult to trade with lately. They are getting worse about everything."

That was true. That was why Minos had compelled Androgeus to go. A show of strength was what was needed to put them in their place. He had hoped that a defeat at their own games would be enough. Androgeus had opposed the idea arguing that a defeat on such personal territory would only rile them further. It appeared that he was right.

"So he won. What then?"

"You must remember that I was not there. I only know what I have been told, some of it by men of Attica."

Minos nodded to get him to continue.

"I was drinking wine with two of my crew in the city. We had struck a deal to trade felted blankets and colored oils for a load of magnesia powder. It was a difficult trade. They are beginning to see that their products are worth more than we have been paying them. So I bargained for less than I could have got last year. While the ship was being laden, I saw a friend which I had lost contact with some years ago. Normally I would stay with my ship while it was being loaded, but it was only powder. Anyone can load powder. I checked it for adulterations of flour or lime before loading and knew that the crew could manage the rest. It was important for future trade that I spend a bit of time and drink on my old friend."

"You are justifying your actions. Tell us what happened to Androgeus."

"A group of drunken revelers came down the lane, whooping and hollering. They had killed the mighty warrior, they shouted. Who was the most powerful now? They were calling to all men of Attica to rise against the parasitical men of Minos. That is what they said, Master. They yelled that the bodies could rot by the roadside and be picked to the bone by black vultures.

"It was my friend that helped us locate their bodies. He was born in Athens and knows every road. He knew where they must have been ambushed. We found them not far from the water. They had been on their way to their ship when the mob had waylaid them. We did not think one of them was alive. Arms had been broken, throats slit. All of them had the marks of being beaten with heavy clubs. Most of them had their skulls stove in. In the darkening evening, the only one we could find with any sign of breath was Androgeus. We did not recognize who he was at first. His face was covered with the dirt of the road where he fell. My friend washed his face with wine and rubbed it clean, and only then did we know who we had. Androgeus's companions were all dead, we were sure of that. We heard the mob coming back, and we shouldered Androgeus amongst us and ran back to the beach. I was going to take him back to his ship, but as we neared I saw that even his crew had been killed. They had murdered them too. One was slumped over the gunnels, and I could see him. I told the three to take Androgeus to my ship and set into the Harbor. It didn't matter about the magnesia. If they were pursued, they should keep their distance. I didn't think I would be long.

"Androgeus's ship had been looted. The guards had been taken unawares, I could tell that. Their weapons were still sheathed. The Atticans must have allowed themselves to be invited aboard in friendship and then turned on them unexpectedly. Strong wine and oil were spilled and their containers smashed." He paused and looked terrified. "I'm sorry. I have to tell you what I did. I was afraid that they would pursue us in Androgeus's ship. We never could have outrun them. I took the lamp and set fire to her. With the spilled oil she caught fast, and I jumped into the water and swam to my ship which was casting off."

"You burned Androgeus's ship? It was one of our finest."

He quaked. "Yes, Minos."

"Extraordinary judgment. How did you get back to Kriti so fast?"

"We rowed the whole distance. As well, we had favorable northerlies. I was in fear that we would be struck down with a meltemi, but we kept going. The gods were with us Minos. Any other time the winds would have made us take refuge."

"And Androgeus, this whole time?"

"He passed in and out of consciousness. When awake we could not understand him. We padded him as comfortably as we could. No one slept. We have not slept for days. We watched him in turns. That was our only physical rest. He was fitful. We gave him water sponged into a rolled towel to suck, but he could take no food. All we could do was keep him shaded in the daytime and covered at night. It is miraculous that he survived. I left my crew in Amnisos, but I had to come myself the rest of the way. Volunteers from there were able to carry him here with great haste. We came as fast as was humanly possible without killing him."

"You have done all anyone could do. I will see to your reward. Now leave us. The physician has all he needs."

The aged doctor was working his way down Androgeus's body. He called for his servant apprentice. Polyeidus, a man in his thirties, entered the room with a carry-box of assorted medicines and instruments. He set them upon a table and spread them in orderly fashion while his master finished a thorough physical exam. The apprentice laid each instrument in the manner prescribed by years of teaching; the forceps, drills, scalpels, a large and a small dilator, and specially shaped pieces of stone for grinding pharmaceutical ingredients. Aromatic herbs of mint and wormwood perfumed the air. He placed the calendar and astronomical chart behind the surgical tools and drugs.

The physician lightly felt and then palpated every muscle. He inserted probes into every orifice. When he had finished he ordered his assistant to light a cinnamon candle. The rare spice filled the room with its redolence.

Asclepius called again, "Two balm sticks."

Polyeidus brought two rolled lengths of papyrus, about a foot long, which had been scented with the extracts of thyme and rosemary. One end of each stick was narrower at one end than the other. A very thin coating of beeswax permeated the paper and held it in its slightly funneled shape. He placed the narrowed ends in each of Androgeus's ears and laid a ceramic tile between each and the bed covers. He set fire to the wide ends and let them burn half way down before blowing them out. Smoke from the smoldering tubes rose thick into their faces. Minos inhaled the fresh vapors. They had an immediate rejuvenating effect.

The physician removed the sticks after a few minutes, when the smoldering had stopped, and peered closely at each end while holding them close to his eye as if he were trying to see down their inner length. The half-burned tubes were almost full of wax, a large portion of which had to have been drawn from Androgeus's ear canals.

"Now some ambrosia."

The assistant, Polyeidus, passed him a tiny jar of especially pure, very clear honey. In it had been mixed a tincture of royal jelly, the viscous secretions from the pharyngeal glands of the worker honeybees fed to all larvae during their first few days and afterward only to those larvae selected to become queens.

Asclepius very softly, very delicately, massaged Androgeus's skull deformity and its periphery with the balm. When he was done he rubbed the excess into his own fingers.

He felt for pulsations and looked closely for raised areas or bluish colorations indicating the presence of subsurface arteries or veins. He made a cut with his bronze scalpel below the injury and drew the blade behind and up in a wide arc, much larger than the actual size of the injury. The incision began to issue blood. With wide tweezers he lifted the flap gently, teasing the skin away from its connective tissues with the scalpel, making short brushing sweeps as necessary. White bone underneath glistened between little rivulets of red blood as he folded the flap back.

"Pin it there," he ordered. His dispassionate voice, to his assistant, was as a demand shouted by a military general. The younger man leapt to the instrument table and took a bent pin, much like a barbless fishing hook, from the inventory. He was back in an instant and pushed the sharp end through the flap and through the still fastened scalp, securing it in place. The physician gave the flap a little tug to make sure.

"Give me the wash." He was handed a bottle of proofed wine, a special concoction boiled from white wine and distilled from its vapors into a water-cooled leather bag. Used only for medical purposes, it was quite unpalatable, it made the perfect wash for clearing blood from wounds. He drizzled some onto the broken bone and cleared it to view. There were two pieces of bone pressed inward and twisted askew, jammed together in unnatural positions.

"Hooks."

A small kit was rolled out on the bed. The physician reached over his patient and selected two pencil-sized tools like dental picks. One had a straight point and another curved. He dipped the points of each into the honey balm and pricked them into the cracks between the fragments. He captured one piece, the most depressed, and gave it a tug. It moved. Using a bit of leverage on the straight pointed tool he pried it into its proper orientation and place.

A bit more blood was stemming from the laceration he had created. He poured more wine onto the surgical site. Able to see better he observed that the area bulged. Carefully, slowly, Asclepius pried back the fragment of skull he had been working on and tilted it up, opening a gap between it and the other broken piece. Another few drops of wash and he could see a small portion of the outer membrane of the brain, the dura mater, the first of the three layers of meninges. It was swelled and pressing the fractured pieces outward. The jammed fragments had been holding the pressure back, contributing to the damage caused to Androgeus's brain. The physician pushed the point of his straight instrument into the glistening membrane. It resisted. He pushed harder, making an indent in the tough integument. Of a sudden it gave and the point pierced into the sheath, it having sprung outward to envelop the tool. He worked the instrument in the limited space that he had, pulling it side to side and up to down, careful not to let the point touch the unseen underlying brain.

A small bead of blood formed around the shaft of the little spear. He had his assistant hold it for a second while he found another tool, a sharply pointed scalpel quite different from the other. He dipped it in the balm then wedged it into the space beside the point and told the assistant to let go. He mumbled something profane as more blood leaked out and obscured his view and asked his helper to lavage the area again.

He could see this wasn't going to work. He took the curved pick and inserted it into the fissure, his face not a hand width away. He held the scalpel handle with his mouth while he manipulated the two picks. He managed to get the sharp curve into the same hole spiked by the straight and pulled back hard. He removed the straight one and resisted the urge to flick it across the room. A short spurt of blood followed the point it as it came free. He pressed the point of the razor-sharp scalpel into the integument, pushing with one hand against the pull of the other. He put his face to the side as he penetrated the tough membrane.

A shoot of red gel erupted out onto his hand and engirded the blade. He continued his sawing cut as his assistant squirted the area, making it as long as he could. Polyeidus held the tools for this part of the surgery, two curved picks to elevate and pull apart the two pieces of bone while the physician hooked away the rubbery clot that had been pressing against Androgeus's brain. The coagulation had been lodged between the layers of meninges covering and protecting the jelly-like organ. Asclepius worked delicately and slowly, seemingly taking forever, separating the clot from the inner meninx and easing it out with the utmost care. With this huge clot removed, or the better part of it, Androgeus should hopefully make at least a partial recovery. The physician wedged the broken fragments into their proper place and tapped them lightly, locking them firmly into their rightful places. To leave one or both of the fractured pieces out would leave too much of a chance of the sharp, bony edges causing further lacerations. With the pieces together the healing would take place much faster.

He used a trephine, a drill, to bore a hole just offset from the joining crack between one of the broken fragments and the whole skull. This would serve to relieve most of the pressure should it start to build again. He used a scraper to hand-finish the hole, carefully rounding its inner edges. As the assistant lavaged the trepanation, the physician sucked the fluid from the bottom of the hole with a reed. There was no longer any coloration to the fluid, it was running clear, indicating that all bleeding had stopped. All of the minute slivers of bone created by the scraping and drilling he removed by this method and spat onto the floor.

He gave the whole area a final cleansing and smeared some of the honey balm onto the exposed bone. Then he released the clip holding the flap back and pulled it down. He sewed it with a fine silk thread right around. He considered, for a moment, leaving a small opening in the suture line to allow for drainage but decided against it. He could tell if the pressure was building now by an increase in the size of the bulge over the surgical site. He would not have to go under the bone anymore. He could just make another incision if he had to and go under the skin to pull out any forming clots.

One more smear of honey and he was done. He had no idea of the complex chemistry involved that sped healing by combating infection but he knew from generations of experimentation that it worked. Enzymes from the bee's laryngeal glands reacted with the glucose of the honey now exposed to oxygen and created disinfecting hydrogen peroxide and the antibiotic gluconolactone. Moreover, honey is hypertonic and thus absorbs water needed by pestilent bacteria to live. They don't even get a foothold in the wound. All that was far beyond the physician's grasp. It was enough that he had witnessed for himself honey healing open ulcers that had defied other treatments for years, that it made new skin grow at double the rate of normal healing, and that, left on its own, honey seemed to defy decay, staying golden and sticky forever in a jar.

He left the cleaning-up to Polyeidus. He washed his hands and dried them on a cotton towel.

"I have done what I can," he told Minos, who had been watching in fascination and silence. "Bless him and pray for him in Council. Mostly the matter rests in the hands of the Gods now."

He left, picking up his long staff on the way. Minos watched him exit through the door without closing it behind him. The apprentice scurried about, quickly gathering instruments and bundling them for washing at some other place. After he had done that he called for a maidservant. The two of them moved Androgeus's body enough to remove the bedclothes and slip in clean ones. Polyeidus gave one final anointing of honey balm over the surgical site and they, too, were gone.

Minos was with Androgeus alone. He sat on the edge of the bed watching him breathe. How foolish his brother looked without hair. How sick. His rage boiled inside.

His dream. Now it all made perfect sense. Androgeus had died, effectively. But the doctor had revived him. Not even that; it was he, Minos, who had called for the doctor, taken Androgeus in when all could have been solved, any danger of truth leaking out, by simply letting nature take its course. He hadn't done that, had he? He had shown compassion and had saved Androgeus. They were the two snakes. The two brothers. And the look the two snakes gave him once again filled him with the greatest foreboding and dread. His dream would haunt him again. If only he could never sleep.

It had come to this, then. His life once again in the hands of the Gods.

A promise made so long ago; an oath made.

Androgeus was the real Minos.

The Chosen.

* * *

Daedalus had been given a supply of clay and the job of making ceramic bells. His mean room was dark with the only light coming from a small window far too narrow to climb through. Hanging from the lintel was one of the creations he was to duplicate in bulk.

Many crafts were made in the Temple-palace. The most superlative faience, glazed earthenware pottery, was manufactured here and, to a lesser degree, at other Temple-palaces. All silver and goldsmithing was done here at Knossos, and all jewelry.

Bells had been in use in religious festivals on Kriti for hundreds of years and were now becoming popular among the general population as wind chimes. They were unique to Kriti at this time, in fact not existing yet anywhere else.

Daedalus had been offered a small potters wheel but had turned it down. If he was to be forced to work for his welfare, he would work his way. He knew Minos was intentionally humiliating him by reducing a sculptor and architect of his renown to a common potter, but he was determined to make the best of it. If he didn't complain, and if he did his work with the quality he was celebrated for instead of creating faulty bells on purpose, then he just might be able to win back some favor. Then he could outwit Minos.

He had made a few bells and selected one with perfect pitch; the one he kept hanging in his window. Every time the wind blew, its chime reminded him of his inventive genius. He wasn't being self-congratulatory, he was being true to fact. There was something else about the way the bell rang that gave him hope and inspiration, though he didn't know exactly what it was yet. It would not be long before the thought would creep into his mind that Minos might control the land and sea, but he did not control the wind.

Daedalus had devised a way of pressing the bells into shape in a way that no one had previously thought of; a way of preserving the perfect profile and weight that he found contributed everything to the distinct ring of the bell.

He had a balanced platform, a small one, beside his clay pile. One side had a measured weight exactly the weight of his bell in its wet clay form. Onto the other side he added a clump of clay, which tipped the balance in the other direction and from that he picked off bits of clay until the balance struck the middle. The measured weight he used was a little heavier than the painted bell to allow for water loss during firing. It had taken some trial and error to get it just right, but he had achieved it in only a few days.

He had another smaller bell, an inverted cup really, like a Shriner's hat with a small hole in the top, that he over-fitted with a thin leather cover that he had oiled. That prepared and set aside, he rolled the clay ball into a thick pancake and pulled the sides up, flipping it quickly onto its side as he rolled the now folded sides flat with his rolling pin half inserted into the open end. It only took him a couple of minutes to get the clay into this preparatory shape, thinning the walls of the work and smoothing them by the pin on the inside and the table on the out. It was awkward work. The hat-shaped clay had to be kept moving or the upper walls would fall inward and ruin the piece. Eyeballing it, he gauged that it was almost the right size. He stood it on end and dropped the leather covered mold inside. Then he rolled and tapped the whole thing until it was perfectly smooth and a lip of excess clay was worked out top and bottom. That at the top he worked together, one little upturned wing on either side. He trimmed off the excess clay at the bottom and shaped it into a snake, a cord, which he fastened to the top between the wings in an arch that would later be used for a place to fasten the hanging string. He used a roll of stiffened parchment to maintain the arch of the clay hanger as it dried. Just one last thing to do; two holes in the top to hang the clapper. He pushed a flat-ended peg hard into the two places between the arch and the two wings on either side. The clay was squeezed out from where he pressed the peg through and forced to the sides, leaving nice round holes. He licked his finger and with his saliva as lubricant smoothed out the bumps and imperfections. He laid it aside.

He picked one of the bells he had made yesterday and set it on the table. It was dry enough. He rapped it a few times with his knuckles to loosen it from the mold. He pushed a pipe into the single hole at the bottom of the inserted cup and blew into it. The cup jostled and peeled free as pressurized air separated the insert from the leather sheath. He gently tipped it out into his cupped hand then peeled out the oiled leather. The remaining bell, flawlessly formed, he set back on the table for another day's drying before he would abrade it with fine sand and send it off to the kilns.

A few painted bells had been returned to him for completion. By completion he meant testing. Young women with long, supple fingers were needed to finish the suspension of the wooden clapper within the bell. They had the dexterity his fat fingers lacked. He couldn't manage the tying of the invisible knots that fastened the string ends together. He rang the bells one at a time, impressing himself with their lovely tonal resonance. Only the perfect would he send to Minos to do with as he would.

A tink of metal on metal alerted him to someone unlatching the door of his little cell.

The door swung outward, which prevented the prisoner from removing the hinge pins. It was Icarus, his son. He didn't get up either as the youth entered or as the door closed behind him by way of an unseen hand.

"I have brought you this." He held out a rock-crystal lens.

"How did you get this?" he asked as he took it.

"I appealed personally to Minos."

"To Minos? And he gave you this?"

"Yes. I told him it was not fit that you who had built this great Palace, and contributed so much during your life, should be confined to a potter's labors in this prison cell."

"He knows it isn't fit. That is why I'm here."

"It wasn't your fault that Pasiphae died. It was her own doing. I think even Minos realizes that. If he thought that you had been wholly responsible, then he would be dealing with you as a convicted murderer. He's not doing that."

"Are you so sure? What, exactly, is he doing with me?"

"Holding you until he knows himself. Have you ever known a prisoner to be kept within the Palace walls? It has never happened. You are not so highly respected that you would not be imprisoned with other murderers, if that was what you were."

Daedalus was not sure that he liked his son's candor. He knew he did not mean any disrespect and that he was only standing up for his father. He wished he could have more love for the youth, but there was something about him that reminded him of his nephew that he had murdered decades ago. Talos had that same attitude, the same simpering dedication, that galled at him. Perhaps it would be justice if Minos caught him up on like charges; latent but just. He had always known in his heart that he could not escape his nephew's vengeance forever. One day he would have to suffer for his crime.

Daedalus tried to be agreeable. There was really no reason why he should dislike his young son. And no one else was coming by to visit. He fingered the lens and held it to his eye. He held a finger in front of it and moved the glass back and forth slightly until he achieved focus. With a magnification power of seven, the lens showed the clearly defined ridges and swirls of his fingerprint and the minute particles of dried clay caught between them that had looked like dust at normal view. He was impressed with the perfect clarity of the lens. This was one of the better ones. He slowly moved the lens away from his eye and watched the image grow to larger magnification, although its clarity was diminishing. At a power of twenty, the image was so distorted and blurred that it was barely recognizable.

"This is a superb lens. I still find it amazing that Minos would let you have it; that is, let me have it. How did you plead for it?"

"I told him you would be better suited to making gold seals and rings than chimes. He did not think about it long."

"And does he wish me to manufacture gold out of the air?"

Icarus reached into a concealed pocket in his skirt. He withdrew a nugget of gold and handed it to Daedalus. He expected his father to react but he just took it and placed it on the table.

Icarus couldn't stand the few seconds of silence. "I have other news. Bad news."

Daedalus looked at him and waited.

"It is Androgeus."

"Androgeus?" That concerned him. Androgeus had always been his best friend. "What about him?"

"He is very sick. They say he may die."

Daedalus fell back in a slump. "He is dying?"

"They say he may." He was glad, in an offhand sort of way, that this news was at least greeted with an emotional response.

"What is he sick of?"

"He was assaulted in Attica. I believe he was competing at some athletic event and was attacked by a group of villains afterward. He was saved by some brave captain who risked his life rescuing him and getting him here. I have also heard that the Palace Physician operated on his brain."

That news worried Daedalus. Limited were the numbers of very sick individuals who were given that extreme treatment, and fewer there were who lived through or after it. His dear friend. He longed to be at his side.

"Find out more if you can."

"I will. Is there anything else I can do for you?"

Daedalus tapped his fingers on the table. "Perhaps there is." He considered. "How much of my wealth has Minos seized?"

"None, really. He has turned title of everything to me."

"You? He has not seized anything?"

"No." He looked down. "To Minos, it is as if you were already dead."

Already dead. And Icarus, being the only child, got it all. That could only mean one of two things; that he was doomed to be forever imprisoned, or that he would eventually be placed before the bull. Minos would be most inclined to the latter. It would suit his justice to have him die by the same creature who killed his beloved. Yes, he admitted, she was his beloved too. And how many others? How many hearts were crushed the day she passed into the eternities? How many men hated him for what he had done?

Daedalus waved his son away.

Icarus took his queue. He had often tried to bridge the gap between himself and his father but he had long since realized that forcing the issue only made things worse. He would do as he was bidden and investigate Androgeus's health. Daedalus would be most interested in that.

Icarus went to the Council Residential Suites. Androgeus had been moved from Minos's apartment back to his own. The Physician had insisted he be in his most familiar surroundings when he regained consciousness.

The Physician had additional difficulties to deal with other than the pressure on Androgeus's brain, which he had relieved. His patient had been severely dehydrated and malnourished. The quickest way to introduce fluids into his system was through a tube into the bowel. Every hour the apprentice was charged with inserting the wooden cylinder into Androgeus's rectum and pouring in a measured amount of fluid. The Physician had called for a fluid of three parts clean water, into which had been dissolved honey, mixed with one part of boiled seawater. At first, the blend worked as an enema, causing the expulsion of the last remaining bowel contents. The second time though, there was nothing left to evacuate and the fluid was completely absorbed, the salt and sugar aiding Androgeus's condition. He was urinating again. That was a particularly important requirement. He had to get the yellow poison out of his body. The assistant appraised what was micturated and compared it to the volume injected from the rear. Ideally, the measures should be very close.

Icarus passed both medical practitioners in the hall. They were going to another call of some sort. He caught a fragment of their conversation as they passed but could understand none of their jargon. He wasn't sure if they were talking about Androgeus or not.

The door was slightly askew. He peeked through and saw Minos sitting in a chair at Androgeus's bedside. He was holding the other man's hand.

Icarus pressed his eye to the crack, double checking to be sure that there was no one else about. Everyone in this quarter should be at breakfast at this time. He was actually surprised to see that Minos was still here. He could see Androgeus move for a moment, wiggling as if to make himself more comfortable. Minos continued to hold his hand.

Androgeus's eyes were still closed. Minos spoke to him as had been requested by the Physician. He had thought that, now that Androgeus was showing limited signs of recovery, anything that might bring back memories would be sure to help restore his health.

"Brother," he said. "Had things been different. Had the labrys of responsibility fallen to you instead of myself, as it should have. Had these things been so then you would be whole instead of wasting in a coma. How many times have I wished you to assume your rightful inheritance? I have done well; you have always given encouragement and sage advice. But without your aegis, I have not the imperative to carry this station forth.

"Was it not wrong of Minos to pass the labrys to me? What were his thoughts when he sent you to the adoption of the man of Amnisos? 'All things have reason' he said. 'All things have purpose.' He ordained both of us Minos and sent you away. To what end? To be only a member of Council? No. Much more than that. I could not do what I do without you. But even that is not all. You have been ordained beyond what I have. You have been made greater than I. And so you cannot die.

"Oh, the Gods. Why would they not let you know? You must not die. You must not abandon me to myself."

He bowed his head and wept.

Icarus's heart was pounding. He could not be caught here. He turned, careful to make not a sound, and fled running back to Daedalus. No. He had to be more cautious than that. He slowed to a walk just in time. People were returning from breakfast. He had made it to the residential area away from the Royal and Council apartments and did not raise any eyebrows. Greetings still were tethered as he was new, having only just taken over Daedalus's comforts, but he was accepted in this area of the Palace.

There was no rationale in going straight to Daedalus. He was only allowed one visitor each day, and any insistence to the contrary would be like raising a warning signal. It would have to wait until tomorrow.

Daedalus wasn't going anywhere.

~~~~~~

Chapter 15

Psychosis

1898 BCE

Nothing was real. Why was he a child? He wasn't a child. A ball fell from his hand, a ball he didn't even know he had. It rolled away from him, down the hall and under a door. It was so strange. He wasn't walking, he felt he couldn't even move, yet he was following. He seemed to go right through the door, like a spirit, something he knew to be impossible, and yet it was utterly real.

The ball came to rest against one huge pithoi, then vanished into the terracotta. His hand reached out, without any purpose of movement, to touch the decorated surface of the jar, and an indescribable force pulled him in.

He panicked. He was immersed within honey filling the pithoi, and the runny sweetness filled his mouth and lungs. He writhed but the fluid was so thick he could barely move, barely breathe.

Oddly, he could see through the walls of the storage jar, now that he was inside. A dead snake just out of reach struck him as the oddest thing, though it didn't take his mind off of the fact that he still could not breathe. The snake was an evil portent, of that he was sure, as he gave himself up to drowning in the syrupy grave.

He gave up struggling. He was impossibly weak. Another snake slithered into the room and crept along to its dead acquaintance, nudging alongside and ignoring him in the storage jar completely. It had a herb in its mouth, which it laid on the lifeless scales of its mate.

From his vantage point, incarcerated in the pithoi, he watched, incredulous, as the lifeless rope slowly revived, and turned to look at him. Both snakes seemed to stare, to say something, but he could not make out what. He became terrified again, and forcibly made his body move. He was near the end, and fear and desperation gave him one last burst of strength. One last look before he succumbed and the snakes were still staring. Coiling up a physician's staff they flicked out their tongues in unison.

* * *

Minos woke screaming, his skin crawling with the discomfort of ten thousand droplets of sweat sticking his cold flesh to the sheet like a viscid suppuration. The dream had come again, so many times he had lost count, if ever one would want to number such a repetitive torment. His long hair rung damp, adhering to his back and around his neck like thick webs binding an insect as it shrinks from the scything mandibles of hell.

Minos had enjoyed opium in religious festivals most of his life but only in the last year had he been demanding it to relieve his mental anguish. Sometimes he could see his precious Pasiphae dance for his personal pleasure. Sometimes she was real; sometimes she came in dreams. At first he was at pains to deny the opium's domination and capacity to intoxicate, asserting to his doctor and Council what they already knew, that the drug produced a rooted, infallible pleasure lasting, at most, half the day. But before long, under the influence of heavy dosages, he was singing invoked ballads of the limitless powers he felt bestowed upon him.

The converse of pleasant and desirable experiences happened infrequently at first, hallucinated demons that haunted and tormented his sleep. In time he could not sleep at all without the drug; every joint hurt, every muscle ached. He lost interest in management of the affairs of state, preferring to sit in drugged idleness as musicians and dancers entertained him.

Lately, he had not been blessed with any pleasurable visions. Tonight a dozen demons, not gods exactly but made of the same stuff as gods, surrounded him. These fearful intermediaries between the human world and the world of the exalted conjured others of their ilk from every cove and from under every table. Vast corteges assembled in mournful pomp, and paraded lamentably, friezes of never-ending procession conceiving in him wretched melancholy and gloom. He was not merely frightened. He became profoundly and suicidally despondent.

His scream terrified his young consort, who bolted up and fled the room without her robe. Minos's attendant rushed in with a bronze lamp to give light to the frightening dark, to oust the incubi and succubi back to the cracks and crevices of shadow. He crushed a small amphora under his step, the shards of broken ceramic embedding in the fleshy sole of his foot causing him to yelp and hop about, the flame of the lamp dancing wildly in his hand. Two of the tiny pottery jugs, the size and much the same shape as an opium seed pod, had been emptied by Minos as his dinner substitute the previous evening. His appetite for the drug was becoming fiercely insatiable. Neither food nor sex was of any imperative to him without the drug, and with it both fled his thoughts altogether.

Grown and packaged on Kypros opium was fast becoming quite a supplement to the income brought in by copper. Not only was it used in the religious rituals of Kriti, but also Egypt and the islands and coasts of the Aegean. The markup was phenomenal and it was, of course, the Minoans who profited greatest.

There were those who were concerned enough to intimate that Minos was becoming, or had become, a slave to the very drug over which he, by rights, should have held mastery. Completely preoccupied it was all he talked about, his only substantive interest. His intricately designed chequerboard, once practiced to obsession, rested unused for the longest time, its cold gold and crystal and ivory cohesion unwarmed by the touch of human hands. The draughtsmen cones sat invitingly upon the two-cubit by one-cubit board, all bordered by seventy-two daisies in precious metal and stone, but no one would handle them.

As the attendant lit the disparate lamps around the apartment to give Minos comfort another came with a further dose of opium. Minos needed it now as much as ever to relieve his awful withdrawal. The attendant heated the little vase over the nearest lamp's flame to thin the mixture of opium paste dissolved in honey and white wine. The paste had to be adulterated so that it could be introduced to, and later extracted from, its narrow-necked container.

Minos leapt from his bed and snatched the amphora away, heedless of the hot ceramic burning his hand. He tipped it up and sucked the end of the bottle, making frustrated noises in consideration of the lingering, glutinous fluid.

He could not stand the wait. He had not given his attendant enough time for the fluid to thin. He hammered the miniature amphora on the table again and again until it broke in his fist and stuffed the syrupy and bloody fragments into his mouth.

There he stood, eyes closed and face heavenward, tonguing the sweet drug from its jagged shards. His health would be restored, his hysteria relieved.

Perhaps he would even glimpse his beloved Pasiphae.

* * *

Daedalus had one of the rings, the unfinished one, clamped into a small vise.

On the desk was the one he had just finished; the Ring of Minos, made specially to order for the king. Daedalus held it up to the sunbeam streaming bright through the little window and angled the heavy piece before his frame-mounted crystal magnification lens. The ring had been detailed so intricately and with such precision that it could not have been done without the lens, and without the lens being mounted in the frame and the ring in the vice to free up both his hands it could not have been done at all. At the forefront of the scene was a sea-journeying Priestess, garbed only in a skirt, steering a shrine-laden boat with a rear-facing dragon's head. She was enchanting it across a bay as she worked only the extended steering oar. On the rocky shore the boulders were shaped like fruits of the field, supporting three separate shrines, two of which sprouted branches and leaves. Beside the left shrine, a fully clothed presiding goddess gestures at the sacral horns on her altar while a levitating deity watches over her. On the right a naked goddess kneels on her shrine, and holds a branch while her other hand searches for fruit in its boughs. A third goddess, a smaller sprite, plucks fruit from the central shrine and tree, her head back and body curled in sensual fulfillment as an elongated fruit dangles from her uplifted arm.

He slipped it partway onto his finger to hold it steady. It was not small like an ordinary band might be. It was an oval, panoramic picture that required its size to be quite overbearing for a finger ornament. True, it was more than that; it was a seal, too, for stamping the genuineness of correspondence.

The Ring of Minos. The Seal of Minos.

Daedalus handed the signet to Icarus, who would present it to the king. He fingered it and squinted, holding it close to his eye to discern, if he could, the incredible detail. Daedalus had been lent the seal maker's most sophisticated tools; cutting wheels, fast-twirling drills, and gravers of bronze. With the aid of the magnifying lens he had worked extraordinary detail into the variety of seal images, sometimes on rings, but more often on the cylindrical seals used as signatures for the elite. Mostly he worked in stone, banded agate or orange carnelian, sometimes also in ivory or bone, but on commissions as this, the works were of gold.

"What news? my son."

Icarus lowered the ring. "Minos has besieged the city of Athens."

"Because of their attack on Androgeus."

"More than that. They have broadcast rumors that Pasiphae has mothered a monster."

"A monster?" He was incredulous. "How could they spread such slander?"

"Somehow the news of the manner of Pasiphae's death could not be contained. It is hushed within the confines of this island, but still the whispers circulate. One of the sailors must have taken liberties with his knowledge and told. A ransom has been offered for the traitor's name but I have heard nothing of any report thus far."

"But a monster? What are they saying?"

"They are saying that the story of her death is a lie; that it is only a shield to secret the truth of her birthing of a half-man, half-bull."

"Outrageous," he stormed, provoked at the gross affront to the dignity of his love.

"They say that the bull-monster of Minos is kept hidden in the Labyrinth, that Minos has raised it secretly and feeds it those who emigrate here. They say that Minos is evil and that all Minoans are cannibalistic. And you, Father. They say you have been consumed by the flesh eaters."

Daedalus shook his head in disbelief. "It is they who are monstrous. Are they so fatuous that they could think Minos would stand for such insult?"

"You know them best."

"They cannot win against Minos. What fools. He will call into favor everyone who owes their allegiance to him, or at least as many as he needs. They have no chance."

* * *

Morning sun rose with the birds and blinded Minos as he squinted against it. He swallowed another dollop of opium elixir and washed it down with too much wine. His head hurt and he hadn't been able to sleep with the recurring bad dreams. They were becoming more sensual, and more terrifying. He had dreamt that the demons had been prodding him, urging him on toward an unseen but familiar girl of wondrous beauty, not as physically beautiful as his wife Pasiphae but purer and finely virtuous of character. The dark stage play of fantasy performed over and over until he hurt with desire, never achieving what he needed, never being allowed by the object of his yearning to get close enough to make the move. He had lain in his soft bed fantasizing in a half-wakened state between reality and sleep over something that he could not reach, when the comfort girl beside him would have willingly acquiesced to anything he could have asked. But she was not what he desired. He did not know himself who or what it was.

People were beginning to move about in the square below his window. He had forgotten that people could actually appreciate this time of day. The noise of chirping birds struck a discord in his ear and the sun seemed more of an uncomfortable glare than a peaceful light. Across the field, a solitary figure was unhurriedly ambling toward the Palace. Her breasts weren't exposed, the figure wearing the warmer garb of women who were more shielded against the coolness of night air, a belt holding her short dress tight at the waist. The woman had a small pack slung over her shoulder and carried a pheasant by the feet in her other hand. Could she have been hunting? Some women did that but it was rare, especially for the aristocracy, which this woman obviously belonged to. He could tell her standing, when she looked to the side, by the way her hair was tied with the sacral knot behind her head.

He watched with mounting curiosity as she came closer. The opium was taking rapid effect, along with the alcohol, and his headache was vanishing as his interest grew. She was familiar, somehow, and pretty even from this distance. What an unusual woman she must be, a young woman, he could tell

445

that much. His heart stopped mid-beat. It was her. It was the dark phantasm of his dreams. His breath ceased for a moment as he stood there as startled as if he had been struck by a bolt from the sky. He recalled the chase, and the desire he had felt, and his organ swelled against the weight of his skirt. He threw his goblet down and rushed off through the Palace in pursuit.

It had been a lovely morning for Britomartis. Up long before the dawn, she had made her way to the woods she so adored. One day maybe she could build a home there. She was comfortable enough living in the Palace, but there was something about the building that seemed so unnatural, so confining. She much preferred to spend her time out-of-doors, especially when the weather favored it. Other girls her age preferred to while the days away making eyes at young men, but not she, she liked solitude away from their amorous approaches. By the dozens they had tried to woo her with offers of friendship, marriage, rich presents, and even bold offers of sexual favor, all of which she rejected outrightly. She had not the slightest inclination to cavort with men. There was only one she found appealing, but he was far too old to have any interest in her. She had almost spoken to him once as he passed in the Grand Staircase, but thought it more in order to wait to be spoken to. He had passed without so much as an acknowledgment, so she let the matter rest. It hadn't been that she found him attractive as so many of the others had, she just would have liked to see for herself if he was as interesting personally as his works implied he must be. It was silly, of course. No old man was ever interested in just talking to a young woman, especially when she was all decorated and garbed to entice him. She never really liked the restrictive attire of the Temple-palace. It didn't matter how narrow one's waist was, they always expected that it should be trussed thinner. She much preferred to be as she was now, with a simple dress and a comfortable belt to keep the wind from blowing the skirt up past her waist. She kept the sacral knot because it left her hair tied behind her back and out of the way. Hunting was no time to have long hair falling about all over her shoulders and front. She liked the feel of her breasts hanging free and the tickle of the fabric against her nipples when they undulated as she walked. It was a pleasant sensation, but she didn't associate the satisfying fulfillment within her torso as anything sensual, certainly nothing that had anything to do with any man.

She drew the bird she had hunted down up to her line of sight and gave it a satisfied look. Beautiful creatures they were, arrayed in multi-colored splendor worthy of something from the heavens. Most singular that they were the males of their kind. Why was it that only among man was the female decorated more than the male? As if the female wanted the male to chase after her. All she wanted was for them to leave her alone and at peace. She tired of putting them off. In the Temple all she wanted to do was spend time with her little monkey and sit in the gardens. The little fellow would be liking a bit of meat from her bird when it was cooked. A few people were already up and about and she knew the kitchens would have the hot ovens fired up by now. She could put the pheasant in with the loaves. The head cook never objected and she always offered the drumsticks and wings to him, preferring to keep only the lighter body meat for herself. They still looked at her queerly when she brought in her catch. It was more that they knew her method of hunting rather than the fact that she was the only young woman they knew of that hunted. She would quietly sit listening until she heard the rustling of feathers from one of the birds squirming to make itself more comfortable. Then she would creep up, silent as a cat in a garden, to where she was so close to the nest she could smell the gamy scent of the bird nestled in the protection of its bush. Slowly she would move, undetectable to any human, so quietly that she might only rouse enough suspicion in a bird to put it on edge and freeze it in the dark. Eventually, it would calm in its familiar nest and forget that anything other than a passing wisp had stirred up a few dry leaves. Another rustle of its feathers and it would find its neck clutched by a swift hand in the pitch black, followed by a rapid flick of its body and an instant numbness as it passed quickly and curiously into a darkness its tiny brain could not fathom.

A man veritably flew from the West Entrance, bolting in her direction, past the few who gave him glances of surprise as he ran past. It was Minos. Whatever was he doing running her way? He saw her and slowed his pace to a fast walk. He was coming right for her. She looked around behind her to see if he might be targeting something or someone else, but there was nothing. For some reason, he was coming toward her. She slowed her walk. There was something very odd about this. She could hardly run from her king, but a quiet voice was telling her to mind him, to be on her guard.

Minos was feeling the euphoria of opium and wine intermingling in his veins and, in tandem, blocking the undesirable righteousness of the spirit of Rhea. He saw the object of his desire and was bound to have her. Lithe and sinewy as a gazelle the huntress stopped her walk and waited as he came up to her, her legs astride in anticipation of his thrust, her arms masculinely gripping the broken neck of a pheasant and the strap of her pack, her berry-like nipples prodding two little bumps onto the light linen fabric which covered her tantalizingly concealed breasts.

He breathed hard as he stopped in front of her, not with exhaustion for he was still in wonderful physical condition in spite of his addictions and his sedentary lifestyle. It was lust. His dark dreams were taking shape and breathing the breath of life.

"What is your name?" he asked.

"I am Britomartis," she responded. She knew that intoxicated leer, and would have left or made a rude retort had it been any other than Minos before her.

"Britomartis. The name means sweet virgin. How appropriate. It is a fact, I trust."

She could not bear his lascivious gaze, hypnotic, staring, manic. She did not answer, not in defiance but in shock that he, of all people, could be so inappropriately bold. It was the king's place to be the epitome of decorum in public and set the example for the citizenry. She had known of his lust for other young women and knew of the arrangements Pasiphae had made for him to be with them at night. She herself had been offered the opportunity of sleeping with him but had turned the offer down. There had been very few to do so but there was no dishonor in it, being better that Minos should be granted a willing rather than reluctant partner. Now he had come to her directly and she wondered if he would be so easy to brush off now that he had taken a personal fancy to her.

"I can tell that it is true. No matter. Your name means nothing in reality. And after, if you please me, I will give you another name."

Britomartis's mouth dropped open. Was he intending to take her right here? She dropped her eyes and saw that he was rock hard. She started to make a sound, to explain politely that she had no interest in offending Minos but could not possibly entertain his desires.

Minos lunged at her but she was too fast. He was the stronger and probably the faster, but in his drugged state he lost some of his ability. She dropped her parcels and dodged him, deaking to the left as his hand swiped her shoulder. A strong finger caught her dress and tore at it as she pulled herself away and fell to the grass. The linen ripped to her belt as she pulled back. Minos tore the whole upper portion away as she fled backward and screamed.

"You cannot run from me. I am Minos. I am your King," he shouted in rage. He had garnered the full attention of the few who were outside the walls of the Palace, and they all stopped what they were doing to stare. None would dare to interfere.

Britomartis ran toward the city, staying away from the people in fear that they might ally themselves against her and aid Minos in his bent passion. He was hot in pursuit as she peeled through Knossos. The two ran like white rivers through the still waking city, down quiet streets, the only sound being from Minos as he shouted demands for her to stop. Out the south of the city she fled, down the valley to the river, splashing across it and onto the far bank. Still he engaged in the chase. She could not shake him even by the steep climb up the rise. She was astounded to see the bulge of his bobbing organ, still inflated after all this exertion, the unquenchable lust in his eyes not even slightly diminished.

People had gathered behind them on the far bank, some obviously giving chase to the two of them, for curiosity's sake alone, or to assist one or the other of them. She knew not what reason they had followed but could not chance hope that it might be to assist her, and so she ran. She sprinted and hurdled until her legs felt as dead as the neck that she had earlier held in her fist.

Minos contrived to gain on her, but could not. Cursing his age, he rued the day he first took the opium. It was slowing him down. Easy to say such a thing when he had enough of it in his system. The thought hit him like a blasphemy and he prayed for strength, repenting that he ever had a bad thought against the drug so necessary for his dalliances into the under and over worlds. At once he was revived, and he raced forth anew. Britomartis's dress flew up to the belt with every step at this speed, her firmly rounded fundament and tight skin flexing and straining, bared to view and compelling him toward her in craving, yearning exigency. He was almost upon her. She could hear his noisy breath behind her and feared to look lest it momentarily slow her down. A final lunge and a grab and he had her remnant of dress. It pulled through her belt and tripped her as she ran, and they both fell together in the grass. Her fear and momentum carried her farther than Minos and she frantically kicked off the linen tripping up her feet. She was up and running, before Minos could recover, with only the belt still around her waist.

Like a deer she fled. Like a dog he pursued. Away from any roadway, they ran across field after field, hill and dale. Miles they ran. Nothing would stop Britomartis, and nothing short of stopping her would slow Minos. The huntress and the virgin. He had to have her. Naked she was like a raw animal bounding across the landscape, an untamed beast of rippling beauty lent by gods to tempt and satisfy him. He had not known such passion in ages; wondered if he had ever experienced such desire. He had but to catch this gift from heaven and he would have his reward.

Britomartis fled over the top of a rise and down an embankment before she could think what she was doing. She was too spent from the chase to reason properly. The sea was before her and steep rocks rising on either side meant she could go nowhere but down. The way was narrowing and her only real escape to safety was behind and sealed off by a determined madman. Minos had fallen behind, but he was still on her trail and would quickly be upon her. She paused at the edge of the cliff. There was no way down. The sheer face offered no respite. A skiff at the base in the waters of the glassy sea seemed little more than a mote floating as so much litter from an uncaring fisher. She trembled, even under the sun and after her long run. It was all for naught. She would have no choice but to submit.

Minos slowed. He had her. He knew these cliffs and knew that there was no way down. He walked toward her to save his strength in case she made a last second dodge to the side. She was a quick one, she might still have a chance if he wasn't careful, and he was almost at the end of his capacity to run any farther. He swelled again. Her beauty was outstanding, her soaked skin and hard-pumped muscles capturing and reflecting sparkles of sunlight. She turned to face him. To her he was a dark silhouette against the glare, looming larger until he reached man-size. He didn't speak, neither did she. It was inevitable. He was there, she was there, only feet apart, breathing hard, both of them. She saw the silhouette move at her side, and a hand tenderly touched her waist and caressed her flank up to her breast.

"I will not have you," she screamed and jerked back. Minos startled but held his position.

"Not have me?" he hissed at her. "I am Minos, you ungrateful virgin. You should be on your knees thanking me for the privilege."

Minos could not see her tears amongst the droplets of perspiration. To submit to this man, no matter who he was, was a reprehensible conception. She felt again the hand at her breast.

She would not have it.

"No," she screamed, and launched herself backward off the cliff.

Minos lunged too late to stop her, her slippery body sliding through his clasp. Panting in horror, almost losing his footing on the cliff edge, he beheld her career to the water, and the white ring surrounding the place where she splashed through the surface of the sea. In a moment calm had returned, and there was no evidence she had ever been.

Minos shook his head with regret. He had never wanted this to happen, not in his wildest imaginings. How could she have cast away her life like that? All he wanted was her maidenhead.

She must have been mad.

* * *

Minos pushed the large, oblong ring onto his finger. Fabulous, he thought, careful not to let his pleasure show. He splayed his fingers and admired it in such a way as to indicate that he was merely inspecting it. It was such a time as this where he was almost glad he had, at least temporarily, suspended Daedalus's death sentence for his crime against the state. The massive white bull's head hung mounted on the wall behind him. It had not fared as well, a monument to Minos's superiority over even such a creature as that.

He nodded, dismissing Icarus. That nod meant everything. Icarus was satisfied that Minos had accepted the ring. It meant that Daedalus's uses were not being ignored and that he would be kept alive much longer. As long as Daedalus could provide service with more skill than any other, then his reprieve would eventually be assured.

Icarus took his place at the back rank and file while other presentations took place, mostly premiums of precious stones and metal. He did not pay much heed to the rest of the program, concerned as he was with devising ways to curry favor for his dear father. If only there were some way to convince Minos that Daedalus was no danger and that all would be better served by allowing him out of his prison cell.

One of the considerations that did capture Icarus's attention was from Athens. The Captain laid out a small fortune in gold. "This is the presentation from King Aegeus. It is only a partial compensation. More will be forthcoming depending on your demands. He offers full surrender, and we will have our ambassador reestablished, with King Aegeus retained as head of state."

Minos gripped the seat of his chair until his knuckles whitened. His facial muscles tightened around his mouth and eyes in ripples of hatred.

"Partial compensation," he muttered. "Send back his pathetic partial compensation. I will not accept it." The men who had placed it removed it hurriedly. It was most unusual for Minos to reject a presented gift. "They have maliciously vilified a Goddess and will pay greater penalty. Our siege is holding without effort. I will not negotiate with them. How much longer before they fail?"

"They have weakened to the point where they are offering conciliation of a partial defeat. For two years they have been afflicted with drought and, in fact, have been importing our grains to augment their needs for that entire time. Cut from our supply line they cannot hope to survive. They are in a famine situation within the perimeter of our siege and are willing to suffer humility. It will not be much longer before they are ready to offer complete surrender. Perhaps even by the time of my return."

"Then tell Aegeus this; we will keep his gold and he will send me seven times that amount again. He will also send an annual tribute of seven of his finest youths, and seven of his finest maidens. Let it be known that they will be condemned into the Labyrinth as sacrifice, to be devoured by the Bull of Minos. The Minotaur.

"And first, select his own children."

MINOS

~~~~~~

Chapter 16

Escape

1895 BCE

The black-sailed ship, the ship of death, eased up to the berth. Theseus sat shackled, leg and arm, to the bow with his six prisoner companions. At the stern, where the oarsmen could watch them, sat the seven maidens, each shackled only by one ankle. Their hearts fluttered in trepidation as the port of Amnisos seemed to slip underneath them. The ship bumped harshly against stone as it came to a rough halt. The Captain of this ship was a crude man, his crew equally unrefined. This was an Attican ship given leave to ply the seas this one time each year. The crew could not leave the confines of the ship. The Captain alone would accompany the prisoners to Knossos. Allowed only to speak to his escort he would not embark again to report back to his king until he had witnessed that the sacrifices had taken place.

A woman, quite lovely to behold in her unusual garb of a single-layered skirt and nothing else, was paddled past them in a large skiff by her husband. There was nothing inviting about the scene, in spite of the winning attractiveness of the couple. Their forlorn expressions and slumped postures as they slowly passed indicated their unsurety in whatever they were about to do.

The woman held a small baby to her breast, not more than a few days old by the size of it. It stopped suckling, and she held it tight in a hug. The little girl's face turned backward toward the ship, and they saw it. An unusual face, but one some had seen before. A pronounced forehead, a wide face, a protruding tongue, with milk drooling out of both corners of her mouth.

A Priest accompanied them as witness to the tragic event. From the shore, the new arrivals watched as the mother gently lifted the newborn over the side and lay it in the water. Carefully she slipped her arms out from underneath as if she were putting it to rest in a soft bed. The baby looked at her with soft wide eyes, but gave no sound. The cool water made little difference. Her little body sank at the feet, air in her lungs keeping her chest and face afloat. The mother looked grimly at the priest, and he gave her a somber nod. She touched the little girl's chest and gently pushed, sinking the bundle that was her daughter into the empty blue of the sea. A few bubbles rose to the surface with what sounded like a faint squeak. In a moment she removed her hand, and the little girl was simply gone.

There were no tears from the couple as the boat turned and headed for shore. There was no pleasure in what they had done either. Only a downcast acceptance.

The captives were lashed together for the walk to Knossos. There would be no time to stop and regain their land-legs. Those who stumbled would have to help each other or be dragged. A few small girls ran up to them with cups of very dilute wine for them to drink. They were thankful for it. It would be the last they would get until the completion of their five-mile promenade along the paved road to Knossos.

* * *

None were allowed into the fabled city in their unkempt state, not even as meat for the Minotaur. Stripped and scrubbed from head to foot, attendants poured water over their soaped hair while others rubbed them with pumice and fat to remove the years of filth accumulated on these untutored people. Some were being shaved, as they all would be as soon as they could be cleaned. There were looks of horror on their faces as razors perilously closed in on their genitals, but none protested vocally.

Ariadne watched the cleansing from a high balcony. The young men and women were attractive shaved and oiled, there was no doubt. They most definitely were the cream of the Attican citizenry. She had heard the rumors already spreading about that one of these youths was the long-absent son of King Aegeus, a son conceived by a union of the King when he was at Troezon. The lad had been raised there and just returned to King Aegeus, missing the first two tributes. He should have been part of the first.

It seemed such a shame to lose such a handsome man. She had heard so many interesting things about him. She probably shouldn't have been listening at the door when the runner had given Minos the news. He had seen her but he had been too under the influence to care, barely able, she was sure, even to comprehend much of what the messenger was telling him.

The man, Theseus she recalled, had led a life of adventure that only the most courageous captains encountered. Born to the daughter of the King of Troezon he was raised as a prince. His posture bore out his upbringing, proud even under the humiliating cleansing. His skin was not rough and dirty like the others'. His muscular burls were attributed naturally and were enhanced by physical, clean work. His slick, wet skin scintillated in the sun, enhancing every sinuous ripple.

She was feeling something for Theseus. Something that she was expressly forbidden to feel. She contracted all of her muscles at once and

454

exhaled hard through her nostrils. She crossed her arms and tightened them in a strangle-hold, surprising herself that she should be so suddenly aware of them wresting up her breasts.

How had the story gone? His father had placed his shoes and sword under a large rock before the birth of his son and before he left Troezon for Athens. He told Aethra, the name she had taken since confirming his seed sure, that she should send his son to him when he'd grown strong enough to roll away the stone and recover the artifacts from under it. When she thought the time had come, he removed the stone with ease and took the sword and shoes. As the coast roads were infested with robbers, his grandfather pressed him to take the faster and safer route, by sea. But the youth, feeling almighty and within himself the spirit of a hero, determined on the more perilous and adventurous journey by land.

Within a day he had met and killed a ferocious sadist who pleasured himself by tying his victims between two trees that sprang apart. When the savage assailed him he swiftly fell beneath the blows of the hero's heavy sword.

He met another man who beguiled travelers to view the sights from a high cliff, and kicked them from behind into the sea. That one was dispatched as he had the other, flinging his remains over the edge as just retribution.

Several similar contests with petty tyrants and marauders of the country followed, in all of which Theseus was victorious. Having overcome the perils of the road, he at length reached Athens, where new dangers awaited him. The witch Medea had become the wife of King Aegeus. She knew by her wicked arts who the new youth was and, fearing the loss of her influence with the king if Theseus were to be acknowledged as his son, cankered his mind with suspicions against the young stranger. She induced him to present the trespasser with a poisoned drink, but just as Theseus stepped forward to accept it, the sight of the sword dangling from his hip discovered to his father his identity and prevented the fatal draught. Theseus's father acknowledged him and declared him his successor, received as the only living child of the King, the others having been removed to his despair two years ago. News of the horrible sacrifices of his brothers and sisters appalled and offended Theseus. After ousting so much injustice along the road, and feeling still heroic, he insisted that he be sent along with the next tribute to fulfill the honor of his father, in spite of his entreaties, who had covenanted to send his children as fodder for the flesh-devouring Minotaur. Nothing could dissuade him, even though the king had offered openly to hide his son in defiance of Minos. The ship departed under black sail, as usual.

The rest of the story was not told, even to the grizzled captain of the ship.

Concealed in the bilge, under the planking and bagged in a waxed and oiled skin, was a white sail, a sail to signal Theseus's victorious return to Attica; after he killed the Minotaur and delivered his people from their terrible bondage.

Unless he died in the attempt.

* * *

Ariadne found her steps impulsive, uncontrolled. She wandered the Palace for a time, as if without purpose, but her mind had not yet released the image of the young man, Theseus. As she knew she would, she ended at the washing place. The captives had been scrubbed and polished, dressed as natives of the island, indistinguishable with the exception of irons on their legs and anxious countenances.

Except for Theseus. He held himself as if this were an ordinary day. He saw her coming, recognized her as the woman he had seen on the landing above. She was above all beauty with her shimmering, fair tresses. He had not looked at her directly then, not wanting to acknowledge that he had paid her any heed, not wanting her to think he was like other leering men. He watched her out of the corner of his eye and knew that he was attractive to her by the close attention she paid him when she thought he wasn't looking.

Here she was now, just a few steps away, looking at him the way other men looked at her. He hid his shock when she spoke to him. He was surprised that she could speak his language so perfectly, but perhaps even more taken aback that she would be so bold as to come up to him so directly and engage him in conversation. She obviously knew who he was and what he was here for; it was so unexpected that he should be the center of her attention like this.

More surprising still, he quickly found out that she was Minos's daughter. Perhaps she could be of assistance in his cause. The guards were paying them no mind at all. Why would they? She was a princess and, even more as it turned out, a Goddess. Of course she could do as she wanted. No one would interfere with her.

She would be perfect.

* * *

Daedalus was tapping the finishing grooves into the large ring, a lampoon of the ring he had previously smithed to order for Minos.

On his desk he had a small poppy-head jug from Kypros where the flower was grown, its extract used to excess, and from where it was distributed. The poppies had come as seeds by way of explorers who had traversed as far inland as the lakes of modern-day Switzerland. Sacks of the seeds had been brought back to Kriti as a food additive, but the interest was so negligible that none had any use for them. The Kypriots, however, found the texture of the added seeds to their meals highly appealing and took the lot as compensation for their portion of labors in the copper fields. It was not long before they were growing their own flowers and the need for importing the seeds became moot. The transport over land for such a meager and diminishing market was soon not worth anyone's while.

After a time someone discovered that a slit poppy-head exuded a white sap that quickly dried to a powder in the hot sun. They found it to have great medicinal potential reliving everything from headaches, to hunger, to the pain of fractured bones. It even stopped diarrhea. As they spread the seeds and grew the poppies in greater yield, it became possible to harvest more abundant amounts of the powder. They found that, in larger doses, it provided a calm, warm glow that pacified and made everything all right. At copper mines, it took the edge off chronically aching muscles and joints that plagued the miners. It helped them work harder and allayed the hunger pangs that too soon halted work. To some people, it became more important than food.

One of those people was Minos. But he had passed through the stages of everything being all right. Everything was far from the way he knew it should be. His drug had replaced his spirituality so he could not find real inner complacency. His hallucinations, the beautiful and the terrifying, were something far beyond the real, and so gave the real a distaste he considered unpalatable. Everyday life had become irritating, and what was not, was boring.

The ring Daedalus was finishing had been the subject of his imagination for three years. He had pondered endlessly the subtleties of the Minoan ways of life, their self-righteousness amongst their opportunism, their pleasures and passions, their ease of life in a world of strife and conflict caused through their machinations from afar. Their profiteering from bronze weaponry, from mastering and seizing the highways of the sea, from instigating wars between countries that both considered themselves friendly to Minos, from instilling fears into king's minds where fears need not have existed, and from preventing the up-and-coming countries from gaining too much headway by whispering clandestine information into the ears of their monarchs. All caused the growth and wealth of the Island of Minos.

And among this wealth, inside this Temple-Palace which was the wonder of the world, greater not in stature to the pyramids of Egypt but certainly in stately beauty, lay a passed-out Minos inebriated by the residue of a pretty-petalled flower.

The beautiful young woman before Daedalus pled her case as his critical eye peered through the lens at his work. If she had been older, a little taller, and her lips a bit fuller, she might have passed for his love, Pasiphae. But he was not one to be deluded by even a perfect look-a-like. She was not his love, and her presence only panged his lachrymose heart that he had been left with mere memories.

On this ring he had five goddesses, instead of four, to show this ring purporting a superior theme. Instead of exalting in the joys of life they were focused on something they saw as essential to, or even preeminent over, life. None of them were completely naked. All wore the flounced, layered, ankle-length skirts common to the Elect. All had their full breasts deliberately displayed. They held themselves much as this young woman in front of him, confident, self-assured, and expectant. Four of the goddesses paid tribute to the seated principal figure, a goddess of greatness who held aloft three poppy heads in her right hand while her left hand supported her right breast. Above them all were the Sun and Moon held aloft by a river-like band representing the Milky Way, which in their myth spurted from the breast of the goddess Rhea. The sun was eclipsed in a small central section by the planet Venus, or Aphrodite, the planet's rays covering the surface of the sun in rank importance. Opium being prepared from the milky juice of the poppy gave three linked symbols. In the background a small goddess carried high the symbol of Zeus and Minos, the ornate labrys, or double-ax, the holiest of Minoan symbols only carried publicly by the High Priestesses and Minos himself. As well as paying tribute to the central figure the goddesses were expectant that they too might receive of the exalted plant. The opium poppies stayed high and firm in her grip while the flowers offered by the farthest right goddess fell limp. With these five intertwined scenes and themes, the message was clear to any who could see the fine detail. The five represented the five tektites of Minos, and the principal goddess also represented the Goddess who had fallen from the sky, the Mother of the Earth.

What he would do with this ring now that he had finished it was something that he was just beginning to consider. To be caught with it in his possession, assuming any should interpret the symbolism, would certain his death.

"Please, Daedalus. You have to help me."

After completing the ring, and contemplating its derisive sarcasm of everything this society was coming to stand for, he now had the task of dealing with another example of irony of Minos's own creation. Minos had kept her from being with any man, woman, or animal. She was chosen by Minos and his Council to be pure from her birth to her death. She would be alone unto herself, protected, and a curse was put upon her that should she fall for another her days would be numbered low. She would never be killed or even imprisoned, but the gods would cease to smile upon her, and her life would quickly expire as a result of that union.

"You love him, do you?"

She looked down, unable to answer.

The third tribute of youths and maidens had come from Athens, and they were about to be sent through the Labyrinth. The Labyrinth was actually an integral part of the architecture of the Palace, knitted into every floor of the building in such an ingenious manner as to be unseen by any stroller passing time or walking about on business. It was used for intelligence testing, as the original cave Labyrinth had been before its collapse. The goal was to walk from the entrance to the exit that ended at the Tripartite Shrine of the Central Court, the section dedicated to Rhea centrally, with Zeus and Aphrodite flanking either side. The shrine's treble arrangement, a raised cella with the two flanking cellae two cubits lower, with corniced roofs supported by colored columns, symbolized the three realms of the cosmos over which the deities had dominion, the red underworld, the ocher earth, and the blue heavens. Those who could find their way within the set time limit, amidst the twists and convolutions of the intertwining hallways and staircases, were granted advancement within the social hierarchy, provided they were of commensurate physical beauty or could compensate for any lack thereof by way of exceptional skill in some area. In this way everyone had a chance to advance; the underclass of serfs and slaves promoted to the proletariat of farmers, herders, and laborers; they and children of slaves to a middle class of artists, artisans, clerks and lower-ranking officials; and they to an aristocracy of the exceptionally skilled, nobles, priests, and priestesses.

One thing Daedalus did approve of was the better living standards of even the lowest among men compared to that of their counterparts of every other civilization. The crude huts and shanty-ghettos usually associated with slave systems did not exist at Kriti. In fact, slaves here enjoyed the same rights and privileges of law as other Minoan citizens with the two notable exceptions that they were not allowed to bear arms or practice gymnastic exercises. Slaves were still slaves, after all, and it would not do for them to exceed in strength that of their masters.

"Please help us. I know you can," she choked.

It was true. He could. He could lead anyone right through the maze with his eyes blinded. He could be spun to dizziness at any point along the way and still find his path. He had designed the Labyrinth and knew things about it that not even Minos knew. He knew every hall, every stair, every moving panel that concealed another way, not only in the Labyrinth proper but in the rest of the Palace too. If only he had designed into the walls a way to get out of this room. But who could have ever foreseen that he might have ended up imprisoned here?

"Very well. Because you awaken memories of a forbidden love of my own, I will."

"Thank you, Daedalus. I knew you would." Her tears flowed openly. "I could not bear the thought of the Minotaur killing him."

Her statement of the Minotaur as fact shocked him. Not only the prisoners, but she, actually believed in the monster. Minos had a certain genius after all. Even as an opium-eating impostor he still had the proclivity to use the foreign legend to his advantage. Where there was fear, there was power. He hadn't realized, in his little cage, how solidly implanted that fear was, even among the local inhabitants.

The victims were not killed, that much he did know. They were chosen for their looks alone and gauged according to their intelligence by how long they took to pass through the Labyrinth. All of them came to the end eventually. Their value was based on a combination formula of the two. None were killed.

They were spread about the island to the highest bidders, and used for breeding.

* * *

Each of the fourteen prisoners sat isolated in their small, separate cells. None were allowed to make noise or to receive visitors; as if any would come. They were given one meal each morning, a thick soup of chopped lamb organs and broth. With that, if they had remained silent, they received a jug of fresh water, enough to last until the next day. Most of them had discovered that the soup was enough to fend off hunger completely if they didn't eat it all at once. The jugs and crocks were not removed from their cells until they were replaced the next morning, so they were free to eat at any time of their own preference.

Once each day, spaced at hourly intervals, they were taken individually to the toilets. They found it a new experience and had to have their guards patiently explain what it was that they had to do.

The Minoans constructed the most hygienic of all toilets in use around the world. Near the small cells, a toilet in the Court of Distaffs in the Domestic Quarter, used by many, not just the prisoners, enclosed for privacy, allowed for the disposal of their excrement in a way that they certainly had never imagined. The concept was easy enough to grasp. They had, most of them at any rate, defecated into crockery that later had to be emptied somewhere, and this new principal was not far different. They sat on a wooden seat with an oblong hole in it. The wood was warmer than any ceramic seat would have been. Below them was a stone slab-built drain that carried away their offal to the main sewer. The booth was not unpleasant, actually larger than the tiny cells that they were kept in. The walls were of easily cleaned gypsum slabs, worn down in places where attendants had abraded away the odd rude hieroglyph left behind by homesteading users frittering away time in the public facility.

Beside them was a jug of water for washing their rears, and their hands after. The remainder they were to dump down the drain, and then replenish it from the large tub outside the door. After refilling the jug, the guards compelled them to pour its contents down a hole in front of the swinging door. The hole was connected under the floor slabs to the toilet and flushed any solid remains back and down to the sewer. The jug was again filled and left beside the seat. A looped rope was released from its hook and a wooden balance-flap tipped down to cover the drain at its hindmost part to prevent the escape of sewer gasses. The water from the jugs did the job reasonably well in the dry summers. But once the rains came, the drains were washed completely clean by the directed waters gathered by troughs on the roof and guided down the light-wells to the sewers. The powerful flushing action took care of any accumulations over the summer months.

Theseus had just replaced the full jug beside the seat and was surprised when he turned and saw the guard bow low and back-step out the door. He had the common sense to know that the man had not come to any appreciation of his standing as a prince. He was bowing to someone else. He stepped outside of the booth and was shocked to find Ariadne waiting for him. She beckoned him to follow her into the next room. Her voice was hushed, knowing that the guard was out of sight but not out of ear-shot.

"You are for me," she said simply. She stepped closer to him.

There was no man alive who could have resisted her allure. He took her in his arms and she pressed her chest against his.

"And you for me," he replied. "I knew it when we met, as you did."

"Yes." And she wept.

"You know, then, our fate. We have been brought here to die."

"Yes."

"Is there any way out of the Labyrinth?"

She wiped her tears. "I have enlisted the aid of the architect of the Palace. He told me what I never knew; that my Dance is the path through the Labyrinth. A thousand times I have performed it, none but Daedalus knowing the key."

"Daedalus?" He had heard of Daedalus. He was a murderous traitor who had still fabulous marbles at Athens which none could equal. So he was the architect of this place. He would say nothing of that.

"You know of him?"

"Perhaps the name was familiar to me. I cannot say for sure."

"The inlayed floor of the Theatral Area shows the pattern to follow. I trace the steps to take over and over when I do the Crane Dance. I take exaggerated steps as if I am climbing stairs, and likewise as if I am descending.

These mirror the paths and staircases to follow when escaping through the Labyrinth. I have them memorized, Theseus. I will guide you through."

He smiled in a pleasant way and exhaled an amused laugh through his nose. "Your Minos will never allow you into the Labyrinth with us."

"He won't have to. There is a way into the Labyrinth that only Daedalus knows about. It is he who will guide me, and I will meet you inside."

"No. I cannot have you destroyed by the Minotaur. If I fail and you died I would be tormented for eternity."

"Daedalus is arranging something. He will tell me later." She saw the doubt in his eyes. "You can trust him, Theseus, believe me. He has no love for Minos either."

"Why is he helping us?"

"He's not. He is helping himself. He, too, is a prisoner and will escape at the same time. I will guide you to an escape which leads from the Palace."

"You will guide us? What about your Daedalus?"

He will take me only to the secret entrance to the Labyrinth. Then he will make his own escape. It will take me a while to find you, and Daedalus will not tarry."

"I am suspicious. Are you sure he is someone you can trust?"

"I know who I can trust, and who I can't. He is an old man, Theseus. He needs as much time as we can possibly give him to advance his escape. Besides, I have no choice in the matter. He is the only one who knows the secret ways, and he cannot show me until I free him from his cell."

"Then it is to you alone we must rely." He kissed her. "You have my absolute faith. I know you will save us."

"We will have to flee back to your ship. Are your people up to such a run?"

He held her tight. "Mine are among the most athletic of all of our people. That is partially how they came to be chosen. What I must know is, are you?"

* * *

"Is the boat ready?" Daedalus asked his son.

"Yes. It has been finished two days. The shipwright charged an extortionary sum for keeping it quiet, but we won't be taking much with us, will we?"

Daedalus bristled. He had not wanted to take Icarus along at all. The boy belonged here. He was only being naive thinking that the rest of the world was anything like this place. He had no idea.

"You should change your mind about coming."

"You have said that so many times. You know I am determined to be with my Father."

Argument was useless. "Go to the shipwright's building and rig the boat as I have taught you. Keep it inside. No suspicions can be raised. Give the wright as much as it takes to buy his silence. Promise him a note describing the location of some buried gold after our safe departure. That will ensure his lips will not become loose before we leave."

"Of course."

"And stay inside the building tonight. You must be there when I arrive. Have you tested the boat for weight?"

"Yes. The two of us will carry it to the water without much strain."

"Good. Go now. I will be there tonight."

"Until then, my Father."

He tapped at the door, and the guard let the boy out. Daedalus really did not want Icarus to come. It was too dangerous and, he had no trouble admitting to himself, he did not even like the boy's company. But he had to accede that he could not have successfully executed this escape without the lad's help. In that, he had been invaluable.

Daedalus removed the clay plates from under his table. His theory had to work. He was bound now. If this idea failed, he might as well commit suicide. He could not tolerate another single year in this miserable cell. Not even another week. He had been planning for months to bolt at the time of the prisoners treading the labyrinth. Any diversion would have done equally well, but this was the nearest to his time of flight. He had previously planned for Icarus to be the one to do the hardest part and he had never been sure of the lad's ability to dupe the guard. How opportune that Ariadne had approached him with her bold request. He had initially considered deceitfully withdrawing his aid at the last minute, giving Ariadne false instructions on how to find the course out of the Palace, but it served his needs better if the captives really did escape. First of all, they would create a major distraction when it was discovered that they were gone. They should get at least a four-hour lead, and then the chase would be on. It would be assumed that they had gone to their ship, but no one could know for sure. Search parties would have to be sent in every direction. Ariadne would soon after be noticed to have gone missing too. No one would ever suspect that she had gone as an accomplice. It could only be assumed that she was abducted. Still, it would not be long before word got back that the black-sailed ship had departed. The entire fleet would scour the seas looking for them. The heat would be off him, hopefully. He would eventually be noticed escaped as well, but it would be assumed that he had taken advantage of the confusion and fled somewhere else on the island, perhaps settling incognito as a hermit deep in the mountain forests. No one would guess that he had escaped by boat. If he was lucky, Minos would forget all about him. Such hopes. He was only fooling himself. Minos would not forget him after what he had done to Pasiphae. He would be hunted on land and sea with the same vehement zeal as Ariadne and the escaped prisoners.

He pondered his drawings for the hundredth time. The triangular sail was weighted at the bottom edge and fastened only to the mast. The movable boom could be swung to either side of the boat to catch wind from any direction. The third edge, the longest, hung free and bowed to catch the wind. He was sure that this would do the task. It had better. His only chance of escape was in maneuverability. He could otherwise never hope to outrun the fully rigged square-sailers aided by banks of vengeful oarsmen. Once underway he should be able to sail close to the wind for the first time in history. The sail should catch the wind even when the ship was heading almost directly into it.

He checked his drawings. They seemed to work. Everything about them screamed that he was right. If only he could try everything out before he was forced to escape. He scrutinized the arrows pointed at the zigzagged lines of his boat traveling in opposition, the angle of the sheets still snatching a portion of the wind. His life depended on the success of this contrivance. He worried endlessly about the wind bowling him over or slipping the whole boat sideways along the water completely unsteerable. He had added a deep keel to keep it traveling straight and widened the hull to keep it from tipping. He hoped it would be enough.

He wanted to have a ship he could sail alone, so he needed a system whereby he could steer without having to rely on a steering oar. His gimbal system used on the false bull's head to have it waver in every direction inspired his thoughts on the matter, and it wasn't long before he was able to apply the same principals to the steering mechanism. The rudder he invented could be tilted up for shallow water or beaching yet could also be pinned in the down position, penetrating the water's depths farther than the depth of the hull, and still be swiveled from side to side. It would probably be better than a steering oar because it could be lashed into position to maintain a steady course without the endless manipulations usually needed. At least, that was the theory.

One last thing. He had to be as invisible as possible. The sail would have to be dyed a dark color, blue or purple would have been best but that would have been prohibitively expensive. He could have afforded the dye, but it was such a closed commodity that Icarus's purchase would have raised too many eyebrows. Anything else to darken the linen would have to be found. He would just have to trust the abilities of his son to look after that.

He could not sleep, and Daedalus knew he needed the rest before his long walk to Amnisos. He would trot or run as much as he could but he had been in this cell so cursedly long that he feared his health had deteriorated to the point where he could not travel fast anymore. Over the last month he had been doing push-ups and sit-ups, leg squats, and jogging on the spot to strengthen himself. He had been disgusted by his deterioration when he at first tried these simple exercises. He damned himself for allowing his health to play second and to be so completely distracted by his artwork and schemes of escape that he had so withered in fitness.

Time seemed at a standstill. When he, at last, heard the muffled speech of the guard outside his door he knew only a few hours had elapsed since the sun had passed to blackness, but it might as well have been days. The conversation was short lived, as he had expected. How long it would be now, he could not guess. He had no experience in this art. As it was, he had not long to wait.

The sound of a body slumping painlessly to the floor notified him of the drug's success. The door opened moments later, and Ariadne entered carrying a small gypsum lamp. Daedalus rushed to the door and drew the guard in by his feet. He rolled the man into his bed and covered him over. It was a long shot, but might buy extra time.

"What did you give him?" asked Daedalus.

"Opium dissolved in strong wine. An enormous dose for someone not accustomed to it. Enough to make him sleep until morning." She hoped that would satisfy Daedalus. It didn't.

"You know we have talked about this."

"I know," she said quietly. She removed a wooden box, like a ring box, from her robe and gave it to Daedalus.

He unfastened the neat clasp and examined the contents. It contained a sulfur-like compound, which was an extract of the copper refining process. A highly toxic compound which would ensure a speedy death to the unfortunate guard who had drawn his lot for this night. "He cannot awaken to identify you as my emancipator."

He scooped an amount of the powder with a flat slat of wood, careful not to even expose his fingers to the substance. He held the slumbering guard's mouth open and tipped the powder into his lower cheek. "Will that be enough?"

"Enough for a cow, although it would take a few days. For him, he will be dead in an hour."

Daedalus closed the box and pocketed it. "What do you call it?"

"Selenium."

He looked out of his little window for the last time. The Full Moon had risen and was shining upon Knossos. "Of course."

The prisoners would already be entering into the Labyrinth. They had to go.

He fondled the mock ring he had made in parody of Minos's culture and decided to leave it behind. Perhaps Minos would find it and figure out its intent. Perhaps the final mockery would send him to his grave with this, the last of the accumulated insults befalling him over these past years. Perhaps then Androgeus could assume his rightful place as head of state and take this country to its limits of greatness without a fool, admittedly a genius but still a fool, destroying it from within.

They locked the door behind and ran down the passageway, stopping at each corner to listen. The halls were dark and they could not take a lamp with them for fear of alerting someone to their exit. Not far along, Daedalus stopped and felt a portion of a frescoed panel. He removed a horn-shaped rhyton from its stand in the recess beside it and pressed the latch secreted behind the urn. The panel clicked and opened slightly. Daedalus replaced the urn and the two pushed through the opening, quietly closing the hidden door behind them. There would be no one who would discover their trail. The narrow passage was pitch black inside and Ariadne held Daedalus's garment as he felt his way in the darkness, rather too quickly for her liking. He stopped, and she heard his hands exploring the wall for something.

He took another step forward. She heard a muted click, and the wall opened into a dimly lit hallway, the light noticeably perceptible only because of the total blindness experienced in Daedalus's private passage.

They were in the Labyrinth, the maze of languorous delight and hallucination from which many found little desire to escape. It was only the immigrant Athenians who had the terrible fears of the Minotaur thrust upon them. And Ariadne had never discussed the beast with anyone who could have set her straight, except Daedalus who chose to keep her thinking the Minotaur was real for his own purposes.

"Are you determined to do this?" She was beautiful in this dim light, reminding him more than ever of Pasiphae. She was far too young still to stimulate him intellectually, but he was sure she would grow with him where he was going. It was just a thought. He might easily still affect his escape with her at his side, and with the prisoners abandoned in the Labyrinth. "I must give you a last occasion to back out."

"I am firm in my resolution, Daedalus. There is no returning for me now."

"You would give up everything for Theseus."

"Yes. Everything. The world, if I could give it. His presence fills my loins with desire. His voice inspires my thoughts, and his eyes pull my heartstrings. It was meant to be, Daedalus. We are meant for each other."

That was the way it was to be then. He could not help but feel compassion for the girl. Would that Pasiphae have had more of that devoted adoration for him. "Then I will tell you this. There is no Minotaur. Its very existence is a lie."

"How can it be so?" The information, which should have been of intense relief to her, was met with incredulity. Why did Daedalus wait until now to tell her this? Of course, she reasoned. If he had told her before, then she would have passed the information on to Theseus. They would not have had any need to fear the Labyrinth then, and there would have been no urgent need to aid Daedalus in his escape. He was a cunning artificer in more than one way.

"It is a lie used by Minos to instill fear in the people of Attica. By fear, he rules. By fear, he profits. He is gaming with these immigrants to submit them, without qualification, to his dominion. When he frees them from their imagined fate, they will be so appreciative that they will give their souls to him."

"They would never be so afraid. Not Theseus."

"He might. Keep them all from the wine rhytons along the wall. You will see them. They are laced with drugs that, in their current state, will make them hallucinate their worst fears. If they fear most the Minotaur, then that is what they will see." He handed her a ball. "Take this thread. Use it to find your way back to this door. You know the steps of the dance, but you have many choices that might still confuse you. Concentrate and try to remember the dance. I will leave the door slightly ajar, but you will not see it in this light unless you have something to guide you to this very place. Take also this short sword. You may have need of it." He was speaking hastily, not wanting to waste any more time. He had to be off, or he would never make Amnisos by dawn. "Go now. Find Theseus. You are exactly half-way into your dance. Follow your steps backward and you will find them near the entrance. Remember not to touch the wine. It is very fast acting and you would never make it back this far, not with your knowledge, not even with the string. Take a lamp from off the wall so you can find your way down my passage to the outside. There is a simple latch which opens below the Palace near the river."

"I thank you for your help Daedalus. If I can ever come to your aid, I will go to any length to do so."

"Tell also Theseus this; he must spread far and wide the lie that he has killed the Minotaur. He must say that he did battle against it with a dagger which you provided him, and found his course through the Labyrinth by way of the thread which you carry." He began to close the panel. "Minos's stranglehold on the nations of the earth must be broken. You have no idea of the evil he has caused from afar; wars, death, enslavement, misery on every scale, all to serve the isolated rapacity of the people on this island."

He vanished into the darkness again, leaving her alone this time to help the Athenians while he took advantage of a precedent head start.

She wedged one end of her clew of thread into the tight crack, securing it against detachment. She had to retrace her steps as quickly as she could without losing track of her place in the dance. She had to do it backward, something she had never done, and it took some orienting and backtracking at places where she knew she was going wrong due to the impossibility of the options available to her. The difficulty was one of scale. Where she had been accustomed to dancing her route upon a stage, she now had a vast building to adjudicate. Where she should have been going right, she sometimes could go only straight, or left. She was thankful that Daedalus had the foresight to give her the clew. It saved her from confusion on several occasions. She had to slow herself, concentrate on her dance steps. It was the stairs that threw her judgment off most. Her dance was only two dimensional, but she was soon able to transmute the high-stepping motions of the Crane Dance to the places where she would really find stairs.

The fine thread was unraveling fast, dropping to the floor of the Labyrinth by the hundreds of feet as she wended toward her goal.

She heard voices ahead, an argument.

A younger man amongst the captives was ready to come to blows with Theseus. He had little regard for the prince's newfound regency. It meant nothing in this dungeon.

"Pack your ass with old shoes," he shouted at Theseus, an insulting epithet saved for the poor who could only go barefoot. "You cannot keep me from the drink. Do you think you are superior here? Do you think you can rule me when we all are made equal by the awful death that awaits us? At least let me drink and face my death with a smile."

"Keep your voice down, you desiccated testicle. You'll attract the beast."

"Bring it on, I say. Let it do its evil work of us and end our suffering." He was chancing Theseus's temper. There was no way, given any fairness at all, that he could take the man at any physical contest. But this place set him into almost an uncontrolled panic, and it was for that compassionate reason only that Theseus didn't throttle him.

"Even the women do not behave as you. Control yourself like a man. Where is your pride?"

"I will not face death with pride. Pride will not save any of us."

He lunged for the wine-filled rhyton and tipped it back, spilling the red liquid all down his front. Theseus let him have it. What was the use of fighting amongst themselves? If he died of poisoned wine so be it. The clear warning that none of them would taste food nor drink within the Labyrinth was clue enough that they should avoid this obvious temptation. It could not be for their good.

They started on their way. They had spent too much time here behind these closed doors arguing. The thirsting youth was right in one respect; their fate awaited them and there was hardly any point in putting it off. The longer they waited, the weaker and less able they would be to fight it. Theseus had planned to take the monster by force, to brave right in and muscle it down. It might be half-bull, but that meant it was also half-man. There were fourteen of them, all told, and if no one lost heart they should be able to overpower any single thing. They could force it down and break its arms. With their combined strength they could even wrest its limbs from their sockets and disjoin them completely from their host. They would club the creature with its own limbs, their new weapons, and drub it senseless, smashing its thick skull with repeated blows and stabbings of the broken bone-ends. They would gouge its eyes to blind it. They would kick and tear its hanging organs. They would choke and beat upon its throat. If it took ten of them to the netherworld with it what did it matter? Four would survive. Four more than otherwise.

They walked as one, huddled close. They had removed the ceramic lamps from the wall where the fourteen wine-rhytons had also hung to tempt them. The light they carried felled them with the strategic disadvantage of letting any creature ahead know that they were coming, even if they did manage to preserve their quietest footsteps. In spite of that knowledge, the light comforted them.

It was deathly quiet in the Labyrinth, like some cave isolated from the earth above by a mile of stone. The only sound was the soft squishing of the pads of their feet against the stone floor and the heavy breathing no amount of concentration could break.

The walls were distractingly decorated in fabulous frescoed artworks, even more so than the rest of the Palace. Here fantasy was played to the fullest extent. In the corridors of the Palace, the whimsical beasts of imaginary color lifted the senses and built an air of pleasant congratulation of life. Here the imagery was far wilder, decadently austere and foreboding. Every myth and legend of sea monster and sorceress splayed upon the walls in abstract conceptuality. The outrageous images were expressly to enhance the demons of the mind released by the unwitting impetuous enough to ignore the enigmatic warnings to leave the wine temptations be.

The thirsty youth who could not control his craves shrieked in terror. A white apparition was around a corner, and he had spotted her at the end of the long dim corridor even partially blinded by the light they carried. His eyes had already dilated more than the others straining into the darkness ahead, because of the fast acting chemicals laced into the wine.

The others almost fell with the panic of his scream and the realization that it was targeted at something tangible right in front of them and not at some whimsy painted on the wall to terrorize them. But they held their ground stalwartly. None turned or made any move to flee, but all were choking on their hearts.

"Fear not," came the hauntingly familiar voice, echoed ethereally by the sheer walls of the vacuous corridor. The apparition flowed toward them suspiciously. They waited, frozen, unable even to breathe.

Theseus recognized her first. "Ariadne," he spoke, only above a whisper.

His soft calling of her name addressed her ears in a most welcome way, speaking his love for her in a single utterance.

She rushed to him, embracing him bodily and feeling as though she might fall through his skin and into his soul.

"Come with me," she said pulling his hand. With a look, she said to the others that she had a private word to say to Theseus that they were not privy to. She took him around the next corner where all they could make out was an indecipherable hushed muffle. She was aware of the distance voices could travel here by how far away she could hear the group's conversation as she looked for them and so she took pains to subdue her enthusiasm at finding Theseus. She told him in condensed version of Daedalus's plan to let them escape, of his insistence that he try to defeat Minos's puissant authority by claiming to have destroyed the Minotaur, and that the beast didn't really exist. She told him that it was all a game and that they were destined to service men and women for the purposes of procreation, to produce children who would be removed from them to be raised by childless couples.

Theseus experienced a fury he had not known even when first hearing of the injustices wrought against his people.

"Come with me," she said. "Call to your people that you will be back momentarily and that they must not move no matter what they see or hear. They are not to even touch anything. That must be absolutely clear to them. If they go any farther into the maze, not even I will be able to find them."

Theseus shouted the commands to his unsure companions. Most of them held him in enough esteem to obey, and the others were too fraught with anxiety to do other than the majority.

She took him a short way down a side passage, where there was another single rhyton of red wine suspended from a bracket.

"Scream," she said.

"What?"

"Scream like you are in battle. Yell like you are fighting for your life."

He began to bellow like a man savaging a wild animal with his bare hands. She took the rhyton from its bracket and pointed to the metal prop, motioning to Theseus to tear it from its bindings. He thrashed and yelled, ripping the metal frame out by its fasteners and then beat it out of shape against the wall. Ariadne threw the dark red wine against him, staining his loincloth and skin as if by blood. As he cursed and screamed she broke the point off the end of the rhyton and used it as an amplifier of her deep calling. She made deep sounds through the megaphone as a bull protesting in pain.

After a few moments of producing those terrifying battle sounds, she handed Theseus the rhyton. "Stab yourself with these jagged edges. You need to show blood."

He knew exactly what she meant and struck it into his side, lacerating his ribs and begetting a flow of blood that mixed with the dark wine. She touched the dagger edge to the blood flow, coating it, and gave it to him.

"Coat the handle too. This was a hard-won blood battle."

As a final gesture he smashed the rhyton against the wall, shattering it to tiny ceramic pieces. Following that Ariadne snuffed the little lamp on a higher bracket, extinguishing its flame.

They found the other members of Theseus's party huddled together even closer. The group could not tell by the echoes where exactly the sound was coming from, only that an awful conflict had been in progress somewhere near them. Whichever way they could have run lay uncertainty. The passageway back had been closed and would only have served to trap them with no hope of escape down another route. They had stayed where they were at the junction, two options open, prepared to flee at the first sign of peril from either one.

"It is done," called Theseus. "Behold your savior."

As he drew closer they beheld his wound, the blood clinging to his side and soaking his garment and leg, the sword held in victory in his bloody hand, they cheered. They clamored round and almost worshipped him as their protector and champion.

"Come," he interrupted them. "The Minotaur is dead, but we are not free of this accursed place yet. Ariadne has given us the means to escape. Follow us."

Ariadne led them by the clew of thread. They followed as fast as she could handle it up and behind her. Not too fast, or it might break, and even with the torchlight they would never find so fine a strand. She might have been able to make her way unaided, but the stakes were too high. There were too many turns, too many stairs up and down, too many places to go wrong, and there was not enough time.

The thread guided her to the wall where the hinged panel awaited.

"In here."

One by one they were swallowed by the little passage.

"No," shouted the youth who had partaken of the tainted wine. "No," he screamed again in prolonged anguish of mind. He was hallucinating already and, in his mind, he saw the walls of darkness absorbing his comrades. Feelings of absolute dread and foreboding paranoia rushed him. Doom. That was the madness there for them all. Doom. He screamed again his abject horror and fled insanely down the darkened corridors, fearful cries disconsolately fading but never perishing.

They had to continue on. Without a word, the panel closed and locked. They would not sacrifice the precious time to chase after.

* * *

Daedalus wrapped the heavy idol and the two tektites in a padding of soft leather and lifted the bundle into his sack. With this last insult, he hoped Minos would be finished. He had almost forgotten about the sanctity in which Minos held these objects. Hidden in some rock or hurled into the sea they would be forever useless to him.

He left the Inner Sanctum of the Temple as quickly and silently as he had come, through the narrow panel behind a curtained wall. There were voices just outside in the next room and he hoped that whatever ritual they were performing would not take them in here, that they were finishing and going in the other direction. If they discovered this caper before his escape was assured, his life would irrefutably be forfeit.

Down the steep stairways and passageways he went, feeling his way and knowing by the smell that he was getting close. It wasn't overpowering, just musky and unclean. He was careful to feel with his feet, not picking them up as he walked but rather shuffling them along until he found the step. He could hear the trickle of moving water below him and a draft of cool air felt refreshing on his bare skin. He sat on the edge and lowered himself into the sewer system. This was the longest straight passage he would take, a steep cement flue, which he could stand in without stooping. It led to the riverbank below the Temple-Palace. The end was grated to keep children from playing inside it and getting themselves filthy, so there was no escape by that route. The bars were securely cemented in place. Above him was another opening which anyone would have missed. No one looked up in a place like this. He pulled himself up and into a natural rift in the rock that led to a shrine close by. This shrine was almost exclusively decorative, little used with the large shrines within the Temple-Palace so at hand. Its purpose was mostly a venue to burn incense in the summer to mask some of the odors from the sewer. He slipped out the panel beneath the altar and, under the cover of darkness, made his way along the Vlychia riverbank a short way before picking up the road. He wondered how long before the others would emerge?

He was determined to control his urge to run. He had to get away as quickly as possible, but he couldn't risk one of the astronomers turning his eyes downward to relieve a strain in his neck and seeing him fleeing down the road.

472

An astronomer might let him get away with it, not being interested in such things, but he might just as easily set off an alarm. Daedalus kept his walking pace brisk and unsuspicious. He was already feeling the ache growing heavy in his shoulder from the idol in his sack. He clutched it to his waist and broke into a run once he was over the little rise that separated his view from the Palace. It was all downhill now, mostly. A gentle slope on the well built and graded road he could keep up the slow jog for a mile at a time before breaking. He switched the idol from shoulder to shoulder, finally draping the sack straps behind his neck and holding the bag with both arms. He couldn't swing his arms for balance but found it to be an advantageous tradeoff. He was making good time.

It took him the rest of the night to make Amnisos. He avoided the little village of Prasas along the way by skirting the hills. That slowed him further and he wondered if he was being overly cautious but, again, he did not want to be noticed by anyone.

He had to take his chances at Amnisos. There was no way that he could avoid going through the town. He could have passed by fewer houses by walking the shore to the shipwright's workhouse but the fishers were always up early, even before morning twilight, some of them. Undoubtedly some would be out already. He stood a better chance of remaining unseen by coming directly through the center of the town.

The boathouse door was unlatched. He pushed quietly, slipped into the dark workshop and closed the door, moving silently into the darkness at his side so he could not be placed.

"Father?" a voice whispered.

He could not quite identify the utterance. "Say your name," he whispered back.

"Icarus, Father."

"Are you alone?"

"As you wished."

"The shipwright?"

"Sleeping."

"Have you drugged him?"

"Yes, Father." Even with his voice a whisper it was obvious that he was not happy to have done so.

"Guide me to him."

Icarus whispered so his father could follow him to the door leading to the residential part of the building. It still tanged of wood shavings, hide glue, and pitch even in here. The wright was as most of the fishers and shipbuilders, filthy by normal Minoan standards. A trickle of light came through the window opening. It was almost getting too late.

Daedalus handed his bundle to his son. "Put this in the boat. I'll join you in a moment."

Icarus looked inquisitive only for an instant before he left the room. Daedalus withdrew the little decorated box given him by Ariadne. He opened the shipwright's mouth and placed some of the red sulfur-textured powder in the man's cheek. His greed was being rewarded.

Icarus unbolted the tall, double doors and swung them out. The twilight was growing fast. There was enough light to see the early fishers already out, and some of the pit-lampers were on their way back after a good catch. Other fishers were preparing their skiffs to leave on the shore. Enough light came in through the door to let them see the interior of the building.

"Where is my boat?" Daedalus said, a panic in his voice as he looked around the interior. There were several small boats in various stages of construction but none complete; except for some strange creation.

"This is it," explained Icarus nervously.

Daedalus could only gape at the double-hulled catamaran.

"What have you done?" He was sick, his hopes shattered. What horrendous counterfeit had Icarus directed the ship-wright to build? It was as long as the boat he had commissioned, it was a sailboat, and it had the distinctive triangular sail; but it was of two narrow hulls, like canoes, joined by four beams. The mast projected from the two center beams which pinched the mast at the front and back, the mast held upright by four braces forming a pyramid below the boom. The top of the mast was roped to all four corners of the monstrosity, which they must have thought would hold it steady. A rudder was attached to the center of the hind support and was hinged up so it would clear the ground. Two hardwood pegs, one a spare, hung by thin ropes off the rudder pole.

Daedalus was twisted in fury.

They had taken his best ideas and twisted them into this mutant confabulation of, of, what . . ? They had not even stained his sail. It was still white. "This is not what I commissioned." He could feel his face flushing. "You fool. You simple bastard." He strained to keep from shouting. "You have the body of a man and the brain of a maggot. Are you offal? I should have sent you to the depths of the sea at birth you mental-defective squid."

Icarus was crestfallen. His head drooped. Daedalus did not even notice he had shattered his son; or care. He scanned the area for a boat to steal. There was nothing that would suffice. He tore his skirt in rage, inestimably frustrated that he could not even scream aloud because of the imminent danger he was in.

"Father," Icarus said dejectedly. "We must go."

Daedalus shook. He wanted to beat the boy senseless. He already was. The idiot. He fought to control himself. He deep-breathed and grabbed the desperate creation opposite Icarus. The boat was amazingly balanced and light, for all its size. The two of them had little trouble shifting it across the sandy expanse to the water. Daedalus hopped aboard the canvas-strung deck, reluctantly admitting to himself that this was much more comfortable than a hard wooden bench. Icarus pinned the rudder down and turned the pole to his father, offering him the helm. He hopped upon the canvas himself and pulled the triangular sheet tight along the boom, tying it off at the end. He wrapped the thick trailing rope once around a support near the rear within the framework of the left pontoon and slowly let out a bit of slack. A trivial breeze caught the flaccid sail and whipped the boom to the side. It caught on the rope and the sail billowed out, fluttering stridently at the edges. The boat twisted and jumped forward, taking off immediately.

The flapping noise shocked Daedalus out his choler. "Pull back more of the sail," he shouted in his excitement.

Icarus pulled hard on the rope and the instability subsided, the canvas filling centrally in a nice bow. One pontoon came right out of the water as Daedalus steered to compensate and drop it a bit. But to keep their heading they had to keep one pontoon in the air. Icarus pulled himself over to weigh it down and that had the effect of making them cut even faster. They flew over the calm water, the white sail shooting them past the fishers as a bird on the wing. That was the analogy they used when later describing the strange spectacle to the Priests. Two men on the wing of a bird whipping past above the water as if in flight. They were as if on the back of an egret, skimming the glassy surface out of the bay and out to sea. Yet it was no bird beneath them. They had made their own wing.

Behind Daedalus could see the square, black sail of a ship being raised. The prisoners had escaped.

* * *

The Physician bent over the still warm body in Daedalus's cell while an impatient Minos hovered over his shoulder.

"Well, Surgeon?" he demanded. "How was it done?"

He would not be rushed. His standing was high enough that he would stand a fair degree of Minos's buffetings before he had cause to worry. He chose to keep silent as he continued his examination. He pressed the expired guard's chest, expelling the last fill of air still within his lungs. It had an unmistakable garlic odor. That was surprising. It could be a coincidence. More than likely the guard had kept a private cache of the bulb for his own use squirreled away somewhere. Most unusual, though, for someone to do such a thing. Everyone of his class ate together at the central mess and as far as he knew they hadn't had garlic in some time. There were no other remarkable signs on his body, not even rigor mortis yet. Death could not have taken place

475

more than a few hours ago. One thing he did find curious was the particularly rich purple of his fingernail beds. Typically, in death, he would have expected them to be a much darker color, a dark interfusion of the colors purple and blue. These were unusually bright. He checked the guard's toenails. They were discolored in the same unexpected way, though not as conspicuous. He was at a loss.

"I must draw your attention to this observation, Minos." Asclepius elevated the guard's hand.

Minos took a hard look. It took a moment in his intoxicated somnolence to register the image. Then he blanched. He understood. "His breath, Physician. Did you smell it?"

"Garlic, Minos. Quite unmistakable, though I cannot fathom where he would have procured it."

"That is the point, Physician. He did not." Ariadne. Only she had the use of the sacred toxin. Only the Mother Goddess. Not even he was able to use the great secret. It was astounding that she would use it to free Daedalus, and only she could have. What hold could he have possibly had over her? They did not even know each other. Not like . . .

"Find Ariadne," he roared. "Find her at once."

The Captain of the Guard repeated the order to the dozen with him and added that every part and passage was to be scoured. If she was not in the Palace then the town was to be searched. They had fifteen minutes. Every guard and every Priest and Priestess were to aid them. He had suffered Minos losing his temper before but never observed his face turning as flaming red as this. He rued his responsibility to remain at his side.

Minos picked up a ring left on the small worktable. Daedalus. He didn't even take this bit of gold to see him through his escape. But then why should he? It would be incredible if he was even able to get outside the walls of the Palace. Even with her help.

He placed the ring on the first knuckle of his finger to scrutinize the depiction. Another of Daedalus's perfect works. Flawless, as the ring he wore on his left forefinger. The same dimensions actually, and the same fit. Odd. He hadn't commissioned this. He looked for the magnifying lens. Daedalus had taken that. Why would he have left this valuable gold?

He decided to wait here in the cell for news of Ariadne. He wanted to confront her here, in the very place where her crime of aid had been perpetrated, so she could witness what her beguilement by Daedalus had produced; the murder of another innocent life.

The doctor was still examining the guard's body, wondering what had sparked Minos's outburst. He might ask at some later date, but not today. Perhaps he might find out himself before then.

The terrified Captain of the Guard stood outside the door, just beside it, only his arm visible from inside the room. He wanted as little to do with this as possible. He would stay out there until another guard came running with news of Ariadne.

Minos wished he had brought a vial of opium with him. He needed more. To pass time while he waited, and he wouldn't be waiting too long, he tried to decipher the ring's engraving. He was an expert at divining meaning in pictures. And with the shortsightedness that had been developing in one of his eyes over the last two years, he was able to make out most of the tiniest of images.

The usual goddesses were there; magnificent breasts on the larger ones. The Star of Aphrodite was eclipsing something; was it the sun or the Moon? It could have been either. A quarter Moon was to the left of the other round image being eclipsed. Perhaps it was the Sun after all. Could he be saying that Aphrodite was more esteemed in the Godhood than Zeus? Was Daedalus mocking him? That would mean the Mother of the Earth, the Moon, was also being denigrated in this picture, represented only as a quarter while the Star of Aphrodite was refulgent with sixteen rays. A smaller goddess in the background carried the symbol of Zeus, the double-headed labrys. Or was it a goddess? He could not see close enough to make out its breasts. He wasn't sure if it had any. Could it be a male? It didn't have legs either under its short skirt. Was this another mockery? A diminished male, legless, representing him? The Milky Way. The milky breasts. And what was this? Poppies? This was mockery. He counted the imagery; five objective personages; five subjective ideals. He was insulting the Five. Daedalus had insulted every sacred ideal of their culture.

He threw back his head and wailed. The doctor jumped back in fear that Minos would strike out at him. The Captain leapt into the cell.

"Find Daedalus." Spittle fusilladed out of his mouth. "When you find him, kill him as he stands."

"But Minos," started the Captain. They could do no such thing under Minoan law.

"Do it," he yelled and fired the ring out of the little window.

A runner chose that very inauspicious time to arrive.

"Captain," he addressed his superior properly, not speaking directly to Minos. "Ariadne is not within the walls of the Knossos Temple-Palace. Neither is Daedalus."

Minos squeezed his fists and compressed a roar of anguish.

"There is more, Captain. We searched the Labyrinth as that is an integral part of the passageways of this structure. The prisoners are also gone."

"Find them." Minos was exploding. "Kill them. Even Ariadne. Bring me their blood. I want it now, do you hear me?"

They all fled, leaving Minos in his rage kicking and assaulting the dead body. There was only one place for him, a place where he might find peace in this temperament. He fled down the halls until he came to the Outer Sanctum, the guardroom where only the High Priests and Priestesses of the Council could come. Not even the guards would have extended their search in here. Beyond the veil was his place, his sacred place; the Inner Sanctum, the Adytum. It was his alone, to be shared at his discretion with the representative of Rhea, the Earth Mother. Not even the present one, Ariadne, had been in here with him. None other since his beloved Pasiphae.

He parted the veil and took long strides to the center altar where he had more opium. He wheeled in shock. His eyes had seen something amiss, out of order, but his conscious mind had not registered. The iron Goddess was gone. And the tektites. The very seat of his power.

His passionate fury rose to unbounded heights. In his rampage he flailed the veil and cast himself out of the despoiled room, beating his fists on the altar of the Outer Sanctum. "I have been betrayed," he howled. "Betrayed by another treacherous woman. I will not have them anymore. I will not have any relationship with any of them." He thrust a horrified Priest out the door. "Bring me a boy. I will have a little boy. I will never trust another woman lest it be to my death," he raged.

He rent the air with weeping, wailing, and gnashing of teeth, and the stone walls of the Sanctum could not contain it.

* * *

Icarus had stocked the boat with enough to keep the two of them alive for several days. In the pontoons, he had fresh water, wine, food, and gold. He had brought some light wool blankets in case the weather turned sour at night. Even two paddles in case the wind died or the sail ripped.

Neither of them had spoken other than to say, 'pull the rope,' or 'slacken the rope.' Both had been embarrassed over the incident at the boathouse. Icarus knew his father had been desperate and, after years of confinement, who could fault him? Things were better left unsaid.

Daedalus was very quickly getting used to maneuvering the little vessel. It sailed as he had envisioned, racing across the wind at high speed, cutting into it at low. But the point was that it could penetrate the headwinds, something never done before with sail. It was astounding. Icarus didn't seem to appreciate that fact, probably didn't even notice they were doing it. The boat became very stable while they were sailing hard into the headwinds, just as an experiment when he knew they were safely away from Kriti, but the slow going made Icarus bored. The impatient youth was making comments like "Let's go that way," remembering that by going that way the boat traveled so much faster. He had no appreciation for tactics or strategy. He was unsophisticated for all his upbringing.

Daedalus still seethed inside about the boat. He had accepted right away that the design was a success; that was not a matter of question. It was the audacity of the young upstart to design with the shipwright this deviation from his plans. What if they had been wrong? It was bad enough that he had been so unsure of his own plans. For those inexperienced crusts of burnt fat to have subverted his plans in such a way was unforgivable. That they were right was no excuse. He had killed the wright because he had been privy to the design of the sail. It was his sail, and no one was going to profit by it except him. There was imperious wealth to be made here.

Icarus was taking chances. They were into the end of their second day and when at the helm he was becoming too confident in leaning the catamaran up on one pontoon. Daedalus occasionally gave him control and Icarus always heeled it over to capture the exhilarating speed. Daedalus would rest on the high pontoon to give it the extra weight it needed and he would transfer the few things they carried to that pontoon as well. But Daedalus was short-tempered and getting fed up with his son's antics. His youthful recklessness had no place out here where they could barely see land.

"Lay us flat," he shouted when the boat heeled over so far that it almost capsized. "You are not fit to steer."

"I'm sorry, Father. It was a gust. I wasn't expecting it."

They changed places and Icarus sulked. Nothing he could do seemed to please his father. He took his place on the right pontoon and they sailed on, more reservedly than before, into the setting sun. They couldn't see ahead from the glare but that didn't matter. They knew their direction and they would carry on.

Of a sudden, a strong gust heeled the boat hard up on its side so far that the rudder tip left the water. Daedalus was immediately aware that they were out of control and that they might capsize. The wind was within a hair's breadth of causing their death. He threw himself up on the canvas mat and pulled his way up to the highest pontoon. Icarus was already hanging over the side, using his weight to leverage the boat back down. Their combined weight probably saved them from disaster and craft leveled off enough to put the rudder in the water again. Icarus was dragging his legs in the water as he struggled to pull himself back aboard. He looked panicked as his fingers clung to the pontoon.

"Help me up," he strained.

Daedalus had slid down to the rudder to regain control. He steered it away from the wind and dropped the pontoon hard to the water, slowing the boat and causing the sail to flap. Daedalus was breathing hard and his heart was racing. He winced and squeezed the salt spray out of his eyes with his fingers. His eyes stung when he pressed them. He heard a cry behind him. He whipped round to see someone in the water flailing his arms. He turned forward; Icarus was gone. He had lost his grip when the pontoon dropped and slipped off. Daedalus turned back to witness the horror expressed on his son's face as he splashed and flailed, his mouth filling with water as he spat and squeaked and sputtered his pleas.

It was the last Daedalus would see of his son.

He turned his back and steered to fill the sail, deaf to the beseeching supplications behind him.

* * *

The crew of the black-sailed ship had stayed the night onboard, as they had been required to for the last several nights. Some hospitable locals had offered to bring soft bed and comforts for them, but they had refused out of principal. Only food was accepted and, although it would have been provided freely, they paid with pieces of gold. The crew would not accept any gift from a people so abominable. They did not stray from their ship at any time, disgusting the inhabitants by urinating and defecating over the side of their vessel, No one would have reported them if they left to use the public facilities but they refused, not having the slightest inkling of what was being referred to. Gross, hairy people. Misshapen faces, peeling shoulders, balding pates. Nothing like the handsome ones brought as tribute. Even their ship was grotesque with its oversized, black sheet. It was a wise judgment of Minos's to demand only seven fine youths of each, male and female. It would have been impossible to find any more in one year among such loathsome canaille.

The ship even smelled bad to the fishermen starting their day, a musky, unclean odor drifting over the harbor on top of the smell of the fresh salt air. It was another beautiful day, clear and warm, just a light breeze here on the shore. The rippled water outside the harbor signaled the presence of a windier state out farther, however. That was good for the fishermen. The unsettled water would excite the fish and bring them closer to the surface. This might be a good day for fishing.

A group of well-dressed young people were coming to the waterfront, handsome with oiled skin so early in the morning, heading for the quay where the black-sailed vessel moored in isolation from any other ship. A beautiful girl was among them who looked like the Priestess Ariadne. Of course it wasn't her, but they were sure that she was the only one outside of legend who had been blessed with blond hair. Perhaps it was a girl of some lesser standing unfamiliar to this town. One of the watch on board the black ship saw them and gave a cheer, waking all of the sailors asleep on the benches. The fishermen thought they must be making crude remarks in their loutish and unrefined tongue.

Typical for such gross men. How they stayed aboard that stinking vessel no one could guess, but it was just as well for Amnisos.

It looked like one or two of the approaching group was holding back the urge to run, taking quick jumps forward only to be latched onto by a confrere and restrained. In a moment the entire crew of the ship was jumping and cheering the arrival of these people. Theseus wished they would shut up but in a moment he, too, could stand it no longer. As a whole they broke for the ship, sweeping Ariadne along and shouting their unhidden jubilation at succeeding in their elusion. They leapt aboard and cast the mooring ropes aside, dancing about the ship in a display of mad disorder while raising the unsightly sail. It filled instantly and they were off, hooting and calling in their own tongue, the fine seeming to enjoin the unsavory as if they were family. None of the witnessing fishers could understand what was taking place. A lone figure, a woman, sat amongst them, different by her decorum, uncelebratory, unlike the rest. Understandable, really. She was of a higher cut than even the prettiest of the women on the ship, prettier than most of the local women as that went. Dressed in fine purple linen she could have been a Priestess. Whatever was she doing on that obscene ship?

"We have escaped," Theseus rejoiced. "We have escaped the stranglehold of the evil Minos. Row, men. Dig your oars deep into the waters and aid the winds in carrying us far and fast from this island of venal malevolence."

Wine was brought out, wine to drown the sorrows of the sailors on their way back to Athens, wine now raised to their lips to lighten their already exalted spirits.

Ahead was a strange apparition, unknown to them and something that could have only come as a sign from the gods. A white point indicating the direction they must go. Once observed it changed course and sped sideways to the wind at an incredible speed. The message was clear. Go in the direction the symbol had indicated.

Everyone participated in rowing, even the women. They were becoming drunk on the wine and in such were given more strength. It did not matter where exactly they were heading, it was more or less in the direction of Athens. For today they would just run with the wind, letting it take them just as quickly as it could, wherever it would. Anywhere away from Kriti.

The celebration lasted the day. Rowing and cheering the wind and oar carried them far and never let up.

As night fell, they found refuge in the hidden cove of a small island. They needed rest after such sustained labor and, while they could have slept aboard, they decided that screening themselves in this natural hideaway was the best strategy.

Only the nose of the ship was beached on the tiny patch of sand at the end of the bight, tied by rope to a solid and solitary tree growing out of a rock crevice. They could be away in minutes if the need arose. A watch was set on a high prominence to look out for pursuers. That they would come, there was no doubt. But they would never be found in this little crag on only one of a thousand islands. The whole Minoan fleet could not find them here given a year, though they could never survive that long on this waterless, barren island.

All settled, Theseus took Ariadne by the hand and led her apart from the others. She was lovely. And to add to her beauty she had sacrificed everything for him. For all of them. They shared a debt to her that they could never repay.

No words were expressed between them as he took her for the first time, a bliss she had only imagined. How could this thing have been kept from her? It was unconscionable that she should never have partaken of this sensual delight, time after time until they were both spent and fell into the deepest slumber.

With the soft, fleecy blanket wrapped about her, she slept as she had never slept, dreaming over and over again her newfound pleasures and her love and desire for Theseus. How different her life was going to be with him, so different from her sterilized life at Knossos where she was revered as the embodiment of the Goddess Rhea, Mother of all gods and man, the Earth Mother.

Guilt began to toil on her conscience. Had she betrayed an entire people for a single man? Or, worse, had she betrayed an entire people for her own selfish desires? Under the progressively chilling fleece she curled into a ball for warmth. The memory of a curse played in her dreams like a majestic, invisible demon, pursuing her down halls she could not navigate although she knew the way. She circled in the Labyrinthine corridors like the river Meander, endlessly flowing toward and then away from the sea in an impossible circuit, returning on itself without beginning or end. She twisted in her disturbed sleep with every turn of the passageways of her dream. Growing darker and colder, guilt and fear built with every slowed footstep. Soon she could walk no more, her legs disobeying her will to move. She clung to the wall and tried to pull herself along, frozen with the fearful, growing anxiety that something was pursuing her and that it was right behind her. She was afraid to look, but her vision, without her eyes beholding it, saw the beast.

It was the Minotaur, the hideous bull-headed monster with the body of a man. Its hand reached out to her and touched her breast above her heart. She could not even inhale a breath to scream, her paralysis absolute. She should not have been afraid, she tried to convince herself. Through the bull's face he seemed to have an implicit smile, as if he was not dangerous. He made no moves to hurt her. It was as if he was showing himself to be gentle. What was it about his face that she recognized?

No, not his face. His body. It was his body that brought the familiarity. She knew the body, knew it intimately.

She was choking on recognition.

It was Theseus.

"No," she screamed, flinging off her covers and waking from her horrible nightmare. "Theseus."

She threw herself out of her bed and stood trembling, wondering if she might still be inside her Temple walls. The cool night breeze snapped her quickly to her senses. She was still where she knew she would be, on an island somewhere far away from home.

Theseus was not with her. His blanket was also gone. She twisted around and looked in panic for him.

"Theseus," she cried. "Theseus where are you?"

She ran back to the stony hideaway. No one was on the rocks. No one at all. She ran the last few steps to the water.

The ship was gone. It was gone.

"No," she wept. "No."

Through the gap in the rocks at the cove entrance she could just discern a square darkness, blacker than the night, departing.

* * *

Minos had kept himself temperate enough to make the journey to Amnisos. He had been carried by chariot behind fast horses along with the Physician. Minoan chariots were the fastest of the time; light, four-spoked, double-wheeled affairs that were perfectly balanced and as maneuverable as the horse that pulled them. Minos had been informed of a death, and he wanted to see it himself and have it checked out by someone with superior medical abilities.

"It is the same, isn't it Surgeon?"

"Yes. The nails, the breath. He is worse though. He has vomited and had an explosive diarrhea. But I do not know what it is that killed the two men."

"It doesn't matter. I do."

He stepped into the light of day. "And what have you found, Captain?"

The Captain of his Palace Guard had interviewed every fisherman who had been at the beach or who had been out on the water at dawn. The stories were the same.

"Two men left on a wing that carried them above the water with the speed of a bird, even faster than the wind itself. They were seen removing it from this building." He indicated the boathouse.

483

"Two men? Are they sure one wasn't a woman?"

"No one said anything about a woman. They said two 'men'."

"Go on."

"After they left another group came to the beach. There were fourteen by the best count. Both males and females."

"Fourteen?" But one of the males was found burbling incoherently in the Labyrinth. "Are you sure?"

"I can only go by what I have been told. There were six men and eight women. They departed aboard the black-sailed ship."

"At the same time as the winged craft, you mean?"

"No. All agree that the prisoner's ship left afterward. There seemed to be no tie between the two."

It hardly made sense. Ariadne could not have gone with the barbarians. "What was their heading?"

"Both started north. The black ship kept that direction, but the other deviated and flew northwest."

"Assemble the fleet. Send word to all ports that these vessels are to be hunted. The winged vessel can only be a creation of Daedalus. He must be found and returned. Failing that I want his corpse."

"Yes, Minos.

"If the second person aboard his wing was not Ariadne then it must have been his son Icarus. I never trusted him. I should have never allowed him in the Palace. He must have been feeding Daedalus information. He must have been involved in the building of the creation that cost the builder, this shipwright, his life. Notify every mariner that there is a price on Daedalus's head. They will also notify every emissary and ambassador in every port of the same. Search Knossos again. If Icarus cannot be located then we can assume that he was indeed the companion of Daedalus. He will also be worthy of a great reward."

"At once."

"No. Not at once. You will also pursue the black-sailed ship. It will be returning directly to Attica. You will find and apprehend the thirteen escapees. Ariadne will be with them. You will also bring the King Aegeus to Knossos. He will bend the knee before me. He will rue the day he thought to make me an enemy.

He will pray that I grant him his life."

* * *

King Aegeus had not left the coast since his son's departure, hoping against hope that Theseus's optimism would win out, that he might defeat the Minotaur and subvert the oppression imposed on them by the inimical Minos.

From his high vantage he could see the waters far distant, waiting impatiently for any sign of the ship returning with its square white sail rejoicing the good news.

The ship should be returning today if all went as hoped, any time now if the winds were as favorable at sea as they were here. He stood at the portico atop the highest hill, a shrine that had been commissioned by order of the Minoan ambassador but had seen no use for at least a decade. It was nothing more than a picnic place, a shelter from the rain or the too-hot sun.

He stood alone, a king without a cadre or retinue. He was in hermitage until his son's safe return. The hill was abandoned, at his express command.

His eyes filled with tears. There was the ship in the distance. It was unmistakably different from any other ship in shape regardless of sail.

The black sheet veiled the ship like a black cloud of death. His son was dead. At that moment, inside, he also died. His disappointment was transcendent and incomparable. No posterity, no succession, his was a prodigality. He was a waste of skin. He had let down his nation. He had been responsible for the destruction of his family and the suffering of his people and had set the interminable path of travail and deprivation forever.

Theseus's optimism had only given him temporary reassurance. He had that to thank him for at least. Now he would join him in the next world. They could comfort each other there.

He bound the cord to an inward curving section of a supporting pillar and stood on his toes, wrapping the remaining length tight around his neck and knotted the last strand. He could feel an expansion pressing outward within his skull as the pressurized carotid arteries fought successfully against the restriction. His veins bulged and his face flushed red, then slowly purple. His temples throbbed. His feet weakened and began to relax. He could no longer hold his weight upon his toes.

The cord stretched tighter as his weight pulled against it. His heels could not quite touch the floor. He couldn't breathe, but somehow that didn't bother him. He had lost all interest.

As his vision fogged he thought he saw the ship drop its black sail and raise a white. A wish fulfilled, he thought, a pleasant hallucination of something most desired. It was merciful of the gods to grant him a parting vision of a thing so hoped for. He could let his soul pass restfully seeing such an illusion.

The gods were kind.

MINOS

Chapter 17

Restoration

1890 BCE

King Kokalos, king of Siciania, wet his lips on the rim of his wine goblet. "I want you to take Daedalus as a husband."

"As husband?" Trapsea was thrilled. She had one hand on her chest as she looked for a reaction from her younger sister.

"I have not broached the notion with Daedalus yet." His daughter's face fell. "I wanted to get your reaction to it first. I can see that you would not be opposed to the idea."

"Oh, Trapsea. Daedalus for a husband. You will be the most envied of all women of Siciania." She felt a combination of envy and admiration for her sister.

"He's so much older than I am, Father. He probably wouldn't want me." She held her hands in front and twisted to the side, keeping a turned eye on her father.

King Kokalos smiled at her. She had so much to learn about men. Of course, it hardly mattered what she thought of the possible union, but it always made things so much smoother when women agreed enthusiastically to their arranged marriages. Daedalus was old, even older than he was, but that would make his daughter even more desirable. What man could turn down the offer of such a beautiful girl now that she had fully flowered?

A sentry entered the room and stamped to attention. "King Kokalos. An emissary from Kriti has arrived. He desires your consideration."

"Ah, marvelous. Send him in at once. Girls excuse me, I have business to attend to. We'll discuss your futures later. Off with you now." He waved them away.

He didn't see enough of the Minoan representatives. They brought the most wonderful trappings for trade and he always felt that the people of Siciania came out far ahead in the game. So far they came, traveling the dangerous waters like anyone else would walk a path. Naturally, King Kokalos considered his island kingdom at the toe of the Mediterranean 'boot' to be the most important civilization in existence, but that was only because he had never been anywhere else and the only contact he had with the outside world was through the Minoans. They chose carefully what they told him and kept him blissfully in the dark with regards to what was going on in the world around him. Only gradually did they impart information to him, a little tidbit every visit that helped shape his perception that the Minoans were mightier than they first made themselves out to be.

The guard reentered and stamped again. "Samos, from Knossos."

"Samos." King Kokalos stood to receive him. "The island of Siciania rises in your honor. May the graces of Minos be ever upon us."

"The graces of Minos will always be upon you, and your island. It is his great delight to engage in trade for the edification of both our countries. Should his special blessing ever be required on your behalf you need but ask."

This slightly veiled offer of military aid was unexpected but gave the king the assurances that his little nation was considered worthy of alliance should the need occur. One could never have too many friends.

"And please be sure to make our offer of contribution in similar circumstance known to Minos." Although Siciania had nothing that could be remotely compared to the armies of Egypt or Babylon it nevertheless was little alliances like this that the Minoans exploited and turned to their benefit. All told, a hundred little armies and economic affiliations were of greater consequence than any single association.

"I thank you on his behalf and will assuredly make it known."

"Will you be seated and take wine with me?"

"Your hospitality is appreciated after so long a voyage."

"Please enjoy. Now, to what end are we privileged to receive this visit?"

"Some trade, of course. But I would leave that to later. I want to show you something first." He released the drawstring of a sturdy bag and withdrew a large conch shell. "I am looking for someone to solve this riddle." He passed the shell to Kokalos. "Should you find the answer to this mystery you will have Minos's undying gratitude, and," he placed a hand over his mouth and cleared his throat, "I might add, a considerable prize."

Kokalos took the shell and furrowed his brow. He flipped it in his hands wondering what the riddle might be. It was nothing more than an ordinary shell, a small hole filed off the point that was too small for trumpeting through.

Samos could see his perplexity. It was nothing new. He had plied the sea for almost five years, stopping at every port, every seaside village, searching out his quarry. He had been to every island in the populated seas north of Kriti, he had combed Attica, he had even searched as far east as

Kypros. Daedalus's little craft, as ingenious as it was, could not have gone farther east without being seen, neither to the south where the waters were too vast. Samos had been working his way west for the last year, the only way left to him. Daedalus was so cunning. He had been seen escaping to the east but those with wisdom thought he was decoying them by allowing himself to be seen going that way. A man as smart as that would double back and slide throughout the islands unseen, probably at night. He could have stopped at any one of a hundred islands, or stepped off on any of a thousand miles of mainland coast. That he would go this far west was as far from their minds at the first as anything could be. But every other place had been searched. It was a long shot, as unlikely as any, but what else was left? Samos had sworn an oath to Minos that he would find the malefactor, and his honor bade him continue until he had word of the man's capture or concrete evidence of his death. He could never hold his head high on Kriti as long as his oath remained uneffectuated.

"The riddle is how to thread the shell," he instructed Kokalos. "I will leave it with you while I enjoy your island. I need a rest from my travels. Trade can wait, I'm sure you will agree." Samos stood to leave after finishing his wine in a few impolite gulps. Save the graces. He knew Kokalos would not be offended or even notice.

"I will give it my direct attention." How hard could it be? "The island is yours. Please enjoy every hospitality."

Alone, Kokalos toyed with the shell, completely absorbed. The task was proving to be frustratingly difficult. He tried everything to get a string through it, pushing it from the small hole, pushing it from the wide end, all to no avail. He dropped wound spools of the string in and twisted the shell in such a way as to get it to thread the curved path, round and around, but it was no use. Every attempt failed. He wanted Minos's promised gift but he felt it slipping from his fingers. How would he receive his reward?

Daedalus.

* * *

Samos admired the natural beauty and ingenuity of the shrine on Mount Eryx. A perfect honeycomb, six sides, six equal angles, it reminded one of a beehive immediately upon beholding it. Honey offerings had been laid out on the inner altar and wild bees came and went as they pleased, drawn by the windward scent. Worshippers, too, came and went, undaunted by the bees that ignored them.

He spoke with some of them, after they had paid their oblations. They were worshipping the Morning Star, Aphrodite. How unusual that they should worship a goddess of the same name. They hadn't last time he had been here. This shrine hadn't been here either, six years ago.

* * *

"Are you jealous, sister?"

"Jealous? No, I . . . How could I be? I'm happy for you, Trapsea. You'll be a fine bride for Daedalus."

"Reatha. You are not being honest with me and you know I can't stand that. Daedalus has been so kind to both of us since he came. I know you love him as I do."

"It is hard not to love such a man," she conceded, looking at her feet.

"I knew it." She placed an arm around her younger. "Don't hold it against me. I will never marry if you do."

"Never? How could you refuse marriage to Daedalus?"

"I would refuse. I would run away. Anything, but not offend you."

"How you talk. How can I believe anything you say?"

"How can you believe what I say? You ask me that? After you lied to me?"

"I wasn't lying. Not really." Her smile faded perceptively.

"You do love him as much as I do."

Reatha's tears began to flow in two silvery rivulets. "Yes. Yes, I do." She wrapped her arm around her sister in return. If only she had been born eleven Moon cycles sooner. Then she would have been the eldest and have this great privilege. How selfish. She shouldn't even have such thoughts. She was happy for her sister; really happy; she wasn't just saying it.

"Do you remember when he made us that toy? The year he came, remember? I was in my twelfth year and you your eleventh. It seems silly now, how we played with that thing, even fought over it. How many toys has he made us since then? Dozens I suppose."

"Fifteen."

"Fifteen?"

"Yes. Fifteen."

"You counted them? You remember each one?"

Reatha nodded. Her nose was running. She sniffed and looked about for something to wipe on.

"Oh, here," offered Trapsea, bending her knees higher and giving a fringe of dress to her sister. The girl really should take a cloth with her. Such a sentimental type.

"I wish we could both marry him," she said after wiping.

"Both of us? I don't think Father would allow that. He probably wants to marry you off to one of his enemies."

"What? Why would he do that?"

"Maybe not one of his enemies. Maybe one of his friends. Who knows. Are you serious about wanting to share him with me?"

"Yes. I don't want to marry anyone else. There is no one else like Daedalus. Are you saying you don't mind sharing? You wouldn't want him all to yourself?"

Trapsea pressed her lips together in a weird sort of grin. "I suppose we've shared everything else. Why not a husband?"

"Do you think he'd mind?"

"I don't know. We look like twins. We aren't much different in any other way, except you're blubbering all the time."

"I am not." She leaned away and swatted her sister.

"And violent." She swatted back.

"Oh. You . . . " They took salvos of harmless blows at each other, wrestling in the grass. A gust of wind blew Reatha's long skirt over her head and she fought with that as Trapsea pinned her and found herself looking overlong at what was revealed.

To share a marriage with both Reatha and Daedalus. How inviting. Would their father ever allow it?

* * *

"You need this shell strung with thread?" confirmed Daedalus. It was an odd request.

"Yes. I want to see if it can be done."

"No other reason?" Kokalos never did anything without a reason, but it escaped him as to what it might be. He was annoyingly evasive about it.

"Curiosity. Nothing more. Can it be done?"

"The only limits are time and expense. I have said that about everything."

"How much time or expense could be involved in this?" Kokalos was sure Daedalus would not purposely stall, but he had to realize that time was of great importance.

"No expense, King Kokalos. I was waxing philosophical. As for time, well, this is a difficult puzzle. You do not make things easy for me."

"A lesser challenge would be beneath you."

"You always flatter me into obeying your will. I'll take the shell to work on in solitude. I need to ruminate in isolation on this one."

"Of course." It was as difficult as he thought then. Good. Samos would be all the more impressed when it was completed. It was time to make Daedalus the offer. "Another thing. I have considered your position with us these last years. I would like to see you integrated into our society more fully. My daughters are in agreement." He sprung his proposal. "They would have you take them to wife."

"Both of them?" It was rash to say it like that but Daedalus was astounded at the offer. He knew he was in the king's favor but this was a high compliment indeed. Kokalos was not being very wise about it though. He should keep one in reserve for a political alliance of some kind. That was the way among royalty in most countries. Still, one could not object. Loneliness was besetting him, and getting worse, and he was fond of both girls. They had become very attractive this last while.

"It is their wish that it be so. They have always been inseparable."

"And your feelings on this?"

An architect and genius like Daedalus sealed to the kingdom by marriage? It would be a coup for the entire nation. In time they, too, could have buildings like the ones spoken of by Minos's ambassadors. Perhaps they could be just as great. "You have been like a brother and a son to me. I wish you to be part of my family. You would honor me by this union."

Five years. In five short years he had risen to the top of society. Minos never offered him a marriage of such standing. He had never even been considered an equal under Minoan law, although his son Icarus had. He pushed the grim thought to the back of his mind.

"King Kokalos, I need not even time to think. I accept your most gracious offer."

* * *

This is infuriating. Daedalus rested the weight of his head in his hand. He had tried everything, thought everything actually, but it was the same thing. He twisted the shell in his mind as he stared at it. He knew the structure of a shell and knew the winding, narrowing passage inside. Nothing could work. The only physical attempt he tried was to fasten a small weight to the thread and let it drop into the wide end. He jiggled and turned it but there was a point where the string would go no farther. He marked the string and pulled it out. It probably hadn't gone half-way.

It was hopeless. This might very well be an impossible challenge.

He shook his head in defeat. It was his age creeping up on him. In his younger days he might have had the clarity of mind to solve such a riddle, but not now.

He needed to rest his eyes. He had been concentrating too hard on one thing and they were beginning to blur. An ant carried a moth across the floor. Such gigantic powers those little creatures had. The task was made to appear all the more remarkable by the illusory mass of the moth, lighter than most creatures of its size. The ant was able to raise it easily above its head instead of dragging it like it might have a hard-shelled beetle.

If only he could have the strength of an ant, comparable to his size. What accomplishments, what miracles he could perform. He could stack blocks of stone without assistance and build temples and palaces in days instead of years. Funny how ants could not build anything of decency when they had the ability. Stupid creatures. It might have something to do with the size of their brain but he didn't think so. Otherwise, elephants and whales would make greater creations than man. If he were an ant he might keep his intelligence, and wouldn't that be something? He would astound the world with his miniature creations. In a second he had made the association. Why, if he were an ant he could drag the string through the shell with ease.

He dropped the insect, moth and all, into a jar and put the lid on top to keep it from escaping. Glue. He needed glue. And honey.

Both were easy to find. He spread a blot of honey around the wide opening of the conch with his finger and pressed his lips to the little hole at the tip. He inhaled slowly until he could taste the sweet vapors, vapors that would attract any ant.

He lay a small snake of wet clay across the ant's thorax, pressing it gently and pinning its body and legs to the table. The ant strained against its constraints, its bulbous abdominal segment squirming limited protest.

He picked at the end of the thread until it frayed into single, whisper-thin fibers almost too fine for his aging eyes to see. He rubbed some of the hide glue on the ant's back, laid the fibers onto it, and worked another layer of glue on top of that, pushing it forward with the strands, incorporating the fibers right into the glue itself.

The wait was interminable. He blew on it to speed the process, but any rush would end in failure. He had to have patience. He moved the table closer to the window so a sunbeam could fall on his little colleague, anything to hurry things along.

Should he chance it now? He spent a few minutes unwinding the thread into a straight line on the floor. Any little knot could get hung up inside the shell and prevent the ant from completing her mission.

The hole wasn't much larger than the ant, and he had a hard time persuading it to go inside. Its legs seemed to be getting stuck but in the end, with a few unpleasant pokes to the rear, it escaped to its freedom inside.

The ant wiggled her antennae in the darkness, registering the scent of food thick in the air. She set off in search of it, her diminutive brain zeroing exclusively on her incessant objective; to bring food back to her nest. But first she had to find it. Daedalus had tipped the shell up so the long spiral would be downhill for the ant. The going was easy at the beginning, but something was impeding its progress as it curled around and around in the slowly broadening passageway, slowing it, tugging at its backside, causing its hooked feet to slip on the smooth, nacreous lining. Straining harder, the something began to annoy it. The ant turned and bit at the thread, clasping it with its huge mandibles and pulling it like a robin yanking a worm from its hole.

Daedalus fed the thread into the hole as the ant demanded it, easing its work, and thrilling him. He was an inspiration to himself. He should be king of this island, not that insignificant sovereign Kokalos. In time. But he would not let things go on interminably as he had done on Kriti. Tied to the royal family he would impress the people with his works as he did there, only this time, with his past experience, he would assume the throne.

There it was. He saw the ant's waving antennae and spidery legs gripping on the glossy, inner shell. A few more tugs against its restraint and it was at the honey, only to be plucked from its prize by fat, pink fingers.

Daedalus tore the ant from the abdomen affixed to the thread and dropped it to the floor, its legs and jaws working in silent pain. He saw it squirm and squashed it under his foot. At least he could show it that much mercy after what it had done. He drew the delicate thread through the shell slowly and carefully, as if he were afraid at first to break it, but found that it could be pulled back and forth easily along the sleek lining.

Outstanding. He pinched off the ant's abdomen so no one would ever figure out how he had solved the riddle. The great Daedalus had done it again.

Was there ever any doubt?

* * *

Kokalos had to show Samos right away, time being an important factor in how impressive the achievement had been. He had the emissary hunted down and brought to him in time for a mid-afternoon refreshment.

Samos was immediately pleased to see Kokalos's smug look.

"Have you succeeded in solving the puzzle, King Kokalos?" He was suddenly breathless with hope.

Kokalos smiled imperiously, his head a little higher than usual, and set the conch before them, the thread dangling out of either end. Kokalos demonstrated that the thread could move through the conch by carefully pulling it back and forth, confirming that no trickery was involved.

"Wonderful." Samos stood and bowed before the king. "You have accomplished what no other has been able, both small and great, in five years of challenge."

Kokalos grinned. He had succeeded in gaining the highest respect of the Minoan ambassador. Minos would share in granting that respect when he heard.

"I must ask one thing. Excuse my forwardness but it is a requirement that I ask. Did you have any help in this task? I am so sorry, but I must ask."

Kokalos could feel some of the proud blood draining out of his face. "Help? What kind of help? Of course not. What do you think? That someone else did this?"

"No, no. Please forgive me. You must understand that I must be absolutely sure." He was sure now. The liar. "I beg that you not take offense. For such a reward that Minos is to endow, well, it must be endowed to the cunning artificer who is able to do this and none other. You understand."

"Thank you. Yes, I understand." Kokalos hoped his face wasn't revealing anything untoward.

"Very good. Then I must be going. My ship awaits, and my crew is in preparedness. I will take this shell as proof to Minos that the riddle has been solved." He would have asked how it had been done, but too much probing might set the warning. Daedalus probably wasn't even told why he was performing the challenge. If Kokalos had even mentioned that the Minoan ambassador was around, he might have taken flight. He definitely wouldn't have complied with threading the shell. That was a certainty. He had to make his leave before he scared the wanted man off.

King Kokalos escorted Samos to his ship, talking about everything other than the shell along the way. Samos kept swinging the conversation to that most impressive shrine at Mount Eryx, the honeycomb structure with the most artful architecture. There was nothing else like it anywhere on the island. Surely the artificer was one to be treasured.

Indeed he was. Indeed he was.

* * *

Minos received the ambassador Samos in private. He writhed with hatred as he pulled the thread back and forth through the shell, stifling the insufferable urge to tear it out. The thread was of the same type of thin, silken thread used by Ariadne to lead the prisoners to safety from the Labyrinth. Hers had been doubled over and wound from the same filaments. The people of Siciania had no such capabilities. Minos's mind dredged the horrible memories. He had found the panels and the secret passageways, and the clew of thread Ariadne had dropped at the panel. He had found their way through the darkness of the sewer and the exit from the shrine. The treachery of it all, the evil machinations conspiring against him. Daedalus must have planned this all from the very inception of construction. It was too outrageous to fully contemplate. He released the thread lest he do it damage.

He twirled one of the two iron rings on his finger, made as a replacement of the iron icons stolen from the Sanctum. It was all he had to connect him to the tektites. These pieces of mock fluff from the far coasts of the Inhospitable Sea were a poor comparison but they gave him something to cling to, although they were no substitute for what Daedalus had taken. Iron was very rare, albeit completely useless for anything other than a rough form of ornamentation, so not very valuable. These rings were such poor forgeries of the tektites that they eternally reminded him of the fact. That is why he wore them. They would preserve his hatred. He twisted the ring harder, the thought poisoning him. It would not pass his swollen knuckle and he returned to spinning it irritably.

Daedalus had been his bane for so many years. The mere intimation that he might still be alive set him off. But he knew in his heart it was true. He greatly feared that another monarch would have the services of so brilliant a man, as capable of building warships or strongholds as palaces or shrines. To a great extent, the prestige of a ruler depended on the possession of a palace more impressive than other rival's or monarch's. Minos could not tolerate such an eventuality. Anyone could build something larger and more imposing than another country if they wanted to dedicate the resources, but who could build with such architecturally inspired style and grace as Daedalus? He would have to be dealt with. No shore of the Great Sea would be safe haven for the renegade. He, Minos, would not permit it.

"Siciania. How could he have sailed so far?" he mumbled to himself.

The ambassador knew he would be better off not speculating.

Could it have been anyone other than Daedalus? The ambassador had done the right thing by not inquiring overly close. If Daedalus had gotten wind that he'd been found, then he would fly as surely as he had the first time. There would never be a second chance. Everything pointed to him being the one. The wonderfully designed shrine, so closely imitative of the Temple Tomb just south of Knossos, built only in the last few years, was tantamount to a dead giveaway in and by itself. That the simple king so obviously tried to claim he was the one who had solved the riddle clinched it, making speculation fact. Only one other had ever been able to solve it. Androgeus.

He assembled the Council in the Outer Sanctum.

"Five years ago our nation was violated. This Sanctum was violated, the most sacred place on Earth." He reeled from the heavy dose of opium, almost hallucinating. The white-loined men and skirted women swayed and wavered with him as if in a stepless dance. "An evil was perpetrated against us which we owe the Goddesses and Gods to avenge. Murder was committed. Virtue stolen and beguiled into committing the offense with sacred potions. Human tribute released and our reputation vilified. The final blasphemy was the stealing of our most sacred treasures with which our society was built and without which our society is doomed. Every place gifted with one of the sacred seeds has bloomed to serve us in strength and wisdom. Without the Goddess, we see the mastery rightfully granted us fading to gray. Soon all will be blackness. Today it has been revealed to me that the source of that wisdom has been taken to Siciania. We have seen the building of temples impossible to that nation but a few years ago. They make false worship of Aphrodite without legitimate Priesthood. They were never meant to have the icons. Never. The

496

two remaining sacred seeds are meant, according to legend and history passed down for millennia, for the Atticans and the lost lands of the Endless Sea, when they are ripe to receive them.

"We must recover them along with the Mother Goddess. The holy relics rightfully belong to our people," he shouted with acrimonious fervor. "The people of Kokalos have harbored an egregious criminal, a treacherous beast that we took to our bosoms in the light of friendship and trust and who broke every law in return. He has been granted every mercy and repaid us with the ultimate betrayal. He has sought and obtained refuge from a treacherous people who have wantonly become steeped in his lies. The people of Kokalos must make the uttermost payment for their continued collaboration. They will suffer our vengeance." His voice rose in fury.

Minos tore out the thread and smashed the shell against a stucco wall.

"They will suffer us in war."

* * *

War.

The Minoans had never touched on the bloody contest of man against man in the unforgiving battlefield of war. They had been directly involved in almost every conflict of importance for the last thousand years, but only in the auspices of advisors and arms suppliers. Never, not even once, had they entered into combat on a national scale themselves. Their role as warriors had never had to exceed that of policemen patrolling the sea against pirates and budding navies, both of which were considered in the same league.

The Minoan fleet filled the bay of Kamikos before dawn. They bore no lights and were simply 'there' when the first break of day woke the inhabitants. Samos led the infantry troops, girded in battle armor of bronze reinforced tunics, corselets, and helmets, and outfitted with shields and long swords, to the modest building Kokalos regarded as a palace. The people did not know whether to watch in fascination or flee. At first, they greeted the Minoans with celebratory waving and cheers as they paraded into town, but it became all too apparent by the fierce expressions fronting their carapaced heads that this was more than an ambassadorial mission. They pulled back and watched in trepidation from the corners of buildings as the soldiers, with their skirts sewn up the middle into shorts, marched past. Many fled taking their families and a few necessities away from the town as fast as they could walk without showing outright cowardice. Most stayed, out of sight, fearing loss of pride as much as the terror of what might, unthinkably, be occurring. In their island community, they had enjoyed the same refuge against battle as the people of Kriti. None had ever known warfare but, now that it had come, they knew it when they saw it.

497

Doors were slammed open in the king's palace. The sailors, none having been on a military campaign, made a great stamping of boots and posturing within the building to terrify the enemy. None of them harbored any fear in his heart, such was the excitement of the moment. These people were so obviously unprepared that they had no hope of defense.

Samos sought out Kokalos and trapped him inside his room until Minos made ready his entrance.

A single shout of "Minos," from the soldiers signaled his arrival. Samos opened the door and pulled Kokalos out by the collar, demeaning him and humbling him as the soldiers filling the interior of the celebratory hall parted in two waves and allowed Minos an isle of passage. The king of the Minoans swept in wearing a cape of gold and silk fabric over his bare torso, a brightly burnished golden sword of intricate inlaid design slung from his waist with a glorious pommel of turned agate rebounding against his richly embroidered battle skirt. His long black hair cascaded like a dark waterfall over the back of his royal cape. The sea of stony clean-shaven faces brooking cold eyes terrified Kokalos as he trembled to stand, fearing his life. To each of Minos's solid footsteps, the soldiers slapped their blades against their thighs. Kokalos could only hear the sound of his heart beating in his ears.

Minos walked to within a foot of Kokalos, staring him right in the eyes. The throng erupted in a mighty shout. "Minos. Minos."

"Kneel before your master," shouted Samos over the tumult into Kokalos's ear.

The king collapsed in fright and pressed his forehead against Minos's boot. "My kingdom is yours," he quailed. "Please. Spare my life and those of my family."

Minos let the pathetic creature kiss and grope his calves for only a moment more before his simpering became too bilious.

"Get up, perfidious wretch. Your truckle sickens the Gods."

Kokalos had to be pulled up by the collar and held there by Samos. He kept trying to fall to his knees. "Why am I deserving of this my Lord? What have I done to offend thee?"

"Offend me?" he roared. Minos almost pressed his nose into Kokalos's, the wayward king's head now held steady by Samos's hand wrapped into his hair. "Offend me? You have not offended me. You have offended the entire world. You have insulted the Gods. You have disparaged every living being with your insolence, down to the most inconsequential insect. How could you, a king, besmear yourself with a muck so foul?"

"But what have I done, Lord Minos?" He was truly at a loss. He had believed that Minos was coming to bestow glorious riches upon him, but when he observed the threatening troops marching just outside the doors of his palace he knew at once he had been deceived. It had been too late to escape, but he still wondered what it could all be about.

"You harbor the evil Daedalus. You shield him."

"Daedalus?" This was about Daedalus? Impossible.

"Daedalus. You have given him refuge for five long years."

How could he have known? It could only have been Samos. The spy Samos. That was why the riddle of the shell. This is the reward. Oh, the Gods. His daughters. His friend. "But what is Daedalus to you, Lord?"

Minos seized his beard and breathed the words into his face.

"He is anathema."

* * *

"Oh, Daedalus. What are we to do?"

The palace had been seized, guards staked around Kamikos, and Kokalos sealed in a cellar storeroom. He would not be freed until his people, or Minos's soldiers, acquired Daedalus.

"Calm yourselves. Sit at peace while I think."

Trapsea and Reatha huddled together and wept. It was cold here in the darkness of this isolated cave. At least they would be safe for a while.

"You will kill Minos," Daedalus said matter-of-factly.

Reatha fell back against the wall in horror. "Kill him? We could not kill him."

Trapsea was more confident. "We'll do anything to save you, Daedalus. We are betrothed. Guide us and we'll do your bidding."

Reatha could not help herself. After her reflex expostulation, she could only agree with her older sister.

They could kill for Daedalus.

They would.

* * *

"Relax yourself. Slacken your limbs. Close your eyes and think of nothing but the blue clarity of a summer sky. Let the tranquility of all that is beautiful surround and envelope you."

Minos had taken an extra dose of opium and was finally letting the tension of the last couple of days dissolve into oblivion. These two girls were masterful in their arts. He would have preferred they not wear so much in the way of clothing. On second thought they could hardly be as attractive as the women of Kriti, although here they were quite exceptional by any local comparison. But they probably still sported the hairy armpits and pubis so favored by barbarians. It was better that he didn't have to see.

He lay naked on his stomach as they massaged away his stresses, one working on his neck as the other dexterously squeezed each muscle on his back. The combined effect of his drug and the blissful rubdown were putting him to sleep.

"Come now, King Minos. You mustn't pass out on us." Trapsea ran her fingers across his cheek. "You'll catch cold on this table. Come to the bath."

He let himself be led to the fleece lined soaker tub, already partially filled with hot water. Such comfortable luxury he had not even experienced in Knossos. The idea was simple and brilliant. The wool soaked up the warmth and distributed it softly at every point. Oh, he was in heaven. One of the girls, Reatha she said her name was, continued to rub his neck and shoulders as he fell dreamily to sleep.

Trapsea left them and climbed the steps to the level above, the false smile now struck from her face. In a small room was a sizable trough, one end raised above a bed of blazing coals, filled with boiling olive oil. At one end a wide wooden plug had been pressed into the hole, swollen to a leakproof fit by the hot liquid. A rope ran up from the plug to its tie on the ceiling. She gripped it tight with both hands and leaned against her arms. To take a life. A spike of apprehension stabbed her heart. She didn't even know Minos. He had mumbled a few things to them while they massaged him, but he hadn't seemed the vile man Daedalus averred. Hot fumes drew beads of sweat from her skin as she swung her weight from side to side. She closed her eyes as she contemplated the inevitable. Minos wanted to kill her love, he had as much as declared it openly. She felt her hands tighten ever harder around the rough hemp. It had to be now. If Minos, for some reason, rose from his bath, the chance would be forever missed. She had to do it. She had to, for her husband, her sister, and herself.

The bath. Ah. In a few minutes they would have it filled with warm water. Unusual for barbarians to have baths. Unheard of, actually. Minos's mind was intangibly troubled by the thought. What would a bath be doing in a place like Kamikos? Maybe Samos had the king build it. Possibly. Siciania wasn't much of an outpost though. Daedalus. Minos's eyes snapped open too late.

Trapsea gritted her teeth in forced hatred and jerked the rope, amazed that it didn't come free with her first attempt. The plug had swollen so much that it was stuck fast. She yanked again, pulling sideways and throwing her whole body weight into it. The plug tore free and she slid back off balance, fretting her palms on the scabrous twine. The wide plug splashed out of the oil spaying droplets of blistering liquid on her arms and clothes. She fell back, cursing the stupidity of her action. Little scalds appeared instantly on the spots where the oil had touched her. There wasn't even any water to cool them. She spat on her wounds as her only resort.

The bulk of the oil coursed into a trough, flowing a few feet to a wide hole. Hideous shrieks of pain from below sent her flying from the room.

Minos had received the full barrage of boiling oil onto his chest. It filled his tub in an instant, the exquisite agony snapping him free of his sedation. He jumped up and fell back into the tub, slipping on the lubricant and splashing the assailing oil all over himself again. The worst was that splashed on his face and in his eyes. He leapt from the tub again, howling anguish. Whitened skin peeled from his body in a huge blister, half of his chest and back draped around his hips, his thighs torn open and hanging loosely over his calves like poorly fitted stockings. He stood, frozen like an anatomical statue, afraid for his life, afraid any movement would make whatever this was worse. Where were the girls? Where was everybody? His neck tightened and he let out a siren-like scream through clenched teeth.

Four of his guards thundered down the steps into the room. Stopping, they were unable to comprehend the hideous apparition. The face was so tortured they could barely conceive that it might be Minos. Below the neck, exposed red flesh glistened and shimmered with every point of light. Bags of white skin, folded about in all the wrong places, sent them reeling into a nightmare state where nothing seemed cogent. What was this? What had happened?

Was this monster even real? It wasn't moving. It was just standing with its teeth barred and its arms out to the side.

They made a move forward as if to touch it.

"No," it screamed through its teeth. "Get away."

Massive blisters filled under what skin remained intact, as they watched in horror, fluid leaking from his damaged or destroyed capillary beds.

Minos fell to his knees as consciousness faded. A jolt of pain brought him momentarily around. but his head spun with hypotensive vertigo. His blood thickened as the plasma constituent poured unchecked through the semi-permeable capillary membranes. The microscopic pores were still too small to allow red blood cells to pass but were still enlarged by the burns to the point where there was no hindrance offered to the simpler fluids of the blood. His blood pressure plummeted, his heart racing as it pumped to no resistance. He toppled onto his side, the impact sloughing more skin from its underlying tissues, a red-tinged ooze like the slime from a garden slug creeping out from the edges of peeled back fissures. Capillary pores had dilated enough now to let the red blood cells pass freely and the ruddy seepage was covering him like a sweat. That final harrowing affliction rose like a fountain, driving him insane with agony and willingly to the only release of death.

The four soldiers knelt beside the grimacing corpse. It was Minos. They had no doubt of that now. His clothes lay draped over a rod against the wall. One of them pulled back the blister almost enveloping the iron ring on his finger. The ring was still hot, the skin slippery like fat from the spit. He must have been boiled in the cauldron, still percolating with hot steam bubbling through the oil from the settled water underneath.

"Seal the palace. Let no one escape." They sounded the alarm. In minutes the palace was cordoned off, the inhabitants ushered roughly into the main hall. The daughters of Kokalos were not among them.

King Kokalos knelt quaking before the Captains, as much from the cold as from fear. A chill wind blew audibly through the open doors and windows. A sudden storm was blowing hard upon them, howling against building walls, from the north. He wished for a cloak so he would not tremble so, but the appearance of such trembling contrition helped sway the hearts of the Captains so they agreed that he really did have nothing to do with the slaying. They had found out how it had been done as they sealed the building. Kokalos might have been able to arrange for an ordinary assassination, but this had more of the nefarious originality and perfection of Daedalus.

"Please, majesties. I have surrendered the island. What was mine is yours. If I could find Daedalus or avenge in any way the death of King Minos, I would. Tell me how I may be of aid to you. All you need do is ask."

There was nothing he could do. Active support was the only thing. They released Kokalos to the streets, to go as he saw fit. He was no danger. He would only benefit their takeover by associating freely with his citizens. They would watch him though, just in case.

The Minoans had no experience with military acquisitions on their own behalf. All previous had been done by other countries assisted with their expertise and weaponry. It had never been necessary before to make direct invasions. Many had bad omens regarding the attempt. It did not bode well with the astrologers. Minos had ignored them. What had they known? The town was taken without bloodshed, quickly, easily.

Now Minos lay dead.

The westerly squall of the autumn meltemi fell upon them with a suddenness and fury known only in tales. The merchant ships, temporarily modified for military conflict, were being torn from their anchorages in the bay. Minos had not had them beached because of fears of sabotage. With most of the soldiers away from the ships the few remaining guards could have easily been routed and the ships destroyed. Now white-capped waves snapped their lines and wind blew the piteous crews against the rocks. Only two ships still with captains aboard managed to battle their way farther out to safety as they watched helplessly the floundering and destruction of their entire navy. Many sailors died on the rocks, smashed or drowned in the breaking seas. Of those who survived, most were grossly wounded, lacerated on barnacles, arms broken against wedged rocks.

The Minoans watched the destruction from the shore, many of the captains weeping openly, their tears mingling with the dark rain as they witnessed their ships cracking and spilling open like eggs.

The storm tossed their two remaining ships like corks upon the high white froth. All prayed the minimal crews would have strength to maintain their position against the rigorous seas driving them shoreward.

They were fortunate. The nonpareil storm was a phenomenon lasting barely the day. By nightfall, the waters had calmed enough to heel the ships ashore. The crews thankfully landed. Even seasoned veterans appreciate terra firma after weathering a storm such as that. A meticulous inspection of the ships revealed no damage. The two captains and their minimal crews had performed flawlessly.

The two ships were filled with the most experienced and skilled crews. They over-manned each one to make the voyage to Kriti in record time. They would be rowing non-stop the entire way. The Council had to be informed without delay. Siciania was taken, Kokalos subservient, Minos murdered, the fleet with the exception of two destroyed, and Daedalus still fugitive.

"We need reinforcements before the islanders realized they have the upper hand and marshal a retaliation."

* * *

Kamikos was in sight. The fleet destroyed by the sudden meltemi at Siciania was far from all the ships at Kriti's disposal. They were merely all that could be mustered at the time. Since then many had returned from trading missions and had been pressed into military service. Androgeus ordered the fleet to a full speed onslaught of the bay. They drove the ships straight onto the sand and came off running, shouting, and blowing horns. In case any islanders had taken the idea seriously of staging battle against the men left behind he wanted it known with a surety that none would stand had any been harmed. There would be ten men slain for every death suffered by a Minoan.

The few people seen on shore from the water vanished by their arrival. They ran up the grade to the palace guided by the worried crewmen who were of the original raiding party, who had left their friends behind. Had any been harmed they were bent on vengeance.

Their fears were unwarranted. The surprised Minoans inside the palace simply stared at them during a moment of recognition as the invading force burst through the doors en masse, then jumped to embrace them. The cheers and felicitations became riotous as they clapped and rejoiced with old friends.

The Captains had wisely retreated to the palace and taken Kokalos and his family, and his most influential advisors, with them. With the most powerful countrymen sequestered from their own people and held, as it were, hostage, they virtually guaranteed their safety for the two weeks without sea support.

King Kokalos had told the locals, from his rooftop, that everything was business as usual, that he was still king, and that Daedalus had a huge price on his living head. Any excursion from the palace by Minoans was of the most polite and diplomatic sentiment. They resorted to taking the island by economic control rather than military. It was not the least curious to them that the people responded well to this, not seeming to have as much concern for Kokalos as for their assurance that they had the freedom to fish and raise their sheep as they always had. They worried about the rumors of additional imposed taxes and were assured that things would remain as before. If Kokalos collected a tax, that was his prerogative as King. The only interests of the Minoans were of trade and finding Daedalus.

The word had spread so far and fast that Daedalus had no way of escaping the island. Everyone wanted in on the reward. All boats, no matter how small, were watched in hopes of catching him and collecting a bounty.

"We are not going to find Daedalus." Androgeus was resigned on that issue. His old friend was far too clever for that. He might not get off the island, but he would never allow himself to be caught on it. There was a better way. "I am offering him amnesty."

"Amnesty?" The protests were singularly of shock. How could Androgeus offer freedom to a murderer of so many counts?

"As for murder, that has yet to be established. He has been accused of many things, including the murder of Minos. If his hand has been involved in these offenses, he will be dealt with according to law. But that cannot happen until he is in custody. He is too valuable a man to be wasted without just cause. I must find out the truth. Make the offer known far and wide. The offer of reward still stands with whoever locates or brings him to us. Only this time, news of his freedom, should he come willingly, will be published. Use my name freely. He will come to it. He will know that Minos is dead and will not have need to fear as he did before. All of you are ordered, by decree of the Council, to adhere to this command. You will preserve the life of Daedalus and bring him to me.

"And now, take me to Minos's body."

They had preserved Minos in the manner of the Egyptians, cleaning him and filling him with preservative honey and balms. They covered him in strips of canvas wrap from the sails of the wreckages and bound him tightly. It was not the manner of the Minoans, but they were presuming that Minos would be transported back to Knossos to be laid to rest with his antecedents. It would not be proper for him to be the only one separate from the long line of Minoses.

They had to wrap him and preserve him, not only for the long time he would be without burial but also because of his appearance. Only a few knew the extent of the damage done to his body. All knew of his death, within the Minoan encampment, but that is where it stayed. Only a few of Kokalos's people knew, and they were also inside the palace, sworn to secrecy on pain of death. The name Minos was one thing keeping the intruders safe. Had he been widely known to be dead anything could have happened.

Androgeus listened as the Captain gave his full report in private of the awful event. One by one, each of the four guards gave their description of the awful event and were then dismissed, each again with a continuance of their oath of silence.

Androgeus did the same with the full Minoan compliment, swearing them collectively to remain mute, even amongst themselves for the time being, regarding the death of their fallen king. For now, it was imperative.

* * *

"Daedalus, they are looking for you." Trapsea was distraught. Guilt had been eating at her over the killing. She remembered Minos's tranquil face, asleep in the bath, before pouring the oil down the hole. As much as she tried to convince herself he deserved it she still had reservations. What a cruel way to die. They should have slit his throat or stabbed him. Then he wouldn't have screamed so atrociously. They had almost panicked at his outburst, barely enough time to escape before the doors closed. Oh, how they ran, ducking behind houses and fleeing down lanes like the collective host of the netherworld might spring upon them at any moment. But the Minoans had been caught completely off guard, just as Daedalus said they would. And none would have ever suspected that two girls would mount an attack on him; never a successful one.

"Calm, my beloved. Calm." He took her to his bosom. "What could be worse now than before?"

"Now they try to trick you. They cannot find you and take you by force so they plant deceit, offering rewards and forgiveness. It is all a ruse, Daedalus. Don't believe them," she pleaded.

"What do you mean, 'forgiveness'?"

"They are spreading lies to draw you out. They are lies."

"What lies?" He directed the question to Reatha, standing coldly by herself while Trapsea cuddled. "Come here and tell me."

Trapsea made room for her sister. Reatha burst into tears. "They say you can come back, that you will not be harmed. Anyone who harms or kills you will be treated in like manner." She gazed into his eyes. "I don't believe them either, Daedalus. I think they still want to kill you."

This was a new strategy, most atypical of a simple captain. "Who is new in Kamikos? Have reinforcements arrived already?"

"Yes. Many ships. I don't know how many. They are spreading the name Androgeus around."

"Androgeus?" Could he be here?

"They say you are to be told his name. They say you will be assured of your safety when you hear it."

"Did you see him?"

"We messed our hair and wore poor clothes. No one recognized us. We did get close enough to see him."

"Tell me how he looked."

"He is a large man. Not fat. Tall and very strong. He has no beard, like all of your people." All of his people. Daedalus almost laughed. He kept his face shaved because that had been what he had become accustomed to. He had never mentioned that he was not a Minoan native. "He had a strange face, like I have seen on old people."

"Wrinkled?"

"No. Not wrinkled. It was crooked. Fallen on one side, without expression, like it had ceased working. The eye on that side was half closed, like it might fall asleep independent of the other."

So. Androgeus had recovered from his injury. Mostly, anyway. This was joyous news. It was almost too good to be true.

"We will go at once."

"No," both girls pled.

"He is my friend. Perhaps my only friend," he added pensively. "If there is one person on this world who I would entrust with my life it is Androgeus."

* * *

"You knew I would come."

"Yes."

"For you and no other."

"Yes."

They sat quietly for a few moments, reflecting on the sad course of events that had led them to this place. Androgeus sipped his wine in the smallest amounts, holding the cup to his lips on his paralyzed side so the wine could be caught before it dribbled to his chin. They had taken a small room in the palace where they could be isolated from everyone else and discuss things in complete privacy. The girls had protested, unabashedly accusing the Minoans of a duplicitous conspiracy to kill Daedalus. Even his reassurances could not quell their insufferable comportment and they had to be taken away by force. Daedalus was reluctant to see them off this way but he had no alternative recourse. He needed to be alone with Androgeus.

"Tell me what you know of Minos."

"I know you killed him, or had him killed." Androgeus struggled with the words. They slurred because of his partial paralysis but he had, over the years, practiced enough in the privacy of his room to make himself understood. He had been reluctant to ever leave the room, his imperfection embarrassing to him. When he did leave it was to go on long walks, often lasting for days, where he would travel the mountains in solitude and build his muscles to their former strength. In isolation he would commune with the gods, gaining confidence and spiritual vitality. In some ways he thought himself a better person than ever before, but each time he spoke he was reminded of himself and his imperfection. He could not even bring himself to look in a polished mirror anymore. The appearance of his face broke his heart.

"Do you know why?"

"You feared for your life."

"No. I will tell you why. He was not the rightful Minos."

Androgeus was shocked. "What do you mean?"

"He had the Mother Goddess, and the remainder of the Five, but he was a temporary keeper, a confederate set by the previous Minos, until the real Minos could come into his own."

"Where did you hear this?"

"You heard it yourself, while in a coma. Minos said it to you."

Androgeus gasped. He had thought it all a dream. Yet no one could have known his dream. Daedalus spoke the truth. But he had not told all. "How could that be? Minos could not have been appointed without the blessings of the Council. They would never have sustained a fraud."

"They would uphold the appointing of any chosen by their king. And because they supported the decision, he could hardly be called a fraud. He was only temporary." He took another pull from his mug. "Androgeus. Consider this. The universe is a place of order. The sun rises and sets every day in a predictable pattern, the stars are the same always, the planets and Moon follow certain paths, the seasons are known before they come. The Gods control it all. The Minoans are the chosen people of the gods as surely as any of these. And Minos is their chosen leader."

"And you had him killed."

"It was the way things were meant to be. If he had not died, the real Minos could not have taken his place. The time is now. With or without approval of the Council, the next Minos is already chosen and approved of the Gods."

"There cannot be a Minos without the Sacred Mother and her Seeds."

"I have that which are needed. I will return them to the rightful heir."

"Personally?"

"Yes. I will restore them only to he that rightfully deserves."

"Then we can no longer talk. You must leave. You cannot be accepted back, even on my order, unless you return to me what has been stolen."

"I will return them to you. That is what I have been saying."

The full light of what Daedalus was trying to express struck Androgeus like a thunderbolt. He, the Minos? It all came together. The dream he could never fully remember. It was true. Minos had spoken his regrets while he was in that dreamlike existence between life and death. Enough was remembered that he could rule out any chance of lying on Daedalus's behalf.

"Me. The Minos."

"At last." Daedalus appeared relieved. "You must accept that it is true."

Androgeus shook his head in shock. Normally he could think clearly, but this was overwhelming.

"But my Father . . . my Uncle?"

"The man you threw a rock at was not your father, neither was he your uncle. You were adopted out to him in your infancy. The secret of your whereabouts was kept even from the Council, with the exception of a few senior ones who died with their lips sealed. Only Minos, your brother, was left with the information. Not even the man who raised you was given the whole truth. Your brother was to abdicate when you became old enough, but he quickly became so corrupted by his office that he refused to hand over the reins of power, so badly had his lust of it grown."

His brother. Yes. He could remember Minos's voice saying those words. "How could this be so?"

"Blame not your brother. It is the time within which we live. It could have as easily been you. Your grandfather knew ahead what was needed for your society; what was best. You were taken as a member of the Council in your childhood at the time your brother was advanced so you could learn firsthand the ways of the sovereign, to see from the outside the pitfalls of one with absolute power who could be led down evil paths. Your experience has led you to this day. Do you understand? Whichever road you follow will be the correct road." He paused for effect. "Are you pleased with the people of Kriti?"

He was about to answer 'Of course,' but hesitated. "No. No, I am not."

"Why?"

"They have corrupted themselves. They seek only riches for themselves instead of improvement for the world. They drug themselves as Minos did, ruining their health, slowing their work, sending our wealth overseas. What joy they have is a falsehood, a lie."

"And you will change that."

"I will change it? It is a place of great achievement and beauty, all restored since the last great quake by Minos's hand; by your hand; but the people are becoming greedy and corrupt. They followed the example of Minos, and he has led them down a fearful path. Since your flight, the country has failed. His obsession tracking you down left him little time to attend to religious duties or needs of state. Many of the Elect have been taking advantage of the weaker orders and have not met with rebuke from Minos. There have been a number of us in the Council who have tried to maintain the old structuring and discipline, but we have not the backing needed to achieve that. Several of the Council have thrown up their hands and do not even attend meetings anymore, preferring to stay in their cities isolated from Knossos and Minos. There are those in Kriti who even laugh openly at us now. All in a few short years by the actions of one man. The gods could not change the damage Minos has wrought upon our country. "

"Don't be so hasty as to presume anything the gods can or cannot do. Perhaps they have no intention of repairing your island. Perhaps they would have you set out on another." It was almost shocking to Daedalus to hear himself talking in this way. He no more believed in gods than in stones turning to gold. But he had no doubt he would be better off with Androgeus, building some new society, than anywhere else on earth. Certainly he would be better off than here, with the imbecilic people of Siciania. It was a miracle they were ever able to build the hexagonal temple, even with his coaxing and instruction. The people of Kriti could have done the same thing, and three times more, better and in half the time.

"Another island." The thought was tantalizing.

"One not far from Kriti, where economic control could still be maintained, where religious formality could once again be central in the lives of the inhabitants; where inhabitants could be selected and maintained according to dictum, all others transferred to Kriti where they would retain close ties and still be considered part of the citizenry. The new island would be of a higher order than any that has before existed, separate, exclusive, like Knossos was intended to be but cannot because of its lack of isolation. The new island would be truly the island of Minos."

"You speak flattering words."

"I speak only truth." He stood to leave, without the permission of his king. "I will bring your icons in the morning. At that time you may confer the kingship upon your own head. You have no need of the Council's endorsement. You are Minos."

* * *

Every Minoan gathered before the dawn at the honeycomb-shaped structure. The Star of Aphrodite radiated brightly, solitary and alone in the predawn, bluing sky. A few captains had protested the danger of leaving their ships untended, but Samos assured them the inhabitants knew better than to tamper with them in any way. They would be destroyed if a single ship was damaged and they knew it.

Central to the ceremony was a simply laid out body wrapped in white linen. Inside the wraps Minos's body lay at peace; peace from the pains of his vicious death; peace from the mental torments of opium addiction; peace from the burdensome guilt he bore from years of carrying the mantle of power unrighteously; peace from the knowledge of possessing his power unjustly from the brother whom he jealously thought might usurp the throne, the brother he loved.

Minos was being interred here on Siciania, the island later to be known as Sicily. His preserved body smelled sweet from the herbs and balms, belying the ghastliness of his blanched and ravaged integument. Here he would remain, occupying the concealed tomb beneath the center of the temple of Aphrodite, interred in the very heart of the one he cherished to the point of worship, his beloved Pasiphae. He would lie here at Mount Eryx outside of Kamikos one thousand years until, in the 5th century BCE, his bones would be exhumed and returned to Crete by Theron, the tyrant of Agrakas.

The ceremony was employed with great pomp, grand eulogies read, the most regal clothes available worn. Maidens spread honey on all six tholos walls, attracting bees to their namesake.

Daedalus inwardly cursed the irony of the funeral. He had built the shrine as an offering to Aphrodite, his beloved Pasiphae, not Minos, for aiding him with her influences to escape Kriti and find safety and hospitality in a strange land.

Local inhabitants grieved and celebrated alongside the Minoans as if they had known Minos personally and had adored him. Great lays of food were spread in preparation of the finale. After Minos was laid to rest and the seal stone fitted into place the concourses gathered close. Leagues of Minoans came to their place at the front and Androgeus stood higher than the rest upon a marble block, wearing the formal clothing of Minos, a golden cape flapping in the breeze behind him. No one knew quite what to make of this.

"Behold, the new Minos," Daedalus shouted. The silence was deafening. Gaping mouths were all around. "Behold your new Minos," he roared again.

King Kokalos started the cheer and shouts of approval came from outside the ranks of the Minoans. The locals were jubilant at the news, the ramifications. Androgeus was someone they could grow to love without any difficulty. All he seemed to want was prosperity for everyone. He seemed to have no intention of subjecting them to dictatorial rule, instead he was sympathetic and amicable to all of their concerns.

Cheering spread among the natives and from them to the unsure Minoans. They were slow to catch on because of the irregularity of this declaration. He must have been ordained to the Seat of Minos while on Kriti, before coming here. But, no, the ones who came with him thought. There was no such ordination or celebration. Could it be that Androgeus was seizing power of his own accord? It didn't matter, they decided. Androgeus was a good man and had led them to a bloodless triumph. He would be a relief after the disorganized Minos just laid to rest. The corpse had been an embarrassment and liability in life. No wonder they didn't want him returned to his native land. They cheered with the best of them. If Androgeus was seizing power, it could not be done by anyone better or more respected, even if he was a bit physically defective. They could look around such minor trivia as a mouth that didn't entirely work properly. After all, he was a member of the Council. And it wasn't as though he was born that way.

As the ovations subsided, Kokalos took his queue again. He was not about to be left out in the cold this time around. It was his great fortune to be rid of the other Minos, who terrified him, and now he had to win the approval of this one.

"People of Minos. People of Kamikos. Hear me." The hue and cry was dissolving of its own volition and he helped it along. "I have pledged my allegiance to King Minos. I have pledged your allegiance to King Minos. It is my intention to pledge and dedicate a new-founded city to King Minos. I do that now with joy in my heart. I dedicate any part of this island Minos himself may choose, for his own city, to be named Minoa in his honor. What say you?" he shouted.

The staccato tumult of approval erupted in a deafening outburst. The Minoans banged their swords together, the Sicilians slapped their legs and hands. The celebration became a near riot.

The new Minos had been confirmed.

~~~~~~

Chapter 18

Kalliste

1886 BCE

Androgeus, Minos, rubbed the polished head of the iron Goddess with his finger, reflecting on his new fortune. He had emblazoned on her back the symbolism of the ages; the five dots in a "W" shape representative of the five tektites and the constellation Cassiopeia, and above them five rings, interlinked as if holding hands, with a dot in the center of each in the same configuration as the "W" below. Lastly, above them all, was a single circle with a dot in the center symbolic of the uniting of the "Five" in one.

How outstanding that the Council should have accepted him as the Minos without any murmur of dispute whatsoever. There was not a single dissenter. No one brought up the old taboo of residence on this island. As far as he was concerned it had been preserved for his day. But then he did have the icons, the physical keystone of their religion. They would have known at once that they were powerless against him, especially with the icons still so far removed from Knossos.

Knossos. Still the wondrous beauty of the world. But not for very much longer.

Minos contemplated the expansive view from his perch on the summit. The sky was so clear he could see the three distant peaks of Kriti emerging unfettered from the waters as a trident clutched by a predominate god. How great was Kriti. How much greater will be Kalliste.

Daily ships arrived on the westernmost coast of the round island, the island named after the planned city.

Kalliste.

The "Most Beautiful."

Renamed from Strongyle, the "round one," the island now hosted the center of Minoan leadership. The Council. Each couple still held the reins and responsibilities of power on the island of Kriti as Koreters, or Governors, each presiding over one of the ten temple-palace bureaucracies that, in turn, administered the nine towns and cities in closest proximity. Deputy Prokoreters administered each of those populations. Ninety cities on the mighty island of Kriti, that was the declaration spread far and wide. Ninety cities populated by a powerful and mysterious people, with ten capitals overseeing nine cities each, and mighty Knossos, being the greatest of all, in authority over those capitols as well as its nearest nine. One hundred cities tolled.

This mass excursion from Kriti was transpiring at a most opportune time. The population of Kriti was such that it could no longer employ everyone effectively. Methods of birth control had been tried and abandoned, nothing seeming to work. The former Minos had encouraged older men who had sired their children, especially those of inferior stock, to consider taking in boys as resident apprentices. The men would no longer live with their wives, although they would still remain sealed to each other. They would live in separate quarters with their young charges, teaching them valued skills and trades, teaching them manners and culture, arts and social distinction, taking responsibility for all aspects of their upkeep and education. And at night they would lie together, these older men and young boys. Their needs would be fulfilled and no child would come of the union. It was completely normal for teenage boys to be courted by older men and, after the required exchange of gifts and formal greetings with his parents, for the boy to go off and live with his lover. It wasn't until he was actually in his late twenties or thirties that a man's thoughts were to turn to marrying, settling down, and having children.

Many of the women protested that they were no longer the objects of their husband's attention. As many rejoiced to be given their homes to themselves, free of husbands and sons. Wives were provided maintenance as they were entitled by law, their sons were taught a trade which would see them comfortably into old age, and they would still be granted progeny when the time was ripe for their sons to take wives.

The rich population of skilled Minoan builders and artisans was ready to be harvested. Tens of thousands had already been moved, brought along with any personal belongings they could pay to transport. Only stable families were invited to come, only ones of the highest breeding. The population of Knossos itself was depleted by twenty thousand, almost half of its burgeoning population removed to Kalliste. Similarly the most cultured, most beautiful, and most intelligent families were transferred from other temple cities and brought here. There were exceptions to the 'family' rule. There were, in fact, many single people, male and female, who were allowed to come if they met the criteria and were given the blessing of their families and the Council. As single people, they had one cycle of the Moon to find a mate and have themselves sealed. That was an easy task on Kalliste with everyone in the same pressured situation. Rare were the youth needing deportation for failure to comply.

Along with the families came a few children who were not turning out as hoped. Some had destructive or even criminal tendencies, which may have been tolerable at a more lenient time but were entirely unacceptable at this intense stage of development. There could be no tolerance for any unconventional behavior. One substantiated delinquency and the offender found himself speedily aboard the return leg to Kriti. Family protesting their relative's innocence on the grounds that he or she "could never have done such a thing" were promptly loaded aboard the next ship. There was no time to waste debating the finer respects of guilt or innocence, neither could the social order spare the resources nor endure the disruption.

Building was proceeding with a fury. A ring of towns was already established along the perimeter of the circular island, spaced every half-day walk so that even old women or families with children could get to the next town in a day. Roads easily joined them along the plains abutting the coast. Sheep and cows grazed blissfully in the lush green fields between and behind. Water was abundant to every town with rivers and creeks fanning from the central four-thousand-foot peak. Every need was met here, on this island set aside by the gods for this transitional time in the Minoan's history. The few native people who had lived here were easily evicted, rounded up without a fight and removed to lesser islands. A rough looking, rather ugly people, they were not given the opportunity to challenge their worthiness to remain even as slaves. They were treated humanely though. They were compensated with tools the likes of which they never could have afforded, and loaned craftsmen for a short time who showed them how to construct better dwellings than they had previously lived in. They were given quality sheep and goats to breed with their own stock of inferior domestic animals, animals that had to be rounded up and evicted along with the inhabitants.

This island was for the elite, as Knossos had been intended before it was diluted with immigrant workers and imperfect children. The laws had been too loose. Knossos was beautiful, but how much more so could it have become if high standards had been maintained? How much purer could it have been if the likes of the previous Minos had been made impossible?

But if that had been the case then there would never have arisen the need to venture to another place. The gods were inexplicable in their methodology.

There would be no drugging here, no debauchery. Wine would be weak, but thoroughly delectable. Food would be unblemished and piquantly prepared with the freshest spices. Only the perfect for the perfect. The criminal would not be kept, neither the deformed child of man nor beast. Pariahs would be taken where they may, to be sold for whatever their worth may be, or slipped into the sea if they be deemed worthless even for sale.

A greater number of the new population were not accustomed to the brutal physical toll they were exacting on their bodies. But with the religious fervor of pioneering missionaries they persevered, butting their hearts and souls, straining every muscle and sinew, until their jobs were done, and then begged for further opportunity to serve.

With the pride and gratification of an ancient pilgrim to Knossos, they suffered any hardship for the collective good. This was their calling and election, and they were endeavoring as hard as they could to have that calling and election made sure.

Samos ascended the burgeoning cone of Mount Kalliste to where two men surveyed the low-lying plains to the south as they talked. He was in the prime of physical condition but the air at this altitude was a bit thin for such a quick climb. Not wanting to slow now that his king had caught sight of him he actually picked up the pace a little, winding himself in the process.

"Hail Minos," he respired. "Hail Daedalus." He felt embarrassed standing before these older men, both of them quite at home at this altitude, fighting his instinct to breath hard.

Minos repressed his urge to jest with Samos about his poor stamina, a comment about his wife coming to mind. "Good of you to join us, Samos. Daedalus is just planning the fifth, the central, zone. It is all coming together at last, Samos." He was obviously elated at the prospect of beginning work in the near future.

"The fifth zone. It is a dream so long awaited. Would that I might live long enough to see it complete."

"You may, Samos. You may. You are not old like we are."

"You have many good years left, Minos."

"Yes, but not many enough. I suppose even Daedalus regrets not having enough time in his short life to see his greatest work come to completion."

Daedalus postured. "I'll be happy just to see it started."

Minos laughed the musical laugh Daedalus had initially heard in his first moments on the Amnisos waterfront. "Patience, my friend. You are visionary enough to see it to completion in your mind without even the first divot of sod upturned. With your drawings, even I can see it. I can live it. It is all around me just as if it were really here. Tell me you can see it too."

"I can see it. But my imaginings are not as good as the real thing." Always the realist.

"Then it will start at once. Samos. How many could we spare from other works to begin up here?"

The question excited Samos. Since the first conception of the idea, he had been among the strongest advocates. He had dreamed of the world palace and the temple of the gods in every waking moment as well as in his sleep. Greater than the pyramids in distinction, greater than Knossos in intricacy, higher than all in elevation, it would become the most magnificent monument ever celebrating the achievements of man.

"The first zone is finished. Every shore town is complete, and the lighthouses are to be illuminated tomorrow night. Everyone is set to begin work on the second zone immediately, without a break in activity. Much of the preparatory work has already been started. Many sites have been excavated in preparation for building foundations. Those workers would be among the first to be required here, and since much of the work is done we could spare some of the crews. We would have to take from that project to work here."

"Let it be done. Without affecting the second zone inordinately how many could be transferred to the summit?"

"We would need surveyors. There are only half as many towns in the second zone as the first, so we could take dozens if necessary."

"Ten should do. We won't be expending our fullest energies up here. Not yet."

"None of the highly skilled workers will be needed right away. Mostly laborers and rock breakers. Again, we had planned on having the second zone built in half the time of the first with the number of workers we have, but we can relax the proceedings and bring as many as necessary to the summit. They will have to be the youngest, strongest workers. Food porters will be needed to make the climb every day. The trail will have to be improved to a road. Several thousands will be needed, I expect."

"They will begin at once. I want the surveying to begin the day after the inaugural illumination of the lighthouses. The laborers will prepare their tools and food enough for a week. I expect three thousand of them up here the day after. Another two thousand can begin the roadwork improvements. Assign another ten surveyors to that team. The surveyors should finish laying out the basic route in a few days and can return to the second zone. They can return after the clearing has been completed."

"Yes, Minos." With newfound energy, he bounded off down the slope like a young gazelle.

"You've excited him, Minos."

"I hope to excite many. It has been hard for our people over these last years. They work with such earnest devotion, but I sense that many who have been here the longest are finding it all a bit tedious. They are the ones who especially need something new, something wonderful, to once again drive their enthusiasm."

"Temples and palaces will do that."

"Yes. I remember." Minos reflected on the construction of Knossos back when they were both young. How the people had rallied. How great was their reward just to be in on the construction. It was as if their souls were being cleansed free of all stain just by their presence on that hallowed ground. "Would that I could see the flame of such passion rise within you, Daedalus."

"I'm old. I've been feeling it more strongly as of late. Not even my young wives are able to raise a flame within me anymore."

"Say that not too loud. There are perhaps men of younger age who might take advantage should they be made aware," he japed.

"They would know better. And I doubt Reatha and Trapsea would want another since giving children. Three each." He wagged his head. "By the gods, what a woman goes through to give offspring. Hardly any wonder their passions have waned."

"Fortunate for you."

"Alas, that is the way of it. I'm teased with many thoughts and chafed with few abilities."

"Abilities enough to conceive the greatest accomplishment in the history of man."

Not quite. He would never be the Minos, the greatest desire of his heart. He had finally accepted that fact and was doing his best to live with it. The Minoans would never accept him even into the Council, although he lent much weight to many decisions through Minos and several others. With all his genius, with all his guile, he could never be given the most sacred station on Earth. It just was not possible and it would continue eating at him until the end of his days. He would do the work they asked, he would create his own vision of the perfect world, with the blessings of Minos and the others. He would live in immortality in and through his creations. It was his lot in life. The gods, whoever they really were, had proclaimed it.

He would do the work, but he knew that only here would he be given credit for his expertise. The rest of the world would never even know he had lived.

* * *

Through darkness, numerous boats bounced among low ripples of night-blackened deep. Hundreds of little canoes, each with two men stroking the sea, drove invisibly in the moonless night toward the Round Island. From the mainland coast just north of the island of Rhodes they came, where two peninsulas jutted far into the sea, a dogged area populated with wild men, fierce and untamable, ignorant to education and prosperity. The people of Cyrbe. Worse than pirates they set out on massive raids like marauding locusts, fortunately few in frequency, raping and killing man and woman alike, bludgeoning young girls to unconsciousness to carry back for slaves and wives.

Only a few girls ever survived a return voyage, most dying of their head wounds along the way. Shark food. A savage occasion calling for more plundered drink as the corpse was stabbed and sliced before being heaved roughly into the water. They loved to run their bloodied hands through their hair, letting the slime clot and scab over into a demented hat. Not large men, they were nonetheless a terrible contest in battle. Any one of them would fight to the death and call to their comrades to eat their body when the moment came.

They were immensely superstitious, cautious of evil beasts of every description roaming the earth and plying the depths of the sea, thus at least a part of their reasoning for raiding. The slaughter of many upon the land was as a votive offering to gods who would ensure good hunting and better crops. The girls dropped into the sea safeguarded their passage home. Their raids were so rare, so unpredictable and swift, that no Minoan vessel had ever caught them in the act and therefore they could never establish which people were responsible for the genocides of entire village populations. No witnesses were ever left to guide avengers who might return the offensive. The killers, when they returned to their land, appeared innocent enough, incapable of executing such murderous attacks from so far away.

They were nearing their destination, the rising cone blacking out stars that should have been in the sky. They had been here before, how long ago no one had tracked, and found the natives an easy mark, timid and fearful, barely mustering up any kind of opposition. The old one. He remembered. But none of them counted years or cycles of the moon. They had annihilated one village, that was all that mattered, and it was easy. There had to be another.

Just then lights began to wink on at specific intervals along the coast of the Round Island. The barbarians brought their flotilla to a halt. This was an ominous sign. A light on a shore signaled a village begging the garrote, but it was impossible that the fires should be kindled at one time in such a diverse spread. Could it have merely been a cloudbank low to the sea that lifted all at once exposing their lit fires? That must have been what it was. Still, they proceeded, with greater caution than before, uneasiness befalling all.

The lights spread as they made their way closer. They should have been wrapping up their attack by now, despoiling the natives, guzzling their drink, and flaming the buildings. Some began to murmur aloud at the excessive caution they were so unmanly exhibiting. The murmur spread and the speed of the attack galvanized. They drove their paddles into the water, splashing inefficiently as they pressed their little crafts forward. The sky was lightening and a yellow rise was lifting behind them. It would be too late now to surprise them under cover of darkness. They would have to be all the more fleet of foot before the women found time to flee in horror before their might. This was so disruptive. They preferred the sneak attack.

* * *

"Samos," called the watch. "Come quickly."

Samos rubbed the sleep out of his eyes and walked as quickly as he could to the landing on the lighthouse. This was the second time he had been wakened by the man. The first time could only have been an hour ago when the youth thought he saw some aberration far out at sea, some disturbance in the water that affected the way it reflected light from the stars. At least he was genuinely keeping watch, not just gazing mindlessly out to sea like some love-struck puppy. False alarms were annoying though. If this hadn't been the first night of the lighthouses being in operation he wouldn't even have been required to be here. Tomorrow, he thought. Tomorrow he can get back to administering more important things and leave the imaginations of overzealous youth to someone else.

"What have you seen?" He almost tripped on the last step.

"Samos, look. I can make them out now, a host of canoes almost upon us."

Samos squinted, then rubbed his eyes furiously. There were too many canoes to count at one glance. "Sound the alarm. No. Wait. Come with me."

The keeper ran down the steps on Samos's heels.

"Where are we going?"

"To wake everyone from lower down. The alarm will carry if we sound it from up there. Our advantage will be in letting them surprise us."

"What?" He could not believe this. "How could that be to our advantage?"

"Never mind. Just wake as many as you can. Have them wake their neighbors. Tell the men to bring their knives, axes, anything they can use as a weapon. And we need the women to leave their children at home and to bring any makeup they have. Everyone will meet at the beach. Go."

Samos split from the youth and hoped he would do as instructed. He must have been gifted with superb vision, He hoped he was also gifted with quick sense. Damn. He should have heeded the first warning. They could have used the extra time. These raiders had been here before, attacking the people that the Minoans had displaced only a few years ago. Well, they wouldn't find things so easy this time. With luck, there wouldn't even be bloodshed.

With luck.

The word spread faster than Samos could have hoped for. In only minutes the full population of youth and adults had met at the beach and were awaiting instruction. Samos organized them quickly. Faces were painted in the fiercest colors, streaks and stripes smeared on with little regard for artistry.

519

Both men and women piled their hair on top and tied it out of the way. They painted a wide and angry looking eye on the nape of their necks, this time taking it a little slower and making it look as real as they could. They had until the invaders attacked.

The lighthouse sentry was sent back to his station to begin the signal the moment the invaders spotted the townspeople. It was still just dark enough that the signal could be seen by both neighboring towns. Too bad that they didn't have a harbor at either one. Ships would have to be dispatched from farther south. Maybe there was even one nearby at sea that could lend assistance. The invaders would have to act fast for Samos's strategy to work. If it got too light . . . He saw them. They had paused to . . . to . . . to do what? It was almost as if the invaders were unsure about something. But an abrupt move by one boat led the way and the others followed in a precipitous attack on the shore. The watchtower sentry flashed the light with a blanket, first on one side and then the other, repeating it over and over until his arms tired and the daylight grew too bright for anyone to see at any distance. And he kept at it.

The invaders leapt into the shallow water and pulled their skin canoes skillfully onto the rough rocks, careful not to tear the material. This was the only moment of their raids that they ever took to slow down. With their crafts safe they were now bent on havoc and devastation.

Up the beach they surged, no order their attack. One more rise to go and they would pour into the town like an anarchy of red ants into a helpless nest of termites.

Samos blew a horn. The Minoans stood up, both men and women showing their fiercely adorned faces over the bluff, and the few who had axes and swords, shields and staves, waved them above their heads.

The invading force came to a crashing halt. This was not what they had prepared for. They were outnumbered at least by two, against outrageous creatures with solid weapons more vicious than any stone tool they carried.

Samos was the first to turn, a courageous move that none of the others were too sure about emulating. Turning their backs on the invading enemy was just a bit brash. But one by one the men followed his lead and as they did so the dread that fell upon the enemy overwhelmed them. The witless barbarians howled in terror, the third eyes of the invincible gods peering at them over the rocky hump. They could never be assailed from behind. As the last exposed their posterior eye, the attackers turned tail and fled.

The Minoans cheered and danced, making a terrible noise as they saluted Samos, spinning their still visible heads from front to back to throw a final scare into the horrible men who had designed evil against them.

A ship had been in the area patrolling the coast and seen the panicked signal of the lighthouse guard. The semaphore had been wrong, but the captain had rightly assumed that the new sentry had tried to raise the 'under attack' alarm and was frightened. His ship cleaved the waters and bore down on the little canoes filled with dirty little men, exacting vengeance for their bold affront on his peaceful people. The captain knew, as Samos had surmised, that this could only be the brazen people who raided and murdered indiscriminately and who had never been caught. Well, he would see to it that this was the last time that they would ever harass the people of these waters.

One by one the captain rammed them with his ship's nose or capsized them with its huge oars, pursuing each canoe turn with the fast triangular sails used only in secret waters away from the eyes of prying nations. The way they splashed he could see that they were terrible swimmers and they hadn't a hope of reaching shore. Many clung to the overturned hulls of their canoes as their paddles floated away. Many more floundered helplessly in the water as their ripped canoes sank beneath them. Not all of the little canoes were destroyed though, not even half. They scattered so widely that the heavy ship could not possibly maneuver and accelerate after all of them. As the day went on the game of cat and mouse continued until the little canoes vanished into the distance. The ship could still be made out, assumed to be pursuing the enemy, not willing to let even one get away that could be caught.

The ones, the very few, who managed to elude their pursuers and return to their homeland told tales that chilled the spine and forever quelled any misdirected urge to set forth upon the deep. Evil Triamates, the three-eyed ones, had established themselves in the islands of the sea. They had taken the islands at the mercy of any casual invader.

Now the islands were untouchable. Never again would they venture away from their lands.

They would remain at home, content to stay on land and tell fireside tales of the Triamates, the three-eyed monsters, and their wooden dragon who had taken the isles of the sea. The waters were now more dangerous than ever with those malevolent, pernicious eyes sweeping for victims.

The people of Cyrbe would be content where they were. On land they would be safe. No onslaught from the sea could get them there.

521

Chapter 19

Atlantea

1628 BCE

A sunlit cloud rested quiescently on Mount Kalliste's peak, obscuring all but a shadow of the gilded palace and temple within its heart. From the lower elevation of Akrotiri, the summit looked like a dream station exalted from the rest of the earth by a brume of radiant mist illuminated from within by golden rays reflecting off shrouded opulent buildings.

"Is it not a magnificent sight, Rhadamanthys?"

"More so veiled than unveiled, like a woman, teasing with what is not seen but almost seen."

How like Rhadamanthys to speak of women. He'd had two previous wives in his time but, blessed with the poorest fortune, they had each died in first childbirth, along with the infants. Each had been intensely beautiful, but none as much so as his present wife who was known for her particularly anemic complexion. He had taken her at twelve and she had borne him a son at thirteen. The ten-year difference in their age did not mean much now, but at the time it caused a sensation. Seventeen years it had been, and she had not been able to bear another, but that didn't matter to Rhadamanthys. He loved both his wife and son like nothing else. Some said he worshipped them as much as the gods.

Minos had come to the shore town of Akrotiri as part of the dedicatory ritual of the Atlantean Games. The island had been renamed upon completion of the Temple and Palace to that of Atlantea. Here on the coastal plain, the wide flat spaces gave the contestants plenty of room to compete, and they could be seen from the stands even in the distance. Each year the competitions were held in a different town, offering new challenges and new strategic advantage. The higher towns offered rocky terrain and thinner air that tested endurance to the maximum, but down at this elevation, beside the sea, the competitors could exercise their greatest strength and speed without tiring. Athletes prepared all year for these events, some sacrificing learning and wealth so they could stay through the eliminations to the last day, the day when the finalists would be stood apart from the minor and intermediate competitors and given accolades by the gathered masses. It was also a great day for the people of any social standing, a day when they were free to visit areas normally restricted from those of inferior order.

The cloud hanging on the mountain peak lifted on the warm, rising currents. A shaft of sunlight glinting off the metal skin of the Palace beamed powerfully down to where they observed, so bright they had to raise their hands as shields. In only another moment the sun changed its degree of arc enough to release them from its glare, and the beam continued on its slow chase across the landscape. Even from this distance they could see the huge gilded rings blazed on the temple side, five rings linked together in the 'W' symbolically representative of so many things; the five tektites spread across the earth yet inseparably joined; the five orbital points of the planet Aphrodite, at last recognized to be the same planet in the morning as in the evening; the constellation Cassiopeia, the mother of Andromeda; the three-pronged trident of Poseidon, great god of the waters upon which the Minoans were dependent; the three mountains and two valleys of Kriti; and the five fingers of the right hand of Minos, whose hand was in all earthly things.

Minos stood to the lectern as below the gathered masses looked to him. He stood upon the dais above a silver representation of the joined rings. Allowed only at towns that had been granted the status of 'host' for the Games the sacred symbol, solid silver unlike the imposing rings of the temple, solicited the blessings of the Priesthood upon the event.

The citizens of Akrotiri were proud of their acceptance as this year's hosts. The sacrifices they made by building and giving of their personal wealth to improve the town and make room for the masses joining them for the week had been an enormous undertaking. Every evening without fail there had been work parties, from the oldest to the youngest, male and female, all assisting in whatever possible way they could. Nearby towns showed their goodwill by financing workers to assist on short-term projects. Small tariffs were added to produce shipped through the port, and not even the tightest captain complained. New buildings had been struck and completed, old buildings had been scrubbed and polished to new condition. The whole town sparkled without a flaw to be found.

Minos's role was itself mainly symbolic. He had a short, inspirational speech to give, and then came the announcement people really wanted to hear. "Let the Games begin," he shouted. The gathered cheered as the words were spoken, the same four words as every other time as long back as anyone could remember. It was a spiritual moment, and everyone felt the excitement.

Minos's queen, who had taken her name from the Goddess Selene, held aloft a large crystal disk the size of a wide outstretched hand. The lens was imperfect, whitish in hue with a few small flaws, and in the right light looked for all the world like a Full Moon. The lens was the largest of any in their possession. It went back only a hundred years and the hard rock crystal had required almost five years of patient and skillful grinding to bring to shape. Its appeal and value lay in its imperfection, for the Minoans were a people steeped in symbolism and the fact that it bore a resemblance to the embroidered Moon gave it great religious significance. As the Moon captures the light of the Sun and reflects it to Earth, they knew this now, so the lens would capture the sun's rays and strengthen them, adding its own magic and focusing the light onto a small point where, even through the clouded crystal, the heat would be far in excess of combustion temperature.

Selene carefully held the outer rim of the lens above her head and turned so all might see it, so they might feast their eyes on her as well, the lithe beauty who kept herself reclused at the temple. She stood with her tanned body upright and her back perfectly straight, her breasts supported firmly over an inflated ribcage. When she had turned once around, she spread her rippling legs and pulled her flat tummy in tighter. She wore only a short, white skirt, a weave of silver thread and linen that scintillated as she moved, sending flashes of multicolored light into the eyes of her beholders.

The crowd became silent as Selene provocatively swept to the high torch, still holding the lens high above her, up the stairs that led to Minos, and past him to the higher landing where a golden bowl filled with olive oil was wicked up by a fat stem. Selene positioned herself between the sun and the torch and focused the brilliant point of light onto the side of the central wick. In seconds the concentrated energy of the sun had it smoking and, with equal suddenness, a flame erupted and spread around and up the torch stem. The oil had already been heated by the sun's warming of the golden platter, and other smaller wicks laid in rays from the center picked up the flame and carried it outward.

The crowd ripped with prodigious lusty cheers as the flame caught. This magical moment was even greater than Minos calling out "Let the Games begin."

Selene posed beside the flame as she accepted applause from the concourses, the lens held tight against her hard belly with a tapered edge slipped invitingly under the belt of her skirt. Against her skin, the unfocused rays of the sun would do no accidental harm. She had ignited the Flame ten years running, and among all of her public duties and privileges this was her highest honor. She could feel their loud accolades right through to her bones and they resonated up and down her spine like the hard-plucked strings of a lute.

524

Musicians received their cue and struck up chords as contestants circled the exercise area, strutting and posturing, displaying their near-naked bodies, both men and women wearing only the competitor's loincloth.

"Fine examples of physical perfection once again, Minos. And more of them again this year. I've never yet been let down by a decrease in the physical attributes of our youth."

"As it should be, Rhadamanthys. Would you that there were less?"

"Gods forbid it."

"Well, then."

"Very well indeed." Rhadamanthys's eyes turned to Selene who was standing above and to the side of them. He noticed that a great many on the ground were also eyeing her, at the expense of the parading athletes. "Selene puts them all to shame, of course."

Minos could not quite hear everything Rhadamanthys said over the din, but he knew what he had referred to. His wife was beautiful, and he was glad everyone thought so. He loved her more than he cared to admit and would be sad when it came time for her to chose her own replacement. She would still stay on as his wife when that time came, she would simply share the title with another. He wasn't sure what to think of that. It was a titillating idea in a way, but he really was happy just with her alone. It would be a long time yet. Look at her. Absolutely incomparable.

The opening celebration went on for the remainder of the morning, with drinking and feasting until the mark of high noon was reached. Then a great to-do was made over the drawing of lots for the first competitions. There were no acknowledged professionals in these contests. It did not matter if one had practiced for the full year or only the last few weeks. It did not matter if one had an occupation from which they gained wealth or if they rarely worked and spent their entire time doing nothing other than train. Neither did it matter from which of the five levels one belonged. During this week, and this week alone, every citizen of the island of Atlantea enjoyed equal status in the competitions. Among competitors, they were as one. Further, the possibility of advancement from one station to the next was possible. This was an aspiration everyone shared. No one would ever be sent back a level because of anything that happened in these Games, but the possibility of advancement was a desirable carrot that motivated everyone to strive exhaustively all the more.

Lots were drawn, the first contenders chosen. Not only the order of contender, but the order of contest was drawn, the first pulled coming out first today. Boxing.

Minos liked boxing, one of his favorites. He won the championship when he was younger, just a month before he was set apart as the reigning Minos upon his grandfather's death. If only he hadn't been so preoccupied right now with other things, vastly more important things, he might let himself be drawn more into the spectatorship.

"Have you decided to go through with it Minos?"

"Mmmmm?" His wandering thoughts were broken. Although he had been staring at the fighters below while standing at attention, his thoughts had been miles away.

"The renaming? Are you sure you want to go through with it?"

"Yes, Rhadamanthys. I have considered it to death. There is no more to be said. At the conclusion of the week, at the closing ceremony, I will make the formal declaration."

* * *

One solitary runner pounded down the ring road under a sweltering sun.

The road used for the final meet, the only event not left to selection by lot, was the road that encircled the island in almost a perfect circle. This road, with short feeder roads to the coastal towns, was the boundary between the first and second levels, a forty mile circular route beyond which only those with higher license could pass. Anyone could use the road, but only those of greater office could pass higher in elevation to the area circumscribed. The same was said of the next ring road; those of the second level and higher could use it but those of the second level could not pass above. Likewise was the pattern established on the island unto the fifth level, which was not a road, but the walls of the Palace and Temple themselves. In all then there were three ring roads on the island separating the four levels to which the inhabitants more or less confined themselves. Only the Elect of the fifth level could enter and reside in the Temple or the Palace. Any citizen could at any time condescend to associate with lesser citizens but could never, under any normal circumstances, make overtures to associate with the greater.

A murmur rose in the crowd. Two more runners appeared and were running faster than the man in the lead. They might just have enough time to catch up. If so, the race would be very close. That is what the assembly enjoyed seeing; a close competition, a hard-won victory.

The lead runner apparently didn't know that he was being pursued with such intent. He kept his pace steady and even, while the runners astride each other behind him had broken into a sprint. They were very quickly narrowing the gap. Someone in the crowd started to shout and right away others joined in. In a moment everyone was calling at the tops of their lungs for their favorite athlete to unleash his strength and fly to the finish ahead of the others.

The lead runner glanced over his shoulder. He could see what the raised voices of the crowd were calling about. Steeling himself for a final burst, he shot ahead and kept his pace unrelentingly. At first he only managed to keep his distance, but his pursuers fell behind as their stamina ebbed. They had misjudged the distance and now had squandered their energy. It would be impossible to catch the lead.

The crowd roared in exuberant admiration as Minos flew barefoot into the arena, right up to the finish marker at the far end. He held his breath and with a final effort actually accelerated as his head swam and his lungs threatened explosion. Minos collapsed at the finish mark, his chest heaving to the resounding noise of the felicitating crowd. He was mobbed and held above their heads, passed bodily from one hand to the next in this irreverent show of praise for the man who was more near to the gods than any of them.

How right that he should win the longest race. How right that he should have shown them that he could. There was no requirement that a Minos should ever perform, it was assumption that they should be able to excel at anything. But to have the privilege to witness such a demonstration was not an annual occurrence. It almost never happened. What honor he had blessed them with to see the corporeality of his supreme capacity firsthand.

The crowd spread apart as the next two contestants rushed the gate. Another cheer erupted. The two men charged through the separating press that parted just in time to let them pass unhindered. Both were almost blind from exhaustion, and there was the finish line in sight. A second was still a worthy position, and far more prestigious than a third.

Minos beckoned to be let down, and stood at the finish line. The two runners were almost upon him. They were so close it was impossible to guess which might beat the other. The tumult of noise was deafening. The enthusiastic spectators cheered as if the two men were vying for first. Neither seemed to have the advantage. Both were too spent to rocket forward at the last moment as Minos had, but both held on defiantly in the same manner, not willing to concede defeat to the other. Both crossed the line at the same time and Minos could proclaim neither ahead. They had crossed at precisely the same moment.

"It is a tie," he declared.

He led both men up the steps to the podium and stood them together. It was all the young men could do to climb the steps, so entirely spent were they. Chests heaving, naked bodies dripping with sweat and glistening in the sun, all three stood there saluting the crowd. All three of them had been so far ahead of the pack that still not another racer was to be seen.

"What are your names?" he asked the two men.

"Aeacus, Minos."

"Ryata, Minos."

He turned to the cheering masses and signaled for silence. Although he commanded absolute power, they still took their time quieting themselves.

When at last he could, he called down to them. "I proclaim Aeacus and Ryata equally titled as first place champions of the longest race. They shall share the title between them until next year when they may rise against each other again and, perhaps next time, one of them will vanquish the other."

The crowd laughed and applauded. But what was he doing? Minos had come first, not these two. He was humbly refusing to take the honor to himself in favor of these younger men. As the audience clued to the gesture that Minos was declining to acknowledge his right to the acclamation of the prize, they went into a frenzy. Such a tumult of acknowledgment and jubilation had never been heard from a crowd of any size.

Someone started chanting his name. "Minos. Minos." A few more joined in on the same cadence, then a few more. The shout amplified and spread and in a moment all present were calling his name. The volume was so great, the meter so perfect, that even the podium felt the robust pulsations of adulation.

Minos had crowned Aeacus and Ryata in humility, and they had adored him for it. His concern was never in a meager crown of glory for a race easily won. His position was profoundly improved by passing it by.

A greater crown interested him. A crown yet to be made, of a glory greater even than the mantle of Minos.

Tonight.

Tonight they would find out all about it.

* * *

The closing ceremonies were wrapping up. They were hardly different from the opening ceremonies except that Minos could list the extraordinary accomplishments of the winners of every competition this last day, the most celebrated being the tie between Aeacus and Ryata. Many winners would be moving up the social ladder because of their triumphs, and this was also announced to heartfelt applause. Jealousies over such things were always discouraged and kept to a minimum. Everyone at least tried to go through the congratulatory motions of being pleased for any who had been deemed deserving of advancement, wishing with all their hearts it could have been them.

Minos had several announcements of major importance, and started with the least of them. "In honor of the rings joined in unison before you I do solemnly declare that the Atlantean Games will be now and forever known as the Olympian Games." There was a buzz and then a rousing applause from the congregation. There had been rumor of the change, spread purposely for days to test the waters, and there had been general approval. The 'O' was for 'omega' which was synonymous for 'last.' It stood for the circles joined together. It stood for the never-ending, infinite universe and the endlessness of the spirit, a continuous, eternal round. Predating the Greeks by eight hundred years, the word would live on until the end of time. That was its destiny.

And now for the bombshell. Minos was gambling everything on this, not just his own leadership, but the whole of civilization as they knew it. The mood of the crowd was right. This was the only time it could be done.

"On this island of Atlantea I am known as Minos." His voice resonated over the hushed concourse of people. "You know that the ten Councilmen who I sit with are also known as Minos on the island of Kriti. From their own thrones, they sit in jurisdiction as Koreters over the ten provinces. This is right. It is as it should be. In this way the people of Minos have distinguished leadership at all times and, as priest-kings of Minos, are of one mind. Constancy. Neither do the people have to wait eternities to receive guidance and leadership. Every citizen has access to their kings within a few days walk. Justice is always served and laws are fully upheld. The society there is, again, the envy of the world, and it is our place to assist them in all ways.

"We are their elite," Minos shouted. The crowd stamped and slapped their thighs, cheering as Minos began to inflate their egos. "It is our place to lead them, the people of Kriti, in all things. From any of you can come a Minos. No one is restricted from holding such office." The cheers rose louder. Minos was crying out to be heard. He held his hands out for silence. "And as you are the select body of the people of Kriti, who are themselves the elite of the people of the world, so too am I the elite of the Minos kings. Here on Kalliste they are called, simply, Councilman. I want them to share more fully in my glory. I want them all to be known here as they are on Kriti. From this moment forth they shall be known to all as Minos, each of them, as is required of their office."

Minos glanced at the four Councilmen in attendance, and their Priestess wives. No objection there. They were concealing smiles beneath their hard-set expressions, the women more loosely exposing their true feelings. This announcement was highly irregular but flattering in the extreme. The title of Minos conferred upon them? That title had stayed with one person at any given time throughout history, for one and a half millennia. To change things now, out of the blue like this, was extraordinary. But they had not attained their positions by being unaware of the less than obvious. If they were to be called Minos, what would set him apart from them?

"For myself, I will take the title of Chronos. Chronos. King of all Priest-Kings. The master of Heaven and Earth."

The crowd reacted with pandemonium. They clamored and cheered and everything was thrown into the air.

"Chronos. Chronos," they shouted and repeated. They adored him. They idolized him.

He had chosen the perfect moment.

* * *

Kalliste. The Fair One.

Bathed in sun above a low-lying cloud an observer looked out upon the bright cottony tops of the nimbus vapors that obscured everything below. It was as if the great temple had been translated to the heavens and had forever left the weighty earth behind.

From this height, on a clear day, even Kriti, sixty-eight miles to the south, could be seen. But not today. Today it was as if they were alone in the universe. And how appropriate.

The ten Councilmen and their wives, the ten High Priestesses, assembled in the great chamber concourse for this extraordinary meeting of the whole. Not even the glory of Knossos came close to this. This Great Temple was far more sumptuous. The entire exterior was leafed with silver foil, and the pillars with gold. The island was obscenely rich with silver and gold, which for eons had percolated up through steam vents all around the island. Inside the temple, the ceilings were of ivory, taken from the last of the now extinct pygmy elephants of the coasts and islands of the Mediterranean, curiously wrought everywhere with gold and silver and orichalc. The walls and pillars and floor, all other parts, were also coated in orichalc. Throughout the temple statues of gold adorned every corner.

In the auditorium where they waited there was a new god, a god of gold, posing erect in a flaming chariot - a charioteer with six winged horses - and of such a size that he almost brushed the ceiling with his hair. Surrounding him were a hundred Nereids riding on dolphins. The scene half filled the vast chamber.

Opposite the new god, where it had been since the Temple's construction, was the First Pillar of the Orichalc. Made of prized and highly valued brass, orichalc, it was all the worth of gold. On this pillar were inscribed the system of laws handed down to them from the ages, the laws from which the lineage of kings known as Minos had ruled and whose justness commanded universal admiration. So many generations of Minoans and Atlanteans had lived under the banner of peace with this system of laws that the numbers no longer made sense. It was hard to believe that people had been under this wonderfully successful system for so long. And yet it was true.

One by one Minos called up the Councilmen, starting with the one from Knossos. Minos and Selene laid their hands on his head as he knelt before them and spelled a blessing upon him.

Minos spoke first. "Councilman Eatoas, by the wisdom and power of the Great Earth Mother, we ordain you to the office of Minos, to be forever known as such at Kalliste, on the island of Atlantea, on the island of Kriti, and everywhere abroad. Your station of power shall be at Knossos and the Province of Knossos, never to be taken away, even upon death."

They removed their hands from him, and Selene drizzled a few drops of pure olive oil onto a small thumb-sized patch shaved from the top of his skull. They replaced their hands on his head, this time with Selene's first, and she spoke.

"Great Minos, king and sovereign of Knossos, faithful protector and defender of the Great Earth Mother, anointed ruler and crowned potentate, I seal your increase upon your head and forever bless you with the greatest powers of knowledge and wisdom available to the ancients. In all things will you be as wise as Minos, and worthy to bear the mantle and the name. As the kings of old, down to the very first, you will carry the banner stalwartly and with potency. None shall prevail against you except the very gods. Rise up in strength and vigor, let it fill your veins and steel your sinews. Feel it enter your spine and your loins. Stand now, and receive your blessing."

They freed their hands from his head and allowed him to rise. His eyes were still closed and he pulled a deep draught of air, filling his lungs to capacity. He could feel it, the influx of power and majesty of the Earth Mother filling his marrow. He stood with his head back basking in the glory sensation until an unsaid prompting to take his place and witness the rest of the ordinations prevailed upon him.

Each of the ten ordinations were similar, though they differed slightly as Minos and Selene were moved to speak according to the spiritual dictates of their Earth Mother.

When the last, Rhadamanthys, the new Minos of Phaestos, had resumed his place, Selene knelt her own husband before her. With all the refinement of the most regal nobility, she took on the airs of the world queen she was.

"Great Minos," she spoke as she lay her hands upon his head. "Worthy have you been to hold your office these years. Through the ages, from the very beginning, the world has waited in anticipation of this day." She poured a tiny amount of the sacred oil on his shaved crown, watching as it puddled and disappeared into the roots of surrounding hair. She replaced her hands as she spoke again. "Receive this, the crown of the highest station of man, the pinnacle of his achievement, the vertex of his possibility. Stand above all, above the world, above every living thing. Beholden only to the gods alone, none other. Be served in every capacity by the ten known as Minos. They pledge their allegiance to you and swear their very lives on your behalf. Raise thyself now to thy greatest fulfillment. Take upon thyself the name and mantle of Chronos, god of Heaven and Earth, to decree and have authority in equality with the High Priestess, no longer in subjection to her binding dominion but joined as one with her for the greater endowment of united quantification. Bear now the confirmation as each Minos and Priestess lay their hands upon your head and anoint you with their oils and blessings."

Selene opened her eyes and beckoned to the first couple from Knossos to come forth. They held the little pitcher of oil unitedly and spilled a small amount on their master's crown, confirming everything Selene had said and passing the cup to the next pair. All ten couples laid their hands upon Chronos and confirmed upon him his title and office.

When they had returned to their places he opened his eyes, and his being had changed, his eyes full of light and power, his hair with whips of gray that had not been there only an hour before, his sinews exposed in strength, his muscles rippling without having done any vigorous work. His whole form had taken power that could only have come from the Heavens.

He stood and, as he did so, they could see the incredible steel in his legs. He clenched his fists and held his arms outstretched, his hands extended back and his wrists pointed forward at them. They could feel power emanating from him, enhancing their own new capacity.

"This day," Chronos decreed in his sonorous voice, "I have been endowed with the greatest gift of the gods. And whereas this Temple has stood as tribute and example to the Earth Mother so too must the Palace next to it stand as tribute to a god who has served us and is mighty in fact and in deed, a god without whom our Minoan nation could never have stood up in the bitter face of the world and beaten all odds to become the greatest nation of all time."

Chronos spoke of his Palace, which was as richly adorned as the Temple, almost twins to the building. The only difference was the library that was generally acknowledged to be the finest and most complete anywhere. There were to be had manuscripts of every size and type, in every language of the Earth that was written. The Minoans had a change of heart a couple of hundred years ago when the island of Atlantea was being established. It had been acknowledged at last that there was no one, no matter how wise, who could even retain half of all the tales that were to be known, and so books of tales and events had finally to be kept. To keep the culture of the spoken tale, the library was limited to the Palace where anyone of the fifth order could have access, even as a request for someone of a lesser order, as some books were removable though carefully accounted for. Damaging or thieving of the books or tablets was met with harsh penalty, including degradement of position, the worst penalty in the mind of any island inhabitant. Now Chronos was going to alter the designation of his Palace.

"The god to whom we owe so much of our destiny is one who is little spoken of. That is about to change. The god deserves his due, as we have deserved ours. The god stands before you, to be moved to the Palace as soon as you align yourselves with him. The god is here as a visitor of the Earth Mother. They have been together from the beginning and it is fit that they should have temples to one another, side by side."

Every Minos and Priestess naturally assumed he was dedicating the Palace as a temple of Zeus.

"I give you," he waved at the golden statuary behind them, "Poseidon, god of the Sea."

Poseidon. They gasped. Chronos was dedicating his Palace to the god Poseidon? Not Zeus? None spoke. None could. They were struck dumb from the surprise announcement. Several of them batted their lips as they began to express their dismay, but thought better of it in an instant. Selene was dispassionate about the whole thing and obviously a supporter of the idea. She would have known about it beforehand. Why had they sprung everything at them like this? That is why they endowed them with the Minos titles. They had to have received something to soften them to the point where they would let almost anything pass. And this was that something. It had been brilliantly contrived and executed. There was not a one of them who could utter a protest.

As if in concordance with what had been done the earth rumbled deep within its bowels.

Or was it a rumble of discontent?

* * *

Chronos had neatly dissolved a factor of his Minos title that he had never liked. The name Minos hadn't ever been that popular at Achea, especially at Attica. After the scandalous death of Pasiphae, the annihilation of the Minotaur, and the later abandonment of Ariadne as a purposeful insult against the Minoans, the Acheans had embarked on a campaign of maligning the name ever since. Now that he was called Chronos that problem ceased.

Chronos stood enclosed by the low portico walls on the north side of Poseidon's temple. He gazed absentmindedly into a garden of hybrid flowers, crosses of white Madonna and red lilies. He loved flowers, and it was shameful to see them erased of their glory by a gray layer of fine dust. The building had been officially set apart and dedicated after the removal of the Poseidon statuary from the Earth Mother's temple next door and its installation in its proper place in the great hall of this temple. Another dyspeptic rumble emanated from deep beneath the earth's surface. Chronos was becoming uneasy. Not worried, just a bit on edge. These low rumblings had become increasingly regular since the dedication of the palace to Poseidon. He wasn't overly concerned about whether he had done the right thing or not, the astrologers assured him that he had acted in accordance with the dictates of the stars, but he would have been less uncomfortable if he had some answer to why there had been so much activity deep inside the earth.

The shocks had all been very minor, and reports said that none of the little quakes had been felt anywhere other than Atlantea. They weren't even real quakes, more like deep, prolonged, vibrations. But there were so many of them. Sometimes there were dozens in a single day.

He saw the wisp of smoke that had been pouring out from a vent of some sort across the peak of the mountain. It had started as a faint vapor just after the rumblings had, increasing in density since then. The smoke was coming out of solid rock, where no combustible material lay, where it was impossible for anything burning to account for the grayish black column issuing forth into the atmosphere. With each strong rumble the column grew thicker and more ominous, never ceasing or letting up for a minute, not even at night.

People were getting edgy. Chronos was continually reassuring them that it was merely Poseidon revealing his pleasure at having, at long last, his rightful place of honor. But discretely, at very private times, the Minoses came to him and ventured the suspicion that maybe it was Zeus who was demonstrating some displeasure for the slight against him. Never expressed in a forceful manner, they backed off immediately when Chronos brushed aside their intimations. Inwardly, however, he took their counsel to heart. The Minoses were invaluable allies and, as his closest associates and friends, he had always found he could trust in their counsel. But he could not be wrong on this, he just could not be. The ramifications would be too severe. If Zeus had been insulted, if Poseidon had not been pleased, then they were in mortal danger.

He refused to even consider it seriously.

* * *

The ship unloaded its inventory of tin from the distant island of Britannia, a land floating just adrift of the continental landmass in an ocean vastly more immeasurable than the Great Sea itself. The island was named after the goddess Britomartis who Minos chased into the sea.

Britomartis had been caught in the net of a fisher and her body hauled to safety from the ravages of marine life that would normally have set upon her. The legend grew of how she withstood the amorous pursuits of Minos, and Rhea had later confirmed that she had been rewarded with immortality as a goddess for her chastity.

* * *

The Minoan manner of worship was evolving to the devotion of many gods and goddesses, a wide diversity of deities both animate and inanimate, regarding the whole cosmos to be dynamically alive with efficacious deities and lesser spirits of an intangible nature. They came to have names and responsibilities, manifesting themselves in any imaginable form and then disappearing, one moment rising to the rank of a consummate deity, another disseminating into the mystic ether. They were given personalities and personal histories, and they were capable of endless overlapping transformations. Zeus, greatest of males, could manifest his being as anything from a swan or bull, to a spectacle of thunder and lightning, or even a shower of gold.

The shipments of tin from the Levant had become more rare and expensive, and the Minoans had resorted to exploration to find new supplies. Intrepid travelers that they were, they explored far past the pillars of the Mediterranean and found a body of water of impossible size, a body into which many had ventured and incontrovertibly vanished into the distance, never to return. The rare few who had made their way back, after weeks of travel, had only to report that either there was nothing to be found or that any land in that direction was much too distant to reach. But they did find other islands closer to the main continent. A group of small islands clustered around two larger ones, two islands even greater in size than Kriti. And on the larger of the two, they found inhabitants who were willing to work at extracting the tin that lay in their land to the exclusion of almost any other. They were a rough people, unlearned, hunters who lived in skins instead of cloth. But they were extremely hard working when put to a task and, when their minds were made up to accomplish something, nothing could put them off. It was the trade for wine, Egyptian glass beads, and bronze tools and weapons that impelled the inhabitants to labor in the tin mines. All to the great benefit and profit of the Minoans.

The Captain loved the social and diplomatic aspects of long-drawn-out negotiations over the price of cargo with any culture, be they Egyptian, Cypriot, Levantine, or even the less refined British. The passion for haggling is still deeply ingrained in the Mediterranean economy, begun with the Minoan merchants and traders of so long ago.

"Bless the Gods, I love this place," declared the ship captain as he inhaled the sweet air of Atlantea and rubbed a polish onto the small blob of amber he had picked up on the faraway island of Britomartis.

Britomartis. The Sweet Virgin. The Mistress of Wild Animals and Queen of the Wild Beasts. A free hunting goddess her province was terrestrial, the mountains and hillsides, where wild animals needed her protection against the perpetual onslaught of man. She loved the raw nature of the separate islands of the Endless Sea.

But here, on this island of the Elect, could she not love it even more? Every fragrant plant and flower that was pleasing to the senses was grown in abundance everywhere, unlike the crude and unsculpted islands of the sea. Whether the herb be good for food, or just the eye and nose, it was here. His favorite port was this one at Akrotiri where, by law, all buildings had to meet minimum standards and, for the most part, were owned by people who were in a continual contest with their neighbors for dominancy of who had the most exquisitely decorated abode. Hanging pots with draping fuchsias graced the alleyways and lanes. Grape vines grew against walls where light was adequate enough for them to mature. Flowers of every hue and color were set outside the snow-white houses during the day, and brought inside at night to give the sparkle of life to lamp-lit interiors. Wherever he went, frescoes of the most glorious workmanship adorned walls both inside and out. Here a wall of cavorting antelopes confirmed that mariners had traveled to east Africa, the only place of their existence, while swallows shot about like arrows on the ceiling above. Outside of doors was evidence that the stone vase-maker's art had reached unparalleled heights. The dark black-blue serpentine which was popular before was still used a great deal, but now new materials were being used as well. Alabaster, gypsum, limestone, marble, cornelian, and lovely variations of breccia all were sculpted to perfection. Extremely hard rocks like porphyry and black obsidian were worked to such a degree with Naxos emery that no one would ever guess the innumerable hours required in their painstaking creation. Ornamental rocks of the most fascinating variety were imported from everywhere, green speckled basalt from the Peloponnese, a pure Egyptian alabaster, the exotic rosso antico from mainland Achea, and the white-speckled obsidian from Yiali in the Dodecanese. Stones of every origin were used in the purely temple art, sublime crafted gold leafed on the rims and kept indoors. Every house had at least one amphora of magnificence inside the living quarters and another of lesser caliber outside the entrance. The town was magical, the most exquisite coastal town of any, bar none.

He stopped at a table minded by a youngster who was selling wares for his mother. She had assiduously perfected the craft of faience, forming the · brilliant paste into decorative plaques, vases of turquoise blue, polychrome goddesses, and marine reliefs so realistic one could not tell an enamel crab from a genuine fossil.

The Captain, as he preferred to be called instead of his real name, was dying for a drink of some real wine. They had stopped at Siciania on the return journey for a day of rest and some hearty cooked food, but their wine was not to his taste. It was drinkable but hadn't the cultured flavor of a good Atlantean jug.

"Get that cargo out of the hold," he ordered. "We haven't all day to stand about." The men were already sweating as they passed the metal ingots from hand to hand and stacked them on the crowded pier. In another hour the transaction would be sealed with the metal trader, the Captain could pay off his men for their two months of hard labor, and he could take his profit. He would seal the trade for bronze and take the manufactured alloy to Kriti where it could be remelted and poured into molds for weaponry to be shipped elsewhere. The standard sixty-four-pound oxhide-shaped bronze ingots were a sailor's dream to load. They could be tossed with impunity without fear of damage, they were light enough that four could be carried at once between two men's shoulders, and they could quickly fill the hold with as much as the ship could safely carry. Glad he was that they weren't bound for Phaestos where they demanded the enormous five-hundred-pound ingots. Ah, there would be some feasting and celebration among his men tonight.

The Captain glanced up at the summit of Mount Kalliste. No one could come here and resist the spell of its radiant peak. There were always parts of the structures that reflected glaring beams of light to ones' eyes no matter where they might be on the waterfront. As a result, it was rarely possible to make out more than the outline of the two structures. Someday he would like to travel up there and visit the silver temples but, of course, that was impossible. He had rights to the second level, an automatic right for any sea captain, but that was as far he was allowed to go. That didn't bother him in the least as he was most comfortable right here on the coast in his favorite town, as far as he was concerned even more beautiful than the more highly decorated and embellished towns of the second level. They could decorate all they wanted and still never make up for the natural beauty of the coastline. It was just a tug of curiosity, that's all, a curiosity that all explorers had that made them go to unusual and even extraordinary lengths to seek the unknown. He had heard about the incomparable beauty of the palaces up close and the unimaginable splendor of their interiors. Sometime before he died he really would like the privilege of seeing it, but shook off the hope again as a most unlikely aspiration.

The captain noticed that the smoking vent was more active by far than when he broke shore three months ago. It was spewing vast amounts of smoke and steam and it looked to be sending forth ash as well. A drift of haze that seemed to fall out of the smoke rather than deviate to the side clued him to that. It was a wonderful marker really. It signaled the place of Kalliste while they were still hundreds of miles at sea. During the day they were able to adjust their course without any need for the usual navigational indicators. They just followed the plume.

Quick hammering tremors, lasting only a few seconds but strong enough to knock the Captain and a few other distracted men off their feet, pummeled the island. A blast of rock and ash exploded out of the vent near the upper reaches of the mountain peak. Solid gray billowing clouds of ash blew sideways, up and out over the far side of the island, thankfully away from them. Rocks still hurtled through the air as the sound blast struck them. It was almost as terrific as the quake, deafening to the ear, and enough to cause them further imbalance. Rocks rained down on field and town, a cloud of pumice following like gray popcorn drifting lightly behind on the same trajectory. Under conditions within the volcano throat gasses within the lava expanded rapidly, transforming the ejecta into perforated glass foam abounding with tiny air holes. Heeling after the pumice was heavy ash that sifted like a light rain on the northern half of the island territories.

The Captain was glad that he was not on the receiving end of that little explosion. He despised having his ship dirty and knew his crew hated cleaning filth that was not of their making.

The vent was spewing twice the volume of smoke now as it was a few moments ago; at least the column was twice as thick. The force with which it was being expulsed was far greater. It was not merely venting passively like a chimney, it appeared to be under pressure. In minutes the big dusty cloud from the explosion had dispersed and sank down to the sea, and the column was the only marker left billowing into the sky.

"The gods are angry about something," he commented. "I wonder what it is?"

* * *

Chronos picked himself off the floor. The blast had felt and sounded far more acute on the peak than at the seashore. He tried to see through the dust and fine ash drifting into the air of the temple. It was just a light dusting that he was getting, not anywhere near the bulk of the material, but the abrasive particles scratched his eyes, and he squinted. His head was ringing from the blast of the fulmination and he placed both little fingers in his ears and shook them. It didn't make any difference.

Selene came running into the room. She had been on her way to see him, walking through the corridors of Poseidon's temple, when the explosion occurred. Several of her consorts, and two priests, also swept in on them.

"Chronos. Chronos. Are you all right?" they shouted from behind before Selene could get a word out. They gripped each of his arms and he shook them off.

"I'm fine. Do you think I'm some old man?" It was well that they had shouted as they came from behind him or he wouldn't have heard them. "Selene," he said lovingly as he caught sight of her. "Are you all right?" He shot a glance at the two priests. They had better have checked on her health before his.

She pressed herself against him as he wrapped his arms around her. "I'm fine too. I was so worried for you. I could not tell where the sound was coming from. I feared something had happened to you."

He turned her away from the others and swept his hand up, indicating to those behind them that he wished to be left alone with his wife. He took it for granted that they obeyed his whim without turning to check. He knew they would be gone.

"It is time for a solemn sacrifice," he said concernedly.

"I have come to speak with you about that very thing. I have felt the need for some time. I know we have done four to Poseidon since the vent began to spew, but I believe it is time for another." Her eyes fell as she withheld what she had really come to say.

He touched her under the chin and guided her face up where he could see it. "Do you think that the Earth Mother also would benefit from the sacrifice of a bull?"

"Perhaps. Normally a new white lamb is what is required. Perhaps a white bull . . ." Her voice trailed softly away.

"Selene. My love. You know you can speak with me about anything. No subject can be too sacred between us. Tell me what you are really thinking."

"I fear the gods. We have angered them."

"How could we have done so? There can be nothing that I can think of."

She struggled to find the words. "It is Poseidon." She could not say more. He would not understand.

"Poseidon? It is not possible. We have done nothing to anger Poseidon."

She knew he would not understand. He was so fixated on his god of the waters that he had forgotten the god of the lands.

Zeus.

"But you might be correct," he said as she was formulating her words. "I have been considering for years the distribution of the Seeds. Perhaps I have lingered too long. Perhaps that is the problem. The gods could have become angered at such dalliance on my part." He let go of her and paced the balcony. "Yes. Yes, that is the problem. Of course. Any god would be angered. We must see to it at once. Today."

He rushed through the door and she trailed after, wishing she had spoken. The two Priests and Selene's escorts who had been waiting outside took up the pursuit. They were heading for the Sacred Chamber, the place in the Earth Mother's temple where the Goddess was kept flanked by the two remaining tektites. Out the golden door and across the hand-manicured lawns and gardens, to the other temple, they strode. Chronos stopped as he passed into the fresh air, waiting for his wife to catch up and take his arm. By tradition, she had to guide him across the walkway to her temple as an invitation, although she could enter Poseidon's temple freely. The indication was that the Earth Mother, Rhea, was of greater universal eminence than Poseidon who only presided over the waters of the Earth. As they traversed the courtyard they could see through the clearing haze that the profuse column of smoke was also firing sparks into the air. It had ceased being a benign streamer. Fire was becoming a real threat.

That worry had Chronos suddenly lengthening his stride. No wonder Selene had been so upset. She had known that this crisis was only going to get worse unless he abided by the god's wishes and sent off the tektites as he was supposed to ages ago. He just couldn't bring himself to part with them. How stupid of him. He should know always to obey the dictates of the higher deities.

They entered the golden room. It was small compared to many of the rooms in the temple, only enough room to seat twenty-two. The Priests and Selene's escorts were not welcome in here. This room was only for Selene and her High Priestesses, and their husbands. None were here now, none thinking that either Selene or Chronos would have cause to come here at this moment. It would not be long, though, before some entered. The escorts would be sweeping the building looking for any of the High Priestesses, and the Priests would be hurrying back to Poseidon's temple to find Councilmen. None of them were sure exactly how many of the kings and queens of Kriti were with them at this moment, but there were always a few.

Selene led Chronos through the golden room into the Inner Sanctum, the most sacrosanct room, not any larger than a servant's bedroom. Size was of no importance to these hallowed icons. The goddess stood where she always did, unmoving on the altar center. On either side of her, the two tektites rested. This was what made it so hard. Chronos knew that both had been destined to be dispersed at the same time, and after them there was no other. They were the end, the last of a group of five that lived on only in the symbolism of the five linked rings adorning the sides of the temples. Chronos had actually hoped never to see the day where he would have to pass on this onerous duty to a grandson, but the only alternative was to administer the event himself. The thought, even as he stood there contemplating it, broke his heart. He was so loath to do this. No wonder the gods thought him weak and had to persuade him with blasts of fury from the depths and darkness of the earth.

* * *

The ceremony was of consequential importance. Every person on the island was required to be at Akrotiri for the send-off. Every Minos and High Priestess had been summoned. Chronos had been sure that he would be sending the Seeds off the day he stood in the Inner Sanctum, but Selene had stifled his conclusion. She rightly proposed that the gods would not be angered further by doing what was right and ceremoniously dispersing them with the full liturgies that they deserved.

Two longships stood by, the entire port cleared of all other ships and boats. These were two of the largest and most capable ships. For one, it was of ceremonial purpose only; for the other a necessity.

"May the Earth Mother, and all gods, seal this heavenly stone with all the might and power of divinity and immortality." No one had been allowed to know exactly where these tektites were going except Selene, Chronos, and the Council. Two of the Council couples would be captaining the ships, selected by lot so that there could be no doubt as to the god's choice. Further, there were a host of men and women of all trades aboard who symbolically stood for the collective skills and intelligence of mankind. "Take this Seed to Achea, where its aura will fill the Hellene people and bless them with the knowledge and wisdom of the Egyptians and the Babylonians. May their culture and people thrive."

Chronos passed the single round of extraterrestrial steel to Minos of Malatos. He wrapped it in diaphanous purple silk and, without a word, signaled, and his crew cast ashore the ship's mooring ropes. They used the square-rigged sail as they set for Achea. They were in no hurry, and they would be too spiritually distracted to remember to change from the triangular sails as they neared Attica.

As they observed the ship sailing away, oars torpidly assisting the voyage, many in the congregation cried. They wept openly at the beginning of this new era without the tektites. As the second Seed was passed to the Minos of Gournia there were some who had to sit down and grieve. The tektites were of legend and myth, the very soul of the Minoan people. They had come down from uncountable years ago, near the origins of time, and stayed with the people this long, and now these last were being conveyed to other lands. It was the end of an era for them, and the beginning for someone else. They would never again hear of them in this life.

Chronos passed the same blessing on the other Seed with one substitution, the destination, and an addendum. "Take this steel to the unknown lands beyond the Great Ocean. As we are the great island of Atlantea, so too do we name the Great Ocean, and we do so in your great honor. Atlantic. Take the steel to the other side, the distant shores, never before explored nor seen. If there be people, deliver them the tektite as we have yielded the others. If there be none, then you yourselves must become the people." His voice wavered. "In either case, we will never see you again. May the gods bless you and make your voyage one of the highest ascendancy."

Also without a word the Minos Captain received the tektite and also wrapped it in a cloth of purple silk. They used the triangular sails to propel themselves forward, and the oars were not even dipped into the water so quickly did they depart. Oars were held high in salute as the second ship passed forever from the history of the Mediterranean.

* * *

Rhadamanthys, Minos of Phaestos, stood among the bewildering archives of collected works. The greater portion of the Poseidon temple had been taken over by the library. Even the librarian was having a difficult time assisting him in finding what it was that he wanted.

"There is so much dust in here we just can't keep up," he lamented. "We have ten cleaners on duty at all times, at all hours of the day, every day. There is no rest day in the Temple," a fact that Minos was well aware of. "And the light is so inadequate. Normally it is such a lovely place, but we have had to cover the windows with silks to keep some of the dust out. You understand, I'm sure."

It was dark in here, thought Minos, the light stained from the red silk the Minoans fancied to keep back drafts but still let in light in the winter months. Red paper was used in the more humble abodes, but still only during the colder times. How different from before when light streamed in at this time of year and reflected off the polished walls, lighting every isle between the scrolls and tablets. A cleaner was going around to all the windows with a wide reed swatter, beating the dust off the outside of the coverings. Where he struck it, the dust fell off to the outside, and more light penetrated through the sheer fabric. Illuminated dust swirled in and out of the streamer of light, showing them just how filthy the interior air had become in spite of their sincere efforts.

The librarian sorted through the stacks, too slowly for Minos's patience and he was a patient man; so he also began to dig. It was purely out of curiosity. There were so many records here that he didn't really know where to begin, so he stayed close to the librarian. Chronos had made it an offense to keep records of all but financial transactions on Kriti, and those had to be kept on the unfired clay that was of no lasting use to anyone. All fired records, which preserved the clay by transforming it to ceramic, had to be transferred to the Poseidon library, and certainly all records of religious prayer, or history, or imagination. This made sure that all of the most worthy made the journey to the Temple on a regular basis, because part of the search for knowledge and enlightenment always involved researching the written word.

Minos didn't expect to find anything of much interest among the ponderously capacious piles of tablets. He would be better off in the section of scrolls or the section where the leaves of parchment were kept. They were so much easier to finger through. Slowly over time every record would be kept by those methods, he predicted, either one was fine. Personally, he thought that wasting lambskin vellum was a bit excessive for any but the most valued written material. Papyrus was perfectly suited for most things. They had even started growing the reeds on the island to make specialized paper not available from the Nile region from where the majority of papyrus was imported. It was light, durable, and took ink better than vellum. And anything was better than

542

the ridiculous clay tablets. They were so outdated and cumbrous that he couldn't understand why they didn't just transcribe them all to papyrus and dump the lot of them down that damned vent. Maybe that would plug it up.

In fact, scribes were doing just that; transcribing the tablets to papyrus. But it was a long and arduous process, and new material still had to be written. All of the latest text was on the papyrus. The big push for space had become the real driving factor. The library was full. There was no more room at all. A hundred tablets could be transcribed to one large scroll, and that meant a hundred tablets could be moved outside. But things are never as simple as that. There was always someone who protested that the tablets were historical, original, valuable, or sacred, and thus should never be disposed of. Also, there was the problem of mice and silverfish eating the papyrus. The library had to be kept scrupulously clean and lately, to the objection of more than a few, no food or drink was allowed in that might be spilled thereby attracting the little vermin. Therefore there were many hundreds of tablets that had their equivalent in papyrus or vellum, or even both, yet were still archived in the library. The logically illogical argument in defense of the situation was that two or three patrons at once might want the same scripture, even though in reality the chances were astronomical that anyone would want either.

Minos wanted one though. He sneezed out a black smear of snot and wiped it off his face in disgust. He had nothing to wipe it off the back of his hand except his kilt, and so he used that, leaving a dark libelous streak down the side that only aggravated his sensibilities more. He couldn't even keep his own clothing white. The situation had become intolerable. He wiped at his face with his other hand, knowing that the wet he felt on his skin meant that he still had some of the slimy denigration upon him. He scrubbed the area with his palm and his forearm and hoped that he got it all off. The librarian was pretending not to notice and wouldn't look at him. He busied himself picking through another pile of tablets.

"Ah," said the librarian with self-ingratiating satisfaction. "I believe this is what you have been seeking." He handed it to Minos. "I had forgotten that it was on a circular disk. If I had remembered, I could have located it in a fraction of the time. Please forgive me. There is so much disruption with all these workers. And the dust. Well . . . you understand."

Minos waved off the apology as he scanned the surface of the disk. Then he flipped it over. There was writing on both sides, spiraling from the center to the outer rim. Between the lines of separation were the imprints of set hieroglyphic type that had been impressed into the soft clay before it was baked. This was one of the newer styles of hieroglyph, the kind Minos preferred because it was so much easier to read. There were forty-five different and repeated symbols on the disk, two-hundred-forty-one pictograms in all, with lines dividing the sixty-one phrases, all in the most organized arrangement. He was used to this kind of writing and didn't even need to rotate the disk. It was simple enough to let his eye follow the spiraling track and read the imprints from any angle, right side up, sideways, or upside down. It was easy once one got the gist of it because of the regularity of the print, and so much more pleasurable to read than the usual linear script. Stamps carved from wood had been used make the identical symbols, the world's earliest example of movable type. This script was sacred. It was for the temple site alone. Not even Minos could take this tablet out of the Temple. The circular shape designated it as among the most sacred of prayers, a hymn to divinity, to be exercised only by those in authority, of which he was one, and only with the blessings and approval of Selene. He wondered if he could approach her.

Another muffled explosion blustered from the vent. They had become so regular that people were getting used to them, barely paying the minor ones any mind at all. Minos held the disk in front of him as he contemplated it and walked past the librarian who had returned to his station near the door.

The man stammered after him. "Ah. Minos. Ah . . . You really aren't to take that."

"I'm just taking it to my room to study it privately."

The librarian came following quickly behind. "But, ah, we have study areas set apart for, ah, that. Wouldn't you prefer to use one of those?"

"No, I would not. Your library is filthy. I will not stay a minute longer."

"Please, Minos. You place me in a very difficult position."

He stopped and faced the man directly. "I do not. You followed me out of the library. You have placed yourself in whatever position you are in."

"Minos, please."

He was an annoying little stickler for rules. "Look here. This is nothing more than a piece of baked clay. It is nothing. It simply has a poetic prayer impressed into its body that I would like to study alone. You understand, don't you? I know you are doing the best you can under these insufferable conditions, but you must see that they are inadequate for serious reflection. Why, I can barely breathe in there. Would you have it be known that I cannot even breathe in your library?"

"No, no, of course not," he blurted.

"Then what objection can you have? I will return the disk as soon as I am finished with it."

"But it is so irregular," he continued to protest.

Minos squelched the thought of prodding both his thumbs into the squeaker's eyes. "There is nothing that is not irregular these days. We live in a strange time. Kalliste rumbles and smokes and casts filth into every secluded corner. Would you have that continue?"

"Of course I wouldn't."

"Would you accept responsibility for its continuance?"

"Me?" He was horrified. "No. No. How would I ever be responsible?"

"By interfering with things of which you know nothing. Now, if you will allow me to take my leave, I will resume my sacred duties which you seem determined to thwart."

"Sorry. I'm sorry."

"May I continue then?"

"Yes, Minos. Please continue," he said worriedly.

Minos turned and took a few steps.

"But the disk," he heard bleating behind him.

He felt his head inflating with blood and reared back on the librarian. "Is there something you do not understand? Is there something you do not comprehend?" The librarian was forced to walk rapidly backward or be mowed down. "You are charged with running the library, not a collection agency. If you are incapable of such a small feat, as you have shown by the disgraceful state in which you keep the interior, I will have to conclude that you are inappropriate for this station," by which he meant that the librarian was that close to being stripped of his rights to the fifth level. The librarian's mouth opened and closed silently and his lower lip seemed to flap independent of reason. "Now, I wish to continue my work. I do not wish to see you again and I do believe that you will agree that this is for the best." He leaned his face forward as they continued their path back toward the library entrance so their eyes were only inches apart. "Do you?"

"Yes. Yes," the librarian gibbered and fled back to the sanctity of his volumes.

Bureaucrats. If they ever got complete control of those who actually did anything useful, then the world would stop cold. Unbelievable that they could be so isolated in their little circle of responsibility that nothing else could be considered worthy of substantiation. He watched to make sure the blithering pest wasn't going to have a change of heart and take up pursuit once again. Minos wasn't satisfied until the librarian disappeared into the dust of his vaulted chamber, with one fretful, anxious glance behind as he crossed the threshold.

Minos continued into the accommodating garden between the Temples. He chuckled to himself as he thought of the librarian discovering him out here with the disk. It was bad enough that it had left the library let alone the building. The man would have a frenzied conniption. Minos could envision him stuttering and twisting in anguished protestation. How did such a neurotic, peevish type graduate to the fifth level? He must be a very good librarian, but that couldn't be enough. He was an apology of a man. He must know somebody. He must be related closely to Chronos or Selene to have gotten this far.

Minos stood outside the portal waiting to be noticed. This was an irritating matter of form that he had to endure along with every other male. They could not be granted entrance without invitation and, unless they had made previous arrangement, there was often no one near the door to see them waiting. He stood grinding his teeth at the absurdities of protocol he had to put up with. There was no gate to keep him out, he could walk in if he chose. But he knew that if he did he would be the first to ever do such a thing and even though he was a Minos he would be seriously putting his station at risk. Wouldn't that be the living end? That nasty little pinch of a librarian at a higher station than himself? The wobbling cloy would probably get a charge out of that.

To the west he watched the vent vomiting its bilge. Was there no end to it? The exhaling plume was thicker and faster than ever. The air around was dense with it, and the garden had been ruined. Half of the plants were dead, and the others caked in mud where attendants had tried to wash off the dust with water only to have more settle on the damp leaves.

On one desperate flower, a honeybee tried to pick its way through some dust to glean a bit of pollen. The bee was almost as sullied as the flower. It was a despairing act of futility. The Atlanteans were fortunate enough to be able to import their honey, the favored sweetening agent, from Kriti. Syrups from the juices of pressed fruits and dates were also available, but none were so delectable as honey. There was hardly any satisfaction in that. The bee was the symbol of creativity and stamina, hard work and enterprise. Here he was, a great king, at the center of the world and he could not even get local honey. Minos knew that most of the bees of Atlantea had died recently, no longer able to forage a living among the flowers. With the warm weather, they couldn't even go into hibernation. They had to try to produce, It was their nature. And it was their nature that was driving them to their deaths, trying to collect pollen as if it were as precious as gold. All those hundreds of thousands of little Minoses, all dying or dead. Minos set his jaw against the thought.

A priestess walking past noticed Minos and stopped to greet him.

"Are you waiting to come in?" she inquired with a smile. It was good to see someone smile these days. The conditions had put a damper on most people's emotions.

"I desire an audience with Selene."

"Then you may follow me. I will escort you to her chamber."

She led the way with Minos walking a few steps behind. Hardly an insult, it gave him a chance to examine her form under her tightly wrapped skirt. She had a wonderfully waspish waist and tight buttocks. Usually topless at this time of year, the women had taken to wearing light shawls to protect their skin from the irritating dust. The women were even more fastidiously clean than the men, and they could not shoulder the burden of even a light sifting of dirt. The thought alone was repugnant. That it was happening and there was nothing they could do to prevent it was abhorrent.

He followed her to the center of the Temple where the air was heavier and damp. This was where one of the springs rose up from the earth, one of six near the top of Kalliste that supplied them with a steady stream of hot water. Even in here the servants could not keep up with the cleaning. Steam condensed and rolled in trickles down the walls, leaving it streaked and shoddy.

The priestess suggested that Minos should wait a moment. She stepped inside the overly humid room and he could hear several muffled voices.

"You may enter," she informed him when she returned.

He stepped into the mist following the young priestess. Selene sat on the edge of the marble pool at the corner toweling herself. Her skin was flushed from the heat of the water up to a line at her shoulders, above which it was normal of color. A movement on the periphery drew his attention through the fog. Another figure, most decidedly male shaped, withdrew quietly through a side door.

"Come. Sit beside me, Minos."

He set himself on a perpendicular edge of the pool, close to Selene, so that he was facing her rather than sitting alongside. He dangled his calves into the hot water. It was very refreshing. He hadn't bathed since morning and the water against his skin felt very pleasurable. The water in Rhea's temple was considerably hotter than the water at Poseidon's temple. He thought that unusual since it must be coming from the same source. Then he recalled the system of valves that Chronos had designed to arrest the habitually constant flow through the pool. That allowed the water time to cool as it did for the drinking water, although it wasn't allowed to get that cool for bathing. When it got below a comfortable temperature some of it was drained out into the sewer and more hot water was permitted to flow in through the valves. Selene couldn't have been using that method. She must have the water flowing constantly through her pool. He noticed the water did appear to have a current, although it could have been from the way she was waving her legs in the water.

These pools were huge by the standards on Kriti. There they had no natural source of hot water springing so freely out of the ground. They had to heat their water with wood, and then the water had to be carried to the sunken bathrooms common to every palace. The elegant terra-cotta tubs were generally too small to lie down in and were mostly hip baths. A few were longer, but most people thought the longer ones were too indistinguishable from burial coffins that, except for the addition of a lid, also had plug holes. In fact, the coffins were made by the same bathtub craftsmen, for those who had such a fondness for bathing that they had to be buried in one.

How the people of Kriti enjoyed vacationing on Atlantea. A great many had rights to levels higher than the first and took full advantage of their license when they had the opportunity. The baths of Atlantea were one of the main attractions. The island was rife with springs and hot-springs, more so these last few decades. Each kind, be it cold, warm, or hot, were of abundant volume and wonderfully well adapted for use because of the natural taste and excellence of its waters. Some were most pure and others were of high mineral content with pleasing vapors and medicinal qualities. Reservoirs were at every spring site, some set under the open sky, others under cover to supply hot baths in winter or inclement weather. There were common baths for all, and separate baths for women, and others for men. Even horses and other beasts of burden had their own baths in Atlantea.

Another priestess, probably Selene's personal attendant, came out of nowhere just as he was about to speak. She distracted him by picking from the floor a protective sheath. He hadn't noticed it in the haze until her action drew his attention to it. Obviously, Selene had been receiving some attention from the man he had seen hastily departing. Selene was renowned for her fantastic figure, even though she could hardly be considered young anymore. She had preserved it by not allowing herself to have children. Minos's wife used the same method, although it was more because she did not want more than the one child they already had. She was forever telling the joke that Minos produced semen containing serpents and scorpions, and to sleep with him safely she had to insert the bladder of a goat inside herself. While the method she used was true, and faultlessly effectual, the joke she made spread on the wind. In no time even the fishers heard about it, and when that happened there was no one who would not hear. Soon the use of animal gut as a sheath was all the rage among women. It allowed them to keep their men at home, now that the population was growing so rapidly again. Atlantea had stopped taking immigrants so readily years ago. In fact, the numbers of people emigrating, forcibly, from Atlantea to Kriti were increasing every year.

He had the good graces of any of the aristocracy to leave the subject unmentioned. He barely batted an eye as the attendant discreetly retreated with the used sheath.

"I have come to speak about a difficult subject," he started. It was hard to concentrate with such beauty before him, still toweling herself. She draped the damp towel over her head and threw her torso forward. Her long hair flipped onto the towel and she wrapped it firmly behind her head with a twist. Then she threw herself back. The bundle rose up like a turban and cascaded flaccidly over the side of her head, her hair partially in the towel and partially out. She put a hand on either side of her narrow waist and pushed her elbows forward as far as she could, pressing out her chest at the same time as she twisted her head to the side and rotated it. He heard a few audible cracks from her spine.

"Ah, that's better. I've been trying everything to get that annoying crick out of my neck." The attendant was back and placed a bundle of folded towels between Selene and Minos and then left them alone. Minos noticed that the priestess who escorted him in had also discretely disappeared.

Selene flipped out a towel and draped it over her hips. Whatever favors she had given another were obviously not going to be passed along to Minos. He was relieved. For all the times in his marriage he had been tempted, he had never succumbed. But he was not sure he could have held out against Selene. He was glad he would not have to try.

"Tell me of this difficult subject."

He paused a little too long.

"Does it have anything to do with that prayer disk?"

"Yes. Indirectly."

She reached out and touched his knee. He saw her hand coming but his joint gave a reflex jerk against all he could do to suppress it. She smiled and breathed a laugh. "Dear Minos. You have nothing to fear from me. I won't assault you." She let go of his knee. "That man you saw leaving was a physician. He was working on my back when you arrived. I sent him away before he was finished." She twisted her spine again and it popped once. "But now it seems that you have brought me luck with your arrival. I will not need to see him again today. As for the sheath you so fleetingly observed, well, I told you I had tried everything today. Chronos does visit me regularly, you know. In fact," she poked his knee teasingly again, "I will have you know that I am every bit as faithful to my husband as you are to your wife. There has never been a time in my life when I have settled for less."

He wished she wouldn't poke him like that. He felt a little current of sensation ranging from his knee to his groin.

"Oh, I'll stop. Here. You're too distracted to see these." She draped a towel around her shoulders and covered her breasts. "Now tell me what is on your mind. No. Let me make it easy for you. You'll take forever to broach the subject if I don't. And no wonder. It is a difficult one, as you say. You have come here because you are concerned about the vent. More than that you are worried that what has been done by Chronos is not enough, or that it is simply wrong. Am I right so far?"

"Yes." How could she have known?

"You have always been a man of great learning, more so than most, perhaps more so even than Minos of Knossos. Perhaps even more so than Chronos," she added in a disconcerted whisper.

Her last statement astounded him. They were words he barely allowed himself to think and she had openly spoken them.

"You are thinking that it is shocking that I should speak so about Chronos. I have been concerned, deeply concerned, for a very long time. I, like you, have not known exactly what to do." She turned on him with a grave cast. "Minos, I am sealed forever to my husband and want to make it perfectly clear that I am not betraying him. But he is wrong. Both you and I know it. His sacrifices to Poseidon have been futile and have initiated the wrath of the greater. You know of whom I speak."

He said it. "Zeus."

Just then a small tremor shook the Temple.

"You see. You feel it. I knew you would. Even the mention of his holy name confirms it. How many times have I bade Chronos to see, but he is blind. How many times have I spoken, but he is deaf to my supplications. Do not think your fealty wavering because you have drawn the same conclusion. It is right. We are right. Minos, I have prayed for months for someone to come forward. That someone is you. You have felt the spur entreating you to come to me." Her wide eyes moved from his to the disk. "You have delved into the library and have found what it is you need."

She held forth her hand for the disk and he proffered it to her. She scanned it slowly, absorbing every word, turning it over in her mind. At last she closed her eyed and held the disk high in both hands. "Rhea, greatest of all. Great Goddess, the Earth Mother. Hear my words. Bless the words of this holy prayer disk I hold in my hands. Bless these words with recognition and approbation. Bless Rhadamanthys, Minos of Phaestos. Grant him safe passage from Kalliste to Kriti where he may render service toward our mutual exigency. Impart him the courage and wherewithal to conduct himself in the manner beneficial to our cause. Seal thy promise upon him I beseech thee. Amen."

They stayed in silence for a moment.

"What am I to do?" asked Minos.

"A most difficult task. Perhaps more difficult than my own."

"What are you saying? What are you to do?"

"I soon must evacuate Kalliste, all of Atlantea, actually."

"No." Minos was horrified.

"Yes."

Another low disturbance emanated beneath the Temple. The water rippled on the surface of the pool before they heard the noise.

"We must leave. Hurry."

The rumbles became greater. The building began to shake and vibrate visibly.

Selene's attendant priestess ran into the room shouting for them to leave.

Minos also shouted as he stood, clutching tightly onto the prayer disk. "We have to get everyone out."

"I have given instruction to my priestesses to vacate the Temple at the first sign of earthquake," Selene called to him. She was having a hard time standing with the building shaking as it was.

They ran together, the three of them, joined at places by others fleeing the building. Out they ran into the concourse between the Temples. The vent gave a potent, explosive blast that knocked them all to their knees and the earthquake stopped. The western sky had been obliterated with an impenetrable cloud of tephra. The fortunate summer breeze carried the lighter dust up and away, but the heavier rocks and scoria fell upon the towns below. Some of the rocks were red hot and started minor fires that, fortunately, were easily extinguished. The hole was venting more voluminously than ever with its impenetrable column rising to an infinite height.

Selene spoke over the hissing sound of the falling volcanic ejecta. "You have to go now," she told Minos, holding fast to his arm.

He nodded somberly. "You have prayed for me. Now tell me what I must do."

"A sacrifice, Minos. You must sacrifice to Zeus."

"A lamb? A bull? What must I sacrifice?"

"Neither." She could not brace him against her words. "You must sacrifice your son."

* * *

Many small earthquakes trembled beneath his feet as Minos of Phaestos traveled down the sloping road to Akrotiri. None of the paving stones had come completely out of place but so many had jostled in position, one high, another low, that it was impossible for him to take his eyes off where he was walking without tripping. There was little he wanted to see anyway. The scenery of the once green island was now an unappealing and uniform powder gray. Whereas before the differences between the glories of each level were plain to the eye, now they were indistinguishable from one another, with the obvious exception of the size of the buildings. Heralds were proclaiming tidings of the coming general evacuation. Only a few pretended to be shocked. Most had entertained thoughts of the inevitability of this happening if conditions did not improve, and things had only gotten worse. To save time, the populace would be transported to the nearby island of Ios. That way the ships could get everyone off Atlantea quickly, before the final stage where everyone on Ios would have to be moved to Kriti. Selene hoped it would not come to that. She hoped with all her heart that Minos would be successful and that Chronos would come around to her acceptance of the failure of his adherence to the singular worship of Poseidon. It would take a united front of the two together to avert disaster.

How infuriated Chronos had been with her when she told him of the program she had initiated to vacate the island. She had not told him everything, though. She had not told him of Minos going to the mountain of Zeus. He was angry enough without her exacerbating the situation with further news. He probably could have tried to counter the movement to leave if he had been entirely without reservation himself, but he had seen at least a portion of the logic involved. He hated this challenge Poseidon was casting their way as much as anyone, and longed for a way out. He just couldn't find it. But one thing was for certain, he was not leaving the island himself. Others may run, but he would remain, and he would prevail.

As Minos of Phaestos set sail from Akrotiri, those of the fifth level had finished the abstemious packing of their few necessities. Selene's message had been clear; no frivolous belongings, no luxury, no extra weight. The ships would be filled to the cargo line, and a little more. There was no room for excess. Minos's royalty secured him a little extra space, but the ship was very crowded. Because of time constraints the oars were out even at full sail. Only one sailor was manning each oar, and assisting him were two other passengers crowded onto his bench. The center gangway was packed with uncomfortable sitters, mostly women and children too weak for the rigors of the oar, the rest piled up at the bow like nested animals or spilled out to the stern with the Captain and Minos.

The roads were filling with people making their way to all ports; to the largest, Akrotiri, and to the secondary and tertiary as well. The last were fishing towns that had only small boats. But those small boats would do in this situation. They were adequate enough to make the eleven-mile voyage to Ios. That was the shortest possible distance from the north coast, but from Akrotiri on the southern coast it was considerably longer, almost twice as far. It would have been closer for them to go to the island of Anafi, but there they would find no water. It was a barren island. The closest suitable haven was Ios. At least those departing from the southern coast could hug the shore for the first half of their journey. That was a comfort to many. For a sea people, it was astonishing how few had ventured more than a short skip from shore, if they had been in a boat at all.

Many of the lower orders, those who were fishers and farmers, begged to be taken directly to Kriti. After all, it was ridiculous to them to have to go north only to have to go south a greater distance later. They should just get the single voyage over with at once. Many were quite out of joint when their objections were met with stern refusal. Still, they were people of Atlantea and they had the capacity, in the end, to understand that what they were doing was for the greater good of their people as a whole.

They were fortunate that every transport went off without incident, that they met with no meltemi to jeopardize their lives. The odds of meeting a summer storm were slim over such a short distance but, had it occurred, would have grounded the fleet for a while and made evacuation of the remainder impossible. Worse, with so many inexperienced people in overloaded ships, one could easily be swamped. Lives and, more importantly, a ship, which could be used for many more evacuations, would be lost.

The vent was exploding regularly at two-hour intervals since the last earthquake. The earth itself stood still by comparison, vibrating tremors no longer of any account to anyone, but the vent was tremendously active. The western half of the island was becoming obliterated under accumulating ash. Returning ships focused their relief efforts there first. With the air so poor there were many who found it impossible to make their way around the circle road to other ground. They could follow the slope downhill as far as the sea and that was as far as they could go. They grossly overloaded the ships and held close to shore, dropping off numerous people on the northern tip of the island where conditions were not so onerous before continuing on to Ios with their lightened encumbrance.

It took a full week for the ships to transport everyone to Ios. Every seaworthy vessel from Kriti was seconded to assist and, as ships came on trade missions, they unloaded and stayed to help. Not every ship was in the area but, all told, there were over one hundred crafts of varying sizes, not counting the smaller fishing skiffs.

A tremendous earthquake rocked the island as the last of the inhabitants were leaving. With the exception of Chronos, Selene, and a few personal assistants who vowed they would have to be killed before they would leave their sides, the island was devoid of human life. Even the Minoses had left. Minos of Knossos had stayed the longest. He was the one Chronos respected most. He was from the Temple of Knowledge on Kriti. He was wiser than any of them and as such the senior of them all. Minos of Knossos had argued, bitterly at times, with Deukalion, Minos of Zakro about what to do with the iron goddess. He had petitioned Chronos to cast it into the vent with pomp and ceremony to placate the gods. Deukalion had argued that the idea was unequivocally sacrilegious and under no circumstances would such extreme action mollify the angry gods. It would only serve to inflame them further. What should be done, he rebutted, was to melt the goddess in the molten rock that spewed out on occasion from the vent. Oozing red and black against white over the rock landscape, the gently flowing lava could be approached without danger, as long as the vent didn't explode again. The solidified rock slag could be struck off the softened iron and the goddess could be hammered into a sword, or perhaps a grail to toast the gods.

Chronos had dismissed Deukalion's idea out of hand. Minos of Zakro left the island in a huff, thinking dark thoughts about how the two had conspired against his most logical conclusion.

Chronos had almost bought into the prompting of Minos of Knossos though; sacrificing the goddess to the vent; when Selene got wind of it. She vetoed the notion at once, seized the icon from its place in the Inner Sanctum, and kept it secure in her private quarters. It was unheard of for the High Priestess of Rhea to actually exercise her authority in that respect, but no one could refute the right she undeniably possessed to do so. At that juncture, even Minos of Knossos abandoned them for the safety of Kriti.

Chronos once again sacrificed a bull to Poseidon without the blessings of the Council or even notifying Selene what he was about. He had the aid of his terrified personal assistants, improperly abetting in the sacrifice of a white bull, and this last brought on the terrestrial upheaval. Pent-up stresses under the surface had let go at once, having built up for an entire week without requiting. The damage suffered to the island was of intolerable severity. Most noticeable was the demolition of the Temple of Poseidon. There was damage to every building, including the Temple of Rhea, but none were so thoroughly demolished as the Temple of Poseidon. Under its cloak of dust one would never suspect the glory that had once resided on that spot, now reduced to rubble.

Chronos cried in anguish. His fabric of soul was rent. His foundation suffered ruin, matching core to core his wonderful building. He clawed his chest and lamented and drew blood from the strikes left by his manicured nails. Selene attempted comfort but he was having none of it. Bewailing the proclivities of gods he saw that his nurturing faith in Poseidon had been wasted dross. This dawning apprehension gnawed his gut as his mind dealt with the thought that he alone might bear the responsibility of the awful torment and destruction being visited upon his people.

What a fool he'd been. Oh, curse his head. Curse his body to his very feet. He groaned in abject misery and despair and tore at his flesh again. He was inconsolable. Tears and snot streaked his ashen face and drooled like muddy syrup to his chest.

He had conceded to come as far as coastal Akrotiri, and now it was in ruins all around him. Roofs had collapsed, unable to support the weight of fallen tephra and sustain earthquake shocks in unison. Pots had tipped, even the massive pithoi had tumbled over and spilled their contents. In front of him was a stairway of ashlar block that had simply folded in the center, all the way from bottom to top. Most walls had remained standing because of the superior method of wood post and beam construction between layers and columns of rock blocking. Everywhere was the omnipresent pumice, the dust and rice sized crumbs that covered everything to a depth of one or two inches and built up in drifts like snow, feet high in places.

"Look, Selene," shouted her attendant excitedly.

All except Chronos followed her finger to the peak of Kalliste. He didn't care anymore.

"Chronos," shouted Selene. "Chronos, take heed and look."

He pulled out of his self-indulgent sorrow for a moment, long enough to comprehend the sight which had evolved into something so unfamiliar.

The smoke had stopped. The vent was no longer giving off smoke or dust or pumice. It had plugged completely. The earthquake had closed it off.

Chronos could not even speak. He fell back on his rump and sobbed into his hands. All this time. All this time and all he had to do was acknowledge the impropriety of his wrongs. Around him his nation lay in ruins, his people gone. There would be no forgiveness for him in this world or the next for his foolhardiness. Oh, the evils of self-righteous pride. Of all people he should have known better, should have been aware of what was happening to him. Now it was too late. He wanted to die but death was too good for him. There was no pleasure to be harvested from seeing the vent stopped. It was his fault it had ever opened. He had offended every god, every spirit.

There were not words to describe his agony.

* * *

It had taken no time at all for the refugees to see that Kalliste had ceased smoking. They had noticed as soon as the opaque haze surrounding the islands cleared. The mountain peak was easily visible from Ios. They waited another week before venturing back, encouraged by the natives of Ios who found their food and water supplies strained beyond limits. With the population almost overnight increased tenfold they all suffered. But the greatest affront to the Ionians was that they could not believe that in such dire hardship the Atlanteans were continually complaining about no place to bathe. Even if there were, they could not have done so with the limited water supply that was barely adequate to keep them all hydrated in this hot late-summer weather.

The Atlanteans were overjoyed to see that their island was once again safe, but the first to set foot were horrified at what they found. The gray, cadaverous complexion blanketing everything cast a pall on the island so far removed from its glorious splendor that they felt physically sickened. When they grounded and stepped ashore and witnessed the destruction of their homes and shops, and worst of all the damage to the temples which filled their lives with respect and adoration whether they were granted the right of access or not, they perceived a similitude of the devastation Chronos endured.

That did not stop the Ionians from encouraging the rest to return. They tirelessly pointed out that as rough as the conditions were, they still had plenty of water on Atlantea, more than enough. And what was a little dirt? It would probably freshen the crops and be completely covered over with green by this time next year. As for the buildings, well, who hadn't had earthquakes in their history? They would manage just as everyone else did. They would rebuild.

The Atlanteans were far from fools and knew the spirit tailing the reassuring suggestions. All the same, they retained their composure and thanked the Ionians for their hospitality in this desperate time of need. They themselves would be glad to see the last of this inadequate island. They would see what awaited them on Atlantea but, from all reports, they would probably not be staying. Their ancestry resided on Kriti. They would again settle there.

Ship by ship, in reverse, they returned to Atlantea. The ships were not so full this time as the crisis seemed to have abated. Their stay was short. They were only stopping to claim their belongings. They emptied their homes and stores of anything of value or of sentimental worth. Captains were making a fortune on the relatively quick hauls between Atlantea and Kriti. Under full sail they still lowered the oars and drove the ships faster. At each end of the leg they had arranged fresh crews so the others could rest. The ships were working non-stop twenty-four hours a day.

Inhabitants of the higher levels were paying extortionist's wages to carriers who thought they might be risking their lives by staying. They were as nervous as anyone else about staying long on the island. The carriers demanded as much as half the inventory they conveyed. They had to charge that much because it was what the captains were charging them to get it off the island. The captains were securing half of the inventory for themselves, storing it in warehouses at the northern ports of Kriti. Passengers thought themselves lucky to get away with so reasonable a fee. Better to lose half than have to leave it all behind. The gray rafts of ash and pumice, tinted reddish-brown in the light of day, floating in huge blankets on the water ,would have completely bogged down smaller craft. In this way, by large ship, almost all of the valued goods from the lower levels of Atlantea, even down to kitchen utensils, were removed from the isle. Only the huge pithoi, the man-sized pots for storage of bulk foodstuffs, were abandoned.

No one had seen or heard tell, even in legend, of anything like these gray blankets interfering with traffic. Smaller ships had to skirt the edges of the thick rafts, still traveling through the thinner portions of the floating ejecta, impossible to avoid altogether, but adding miles to their course by the forced detours. The rafts had mostly settled on the western side of Atlantea, but the

556

water currents were carrying them south and east, maneuvering them directly in the way of ships going back and forth to Kriti. Had any of the Captains been maintaining their usual routes they would have witnessed the course of the mats of the glassy froth bumping up against the island of Kuprios, long in the distant past known as Kypros. Uncountable millions of tons of buoyant pumice stone spun off in many directions but mainly washed up against the shores of Kuprios, terrifying the people of that island who had no idea from whence it came or what it was all about. The floating stone mats devastated their fishing industry, driving them to migrate inland where they could hunt.

Chronos had taken residence in the Temple of Rhea while this final evacuation of material was occurring. Five of the ten Minoses of Kriti, along with their Priestess wives, had also occupied it with him. Selene had granted the men unconventional access in these unique circumstances. The men still grieved over their fallen temple, which they had held in such high regard. Now it was a pile of broken stone and not even the most optimistic could envision a rebuilt glory such as the one they had known. Not even the gold and silver foil showed through from under the dust. But even with this unequivocal indicator of the unrighteousness of the Poseidon Temple, some of the Minoses still murmured.

"The sacrifice was not done according to the satisfaction of Poseidon," ventured the doughty Deukalion, Minos of Zakro. "Look at the temple. It lies in shameful ruin because of our lack of resolution, because of our faintheartedness." He was aware of Chronos giving him a petulant eye and quickly spoke to soothe any misunderstanding. "There was nothing anyone could have done to prevent it. It was inevitable, a trial that people have always faced to gain guidance and instruction. Knowledge is only obtained by trial and trials by their very nature are adversarial. Let us look on this as opportunity to gain wisdom, not as an eternal punishment for misunderstanding what was only vaguely before us."

Where was he leading them? "What are you suggesting, Minos?" He had piqued Chronos's curiosity.

"I am suggesting, Chronos, that placing Zeus above Poseidon may not be the wisest of moves."

"We have been over this before."

"Yes. But consider. We are people of the sea. Our ancestry, chosen of the gods, has always been an island people. We live surrounded by the sea whereas others are land dwellers exclusively. We control the seas. The sea feeds us and protects us. By way of the sea we have become wealthy beyond measure. We are never afflicted by the onerous droughts and pestilences of the land dwellers. The sea, again, protects us. And the god of the waters is

Poseidon. If his temple has fallen it is because he alone is displeased, not some other god."

"Do you not feel that Zeus could destroy the temple as easily as Poseidon?"

"Yes," Deukalion replied carefully, "but why would he? Why would there be conflict among the gods? It defies rational thought."

There were nods of consent around the circle. Deukalion had done his job well. He had solicited those Minoses who were of like mind and taken them along to Kalliste to lobby Chronos. It was working. Without Selene sitting beside him twisting his mind he was going to be swayed.

"Then we need to alter the sacrifice," Chronos confirmed.

"Not alter the animal, Chronos, just the method."

"You are correct, Minos of Zakro. In my mind I have seen what you speak of. I am shamed to say that I have been misled and have allowed myself to be so. Forgive me, each and every one of you. In time, it will be the people I must beg pardon from. It is they who have suffered most."

"Repent not, Chronos. As you say, you were misled. There is no soul alive who would not have been."

Chronos stood abruptly. "Arise, all of you. We will take this matter to hand immediately." He called out the door. "Priest. Come at once."

A younger man rushed to the doorway. He had been kept out of earshot during these sensitive talks. "You are personally charged with bringing a prime bull here to the temple."

The order registered at once and the Priest raced off. A bull to the temple of Rhea. What next?

The stable of sacred animals had collapsed during the last quake but, fortunately, only a few had been killed or injured, and fewer had run off in panic. The finest bull, a gloriously handsome white beast with sharp, upturned horns, had escaped even a mark. He was the purest of his race, descended from the first bull brought to the shore of Kriti by Poseidon himself over one thousand years ago, a perfect reincarnation of the selfsame animal. The priest required twenty of the strongest men, devoted priests who attended to the needs of these sacred animals, to bring this one into submission. There were looks of disbelief as they piloted the magnificent contradictory animal through the front Temple gate.

Chronos met them at the entrance. "Set him free," he ordered.

The priests moved with circumspect attention as they cautiously untied the bull. Backing away to safety Chronos closed them out of the Temple. The bull was free. He sniffed the air suspiciously and gave a hard stare at Chronos through his prodigious glassy eye before wagging his head, as if to shake off the insignificant human's presence, and sauntering down the corridor.

"Are all of the entrances sealed?"

"Yes, Chronos."

"And the women?"

"We have sealed them in the Inner Sanctum. They will be safe there."

"Did they protest?"

Deukalion tipped his head. "Not loudly, Chronos. And none were harmed."

"Very good. Let us proceed then. I do not believe we have much time."

They gathered the ropes which had been used to bind the bull and blessed them according to dictate. As they prayed that they might capture the victim that they knew would be acceptable to Poseidon they felt a rumble at their feet. Either it was opposition from Zeus, which was something only considered for a moment in their minds before being pushed to the back of all possible considerations, or it was approval from their master, Poseidon.

Each taking a rope they fashioned nooses to the end of long staves in preparation for the hunt. With Chronos in the lead of the five kings of Kriti, they hunted the bull now roaming free in the confines of the temple. Had Selene known what they were doing she would have condemned this activity as penultimate blasphemy, second only to the willful destruction of the Temple itself. They stalked the beast, hearing its snorting echoing down the quiet passageways as they silently crept in pursuit. This temple was orderly, contrary to the Labyrinth of Knossos, and relatively small for all its apparent magnitude from lower elevations. Much of its size was optical illusion. The six men of the highest priesthood tracked their prey in minutes to the large meeting room and surrounded it.

These men, for all their age, were still among the strongest of the Minoans. Very few of the most puissant youth could match these men in speed, and almost none in a contest of strength. They were the peerless examples of physical attribute, and these six were pitting themselves against the first among bulls.

They spread thinly around the beast, confusing it. It took short charges and Deukalion got the first loop around its back hoof. He yanked hard and the bull spun his head to see what was going on behind him. Chronos jumped forward and slipped his noose under the bull's front leg as he took a step. As it reared up at the front another noose was slipped under the other leg, and others over each horn. The last was tightened around its remaining hind leg and the men dropped their staves from the ropes and pulled in unison, those of the head one way, and those of the hooves another. The bull reared up and with his weight off of his front legs, the combined twisting force of the men on their ropes pulled him hard to the ground, the impact forcing an explosive grunt from the bull along with an evil discharge of snot from his nose. As he kicked, they allowed a bit of slack to tangle in his legs. The harder the bull struggled, the more entangled he became, his horns wrapped tightly into the knot forming around his legs. It had only taken a minute. The small cadre of men, whose combined strength was not but a fraction of the bull's, had outmaneuvered and outwitted the powerful beast.

They winched the imposedly placid creature to the Pillar of Laws and tied its horns securely to it. They could free it now, untie its legs. All it could do was stand and ride the pillar up and down, shaking its head in frustration and futility. The strength of the bull's neck was nothing as compared to solid rock.

"Hear us, Great Poseidon, Master of the seas and waters of the Earth." Chronos was sweating profusely from the paramount cascade of energy he and his kings had poured into this feat. The danger had been so substantial that it confirmed the miracle of protection that had been afforded them. Not one of them had been hurt. He withdrew a polished blade from its waist sheath and held it to capture a glint of sunlight. He reflected it into each of the bull's huge, black eyes, back and forth until the creature began to squint and blink.

Blinded, with water running down its face, the taurus was now safe to approach. "Poseidon, accept our sacrifice. Take this creature's soul into thine own." With those words, he slashed the razored blade across its throat. Its carotid arteries sprayed the sacred inscriptions of law on the pillar, darkening the gilded overlay with blood as it thrashed its head. Blood gushed both from artery and vein, pooling on the floor in a greasy red collective. The bull slipped on its own slime and crashed to the floor, too weak to do more than lift its head. It looked around the room at its antagonizers as its chest heaved and bubbles of red burst from its mouth, nose, and neck where its trachea had been severed. In a moment it had lost even that lingering remnant of strength and its head fell back, horns clattering and scraping as they struck the floor. Another moment, a final exhalation, and the bubbling stopped. The bull was dead.

Two of the Minoses had passed on the dying scene and had retrieved the fire needed to complete the sacrifice. They took anything of wood in the Temple near at hand and piled it on the fire set in the middle of the floor. The others set to work severing the bull's limbs from its body and when the fire was raging, lay the legs upon the flames. Chronos filled a bowl with wine and cast in five clots of blood, one for each of the assisting Minoses.

Chronos took the bowl of wine and blood and sprinkled it around the fire, purifying it, and did likewise to the column to which the bull had been tied, swearing aloud with his kings to forever judge according to the laws on the pillar.

They cast more wood and furniture upon the fire and still the flames grew hotter and higher. They ritually carved the bull to pieces and cast each piece into the fire, including every entrail. Then they each drew golden cups, partially filled them with wine and once again added clots of blood. This was their libation, their swearing of fealty to Poseidon, irrevocable, which they cast upon the flames. But not all of it.

Each left something in the bottom of the cups for themselves.

To drink.

* * *

Rhadamanthys, Minos of Phaestos, agonized over his failure to carry out his appointed duties. He was not a cowardly man. There were those who would attest without hesitation to his veracity and rectitude. There was no foe or issue at odds with him from which he would back down. Even when pressed recently by the powerful Minos of Knossos, he still held his ground against daunting leverage and maintained his stand that Zeus was supreme and Poseidon should be dismissed as a lesser god. He had withstood the wrath of the lobbying force, a last tactic of the desperate, and sent them on their way knowing that if he was wrong he would soon find that he would be replaced. This was a very difficult time for Kriti. The kings were dividing along parallel lines, lines which could never come together. He felt a great foreboding that if this situation with Atlantea could not come to a resolve, then their civilization could be destined to end. And as much as he tried to eschew the decision he had already sworn to carry out, he knew within himself that he would have to soon conclude it.

He did not even enjoy sitting on his high balcony any longer. There was no pleasure to be found anywhere.

"Come sit with us, Minos," soothed his wife. The High Priestess had been told about the nature of Rhadamanthys's gloom by Selene herself. She too recognized the need for acting on the revelation but could not yet bring herself to commit the sacrifice. They had not told their son yet, in fact, had barely spoken of it between the two of them since returning to Phaestos. They had memorized the prayer of the disk and daily recited it in their minds. The time would come, they knew. The time would come.

Rhadamanthys leaned over the balustrade of the temple-palace and quietly pondered the spectacular views from his vantage point on the precipitous hilltop. The long Messara Plain stretched east before him, waving its fields of rich grains in uniform undulations. He ran his fingers down the length of an enormous elephant tusk. Many said that the Phaestos Temple rivaled Knossos in splendor, not in size or lavish decor but in idyllic location and compact perfection. He wondered whatever happened to that peevish librarian who had almost succeeded in refusing him the disk. He wondered if he had died in the collapse of the Poseidon Temple or if he escaped with his life. Perhaps he managed to save some of his precious scrolls from the wreckage. Rhadamanthys wondered if the administrative blight had heard he had slipped away from Kalliste with the sacred disk and whether he agonized over the loss. Thinking such thoughts were the only things bringing any pleasure to Minos these days, and overall that offered minimal relief.

The High Priestess took her husband by the arm and led him out of hearing range from their son.

"Your thoughts are deep and dark. Why don't you talk about them with me?"

"You know what I dwell on."

"Yes. My thoughts continually ponder the same thing. Remember, our strength is in togetherness, as it always has been. Together we must do, or not do, what is required of us. I will stand by you, my husband, in whatever you decide."

"It is not a kindness you pass to me in consigning your authority."

"He is my son," she wept. "I cannot sanction his death by myself."

"He is my son, too."

"I know." She embraced her husband and pressed her wet face into his bosom. "I have never forgotten."

Together they held each other and cried a long time. They both had made up their minds and the conviction was too painful to deal with all at once. Weeks had passed and they had been derelict enough as it was. The trial was made all the more difficult by the news that Kalliste had sealed herself and was no longer sending forth ash. Had the Temple of Poseidon survived the last earthquake as the Temple of Rhea had they would have taken that as a portent that they had been wrong and abandoned their intentions. But that was not what happened. The Temple of Poseidon was crushed like a child's sandcastle and right next door the Temple of Rhea stood as a beacon lighting the way of truth.

They looked at each other, beholding the anguish of soul in one another's eyes. Rhadamanthys could not speak, so his Priestess did for him. "We must take our son to Juktas."

All Rhadamanthys could do was nod his confirmation.

* * *

"How shameful that Zeus's home should be left to disintegrate like this." Katreus had been raised by his parents to have the deepest love and respect for all deities, most especially Rhea, but secondarily Zeus. He had never thought much of Poseidon, considering him more of a convenient imagining of man rather than a true god, perhaps reflecting the subliminal thoughts of his parents.

Rhadamanthys, his Priestess wife, and their son, gazed upon the ruined temenos foundation walls. They were all that remained of the tripartite shrine after the last earthquake destabilized the slope and collapsed the building. The long iron rods had long since been taken away and anything of value appropriated for use in Poseidon's shrines.

"Our son speaks the truth, Minos." She maintained the formalities due this austere occasion. "How could this gravesite, among all others, suffer such neglect?"

"There have been many who would repair it and even restore it to its original glory of old. But the Minoses of Knossos have held this territory as their own and prevented all works not of their initiation." He picked up a rock and, after examining it, pocketed it.

From their vantage they could see Knossos quite clearly, four miles north. It was the largest city on Kriti, the most populated city of the entire world, amassing a population of more than eighty thousand. And it was sure to grow more populous than that with the influx of citizens coming from Atlantea. They were used to living in splendor and Knossos was still the most effulgent of all the temple cities.

"It isn't right, Father. No sacred place should be left in this state."

There was no argument. Zeus's cairn would have been the most appropriate place to do what they had to do. Even Katreus felt an attaching spirit about the place. But they could not sacrifice here, not properly. Without the correct rites and prayers, without the libation cups and rhytons, and without a suitable setting, the sacrifice would be unrecognized and tantamount to murder.

Katreus had not been informed of any reason for being with his parents. As far as he was concerned he was just along for a vacation outing. He enjoyed their company and wanted to know everything there was to know about them, especially their callings as Minos and High Priestess of Phaestos, and this was a great opportunity for him to find out more. Except they were unusually quiet and introspective on this trip. It was a great honor to have them for his parents and he was the envy of most of those he knew. There was always someone who had nothing nice to say about anyone of authority, be it theological or governmental, but they were easy enough to ignore. The people he was closest to venerated his parents, as did he.

They went down near the base of the mountain where a small village known for its herbs lay. Aminospilia, they called it. Pungent scents perfumed the air as they came along the neighboring farms. The wild rose grew at this lower altitude. Prized for the labdanum it exuded, it was protected by law and gathered for use in perfumery. Other wildflowers grew prettily among the roses; asphodel, milkworts, and pinks. Katreus wondered where they grew before all the forests were wiped out. Aleppo pine forests were common, they said, in olden times, especially in the east. Now there were only a few scattered copses, almost completely gone from reckless felling, overgrazing, and soil erosion. Farmers had finally come to understand that trees were not their enemies, that they preserved topsoil from wearing away by both wind and water, that they were an investment in the future and would be profitable for building, or for firewood, at some time as yet unseen. The trees only added to the beauty of their farms and pastures. They had taken to planting varieties of native trees in organized synchrony, contesting with their neighbor over who could be most artful. Juniper, plane, willow, oak, and useful trees usually kept back from the property perimeter like olive and citrus, graced the landscape like an orderly renaissance painting.

Katreus thought that there was much lost in urban city living. They smelled of people no matter how efficient the sewers and street cleaners, and the oneness with nature was lost regardless of how they tried.

This was a choice place on all the island. The sea sparkled as always in the distance, azure in the brilliant light of mid-day, sherry-wine in the beam of the setting sun. Baying donkeys vociferously lamented their loneliness or serenaded their loved ones, and roosters ruffed up on posts enounced the rising sun of every dawn. Here in the open air there was life, a joie de vivre that came from a mountain on one side and a sea on the other. From here he felt the enchanting sense that he could see into eternity.

No wonder Knossos was chosen to be near this section of the island over all others.

A drilling sound like a forest fire came from a group of workers in a field on the outskirts of the village. Silkworms made the irritated tone as they quashed their way through mulberry leaves covering them in their boxes. There were more boxes than could be easily counted and the combined numbers of worms, innumerable populations, produced the eerie noise of invisible cause, unless one knew beforehand what the people were doing. Flaxen yellow, butter soft loops of raw silk were being drawn from hissing cauldrons and twined slowly and piously onto hexagonal frames of wood ready for the looms. How ancient can this art be, wondered Katreus? So intent on their task, the workers did not even notice the three passers-by as they made their way along.

A peasant traveling opposite to them reigned in his donkey and gazed at them in quizzical recognition, and then at the green valley descending below.

Turning back to them he said prophetically, "You have chosen the right place to work. Here the partridges sing more sweetly than anyplace else," words uttered before, and that would be echoed by another in thirty-four hundred years.

Their eyes followed him in unison as the elderly man rode his donkey down the hill. His words had an ominously hollow ring for all that he said. Katreus would have liked to have struck a conversation with the old fellow but he had sensed an urgency in what his parents were doing and knew they could not afford the time. Instead, he let his eyes take in what the man had been referring to, the lovely green valley at their feet worked for countless years by the people of the area. Beyond the silk workers were the saffron fields, the crocuses blooming in all their glory. A powerful aphrodisiac, it would still need a doctor's prescription on Crete into the twenty-first century. Katreus still had not experienced the potent drug. He thought about it. He knew enough about sexuality from what he had been told, but had not yet availed himself of the opportunities that awaited him by way of many inviting girls of his age. Later, he had always thought. And as his parents had always instructed him, the world is too large, too interesting, too curious, to waste one's short youth on such frivolous base things such as that.

Large outcroppings of rock cleaved the landscape, hewn with shallow caves. Anemospilia, they called the village, 'the caves of the wind,' because of an ancient belief that the caves pocking the rocks were carved by fierce meltemi gales.

The shrine was easy to find, the largest building in the little village and the only one constructed out of substantial stone and surrounded by a small walled plot known as a temenos, or sacred enclosure. It stood upon a ridge overlooking lowlands that draw the eye to a focus on Knossos. Above the three doorways of the shrine were the usual horns of consecration.

"I am Minos of Phaestos. I require the use of this shrine." He spoke with authority to the surprised priest.

"Yes, Minos. Please enter." The priest stepped aside until all three had passed into the north-facing entrance and then followed after. "May I offer myself to be of any assistance? There is no one else here and I am not currently required for anything," as if that made any difference when a Minos was paying call.

Rhadamanthys almost sent him away, desiring only privacy, but then thought he could be of some use after all. The priest was of fairly high standing among shrine keepers. A handsome man, his hair descended in a thick braid past his shoulders. His neck, ears, and waist sparkled with jewelry, and his costly robe was embroidered with a graceful quatrefoil design. Aristocratic, he would be proudly privileged to serve one of his kings. "You will escort us to the sacrificial room," he was advised. "Then you will provide for us all the necessities required for immolation."

This was wonderful news, thought the priest. A Minos sacrificing in this shrine. Minoses never came to shrines. He might leave a great oblation, or send one later if he received the service he required. When the news spread, and he would see to it personally that it did, others would recognize the greatness of this shrine and come flocking. The priest was exultant. This could become a rich sanctuary, depending on how he handled these people today. He was merely a subordinate, but it bothered him sometimes that the ritual contents of the shrine were so antiquated. Some of the pieces appeared to be hundreds of years old. Perhaps that all might change. Perhaps he might be given presiding priesthood authority over the shrine after this.

The woman didn't speak but he had to presume she was Minos's wife, a High Priestess. She dressed like one. The circlet of small gold ax blades she wore as a necklace, layered with a second of imported stones and a third of blue glass rosettes revealed her rich standing. He had no idea who the young man might be and, for his part, thought it best not to inquire.

He left them in the vestibule, the foyer separating the three worship chambers from the outside. Along the upper edge of the walls ran a limestone frieze of piquant triglyphs and half-rosettes. One wall was done up in a panel of spirals and frets on a surface painted to simulate marble, another carved in high relief and living detail the contests of man and bull. Here, as in all shrines and temples, the Minoan artisan spread all his lilting glories of buoyant art. Ladies in blue with classic features, comely arms and comfy breasts, caught chatting in an anteroom. Fields of lilies, lotus, and olive spray, ladies cozy at the opera, and hovering dolphins lingering motionless in the sea. The aristocratic and slightly androgynous cupbearer, cocked and strong, conveying precious ointment in a slim blue vase, his face sculpted by breeding as well as by art. Into the dark hall the artists had brought the vivid splendor of open fields. Plaster sprouted lilies, tulips, narcissi, and sweet marjoram. The Saffron Picker bending eagerly to pluck the crocus, colors warm, blossoms abiding fresh throughout the year. No one viewing these blissful scenes would ever again suppose that nature was discovered by any Renaissance artist.

Dim light from a single oil lamp lit the vestibule as the priest came out of the first of the worship rooms with another lamp still unlit. Igniting it off the first, he conveyed the flame to several lamps placed exactly about, bathing them in a warm glow. Into each worship room he vanished, one by one, light growing in each as he lit every lamp previously prepared with a full supplement of scented oil, augmenting aromas of honey offerings in the east room.

"The right chamber is where the sacrificial table is. The central chamber is where the deity resides. But why am I telling you these things? Of course you know." It was the standard layout. He worried that he might have been a bit too obvious by not mentioning the left chamber, which was where patrons were expected to leave their oblations prior to commencing worship, and afterward as well if they had a particularly spiritual session. He wished he hadn't said anything at all.

"We will require your assistance, Priest. Is everything in order?"

"Yes, Minos." He was getting nervous. This was a holy place but neither Minos, nor his Priestess, gave any indication that this was going to be anything other than the most dour sacrifice. While he was on that thought, he wondered what they had intended to kill? They had brought nothing with them. It was most likely that they would send him out to secure a nice lamb.

"You may lock the entrances then."

That was a most unusual request. The priest had never heard of such a thing. "Yes, Minos. As you wish." He was taken aback. To lock a place of worship? And such an order coming from one of the Highest, whose second abode was Atlantea, an island known for its obedience to law and a tradition of keeping every door unlatched. He couldn't puzzle it out.

"You will assist us when you are done."

"Of course." He was almost hoping to be released from this suspicious service. How bizarre. A sacrifice without a sacrifice. Behind locked doors yet.

They stepped into the central room, narrower than it was long, with lamps and large and small eggshell-thin polychrome pottery arranged on either side, decorations of octopuses, fish, dolphins, starfish, and argonauts in background settings of shells, sponges, corals, and seaweed. On vessels thinned to a millimeter's thickness, the artists poured out upon them the motifs of their rich imaginations. At the far end was a low stone altar, raised only a few inches off the floor, on which stood a life-sized xoanon, a statue, of Rhea the Earth Mother. While it was a shrine of Zeus, it was usual for his beloved wife, the only creature he held in higher esteem than himself, to be given the exalted position in his consecrated sanctum. Its feet of fired potter's clay were the only immutable part of the figure. The rest of it was a light framework of wood, topped with a perfectly carved, close-grained soapstone steatite head. The frame was cloaked ardently with a fabulous mantle, which must have been equal in value to the entire structure of the shrine. Flanked on either side of the deity were a labrys and a shallow dish of oil in which floated a flaming wick.

They stood in silence contemplating the figure while the priest noisily secured the doors in the outer vestibule.

Rhadamanthys placed the stone he had carried from Zeus's burial site beside the large unhewn stone in front of the low altar, the stone which symbolized the earth, which with the sea and sky the Minoans considered eternal elements of their world.

"Father. Are we offering sacrifice to Zeus?"

"Yes, my son," he said softly to his eighteen-year-old.

"But where is the lamb?"

"He is here, my son."

The boy looked quizzical and looked to his other parent. "Mother?"

Tears were flowing from her eyes. She wiped them with a small cloth and began the prayer of the disk. They had memorized it and left it at Phaestos in case their son discovered it and brought up questions that they did not want to address on the way.

"Arise, Savior. Listen, Goddess Rhea," she intoned. "Giver, Redeemer, Savior, Mistress." She paused.

Rhadamanthys took his queue. "Arise, Savior. Listen, Zeus, husband of thy lover. Giver, Taker, Redeemer, Destroyer."

Katreus had a dawning realization of what was happening. "I am the sacrifice," he breathed in graceful acknowledgment.

They each touched a shoulder and, without another word, led him into the west room. Without urging he lay himself on the altar, submitting himself consummately to the requisition of his parents. Rhadamanthys tied his hands as he lay on his right side. To the sound of the priest closing the last door and securing the last lock, Rhadamanthys bound his son's ankles and drew them up behind him, trussing them tightly with his right heel nearly touching his thigh.

The priest entered the room and almost staggered to his knees. The situation could not have been more clear. A human sacrifice. Such things had been only spoken of as heathen forms of worship, practices reprehensible to the sacred priesthood. There had never been a human sacrifice on Kriti. He was terrified. Rhadamanthys was so far above him in authority he could not dare speak his mind. Such open challenge would invite Minos to strip him of his priesthood and cast him out in disgrace right then and there.

"Come, Priest," said Minos quietly. "You can see where you are needed."

He could. He took his place at the altar side and straddled the shrine's most sacred vessel, the spouted bucket-like vase for pouring blood libations. A trough led to its opening where it would receive the life force of the offering as it dribbled from the altar. He felt hot and he knew he was sweating. He could feel beads forming on his brow and his eyes watered and stung from the salty perspiration wicking into them.

Rhadamanthys felt sympathy for the priest. He could see that he was rent between his fear of what he was doing and the loyalty of his faith. He was glad the priest hadn't bolted. He was reluctantly prepared to kill him if need be but would have loathed having to do so.

The priest watched Minos's hand, adorned with two of the symbols of his office, the silver-iron ring and the engraved stone wrist-seal decorated with a slender boat poled by a muscular man. Rhadamanthys withdrew a bronze blade of the most perfect quality, sixteen inches long and incised on either side with the fanciful rendering of an imaginary beast with the snout and tusks of a boar, ears like butterfly wings, and the eyes of a fox. The alloy was of such superb caliber, substantial and enduring, that it would retain its razor edge through to the twentieth century. Its black ebony handle had been polished to such fanatical luster that it even caught the light of the oil lamps. Rhadamanthys held it above his son and gazed at the ceiling as the High Priestess played a somber melody on a small flute.

Rhadamanthys repeated the mantra over and over as she played, the back of his right hand on his forehead in supplication. "Arise Zeus. Arise, Goddess Rhea."

When the music stopped they raised their palms with their fingers spread, intoning the mantra of the disk in unison.

"Arise, Savior. Aia, redeem. We offer sacrifice, Holy One, Lady of Youth. Arise, Savior, Earth Mother, Rhea. Come, Goddess of Growth. Be gracious, Goddess of Growth. Great, thy grace. Accept. We play the flute. Arise, Holy One, Mother of Waters. Lo, hasten, Rhea, Goddess of Herds. Arise, Savior, Holy One, Lady of Might. We offer sacrifice. Hasten. Receive. Bestir thyself. Behold. Lo, we call. Arise and listen, Goddess. Be swift, redeem, accept. Arise Mistress, Mighty One, Shining One. Put forth thy strength, Savior. Listen, Goddess, to the flute. Listen. Listen. Accept, Giver. Redeem, Goddess of all."

The High Priestess raised the flute to her lips as she watched her son close his eyes. There were no tears, no supplications for liberation. He was at peace. His parents would never steer him wrong.

High-pitched music rang clearly from the slender flute. Rhadamanthys lowered the blade to his son's throat and touched the point to his skin. His son barely winced. He slid the blade forward and then quickly drew it back, deftly twisting the point down into the space between the trachea and the thick trapezius muscle, severing both the left carotid artery and jugular vein. His son hadn't even moved. Rhadamanthys rested the blade flat, just over the incision, keeping the pumping blood from spurting across the room. The blade rose and fell with each pulsation of the sacrificial lamb's heart in ever-weakening quivers, blood pouring out of the wound over the youth's neck, down the trough, and into the receptacle. Katreus opened his eyes, just before the end, and rolled them up to see his father and mother. His mouth opened and his jaw fell, as if he was about to say something, but nothing escaped his lips except a faint gurgle. His expression said enough. He bore no ill will. It was what he wanted, too.

Rhadamanthys closed his son's mouth, which had sagged open in death. He placed his hand over his eyes and slowly, gently, closed them. To him, it had felt as if his own life had ebbed away in his son's passing. He no longer felt that life was worth living. There was nothing for him anymore. Not even his wife of many years could make him desire this existence. He had done as the gods had commanded and no longer wanted any part of his priesthood. They could take him now, if they wanted. He was ready for them.

Rhadamanthys touched the shimmering blood on the table and wiped a stripe across his forehead, repeating the sign on his wife. They choked back their emotion as the priest carried the blood vase to the central nave. He would wait thee until Minos came to pour it over the unhewn rocks before the xoanon of Rhea.

The priest stopped in the corridor as the odd sensation traveled up his legs. It could have been a minor quake. Then a shock wave slammed into the shrine, deafening them even inside the rock shelter. The concussion could only have been supernatural. Originating eighty miles away they had no idea of its true cause. But that cause triggered a waiting quake, a binding of rock below the surface that had been waiting for a massive release of energy. Straight up from its hypocenter, the wave lifted the shrine six feet and slammed it back down. Every pot smashed as the roof began to fail above them. Oil cascaded across the floor. Bolts of fabric, also offerings of oblation, rolled out as the building rebounded and soaked up the oil. Fire from tipped lamps spread to the cloth, now a perfect wick.

The priest was the first to fall, unable to step even one foot into the central room of the deity. Panicked, he turned to flee, and in terror realized that there was no way out. Even had the door been open he would not have escaped. The wooden beam above his head fell away from the crumbling wall, driven down by another shock. It struck him a full blow on the back of his head, knocking him flat on his face and throwing the libation vase from his grasp. It smashed brutally, its sanguinary contents spilling uselessly on the floor, the sacrificial offering aborted. The collapsing roof hammered his bones to pieces and so marred his body it would never be known if he were man or woman.

Katreus had died in vain. His bubbling death rattle scarcely terminated, the climactic temblor that dropped the shrine roof reduced the massive walls behind it. Tumbling blocks of stone fell excruciatingly against Rhadamanthys, knocking him flat on his back to the ground. As the massive stones fell, he raised his arms to the boxer's position to protect his face and ward off the falling debris, but neither the strength of his powerful six-foot frame nor his fervent pleadings to the gods were to save him here. He wasn't ready for them after all, and felt profound embarrassment as he shit himself and died.

His beloved wife, the High Priestess, suffered a slower death. Trapped in the corner with no way of escape she lay prone, her legs splayed and paralyzed, pinned beneath the heavy oak beam that had snapped her back. The weight of it, supported entirely by her body, leaned into her like a mountain, squeezing the air and life out of her lungs. Too slowly, quietly, she asphyxiated, her flesh turning blue under a pestled coat of dust blocking every pore. Only tears streaked her face. Not for herself or husband, but for the life of their son that they had slain for naught.

* * *

Chronos stood nearest the castoff heap of shells from the land snails they were consuming. Minos of Knossos had brought them along as an offering of dedication and devotion to Chronos, knowing that he loved them and could not find them on Atlantea. All of the Minoses, except one, had come. They had come with their wives but had allowed them to go on to Kalliste, to the Temple of Rhea, while they stayed behind in the ash-filled coastal city of Akrotiri.

"There is nothing for us here," Chronos declared. Atlantea is in ruin and I do not know when the gods will allow us to occupy it in peace again. The city is empty, the island likewise, there is nothing left. Only the Temple of Rhea has been left any glory, and that too is fading. Our people have evacuated. Only the looters are still rummaging through the cities looking for abandoned valuables, and there is nothing that can be done about it."

"We will come back, Chronos," spoke Minos of Knossos. "We will reclaim this island from the evil befalling it. In time Atlantea will rise from the dust and blossom, once again, like the rose."

"In time, it will. But that time is not in the foreseeable future. For now, you will take yourselves to Kriti and continue with the faith. I tell you solemnly your salvation will be in Zeus as well as Poseidon. Let the women attend to Rhea. They worship and revere on Kalliste. That is their place. Leave them to it. Go now, and save the civilization of Kriti. Minos of Knossos, I charge you with leadership of your brethren. All present witness that I anoint you 'Chronos' in my absence. When my time comes, and it speedily does, you will take sovereignty."

"You speak hastily, Chronos. I do not seek your position, only the reverence of the gods as they stand in order above us."

"And in what order do you place them?"

"You are representative of Poseidon, Chronos. I speak for all when I give declaration that we all stand by you."

"I am adjuring you to give yourselves to Zeus. Poseidon has failed us. I will hear no argument. It has been an anguished epiphany, full of anxiousness and distress. I command you to go at once. Take the ship, and send another back to wait here for the High Priestesses. How long they will be, I know not."

"Then you must come with us," implored Deukalion. "You cannot expect us to leave you behind."

"When I come, I will come with the High Priestesses. Go now. My patience wears thin."

"But Chronos . . . "

"Go," he commanded.

Slowly they filed away. Minos of Knossos tarried longest, and then he too turned his back and departed. This was bitter ale. Kalliste had been their second home, their haven and refuge from the ordinariness of the world. They suffered their departure with obdurate contrition. Their temple-palaces on Kriti were stations of respect and they personally determined the spiritual asseverations of their communities, but who now would see to theirs? No Atlantea? They had to rebuild. They would. They determined in their hearts, as if of one mind, to do so. Not tomorrow, not next year, perhaps not even on Kalliste, but sometime, somewhere, it would be done.

* * *

Chronos was a solitary figure wandering the streets of the western shore. He had left Akrotiri to merely wander. He had kept a fast pace for someone in his frame of mind, and carried on through the starless night without a thought to time. The sun was warming him now, through the dismal haze. He kicked at some gathered dust on a Minoan threshold stone, a slab of green limestone decorating the entrance of a new home, as he despondently toured the abandoned city. All was still, the earth, the sky. Between the buildings there was not so much as a current of breath. It would not remain long, this peacefulness. He could feel the coming meltemi. He could smell it in the air. Soon the gale force winds would come. He would be safe here. No, that wasn't true. But his kings should make Kriti if they hurried.

"Why? Why is it thus?" he queried, to no one in particular. "Why does it end?"

"Because it is incomplete and cannot stand." The voice was within and he recognized it, somehow, female, warm and abundant with love. His thoughts swirled around him just as the dust of the volcano.

Incomplete, the soundless voice had said.

Not one single domestic animal remained, not a horse, nor a donkey, not even a chicken. Perhaps there were some wandering or penned at higher elevations but all had been stripped from the coast, loaded aboard ships and taken away. As he perused the city he made an odd observation. It was something he had seen continually but, until this moment, it had not registered. After the blanket destruction caused by the earthquakes, after the valued possessions had been sorted for removal, even while the removal was being executed, even then people had been tidying up. In many of the rooms Chronos peered into, he noticed that pottery, furniture, everything abandoned really, had been righted before they left. As the departing refugees sorted their belongings, recovering their most essential, they were apparently possessed by a bizarre, irrational kind of behavior, inborn perhaps, totally spontaneous. Had they been made aware of their own actions they likely would not have been able to explain themselves. Chronos checked the storehouse along the meandering road. It was one of the storage buildings stocked with pithoi containing the most select grains. Evidence of the quake that had toppled them had all but been erased. Every vessel was standing neatly and they had been rearranged in banks of ten. He had to see inside. Astoundingly they were still brimming with food. Why did they bother? Either take the food or leave it on the floor. It seemed such a waste of time and energy at a time when they could least afford that luxury. But that is incomprehensibly what at least some people did before making their final departure. Chronos wondered if this was a normal rationalization that people encountered when forced to leave a cherished home? He knew for a fact that this situation was hardly unique, invading hoards were always at it in foreign lands, often using the tools of war provided by his own foundries, and that the invaded were often given advance notice of the invasion. Did the women clean beforehand? The thought was preposterous. If they had any sense they would have destroyed their villages ahead of time to keep their food and wealth from the invaders. This was different, though, this invasion by the unseen forces of nature. Maybe there was a different outlook on the whole. But who could explain people?

Across the avenue, he had to poke his nose into just one more home. He slid the wooden door along its track and peered into the shadows. He had been unaware of the old lady who had been resident taken from her home flailing and carrying on, stridently protesting that she be granted just a little more time to whisk a few more pans of ash from her floor, so vital was her instinct to leave a legacy of cleanliness, decent for the next presiding drift of ash. The woman of this house had been a bit different from many others, of that no one could dispute, confidently expecting to return. That was good, he agreed, for hand-in-glove with such an expectation was hope. She had left her kitchen in immaculate order, the bronze utensils of knives and saucers, pots and pans. All of her culinary tools were there, mortars, millstones, stone vases and weights, even dry staples. He took her broom to use as a walking stick and felt a brief pang of guilt, as if she might one day find it missing. This woman was sure of her return. Her husband must have been a fisher, for also there were abandoned fishhooks aplenty and a fearsome awl. A small minority of Atlanteans would probably yet be here, he mused, if they had been allowed. He pictured a young child nestled comfortably on the short rattan bed in the corner, dreaming happy dreams. Mothers busied with their work, still sweeping their homes, while their offspring clung like nervous chicks refusing to open their wings and leave their nests.

He walked to the stadium where the name Chronos had first been proclaimed with unanimous acclamation. Where multitudes had gathered and cheered, he beheld only static desolation.

A small glint captured his eye, something from the podium under layers of dust. He tapped at it with the broom handle, and some of the dust fell free. It was the symbol of the linked rings. He brushed it off with the straw end, and the silver reflected brightly in the sunlight, contrasting pointedly to the somber shade of the ubiquitous volcanic pellicle.

Chronos stood as if mesmerized, fixated, staring tenaciously at the representation of the 'Five.' The promise of the gods. A later age after many civilizations had risen to greatness and fallen. The promise that sometime in the future, who knew how far off, the tektites would all come together again and reign in the onset of the most glorious civilization. The covenant of the gods? No. Just one god. The Goddess Rhea, the Earth Mother, the ancient Selene, the Moon.

Here on the island of Atlantea they had possessed every true spirit, uniting gentleness with wisdom. Here they were isolated from the world, in it but not of it. They used the world as a means to an end, but not as an end. They scorned everything but dignity and honor, and attached little importance to their present state of life, thinking lightly of gold and other property possession which was often more of a burden to them than an aid. But with time this divine apportionment had faded within them. Human nature got the upper hand and they, being unable to bear their fortune, behaved unseemly and, he with an eye to see, grew visibly debased for they were losing the fairest of their precious gifts. For those who had no eye to see true happiness, they still appeared to be glorious and blessed at the very time when they were becoming tainted with unrighteous avarice and power. The god who ruled according to law, and able to see all things, perceived this honorable race in woeful plight, and had to inflict punishment on them only that they might be chastened and improved.

Chronos had been wrong, he realized. It was not Poseidon, nor Zeus, who had been punishing them. It was Selene. They had forgotten her, not completely, but they had neglected her even with her temple, and relegated her to the auspices of a secondary Goddess. The ancient writings to which he had paid little enough heed came flooding back into his mind. Why had he not ever put them all together? Why had he not ever given the Highest of the Priestesses, his own wife, the credence she deserved?

From deep within the earth came a muffled rumble, intermittent at first, but soon continuous. It didn't matter. His Minoses had escaped by now. The linked circles of silver dropped out of their previously loosened inset with the first tremors, and fell mutely to a cushion of ash. The short release of energy was just a prelude to the liberation that was coming. Chronos picked up the silver insignia and carried it with him as he continued his perambulation through the city. He wiped it on his garments and held it in front of him, as one might a book while walking, examining every curve and detail and pondering the meaning of the symbol. It was hard, weighty, and cold in his hands. The silversmith who had made it had worked and polished the back surface as well as the front, burnishing it to a high gloss and varnishing it with a clear baked-on glaze to preserve its sheen. Even after all the years in its weathered niche, it looked like new. He held it up before his eyes and the peering stare of the Full Moon, now risen high in the daytime sky, looked back through the central circle. He welcomed its gaze and knew his wife and her priestesses at Rhea's temple were actively engaged in beseeching the Goddess's aid in their cause. But the Moon was more remote and abstract than his held ornament of silver. How he loved the beautiful creations of man. Could it ever be the same on Kriti as it had been on Atlantea? He had never been there, never voyaged anywhere as other kings had. The thought of leaving was in itself too much to bear. To actually leave might be impossible for him. He had traveled the world vicariously by way of reports and narrations from his captains and kings. Through them he had seen the pyramids of the Egyptians and their grand treasuries; the massive blocks of the Stonehenge in Britain, its tombs filled with the Egyptian beads they so fancied; the waters of the Tigris-Euphrates and the wonders of Babylon. There was nowhere he had not been. And having seen it all with the eyes of hundreds he still, even now, preferred his island of Atlantea, Strongyle, and the watchful Kalliste. From here he was Chronos, all-seeing, forever in time. If this was where he should die, then die he would.

Death was nothing.

He would return. There would be none to stop him.

Chapter 20

Armageddon

The sands of change slowly flowed through the hourglass of time, sinking into the center hole while the rim of grains adhering to the sides of the glass stayed, mounting inexorably, until their own intractable weight dislocated them at an instant. Those volatile sands of time diverted the inestimable potential of the Minoan civilization to the realms of oblivion.

Above the Mediterranean, two hundred forty thousand miles distant, the Full Moon was recipient to the oblations and divinations of nine High Priestesses and their mistress on Mount Kalliste. Pouring devotions to the One, they implored for the salvation of their people. Their atoms melding as one with the atmosphere, had the focus of their worship a distant vantage, the ten could have witnessed, unaided by any lens, the oblong violet sea of the Aegean framed by land. With the smallest optical enhancement they could easily have beheld the nearly perfect circle that was the island of Atlantea, flawless in its outline, its lovely ocher-colored volcano rising central from the tiny island so compellingly that even among the delicate Aegean islands it was outstanding in its jewel-like beauty.

Over the years increasingly large volumes of pumice had surged out from the mountain core, mining a yawning cavity no less than four miles in width and five miles deep. As Chronos pondered his last moments on the surface, the fragile equilibrium act between gravity's unfailing grip and the outward volcanic potency straining to attain its climax, the mountain began its final countdown to failure. This day, it was gravity that won out in the end. In the most violent and destructive of all volcanic behavior, the collapse of a volcanic cone, the canopy crumpled and plunged into the clandestine vault. A phalanx of destiny ejaculated into the wide open skies of the Aegean, and the island of Atlantea ripped through to the fringes of the atmosphere at twice the speed of sound. With the downward pressure suddenly terminated, the fault in the upper mantle had nothing holding it back. A second phreatic charge countered the first in an even mightier explosion of injected energy from the simmering reservoir, the loudest sound ever heard by human ears. A fluid dacite became a gas-charged magma of andesite, contaminated with liquefied gasses under unimaginable pressures. It uncorked from the frank red center, and gas exploded from the lava, shredding it to microscopic particles.

A jet black stain appeared over the Aegean Sea, perfectly round it was, like the island from where it seemed to originate, vast and cloudlike. Everything and nothing, it was as much an absence as a manifestation, a withdrawal as an unveiling. A shock wave faster than sound spread much like a ripple from a stone lobbed into a pond. The pressure and density change of the atmosphere left a visible disturbance on the water surface as it sped outward, creating white clouds that formed and vanished on the edges of the concussion as it passed. The dark miasma was not so quick to follow, taking a full hour to widen to a two hundred mile diameter, another hour to radiate to four. The hemispherical swelling burst up through the atmosphere above the island of Atlantea, which was no more. Ramparts of levitated water hung suspended, parted like the Red Sea by the breath of God, around the rim of a well one mile deep. As the planetary keck discharged from the epicenter of the explosion, seething waterfalls like nothing imagined edged in and filled the gaping maw. A fleet of aircraft carriers might have slid over the vast rim without notice, comparatively smaller than a few suicidal barrels dropping down the white curtain of Niagara.

Central in the rabid tempest was a fiery red agglomeration of air and vaporized rock hotter than molten iron, hotter than tungsten steel drawn white from the alveolus of an arcing forge.

The mountain of Kalliste had changed in a twinkling to plasma under the combined forces of nature pent up against it. The unison of energy of a thousand hydrogen bombs detonating lifted it and disseminated solid rock into particles smaller than the most refined flour.

What had been a round island was now crescent. What had been a proud peak was now a lagoon seven miles across, rimmed by cliffs a thousand feet high and plunging another thousand below the sea. A crater filling like an empty barrel pushed below the waterline.

Chronos had been sheltered, at least in the sense that he wasn't vaporized. The southern spur of the remaining vestige of the island had been protected. Just before the main explosion a burst of ash had blown out of a new vent facing his direction. The pitiful attempt of the mountain, too little and too late to relieve the massive pressures within, had snuffed his life with poisonous gasses and buried him in a blizzard of cooler ash. Peacefully he seemed to lay under his popcorn drift of freshly fallen snow. But it was not snow at all. Not even an insect stirred beneath it. On the disappearing coast, an iron form struck the paving stones very close at hand, its fall cushioned partially by the blankets of ash. The Goddess of the Minoans, the icon of the Earth Mother, had been blasted away from the worshipping Priestesses as they and their Temple of Rhea preceded the fall of the mountain. Chronos, in spite of his revelations, would surely have interpreted its nearby conveyance as a rejoinder that he was superior, after all, in some way to his exalted mate.

Behind the frothy pumice that blanketed and protected the coastal city, a river of water-soaked ash, a cement-like slurry, roared over the town in a burying torrent called a lahar. The flash-flood of sludge sheared away anything not protected by the pumice fall; trees, fences, poles, and higher buildings and towers. Had Chronos only been partially buried he would have been scythed asunder by the shearing forces like a stalk of wheat assailed by the reaper procuring his livelihood.

Thus preserved under the two hundred foot thick bed, still clutching the silver Olympian rings, Chronos missed the effects of the blast following on the heels of the venting.

To begin to grasp the magnitude of rock disintegrating in an instant from the face of the earth one must actually visit the site of Atlantea, or Santorini as it is known now. Only centered in the caldera, floating amicably in a comfortable boat, can one truly understand. Other magnificent tributes to nature are scattered far and wide across the globe, but all took millions, or at least tens of thousands, of years to form. This was an instant in time, a convulsion that shook the Aegean. It happened all at once. Fifty cubic miles of rock sent as an offering of vapor to heaven, like so much incense.

With mind-staggering force the Kalliste volcano detonated high into the atmosphere. A tropospheric meltemi was blowing in at just that time. The prevalent autumn westerlies carried the bulk of falling ash six hundred miles in an east-south-eastern direction. The particulate matter blasted beyond that layer into the stratosphere spread out for a radius of hundreds of miles in every direction, blackening the sun. Driving winds at that height eventually dispersed what didn't fall immediately over the entire planet, causing spectacular sunsets for years and chilling the global climate.

When Krakatoa, in the Sunda Strait between Sumatra and Java, exploded in 1883 the roar was heard more than two thousand miles away in Australia and three thousand miles to the west on Rodrigues Island, and the resultant aerial vibrations circled the globe several times. Dust sifted to earth one thousand miles away. The culminating horror, the tsunami waves, one hundred thirty feet high and with a velocity of over fifty miles an hour, ravaged the nearby coasts of Java and Sumatra. In some places, they raged inland for a thousand yards and still they were thirty feet high. Three hundred towns and villages were erased and thirty-six thousand people swept away. Surges rose on shores as remote as India, Cape Horn, and South Africa.

Yet as colossal as that was, the explosion of Krakatoa released a minuscule portion of the destructive force of Kalliste. In the death throes of Krakatoa only about five cubic miles of the island were lost. Vesuvius and

Mount St. Helens combined totaled only one cubic mile. At Atlantea it was closer to fifty, the loudest and most violent cataclysm witnessed by man.

Had the island not been covered in so thick a layer of pozzuolana, every evidence of occupation would have been totally obliterated. The frescoes, the rattan beds, the flush toilets, showers, and walls honeycombed with plumbing, all were perfectly preserved. When archeological explorers would first tunnel into the side of the Theran ravine, they would have to assume immediately that the gods of good fortune had smiled upon them. They could only gather that they had stumbled upon the royal palace. Where else would be displayed such wealth? Then, as streets and multi-storied, discriminatingly adorned buildings slowly came to see the light of day, they would skeptically determine that this was how the common resident lived. The common citizen with sliding screen doors, personal baths, kitchens, painted ceramics, and hanging gardens? Good God. If they ever found the palace, it would be beyond belief.

On the water, the Minoan fleet at sea, done with the transportation of citizenry, were toiling at their usual merchant business. Around them, the sea turned the color of lead. From wherever their direction, they witnessed the red fireball that quickly turned to darkness, a burgeoning hole of night in the distance bounded by a retreating blue day. Where their sacred mountain had been, they saw only a ball of radiant vermilion. It swelled, tripling in size in a second, tripling again in another. The edges surged through temperate air and turned from red to black, slowed by the resistance of the cool atmosphere and curled down like an ominous mushroom cap, the center still rising and curling, alive with animation. There was no stopping its progress. It shot its bulk upward toward the heavens without impediment.

Along the surface of the earth, a white band spread out from its focal point and seemed to be increasing in height. Rising and diving, coiling as a snake in the throes of a painful death, it undulated as it grew, fading, then coming into being again.

The shock front shredded mariner's eardrums and concussed a great many unconscious. Deafened to one another's shouts of dismay and agony their ears gushed blood. Another blast followed on the heels of the first, felt only as a thump against the chest this time, not heard. They shielded their eyes against the malignant evil rising like an unfamiliar demon from their beloved Kalliste. Brilliant blue lightning arced through the germinating cloud, huge but still only a seed of its potential. Like a tree it strove to meet the sky, an immense trunk projecting into the air with its boughs reaching out to embrace and block the sunlight from all below. The sea turned from wine-dark to malignant-gray as its roots rushed out to clinch them, slashing down masts and capsizing ships. Even as it kindled them spectral fingers flicked the crews from their benches, garroting them and quelching them in the Mediterranean.

Hot air, heavy with ash, cut across land and sea faster than a tidal wave. Around the insignificant Mount St. Helens, three million trees were stripped of their branches and swept down, all fanned away from the center like stalks of wheat in a storm, heat searing the flesh off living things and igniting wood as far as ten miles away. Kalliste was so much greater.

The movements of pulverized rock from volcanoes are essentially bi-directional, dependent on their fragmentary proportions. From the very largest down to granular size, they free-fall, haling slipstreams of air in their wake. Individually each would be meaningless, but as a body the collective mass forges a phenomenal downblast which strikes the earth and diverts laterally, gripping the earth as it spreads unchecked in every direction at far over one-hundred miles an hour. In this death cloud, known as the 'Pelean Phase' after the Mount Pelee eruption in 1902 on Martinique, each particle, large and small alike, sheds its blazing heat. When this surge swept the ground of Saint Pierre it roasted and killed virtually all of the thirty-thousand residents.

But Kalliste was fifteen-million times worse than Pelee.

The insurmountable heat of the volcanic explosion thrusts blistering waves heavenward, ousting the fine, microscopic ash to the stratosphere, driving it aloft in opposition to every influence of gravity. This 'Plinian Phase,' named after Pliny the Younger who witnessed the Vesuvius eruption from a fifteen-mile vantage point, is the rising plume that from all appearances betrays no end.

Kalliste, too, strove higher to embrace the Gods.

* * *

At Amnisos, the port city nearest Knossos on the northern shore of Kriti, families gathered in their groups to comfort each other after the earthquake. Like all other quakes it caught them off guard and they, especially the children, needed the consolation of their family members to regain their composure. Most who were indoors were badly wounded under falling roofs and walls, many succumbing immediately or later to their injuries. Thankfully, the quake struck in the afternoon, and most were outside. If it had hit them at night as they slept in their homes, the loss of life would have been horrible.

"Why must we endure these upheavals?" a woman beseeched her husband as she nursed her child's broken leg. "Are our priests not to supplicate the gods to shelter us from these things?"

"I suppose there is nothing anyone can do about the actions of the gods. They have their reasons for everything even though we cannot always understand."

"You speak as the priests. Always an answer." There was little chance of comforting her as she listened to the bustle and entreaties of the wounded around her. "Why would a god want to inflict such an injury upon our daughter? I can accept this as a random act of nature but, if you believe in the wisdom of the gods, there are so many other ways to visit us with affliction. What need is there to hurt a little girl? Do they delight in a child's suffering?"

He hated reasoning with his wife when she was like this. Always so skeptical of religion. It was becoming an all too common belief on Kriti to have no belief at all. He held his daughter's foot and gently pulled it. He felt, more than heard, a dull clunk inside her thigh as the two displaced bone ends slid into their set position. She was such a brave little girl. He had always been so proud of her. She had hardly cried out during the shaking and had only shed a few tears and held her bent leg in puzzlement after the pillar had fallen and knocked her to the side. Praise the gods that they had spared her life.

"It could have been much worse," he soothed.

"Much worse? It could not have happened at all." The woman was cut off by a noise that split the air, a tumult that hurt and shook their flesh.

Their daughter screamed in surprise. People were shouting all around them, but no one could hear. Another peal following the first was the only noise to register, its volume resounding even louder than the first.

"Now do you not believe in the gods?" shouted the husband, still immobilizing his daughter's leg with a gentle traction. "They are coming for people like you. Fear, woman. Fear for your life and those who have paid no mind to the gods." His diatribe was in vain. She had been deafened.

Citizens fled the town for higher land, fearful that they could not see amongst the buildings and afraid that Poseidon was enacting vengeance from the sea. Fishers and mariners, more at home near the water, stayed with their boats, but they stood along an otherwise deserted beachfront. They forcibly shouted between themselves but could only just make each other aware that they were actually speaking. Only the bulging veins on their necks and foreheads revealed that they were not in a conspiracy to fool their brothers by silently mouthing their words. A few grew suspicious of the orange mushroom-shaped cloud growing like a nuclear explosion in the north. It was unlike anything they had ever seen. It was impossible to tell if it was stationary and growing or if it was advancing toward them like some spawn from the gates of Hell. As sailors, they knew the tales of sea horrors were for the benefit of the land dwellers. But in the backs of their minds, they always carried a burdensome doubt on whether some of the stories might be true.

Some of the fishers began to pull their boats up the beach, terrified that their most precious assets might somehow be in jeopardy. They had no idea what was happening and weren't taking any chances. If that was a storm brewing, they were not going to risk their most valuable possessions.

Even the captains of the trading vessels were getting anxious. It was bad enough losing their hearing, but of far greater concern than their own personal wellbeing was for that of their ships. None of them had ever seen a cloud of such ominous portent. Not the most violent meltemi had ever risen in such swift attack. It was beyond their experience, and if they could have done as the fishers were doing and pulled their huge ships ashore, they would have. One was giving it his best shot by tying onto the boathouse launching skid, but it would probably be impossible for him to labor the ship up the incline without the help of twice the number of people as were presently here.

All of the captains noticed the same thing at the same time. About a foot above the waterline, on the seawalls, was a band of green marine algae. It shouldn't be there. It should be covered with water. There were no tides in the Mediterranean, nothing to account for such a sudden drop in the water level. They watched with fascination as the seawall appeared to raise itself higher above the receding water. Ships that had been moored in adequate depth struck their keels on the bottom and listed to the side.

They noticed some of their cohorts gesticulating wildly out to sea, their mouths working furiously but still muted. It was plain to see. There was a rise in the water at the horizon, an elevation that only a captain would have noticed. The cloud in the sky had grown enormously as their attention had been diverted to the enigma of the descending waterline. A gray swell of water seemed to be lifting to make room for what it was retracting underneath. There was no one to explain the phenomenon, no one who could even make a rational guess as to what they were facing. But they all knew one thing. They were soon to be met with the face of death.

Faster the water receded, making a sucking sound along the way that no one could hear. Puddles under the keels of stranded ships resting on their sides reflected diamonds of sunlight. Further the water level slipped down the incline, leaving fish thrashing in isolated depressions. Had the witnesses not been in a state of psychological shock from the events thus far they would have seized the opportunity to scavenge the helpless bounty. The entire harbor drained into the distance, exposing wet mud and sand that had, only minutes before, lain under four fathoms of water. It returned all too quickly, but before it came a different wave, a pyroclastic flow, a glowing tide of searing gas and talcum ash so hot it consumed everything in its path.

Watching amid the hillside clusters of higher ground the greater portion of the people stood as families, holding each other close, waiting for the onslaught of the boiling demon, waiting to die, if it was the judgment of the gods, as one. It held them spellbound, transfixed. What was it that was so profanely captivating, burgeoning clasps of evil and blackness, the devouring jaws of Hell gaping wide after them? For a moment the chimera seemed as if it had stopped at sea and relinquished its advance, but then a limb of the cloud wildly bifurcated and, with fantastic speed, rushed the city. They needed no auditory capabilities to discern the rumble as it welled up through their legs and body trunks, advancing through the rocks at their feet. A rip of fire cleaved through the barrier of all-surging black smoke and washed onto the island supposedly protected by the limitless waters. Many raised up their hands beseeching the gods for salvation, either temporal or spiritual. But equally as many believed there were no gods and that this eventide was proof, ushering in the world's last unredeemable, eternal night.

Slamming them at two hundred miles an hour, too hot to breathe, too thick and too corrupted, blackness darker than coal enveloped them, blew them down, and choked them out with microscopic dust and sulfuric acid gas. Through the painful acceptance of unknowing inevitability, people accepted their fate. Only a few could not pass quietly. The girl's mother cursed to the flailing winds as they sucked and poisoned the life out of her. The little girl closed her eyes to the biting winds, not knowing that she was so well protected between the buildings and against the wall where she lay. It was to her as if a veil of peace was drawn over her eyes as she passed placidly from the confines of her mortal frame. Her father never let go of her leg. Blinded by the stinging ash and wracked with uncontrollable coughing he clung to his daughter, trying to speak, to let her know he was there and would never leave her side.

They had been in a void in the death cloud. A random and rare eddy filled with cool air. Wherever the voids appeared they acted in every way like a protective bubble. It is anyone's guess as to how they form or what features of the landscape keep them stationary for long enough for the wave of fire to pass. Buildings and trees fell like matchsticks, not all in the same direction away from the center of the blast as one would expect, but in the direction of individual eddies within water-dense waves of air. The collective whole painted a graphic image of the myriad channels and unexpected course changes within the cloud. In some places the blowdowns diverged in two directions and parted trees like hair. The capricious cloud weaved and bumped along the varying terrain, illogically and inconsistently. Where the girl and her father peacefully died in an area that got no hotter than a scorched cloth, other places and people seared. Some almost vaporized as they fell, consumed by temperatures of twelve hundred degrees. Thousands of seals and clay tablets were baked and preserved for future ages by the raging fires, leaving an indecipherable legacy of pictographs and scripts hardened against time's tooth by the conflagration's heat.

A captain was picked up and hurtled headlong up the street and trounced by the clasp of an invisible fist onto the pavement, his short sword and a purse with three pieces of gold still belted to his waist. Roof tiles, sheets of stone, and a middle-aged woman sailed like disks and impacted like missiles beside his broken body. The woman's bones shattered in two hundred places as she smashed against the wall adjacent to him.

The unpredictable cloud blasted indoors, potent and sucking as the torrent of upsurging gasses overturned baths and basins, crashing them against walls, paradoxically leaving hanging gardens on the next block untouched. Havens of refuge existed for a short time as the orb of desolation passed innocuously around and overhead. The tumbling cloud pincered the ground like talons one moment, the next rising a hundred feet like a cobra before buffeting the earth once again, sometimes doubling back on itself, traveling the way it had come, assailing the terrified hopefuls who had expressed a futile gratitude for deliverance. Thick shafts of multi-colored lightning, blue, green, and brilliant red, pierced the darkness. Silicates within the ash cloud caused the nightmarish light show, refracting a rainbow of diverse hues from the full color spectrum.

There were small pockets of survivors still with a few moments of life lingering. Those who could speak cried out for water as they blindly felt their way around, or curled under blankets for protection. Those who groped in the blinding ash and found laden jugs found also that they could not drink at all, so badly had they burned their mouths and throats, so terribly that their throats were almost entirely closed by swelling. The devilish cloud did not burn their garments but where their skin was unclothed it scorched inexorably.

A mother sobbing miserably as she blindly held her baby's limp corpse wailed that she would never find a way to bury him decently in a larnax, the clay sarcophagi of paneled sides and gabled lids favored by the wealthy. Elaborately plastered and painted with images and scenes of goddesses and griffins and goats drawing the dead's soul to the peace of the Elysium, the larnax ensured that the occupant would live ever after in the company of gods. Her baby, the life that she was charged to raise and have responsibility for, was condemned because of her to reside for the remainder of eternity in a lesser kingdom.

A notable singer, an aged and very fat woman of the distinguished temple choir, notwithstanding all her scalds and burns, had found her throat clear enough to sing hymns from the altar of sacrifice. Her voice would crack and fade, until she refreshed it with drink and could continue again. An ancient hymn it was, a hymn of loneliness and love, of origin no one could suspect or recall.

In a prison cell, a man jailed for rowdy drunkenness stirred uneasily. He had felt the quakes and heard the murmurs of alarm. When another jolt came he woke to the sound of screaming, and realized with shock that it was him. Hungover, he could not understand what had happened. Hot winds blew things past his window. Through the smoke, here and there, was only ruin and destruction. In minutes all had been demolished. This evil vision compounded a terrible pounding in his head. He tried to comprehend why he himself was not dead. He was in the midst of an inferno, with nothing and no one else alive. He curled his nose to the stench of smoking cinders and burnt flesh, and collapsed and vomited as the realization dawned that the origin of the emanation was his own charred and blistered skin. Fearful of the dust asphyxiating him he urinated on his shirt and covered his face, breathing through it like a mask. Another back-eddy detonated through the upper story of the prison, reducing it to a rubble heap. A guard was beset in a particularly cauterizing clout of dust. Transformed into a carbonized wraith where he stood the gust knocked him down and shattered him like charcoal. The prisoner did not see that happen as the building continued collapsing all around. The debris pile neatly encircling him delivered him from a death as certain as the guard's. He tried to free himself from the wreckage, screaming agony from his bruised and battered flesh, but was knocked back by another salvo of wind. As suddenly as the raging gale started, it stopped, an unholy silence subduing the vicinity. As the poisonous gasses settled around him, he could only hear a dull hue of flames crackling through aged beams and a woman's voice carrying over the wreckage. He thought he recognized an ancient adoration customarily sung in the temple, but it ceased abruptly.

At a popular tavern on the edge of town, the keeper climbed a ladder out of his cool cellar and emerged into the frontiers of a netherworld. The whole upper story of his inn had been torn away and set flaming outside the front door. Every table and chair had been upset or smashed, yet his jacket remained quite undisturbed on the hook where he had left it. As he stumped this out in bafflement, the fabric caught, combusting of its own volition. A woman who had been his patron, and for whom he had gone to the cellar for a special order, was all ablaze in the corner. The little pet monkey still leashed to her wrist was carbon. When he realized what it was burning he rushed over to help, but she leapt up at his approach and fled the building, shedding whorls of flame and billows of smoke. Another patron was on the floor, shucked of clothing with his hair scorched off. He was dead but still moving, wearing what the keeper initially perceived to be a tight red shirt. Still shocked by the performance of the burning woman, he cautiously approached the twitching corpse, the abdomen distending corpulently as if it was being augmented with great measures of poison gas. When inexorably the gorbelly ruptured, tallowy organs pinguid and buttery with fat squeezed out like a gelatinous paste and metamorphosed into a mire of obsequious slime.

Gagging, he retreated from his past beloved tavern. He experienced only the revulsion of the moment, all memory of past delights permanently struck from his mind. Too shaken to more than stagger, he stepped out the door and put his foot into something soft. He slipped, connecting with a kneeling man whose body had already breached, splashing into the puddle of lardaceous viscera settled on the paving stones. Horrified to yet a higher order of magnitude, he stared wide-eyed into the empty eye sockets of an oily debrided head. Formless lips ovalled a grizzled portal and the blackened knurl that was his tongue.

Everywhere he bore witness to the destruction of the city he held so dear. His pearl looked as if it could have been naught but this same malignant landscape for uncounted lifetimes. Of the eight thousand citizens, he could see no vestige of a living being. Straggling through the disrupted and defiled streets, he looked harder at a wide group of smutty heaps not far off. They must have been caught, those poor souls, by the caustic vitiate as they bolted from the shrine where they had been worshipping. Someone had tried to take a terracotta idol in the confusion, before falling dead to the earth. The snake-entwined goddess, with hands raised in supplication to a higher deity, had done her no good. Whether she had been rescuing it, or stealing it, no one would ever know.

Unbelievably, one of the disfigured wraiths began to stir, then rose upon its tattered stalks and advanced toward him. A man, a woman, there was no way to know. He - or she - was carrying a shirt in his hands and the tavern keeper could not understand why anyone would cling to such a remnant. Then he perceived the frightful reality. The ghoulish pedestrian was cradling his own skin.

Beyond the capacity to feel his own wounds or acknowledge exhaustion, the keeper turned and ran, yelling and screaming in terror as he realized that his skin, too, was blistering and peeling. The wheals burst with his sudden movement and the fluids running down washed muddy streaks on his dusty skin. He did not hurt. There was no time for pain. Past the charcoal dead, and still dying dead, he whipped, to the safety of the waters of the sea. Blisters on his back and chest gaped open, inviting the abrasive, stinging dust swirling around him. He did not let it bother him. His blisters would heal. He was thankful that he was still alive. Coughing and choking, blind from dust and darkness, he fled down the embankment. The fervid tongue of death, for now, had granted a moment of mercy.

At shore every ship had ignited, blazing away on land where water should have been. Had the fires of Hell on earth boiled away even the oceans themselves? The masts had been cropped of their rigging and sheared clean off their decks without so much as a tattered edge, cleaved as neatly as cane struck by a honed blade. Lightning shredded the darkness of the ionized dust cloud. Still hot enough to roast flesh the wind dried and assisted igniting spilled oils and paper, wood tables and fallen beams. Buildings flared as winds nurtured the flames, even in the poisoned, oxygen-depleted environment. Beyond the town, sparks rose and then fell on dried timber on the whole eastern half of the island and set massive forest fires raging uncontrollably. Crops caught with manic excitement and, blown by the dry and heated winds, incinerated themselves across the wide plains of Messara.

Fifteen minutes later at Amnisos, when all were dead save the tavern keeper, an unthinkable rampart of water rode up the incline of the drained harbor. At sea it had been a mere hump of water, a long and gentle rise that would have endangered no ship. A vessel far from shore would not have even noticed its passing underneath. Only in the shallows did the submerged land force the pressurized swell of water up from the deep to massive heights. Blotting out the invisible horizon in this impenetrable darkness it did not crest until the resistance of the seafloor dragged the base of the wave back and made the monumental goliath pitch ahead, raging and furious like a rabid wolverine. As lone witness he opened his swollen eyes, mere weeping slits, but capable enough to envisage his destiny. A humid spray wet his face as he felt the sound of his own rasping wheezes overborne by the sub-audible reverberations of the final assault. Behind the sheer curtain a massive white bull reared on its haunches, growing taller by the second. There would be no acrobatting over the horns of this one.

"Great gods of Zeus and Poseidon," he mouthed. "Why do you persecute us?" He collapsed in the sand, writhing in pain as the microscopic edges of salt, ash, and sand gouged his exposed raw nerve endings. For all he knew, he was the last, the very last, human alive. Then a calm washed over him as a comfortable autumn breeze, and his agony dissipated. "Selene," he whispered, giving himself entirely to his sudden revelation. "Mother Selene." He knew. And he grieved, not for himself, but for those who had made their final exit without knowing.

Two-hundred-and-fifty feet high, it towered over the trifling habitation of Amnisos and swept it away like a spider down a drain. The people, their ships and personal effects, all were torn or smashed to pieces in the torrent. A short walk from the beach a wealthy man's summer villa was stripped down to the foundation, the rest of the large building swept off in an instant. The foundation blocks, three feet across, were kicked about like some giant's toy. A quarter of a mile up the road and fifty feet above sea level the buildings were similarly leveled. As the leviathan mass of water receded it sucked and dragged at the rectilinear blocks of an unrecognizable structure. One block was snapped in half and deposited more than three hundred feet away from its counterpart. Theories would abound for centuries over who the invaders were who destroyed the city, but invaders don't do things like that. They rape women and children, murder the men, and they loot and burn. They smash treasures that can't be taken, but they have better things to do than breaking ordinary walls apart and hauling half-ton splits of stone hundreds of feet just for the plain enjoyment of it.

A thousand years later on the Turkish island of Samos, far enough north to escape the worst of the death cloud, almost twice the distance of Kriti to the south, and partially sheltered by other islands, Diodorus, the Greek historian, wrote that those indigenous to the island faithfully observed ancient practice by sacrificing offerings on altars placed at elevations to chronicle the immersion line of a catastrophic deluge from the sea. Their legend gave account, he said, of fire scorching the heavens, and lightnings and thunders blinding and deafening the inhabitants, and seemingly unending darkness. They said Poseidon rose against his own offspring who dwelled upon their island home in the distant west. He rolled the island like a scroll shutting his children tight within a mountain, and dragged it into the depths of the sea, sending forth an inundation that threatened all life across the entire world. Only those moved by divine inspiration to abide at higher altitudes escaped annihilation, and as the recipients of that freely imparted wisdom they ever after offered thanksgiving.

On the island of Kea, one hundred miles northwest of Atlantea, the south facing Minoan city Hetos was stamped flat. The vital currents uprooted buildings. Life-sized terracotta statues of thin-waisted ladies were pounded and scattered and heaped in corners by receding water. At the later request of the people of Kea, the Greek poet Pindar wrote the Paean, which begins, "I tremble at the heavy sounding war between Zeus and Poseidon. Once, with thunderbolt and trident they sent a land and a fighting force down to Tartarus, the sunless abyss below Hades."

The Grim Reaper swept into southern Turkey on the crest of a cascading tidal wave. Two Kalliste-facing peninsulas extending into the Aegean, just north of the island of Rhodes, confining the tsunami as it thrust forward, compressing and funneling it as if squeezed between the jaws of a flagitious vise. Forcing the pile higher and higher, the mass ascended until it spired to the majestic height of eight hundred feet. Then it struck the estuary at the distal end of the firth. A rush of bulldozed wind and a moment of shadow curtaining the low afternoon sun was all the warning the people of Cyrbe had. They had heard the splitting rents, an hour before, of the dangerous gods residing in the Aegean, thanking all holy things that they had been safely inland. They feared the sea and all its horrible entities, dragons, Triamates, Cyclopses. Awful gods. But the hour passed uneventfully except for a storm cloud brewing rather quickly along the western horizon. It probably would not affect them. They had no way of knowing or preparing for the onslaught. There was no time for cognitive thought as the churning upraised monolith swept over them as inconceivably there as if they had been in the heart of a desert. Thirty miles inland it scoured the forest to bedrock and gouged a scabrous vista as devoid of life as the surface of the Moon, leaving in the backwash of its reclining wake an upheaval of mountainous boulders intermingled amongst the sediment.

Uncountable millions of tons of pumice had been spawned over the years from Kalliste. Mats of the floating porous froth had formed and coalesced into huge rafts that followed the currents. One of these largest had finally prodded against the western shore of Cyprus, aided by the sudden eastward gale, the meltemi, which had curled down from the northwest just prior to the mountain exploding. As the resulting tsunami bore down upon it, the raft was lifted and catapulted onto the island to elevations of ninety feet above sea level, in measures sufficient to make mining the material profitable. In the fields below the pumice, a broken town had been randomly elbowed about, like at the city of Amnisos on Kriti. Large stones had been tumbled against one another and cracked in half, and their mating ends moved fifty paces or more, just like at ruins wherever the tsunami struck.

* * *

What was left of Atlantea was buried under two hundred feet of ash and pumice. Debris blown at first by the explosion and then by the meltemi rained down on Turkey and Minoan settlements across the eastern half of Kriti.

Directly in line with the central half of the ash-fall lay the Palace city of Zakro, a natural port on the eastern tip of the island. Wrecked and burned by the incinerating atmosphere the city was spared the cleansing effects of the tsunami. Slabs of stone were battered flat and laid prone across the ground, all oriented along the same point of the compass, blown down by the great wind of Kalliste. Charred bodies of inhabitants black and oozing left such a fearsome impression on those who found them that the full quarter of the island, isolated from the rest by a partition of high mountains, was declared anathema, off-limits to any and all. Having fallen and eventually grown over like a lost city of the Andes their gold and silver and peerless bronze tools, their elephant tusks from Syria, their carved pink granite from Upper Egypt, their copper ingots from Cyprus, all stood waiting for modern archeologists to come poking forth with their shovels and theories. "Looters and pirates," they would say did the damage. But how could that be when everything of value is untouched while destruction was wreaked upon wood and stone? Would even the most base culture waste their time and energy so inanely? All the implements of Minoan life were left behind; bronze tweezers and razors, gold jewelry, and even their most sumptuous perfumes. Premium bronze, cast in the standard yard-long ingots with inward-curving sides that made them easier to carry on the shoulder, sat free for the taking yet was shunned as if it were haunted and damned.

Concurrent to the destruction meted elsewhere, Phaestos, greatest city of Kriti excepting only Knossos, was altogether incinerated on the south coast, left but a charred husk of its former glory. Here was the place where the Minos of that territory had left the prayer disk and taken his wife and son, Katreus, to assuage the gods against censuring them by this very course. Phaestos. Twenty miles more distant than Knossos and shielded by the eight thousand foot mountain of Juktas, it suffered worse than the capital city which had been comparatively spared the complete desolation, the same almighty judgment, visited upon so many other cities. Again the archaeologist would argue, "Volcanic death clouds do not act with such inconsistency; crazy humans do." They ignore what they already know, excavations at Herculaneum where hot volcanic dust from Mount Vesuvius carbonized wood in one room while in the next room, buried under the same ash, not even wax or amber melted.

Downwind of the explosion ships at sea capsized under the weight of falling ash. Those who could still breath could not labor under such harsh conditions with speed enough to save their vessels. Ships at harbor were smashed by tsunamis. So, too, their fleet-based support services of shipwrights and maintenance crews who drowned along with their specialized capabilities. Washed away with them went their docks, maintenance facilities, inventories of marine equipment, seasoned wood for oars and masts, special weaves for sails, stores of rope, and the land-based naval administration.

Under three and four inches of ash, agriculture ceased utterly and the population shifted to the relatively ash-free western island. But even in areas of lighter ashfall crops were ruined. Where it fell only one-sixteenth of an inch deep it blighted and yellowed leaves, adding to the general famine and economic collapse. As far away as Egypt and Cyprus the devastation of the ashfall was felt. Tuna populations fell to impossible levels in the sea, as did other fish poisoned by ashen waters of both lake and stream. Flying birds choked to death and dropped from the sky. Multitudes of rats, protected by day in their burrows, survived only to become desperately hungry. Deprived of vegetation they scavenged meat off the bones of the dead and, in countries affected only by famine, became fearsome pack animals, stalking creatures larger than themselves. Half an inch was enough to cause a slow and miserable death in humans. Observed under a microscope, the ash is exposed as more than a choking wood ash from a fire. It consists of infinitesimal shards of glass, gouging the linings of lungs and working their way deeper with every excruciating breath. The black mass of cutting edges, like miniature obsidian knives, destroyed eyesight with every blink and left the unmasked coughing blood. No natural or medical defense of the respiratory system could dislodge the razored slivers and slowly they would die, an intractable form of silicosis wreaking destruction upon their vital tissues.

At sea washed the bodies of multitudes, killed by fire, by water, by dust. And would they have been given the choice, the same fast death or the lingering diseases with the same eventuality, which would they have chosen?

* * *

Not every ship was destroyed, likewise not every boat. But one place they stayed far away from in their ships was Atlantea, Kalliste, Strongyle, "sunk in a day and a night," a mountain of the sea vanquished and destroyed as quickly and easily as one would stamp down a child's beach castle leaving only an imprint in the sand. "Thera" they would call it. The "Island of Fear."

A generator of weather, on a global scale as is the case with all large stratovolcanoes, Thera's ejecta of dust, ash, and sulfur dioxide aerosols drew a veil across the Earth. Pollutants bending and diffracting light rays as the sun hovered near the horizon created years of brilliant crimson sunrises and spectacular sunsets. Alarmed populations, horrified that the Earth had taken fire, entreated their gods in supplication to put out the raging skyfires they thought would surely consume them. Static charges created by colliding dust particles caused jabs of lightning to arc across the sky in pyrotechnic displays of unbridled power. Pumped beyond the reach of cleansing rains the sulfur dioxide converted to sulfuric acid, dispersed with the dusty haze by stratospheric jet streams. The finest powder, on the order of tens of millions of tons, reflected sunlight back into space and the sulfuric acid absorbed more before the warming rays could reach Earth's surface.

After the Tambora eruption of 1815 the massive cloud slowly circled the Earth and, by the following summer, a volcanic veil of dust shielded most of the Northern Hemisphere. As the summer of 1816 advanced a bitter delineation from the norm began to emerge. Unseasonable cold fronts rippled across North America and Europe devastating all but the hardiest of crops. Enshrined in American folklore, it became the summer remembered as "Eighteen Hundred and Froze to Death." Many a day in New England saw the thermometers barely reaching fifty degrees Fahrenheit and, when darkness fell, the temperatures frequently dipped below freezing. On June sixth a blizzard dumped six inches of snow and, further south on the Fourth of July, the highs in Georgia climbed only to forty-six degrees. But it was not only North America that suffered. Frost, snow, sleet, and ice combined against crops and farmers throughout the world. Famine stalked the people of Europe, and they ate everything from moss to family pets. People took desperate risks and churches had to issue warning bulletins to educate parishioners about poisonous plants. Food riots broke out in France. That terrible year propelled the mass migration of bankrupt Yankee farmers from their homes in New England to the greener pastures of Indiana, Illinois, and Ohio.

Tambora's effects were widespread and devastating, but the eruption of Thera had an even greater impact on history. Dust and ash darkened the heavens over Egypt for days on end raining toxic substances that poisoned cattle and man, and the son of Tuthmosis III. Rivers were stained blood-red with algae blooms, and toads and insects were provoked to frenzied activity. A great exodus led by a man named Moses set out in search of a promised land away from the enslavement which had bound their people for hundreds of years. Curiously, what inspired faith in one religion precipitated adversity in others. The religions of the Minoans and of the Egyptians were in crisis, a meltdown in the case of the Minoans.

With every triangular-sailed ship destroyed, and the only knowledgeable wrights on the islands of Kriti and Atlantea annihilated, the old square riggers were the only alternative to builders who simply did not have equivalent skills. Trade that had flourished throughout the Mediterranean faltered and failed. Economies collapsed. The rich islands of the Aegean, the wealthier coastal cities of mainland Greece, and even the faraway islands of Cyprus and Sicily died. Egypt and Babylon, able to sustain themselves through a few years of crop-failing weather, managed to survive although they, too, suffered terrible setbacks.

During the summer of 1627 B.C.E. a thin layer of dirty, acidic snow was deposited on the Arctic icecap. California bristlecone pines displayed very rare dark cells, indicative of frost scarring from the resultant false summer on their annual growth rings. And King Chieh of the Chinese Hsai dynasty complained about the heavens giving severe orders, the distressed sun, the frosts of summer, and the five cereal crops withering and dying. Disaster followed disaster as floods and freezing weather were followed with seven years of drought. Famine drove many in the northern provinces to desperate acts of cannibalism.

No one else documented the great upheavals of the time as they were actually happening except the Egyptians. "It is inconceivable what happened to the land," begins the Ipuwer papyrus. "The land to its whole extent was confusion and terrible noise. For nine days there was no exit from the palace and no one could see the face of his fellow. Towns were destroyed by mighty tides. Upper Egypt suffered devastation. Blood flowed everywhere and there was pestilence throughout the country. No one sails to Byblos anymore. From where shall we get cedar for our mummies? Priests were buried with objects of foreign trade, and nobles were embalmed with oils from as far away as Keftiu. But the men of Keftiu come no longer. Gold is lacking. How important it now seems when those oasis people come carrying their festival produce. The sun is covered and does not shine to the sight of men. Life is no longer possible with the sun concealed behind the clouds. Ra has turned his face from mankind. If only it would shine even for one hour. No one knows when it is midday. One's shadow is not discernible. The sun in the heavens resembles the Moon." Glass was broken and plaster walls cracked by the concussion waves even this far away.

With the conditions on Kriti so onerous many left the island for better grounds. Many sailed to the oasis west of Egypt from where they kept trade. Others became nobles at Egypt itself, and Babylon, maintaining the longstanding tradition of association at the highest levels of society.

Another remnant, abandoning their ships and islander status for the mainland, renamed themselves the Messapians and built the city of Hyria on Iapygia, the southeast heel of Italy.

Others of the Minoan civilization went southwest to a fertile oasis in North Africa, a people known to the Greeks as the Atlantes, residing under the protection of what they named the Atlas Mountains in remembrance of their place of birth.

Others went to the western side of the Peloponnesus where they converged on a mountain that reminded them of two in their history, Kalliste and Juktas. Olympus they called it, in consideration of their annual games. A small and private sect they kept to themselves and, untraditionally, elected to keep no records. Passing on tradition from generation to generation, they maintained many of their skills. Very powerful they had little to fear from neighboring Acheans. Not until the Greeks wiled their way into their culture did the Olympian Games become part of written history, becoming a national and international celebration once every four years, of such importance that even wars would be ceased during competitions. Mount Olympus became the new seat of the Gods.

Sarpedon of Kydonia, the only Minos to survive the upheavals, forsook the island in disgust when civilization all around him degenerated to the degree that he felt nothing but loathing for his own people. With his family and supporters, he fled the holocaust to the coast of Asia Minor where he founded Miletos.

Welcomed to the Levant, Canaan, the east coast of the Mediterranean, by friendly business associates others set their holdings. The people of Caphtor they had traditionally been known as in this place. They took upon themselves the name Philistine and with ease completely subdued politically the land that they called Philistia, or Palestine, where the coastal city of Gaza had long born the welcoming name of Minoa. Phoenicians they would become, the curious explorers of the oceans. A salvo of refugees simultaneously rallied to the Levant; the exodus of Israelites from Egypt; the fugitive Syrians seeking asylum from the wars of Kir; and the Philistines from Caphtor.

With this overwhelming influx of nationalities and diverse cultures there could not but be conflict. They butted margins and began conflicts that they have obdurately sustained to our own day, never coming to terms with their differences.

Amos the prophet linked the migrations and confusions to the day when lands melted and the sea rose up to terrorize the Earth. "And the Lord God of hosts is he that toucheth the land, and it shall melt, and all that dwell therein shall mourn: and it shall rise up wholly like a flood, and shall be drowned. It is he that calleth for the waters of the sea, and poureth them out upon the face of the earth. Have I not brought up Israel out of Egypt? And the Philistines from Caphtor, and the Syrians from Kir? Behold, the eyes of the Lord God are upon the sinful kingdom and I will destroy it from off the face of the earth."

Jeremiah the prophet beckoned to his kinsmen, "Behold, waters rise up out of the north, and shall be an overflowing flood, and shall overflow the land and all that is therein: then the men shall cry and all the inhabitants of the land shall howl. The Lord will spoil the Philistines, the remnants of the country of Caphtor."

North of Canaan, where the Philistines were establishing themselves, other mass migrations were commencing. Small armed bands inspired by a blood-red moon joined with larger groups and left a legacy of burned villages and broken pottery behind them. Taking what they could carry as they went they fractured and felled the Hittite Empire.

And Moses spoke also; "the Caphtorims, which came forth out of Caphtor, destroyed them, and dwelt in their stead." At this time Asia Minor was rife with change. Secondary to the tidal waves of Thera were the waves of invaders occupying the area, pouring in like floodwaters upon the plain, including even the tide writ large by the Old Testament, that of the Hebrews fleeing the intolerable oppressions of a tyrant Pharaoh.

Epilogue

Over a period of fourteen hundred years the Minoan civilization had spread select portions of their knowledge and wisdom around the world. There was no great civilization that had not benefited or been influenced by their contributions. With the Minoans reduced in number, and with their leaders and most of the educated and skilled located and cut down on the northern coastline of Kriti, there were no realistic hopes of rebuilding. Atlantea, their seat of knowledge and learning, had been obliterated. Even rich Knossos, the capital of the 'island of ninety cities', had to be rebuilt, but with the weakened Minoan's limited resources, and the will no longer at hand, it passed to other ownership. For the same reasons, they were open to assailment from neighbors, adventurers, and rebel bands, who slowly over the years crept into their established territories, taking one island at a time, until Kriti itself was overcome.

The Acheans and Atticans, who were now known as the Mycenaeans, imposed their language and their artistry upon them. The language was the early form of Greek, still recognizable as such today, the oldest surviving European tongue, written at that time in the script known as Linear B. The horizontal pictorial text represented inventories of weapons, chariots and their parts, ingots, the scales in which Minoan talents were weighed, precious vessels and others containing various liquid products, granaries and storehouses on piles, different kinds of cereals, the saffron used for dyes, trees, perfumes, domestic animals, including horses and swine, and the crook sign which indicated sheep. Nothing poetic, no dreams, only raw data. The revered bulls as so beautifully depicted in frescoes were now being tortured to frantic madness by spears and arrows, instead of being merely tormented by acrobats. Brutality extended to every ferocious animal that could be captured alive and brought to the arena, up to and including man.

The Greeks embraced violence in their art and entertainment. The oral history of the Mycenaeans, the early Greeks, was that of a people locked forever in chaos, turmoil, devastation, and campaigns of conquest. Had the eruption of Atlantea never occurred the Minoans might have kept their more pacifist ways and, in time, could have spread their philosophies abroad. The inferiors who they made trade with, gained wealth from, may have eventually come to the understanding, only recently grasped by modern societies, that there is greater benefit in preserving what one has and building on it rather than attempting to plunder and destroy the works of rival nations. But with Atlantea out of the way, and with ownership of one of the tektites, the Mycenaeans gathered strength and communal intelligence and extended their influence into the Aegean world. It was the way the Goddess had meant it to be. Atlantea and the Minoans had failed. They had had their chance, and now it was time for another to try. While it was expedient to do so the Mycenaeans lived harmoniously with the Atlanteans and Minoans, drawing heavily on what skills they could glean to forge their own civilization. Finally, when the Minoan civilization came crumbling down, their defenses diminished, their navy weak, the opportunity for complete Aegean control was open. The Mycenaeans moved into Knossos. They destroyed all of the Minoan sites in eastern, central, and southern Kriti, with the exception of Knossos, that were not already obliterated in the maelstrom of Thera. The casualties of the Thera cataclysm were the palaces of Malatos, Zakro, and Phaestos, the towns of Gournia and Palaikastro, the off-shore settlements on the islands of Pseira and Mochlos, and the great houses at Nirou Khani, Sklavokampo, and Tylissos. Hierapytna was the sole port facing Africa spared destruction for some reason. The sites were left abandoned, or only reoccupied partially, and the era of great material prosperity and notable arts and crafts came to a complete end.

Only at Knossos did the dramatic break seem not to occur. There was no complete severance of palace traditions, but what survived was fabricated, counterfeit, a poor similitude fostered by an invading Mycenaean faction who sought to copy, in a hopelessly inadequate way, the greatness of the civilization they had dispassionately assisted nature in destroying. The spirituality was lost.

In the end, they threw down the walls of Knossos as well. Alpha and omega; the beginning and the end. The walls came down between the Throne Room and the Central Court atop the seven young children, eight yards beneath, unnoticed by the myriads who passed overtop of them throughout the centuries. They were protected now more than ever before. The nearby throne of polished alabaster, useless as a seat of authority, it nevertheless survived man's and nature's threatening violence, likewise never succumbing.

Unspeakable crimes began occurring, that which would never have been tolerated, almost immediately after the conflagration. In poverty one old woman took to feeding others by way of scraping the tender flesh off dead children, disposing of the bones beneath the floor of her house. Considered a savior by the many she nourished, she was never questioned too extensively about where she obtained her meat. The first had been the woman's only sheep, its bones too interred beneath her floor; but the meat kept coming. They innately knew something was amiss but never suspected themselves of engaging in the obscenity of cannibalism. And she never offered an explanation. She did not need to challenge the law. The dead were so numerous as to render an accounting impossible.

Western Kriti recovered quickly in terms of agriculture. The lighter ashfall, which decimated crops the first years, dissolved with rain into the soil and gradually, over the next decade, increased its fertility manyfold. Plants of every kind grew at a tremendous rate and gave unheard of yields. But by then it was too little, too late.

Remnants of the wiser Minoan sects existed, spread all around the Mediterranean, but were unable to hold on to their once inspired, and inspiring, civilization. Their works had reached pinnacles of technical skill and artistry that much of it still ranks among the finest ever produced, and there was nowhere to go but down. They tried to maintain past standards for a while but, without the Iron Goddess at the center of their world, it was impossible. If they had retained but one of the tektites they could have held on, but their world was passing on to other hands. Ionian inhabitants, particularly those of Miletos, the descendants of the Minos, Sarpedon, who left Kriti in disgust, tried most heartily to maintain the ancient wisdoms. However, with so few in number, it was impossible to have full knowledge of every field. In secrecy, they kept their knowledge and did their best to preserve it amongst themselves. There were times when they generously deigned to share it, a hope vain, for without status as a respected world power they were as dust in the wind. Before, they believed, all living things, and all seemingly inanimate things as well, were imbued with the living essence of the cosmos, and therefore something of the divine substance. But without the Goddess, and in the absence of any of the five markers of knowledge, their religion faltered and they became atheist, without spirit.

Insulting the gods came the Ionian scientist Democritus, who, with cautious support from the remnants of his Minoan kindred, openly denied the existence of the eternal spirit of man. Plato himself was one of the suppressors of their revolution in human thought. "Nothing exists," said Democritus, "except atoms and empty space," and then expounded, to the relatively untutored, knowledge inherited from a bygone era of the composition of the Milky Way, a host of uncountable stars, most too small to be seen without the aid of the long-lost eye enhancers. Scientific logic with no spiritual backing. Just one side of a coin.

Plato retaliated against Democritus and advocated the burning of his books as kindling. The Ionians, gaining confidence in their scientific rediscoveries, tried again by sending Aristarchus, a man of milder and less offensive temperament, to enlighten them on the obvious conclusions to be reached from observing the Earth's shadow on the Moon during a lunar eclipse. That proved the postulation that the Sun had to be much larger than the Earth and very far away even though it did not appear at first glance to be so. Further, the observation proved that the Earth was spherical and orbited the Sun and, inferring from Democritus' suggestion, the stars were none other than suns farther away and, if logic were to continue, one must conclude that there were vast numbers of worlds like the earth and the other planets around those suns. Aristarchus, like his predecessor, had failed to defend his thesis and his writings also were consumed by fire. The new present was not ready for the past commonplace. If only they had been able to preserve their religion. One without the other was as man without the woman and can spawn no child.

The skill of the Minoan shipwright was completely lost. Not even the Phoenicians could preserve it. In Greece they built ships backwards, the shell of the hull first, and then fitted the ribbing inside that. The concept of a triangular sail never occurred to anyone, and sailing into the wind was inconceivable.

The symbol of the physician survived, the double-snakes coiled gracefully about a single longstaff, in memory of a nightmarish vision plaguing an opium-addicted potentate.

With the passage of time, while others let the Minoans, known by their various names, fade from memory, legends grew among the people of Mycenae around the vanished isle of Atlantea. 'Atlantis,' the name would be corrupted to. Fair and wondrous, they would say, where fruit was in infinite abundance and where the earth was rich with precious metals, especially of fabulous brass, the iridescent orichalc most prized by the ancients. Magnificent mountains, lush plains teeming with every kind of animal including elephants, canals separating five concentrically circular islands with ports full of vessels and merchants coming from all parts who from their numbers kept up a multitudinous din and clatter night and day; so the legends spread. Through translation errors from Egyptian on the part of Greek philosophers who lived twelve hundred years later, the island would be enlarged by a factor of ten and moved away from the familiar Aegean to the legendary seas beyond the Pillars of Hercules, into the Atlantic Ocean.

Kalliste, with its fast-flowing streams, its lush canopy of papyrus and palms, became the dried husk of Thera, the 'Island of Fear.' From the most beautiful to the most barren, all in an instant of time. Even swallows, plentiful and welcomed before as harbingers of good fortune, never did return to Thera. Wiser than people in many ways, nature had permanently altered their migratory instincts. Birds learn from experience.

The Minoan dead, whether interred in a cave, a jar, a sarcophagus, a tholos tomb, or a corner of an ossuary, always expected a satisfactory afterlife. None ever had a complete preoccupation with mortality. The mystery and portentousness of dissolution was looked upon as a natural event, awaited, expected, never to be rushed but always accepted in the due course of time. The land of the dead fused in the Minoan mind with the fertile soil from which sprang the plants and crops. Bereavement was only an acknowledgment of a temporary parting, of the place that man had in the universal rhythm of growth and decay, the timeless rhythm of the Great Goddess and her lover, the dying mountain god. It was not unreasonable to observe rites of deification of the departed man or woman, gone to their final rest in the full bosom of the Mother Goddess. The distinction between mortal and immortal, between flesh and spirit, did not exercise a differentiation in the Minoan mind. In death, the individual followed the well-trodden path of the Cretan Zeus, whose tomb only the Greeks could not accept as authentic. "Liars," they would forever say of the Cretan people, still hating them for taking so many of their beautiful youth, and for the death of their King Aegeus. And when passing by the once beautiful Atlantea, the most flattering name they could find for it was Nea Kameni, "the New Burnt Land."

How would the present be had the Minoans chosen another place to build their society? A people of promise, they became the most advanced, intellectual people of their time. Collectively destroyed in a blink, they speak to us as a voice emanating out of the ground, immortal, as it were, preserved by the same forces of nature that brought them tumbling from their lofty zenith of perfection. Where might we be now had they survived? Does anyone suppose the twentieth century might have occurred a thousand, or more, years ago?

Today the island of Crete is a pretty, quaint, some would say backward community, judged by the new world standards of our budding twenty-first century. But under the dust of its soil, and that of its neighbor Thera, lie the partially exposed ruins of the first great world power. Mingled with the ashes of the earth lie hundreds of thousands who took inspiration from their faith and let their minds soar to heights uninhibited by greed, political machinations, educational prejudices, or religious persecution. Olives are still harvested where Selene planted her young whips, gifts from her 'Little Bee.' Trees thriving in the droughty clime today are direct descendants from those same young plants pressed into the earth by her hands five thousand years ago, genetically identical because of the olive's unique way of sending forth sprouts from the ground by way of its root ends.

The vast stands of fir, oak, cypress, pine, and cedar have long since disappeared. Pillaging of woodlands started with the Minoans and, by the time of their demise, the greater portion of it was gone. Fires set by Thera after a typically dry summer raged through and decimated the remains. Trees, which helped conserve winter rainfall and kept small rivers running all year without ever drying up, are virtually extinct on the island. Springs which percolated pure, rich water in abundance are now largely wizened and barren. Winter rains, without the protective carpet of green, now gouge deeper gullies and erode the topsoil. With the exception of agricultural areas, the scoured land is little but exposed, arid, ochre-colored rock in the summer. Bleak, but still pretty where tended by conscientious landowners, and still surrounded by the most heavenly sent water on Earth, the Minoans have bequeathed to us the simple gifts of beauty and silence.

Even now, as in Homer's time and earlier, men gather before the fire with their cups of wine and remember the tales of a long passed age of glory, tales of magical palaces where magnificent monsters roamed, mighty fleets of ships plying the sea, and gods walking among men, forging the great race from which the commemorators themselves descended.

Everywhere are groups of children, fiercely loyal to their families, but still at odds with each other as they vie for position as chickens establishing a pecking order. Associating with brother and friend, they battle as jealous enemies. Always it is the youngest and least able to defend himself who is thrown into the anthill.

And so we will conclude at Aminospilia, paying the debt we owe to the Minoans by endowing their memory to the four winds. As time ponders along we will learn yet more of this astonishing and cultivated people. At the ruins of a shrine exhibiting shocking evidence of blood sacrifice, donkeys still serenade lonelylike, and when the hillsides embrace the sacrament of quiet, the partridges return and sing more sweetly than anyplace else.

And the Moon stares down with compassion upon her children.

~~~~~~

Acknowledgments

It's usual for an author to be lost for words when it comes time to acknowledge all those who have contributed to the writing of a book. Some contribute vastly to the academic side while others give a piece of themselves unknowingly as part of a caricature composite. To all I give my thanks for their literary inspiration, but special mention must be made to the following:

Mrs. Shields, a high school teacher who instilled the love of reading into her students; a public library system with wonderful librarians that make research easy; to unnamed friends who offered encouragement, and some disbelief, at what I was attempting; Costas Zouganelis of the island of Mikonos, and Melville Grosvenor, for the story of Petros the pelican (apparently Petros is still alive and well, entertaining tourists and natives alike, although there is some debate about whether or not it is actually the same bird year after year); Homer, for the Odyssey and the Iliad; an unknown Egyptian priest of the goddess Neth who had access to the House of Books in about 590 B.C.E., who passed on the tales of Atlantis to Solon, the Greek statesman; Solon, for recording those tales in the form of an unfinished poem and bringing them back to Greece (unfortunately that poem has been lost to us, and apparently used Greek names instead of the original Egyptian); Dropides, the great-grandfather of Criteaus, who knew Solon and preserved his writings; Criteaus, who received the tales from his great-grandfather almost two hundred years after their composition and passed them to his young cousin Plato; Plato, who had the foresight to preserve the tales in his own writings; Timaeus, a statesman of Athens, who told Plato more (though where he got his information I have no idea); the Greeks who thought Plato's "Timaeus" and Criteaus" worthy of preserving; Sir Arthur Evans for his magnificent publication, "Knossos, 'The Palace of Minos'", a record of the archaeological excavations which he undertook, largely at his own expense (mankind has regained a portion of its lost wealth through his efforts); archeologists Arthur Cotterell, Leonard Cotterell, Reynold Higgins, Rodney Castleden, Jacquetta Hawkes, Joseph Judge, Hans Georg Wunderlich, and James W. Maver Jr., for continuing the work and for contributing most of the academic material for this book; Yannis Sakellarakis and Efi Sapouna-Sakellariki for their research regarding human sacrifice in a Minoan temple; F. Melian Stawell, author of "A Clue to the Cretan Scripts", for his translation of the Phaestos Disk; Nina Hyde for her information on the history of wool; Tim Severin for his experiences with reproducing ancient vessels and as an oarsman on a long voyage; Noel Grove for descriptions and impressions of volcanoes; the victims of the Mount Pelee eruption, and especially the survivors, for their personal tragedies, sacrifices, and testimonies which have left us richer for the telling, but them poorer for the experience (they, more than any others, have contributed to the firsthand knowledge of what it is like to cling to the edge of mortality within the death cloud of a volcanic explosion) with thanks especially to Léon Compère-Léandre and August Ciparis (the prisoner) who were in the middle of it; Ellery Scott who witnessed the Mount Pelee eruption from aboard ship and Mr. and Mrs. Fernand Clerc who witnessed it from four miles away; Spyridon Marinatos who began excavation of the ruins at Akrotiri on the island of Santorini (Thera) in 1967, and to Christos Doumas who continues the work today; to unnamed witnesses of the Mount Saint Helens eruption; Pliny the Younger for his descriptions of Mount Vesuvius erupting from a distance of fifteen miles; greatest thanks to Charles Peligrino, a scholar of the highest order of brilliance, who's research into the island of Thera was most inspirational in creating the latter portion of this book; finally, to the ancient Minoans themselves, who, if they had been allowed by Mother Nature, would likely have ushered in the twentieth century two-thousand years ago.

Apology

I've named King Aegeus after the Aegean Sea, whereas most presume the process to have been just the opposite. However, having to call the sea something, and not knowing what the Minoans called it, I stuck with the current name. Anything else too far removed from what it is now known as, at the risk of offending many readers, might have been confusing. Of course, no one knows what the Minoans even called themselves (the Egyptians certainly called them Keftiu) so everyone calls them Minoan, after King Minos. Likewise, I had no trouble changing names slightly: Crete to Kriti, Cyprus to Kypros. These are close enough to the English so that they are still recognizable, and in fact are how they are actually spelled in some places. No doubt I'll be hearing from many purists on these and many other issues, however, I hope the reader will remember that the purpose of this book is mainly to entertain. If an interest develops that will lead the reader to Crete and Santorini to see those places for themselves, then this will be a wonderful thing. I am comfortable with my logic, and I hope the many doctors of archeology, or other sciences, will turn the other cheek if I have offended their sensibilities. If they have anything to add for future editions, I would be very pleased to hear from them. My greatest hope is that an interest will grow in a demand to continue with the excavation of Knossos, which is still, for the most part, unexcavated. It is pathetic that humanity has had, and still has, such a propensity to spend so much on destroying their present instead of preserving it into the future. We value our past so minimally that barely a pittance is found to fund worthy archeological projects, yet unlimited funds are borrowed to destroy whole civilizations.

Any complaints, suggestions, remarks, etc. can be
sent to the author at
neepness@icloud.com
He'd love to hear from you.

Printed in Great Britain
by Amazon